Peter was working as a salesman when, in the aftermath of the COVID-19 outbreak, a new passion for 3D modelling and a personal battle with depression conspired to unleash an unknown ability from within to write and tell stories.

The entirety of this story was penned during my own personal battle with depression and as such telling this story became my coping mechanism for my own fight with my mind. In hindsight, I was lucky to find a way to manage the power of my own destructive mind but many are not so fortunate. I would like to dedicate this book to everyone and anyone who suffers in silence under the cruel weight of their own mind at the mercy of mental health problems.

Every dream starts with an idea

Peter Harrison

LIFE DOWNSIDE UP

AUSTIN MACAULEY PUBLISHERS™

LONDON * CAMBRIDGE * NEW YORK * SHARJAH

A CIP catalogue record for this title is available from the British Library.

ISBN 9781035846139 (Paperback)
ISBN 9781035846153 (ePub e-book)
ISBN 9781035846146 (Audiobook)

www.austinmacauley.com

First Published 2024
Austin Macauley Publishers Ltd®
1 Canada Square
Canary Wharf
London
E14 5AA

Firstly, I would like to acknowledge my dear wife, Nicola, for enduring my worst lows during my battle with depression and for putting up with my continual ear bending every time I spoke in depth about this book. I would also like to thank the following people for standing beside me and convincing me never to give up and to stand my ground when times became testing. Loren Hornett, Matthew Williamson, Verica Hupe, Bonny Bendix, Ken Vincent, Magnus Strindoem, Tammy McCoy, Scott Lavers and anyone else who didn't tell me to just give up or quit!

Table of Contents

Life Downside Up
Introduction

So, I get that you have gone to the effort of readying this studio for me so you can get those killer shots of me but could we go somewhere less…indoorsy? I feel awkward enough as it is without the lights and that chair ready and waiting for me like an interrogation.

The enclosed space makes me feel on edge and if you really want me to tell you my story then this dark room won't help me tell it. There is a nice spot in the park overlooking the town or by the beach there is a bench, I go there to think quite a lot so could we go there? If we could go somewhere else to talk then I will open up to you and even let you get those studio shots you want? But in clothes! I'm not that kind of girl!

I'm Fae Edwards, 27 years old and I work as a therapist and am a trainee consultant at the Hotel Davizioso, but that isn't why you brought me here today, is it? You aren't that interested in the work that me or anyone else at that place does, are you?

The real reason you have gone to all this effort is that nearly 10 years ago, I made my first visit and stayed at the hotel as a patient suffering from depression and bipolar disorder.

Today I work at the hotel and I am still suffering from both conditions and that is the real reason you have brought me to this expensive studio. On the surface, I look normal, right, but looks are where the normal stops and the abnormal begins and the deeper you go, often the darker that gets.

Some days I'm absolutely fine and nothing fazes me but other days the entire world just crashes down on my head or I become angry, irritable or obtuse and push away everyone or anyone that tries to help me.

Sorry, I'm just not used to people wanting to talk to me about who I am or maybe more importantly what I am? In truth, talking about myself and my past doesn't really bring me much joy. In truth, it's quite painful and sad.

So that begs an obvious question, doesn't it? If talking about my past and myself causes me so many problems then why am I doing this? Well, that's also easy. People like me live our lives downside up and people often see what I am before they even see who I am if they get that far in the first place.

Unfortunately, that is entirely true, hopefully though you will learn that there is far more to me than a few tags or passing judgements which define me as a person. The real reason that I agreed to this though is so that maybe just one day other people like me will be viewed as normal and not taboo? I mean, do I look taboo to you?

So, before we begin, can I ask you a question?

Do roller coasters scare you?

I mean, after that empty no you put out to act fearless?

Do they actually scare you?

But you are scared before the ride?

Being around me is kinda like that!

But you could try to see it differently?

Why don't you try waiting until after the ride to see if it was scary or not?

It's a strange story and it's going to take a while so if you are sure you want to do this then let me begin!

That's why I brought this photo with me, from a holiday with my mum and dad in Monesta, I was 11 years old and they pulled me out of school to take me as they couldn't have afforded to take me during school holidays but that was my birthday treat and reward before I started high school. I remember that holiday well, my dad got sick after trying new food and me and Mum just spent it doing girly stuff together, while he spent the holiday largely in bed.

On the surface and in this photo, I look totally normal, like a cute 11-year-old girl, but a few times Mum caught me just looking into space and oddly subdued. My mum figured it was just my dad being unwell that had made me act a little odd but I remember sitting outside with her for this photo on that holiday. Though, what I really remember about that holiday were the comments she got about me being sweet, adorable and cute, however in just six months' time those words would never be used in a sentence together with my name ever again.

Chapter 1
Shattered Dreams

Growing up wasn't too bad, I had the usual tantrums and moods that all kids do but for the most part it was pretty good, it wasn't until I started to turn from a girl into a young woman that things got more confused. Growing up in the town of Oured which was more of a suburb for the city of Usted just to the north of Oured. My dad worked as a cabinet maker for a local joinery firm, while my mum worked as an office clerk for Oured's council, having previously worked for a holiday firm. Dad was originally from the UK, but moved here when the IT firm he previously worked for ran a team building holiday here.

While on the holiday, he met my mum and discovered a passion for carpentry and joinery as part of their team building exercise. While the rest of his team went back to the UK, Dad stayed behind and eventually quit working in IT, partly to pursue his new passion for joinery.

Partly though, he just couldn't get used to the language here, relying on people to understand him through his deep Yorkshire accent, eventually they married and eventually had me. Mum named me Fae, in honour of her aunt who had passed away just after she had fallen pregnant with me, Mum's aunt had played a big role in her childhood and wanted to remember her through me.

My parents were great together too, they hardly fought and always seemed to be deeply dedicated and thoroughly in love with each other, or at least that was the case until I started changing.

Just before I finished primary school, I had started the growing process that all girls go though, developing and turning into a woman, when I had a strange day where I just sat in my room in the dark, all day. My mum phoned the school and told them I had been sick, unsure what was wrong they just figured it was part of my transition into womanhood?

During the summer holiday and just before I started high school, I had a few more of these days but stranger still was a few times I just seemed to phase out and be unable to function? Sometimes, these moments would just be me being sad, hyperactive or angry but once I became incredibly nervous, seeming to shelter away from everything. These odd moments would last a few minutes or just a few hours, but something was happening and my mum was worried, she contacted a doctor who came out to visit me.

My concerned mum was told it was just the start of me experiencing the beginning of the menstrual cycle that was causing my strange runs, my mother though unconvinced accepted the diagnosis. While these strange little moments happened infrequently, they caused great concern to my mum and dad, though initially both accepted that, 'growing pains' were the root cause of them and soon enough I would grow out of them.

While I started high school, the moments stayed innocent enough, affecting me lightly but just after Christmas, they suddenly started to happen more frequently and sometimes my swings would be very violent. Crashing moods and emotions would conflict and manifest as fits of rage, heightened nervousness or sometimes crushing sorrow and sadness. Gradually missing more and more school, people were starting to want answers from my parents as to why I was so frequently absent for growing lengths of time.

My parents weren't inactive at all of course, they had been taking me to a steady stream of different doctors as they tried to figure out what was going on, for the most part they left each doctor no more enlightened than they had been before we walked through their door. Both of my parents were growing concerned about what was going on and seemingly getting no real answers, they decided to try to find a specialist who might give them some kind of insight into what was happening to me.

After a year of getting nowhere, my mum called in a favour through the council of Oured and had me referred to a specialist in the city of Usted, just to the north of our hometown, Oured. Two days before I was set to visit the specialist, I had a violent turn in school, crashing in a crying fit during lunchtime, falling and hitting my arm, I was sent to hospital as they thought I might have broken my arm.

Dad came to the hospital as fast as he could, collecting Mum on his way, while talking to one of the doctors about what had been happening to me over the last year, they called a consultant in to speak with me and run some tests.

Being quizzed for what seemed like hours, the consultant took my parents aside to tell them that in his professional opinion I was suffering from depression but he wanted to refer me on again to get a second opinion.

That consultant referred my parents to the same specialist in Usted, we drove there in the morning, where I would spend the day speaking with psychiatrists and having tests done. Both of my parents were also quizzed about what had been happening to me as they tried to establish what was really going on, it became obvious that this was far more than just growing pains.

Something became very clear to them, whatever was happening, had been steadily worsening and been occurring for far longer than either of them realised as the consultant started to delve into my younger years. While my parents awaited the outcome of my assessment and diagnosis, they tried to have me given a 3-week reprieve from school, but their request was denied as they were threatened with legal action.

With my swings becoming more extreme, it probably would have been better if the school let me take that time off, as I was sent home 4 times in that 3-week period having either become uncontrollably sad or angry.

Having waited 3 weeks and with me having been suspended from school for a week after an argument with a teacher, my parents got the diagnosis they had been dreading. They drove me back to the specialists in Usted to receive the news that I was suffering from depression and bipolar disorder and in their opinion, it had been ongoing for many years.

That specialist surmised that my bipolar disorder had always been there but the depression was newer but had been caused by the swings that accompanied my bipolar disorder. Mum was utterly distraught, partially because she worried about my future but mostly because the way the news was given made out that she was a poor mother. My dad however was pretty laid-back about it all, he just started to call me. 'Jaffa Cake', as not all things are meant to be one thing or another, putting his usual happy taint on everything. Naturally my parents immediately informed my school, who seemed fairly supportive though not always in the best way.

During my first week back from suspension, I was stood before my classes with people being told to be nice to me, of course with all teenagers the first thing they did was the opposite. Suddenly, the world became different and darker, where people had been supportive or concerned before, now I became a target for bullying and ridicule. During that first year, I suddenly started to become the victim of a seemingly endless tirade of abuse, they called me retarded, of stupid, stuff like that.

Gradually though I started to shut myself off from people, I had a few friends but not many, the problem was my swings were getting more and more erratic and sometimes, I could be totally different versions of myself. School was getting harder and the bullying had started to cause a very different problem at home, with my swings getting more violent, I started to vent at the closest person to me at the time, my mother.

Mum had always been very supportive, though sometimes quite harsh, she always meant well deep down, she tried getting my diagnosis reviewed a few times as she didn't want me to be branded as a problem for the rest of my life. Driving me to work harder to give myself a chance, she became my outlet of choice every time my temper turned, where she was so good to me, she became my natural punch bag each and every time my temper turned, I took it out on her.

We started to argue and yell at each other more and more, my mother would then bring my dad into things and every time his laid-back approach let me off the hook for the things I did and said to her. Slowly they started to argue, at first, they went for walks so I couldn't hear them but gradually they just argued in the kitchen, the problem was my dad backed me up and all that did was give my temper a greater punch.

Just after my 14th birthday was when things started to intensify, my moods shifted wildly and unpredictably, crushing depression and anxiety attacks were slowly tearing away my confidence. Isolating myself from nearly everyone but a few people who I was clinging onto my threads, loneliness was starting to suffocate me in my own little hellish mind.

Dad simply started to brand my varying states as either 'Crashes' or 'Episodes' and almost dismissed my steadily worsening problems and states of mind. Crashes were his name for my depression spikes, where I just seemed to fall eternally further and further down until I reached a point where I could fall no further. Episodes were the name he gave to my fits of rage or hyperactivity, as generally they didn't last very long but were generally pretty violent turns of mood.

While my dad seemed to act as if nothing was wrong or even support my often negative outbursts my mother was slowly watching her daughter fade away. Those days where we had gone shopping together and shared those wonderful moments that mothers and daughters share, had all but faded away into nothingness. Slowly we drifted apart, almost to the point where the only time we really spent together were our arguments.

Most saddeningly though, my worsening state was also starting to affect my parents' marriage, though sometimes it seemed like their very different approaches to me was also a big factor. With Dad almost acting as if there was nothing wrong and my mum thinking that I had just been labelled a problem for life, the differences were starting to pull them apart. Arguing more frequently and their generally pretty solid union began to wither and fray, over time they started to grow distant from each other.

These first few years after my diagnosis were tough for all of us but they would be nothing compared to what would come over the next two years.

School life suddenly became a much bigger part of the spiral downwards that would happen over the next few years, with the bullying turning from abusive to malicious and eventually dangerous. Gradually having lost all my friends due to the moody swings and crushing depression I had been experiencing, life alone made me desperate for some form of human interaction. Desperately, I would try to befriend people and to try and get a few minutes in the sun with people, the problem was the only people that ever took the bait had ulterior motives to do so.

Initially, it started easily just being built up to be knocked down but the thing is that their refusal just made me try even harder and give them even more rope to hang me with. Fake friendships would blossom for a week or so before they would knock me back down, but when I got my first phone, I made doing this even easier for them. Fake friendships also grew to be fake boyfriends too, who would build me up so that their real girlfriends could knock me down.

The first of them was called Toby, he even met my parents to try and seal the reality of the scam but eventually he got his mum to dump me via text. Toby was the first of many, the only difference was I just didn't introduce them to my parents, lying to myself and them to hide my own sorrow and shame at how my life had started to become.

My parents were largely unaware of how bad things for me were until one night just after my 17th birthday one such event changed everything and unlocked a very different side of me. My depression had hit its peak with obvious bullying happening all the time, name calling but that more subtle form of torture was becoming much more dangerous as it tore the fabric of my mind apart.

People would start standing up for me and defending me from the routine bullying, meeting up with me after school but it was all a set up for the big show.

Desperate for human contact, I would head wherever they planned to meet only to find myself spending the night alone with my mind. Such a group had been around me for 3 or 4 weeks and wanted to meet up to celebrate my 17th birthday at night, we were going to meet in a park near the river in Oured. I was so excited as I headed to the park, but of course they didn't show up, an hour or so after they should have been there, I got a text. "We don't want a worthless, stupid, retard as a friend, just die, Fae."

That text sent me into a downward spiral, sitting alone in total darkness in that gloomy park, I had taken all I could as I started to walk to the bridge, I started to think something far more dangerous. "All I have to do is take one step too many." I stood looking over the bridge and down to the river below it, a drop of some 100 metres. "Just one step too many." I started to climb over the railings and stood on the edge of the bridge and took one final deep breath.

Behind me, I heard the screech of car tyres and steps increasing in volume as I started to say goodbye to the world and tell my parents I loved them. Shouting was followed by a violent pull on my shoulder, as I was pulled back over the railings and into the arms of a passing stranger. He looked at me with sheer terror and concern on his face as I broke apart and cried my eyes out, he took me in his arms and just held on.

Picking me up, he carried me to his waiting car, taking me to a park near to my home, sitting me on a bench and sat talking with me for a few hours. Barryn was his name, he was 24 and had been a soldier before being discharged on mental health grounds after a vehicle he was in was hit by a roadside bomb. Barryn came round to discover he was the sole survivor of the 10 people in that vehicle and stricken with guilt he developed PTSD as a result of it.

He worked as a security guard for various nightclubs, he gave me his number telling me to phone him if I ever got in trouble again and he would show up. Before Barryn drove me back home in the morning, he told me to just keep going and never to give up, he told my mum what had happened, she was distraught of course but thanked him for saving my life.

Barryn, true to his word did show up every time I called or text him, my mother wasn't too keen on him being around, but he vanished two months after, it turned out he got stabbed trying to break up a brawl at a bar in Usted. We went to his funeral; he was a rare friend in what was just the start of a hellish nine months which culminated in multiple suicide attempts and my mother and father finally breaking over Christmas.

While my condition was worsening, so too was the previously unbreakable bond between my mum and dad, there were two main reasons why they started to break apart. Firstly, my temper and swings had grown more unpredictable and wilder, my mother actually told me she might get to see her daughter 2 or 3 times a year after I turned 17.

Secondly, my parents' approach to both me and my problems were almost as different as my swings and moods. Mother worked tirelessly to get me help, over the course of three years she tried all kinds of different clinics and psychiatrists but for the most part we both wound up with more questions than answers.

Together, we would visit almost every health facility in Oured and Usted over the course of 3 years, seemingly getting nowhere she started to call in favours from her bosses in the council. Dad however, almost acted as if my problems simply didn't exist, almost sweeping himself under the carpet, he spent more time in the shed tinkering aimlessly than supporting my mother.

Seemingly the only person that understood me, I used to side with him every time my mother bit at him, a vicious cycle had begun. Mum and I would argue and eventually she would argue with my dad, when they finished, I would step in to defend my dad and generally cause a bigger fallout. Defending the only person that seemed to get me, I would stand up for him no matter how right my mum was, the problem deep down was my dad was so far removed from reality that he didn't really understand me at all.

Deep down my mum's biggest concern was that if I didn't do well at school and college then my future would be bleak at very best, this was why she was such a driving force. Dad seemed to think all I needed was one person to see beyond my conditions and give me a chance and everything would work out for me.

Their views and ideas being so different was causing me nearly as many issues as my own mind was and eventually something had to give. Fighting and arguing more and more they started slowly unwinding and their union was shearing and I was driving a wedge right between them.

Christmas was approaching and once again having spent weeks being befriended in preparation for the big fall, once again I headed to that bridge. Barryn was the only person who would have been able to help me that night as

21

after being left in an old building on the outskirts of Oured all night. Spending hours alone in darkness, my mind was once again at breaking point with anxiety tearing away what little confidence I had left; my real breaking point had come.

Mum happened to be out in Usted that night and drove past me while I was walking to the bridge, stopping when she got her first glimpse of the world, I was hiding from her. Over the last 5 months, things had gotten worse with school and in general but I had become quite good at just hiding it from her, my mother withdrew me from school and started looking for a new solution.

While my mum looked for a new solution, my dad took me to get the dreadlocks I had wanted since turning 17, against the wishes of my mum. Though Mum didn't openly disapprove of them, she told Dad that he had taken the last piece of me away from her with those dreadlocks. School would resume for me in the new year and in truth with my state worsening they were being pretty good to me and Mum.

Over the new year while my mum was at work her boss gave her an option, a new facility had opened in the coastal town of Ljianstipol and was offering a respite in a new and experimental kind of healthcare facility. While I sat upstairs, I could hear my mother talking on the phone over the course of an hour, she sounded deeply upset, when I went downstairs to see her. Sitting at our kitchen table with her head in her hands crying, she had spent the last hour discussing sending me away for 4 months to give me a break from my troubles in Oured.

Explaining to me that she wanted to help me and to try and help them save their marriage from falling to pieces, my dad was in agreement with her too. Over the next two weeks my mother arranged with school for me to be away from March until June and she also arranged with the place in Ljianstipol for my visit. Once I sat with her while she spoke to the owners of the place, I could see and hear the fear and desperation in her voice over the course of that hour long phone call.

Despite her not wanting to send me away, she believed that if something didn't change for me soon, she might well be burying me very soon. Her hope was at least they might be able to help me understand what was going on in my mind and help me get some answers finally, her aim was sincere and well-meaning.

While the time for my trip approached our relationship turned sour but not only with my mother with my father too, his dismissive approach was also starting to chip away at me. Dad didn't want me being sent to that place no matter what, especially as I would be there for my 18th birthday. Shrugging off my problems and blaming my mum for condemning me to a life of judgement and misery by sending me away, for once I took my mum's side.

Me and Dad argued for a few hours, I stood up for her defending her for the first at least she was trying something instead of hiding away in her shed, we didn't speak for 4 days after this fallout. Truthfully, the last thing I wanted was to spend my birthday in a strange place with no friends or even family around but with life becoming so desperate for me, I agreed with her, I needed something to change.

During the 2 days before I went away, Dad stayed at work or in his shed, avoiding contact with both of us before it was time for him to drive me to Ljianstipol. Begrudgingly he drove me down and we didn't exchange a single word for the entire trip and it wasn't until we arrived at the venue for the next 4 months of my life that we spoke just to say goodbye. Dropping me and my life in a small suitcase at the doorway of the Hotel Davizioso and the owners Tony and Gale.

Giving me a guided tour of the Hotel Davizioso, they explained that the facility used to be a 5-star luxury hotel as we started to wander its marble clad interior. They joked that there were reviews online from disgruntled tourists who had been turned away from the place, still believing that it was a hotel. Showing me to the different communal areas and dining areas and explaining that they didn't have patients here, just residents or guests.

Residents generally lived in the hotel all year round, many having been passed round the healthcare system that couldn't help them. Guests were generally here for shorter periods varying from a few weeks to 6 months, the residents had the larger rooms at the top of the hotel and guests had smaller rooms on the lower floors. The first order of business was to give me a coloured rubber wristband, the colours indicated to staff my conditions and also could be used as a method of payment in most of the shops in town.

My wristband was purple and deep blue to indicate my depression and bipolar disorder, the bands colours of course also helped other guests and residents identify people with similar conditions to themselves. Leading me to an elevator, they had given me a room on the top floor next to another resident who suffered from the same conditions as me, they introduced me to him as they took me to my room.

Steven was his name though he simply called himself Shanky, though at that time I had no interest in making friends here! The room was nice and enormous, I had a king size bed to myself, a big bath and a living room, to all intents and purposes it was its own self-contained apartment.

Something that I noticed in my early days in this odd place was that for the most part many of the people here quite a lot older than me and many seemed kind of normal? Ljianstipol itself was also quite odd, the quaint town was formerly the reserve of the political elite of the regime which fell towards the end of the last century.

While under the old political leadership the town had been named South Usted, half was kept as the old cobbled walkways which had survived for centuries, the other was paved and designed to be a replica of the former capital Usted. The reason for this split in half design?

The propaganda for the regime could be filmed here in what was a mini replica of the capital, complete with its own political bureau and monument to the leadership. When the regime and the monument fell, the name was reverted back to Ljianstipol, though there are still people here who will frown if you call it that and scowl at you telling you that this place is South Usted.

My new neighbour at first creeped me out a bit, he was a lot older than me, pleasant but at 17 the last thing I wanted was a friend here. My mum and the owners had put me next to him as he had agreed to help the owners to help me, with him suffering from the same conditions as me they hoped he would help me understand my conditions.

The problem was that I had no confidence, self-esteem, I was scared and in truth utterly terrified of the place and the people here, for the most part I just hid in my room.

Only really leaving my room to get food or occasionally to take a walk around the hotel late at night when I was sure nobody would be around. Mum called me quite often and Dad did a few times during my first couple of weeks here, I lied to them telling them I had made friends and felt good.

My mum of course, was routinely being kept informed by the owners about how scared I was and how much time I spent isolated and hidden away from everyone. Shanky, of course, kept trying, "Hey we've got the same wristbands!" He would say sounding excited, in truth I blew him off a lot at first, but he kept trying.

When I left home, I smuggled a bottle of deep blue hair dye with me to colour my dreadlocks, hidden among my clothes so that my mum didn't find it before I came here. After two weeks here, I decided to try and dye my hair, I had been feeling lousy and low all day so I hoped it would perk me up a bit? Shaking uncontrollably, I wrestled with the bottle but somehow, I managed to get it open, fumbling with it and casting the electric blue contents down the sink.

Without logic nor reason, I tried scooping it up with my hands only to watch it all slowly drain away, like my life, the dye was trickling down the drain. Letting out a series of frustrated cries and yells, I wound up laying and curling into a heap by the window near my bed. Laying down and staring at the wall, crying loudly and violently as my teen emotions raged away before the sadness took control.

I could hear muffled voices by my door as the depression kicked in and took hold of me, the muffled voices became thumps on the door. Tony broke the door down, coming in to find me lying motionless on my side, staring emotionlessly into nothingness and the darkening abyss of my own mind.

Fear and terror were in his voice as he rolled my seemingly lifeless body over and revealed my blue hands and red and tears-soaked cheeks. Reaching down to pick me up, the sadness and concern on his face caused me to just break down into tears as he picked me up and held me.

Tony lifted me up and sat me on my bed and rang his colleague, asking him to go and get me some hair dye, tonight he would dye my hair for me. While waiting for his colleague to come back, he started to talk to me about my time at the hotel, discovering that I had barely left my room. My neighbour came in to help him talk to me, he had also tipped him off that something was wrong and that I needed their help badly.

Shanky started to tell me that he would try and help me to understand myself, he waved his band at me. "I've got the same colours as you," before he left me and Tony to talk. Tony explained how they had set up the Davizioso with his business partner Gale, after Tony had lost his son to depression and he said they weren't going to lose me to it either! Something became obvious while we awaited Gale's return with that hair dye.

These people, no matter how strange they were, really wanted to help me and to help me understand myself. Telling me about the phone conversations he had been having with my mother before she sent me here, he told me how ashamed she felt, but like him, she was just being failed by a system that couldn't cope with me or help me.

Tony's son had been passed around the system just like me and most of the residents and guests here had been, before being discharged from a hospice only to commit suicide 6 hours later. While Tony told me a little about himself, Gale returned with hair dye and a girl, his daughter and she was going to help the two men dye my hair for me.

Ellie was her name, she told me that she was 20 and that this time that blue was going to be in my hair and not on my hands or poured down the sink. This was her first visit to Ljianstipol and her dad's business, but he had been telling her about me before she came down to visit. Gale hoped that with her being similarly aged to me that she might be able to reach me more than they could. Gale started to explain to her how I hadn't left my room, Ellie's response was simple, "Surrounded by all you old farts, nor would I." Ellie was 20 years old and lived in Zyvala, a large town near the mountains far to the north of Ljianstipol.

While she dyed my hair, Tony was trying to clean the blue dye off my hands, she sneaked a look at my wardrobe, "You could always take Fae shopping and get her something nice." She smiled at me and sat down on the bed with me and held my hand, "Like a daddy and daughter day just for Fae?" She smiled trying to break the near permanent frown that was on my face.

Eventually, they calmed me down and sorted me out, I sat on the bed with Tony and fell asleep, waking in the morning to find him still there, awake and exhausted. Wincing from time to time where his ribs hurt but he didn't let me go and he didn't leave me in that room alone either, and that morning he was going to start helping me.

Waiting for me to wake up he told me that today I was going to go with him and discover the new land I was in, but breakfast would be the first thing we would do. Tony took me downstairs and through to a backroom he simply called 'Gale's Bar' claiming it was Gale's pride and joy at the Davizioso. Set up to look like an American pool bar, complete with a competition grade pool table and a small seating area, it was where Gale went at night when his insomnia acted up.

Tony ordered us breakfast while Gale played me at pool while we waited and in truth, he was pretty good at his beloved sport. Gale, and Ellie joined us for breakfast, talking and trying to put me at ease and bring me out of my shell just a little bit and to get me ready to explore the world. Tony threw me my hoodie.

"Come on we have a big day ahead of us, it's market day and it's time you saw Ljianstipol," he smiled away as we headed out of the hotel and into town.

We walked along the river and towards the new part of town, stopping to get coffee from a van parked near the bridge into the new town, run by a very Italian man.

Tony introduced me to the concept of global coffee with a Cuban latte, it was really nice but very strong! Over the next two hours we spent our time wandering the shops in this new part of town, getting me a couple of t-shirts and a vest top. Soon enough it was lunch time, before he picked a venue for lunch, he checked my age. "17 but nearly 18, right? What's a few months going to hurt?"

He took me to a diner by the riverbank, sitting by the river we had burgers and a beer and we watched the river flow by. Tony knew I was underage but he lied for me and introduced me to another new experience, crisp and cold beer. Once we finished up here, it was back down the river to the old part of town and its cobbled streets that defined the entrance to the original parts of Ljianstipol. Wandering the shops here my eyes got a big surprise as prices soared in some of the galleries and shops in this part of town.

Wandering the market bustling with artisans and craft stalls, Tony got me a bracelet made from guitar strings before he walked me through the market and into a little park. Claiming that sometimes he came here to think, through the park there was a promenade that led onto the beach, it was very pretty and potentially places to go if I needed some headspace. Tony took me to get one final treat from a boutique shop near the marketplace, the top he bought me was more expensive than everything I was wearing.

The boutique was owned by a strange and quite rude Frenchman, though he did take our picture in the marketplace for Tony. Slowly we wandered back to the Hotel Davizioso, I thanked Tony saying I had a great day, he smiled back at me. "You aren't done yet, are you?" Wondering what he meant as we got back to the hotel.

Tony took me back to my room so that I could shower and get changed, Tony planned to introduce me to something else in the hotel, a place to get away from things? Somewhere within the Hotel Davizioso but off limits to pretty much everyone? Returning to Gale's bar for dinner, to be joined by Shanky and Gale, we had a veritable feast in that bar complete with the biggest ice cream sundae I had ever seen.

Gale hustled me at pool again before Tony led me through the hotel to a security coded door and whispered, "1604," and pointed at the lock. Pressing the code in and opening the door which led to another doorway up a set of stairs, I put the code into the lock here too and opened the door to reveal a huge secret rooftop garden.

Filling the entire roof of the hotel was a Japanese themed garden, at one end sat a pond with a pergola above it and at the other a log cabin with a log stove for the colder months of the year. Tony started to walk me round the garden. "You can come here anytime you want, just keep the code a secret," partway round the garden was a cherry blossom tree with a plaque underneath it. Tony looked at me. "My son David's ashes are inside that plaque, the code is his birthday, I've already lost David once. I don't want to lose him again, that's why it is locked."

I took Tony's hand and looked at him. "I won't tell anyone about here," he smiled back.

"I know you won't, I trust you Fae." Tony walked me down to the pergola sat over the pond and opened a hidden cool box. Hidden within the walls of the pergola, the deep cool box was filled with chocolate and beer, Tony handed me a bottle and took one himself and looked at me. "To new friends," tipping his bottle to me.

Tipping my bottle back to him, "To new friends," we sat and enjoyed a beer together in peace and quiet while the day turned to night.

Looking over at the exhausted man, "Thank you for today," he smiled back, "Just do me one favour, Fae?"

I looked over as he looked over at the last hints of daylight. "Sure, what is it?"

Tony looked over at me. "When you have hit the bottom rung of the ladder, ring me or Gale and we will come and get you! We will never leave you behind and there is always a room for you here, Fae, you promise me?"

Sitting back, I took in what he had just said to me and felt a little glimmer of hope within me. "I promise," sitting back in peaceful silence.

Together we stayed for another hour or so, sometimes talking, sometimes just being quiet, overlooking the day fading away like the start of a new hope in my life. Finally, at least one person understood me and was only too willing to help me to try to understand myself.

Eventually, Tony guided me back to my room and stayed talking to me, he was exhausted and in pain, but he had put a smile on my face and soon enough he passed out with me propped up against him and his arm around me. Through his sheer will and determination he had finally broken that nearly fixed frown and in truth for the first time I could actually trust someone.

Ellie and Gale came to see me the next morning to see the exhausted pair fast asleep propping each other up. Ellie was going back home to Zyvala and left me her number, telling me to text her or ring if I needed to talk or fancied a couple of days away with her and her friends. During the next two weeks, I spent a lot of time talking to Tony, slowly revealing myself to him, Gale and eventually Shanky too. Where I was used to people building me up, so that they could watch me fall, it was hard to trust him.

At first, he sat on the other side of my door, talking to me through it, slowly he moved further and further into my room, before I put a chair at the end of my bed for him. Trying to help me understand my conditions and what they meant for me, slowly building my trust in him up as he walked me through what being bipolar really meant, though I was still wary of him. When one night, he asked if I was scared and frustrated about myself, I knew he meant well and my guard dropped and a friendship started to form.

Shanky was one of the first full time residents for the hotel, having spent years drifting round almost every facility in the country, he found himself in Ljianstipol as his last hope of personal salvation. Not long after he moved to the hotel, his bank lost his money while moving his account, unlike most places Tony and Gale let him stay for free while he got back on his feet.

Shanky tried to repay them what he owed them but they refused his money, instead he started to sell his artwork and place the money he made into a hedge fund the pair ran. That fund was there to give people a good start from which many of the guests, residents and myself included have benefited. Money wasn't what Shanky was gifting me though, his gift to me over the duration of my stay would be far more valuable than money, Shanky started to help me to understand who I really was.

Though maybe more importantly, what I really was, slowly he helped me see that I was a victim of a system which was not truly capable of helping me. Just like Shanky I was on the fringe of serious psychological disorders and just like him in the grey area of the healthcare system. Every evening he would come and chat to me about me and eventually he started to share his past with me.

Slowly he started to unpick my inhibitions and fears and started to help me to recover and eventually develop coping mechanisms to try tackle my inner beasts. Helping me to realise that I wasn't alone he started a small fire in my heart when he revealed that he had tipped off Tony the night he broke my door down, as the stench of that dye had him concerned about me. Fearing I might do something to myself or that I already had, he rang Tony who broke my door down and then introduced me to the world, a new and different world of people who cared.

One night after our ice breaking introduction to each other Shanky sat on a chair looking out of the window at the world and started to tell me his real story.

"Life has never been fair to me either, Fae, like you I've had to try harder to do simple things, I struggled to sleep, bouncing off walls and acting crazy to get people to be around me. I got picked on a lot in school, just because they didn't understand me, same way I guess you have with your school life too? Though your dad seems to get you? For me that was my grandmother, she was my saviour and just understood me, she might have been the only person that genuinely made me feel like there was nothing wrong with me?"

"My problems started early though front the age of 7 when I tried to hang myself from a set of swings I got my diagnosis, your problems started when you hit puberty right? Like you though, Fae, I have pretty much been alone all my life as people struggle to be around me for long periods of time, I keep fighting and getting back up though, Fae." He smiled and looked at me as I started to absorb what he was telling me, just listening to him and taking in his advice and stories.

Shanky came and sat one the end of my bed. "You feel abandoned?"

I looked up and nodded back, "The people at school I expected but not my parents? I didn't think they would send me away, just so that they can argue without me being around? Though me and my mother have been arguing a lot, my crashes and episodes were getting worse and lasting longer, she just became my target most of the time, not intentionally, she just timed anything she did or said just wrong enough to unleash my inner rage. Truthfully though, she is the one trying to help me, my dad acts as if nothing is wrong, but it is wrong and getting steadily worse."

Shanky sat thinking while I told him my first truths, "Maybe they just don't want you to hear them talking about how they struggle with you? Maybe they don't want you to start thinking that you are the real problem in their lives?"

Sitting, taking in his thoughts and beginning to think deeper to myself, "I love them both, I know they are going to break up, I just don't want to be the cause of that, their life was better without me around them."

Shanky took me by the shoulders, "Don't ever think like that! You might be the only thing that is keeping them together! You are the only thing they have to fight for and that is what they are doing every time they argue, fighting to keep you in both of their lives!"

I gave him a huge hug as I started to cry, thinking about how I had destroyed my parents' marriage and their love for each other.

Shanky stayed with me that entire night, talking and trying to build me back up, during our talking I discovered that it was his birthday the next day. We went into town and got him a cake to celebrate, while we celebrated his birthday, I let slip that my 18th was soon. Shanky started to get me to attend some of the counselling sessions that were on offer at the hotel, helping me to unpick the network of troubles that were hindering my life.

Sessions helped to unearth my true problems, Shanky, Tony and Gale though were slowly turning me around, growing confident enough to leave both my room and the hotel. Evenings spent with Tony on the roof helped too, he was pretty good to me and he really helped as did Gale, though in a different way. Some nights when I couldn't sleep, I wandered the hallways and rooms of the hotel, finding sleepy staff or night security wandering round the empty expanse of that hotel.

One night though, I could hear noises coming from Gale's Bar, peering through the window Gale at 2 in the morning was playing himself at pool, he saw me looking through the window and waved me in. Gale offered me a pool cue, "But I can't play?" He smiled. "No better time to learn," for the next few hours we played, he beat me every time, though I got better.

Gale explained he suffered from insomnia and often came to this room when he was restless, confessing that the pool table was at the hotel as his wife threatened to leave him if she came down to that table in their house. Tony came in to find us just after 7 in the morning and asked me to help him with Shanky, fearing the worst for my new friend, I followed him through the hotel and towards Shanky's room. Walking in the door to find Shanky had tipped everyone off about my birthday and arranged a small and private party for me, though I didn't want any fuss, having people care enough to throw this little party meant the world to me.

Held in a quiet room upstairs so that the now 18-year-old, frustrated girl in a care home she didn't want to be in and surrounded by people she hadn't wanted to know, would come to realise that she was wanted here and had friends here.

Those four months I spent in Ljianstipol passed quickly, I grew to like the Hotel Davizioso and the town itself, when I came away from there, I had grown and changed. Understanding myself and forgiving myself for what had happened so far in my life, I had moved along and taken a turn, it was a shame that didn't apply to my parents' marriage. Tony and Shanky kept in touch with me too when I first left Ljianstipol, my dad really didn't approve of that, though my mum really did as for the first time I seemed to have actual friends.

Though for my dad, my new friends were going to be the least of his concerns, my time away had made me realise just how hard Mum had been working to help me. Suffering the worst blows my conditions could throw her way, she had worked tirelessly to get me some real help and real answers where my dad had done nothing to help neither me or her.

Returning home, I was going to rebuild the relationship with her that I had all but destroyed with my fits of rage, my dad started to grow angry as we started to rebuild our relationship. Growing more distant he rarely came in the house and started sleeping in a spare room, isolating himself from my mother and almost ignoring me entirely, now it was him who was breaking them apart. Armed with coping mechanisms and a better understanding of who I was, whenever I got angry or crashed, I took myself away for a few hours to give my mind a break, my days of yelling at my mum seemed to be over.

Taking myself away to look at the moon or just feel the wind in my hair seemed to stop my moods swinging wildly and a few hours alone thinking did my mind good too, returning to my house better than I left. Mum was keen to encourage this kind of thing as I was becoming happier and she openly told me that she felt like she had her daughter back, I just thanked her for her years of work to help me.

Mum took me to find different places where I could go and recharge myself, different parks and places, exploring together to find these places of solace for my mind. What though encouraged my mum for my general state, utterly outraged my dad as he didn't want me to be treated like a freak.

While he started to yell at my mum about what she was doing to me, for the first time ever I stood up for her and my dad was in a state of shock and awe as I defended my mum. Finally, he seemed to realise the JaffaCake he had driven away and the JaffaCake he drove back were almost totally different people and he did not like it at all!

Mum had been working with my school to get them to allow me to take my exams from home, she pulled favours with her bosses to try to help me get some kind of chance. Truthfully the school had been pretty good with her, they gave us a laptop so that I could do my exams from home, so that school wouldn't cause any complications, Mum took the month off work so that she could invigilate my exams.

Encouraging me to go further and further and pushing me hard, it wasn't easy for me or her, we yelled at each other, not arguing but just letting out steam before we would both go and sit somewhere outside to laugh off the red mists that crossed us during the day. My final exam was the hardest and I was really struggling, my dad gave my mum a break, he tried to emulate her and tried to encourage me, though instead of encouraging me he was testing my temper.

Slamming his hand on the kitchen table, "You need to push harder Fae!"

I snapped at him, "I'm doing the best I can!" Yelling across the table at him. Starting to cry, "What difference will it make anyway, it's not like any place is going to give me anything more than a crappy job anyway!" I yelled louder at him, crying as deep down I knew it was the most truthful thing I had ever told him.

Dad vanished outside and just left me sitting at the table crying before my mum appeared and stepped in to help me, she helped me finish the exam before my dad reappeared. When he came back in, she scowled at him, "Why did you leave her crying alone!"

He snapped at her, "She yelled at me!"

My mum went on the offensive! "She has yelled at me for six years and you didn't mind? You just hide away outside and act as if nothing is wrong with Fae!"

He looked at her, "There is nothing wrong with her! She's fine now, she doesn't need those friends she met in that horrible town!"

My mother stopped and held her face, "They are the only people who have helped her understand herself, you have done nothing for her by pretending there is nothing wrong with her!" as my dad went to answer her back, I stepped in to defend her again. I stood in front of her as if to shield her from his words, "Mum is the only one who helped me, she has worked tirelessly to help me, you have done nothing, acting as if I am fine, when I'm not fine at all, while you hid away, I took all my problems out on the only person who was helping me."

Dad backed up, "But JaffaCake, she is making out as if you are broken!"

I looked at the floor and took a deep breath before looking back at him, "I was broken until she sent me away and stop calling me JaffaCake! While she suffered you did nothing to help her! You are an arsehole!"

Dad went outside in silence. Mum hugged me and asked me to go upstairs, while she went outside to talk to my dad, sitting in my room on the floor I heard them argue for an hour before he got his coat and keys and drove away.

Around half an hour after he had left, I went back downstairs to find my mum sat at the kitchen table, crying and smoking the cigarettes that she had given up 2 years earlier. Walking over I spoke to her softly, "Mum are you okay?"

She smiled through her pain and took my hand, "Sit down Fae," she gave me a glass and filled it with red wine. "Whatever happens, I need you to know that it's not your fault, I love you and you were the only thing that kept us together," she poured herself another glass. "It's a shame that he didn't try help you more, but he can't keep pretending that there was nothing wrong with you. I didn't want to send you away but you needed help and badly, I didn't want to bury you, especially as he didn't want to admit that everything was fine, it wasn't fine and I guess you just made him realise that," she started to weep again.

I stood and went to comfort her, "He needed to hear the truth, sorry Mum, I didn't mean to make him leave, but I'm not fine, I'm better now but still not fine."

She put her arm round my side and pulled me to her, "We'll be just fine Fae, and it's not your fault, it's his own fault," we stayed there together for the next hour talking about everything and I started to tell her about Tony telling me about her phone calls to him before she sent me away.

Telling her how hearing about them made me realise how tirelessly she had been trying to help me and how it made me realise that my dad was the real problem at home. My mum was different after that night and we spent even more time together, when to my surprise I got my exam results back and they were good, I thanked her for her effort to help me. While my mum helped me get a place at a college in Oured, my dad grew evermore distant from our lives.

Initially, he visited fairly often, he moved into a flat just outside Usted's city centre, gradually his visits waned and he became bitter and twisted at my mum. Every time he bothered to show up, he would make snide remarks at her and each and every shot he fired set me off, we argued more and more until he stopped visiting. Defending her from his continual tirade of nastiness, his last visit was entirely malicious and a deliberate attempt to break our relationship.

Arriving late, drunk and with a girl in his car, he didn't bother coming in the house, instead he handed me an envelope, "Divorce papers for you Mum, something else you destroyed," he snidely grinned as he walked away, reeling at the remark.

"Dad?" He looked round at me. "Just fuck off!" He laughed and got in the car and it was the last time I saw him. I walked in and broke down at the kitchen table, I rang Shanky and he spoke to me while I waited for Mum to get back from work. Just after Shanky hung up, Tony phoned me too, talking to me about what had happened, he offered to come and get me, but I told him I needed to stay for my mum.

Over the next few months, he would come down and visit largely to argue outside with my mum in a series of bitter and public rows. While they argued outside every now and then, he would look at my window to see if I was watching, in the end my mum signed the papers and the bitter breakdown began. From here on in the only time I would hear from my dad was on my birthday and at Christmas, though most of the time any contact would end with crying or anger for me as we grew more distant.

Outside of my deteriorating relationship with my dad things were pretty good, me and Mum were getting along well and with her pushing me I was doing well at college too. Unlike my time at school, I had started to protect myself from the torment that crushed me at school, people from time to time tried to hurt me, but with an understanding of them and myself, these events were rare.

When they did happen, I had picked a venue where I could be happy alone anyway, so when they didn't show or did whatever they had in mind, I was somewhere that I could employ my coping strategies. When these events happened and I went home, me and my mum would laugh about them while drinking wine or beer. My crashes and episodes hadn't gone away at all, in fact while my dad was being so awful, they actually intensified, but unlike before I could cope with them and a phone call away, I had help if I needed it.

Truthfully my bipolar swings were calmer, it was the crashes of depression that were giving me routine problems now. Rationally my changed relationship with my bitter dad was the cause of those, depression fuelling anxiety would send me tumbling from time to time.

While my parents' divorce battle intensified, so too did the nature and style of my crashes, going from extended lulls of mood, to brutal sudden emotional collapses as my mind started to consume itself. In a frank conversation with my mum about how she was coping with the way my dad was now treating her, she confessed openly to me just how much she was suffering.

These arguments took their toll on my mum and their divorce was going to be long and probably quite brutal, she started talking to me about it and asking if I wanted to go away again so that I didn't get any backlash. Spending a night with her showing me what Dad was now sending her by text we started to talk about just how vicious he had become.

Sending her pictures of girls, he was sleeping with all titled "if only you had been her," he was making sure she knew he was moving on, though each girl was different so maybe he was just flashing some cash to them?

During our chat, I rang Tony and started to talk to him while my mum listened in, he immediately offered me a room again, my same room form before next to Shanky. Looking at my poor mum, I put my hand on hers as I asked to have the room for the next 6 months, she smiled as I took myself out of harm's way.

Tony would collect me in three days' time, Mum took me shopping to get me new clothes for my trip while I spoke to my college and explained where I was going. Sure enough, three days later, Gale turned up at our house while my dad was there, Gale guided me to his car and my dad yelled at my mum for sending me away again. While he yelled, I got out of the car, "I'm sending myself away! I don't want to be anywhere near you while you go through this!"

I walked over to my mum and gave her a kiss goodbye. "I love you Mum," she hugged me as my dad snarled at me. "And what about me?"

I looked around, "What about you?" I got back into Gale's car and he drove me away and back to Ljianstipol.

During our drive down I asked if he had heard from Ellie as I had contacted her multiple times and not heard back from her. Gale explained that she had a new boyfriend and he seemed to be quite controlling and like me he didn't hear much from her either, having not spoken for nearly 4 months by this time.

Gale was concerned about her but his concerns had caused a small fallout between them, which was still ongoing. Gale started to tell me more about him, Tony and the Davizioso during the long drive to Ljianstipol.

Gale was an investment banker but then became a property developer in Zyvala after his own investment firm went downhill. Using his banking knowledge to move money around at just the right time meant he often turned large profits on his investments. Tony and Gale had been friends at school after they got into a fight over a girl, they were both chasing after, neither guy got the girl but they found each other.

Friends through school, Gale moved to Ljianstipol to help Tony recover from the loss of his son David, Tony had been on a self-destructive rampage in Ljianstipol until Gale showed up to try and sort him out. Tony was a former footballer and national hero, scouted early in his playing days after he rose quickly at a small local club before being signed to one of the country's biggest teams.

Leading them as captain and helping them win multiple league and cups trophies he was selected for the national squad, when his playing career ended, he became a coach. While coaching a team in Usted, his son had begun a spiral down through depression caused by the media continually hounding him, until one night David killed himself after being discharged from the clinic he had been sent to. Tony quit football immediately and went into a rampage in Ljianstipol gradually drinking and throwing away all his hard-earned money.

Tony's wife Mona asked Gale to step in and help Tony, who was being shielded by a local resident Fabi who had found the drunken hero in a park falling to pieces. Fabi even hid Tony from Gale, until Gale broke down his veil and helped his friend to repair himself. During a drunken night Tony had spoken about making the kind of place where if his son had been sent, he wouldn't have wound up killing himself.

Tony wanted to make a place where people could send their family members or just themselves to get a break, away from the hardships of their daily lives and conditions. Rather than being like a prison like most places were, it would be a totally open house with people able to come and go as they pleased, almost like an all-expenses paid holiday resort?

Gale had found a luxury hotel near the beach which had been bought and sold multiple times, with each owner failing quicker than the last and it was cheap too? Gale talked Tony into investing what little he had left with him and instead of talking about this dream, making the dream into something very real. Gale's financial wizardry would make it hard to fail when backed up by Tony and his nationally renowned status made him the perfect face of the business.

Two months later, the pair bought the Hotel Davizioso and started to make that dream into somewhere very real.

The hotel had been a former exclusive plaything of the old regime and as such was treated to a no expenses spared approach. Where most places had a marble veneer, the Davizioso had inch thick slabs of marble everywhere, thick rich carpets and the finest architecture in the country. When their proposal hit the town, most businesses were sceptical at best, but as they unveiled their plans and how things would run, most places jumped on board.

During a drunken night celebrating the new adventure they dreamt up a wristband system, a simple rubberised band with two chips inside them. One chip was a tracking device so that they could keep tabs on any guests and their location, the other chip could be used with any card system as a means of payment. Linking the system to every bank and major credit card meant that residents wouldn't have to carry money and if they went AWOL, they could be traced quickly from anywhere.

Once the pair submitted the proposal all the town except a few more affluent businesses bought into the scheme. Those bands of course would serve a secondary purpose by allowing people to quickly identify the conditions that the wearer had by the use of a colour coding system.

Every business in Ljianstipol has at least one reference card showing the colours and what they mean, even if there are multiple colours like my band was. One last stipulation the town had was the name and declaration of the business, the town didn't want the place to be labelled as a respite home or health retreat as it might hinder the town's push for tourism and affluent visitors.

Tony and Gale kept the name Hotel Davizioso to appease this concern, though they still got attempted bookings from people unaware that the place wasn't a hotel anymore.

Stopping at a roadside café along the route to Ljianstipol, Gale phoned my mum to see if she was okay, she was shaken by my dad but just asked him to look after me and to tell me she would ring me in a few days. Gale started to talk to me about a few changes that had happened to both the hotel and Ljianstipol since my last visit nearly two years ago. They had expanded the hotel; a nearby smaller place was offered to them and they bought it up to use as staff housing and for guests on shorter stays.

Most of the communal areas had been overhauled and modernised but Gale's Bar was still the same, he liked it how it was. Ljianstipol was growing in both size and popularity, more tourists had started to visit the town and with its popularity came new ideas and needs. Pedestrianisation was starting to happen with the town's roads being turned into walkways now bollards separated the cars and people.

All the roads and surfaces had been changed to be soft touch surfaces so that people could walk barefoot and sit comfortably on the pavement to listen to bands and buskers that now lined the streets. Even the cobbles in the old part of town had been overhauled and been swapped for the soft touch versions, bands had started playing every Sunday in a large park to the north of the town centre.

Ljianstipol had cemented itself firmly into the hearts of a growing number of daydreamers and bohemian visitors all eager to get a slice of the pace of life and laid-back approach it offered.

They had also dreamt up a new venture to help people in town, new visitors or long-term supporters of them, a simple scheme he called 'Pay It Forward'. A system to repay people for the good things they had done for them since they first arrived in Ljianstipol. The idea started round the home of Fabi, the man who saved Tony from himself, with pedestrianisation coming his coffee van would have no customers?

Eventually, he would have to leave Ljianstipol and take both himself and his new girlfriend Alyssia with him, with him having no influence in the town he was in a precarious spot having to choose to remain in ruin or move away. Tony and Gale listened to him and his problems and having been rescued by the man, Tony wanted to help him, but how? Together they dreamt up a simple charitable business, every member paid in and every member was a shareholder, if the business grew it meant that people in the scheme no matter how small, would have a voice in the town.

The money would be managed and manipulated round by Gale before being drawn down annually and then gifting the money back into the scheme or using it to make change happen. The concept was simple, any member could pay it forward for someone, in exchange the recipient would do the same and create a snowball effect of good deeds.

Many people signed up and the scheme rapidly grew to have around 20 members all of whom now had a say in Ljianstipol and the direction it would take in the future.

Fabi, the man who had saved Tony from himself was going to be the first person to benefit from the scheme, just he didn't yet know it. They had been learning about his dreams to have his own shop, a coffee shop built to look like a British post box in honour of his girlfriend.

Gale found out the base of the old monument was for sale and bought it for him and started having it converted into Fabi's dream shop, without him or his girlfriend aware it was happening. Tony and Gale invited him to see the new place being built at the edge of the town, only to discover that he had been given the business he dreamt of. Shanky would be next to benefit from the scheme, with his health deteriorating Shanky was starting to lose his ability to paint and draw.

Tony and Gale knew that if he couldn't produce his art then his mental state might follow his hands only too soon, so they got him a tablet to draw with instead and a large format printer so that he could produce his art for the market stall.

They respected Shanky and he was a member of the scheme before it really existed, all that money he tried to pay them back, they invested into the scheme for him. His real contribution though was being the ears and mouth of support in the Davizioso, whether they employed him or not, he worked for them, helping others to understand themselves. Helping people just like me and just like he had with me saving them from themselves.

Something that I found strange though was that as much as I enjoyed hearing all these new things and changes, I couldn't quite work out why Gale was telling me about these things? Particularly that scheme they now had running to help people make a start in a new home? Maybe Gale was hinting to me about something? Ljianstipol appeared over the horizon as the journey drew to a close but we drove to Gale's home just on the outskirts of Ljianstipol, from here we would continue via golf cart to the Hotel Davizioso.

Bicycles and golf carts were the only vehicles allowed into Ljianstipol's centre, beyond this all access was via foot. Gradually we arrived at the door of the hotel to both Tony and Shanky in waiting, Shanky smiled at me as I got off the gold cart. "Look at you, Fae! You look better than I remember, but my memory isn't that good anymore!" He laughed at me, I laughed back at him, "I missed you too Shanky," he gave me a hug before it was Tony's turn.

Walking over he just wrapped his arms around me. "Good to have you home, Fae," smiled and gave me an envelope, I looked at it, "What's this?" as I opened the envelope and pulled out an x-ray.

He started laughing. "A memory from your last visit," he pointed to the two broken ribs he got after breaking my door down. "Any hair dye, this time?" He smiled at me.

"No, I found better bottles here last time," he hugged me tighter. Shanky started to walk me to my room, right next to his on the top floor, this time I had a new window which overlooked the old part of town and the beach. This room was bigger than my last one and the bathroom had a shower and a big bath too, like a girl's dream!

Tony and Gale greeted me again and gave me my new wristband, still the same purple and blue as before but Shanky had a new colour, waving his arm proudly at me. "I'm worse than before Fae!" Flashing his new turquoise colour at me.

Shanky sat talking to me as I revealed why I was back, him reasoning with me all night that I wasn't the cause of their problems, I wasn't angry anymore, just sad that I broke my parents up. My dad was bitter, really bitter and he used that against me and my mum, sometimes she deserved it but for the most part she was the only reason I wasn't dead.

Sadly, though I loved my dad and his laid-back approach but just as Mum said, he was making things worse by ignoring the problems we had. As much as I hated hearing my mum talk about how the world would see me, deep down she was right, I was a problem and an unjustified risk and people were cruel whether it was intentional or not, just cruel.

Shanky simply put it that, "We are an easy target for people, like we walk around with it written on our foreheads? To the point where we are scared and hide from people and eventually just shut ourselves off from the world. But once after I woke from a coma, a friend whom I thought would never be there, had been sitting with me the whole time, from that day I gave people a chance to be closer to me. About 1 in 50 are good, the rest are out for whatever they can get, no matter how much it breaks you, hurts you or ruins you, you need to stay open for that one person, Fae!"

This little moment would be one of the most significant turning points in my approach to myself.

During my second stay he remembered my damn birthday too! One evening he came to me saying, "There was something up the street I needed to see." I was suspicious at best but we walked up the road to a pair of houses and through a gated garden. Wandering down a little path into a large open garden to be surprised by Tony, Gale and their partners plus a few new people from Ljianstipol. Beer flowed and spirits were high as we celebrated the end of my teenage years, as much as I was annoyed it was a touching return to Ljianstipol and the hotel, once again I had friends.

College, much to my surprise also did something unexpected just after I returned to Ljianstipol, rather than move my exams back a year, they forwarded my grades and I got my qualification while in the hotel. My mum was elated hearing that I had passed the courses and Tony threw a little party in Gale's bar for me to celebrate with me. Summer in Ljianstipol was seeming like a good move, my mum kept in touch about how things were back home, I missed her this time, we had become good friends again since my first visit.

Dad actually tried to visit me, only to be turned away by a very defensive Tony, my dad of course didn't have good intentions for his visit and Tony knew it too. During the evenings we had spent together in his garden on the roof I had told him what my dad had been like since my first visit and since he had walked out on Mum. Tony who had defended my mum on my first stay at the hotel made no attempt to defend my dad and his actions, Tony seemed outraged—that aside from my birthday and Christmas he didn't talk to me at all.

Times had changed though, and throughout that summer I just grew more and more, growing stronger and learning more and more about myself, I hardly used my room, spending more time in the communal areas, I was like a different person. Attending different counselling sessions, I was learning to control things better and things were good, just before the end of August my mum came to visit me. Proudly showing her round and introducing her to this place and all the strange people who had helped me, she was happy to be here.

Staying in a nearby hotel, we met a few times and I showed her round Ljianstipol for her brief stay, the reason for her visit was to see me and to break the news that the divorce was over. Dad had been pushing to get more money and the house but had been refused by the courts and wound up with the car and some of their savings. Dad was going to move far to the north to a little city called Lyaza with a new girl he had met after they broke up.

My mum sat in tears telling me that it was unlikely that I would see him again, taking her hand I smiled at her, "I've got you still Mum," she smiled and gave me a huge hug. I took her to Tony's rooftop garden the night before she went back to show her where I spent most of my time. Tony and Gale joined us for a few beers before she headed back to Oured the next morning, I would head back to join her in October.

Gradually my crashes seemed to dull as well, almost as if my parents finally parting ways somehow gave me relief in my mind? I did attend a few sessions with mentors to see if I could find a reason why they were so violent and so unpredictable? Anxiety seemed to be the reason they thought they might be so bad and the crashes were the final vent before those anxieties passed through me, Shanky thought so too.

Spending more time with Tony and Gale just heightened how pleasant my second visit would be, many evenings watching the sunset from the roof and the odd pool night with Gale into the morning. Life was good for a change and I was starting to feel different about everything, more like there was a light at the end of the tunnel and less like darkness was all I could or should expect?

While time slowly ticked away, my visit to Ljianstipol was grinding to an end and soon it would be time to go and tackle the challenge of adult life. Working life and school life were to be very different and with a positive charge in me for the first time, I felt oddly optimistic as Gale drove me back to Oured. Shanky stayed in touch, I had taught him how to text during our time through summer and not many days passed by where I didn't get something from him. Shanky wasn't alone either, both Tony and Gale stayed in touch as I embarked on my journey into the adult world of work.

First jobs were easily found, I just didn't declare my conditions on my resume, the problem was that if I had an episode or crash at work, I often found myself redundant fairly soon after. Over that first year in the working world, I just about managed to last 2 months at any job I found, eventually I started putting my conditions on the resume, at least if they knew, they couldn't fire me, right? Wrong! Very wrong! Most of the interviews I had went well, well at least until they saw those words at the bottom of my resume as they read, 'Bipolar Disorder and Depression' my resume was in the bin, no matter how kindly they phrased their rejections letters.

Every once in a while, though I would catch a break and find something, generally lackie work where I was kept distanced from the other people I worked with. A few times I wondered if this was so that I couldn't pass my problems round like the flu, of course with most of these jobs a crash or two and I was job hunting again. While my working life was scraping along, my dad had married some girl he met, the sick bastard invited me to his wedding? Like I wanted to go to that!

My mum was happy he had moved on as at least now he had started to leave her alone; my mum had started seeing a new guy from her office. Ashleigh or just Ash for short, he was pretty cool in truth and they were both respectful about me, almost too respectful in truth as they started courting more frequently.

Eventually, my mum broke the awkward news that rather than have Ash move in with us, she was going to try living with him, not every day but a few days a week, almost grooming me to be at home alone. At first, she would spend a night a week with him gradually this became 3 or 4 nights a week and slowly she started to move out, spending less time at home. Seeing her happy again was nice, even if it felt odd to be home alone so often, but I wouldn't have wanted her to throw away a chance with a nice guy for me!

We had a few heart-to-heart chats and she revealed her plans to me, she would eventually move in with him just after Christmas and the house would be mine unless things didn't work out. Ash was pretty honourable too, he even asked my permission to propose to my mum on Christmas Day, of course I let him, I hoped they would be happy and at 23 I would have my own house.

Christmas Day he popped the question and Mum bawled her eyes out as she agreed and then moved in with him in the new year, they visited me every weekend, taking me for meals or shopping, stuff like that. In the shadows though my mind was ticking away, almost unnoticeably changing, while my mother's new happier life began a new side of my conditions appeared.

Work was the venue for the first of these new spasm like crashes, violent and uncontrollable shakes would send me falling to the floor, like a seizure, but instead of being out of control, I was very much aware of them. During January, a local packaging company had needed an office body, I needed the money and applied, much to my surprise they took me on and soon put me on their sales floor. Only telesales and selling cardboard packaging but it was the best job I had been given up to this point.

My manager had a sister who suffered from depression so he was pretty understanding and knew sometimes that I would just be unable to really work, so I was pretty lucky really. One day during lunch, I had a crash in my booth and just hunched over my desk, unable to function, he took me home and assumed I would be back in the morning.

While he drove away my crash intensified, my mind started throwing itself around and a huge wave of anxiety kicked in as I started thinking about the things people had done to me in my school years. Thinking about the times I was left alone to suffer as my tormentors laughed at how pathetic I was, it set a cycle going in my mind. A cycle which continued for 3 more days, my boss wasn't angry at me for missing work though he did seem quite concerned about me.

When Mum found out, she and Ash came to see me and make sure I was okay, which when they arrived, I was fine, the problem was these new crashes had no start point and no end point. Moments before I would just feel a twitch on my lip or eye and soon after I would be going down, with seemingly no trigger or start point, they were actually quite scary.

Over the next year, they would happen once a month on average, sometimes lasting hours and sometimes days, but my boss was okay with that, or so it seemed? Taking me for a meeting in his office he gave me a business card for a therapist he knew, he signed me up for a free session to try to help me. Seemingly going well, the therapist was pretty good, until I crashed in his office! However good he was at talking, he couldn't walk the walk as he phoned other specialists to try help him bring me round.

Police came and took me home, escorting me from his luxurious office and consultancy room, they left me in my home, where I stayed for the next week. During my low time, I found a website with a forum and started to delve for answers here, my coping mechanisms didn't seem to help with it and they seemed to be getting worse.

Starting to talk to a few people online helped, though sifting through the internet trolls was no fun! People actually signed up to the website so that they could mock people? Really? Buried amongst it all, I met a few people in other countries who slowly started to help me, much the same way Shanky had during my first talks with him. Gradually it seemed likely that the sudden change from a bustling home to an empty and often negative memory box might be a big part of my new strange crashes, coupled with growing loneliness and dropping self-esteem.

Guys had often been something that didn't happen for very long with me, the trail of destruction they left when they dumped me often ran deep. No matter how hard they started out a good episode or crash would generally send them packing and taking what little confidence they had given me with them. I had a few boyfriends over the last year, most faded quickly, some managed to last a month or so until my own anxieties would push them out. Work had given me a few friends who came over once in a while or met at bars, but life was lonely, my only friends really were Mum and Ash, with Christmas approaching we had a shopping day planned.

Meeting her in Usted for a shopping day before Christmas, we spent hours wandering shops together before Ash joined us for lunch to break the news that they would be going away for Christmas. We had a great day shopping and spirits were high as I started to walk to catch the bus back home to Oured, when it dawned upon me that at 25 life was about to get much lonelier!

Chapter 2
A Hope for Tomorrow

Having spent those few precious hours with my mum and Ash shopping before Christmas in Usted, my spirits soon slumped on that bus journey back home to Oured. Unlike any previous Christmas, this year I would be entirely alone, my dad hadn't been around for years, in truth I didn't ever hear from him anymore, since he moved and remarried, I was lucky if I got a card turn up from him, even if she had written it for the bitter bastard. Mum and Ash were going away for the Christmas period, their late honeymoon after they tied the knot during the summer, at least we went shopping though? Having slowly prised my parents apart this year for the first time I would experience the loneliness of an empty and quiet house at Christmas time.

Hours seemed to tick by as I slumped looking out of that bus window, when I noticed a foul smell and strange smell? Amidst my own self-created gloom, that smell seemed to be even worse. All the pretty scenery was being obscured by the rain and the condensation from my breath, what a miserable bus ride! Finally, the torturous bus ride came to an end, the walk home seemed longer due to the rain and my mood wasn't helping either.

My thoughts were clouding me nearly as much as the rain, maybe it was time for a change? Not just a change, a huge change, though that smell seemed to be stalking me? Maybe I had got something on my clothes? Debating in my mind what that smell might be as my journey home was coming to an end.

Finally reaching my house through the rain and cold, well my parents' house really, just now they had flown the nest and left me behind. Opening the door and putting the bags from Mum and Ash on the kitchen table and just slouched on the sofa looking at the ceiling. Exhaling a huge sigh to myself, "Fae, what are you going to do now? You have no one now?" My mind was crushing me and guilt over the past and what I had done to my family was never far from my mind. Slowly running over all the arguments, I had with Mum and Dad, that ominous and noxious smell had grown stronger. I went upstairs and changed my clothes before tossing my clothes and that smell into the washing machine and resumed my spot on the sofa.

Gradually, my mind mulled over that day my dad walked out on us, I remember Mum sending me upstairs while she finally told my dad those home truths that sent him packing in that huge row they had. It wasn't just my mum of course that day was the first time I stood up for her and all she had done for me, when I turned on my dad, he really didn't like that.

I remember waiting to come downstairs to find her smoking and drinking in realisation of what had just happened to her marriage. My guilt at finally tearing them both apart has never eased, they both said it was always going to happen but I never believed that and have never forgiven myself for breaking up their previously joyous marriage. While my mind bothered me that smell came back, I took one of my dreads and ran it through my fingers.

"Maybe these need to change Fae? Are you really this girl anymore?" Talking to myself and thinking out loud. Suddenly, I found the source of that god awful smell! My dreadlocks had been my style of choice for 8 years now and they stank! Even the blue dye couldn't mask that odour, no wonder it had faded!

Washing them didn't help, if anything it made it worse, it was time for a pro's help! Three long hours I spent ringing different salons to have them sorted out but with Christmas just two days away nobody could fit me in. Standing in front of a large mirror in my lounge, I looked at myself, "Fae this isn't you anymore!"

I looked through a drawer, found some scissors and got to work, carefully cutting them out one by one my dreadlocks fell to the ground like little faded blue snakes. Admiring my handy work, it didn't seem too bad, especially after a thorough wash or two, well until the next morning. "What have you done, Fae!" Thankfully my mum got me a beanie hat for Christmas, I guess that present needed to be opened early.

Christmas Eve I was going to meet some colleagues, it should have been a nice evening, only it became obvious that I was being avoided by my boss? Eventually, he told me that I was being made redundant, he couldn't handle the workload caused by my crashes and episodes.

Then again, he wasn't alone in that, my parents struggled with them so I didn't really blame him for giving up on me, he had been good to me over the last nine months. Christmas so far was turning into a total disaster, I got home and just sat on my sofa and cried, I had never felt so alone and it seemed like the entire world was having a party at my expense.

While sitting on the sofa, I looked over at a picture of me with Tony from my first visit to Ljianstipol and the Davizioso. Hauling myself off the sofa, I collected the picture and took it back to join me in my misery. I slumped back and held that picture up, remembering that day 8 years ago only too well, it was the day after Tony broke my door down thinking I was attempting to kill myself. Tony had sat with me all night and helped dye the same dreadlocks I so willingly cut off last night and just talked to me. Tony was exhausted but when he realised that during the month, I had been there I hadn't left the hotel and barely left my room, the next day he changed that.

That morning Tony threw me my hoodie. "Come on, I've got so much to show you!" He took my hand and stood me up before he took me to see Ljianstipol for the first time. Our first port of call was to go visit a strange coffee van parked just outside the market square, introducing me to the wonders of global coffee but then he hadn't slept so who could blame him!

Walking me into the newer parts of town, he took me shopping before we stopped for lunch by the river, only burgers and beer but set against the backdrop of that river in the mid-April sun, it was very pleasant. Next, we headed down the river to the old part of town, the former plaything of the fallen regime. Asphalt turned to age old cobbles in this high-end part of town, with a market in the square, artisans and buskers littered the streets, selling artwork, pictures, craft items along with the hopes and dreams that went with them.

Seemingly spending hours here before Tony got me a bracelet made from upcycled, coloured guitars strings. Introducing me to a seemingly quite rude Parisian, getting him to take this picture of me and Tony on our little jaunt together. Finally, he showed me the beach and a park between the beach and market square with a fountain of thought in it.

What stood out so much about this photo? Tony was clearly suffering from a lack of sleep and his ribs hurt too, but through his sheer determination, I was smiling? Sitting thinking about that first day trip in Ljianstipol and how much he really needed to sleep and of course he had broken his ribs! Tony had been good to me during my first stay at the Hotel Davizioso, he had really brought me out of myself, not just him or course, but he really worked on me. Most people gave up quickly but not Tony, he just kept working on me until I finally succumbed to him. Sitting thinking and smiling about him and that day, it started to dawn upon me. Maybe? Just maybe? Ljianstipol could be the place to begin a new life? A life away from my dark past and this reputation that clings to me? A place to make a fresh start!

Christmas Day, I woke up charged to look for a place to start my new life, Mum said if I moved, I could keep the proceeds from the house and I hadn't heard from Dad since last year, so I guess he wouldn't mind? Hours passed while I scrolled through lists of houses before I found it! Just outside of the town a big three-bedroom house, with a nice garden and maybe 10 minutes' walk to the pedestrianised town. Maybe Christmas alone had turned out to be a good thing, but I wanted to see what they both thought, it had been a year since me and Dad last spoke.

Shaking at the thought of what he might say I called him and he answered straight away, "JaffaCake! Merry Christmas!" We spoke for half an hour and his response was typical of the man I used to know, "Go for it JaffaCake! You might even have something left over afterwards." Though that laid-back and carefree style might just be what really broke him and my mum apart! Mum was supportive too though had the usual loving apprehension I adored her for. "Maybe a fresh start wouldn't be a bad thing?" Though she did seem quite happy when I sent her a picture of my new hairdo! "I've got my girl back!" She laughed as her and Ash rang to wish me Merry Christmas.

Suddenly, amidst the despair of spending Christmas alone, deep down I found myself dreaming and hoping? Both feelings I had long forgotten since my visits to Ljianstipol and the reality of living in a world that simply saw me as a problem had kicked in. The entirety of this town knew about me and my problems and dark past and they seemed to haunt me wherever I went. Maybe in a town slightly more understanding I could finally get a break from that and maybe if I was lucky, I might even get the chance in life that I so desperately needed?

Christmas Day was my break point, I had set my mind to moving away and starting a new life. Ljianstipol wasn't exactly unknown to me and I remember fondly it's laid-back and calm environment. When the morning came, I was going to contact estate agents and begin the process of escaping this place and starting afresh in Ljianstipol.

Dreams are strange things though, they can introduce us to new thoughts and ideas, however they can also remind us of our deepest fears. I spent the last few hours of Christmas Day starting to pack my past away into boxes, readily awaiting the next morning so that I could begin my escape. My bedroom wall was still adorned with pictures of people that I thought were my friends from my youth. Carefully unpicking them from their wall tack, I found myself gradually filtering them into the bin.

I won't let this happen again, I thought to myself as I dreamt about some of the awful things these people had done in the past. Nights sat alone in awful places with no company but my tortured mind tearing away at my self-confidence and self-belief as these people led me to places only to see how far I would fall when it dawned upon me that I was totally alone.

Most people never knew the full extent of how much these people tortured and tormented me over the years, not even my parents really knew, though it wasn't like I wanted people to know just how deep the cuts they gave me truly were. Ljianstipol wasn't going to be like that though, deep down, somehow, I knew in my heart it would be different, now I just had to convince my mind of that fact.

While I packed my life away into boxes, forces in the background seemed to conspire to help me as I got a phone call from the estate agents. On 30 December, I had three people come to view the house and soon after a little bidding war began between them. This former family home situated just outside of the city was in a prime location for the slightly more discerning homeowner or businessman that wanted to be near the city but far enough away to escape the noise, dirt and congestion.

On 2 January, that bidding war culminated with the house selling for 20000 euros more than it was on the market for, that same day I put in an offer on the house in Ljianstipol and fortunately for me it was accepted immediately.

My new home had cost me 35000 euros less than my house sold for so not only would I be moving to Ljianstipol, I would also have enough to be able to gradually find work instead of just taking the first job I might get offered.

Hours after my offer was accepted, I phoned Mum and then phoned Dad, both were happy for me and offered to help if I needed it, but I wanted to do this alone, this was going to be my first 'Fae' thing. I spoke to the new owners a couple of times to see if they wanted all the appliances that were in the house, they were a young couple with a baby on the way, it seemed they could benefit from them? They offered to pay for them but I told them to accept them as a housewarming gift.

When the removal vans turned up, they packed what was left of my family life into the back of two vans and headed to Ljianstipol with my keys in hand. I stayed behind and had one last walk around my family home and it's tainted past, measuring myself against the height chart on the door frame my parents had made, as it turned out, without dreads I had grown an inch?

I left a little card on the kitchen worktop for the new owners, wishing them good luck with their baby and marriage. As they arrived on the driveway, I was weeping inside as I gave them the keys to my family home and with it my past. They gave me a lift to catch the bus to Ljianstipol. They were nice and I hoped they would be happy there, just as happy as I would be in Ljianstipol and my new home.

Waiting for the bus to Ljianstipol in the sunshine for half an hour seemed a fitting end to my time here in Oured, this bus journey would be the shortest five hours of my life. Sitting alone looking out of the window, I struggled to contain myself and my joy as the bus wound its way through the streets of Oured and out into the countryside.

Crossing the boundary out into the new world a deep smile filled my face as the thrill and happiness of this new life and new hope I was creating for myself finally dawned upon me. Mile after mile, my mind had become enriched and a deepening happiness was filling me. Halfway through the journey we stopped at a roadside service station, even the filthy toilet floors couldn't dampen the joy saturating my heart.

Though maybe I shouldn't have got a burger and takeaway sandwich from there, it turned out their mayonnaise might have seen better days! My stomach definitely churned after eating that chicken and mayonnaise sandwich, at least they couldn't pollute the bottle of cola I used to wash away their sins.

After a few more hours on the coach, in the distance, I could make out the coast and the town which was about to become my new home. Ljianstipol was growing closer and as we drew nearer; my excitement was exploding throughout my mind and across my face.

Passing by farms on the outskirts of the town as we began to venture deeper into the curious south coastal town, passing by parks and beautiful homes as the bus station on the fringe of the town drew closer. Practically leaping off the bus, I collected my suitcase and started to try and navigate my way towards my new home.

Rapidly I discovered that my inbuilt intuition wasn't quite the navigational tool that I hoped it was, thankfully a kind barista pointed me in the right direction. Fifteen minutes walking and I found myself arriving at my new home with the removal driver waiting for me. My first steps into my new life were joyful as he showed me what they had done with my furniture, handed me my keys and left me to start my new journey.

Colour schemes and plans started to fill my mind as I took the first views of my new home and life. Venturing into the garden for the first time, far down the end was a blossom tree with its pink flowers just starting to appear. One useful thing I did get at that stop on the bus journey was some beer, I sat outside and watched the sky turn orange as I toasted to celebrate my new life in Ljianstipol.

Maybe for the first time in years I felt the glimmer of hope again and excitement at the prospects of my new life. A life away from the stigma and prejudice that had marred my life, an open doorway and a fresh start. Christmas on my own as it turned out had proven to be one of the best things that ever happened to me.

I woke in the morning just in time to see the sunrise over Ljinastipol, it was almost as if the universe conspired that morning to tell me I had done the right thing. Looking out the window to see the shadows gradually vanish as the sun casted it's glow across this new and wonderful land. Light dancing across the buildings and streets with the beach glistening in the distance, what a day to be alive!

Ljianstipol had been changing since I last visited, having become a popular destination for tourists and dreamers, dreamers just like me today. Dressing myself eager to go and explore the town and see just how different it was to what I remembered, I couldn't wait to get stuck in.

Casting one last look in the mirror before I started my adventure, I put my beanie hat on, I wasn't brave enough to confess to a hairdresser why my head looked so strange. At first, it didn't seem too bad but as time passed my hair grew oddly and in clumps, I needed to get that fixed too, even if it meant telling someone why it looked so strange! With my shroud on my hair, I set off down the street to begin my new adventure in my new home, my first port of call was a cup of coffee!

Walking through the streets and towards the start of the pedestrianised area, I came across a coffee shop just inside the bollards and like a gateway to the shops. Leaning up against the wall smoking a cigarette was the barista that had given me directions!

He looked up and smiled. "You found it then?"

Smiling back to him, "Yes thanks, I was totally lost!" He laughed.

"Yeah, no problem, what can I get for you?" I studied his menu.

"Can I get a mocha please? And thanks again!" He started to make me a coffee, "So are you new to Ljianstipol?" I leant against his counter.

"Yeah, I just moved yesterday from Oured," he popped my coffee on the counter. "Nice to meet you I'm Fabi and welcome to Ljianstipol," he put his hand out to me.

"Nice to meet you Fabi, I'm Fae," I shook his hand. Fabi walked round the front and offered me a seat and sat down to introduce himself and the town to me. "Have you visited before, Fae?" I came over shy.

"Yes, twice before, I was at the Hotel Davizioso."

He looked at me. "There's no shame in that Fae, welcome back! Was the town pedestrianised the last time you were here?"

I felt good knowing at least to this one person my past wasn't an issue. "They had just put the bollards up; this shop wasn't here though? What is it?"

Fabi stood up and patted the wall. "It's a British post box, my wife Alyssia is British so it's in her honour!" The red and black coffee shop stood proudly at the entrance to the town and clearly it looking as it did meant a lot to him, "My wife runs the gallery in the market square, so if you get lost, go there and say hello and introduce yourself to her." He smiled at me.

"Thanks, how much do I owe you for the coffee, Fabi?" He raised his hand to me.

"No, this one is on me, welcome to Ljianstipol and it's nice to meet you Fae," I offered money and he refused it, instead he gave me his phone number? "If you get stuck or need anything, just let me know Fae."

I sent him a text and he sent one back and sent one to his wife. "I've asked her to keep an eye out for you Fae, so drop by and say hi to her!" Fabi shook my hand once again as I headed to explore the town.

Wandering the new part of town, this seemed largely the same, different shops and more eclectic cafes and restaurants but the same kind of feel as it had before. All the shops were quite nice and the now car free streets had buskers and odd pop-up shops along the main walks.

Spending a few hours here I stopped to get a sandwich before walking to the old part of town. Walking along the river had changed, the railings had been swapped and looked nice, twisted and rusted metal had been replaced with soft and smooth concrete walling. Easily I could imagine sitting on there overlooking the river as it gently flowed by below with birds and fish fuelling the imagination even more.

The bridge crossing the river had also changed, as sculpted concrete and railings filled with padlocks had replaced the rusted metal of my previous visit. Wandering down along the river, even the paths had been updated and little spots to sit and think or for couples to show their affections had been created, it was quite serene.

Walking up the steps into the old part of town even this had changed, the cobbles were fresher and that market square now had a little fountain in it. Walking in and out of the hidden alleys to unveil more unusual and quirky shops, though down here window shopping was my option!

While wandering the cobbles, I did see the gallery Fabi had mentioned but it was busy inside so I headed back home instead of bothering his wife. Though it was nice to have met someone so early on, deep down I wanted to start unpacking my boxes that sat in my home.

Wandering slowly back through the streets and out of town towards my home felt exhilarating and I didn't know why but somehow, I just knew I would be happy here? During the evening I began the process of unpacking all the boxes which contained my past into my future. Combing through my old books and photo albums, photos of my family life before my problems even began.

Each childhood memory gave a glimpse of the life and the Fae that only me and my parents remembered. Pictures of me and my mum before my problems began and before they slowly tore my family apart.

Dwelling upon those fond but distant memories of being a happy 11-year-old girl in a picture of me on a bench at night, my mum loved that picture. Though that picture was also sad for her as it was the first day, she got a warning sign that things weren't right. We had gone on holiday, Dad felt unwell that day so we spent the day together, Mum worried I had the same illness as Dad as I was just off all day, distant from her.

Mum said I just wasn't really there with her that day, almost lost in thought and oddly subdued all day until she took me to sit under the moonlight, then suddenly I perked back up. Mum always said the only thing she really lost when my problems began was her little girl, those sweet cheeks and cute hair.

Maybe now in a new life I could bring that girl that my mum missed so dearly back? Not just for her but for me too, I would love to be that girl again and maybe get that hairstyle again someday. Ljianstipol had saved me from myself before so maybe this time it could help me to rediscover someone so long lost that only my mum and me knew she had ever existed.

A rare opportunity to reimagine the girl I had become over the years and just change everything that I had lost over the years. I gave that picture Mum loved so dearly pride of place on my sideboard in my lounge and sent Mum a picture of it sat proudly in my lounge, she responded of course, "I always loved that picture," and I replied back to her, "I always loved you Mum." Rebuilding my life in Ljianstipol was going to be a challenge but one I welcomed openly and readily wanted, with what little pieces of my past I had brought with me unpacked it was time to begin that new chapter of my life.

During my first few days I explored more of Ljianstipol, finding a small park near my home and a hardware store just outside the main town. Decorating and reshaping my home would be all I really did for a couple of days, though I did make visiting Fabi for coffee my new morning routine. Fabi was the first person I met after moving and his coffee shop wasn't far away either, his coffee was legendary too.

His shop which was made to look like a British post box stood like a beacon in the street and once he got to know people, he would have their coffee ready and waiting for them. During my first few days, I spent an hour a day just talking to him and learning about him and how Ljianstipol had changed since I last visited.

A few days after I met him, he surprised me as he gave me a cup with a green ribbon on it and in support of mental health charities. Unlike many businesses which just expanded, Fabi used his success to do charitable things and those cups and mental health charities were now going to receive cuts of every cup he sold. Every morning though in those early days something perplexed him, even in near 30-degree heat, I wore that beanie hat? Every morning he would ask, "When am I going to see those gorgeous locks, Fae?"

Naturally I didn't want to tell him the truth or show him what I had done to myself and I hadn't found a barber shop here yet.

April had turned to May on my fourth day of my new life and this morning was hot! Really hot, yet as always, I walked to see Fabi with my beanie hat covering my shame. While I walked down, there was a woman standing with him this morning? Leant up against his shop smoking and talking to her, he waved as he caught sight of me walking towards him and his coffee.

Fabi introduced the slender and blonde-haired beauty to me as his wife Alyssia, she was a magnificent looking lady too, tall and fair skinned. Alyssia began to talk to me as Fabi prepared my coffee, she had been keeping an eye out for me in her gallery after being told there was a new friend in town.

While I introduced myself to Alyssia, Fabi swiped my hat off my head revealing the disaster I had made on my head. Truthfully, I would have felt more comfortable standing in that street naked than I did with that awful hair on show for the world to see.

Alyssia scowled at him, "Fabi! Give that back, you've upset our new friend!" Clipping him round the ear.

"Sorry Fae, he's a twat!" as she apologised to me for him.

While I stood waiting for his laughter, I noticed he was analysing me, stood with my hat in his hand, "Did you do this to yourself Fae?" I shyly nodded back at him.

Pressing his hand to his face, "We can fix this, Fae? Then your hair will match those pretty eyes?"

Feeling encouraged, I nodded back at him. Fabi asked me to meet him at his shop that evening and they would help sort my disaster zone head out for me.

Having spent the afternoon in my garden I wandered down to meet Fabi at his shop, he walked me to his place just out of town to meet his waiting wife Alyssia. Walking into their kitchen to be greeted by her with a beer in hand and one waiting for me, she sat me on a chair. Naturally expecting Alyssia to be doing my hair, she pointed to Fabi as he wandered in the room with scissors and a trimmer in hand.

Fabi started to cut away at my hair explaining he was a barber before he developed a deep love for coffee, pastries and talking. While he got to work, Alyssia started to talk to me about my past and where I was working, as I told her about myself, "Ah you are why he has got those new cups!" She smiled.

Fabi was still cutting away as Alyssia vanished? Returning to question me. "Did you want an interview at the Hotel Davizioso, Fae?"

I smiled back, "Tomorrow? Sure!"

She started talking and arranging for me to go for an interview on Thursday. Alyssia returned, "Do you have a jacket or suit Fae?"

Before I could say a word, "Ah just go as you are Tony and Gale don't care about fancy clothes, they care about people," Fabi butted in.

Alyssia rolled her eyes at him, "A good impression never hurt, Fabi."

Fabi finished my hair, having shaved the sides and cutting an intricate flower into one of the sides. Fabi started to colour my hair for me in purple, blue and turquoise while Alyssia started to offer up blouses for me to wear to my interview. Alyssia handed me a blouse and jacket. "Do you know where it is, Fae?"

Feeling embarrassed, "Yeah, I kinda stayed there a few times," she smiled. "At least you know what others are going through, Fae," reassuring me. Fabi finished my hair for me and as I left asked one sole thing of me. "Leave the haircuts to me next time Fae," he and Alyssia wished me luck for my interview.

Walking home with my hair proudly on show for the first time in six months felt incredible, as the warm air and sea breeze blew my locks round my face. Life in Ljianstipol was already seeming to be very good, though I was nervous about my interview tomorrow, I hadn't expected to be thinking about a job yet let alone working at the Davizioso.

Wondering if they would recognise or remember me? As I made my way through streets and back to my home. Carefully hanging the blouse and jacket that Alyssia had given me up so that it didn't get crumpled or creased. Dreaming to myself as I sat in my lounge and dwelt upon my fond memories of both Tony and Gale, just maybe that dream was going to be reimagined and start all over again?

Morning soon came and with it an unexpected phone call from my dad! I started to show him pictures of my new home and my new haircut too. Dad as always was filled with that usual laid-back optimism he always had and when I told him that I had an interview at the Davizioso, his reply was touching, "You are as qualified as any to work there, Fae."

We had gradually been talking more and rebuilding the bridges between each other that had crumbled away over the years, it was good to speak to him too, as just like my mum I missed him. Before I headed for coffee and my interview, I rang my mum too and gave her the same tour of my home and my hair. "That looks more like my little girl," she happily told me on the phone.

Wishing me luck with my interview and shedding a tear as I showed her where I had put the photos of us from my childhood round my home. Meeting Fabi for my morning coffee, he gave me back my beanie hat.

"Hopefully you will only need this if it gets cold now Fae," he smiled as I thanked him for sorting my hair out. Wishing me luck as I walked down the streets and towards the river for my date with destiny. Excitement and fear both filled me as I wandered along the river towards the Hotel Davizioso, the last time I saw this place was as a patient.

Walking through the doors and heading to reception, I was greeted by two young girls, a shy looking girl with glasses came out from behind the desk to lead me. Walking the old halls of my past as she guided me to a large foyer upstairs, she took up position behind a desk as I sat on a chair waiting to be called in.

When called, I walked into the room and there at the back sat two guys, one with a half open white shirt, cargo trousers and sunglasses, the other in a short sleeve shirt, jeans with slicked back hair. The guy in the white shirt pointed at his friend.

"He's Gale and I'm Tony, did you want anything to drink before we start?" He opened a fridge and took out 3 beers, opened them and offered one across the table, I took it for liquid courage!

Gale was looking through my resume when he paused and showed it to Tony, pointing to the bit near the bottom of the page. My heart began to sink as they pointed, this was how all my interviews went, they came to my health problems and my interview was over. Whether they told me at the time or not the interview was over and I was used to it happening.

Tony took my resume and leant back to whisper to Gale, looking round and dropping his sunglasses to look over the top. Gale took one last look at Tony and leant back to whisper to him again, looking back round at me before they both settled back down.

Tony started removing his sunglasses, "What happened to your dreads Fae?"

Gale leant in, "Didn't you have blue dreadlocks, Fae? Though I know that was nearly what 6 years ago now?"

Calmness came over me. "You remember me then? They started to smell when it rained so I cut them out," exhaling my fears as I spoke to them.

"Now you have a Fabi special?" Tony asked as he chuckled at me.

"It suits you though, Fae."

Gale took my resume back, "I suppose you thought that this was over when we read about your problems?"

I nodded back, "It's how they normally go, they see I'm bipolar and depressive and I go in the bin."

Gale frowned, "We know, we don't want people who are good on paper, we employ people and you have a set of skills which make you unique here, Fae."

Tony joined in, "You took the beer too, so we know we can break bread with you, you know what some of our patients are going through too and you have first-hand experience of mental health conditions and this place. You know first-hand what we try to do for people with problems," he sat back and smiled.

"Do you remember the code for the garden?" I sat back thinking about the code to his secret garden he had given me eight years ago.

"1604," he smiled. Gale stood up and Tony joined him too as I sat puzzled.

"It's nearly 35 degrees in here, it's sunny outside and we have cold beer, you really wanna sit here in the dark alone Fae?"

I stood to join them, they took more beer and led the way, "If the code is right the job is yours."

Tony smirked as he led us to the garden. We approached the coded door Tony pointed at it, "Moment of truth Fae!" My fingers were sweaty with fear.

"You nervous?" Tony said, as I punched in the code.

"How could I forget the date of your son's birthday?" I smiled at him as I pushed the door open.

"Lead the way then, I don't wanna drop these," Tony said as we walked out onto his rooftop garden. Walking us down a bamboo pathway my memories of this garden started to flood back of the evenings we spent here watching the sunset. Walking down the path to that pergola sitting over the little pond.

"Take a seat, Fae," Gale opened his arm and guided me to seat.

"It's just as beautiful as I remember," I smiled as Gale handed me another beer.

Gale sat down. "You were our first young guest Fae, we hadn't been running long when you first visited us, did your parents ever work things out?" I sighed. "No, they never did, they still talk but only if they have to."

Tony looked at me. "Sorry to hear that Fae, they were good people."

Gale looked over. "How long have you been here, Fae?"

I smiled. "Under a week, I moved away to make a fresh start for myself away from Oured and my history and reputation."

Smiling to them both, "Well then today is going to be the first day of that new start, is Monday to Thursday good for you? Say 8 until 4 with an hour for lunch?"

Tony dropped his glasses to see my reaction. As his words sank in, I just pointed at myself in shock, "You mean it? You want me to work here? Me? But what if I have an episode or crash?"

Gale looked at me. "Then send us a text with a frowny face and stay home, send us a smiley face when you are coming back in," Gale gave me their numbers and we sent each other a text to make sure we had them. "Monday then, Fae?"

I nodded at Gale and shook their hands, "Thank you so much for this chance, how will I repay you for this?"

Gale shrugged his shoulders, "Easy, repay us by using your experiences to help other people?"

Tony nodded and patted me on the back, "Welcome back Fae, we should toast to celebrate," they clinked their bottles with me.

"Cheers," both smiling away. I sat with them bursting at the seams with excitement that someone had given me a chance and overlooked my problems. Not just overlooked them, but here they were seen as a potential strength, no matter what I wasn't going to fail myself or their faith in me.

Just as we finished our toast, Tony asked, "You heading back to Fabi's on your way home, Fae?"

"Yes, I walk past his place to get home, how come?" I asked back.

"Would you take him this bag of coffee, it's way too strong for me! Unless you want to try it?"

Tony handed me a large bag of coffee and shook my hand, "See you Monday Fae, text us if there are any problems." Gale shook my hand as I left.

Heading away shocked, excited and with a jump in my step, for the first time someone had seen beyond my problems to the girl underneath. Those guys were totally different to what I had expected but their faith in me was a turning point in my life.

Walking through the town to Fabi's shop, but he had closed early? I headed to their door and Alyssia opened the door with a pensive smile on her face, "Well?" She said nervously. I looked down at the floor, she leant over to give me a hug.

"They gave me a chance!" I screamed at her in excitement, she grabbed hold of me. "That's wonderful news, Fae!" She yelled upstairs.

"Fabi, get down here and buy this girl a drink to celebrate!"

I could hear him running down the stairs. "You got the job, Fae!" He came out and hugged me too.

"I'll get my coat; you deserve a beer or three!" I handed him the bag of coffee from Tony. "Hmm you can try that in the morning but tonight we celebrate your new start," he popped the bag inside the door and off we went into town.

Heading down into the town and towards the river and its selection of nice bars that adorned its banks, Alyssia picked the place and we enjoyed some beautiful crisp local beer. Not only had I now found some friends and found a job but I was also starting to create the new life for myself that I hoped this move would give me.

Alyssia winked at me. "You better keep hold of that jacket and blouse, you might need them on Monday," as we sat talking and breaking bread as new friends in Ljianstipol, my new home.

Friday morning, I woke with an untameable smile, I looked in the mirror and saw that same happy girl that Mum missed so dearly looking back at me. Someone had given me a chance, not just a chance but a huge opportunity to prove myself. My head was a little sore thanks to Fabi and Alyssia but in a good way, it felt good to be heading in the right direction, but one thing was troubling me? What did I need to wear for work? I didn't want to text Tony or Gale to ask them, how silly would that look? So instead, I headed to see Fabi for coffee, maybe he would have an idea?

I headed down the street in the morning sun feeling optimistic and hopeful, this wasn't a feeling I was accustomed to but I hoped it would become common. As the shadows began to vanish amid the sun's rays, I began to walk to Fabi's odd coffee shop, he was leaning against the wall, one hand in his pocket and a cigarette in the other.

He dipped his sunglasses to me. "Morning, Fae! How are you feeling this morning?"

I shook my head at him, "You seem to have coped better than me or Alyssia," he started to laugh as he made my coffee.

Fabi suffering waved his hands at me. "What are you up to today, Fae?" Clearly suffering from alcohol intake. "I'm going to try and find something to wear for work, though I'm not sure what to wear? I don't want to ask and look stupid," I said back leaning down to put my head in my hands on his counter.

Pausing he put his glasses down to think, "There are some good clothes shops down by the river? Or that place near the gallery?"

He pointed down to the river, "Wait I know what to do," he pulled out his phone and rang Alyssia, "Hey hun, can you take Fae shopping, she needs something to wear for her job on Monday, you know what my shopping is like!" He put his phone back in his pocket and put my coffee on the counter.

"She will be here in 5 minutes, Fae." Give him credit where it was due, his coffee was something else, nowhere in town was anywhere near as good as the quality of his coffee.

Alyssia's silhouette appeared walking down the street towards us, her slender and tall brunette figure, originally from the UK, she had met Fabi after a hair emergency while on holiday. Fabi called it love at first sight, though she says that she went on a date with him to shut him up but they have been together ever since, she is a curator at one of the galleries in the old part of town.

"You are hopeless, Fabi, give me your card! Or were you going to send her to that awful place near my gallery?" She didn't mince her words either!

"Come on Fae lets go get you suited and booted, don't worry, he's paying!" Alyssia took my hand and started slowly guiding me towards the river, "So what sort of thing are we looking for Fae?" She asked shielding her eyes from the sun.

"I'm not too sure, I didn't really notice any staff apart from the receptionists," she stopped. "Ah okay? Wait I have an idea," she pulled out her phone and began ringing someone? Pacing up and down waiting for them to answer.

"Hey Tony, why didn't you tell Fae what she needs to wear on Monday! I mean, come on Tony that's not a good impression to make with a new member of staff!" Scolding him in a heavy British accent.

Pacing angrily round, "So nothing too formal but not revealing either, no suits? Definitely no suits, fine! I will do your job for you, Tony!" She hung up the phone as I stood in awe.

She smiled as if nothing had happened, "Now I know where to take you, come on let's get you something special for work on Monday," her confidence was truly enviable.

Guiding me up some steps to the cobbled part of town where I avoided as the shops here displayed goods that I could only dream of owning. Walking me towards an outfitter run by a Parisian called Francois, he would often pose against the wall of his boutique, scowling at the awful attire on most women, he was friendly but very fashion aware.

"Francois, I have a job for you! This is Fae, she's new in town, she needs to look casual but formal, not exposed but flexible, nothing suit like either!" Alyssia commanded him as he sucked away at his cigarette. He looked at me strangely, like he was dissecting me with his eyes? Before he threw his cigarette to the floor and stamped it out, he pulled out a little tape, casting it towards me.

Walking round me huffing and puffing, "Hmm, no, no that, won't do?" My mind wandered as he circled me with his little yellow tape before he stood back and twirled his finger, commanding me to stand with my side facing him. Pausing and holding his chin, stroking his little beard, he lifted his finger before slowly recalling it and huffing a little more while he rested his finger back in his beard. He looked at me through his eyelids, waving me towards him, as I started to walk towards him, he raised his hand to tell me to stop before waving me backwards?

"What the hell is this guy doing, Alyssia?" I whispered to her, she smiled and waved her hand.

"Just wait," he continued to look at me, when suddenly he waved me forwards again, "Slowly this time!" He said.

As I started to walk towards him, he walked backwards through his shop door ushering me along, his gaze was so intent as he watched me walk through the door. "You can stop now," he said.

Frantically he started pulling out fabric and shoving them back in, swearing at himself as they fell down, in a deep French accent he spoke to me. "I needed to see how you move and walk, the fabric needs to morph and work for you perfectly otherwise you will look like a bag of shit!" I stood slightly bemused by him as he pulled down different bits of fabric before he started to work his way around me with his tape measure again.

Francois started to measure me. "Someone with your figure can't wear the wrong thing, you are beautifully shaped and the fabric needs to show those beautiful curves off so that when you walk you will float and make all the boys happy!" He winked at me and I blushed a little.

While he was speaking, Alyssia stood outside laughing as he worked his magic, I went outside briefly, "He is different but he is a magician," she said winking and laughing.

"Hey get back here! How can I work without my muse?" He called out. Francois lifted a little template and offered it to me before he took it back and reworked it.

Alyssia walked into the shop, "Well Francois?" She questioned him.

"Let me work, will you? Blue would bring out her eyes and show that wonderful figure too but with white collar and cuffs, do you keep this hair colour?" He asked.

I looked over and he was scratching away at a piece of fabric with a pencil. "Yeah, I keep it this colour," I spoke softly back to him, he looked over his glasses. "Hmm your voice is quite beautiful too!" Making me blush again. Francois lifted his template and offered it back against me, his eyes lit up and a smug grin came over him, "Perfection!" He declared as he pulled down a deep blue fabric. "Come back this afternoon, you need how many?" He looked at me but Alyssia answered.

"Three, make three for her, but can you make one with a purple collar and cuffs?" He snorted at her, "Fine, be back, for, say 2pm?"

As we left, he shut the shop door and bolted it closed. Breathing a sigh of relief, "He's insane but trust me he is a magician when it comes to clothing, plus the gallery is paying for them, they have a strange deal with him, so enjoy them!" Alyssia was certainly not shy of street smarts either.

Alyssia smiled at me. "Underwear? Or are you good on that?" She asked unashamedly, I blushed a little. "We better go and get that too," she chuckled leading me down an alley to another shop.

Wandering the aisle with her, "Black and purple okay for you Fae?" as she waved some bras in the air at me.

"They are fine," I chuckled back. Alyssia was a total livewire, she just didn't seem fazed by anything in truth, I was in awe of her, both envying and admiring her all at the same time. Once she had sorted my underwear situation out, we left to head back to Francois. Feeling anxious, I asked, "Can I ask you something, Alyssia?"

"Sure?" She replied looking at me. "Why are you doing this for me?" She stopped and took my hands.

"Someday Fae, you will do the same that I am doing for you today for someone else, someone who hasn't been as lucky as you, when that day comes you will remember this exact moment when you give them all you can, in the same way as me and Fabi are giving to you. Fabi and me have been lucky but we have been helped along too, whether you take them to Francois or anywhere else you can call this, 'Paying it forwards'." Alyssia spoke calmly and without letting go of my hands before she gave me a hug.

"Now come on, let's see if Frenchy has worked his magic for you!" We walked towards the boutique where Francois stood casually smoking away, he saw us and that grin returned, "My muse has returned," he cast his cigarette away and opened the door.

He pointed at my top. "Take this off and close your eyes," I obliged as he drew my top over my arms and pulled it down over at me. "Open your eyes and look at this marvel!" He pointed me towards a large mirror. I turned and looked at the beauty of his work, neat stitching and little pleats all finished off with a V-neck which ran gently down my chest, trimmed with crisp white cuffs and collar. Francois looked over at me.

"Black underwear only," he called as Alyssia threw him one of the bras, I looked at him in horror.

"Come now, I'm French, you think I haven't seen breasts before? Turn around!" Speaking softly to reassure me. He lifted my top off me and swapped my bra for one of the black ones Alyssia had thrown him before he pulled my top back down.

Pointing to a large mirror at the end of the shop, "Watch your top as you walk," he ushered me along as I walked the top moved seamlessly with my body, showing all my curves but not creasing or riding up. I turned to him with my face alight. "This is what perfection looks like!"

His smug grin resurfaced. "It's so beautifully made," he looked and smiled at me.

"Paying it forward Alyssia?" She nodded at him.

"Fae, isn't it?" He looked at me through his eyelids again.

"Yes Fae, thank you!" He smiled. "I'm Francois, come and see my anytime you like, this is also for you, it is how you say? Welcome gift!" He handed me a bag and gave me a little hug.

Heading back to Fabi's coffee shop with my face beaming and Alyssia was pretty happy too, Fabi leaning against the side of his shop just as he was when we left him this morning. Looking over he removed his glasses standing in awe, "Well look at you Fae!" Nearly as excited as me.

"Francois really worked his magic on you!" I nodded at him grinning from ear to ear. "I have never looked this good!"

He laughed, "Well get used to it, Francois won't see you in anything less than this now!" Together we headed for another celebratory drink, though still suffering from the night before we were more reserved this time. Walking home with my bags of goodies in hand through the evening sun, smiling and thinking how lucky I have been to meet such good people.

I wondered if someday I might be able to pay it forward and help someone on their journey of life and offer the same incredible friendship and kindness that these people have shown me.

I spent most of that evening thinking about what had happened during the day, this sudden acceleration of a life of any kind, not just a life though something more meaningful than just existing in the world. Suddenly, I found myself surrounded by people who cared? Not just cared a little but people who wanted to help me out in life and give me the start and chances I had dreamt about in Oured.

Francois didn't even know who I was and yet he quite willingly had gone to great length to make me feel welcomed and special? Tomorrow maybe I should go and thank him and formally introduce myself to him? Afterall, I'm sure his work isn't cheap and he as far as I could tell had willingly given his time and skills to me for free without so much as questioning why he was doing it. Feeling deeply happy before I went to sleep that night, tomorrow I was going to go and thank that strange and eccentric Parisian for his gifts.

Walking to Fabi that morning felt different? I couldn't really understand why but somehow Ljianstipol had gone from a new town to a deep and meaningful home? People had warmly welcomed me and within a week of being here I had friends and on Monday and much to my amazement a potential career opportunity ahead of me.

Where in Oured I got what job, I was lucky enough to be offered and only for a matter of months before my health would help me find my way out of the door, here I was almost a better candidate because of my issues? Heart-warming gestures had been thrown my way from day one and with no reason for these people to extend their hands to me, I felt utterly in debt to them.

Francois had been at the forefront of my mind for most of the last evening, he hadn't just made the three tops as Alyssia requested, he gave me another bag, a gift from him. It wasn't until I got home that I discovered that he had also made me two pairs of trousers, another top and some underwear too.

Having never really met him, yet his generosity was astounding and touching, though I knew he would refuse any attempt of payment, maybe he would at least accept my thanks and maybe a pastry or two from Fabi?

Wandering down towards the old part of town with a sweet smile and the odd chuckle to myself, as I thought about my experience with Francois at work.

Those old cobbles felt different this morning as I wandered towards the market square to give my thanks to that curious Frenchman. Poised and ready Francois stood against the wall of his shop with a cigarette in hand and those scathing eyes scouring the horizon for the badly dressed.

A strange smile donned his face as I wandered towards him with my gift of pastries in hand, casually he stood to greet me as I walked towards him. Leaning towards me, he gave me a hug. "Now today will be good as I get to see those beautiful eyes, Fae," he smiled as I offered him my gift of thanks. Francois took the bag and smiled again as I looked at him, "I just wanted to drop by and say thank you for what you have done for me," opening the bag he offered me a pastry.

Standing like an apologising child, he led me into his store and pulled out a seat for me to sit and talk with him, he was quite the gentleman really. Francois pulled up a chair nearby and brought through a coffee pot and two mugs.

"It's not quite Fabi's coffee but it is pleasant enough," he offered a mug across the table to me. "I wanted to thank you for what you did for me yesterday, Francois, you didn't have to do what you did and I really appreciate it." Francois sat back and smiled. "You're quite welcome Fae, though I suppose you wonder why? No?"

I took a sip and nodded at him, "I do keep wondering why?"

Francois leant forwards and smiled at me. "We met before didn't we, Fae? Do you remember?"

I thought but couldn't recall. "Tony got me to take that picture of you in the marketplace, though you look better now than you did back then, that was your first day in Ljianstipol no?"

I smiled as I started to piece together who I found myself sat with. "It was, I hadn't left the hotel at that point."

Francois smiled at me. "You still had those pretty eyes back then, I cannot answer for others but my reason is simple, I like you and I want to see you have a good chance here in Ljianstipol. I don't know all your story and no doubt you will tell me someday about it when the time is right and when that time comes, I will listen all day," I smiled back at him.

"Someday we will talk about it, your work is incredible though Francois." Looking over at the wall adorned with his garments, "They are not too bad, but you should see my wife Colette's work, her work makes mine look awful!"

Partly shocked, I said, "Where is your wife's shop?"

Francois pointed to an alley, "The little haberdashery down that alley, her work is beyond anyone's and she is quite beautiful too."

Smiling as he spoke of her, "Just promise me one thing Fae?"

I looked over at him, "One thing? What is it?"

Francois took my hands, "Remember you will always have friends with me and Colette, if you ever need us, we will be here for you," I held his hand in return. "I will and thank you again Francois for everything you have done."

Francois shrugged his shoulders, "They are just clothes Fae, though I hope they help you feel as great as I think you are," I gave him a hug.

"No, they are more than that and thank you again." He held me in return. "Now go and say hello to Colette and we will speak again soon," I smiled as I headed out of Francois' shop and to the alleyway, he had pointed out to me.

Walking down a slightly tormented and darkened back alley eventually I found the strange looking haberdashery Francois spoke of. Windows clouded by laces and fine linens it didn't seem like it would be the home of a master seamstress? Opening the stiff and misshapen door, I wandered into a wonderland of fine fabric and garments which were so beautiful that I couldn't believe my eyes.

Touching some of the fine dress wear on display, my hands had found heaven in the soft, luscious fabrics, stitching so beautiful I couldn't believe my eyes. Behind a little desk sat a soft and small lady, smiling sweetly with short silver hair. "You must be Fae? Francois said you had beautiful eyes, but he didn't say you were this beautiful," she rose to meet me so majestically that I became transfixed upon her.

Wandering gracefully towards me, she was tiny but stunning to look at, she opened her arms to me and gave me a kiss on each cheek, "Welcome to Ljianstipol Fae, I'm Colette, it is good to meet you," she held my hands, "It's nice to meet you, Colette," guiding me to a chair by her little desk.

Sitting in this wonderland of fine fabric creations she smiled as I sat down. "Your hair is quite majestic Fae, like a peacock," she started to hum to herself as she took a piece of ribbon and started playing with it. Wandering round, she continued to hum to herself, "You have been here for a week so far, Fae? How are you finding life here?"

I sat back on the chair she offered, "I love it, the people have been so kind to me and it's good to have a good home."

She looked over and smiled sweetly as she toyed with the piece of ribbon, "I'm pleased to hear that Fae, you can come and see me anytime you need me," she waved me to come over as she held up a little garment, "You would look wonderful in this Fae, it would bring out your eyes," she offered me the top she held in her hand.

"It's quite beautiful, Colette, but I can't take this, you people have given me more than enough already."

Colette smiled and took my hands again, "I understand that, but please do take this for me, could you lean down?" As per her request I leant down as she threaded the ribbon flower she had made into my hair. She smiled as she finished neatly arranging the ribbon, "Perfection," she gently stroked my hair back to sit correctly and pulled out a little handheld mirror to show me my little flower.

"That's beautiful, Colette, thank you," I smiled at her as I looked at her handy work in the mirror.

"You're welcome, Fae, welcome and I hope we get to know each other very well in time, did you wonder about my garments?" She held up another dress she had made, "I may not be cheap but all my garments come with a guarantee like no other, as long as I can still use my hands then I will adjust and repair the garment for its entire lifetime," she smiled as she gently placed the dress back on the hanger.

Colette bid me goodbye with a traditional French peck on the cheek as I started to make my way home to relax and prepare myself to make a flying start on Monday at my new job.

Spending most of the weekend trying on my new clothes almost every single hour as I readied myself for the big day on Monday. Feeling encouraged, I even did a few trial runs to find the best route to work and to see how much time I would need to complete my journey, including a stop off to get coffee from Fabi in the morning.

While the dust from the weekend settled on Sunday, I struggled to sleep through excitement though going to bed quite early possibly didn't help me with that. Waking up extra early I leapt from my bed and got myself dressed and ready for the day, sitting at my kitchen table drinking a cup of coffee and begging for the time to tick down so that my new life could really begin. While time dragged and I started clawing at my face in desperation as I willed those hands to move quicker, I even took my shoes off a couple of times just to pass a few minutes.

Unable to wait any longer, I just decided to walk slowly down to work, at least in my head that was a plan just my body wasn't quite sticking to this plan. Rapidly I found myself at the counter of Fabi, eager to get another taste of his coffee, Fabi was quick with his coffee, but even that felt painfully slow as I impatiently waited.

Without even a single second elapsing before he released my cup, I had gotten hold of it, dumped some money down and headed away, "Thanks Fabi!" He smiled. "Eager, hey Fae? Have a great day!"

Wandering down the route I had practiced a few times, at the start of the town there was a bridge over the river, adorned with padlocks along its railings, from there a little set of steps led to a long path beside the river. Wandering alongside the river down a neatly cut and coloured concrete path all the way to another bridge with a set of cobbled steps which led up and into the old part of town.

Heading up the steps one way led to the marketplace, beach and all the fancy shops that I would never be able to afford to shop in and the other led straight to the Davizioso. Walking seemingly faster and faster with my confidence building up as I finally stood before the heavy doors of the Hotel Davizioso. Taking a moment to check my hair and adjust my blouse in the reflection off the glass in the door, I took a deep breath and composed myself, placed my hand on the door handle and opened the gateway to my new life in Ljianstipol.

Wandering into the reception area confidently I approached the desk, two young girls were behind the desk, a blond and tall girl came over to greet me. "How can we help you today?"

I looked at the tall girl and confidently responded, "I'm Fae Edwards and it's my first day of work today."

She huffed slightly, scanned me up and down before she replied, "Hmm I didn't realise that we employed patients now?"

The other girl turned around, "Leanne! Why don't you go and check the main congregation room," she wandered over and came out from behind the desk, a slightly shorter girl, with glasses and an oddly shy and nervous demeanour introduced herself, "I'm Abby and it's nice to meet you Fae, if you follow me I will guide you to the conference room where you will meet to start you first day," she spoke politely but with an odd soothing tone.

"Thank you," I responded quietly to her. Awkwardly I looked at Abby. "I can find my own way there if you are busy, I kinda stayed here a couple of times before?"

Abby smiled back sweetly, "I will guide you anyway, you worked here before?" I shook my head at her as she started to walk me through the hallways.

"Oh well, then welcome back and just ignore Leanne she is just still quite immature for her age," I settled a little after that initial shock hit me.

Abby escorted me to the awaiting Tony and Gale by their meeting room door. "Fae! Come on, we've been waiting for you!" Tony smiled at me and recharged the nerves I had lost during that first moment at reception Abby spoke to Gale quietly, "She said what to her! Thank you for telling me, Abby."

Abby smiled at me. "I'm at reception if you need me for anything, Fae," she shut the door and headed away.

Gale looked at me and hung his head. "Sorry about Leanne, I keep hoping to catch her saying those things so that I can get shot of her but she hasn't given me the chance just yet, she hasn't put you off, has she?" I felt awkward but shook my head.

"No, it wasn't how I expected to start my first day but it's tame, compared to the insults I am used to."

Tony smiled. "We know but that doesn't make it right! Anyway, we need to do some paperwork and you get to watch a really boring video alone for half an hour before you can do much more than use the toilets here, okay?"

Gale looked around for a cloth. "Here let me clear you a space to write," Gale just used his shirt sleeve to clean a spot on the conference table in the room.

"Sorry we don't tend to use this room too much; can we get you a drink?" Gale opened his fridge. "Uh it's not even 9 yet?" I said back to him as he chuckled and pulled out a bottle of cool water for me.

"Hehe that's why we liked you!" He chuckled and handed me the bottle of water. Sitting at the desk we started to fill out different forms and documents ready for the video that both claimed would be so awful. Tony helped me with the forms and checked them over while Gale tried to figure out the TV in the room, eventually he gave up and just handed me the control.

While I flicked through looking for the video, he was looking for I couldn't help but notice that although he was playing with his phone, Gale's attention was firmly on me. Finding the video, he sat down next to Tony.

"Hope you are ready to be insulted Fae?" He chuckled as the video they had to show me played on.

Periodically they would yell, "As if anyone is dumb enough to do that by accident," at the TV laugh and pat me on the shoulder, this was more like a strange reunion than my first day at work.

Lunchtime rapidly approached and after the mentally insulting video Tony asked where I was going for lunch, my blank look answered that question before my mouth could. Gale rang the reception desk and ordered some lunch be brought up for me by Leanne!

I sat back feeling slightly nervous as she walked in with a grimace on her face with a tray of sandwiches and snacks. Gale smirked at me. "Offer them to her, Leanne, she's a new member of staff!" Begrudgingly she held the tray for me to select something from it, I took a sandwich and some crisps.

"Thank you," she grimaced again before leaving. Once the door closed, Gale erupted laughing. "Spoilt brat! But I will catch her one day!"

Tony joined in, "Not a member of your fan club then, Fae?"

I shook my head and chuckled, "Guess not?"

Gale sat back and offered me another bottle of water, "Unless you want something stronger, it's later now!"

He laughed as I took the bottle of water, "Not yet, but maybe after another video I might change my mind," I chuckled at him again.

Tony pulled out his phone and looked at Gale. "Is it ready?" Gale nodded his head. "Everyone but Leanne is in it."

Confused, I looked at the pair as Tony sent me a text message, just a smiley face? Within seconds my phone lit up with more smiley faces. "Everyone in the hotel staff is in this group, if you ever crash or just feel low, send us a message in here and well I'm sure you can figure out that everyone will be there for you, Fae." Gale smiled at me as he replied to Tony's message.

"I figured you wouldn't object to Leanne not being in this group?" I shook my head, still slightly surprised by them.

"We know at times you are just going to need to be away in your own space Fae, but let us know when you need to, just so we know you are, okay? Alright?" I nodded at Gale and Tony.

"Of course, I will, but why are you doing this?" Tony took over. "You witnessed on your first day of work how people still see you, even though you are on your first day of work she just couldn't see beyond the obvious, we can see beyond that and we know you will become one of our biggest assets here and in truth, Fae, you deserve a good chance and we happen to be able to give you that chance," I cried a little at his gesture.

Tony walked and stood beside me. "Come on we have another afternoon of fun meetings ahead of us, though maybe this afternoon we could go somewhere slightly less indoorsy?" Tony winked at me, almost recounting an exact sentence that I had said to him when he started to unwrap my mind during my first stay at the hotel years ago.

Gale and Tony led the way to the garden on the roof and guided me to their pergola at the end of the path and handed me a beer. "Welcome aboard, we have partnered you up with a couple of people for the next couple of days just to help you find your feet, but worry about that tomorrow, Fae," Tony declared as he offered me a seat.

"Just enjoy me filling out your paperwork while you both enjoy a drink and maybe Tony will take you for a walk," Gale laughed as he sat himself down and pulled out a pen and some documents to fill in. Sitting quietly listening to the scratching of Gale's pen I sat confused but quite content with a nice cool beer on a hot day, though it wasn't how I had expected to spend my first day at work? As the afternoon wore on, I started to fill them both in on the years between me leaving the Davizioso and the events that had brought me to Ljianstipol and back to the hotel to start work.

Both seemingly saddened by the ongoing troubles that continually marred my life in Oured, it did seem at least that I had made a very fortuitous decision to finally leave and move here to stay. While the afternoon wound down, they let me head home early ready for tomorrow when I would get my first taste of life working in the hotel, readying myself to start using my own problems to help other people.

While that first week ticked away, I was partnered with two different people who worked on the floor of the hotel, going round talking to people and guiding them to and from therapy sessions if they needed. Shadowing them, I was reunited with Shanky who gave me a huge hug before taking me to his room to show me what he had been working on since we last saw each other nearly 6 years ago.

Filling him in on the time between our last meeting, he seemed kinda sad how life for me had been but was more than happy to see me back at the hotel, especially as a member of staff. A few residents had opened up to me about their lives and ongoing problems and I had willingly sat and spoken to them for a couple of hours about them and talked about myself to them. My mentors didn't seem to mind at all, as this was part and parcel of the life working the floor at the hotel, someone however unknown to me was keeping an eye on this part of what I was doing.

On Thursday afternoon, I met with Gale to discuss how I was finding my first week, I happily told him how thrilled I was and enjoying myself at work, he seemed happy enough. Gale then asked if I understood the beer at the interview yet?

Being quite surprised I couldn't really even throw out a bad guess for him. Gale went on to explain that he was terrible at sourcing staff, he always had wound up with bad eggs somehow, indeed Leanne was a member of staff that he alone had recruited Tony however understood something that he didn't.

Tony drew on his football coaching years to work out how to find good staff, Tony understood that good on paper never often transpired to being good on the pitch. Tony suggested a simple concept to Gale, if every applicant was offered a beer no matter the time of day, the ones that would understand the way things need to be in the hotel would accept the offering to become part of their team.

Those who refused wouldn't be likely to step in and help residents or patients when they might be at their lowest, they needed people that would openly become a part of people's lives not career hungry hopefuls. Gale simply put it to me that if someone offered me a bottle of blue hair dye that I would dye their hair for them and not just look at it and hand the bottle of dye back to them.

Gale wished me a good weekend and sent me on my way, having partnered me up with two different members of staff for the next week, I couldn't help but feel he was planning something though?

Most people were pretty good to me in that first week, Leanne was still very stand-offish but that was no real surprise after Gale humiliated her in exchange for what she had said to me during that first morning. However, Leanne's hostility was expected but another person was kinda strange with me, this girl though I didn't suspect to be quite so off with me?

During that first moment at work Abby had stepped in and been quite pleasant but from that morning onwards she hadn't exactly been rude or anything just kinda distant? She greeted me every morning from behind the reception desk but that was all she ever said? It felt kind of like I had gotten her in trouble with Leanne or something? I couldn't really think how to explain it as she was neither rude nor stand-offish with me?

I wondered if maybe she just didn't like other people as she was still quite young though she seemed pretty mature the way she stood up for me against Leanne? Part of me wondered if she was just kind of shy, as she always seemed slightly on edge?

Either way I was utterly staggered when late on Thursday night I got a message from Abby asking me if I wanted to meet up with her during the day on Friday? It wasn't like I had anything better to do so I agreed to meet her by the bridge at around 11 in the morning. Abby was going to show me around Ljianstipol a little bit more and I guess maybe I might find out why she seemed to be so distant during the week?

Either way I headed down to the bridge to meet Abby for 11, I stood keeping an eye out for the normally quite well-dressed receptionist, startled when she placed her hand on my shoulder to greet me as I had utterly missed her as she approached. Without her glasses and dressed almost underwhelmingly with just a pair of knee length trousers and a short top on, however she left just enough showing to make the guys double take as she walked past them. Awkward first moments were quashed when she took a look at me and said, "You don't strike me as the new part of town kind of girl?"

Abby started to walk me by the river in the new part of town to an odd cafe she liked. We sat down in her venue of choice and she began by apologising to me? "Sorry, I haven't spoken too much, I'm not quite so brave when it's someone new."

My heart broke at the thoughts I had about her, "Sorry too, I thought you just didn't like me or I had gotten you in trouble with Leanne, thanks for standing up for me by the way!"

Abby smiled. "I can't stand her saying things like that to people, she is like that with me because I'm kind of a big nerd, but they will catch her out one day!" Abby smiled a little as she thought about that.

Lunch arrived and we started to get to know each other a little better, Abby began proceedings by telling me the reason why she was so quiet at work. Sitting up almost bolt upright, she admitted that she wasn't the best for getting to bed early, confessing that she was a bit of a bookworm and quite enjoyed gaming.

While my mind conjured up pretty accurate images of her happily reading books late into the night, I wasn't fully sure what she meant by gaming?

Abby was the youngest member of staff at the hotel and she was quite nervous around people, especially new people. Gale and Tony though had briefed everyone about me though not gone into too much detail so I filled Abby in with a brief version of my history. Abby smiled apologetically at me.

"Sorry about the way Leanne treated you," she looked at me again, "You like different things yeah?"

I nodded at her, "Yeah I'm bit of a hippy girl at heart Abby," she leant over closer to me. "You want me to show you somewhere you might love? I get a lot of my stuff from there?"

I felt curious but was only too happy to follow her lead. "Yeah sure?"

Abby perked up, "Great! Come on, we'll go there instead of the new part of town!"

Leading me out of the town itself and through a seemingly never-ending set of different roads we started to head far out of town. Abby kept talking all the way about finding treasures for her book collection and some cool clothing somewhere? But she was leading me towards a supermarket for some reason?

Confused but equally intrigued, I followed her quite willingly into the car park of a supermarket as we walked past the large store and round it's far wall to the huge thrift store hidden behind it. Automated doors opened to lure us both in, Abby was pretty pleased as we wandered into its aisles filled with goodies just waiting to be found.

Staggered by the sheer volume of the store, I did wonder if my mouth was open going by the look on Abby's face. While Abby hunted for books, I wondered if maybe I might just get lucky in the clothing section and just like Abby, I wasn't going to be disappointed. Both of us found treasure and departed with bulging bags and large smiles as we walked back to the town.

Feeling quite happy that I seemed to have found a new friend at work and wanting to thank her for what truthfully was a very nice day; I invited her over for dinner and to stay for the night if she wanted to. Abby didn't hesitate to agree to come over for the night, rather than head to her home she just brought what she had found during our shopping trip together round to mine for the night.

I gave Abby a little tour of my home and let her pick whatever spare room she wanted for the night before we headed back downstairs. Sitting on the sofa I realised that I didn't actually know anywhere that did deliveries yet? But thankfully Abby had a phone which was full of saved numbers and ordering options, Abby picked what we would be indulging in tonight and I paid as thanks for the day out.

While I placed a memory box, I had found in the thrift store next to the picture of me and my mum Abby saw the picture and was keen to learn more about it.

"That's me and my mum on holiday in Monesta, I was 11 years old, my parents pulled me out of school so that we could afford the holiday, they made some excuse so that they could take me to that luxury resort in the countryside for my birthday, they couldn't afford it during the school breaks as the place hiked the prices out of their reach. During the first couple of days my dad fell ill, he tried shellfish and discovered that he had an allergy to it, undeterred me and Mum spent the next few days together."

"Mum noticed though that a few times I just seemed off? She couldn't say why but I just seemed distant and subdued? A few times she caught me staring aimlessly into the distance, she thought maybe the main area of the resort combined with worrying about my dad was playing with my mind. She got me that cool bracelet in a bid to shift my mood but it didn't work, it was a nice bracelet, I still have it somewhere in my boxes of stuff."

"Feeling slightly nervous, she took me outside with her to sit alone, much to her surprise sitting under the moonlight for an hour seemed to stop whatever had been bothering me. Most evenings, we wound up sitting there with or without my dad as his ailments repeated on him. My mum still has this photo in her purse almost 15 years later? That was when she loved me the most, her little Fae. It's sad for us both though as she witnessed my first depression crash during that holiday and that crash was just a warm up for what was to come during the next few weeks and carry on for the rest of my life."

"It's not all bad though, she did accidentally discover a coping mechanism for me, it's just a shame that she lost her sweet and cute girl somewhere over the years. Maybe someday I could get back to being like that girl you know?"

Abby smiled at me. "Maybe someday, Fae, but then you seem pretty good now?"

I sighed back at her, "One hasn't happened here yet, but it will and when they happen, they can be utterly destructive."

Abby patted me on the shoulder. "I'm sure you will be okay and there are good people here too."

Abby looked around my living room and paused, seemingly surprised by something. "Do you game?" She quizzed me, I looked at her and shrugged my shoulders.

"Not really, there is a console in my boxes somewhere but I don't really play it too much." Feeling slightly curious I took Abby to the room where I had dumped all the boxes that I hadn't sorted out yet. Buried underneath a load of books was my old game console, I pulled it out, "I'm sure the leads are in here too? Well maybe, I might have thrown them away by accident?" I said continuing to sift through the box.

Abby started to look through another box and found something. "Uh, you might want to sort this box out?" She started to giggle and threw me a pair of my underwear, blushing and embarrassed, "Sorry about I forgot about that box!"

Abby laughed back, "It's okay, I won't go any deeper though I don't want to make you go red again!" Finding a console but no leads was slightly embarrassing. When Abby looked round at me again as she found some books, she was keen to read, "Ooh you like reading too?"

I smiled. "You can take these if you want? My mind is more than capable of creating enough fantasy worlds without help!"

Abby chuckled, "Hey do you want to come and stay at mine tomorrow night?"

I looked at her smiling sweetly, "Sure, if you didn't want to meet your other friends or anything?"

Suddenly, she became very shy, "Hey what's wrong?" She looked up, "I kinda don't have too many friends here, you maybe but that is kind of it?"

I looked at her looking so saddened. "Really but you seem pretty cool to me? How about tomorrow you meet some of the friends I have made and then we can spend the evening together?"

Abby smiled a little but still seemed pensive, "Are you sure? I'm kind of a big nerd?"

I rested my hand on hers, "If people can like me then they will have no problem liking you!" Abby smiled before we headed back downstairs to finish our evening together.

While we talked during the evening, I couldn't help but wonder how such a nice girl could have no real friends, though she did claim to have friends of some kind just I didn't really understand what she meant. Feeling certain that both Fabi and Alyssia would be a good starting point for her, I texted both to see if they were happy for me to bring a new friend into the mix for our meeting at the bars by the river during the afternoon.

Either way, part of me admired Abby's bravery to take me out for the day when she had no clue whether we would get along or not, though maybe that bravery was just loneliness? And I knew exactly how crippling that kind of loneliness could really be, after all we were both sleeping in a house I had moved to because of loneliness.

During the morning, we slowly got ourselves ready to venture down by the river, Abby was quite talkative during the morning, that shy veil slowly falling away from her as we spoke more. Walking down town together, she spoke openly about how excited she was to meet some new people, I felt happy for her but sad at the same time wondering just how long had she been here alone without a single friend?

We reached the bridge and I guided Abby to the bar overlooking the river where Fabi and Alyssia would be waiting for us.

Abby was slightly nervous as we walked into the bar and were greeted by Alyssia getting drinks ready to meet us outside. Alyssia soon introduced herself to Abby and broke the ice with her before getting us a drink each and escorting us to the waiting Fabi. Sitting together overlooking the passing river, they both started to introduce themselves to Abby and invited her to their garden tomorrow for a barbeque.

Abby couldn't mask her excitement at being invited over and almost desperately accepted their offer, just like they had with me just weeks ago they had no apprehensions about opening a door to Abby.

One thing did slightly concern me though, we weren't the only ones going to the barbeque Colette would be there but I knew she would be fine with Abby, Francois might be another matter though. Francois was almost legendary for being slightly unpleasant with people, his comments were often barbed and venomous and he had no apprehensions about targeting anyone.

I either hoped he would be kind or maybe that Abby would bite back, though Alyssia would be there to keep him in check along with Colette so maybe I was just worrying for the sake of it? Either way as the afternoon wore on the welcome that Abby was given by Fabi and Alyssia meant a lot to her, we walked back to mine to get a change of clothing for me and then onto Abby's place.

Through the newer part of town, we wandered towards a large selection of apartments, very expensive apartments, we both felt equally out of place here.

Continuing on, Abby stopped at a door and opened it to reveal possibly the largest TV I had ever seen inside her living room.

Welcoming me into her lounge with blackout blinds down and two large plush sofas, her living room was huge! With an open plan connected kitchen integrated into the lounge and a set of stairs at the far end of the room hidden behind a door. Though I couldn't help but notice that Abby's lounge felt kinda lived in? Not particularly messy or anything like that, just it felt like she stayed here a lot, and there were odd foot marks on the front of her sofa?

Abby took me upstairs and offered me the spare room and showed me her room and the bathroom, I left my change of clothing on the bed and we headed downstairs. Abby ordered our dinner for delivery and showed me her book collection, her vast book collection, like a small self-contained library covering almost an entire wall near her stairs.

Looking through her books she had all kinds of classics and the odd slightly less classic modern book buried amongst them. Abby then showed me her game collection, her equally vast game collection, in a cabinet nearly as big as the enormous TV sat upon it, she was pretty keen on this stuff. We sat on her sofa talking and eating our dinner when just after finishing she fired up her console for us both to play but I wasn't ready for what came out from within her.

Initially, she was pretty calm but as the bodies in-game mounted, she turned into an altogether different kind of animal. Shouting, screaming and taunting her way through a mass of victims, Abby danced round her living room to celebrate each and every kill that she gained. Menacing and taunting her way through a tidal wave of noobs on her path to glory, at work a shy and reclusive receptionist but online a domineering and terrifying cyber vixen.

Almost stunned into utter silence as I sat watching her in both terror and awe, behind the safety of her console Abby was oddly inspiring in an odd way. Commanding respect and fearsome, like a warrior of some kind, bashing and smashing her way through anyone that stood in her way. Once Abby finished playing, she went back to being her more usual self, polite and shy again but I had found an odd level of respect for her.

Lying in bed, part of me couldn't help but giggle to myself thinking about her dancing round her living room and taunting wildly at a whole army of guys. Whether out of respect or fear, guys gravitated towards her online and she admitted that she had actually met a few of her opponents for dates.

Heading to the barbeque at Alyssia and Fabi's, I saw her in a slightly different light, she was still the shy receptionist for the most part but in truth she was pretty cool to me. At the barbeque, Abby slowly opened up and was almost confident, as the day wore on though I did wonder if liquid courage helped her with that.

People liked her and she seemingly had become part of the odd tight knit group that I had been welcomed into just weeks before. Heading back home before going our separate ways for the night we agreed to meet up during our lunch hour at work. Abby over the course of the weekend had become an unexpected but very much liked and welcomed friend.

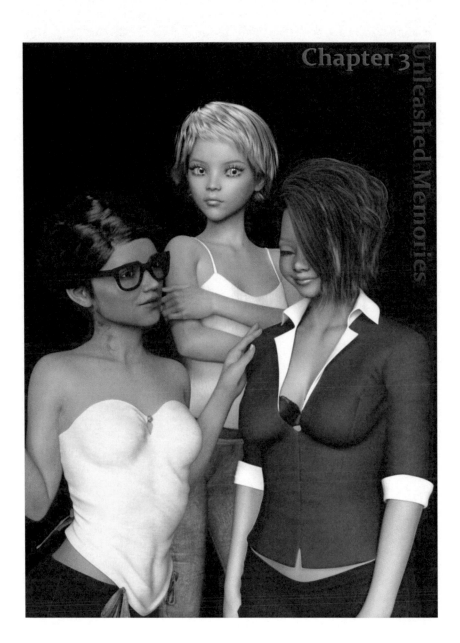

Chapter 3
Unleashed Memories

I had been in Ljianstipol for just over three weeks and life was good, I had made friends and felt a renewed hope for life that had come along with them. Working life had turned out to be just as promising too, with the exception of Leanne everyone seemed to like me and Abby had become an unexpected friend. However, today I was going to explore my new town alone and check out a few places that my new friends had told me about. My only real concern was just how long these people would stick around when either I crashed or had an episode?

Walking around the market square, Alyssia spotted me and invited me into her gallery for a chat, inviting me to a gathering with Fabi and some people they were keen for me to meet. Feeling optimistic, I agreed to go that evening and left the gallery with a nice thought in my mind that kept bubbling away during the day as I explored Ljianstipol further.

Getting myself ready for the evening felt pretty good but the only person who I knew wasn't going to the gathering was Abby, she had a hot date that night. Dressed up as best as I could manage, I headed to Fabi and Alyssia's place excited and content. Fabi greeted me at the door and took me inside to introduce me to everyone.

Slowly being introduced to a host of different people Shaun and his wife Jane who owned the thrift store that Abby had introduced me to. Francois and Colette arrived soon afterwards and we all sat around their kitchen table happily talking and sharing stories. Colette was going to great lengths to speak with me and keep me involved in the conversations surrounded by all these new people, she was quite sweet really.

Jane and the guys started to play cards while Colette, Alyssia and me headed to watch tv and talk some more. Slowly revealing myself to my new friends felt good and it was a nice evening and life felt good. I was in the bathroom, thinking to myself about how my life had transformed so quickly after moving to Ljianstipol and being in the company of these new friends. Looking in the mirror and smiling at myself thinking how lucky I had been since I moved to this new place, just as I stepped over the threshold of the bathroom it happened.

Have you ever had one of those moments where your brain convinces you that there is another step on the stairs? Tricking you into believing that there is some kind of terra firma there that simply doesn't exist? That moment of uncontrollable fear, terror and shock as your foot thumps down onto thin air and through to the ground below with your mind having misled you? That moment where you suddenly lose control and fear your very existence? This was how my crashes started but instead of taking that deep breath of shock and a sigh of relief, I just kept falling.

Falling deeper and deeper until eventually I would find myself falling through the darkness and abyss of my own mind until eventually landing at rock bottom. Surrounded and trapped by total darkness in the deep and black abyss of my own mind.

Once I hit the bottom of my fall, I curled myself up in a corner near the bathroom, wrapping myself up in a heap on the floor and tucked aside so that people wouldn't notice me as I fell into this strange realm that only I could see or feel. Unable to speak or move with my mind collapsing in on itself as darkness had taken full control of me. Alyssia had come looking for me, she found me in a heap on the floor holding myself and staring vacantly into nothingness.

Sitting beside me she held me as I began to shake uncontrollably, falling to pieces in her hands, "Fabi! Get up here Fae needs help!" She yelled so loudly that most of Ljianstipol probably heard her.

I will never forget the look on Fabi's face as he came upstairs and saw his normally smiling and coffee loving friend crumbling in the arms of his wife, his look of utter terror and disbelief. Fabi took my phone and sent a crying face to Tony and Gale with the message "Send help! Fabi," following it, within moments my phone was ringing and Tony spoke with Fabi as he paced around the house.

Gale phoned Alyssia and started to talk to her and give her advice to help pull me back out of my dark hole, Colette sat with me softly stroking my hands. Fabi showed my phone to me, a message on the group Tony and Gale had set up just said, "I'm there for her." We could hear someone run down the street and knock at their door.

Abby came bounding up the stairs having ditched her hot date to come to my aid, finding me in Alyssia and Colette's company, Francois and Fabi stayed downstairs out of the way. Abby nearly pushed both of them out of the way, there was no shy and timid receptionist in that girl tonight. Gently putting her arms around me she began whispering to me, "Come on, Fae, come back to use, we've got you, Fae, come on," commanding both Alyssia and Colette to help her get me into a spare room and lay me upon a bed.

Laying on my side curled up like a terrified kitten, Abby sat on the bed with me and started to talk to me about how she ditched her date. Smiling and laughing as she revealed how she just stood up and left him clueless as to why she had just walked out on their date.

Abby was exhausted after spending all night with me on that bed talking to me and trying to bring me round, Alyssia came in to check on us. Alyssia asked Abby how I was doing and when Abby shook her head, she phoned her boss there and then to tell him the gallery would be closed today, no explanations and no questions, she took the day off to relieve Abby.

Alyssia took Abby's spot next to me and started to tell me about the UK, what it was like and how her and Fabi had met in Ljianstipol. While she told me her story and without warning my mind took me back to a childhood memory where people had lured me out for the night only to leave me sitting alone in darkness. Slowly being consumed by my own thoughts, *Why did they leave me alone?*

Alyssia looked confused, "Who left you alone?" She looked at me concerned, as I began to ramble to her about being ditched in dark places. "We aren't going to do that to you and we will never let that happen to you Fae," she was growing stern in her strong British accent when there was a knock at the door.

"Just give me one second!" She yelled. "I will be right back Fae," she rushed downstairs and returned with Francois.

"Fae! I have a gift for you," he popped a little cup of coffee next to me on the bed and sat beside me. "Alyssia, can you help me get her into your garden?" Alyssia looked confused but she took one arm and Francois took the other and lifted me up, "Not as heavy as I thought, hey Alyssia?" He winked at her and they carried me carefully through the house and out into the garden, sitting me on a concrete bench.

Francois walked back into the house and returned with that little cup of coffee and sat it back next to me after offering me a sip.

Sitting down next to me, he lit a cigarette and sat puffing away and admiring his fingernails. "Your coffee it has my best cognac in it," he smiled and started to hum to me. Without warning, he gently laid me on my side with my head gently resting in his lap and softly resting his hand on the side of my head, he gave me another sip of that coffee.

Gently he stroked the flower shaved into my head. "Have I ever told you how me and the wonderful Colette met Fae?"

Though I didn't reply, I simply shook my head gently as he lit another cigarette. "We both worked at the same clothing company in Paris, she was the head seamstress and finalised any designs to be manufactured, I worked in the design department. During the winter, they gave me the job to design a new dress for summer range, I had so many ideas and concepts, I worked with Colette on them. The big boss liked my design but rejected them in the end as they couldn't be produced cheaply enough to be sold in mass, they wanted things that didn't last, I wanted to create something that people would love and cherish."

"Simple elegant pieces that would make even the curviest of girls feel as beautiful as they are, not something that only looked good on the mannequin. Eventually, after many arguments the boss took me off that design team and relegated me to colour selection only. Of course, this is why I am so angry about the bad things that wonderful women wear, they all deserve to look wonderful no matter their shape or size."

"Colette was quite supportive while I argued with the boss about my design, we met up a few times and went for coffee or walks in the parks around Paris. Colette came on holiday with me to this place and when we arrived, we fell in love with the place, at first, we had a shop together but we couldn't work together, we argued too much at work. Colette kept the shop in the backstreets and I moved into the shop in the marketplace, though Ljianstipol wasn't too popular when we arrived but it is now."

Francois gave me another sip of that coffee and he started humming to me again, "Do you like the park Fae? Hmm?" His voice was soft and comforting, but I couldn't find words to answer. "Colette, she likes the parks, there is a big park just out of the town, maybe you could both go visit? Eh?" He gently stroked my head again to soothe me.

"Maybe we could take you tomorrow?" He gave me another sip of that coffee and the cognac in it hit the back of my throat.

Humming again, "Colette she is worried about you Fae, as we all are, we all want to help you as much as we can, we are your friends and we are here for you," he lit another cigarette and sat happily humming to me again. While he sat humming to himself with my head resting in his lap, calmness began to soak into me and he looked down cracking a strange smile, "The French charms have won you over no?" I could feel a tear beading down my nose. "The cognac," I uttered back softly, he looked down at me.

"The cognac? Ah you women!" He smiled as he continued to hum away, gradually easing my crash in the process.

"Thank you," I whispered interrupting his humming.

"No such thing is needed Fae; you have spent much time alone yes?" He whispered back. Weeping a little I nodded at him, he looked down the garden, "No longer, Fae, you have friends now and we are here for you." Francois pulled my phone out and opened it to show me all the messages of support I had received, "We are here for you, Fae," he carried on humming and stroking the side of my head.

Colette came walking down the garden, almost floating as she wandered towards us.

"Francois really? You gave her cognac? No wonder it has taken her so long to smile!" She knelt down and ran her finger down my nose and gently poked the tip.

"You can take me and her to the park to apologise tomorrow!" She scolded him, "Have you been blowing your smoke over her too? For that you can treat her to lunch too!"

He smiled at me as she laid into him, "Has he been telling you that story about how we met?"

I nodded at her, "Did he tell you why he got fired?" Colette looked at Francois, "Well?" He shrugged his shoulders, "Well not yet?" He smiled at me again.

Colette looked at me. "He called the boss a bombastic bastard among other things, in an argument over that dress he didn't like!"

Francois smiled at me. "He is a bastard."

Alyssia came walking down the garden looking at me laid on my side, kneeling just in front of me. "I'm glad you are okay Fae, you gave us all a mighty scare but at least you were with friends and not alone," she pinched my cheeks.

"Stay the night so that we can make sure you are okay before we go to the park tomorrow," she gave me a little peck on the forehead. "You really want to take me to the park tomorrow after all the trouble I have caused you?" Alyssia laughed.

"What trouble? You are our friend, Fae and you shut Fabi up for a couple of hours!" Her sense of humour kicking in. Francois kept me laid on his lap humming away while he fed me more coffee and cognac, each sip he gave me got him told off by Colette or Alyssia. An exhausted Abby came walking down the garden with Fabi, Tony and Gale.

"How is our girl doing?" Fabi asked as suddenly I found myself surrounded by a whole party of people here to see if I was okay? "I hear Francois is taking you for lunch tomorrow." Tony smiled at Francois who just waved his hand at him, Gale leant down. "Well as long as Fae is okay, how are you feeling Fae?" He looked down upon me, as a smile finally broke through my frown.

"Good to see that smile again, we will see you in the park at 10?"

I smiled back at him, "Yes and thank you."

Francois put his finger over my lips. "Nous sommes vos amis, petite fluer Fae," he smiled at Fabi. "Can you give me a hand helping her back indoors, the cognac has made her heavier."

Carrying me gently back into the house and laying me back on the bed, where the exhausted Abby joined me again so that I didn't spend the night alone.

Exhausted Abby sat talking to me but she was fading fast, dozing off as she spoke to me having spent all night awake with me then doing another shift at work, she needed to sleep. While she was trying to talk to me, I just told her to get some sleep, initially she seemed reluctant but when I told her again, she eased back and fell to sleep, her glasses hanging off her face and her head drooped to the side.

Gently I rolled her onto her side and took her glasses off and put them aside for her, relaxing she soon looked carefree as she slept. While Abby slept, I sat awake thinking about her, she was odd, during my first week at work I thought she didn't like me as she never spoke beyond an awkward morning greeting.

Hiding shyly behind her glasses with the odd forced smile, I remember the shock and surprise when she invited me to go shopping with her and to spend the night. Yet somehow this girl had appeared when I needed someone the most? Without so much as a thought, she even abandoned her date that evening to come to my aid?

Truly she was curious but we had become friendly over the last week by spending our lunch breaks together, whatever the case I felt lucky and honoured to have met her.

Thinking about what tomorrow might bring, I wondered if my bipolar disorder would give my friends a shock when we ventured to the park. Depression and bipolar for me was often like a wave, surfing high among an ocean of happiness and stability but no matter how long that wave runs, it breaks at some point which would lead to my often-violent crashes. Sometimes however after a crash something would happen, something very unusual, once in a while after a crash the old Fae would come out, the Fae my mum missed so sorely.

Somewhere buried within me that cute and optimistic 11-year-old girl was still alive and well, the Fae whose dreams hadn't yet been slowly crushed or smashed out of her. When 11-year-old Fae came out, people loved to be around me, I would become ecstatic and jubilant, the world was my oyster, and I would float high amongst all and conquer the world with her optimism.

My mum loved it when those brief moments happened and in truth so did I. It was just a shame they were rare and where generally I shut myself away for my crashes, it was even rarer that anyone got to see this side of me.

I tried to rest but couldn't as I kept running over the afternoons events and how much Francois had astounded me? Francois was genuinely one of the most unpleasant people I had encountered, his comments were vile and biting, though he was quite charming. However buried underneath all that was a very kind and caring gentleman, truthfully though he largely just talked at me, he had genuinely slowly helped ease my crash.

I said it was his cognac that helped but it was his odd stories and humming that had pulled me back from my nether. Soothing tones that he hummed in had almost hypnotised me out of my slump and his odd thoughtfulness had calmed the darkness within me.

Colette and everyone else had helped but his strange mannerisms had really done the job, though I wondered if his stories were true? Were the comments he made purely a disdain for bad clothing? He was very passionate as he spoke about wanting to make women feel good about themselves so maybe it was all true? Whatever the case was tomorrow, I was going to try and thank* him personally for his help, whether he would accept it was another thing as he didn't seem to help me to gain thanks.

Trying to get some sleep as Abby rested so peacefully, but instead I just watched over her almost as if now I was keeping watch of her in exchange for what she had done for me.

Though I did manage to drift off just for a few hours, waking slightly bemused as Abby rolled around the bed seeming to have some kind of dream or nightmare. When sunlight began to soak through the curtains, I knew it was going to be a good day and 11-year-old Fae was here today, the only question would be how long for?

Alyssia was up early and came in to check on me and the dead looking Abby, she took me downstairs to chat with her and have a cup of coffee before everyone else woke up. Alyssia started to ask about my crashes and how often they happened, feeling reassured I told her that they were fairly irregular, sometimes a couple a month other times I could go a couple of months without one but normally when that happened the crash would be a big one.

Explaining that for the most part people didn't get to see them as in Oured I didn't exactly have any friends to see them and if they happen, I tended to shut myself away until they passed. Alyssia also asked about the memory I spoke about during my crash and I started to tell her about what people used to do to me when I was growing up, all the bullying and other things. Even recounting Barryn saving me from throwing myself off that bridge, it was the first time that anyone beyond me and Barryn actually knew what had happened that night.

While telling her about the friends, I told her about the boyfriends I had that had been no better or worse, generally getting used to make other girls jealous or for a quick laugh. Confessing that for the most part my self-confidence was nearly non-existent and that I had trust issues along with questionable self-doubts. Seemingly disgusted by what used to happen to me, she made a promise that if I needed her all I had to do was text her, she was also going to ask Tony and Gale to let her and Fabi join the messaging group so they would know if anything happened to me.

Tony and Gale, if they argued with her wouldn't stand a chance, she was quite fearsome when she was stern and her voice commanded respect. Alyssia though was happy that I had come to Ljianstipol and found a new way forward and admired my bravery for moving here alone.

Abby was next to join us walking downstairs still looking shattered, she piled a coffee into her to help her wake up as she slouched at the kitchen table. While she sat and joined us, I carried on telling Alyssia my story and in particular why I decided to move to Ljianstipol. Telling them about my early working life in Oured, where most jobs I found would last maybe a month or so before a crash or episode would soon help me find my way out of the door.

Explaining that it was almost impossible to find work as for the most part, the moment any potential employer saw my conditions on my resume, they would write me off. Sadly, though my last employer in Oured had been pretty good, moving me round the business and adapting things to try and help me, it was just a shame that budget cuts made me the easy one to let go just before Christmas.

Alyssia and Abby both sat subdued but very intently listening to my more fractured past, Fabi came and joined us but both hushed him as he sat to listen in with them. Moving to explain how that Christmas I wound up alone and lonely, unemployed and with no real hope of any kind, I decided to change everything in a ditch effort to try and give myself a life somewhere.

Telling them how I had cut my dreads off in a breakdown over my appearance and then found myself smiling at a picture taken when I was a guest at the Davizioso, I had decided to move to Ljianstipol. Admitting to both that when I moved down, I had never expected to find either friends or any kind of job so quickly but had been lucky to have met good people who had helped me out.

Abby just sat looking at me while I told my story before gently cupping my hands, "It's good to have you here Fae and maybe you just need the right people around you?" Her soft and sweet sentiment was carried by her eyes too.

Time ticked away as we sat talking about my past and before too long Francois and Colette arrived at the door for our day in the park. Together we walked through the streets of Ljianstipol and stopped at Abby's so that she could get changed, she lent me some clothes too. Freshly adorned in her best streetwear, we headed out of the town and up to a large park not too far from my home.

Walking along neatly cut pathways towards a large open lawn in the middle of the park with two large plazas at either end of a long winding set of paths which ran through gardens. Down the end of one of the plazas was a stage area where bands sometimes played during the summer and a children's play area nearby. Sitting in the warm sunshine in the park with these new friends, I found myself surrounded by, Colette came over to me and offered me her hand, I took her hand and she took me for a little walk with her.

Wandering slowly through a small pathway which wound through ornate bushes and trees she started to ask if I was okay now and began to confess that she was worried about me.

Talking to her, I began to tell her my story just as I had told Alyssia during the morning, however she stopped me from doing so and just said, "You are here now and those things will not happen to you while you are here, me and Francois won't let that happen to you," Colette began to tell me how her and Francois had met, strangely enough it turned out Francois had been telling the story completely truthfully!

Colette even admitted that his normally quite barbed comments were his frustrations at an industry designed to make women feel awful, seemingly he was angry at fashion and not people? Colette did make a simple promise to me as we wandered around the park, whenever I had a crash or episode, she would come and see me a few days afterwards. Strangely motherly as she made this promise to me, she had also spoken to Gale and asked them to set up a different group so that they could all see if I needed help.

Feeling touched by the sentiment of her I soon gave her a hug and she didn't hesitate to reply in kind and tell me. "You know where me and Francois are if you ever need us." She let me compose myself and we walked back to the group sat in the park, which seemingly had grown larger?

Tony and Mona had joined the group and just as me and Colette got back Gale and Anna appeared to join us too. Sitting merrily in the sunshine we sat with conversations flowing and spirits running high, my new friends were keen to learn some more about me. Despite my fears, I started to tell them the stories I had been telling Alyssia and Abby during the morning, slowly talking them through the destructive path that had brought me to Ljianstipol.

Seemingly disgusted and outraged by some of the problems that had gone on in my past though there was a sense of hope today as I began to talk about my new job. Sitting and openly confessing that if it wasn't for the Davizioso and the staff helping me all those years ago that I probably wouldn't be around today.

Admitting to the entire group that I was still amazed to now find myself working at a place where I once stayed as a patient and that I hoped to help people the same way I had been helped all those years ago.

Hoping that maybe I could use my experience and understanding of my own conditions to help other people with their own problems, I felt an odd sense of pride as those words came out of me. Fuelling a high of passion and self-belief as I sounded resolute that I would help people understand themselves and help them, I didn't quite notice just how much attention Gale was paying to me.

Gale applauded me as I concluded my speech. "But before that Francois owes you dinner," he laughed at Francois who just shrugged his shoulders at him, "And not some cheap restaurant Francois!" Colette bit at him too.

Francois waved his hands at her, "Of course I will take her?"

Colette shook her head at him, "Give me your card, I will take her somewhere nice!"

Francois handed her a card and she tucked it into her purse, "What are you doing on Wednesdayes evening, Fae?"

I sat awkwardly before shyly answering, "Going to dinner with you?" She smiled.

"Correct, meet me at the gallery at 6? Is that enough time for you to be ready after work, Fae?"

I looked and wondered, "Ah make it 7 then Fae," she smiled at me. Our little group agreed to meet every Sunday afternoon during the warmer months of the year, either at the park or we would go round each other's houses and just sit in the garden. Seemingly generating a small congregation of friends around me when Tony asked me a sincere question, "Do you like BBQ's Fae?"

Taken aback by his question. "Of course?"

He smiled at Gale, "We hold a get-together every year at the end of June, we'd love you to come along this year?"

I paused, stunned by their offer. "I'd love to come!" Both smiled back before they stood to leave.

Francois sat next to me and spoke to me briefly, "Colette has she spoken to you?"

I nodded at him.

"Ah good, she was very worried about you Fae," he smiled oddly at me. "She is quiet but she is very caring, we will take care of you if you ever need us to," his softer side was incredible, it was almost a shame that he was tainted by the insults he threw around.

Energy was surging through me as I ran to play on the swings in the play area, I guess 11-year-old Fae was here today after all! Jumping on the swings and trying to get as high as I could before I felt sick, Abby came to join me too, neither of us had strong stomachs though. Colette led Francois home as the afternoon drew to a close, soon enough Alyssia and Fabi left too and me and Abby found ourselves sitting in the park together.

Talking while sitting on the swings again she started to ask about my past a little more, seemingly in disbelief about how I had been treated in Oured and in school in particular. While I told her what she had missed out on hearing while she slept, she seemed upset at how people had treated me and promised to be there if I ever needed her. Walking back, she left me back at my home, I did invite her in for the night but she confessed to needing her bed tonight.

Sitting on my sofa thinking how fortunate I had been to find myself in this new place with new people and yet somehow, they didn't seem to mind my issues and problems? Feeling slightly overwhelmed by the generosity and compassion that they had demonstrated over the weekend; I wondered how this weekend would have been had I still been in Oured?

I would have spent it alone and locked away in my old house with nobody around and certainly no one who would have come rushing to my aid? Wondering where Colette planned to take me for the evening out with her, I did hope she wasn't going to go crazy on the venue.

During my first day back at work I once again was shadowing another member of staff but with a different aim to before? Rather than just following them during their daily rounds seeing different guests I was partnered with one of the therapists, sitting in with them during their therapy sessions and mentoring sessions.

Spending the first day listening and just watching as she carefully and gently unpicked the past of different patients, it was almost as if I was being groomed, just I had no idea why that was? After lunch I rejoined her in the room she used for her patients, but instead of a patient coming in she sat me on the chair and began to talk to me about my crash over the weekend. Over the next two hours, she worked her magic on me and my mind, slowly unpicking the years of torment that were all still very much a part of my reality.

We discussed my trigger signs in particular, we sat sifting over the days before my crash and she pointed out a few times when I had been giving myself warning signs that something was coming. Though it felt odd, she was trying to help me to spot my own warning signs so that when things started to build up or were starting to turn, I could take myself to somewhere that might help me out.

Leaving work an hour early she took me to a few places that she thought might help me for the next time my warning signs started to show up. Walking me to a spot on the beach and to a park not far away from the beach where generally people didn't tend to go so, she thought they might be good places for me to head if I needed them.

Walking home that evening was odd, it felt as if a weight had been lifted off my shoulders and maybe I just needed to learn a bit more about myself again to prevent my problems ruining my life? Over the evening, a new group appeared on my phone, with people from work and my new circle of friends, all now able and willing to help the next time I had a crash, slowly I was being surrounded by supporting hands.

During the evening, Abby popped round to see how I was, with her not seeing me during the day she was concerned I had crashed again and had come to make sure I was okay. Taking a keen interest, she seemed eager to try and understand more about me and my ongoing conditions, we sat in my kitchen discussing my past in greater depth than before.

Seemingly, I had made a good friend in the shy and reclusive girl, sitting she took mental notes as I went into greater depth about the different troubles which had marred my past. Feeling rude as I had never really asked her about herself, she was apprehensive to mention too much until she started to talk about how she wound up with a nice apartment in town at such a young age.

Abby hadn't been at the Davizioso long before her parents needed to move away, her father got a job far to the north and they would be relocating, saddened as she was enjoying her job at the hotel, she reluctantly handed her notice in, but Gale refused to accept her resignation unless she told him where she was going. Slowly, Gale extracted from Abby that she didn't want to leave but couldn't afford to live on her own in Ljianstipol, she was only just 19 at the time and hadn't saved enough to rent anywhere let alone buy somewhere to live.

Striking a deal with Gale, she moved into the hotel and lived in a downstairs room round the back of the hotel while Gale had started to work her money for her. Around a year later, Gale handed her a set of keys, he hadn't been able to fully buy anywhere but he kept some money aside to keep working his magic on and Abby had a place to live.

In exchange for his hard work, Abby agreed to stay at the Davizioso indefinitely though she admitted that was her choice and not something Gale or Tony had asked of her. Slightly inspired by her odd story, I slept pretty well that evening and wondered why I had been partnered with the therapist at work? Were Tony and Gale grooming me or just simply trying to help me once again?

During the next two days at work the same thing happened, I spent the day attending the therapy sessions that my mentor ran before we had a one-to-one session at the end of the day. Slowly, I was learning a few things from her, she dropped the volume of her voice just slightly and spoke with a soft and an almost hypnotic tone as she gently eased her way into people's minds.

She even came to lunch with me, escorting me to a few places round town that she hadn't yet shown me, peaceful and tranquil places which recharged my mind from the things I had heard from her patients.

Before I left on Wednesday, she gave me a small book about mental health therapy, implying that it might help me in the future with my problems and that it would be a good start point to learning how to try and control my mind. Unsuspecting, I sat reading a little before I met Colette for my meal at Francois' expense, meeting her in the market square near the gallery.

Dressed in a simple top and trousers she looked mesmerising as she escorted me to a very plush bistro through the back streets of the market. Staggered by the terrifying prices, I offered her to just take me to somewhere slightly cheaper by the river, however she insisted that as Francois was paying, then no expense would be spared tonight. Colette was a curious person, she barely spoke most of the time, just softly smiling or listening in the background, but from time to time she came alive.

Sometimes I wondered if maybe just the sheer extroverted nature and flamboyance of Francois was part of the reason for that, but she was unashamedly caring and considerate towards me. Having had a wonderful meal she took me to her shop to show me something she had been working on, a simple hippy style top, which wrapped over the shoulders with a split down the middle like a jacket.

Lushly adorned in beads and silver clasping it looked incredible, she asked me to test it out for her, she guided my arms into the top and closed me inside it. Guiding me to a mirror she showed me what I looked like in it, it looked incredible! It was subtle but enticing, concealing but dazzling enough to draw attention, she started to adjust the straps to support my breasts, when she announced something to me. Having previously turned down her gift she had made this top just for me? Feeling stunned, I once again attempted to refuse her generosity but this time she wasn't letting me walk out of her shop empty handed.

Simply, she told me that I now had a new life and this top was the start of my new life, I couldn't refuse her again and she was more than happy to walk me back home with my new top on. Feeling humbled by her once again I just thanked her again and again as she walked me to my doorstep, she shared a little hug with me before she walked back to Francois.

Excited by the kindness and generosity of the people of Ljianstipol I had found as friends I spent most of the night struggling to sleep through excitement. Sitting at my kitchen table I started to read the book that my mentor had provided me with, casually thumbing through the book during the night.

Waking at my kitchen table, it was obvious that my days of staying up all night were long gone, luckily, I had only dribbled down my own arm and not over the book I had been supplied with. Thinking that I was late I rushed around the house and got myself ready to go to work, racing down the streets I didn't stop to get coffee this morning as I was late enough as it was. Bounding up the cobbled streets and through the door of the Davizioso to find the night staff were still here?

Had I looked when I passed Fabi's shop, I would have noticed that he wasn't even open and he wouldn't be for another hour. Rather than walk home to come back in two hours' time, I went and sat in my old room and read some more of that book when Tony came and joined me.

As per their promises all those years ago my room was still here and still right next to Shanky, I sat on my old bed laid down slowly chewing my way through the first chapters of the book my mentor had given me.

Tony sat beside me as I continued reading my book, "Does it feel strange being back in this room Fae?" He asked in a strange voice.

I turned and looked at him, softly smiling as he recollected the past. "A little strange, did you really keep my room for me this whole time?"

Tony softly patted my back, "I promised you a place to stay if you ever needed it and I keep my promises! How has this week been for you?"

I rolled onto my back and sat up next to him. "Pretty good, it's strange to hear stories similar to mine but it's helping me, this book is interesting, it's a shame I didn't have this before!"

Tony took the book and looked at the cover. "It would have made things easier?" I thought about his question, "Possibly?"

Tony handed me back the book, "You will be with Joanne again next week, we have some new guests coming over the weekend too, so be ready for a fun week!" Tony stood to leave and looked round at me. "Hey Fae?"

I smiled at him.

"You don't have to be here two hours early to impress us, just be yourself instead, okay?" He winked and walked away as I thought to myself, *If only he knew why I was so early!*

Joanne arrived at my door to take me down to her room, she was surprised to see me at work so early and reading the book she had given me. "You find it interesting, Fae?" She asked as we walked through the corridors to her room.

"Pretty interesting, I wonder if it would have helped me when I was younger?" Joanne chuckled, "Would you have read it when you were younger?" She ushered me along chuckling as it dawned upon me that there would have been zero chance, I would have read the book during my teen years.

Offering me a coffee we sat and chatted for half an hour before our first patient arrived for their session with Joanne, however Joanne had slightly different plans in mind. While the patient got themselves comfortable, she started to talk to them and told them that today I would be asking them their questions! I looked at her in total shock and questioned her, she smiled back, "Let's see how much you have really been reading?"

Flummoxed slightly, I started to think about what she had been saying during the start of the sessions during the week I had been present for. While the patient watched me patiently, I began to recollect how she had started her sessions, slightly panicked, I blurted out my introduction and looked round nervously.

"Take your time and be calm," Joanne just smiled sweetly and encouraged me, I stepped back and thought about walking away but the patient's soft smile made me think again. I stared at the wall and took a deep breath and composed myself before I turned round and started the session again, calmly and composed I introduced myself and began the session. Soon enough the patient responded and it eased my nerves and an almost word-perfect rendition of Joanne's sessions began.

Joanne sat writing down notes and keeping an eye while I began to engage with our patient and the time soon flew by as I became engrossed in this odd exchange. With the session over, the patient thanked both me and Joanne and left us behind, she turned and smiled at me. "Did you enjoy that in the end, Fae?"

I couldn't lie to her, "I loved that!"

She smiled at me. "I know, so you're going to do the next one too?"

I smiled at her, "If you are happy with that?" She smiled at me again to say yes.

Hosting the next session was easier but still I was cautious as I proceeded to deliver it, carefully reciting Joanne's exact words but this time smoothly and without having to stop and think too much. Rewarding me by taking me for a drink by the river during our lunch hour, she told me that I would be conducting the last two sessions of the day too.

Though I didn't think until the final session came, Joanne was getting me to perform my final session on myself? Calmly talking to myself for just over an hour talking to myself about my own problems and answering myself about them while Joanne sat quietly keeping notes. Feeling slightly bemused as the session drew to a close, she offered a simple insight as to why she had gotten me to perform this odd task.

"Your own mental health is the single most important thing you have Fae and the more you understand your own the easier it will be to look after yourself," Joanne's words hit me deep within and as I stood thinking about what she had told me as she offered me another book, "Something for the weekend, Fae?" She handed me a far thicker book.

"See you again on Monday Fae and well done," Joanne waved me goodbye as I headed home filled with joy over what I had spent today doing and thinking about what she had said to me at the end of the day.

Sitting at my kitchen table, I processed Joanne's words of advice and thought deeply about what she had said and started to look through the large book she had given me. Losing all track of time as I engrossed myself in this tricky and complex world of psychological disorders to look up and see it was nearly 2am! Heading to bed her words kept floating round my mind as they started to seep into my conscious thoughts about myself.

Spending almost all of Friday reading and digesting more and more of the books she had provided me with when she sent me a text message, "Great job this week, Fae, you'll be even better next week!"

I smiled to myself as I read the text and replied to her, "Thank you, chapter 4!" She just sent back an x.

Spending all day reading and thinking about the previous day almost becoming transfixed upon understanding myself, I decided to try and replicate our final session yesterday.

Laying myself down on my sofa, I started to replicate the way in which Joanne had run her sessions upon me, talking myself in and out of the memories and terrors that haunted me. Lying with my eyes closed talking to myself I didn't even notice until I opened my eyes that I had an audience.

Fabi and Alyssia were sitting on the sofa opposite quietly just watching as I talked to myself and provided myself with therapy and reassurance. I looked at both of them wide eyed and stunned that they had been watching me. "How long have you been there?" Alyssia smiled at me.

"About half an hour now," I sat myself up.

"How come you didn't say anything?" Fabi smiled at me.

"We didn't wanna interrupt you, it sounded deep!" I smiled awkwardly trying to think what they had just heard me talking to myself about. Alyssia looked at the book on the table near their sofa, "Pretty deep stuff, Fae, but we can help with what you were just talking about?"

I looked shocked and worried. "What did you hear?"

Alyssia walked over and whispered in my ear, "You want a boyfriend? We can take you into town to find someone for the night if you want?"

I went bright red as they had stumbled in to hear me talking to myself about all the jerks who had built me up and then dumped me for a quick laugh. "Sorry about that! I'm practising giving myself therapy."

Alyssia laughed at me and hugged me. "We kinda guessed that, why though Fae?" I started to explain what had happened the day before when Joanne had forced me to run some therapy sessions with her.

Proudly recollecting almost every single detail of every single second of the day they realised that I had a great day at work yesterday. Confessing how scared I was, during the first session before Joanne had gotten me to conduct a final therapy session on myself to try and help with my own health. Both seemed to listen intently as I grew more and more excited as I spoke about the new twist to my job, though I admitted I was worried about Thursday and finding out whether I would be staying at the Davizioso or back on the prowl for employment.

Alyssia saw that I was worried and that I seemed to have found my career, she spoke to me about it openly and frankly asking Fabi to go home so that we could talk properly. Alyssia assured me that if what I said about yesterday was remotely true then the Davizioso would be stupid to let me go, though her words were sincere, they didn't stop my concerns.

Sitting for two hours, she reassured me that I wouldn't be looking for a new job next Friday and that Tony and Gale would know that I was a good member of staff to keep on. Alyssia came to leave having rebuilt my confidence slightly, as she headed away, I grew a deep determination for Monday morning, I was going to spend all weekend studying and practising so that when Monday arrived, I would be ready.

Spending nearly all of Saturday reading through the book that Joanne had given me I started to look deeper at myself to gain a better understanding of what I was reading. Starting to keep notes on what I discussed with myself and writing down my root causes to my ongoing problems, I found an old book to write them into. Saturday night, I read more of the book before I laid on my sofa to run through another session with myself, once again keeping notes when I finished.

Sunday was a wet and windy day, so there was no park meetup or garden party today, but it was just as well. I was so engrossed with this book that by Sunday afternoon I had worked my way through nearly three quarters of its pages. On Sunday night, I tucked the book and my notebook into my bag ready for work tomorrow morning, I was looking forward to the week ahead.

Walking down slightly early, I wanted to meet with Joanne before our day began, Fabi was still setting up when I arrived at his shop early for my morning fix. Cheerful as ever though still slightly asleep he introduced me to a new coffee he had obtained from Haiti. Walking to work with my fix in hand I discovered that it was quite a bit stronger than my normal coffee but oddly smooth?

Joanne was waiting for me in her therapy room, greeting me with a smile she laughed when she saw the bookmark in the book, she had given me for the weekend. Joanne briefed me and talked me through patient notes, explaining what they meant and what to do with them before we began our first session of the day.

Two new guests had arrived over the weekend, young girls both suffering from anxiety and depression, as Joanne guided me through the notes on them, I got a big shock to see the root cause of their problems.

Both patients had listed social media and the internet as being the source of their problems? Joanne confessed it was a new problem but rapidly growing and becoming more virulent among applicants for care at the Davizioso. Joanne was going to host the first session and then I would host the second as our first patient walked in and strange issues arose.

Joanne began her session as usual introducing herself and calming the patient to sit and make themselves comfortable but as Joanne began to try prying the patient locked up? Joanne tried to coax her into talking in that soft and hypnotic voice but the more she tried the tighter the patient held their tongue? Looking at me, Joanne shrugged her shoulders as the patient avoided any form of eye contact with her, a generational void had emerged and was growing larger.

Sensing Joanne's frustration at being unable to form any kind of bond, I asked the patient what their favourite internet site was and suddenly they looked at me and just opened up.

Spilling every tale, they had about their problems after becoming addicted to social media how it had set off a spiralling reaction of negative emotions and self-loathing. Joanne made notes while I spoke to the patient keeping the momentum running, soon enough the session drew to a close and Joanne patted me on the shoulder as the patient left.

Joanne took the lead on the next session and this time the patient responded to her while I kept notes, the morning was whizzing by so fast that we spent lunch talking in Joanne's room. While she looked through the book, she had loaned me she came across the notes that I had made about myself to use as a bookmark.

Quizzically she took the note out but left an envelope on the page to mark it for me, she sat scanning the notes I had made before quietly pausing and heading to a filing cabinet. Sifting through files she removed one and handed it to me, quietly I sat reading through the notes when she handed me back my own notes, looking them side by side. "They're identical?" Joanne nodded at me.

"Yes, they are, do you recognise the patient just from the notes?" I sat looking through them and trying to think who it might be before I gave in.

"Who is it?" Joanne turned and handed me the file the notes had come from, I looked at the name on the file and looked at Joanne. "It's you Fae, when you were 17, you have just accurately self-assessed yourself," I held the file and compared my notes.

"I haven't improved either?" Joanne looked me in the eye.

"Not yet you haven't but you haven't gotten worse either!" I took solace in that fact.

Joanne let me lead most of the sessions throughout the remainder of the week, partly to distract me from the terror of my meeting with Gale and Tony on Thursday when I would find out if I was staying or going. Joanne told me I was improving every day which was a nice thing to hear from her, she gave me another book after I consumed the second book she had provided me with.

Wednesday night I was a bag of nerves and Joanne knew I would be, she texted me a few times to make sure I was okay, she was supportive and stewardly too. During Thursday morning she allowed me to lead during the morning sessions before she took me for a drink by the river for lunch.

Sitting on the river's bank, she started to talk to me about what I wanted to do in the future and soon enough I spilled my heart out about hoping to become like her and use my problems to help people.

Joanne told me she had put a good word in for me with Gale but only I could decide my own fate in the long run, but she did her best to keep me calm before my meeting at 2. Joanne walked with me back to the Davizioso and guided me up the stairs to Tony and Gale's meeting room, she wished me good luck as she went off to resume her afternoon sessions.

Sitting in a chair near their meeting room as minutes felt like long and nail-biting hours, soon enough Abby appeared. "Hey Fae, Gale has moved the meeting upstairs and outside if you don't mind?"

I nodded at her but before I headed up a strange notion came over me? I went into their office and grabbed two bottles of beer from the fridge and then proceeded to my date with destiny? I'm not sure if I hoped to blackmail them with their own beer but it seemed a good idea in my head if it was too hot to sit in the meeting room then I was sure they would appreciate a cold beer. Walking up the stairs to the hallway and entrance to the garden felt like climbing a mountain and the sun blinding as I opened the door and ventured into the garden.

Fearful and trembling I walked round the winding paths of the garden to see Gale sat alone on the pergola over the little pond. Gale sitting alone set my nerves off even more as maybe this was goodbye if Tony wasn't here? Though as I approached and offered him a bottle of cold beer he did at least smile as he took it.

Gale offered me a seat beside him and pulled out a large paper file and began to look through it while I sat waiting for the meeting to begin. Looking up as he read through the files, he spoke, "Tony won't be joining us today Fae, he isn't so good at this side of things," as he thumbed through different notes.

While he sifted paper, my mind and imagination went into overdrive. "Why no Tony?" I sat imagining all the reasons Tony had been excluded from the meeting when Gale laid the papers down and began the meeting.

Passing me the beer I had brought with me for Tony he began by asking how I was feeling following my crash a few weeks ago. Telling him I felt fine and since being paired up with Joanne I had learned to spot a few warning signs that I had given off before my crash happened.

Gale then asked how I was finding working as a carer at the Davizioso, naturally I told him that I loved it and enjoyed spending time with the guests and residents of the hotel. Gale started to tell me how I had been as a carer before being partnered up with Joanne for the last two weeks. Though he wasn't disappointed, he did note a few places where I could improve but he then let out a big sigh which sent my heart crashing.

Gale sat up and looked at me. "Fae, the problem is we can't see you as a carer, it's just not you, you are attentive and do care but your heart really lies elsewhere, and we know that."

Looking down I sighed back at him, "I can get better?"

Gale sighed and sat next to me. "Look Fae it's not that simple, you just need to do what you have a bigger passion for." Gale put his hand on my back, "Is this the end then?" Gale didn't say anything, he just sat waiting for something?

"Is this the end, Gale?" I asked again and he leant back, "Do you remember something you said in the park after your crash Fae?"

I thought hard to myself, *Not really?* Gale sat back up, "I remember your words exactly. I want to use my problems to help people, you remember saying that?"

I sat and thought and remembered talking to Abby or Colette about that, "Yes kinda."

Gale patted me on the back, "That's why I partnered you with Joanne, we like people who do things rather than talking about them, how many books have you read, Fae?" Sitting up slightly bemused, "Books?"

Gale replied for me. "Two books, and didn't you do this assessment?"

I nodded at him and he pulled out a copy of the notes I had used as a bookmark. "It's identical to your old one from when you were 17, you couldn't have copied it as you had no idea, we kept them?" I nodded again at him, still confused about what he was getting at?

"Impressive stuff Fae," he smiled at me and handed me another beer. "You aren't going anywhere, Fae, just we are changing what we will be employing you to do. You have thrived under Joanne's stewardship and even hosted some of her therapy sessions?"

I nodded feeling slightly concerned still.

"You have read through two text books and learned enough about them to host sessions when Joanne couldn't get through to a patient?"

I nodded to him again, though feeling less concerned by now. "You even have done a perfect assessment of yourself with no training and no option to have copied this document?"

I sat up to respond. "Yeah, though maybe I should have kept it hidden?"

Gale sat back opposite me and leant back, "Fae we won't be taking you on as a carer full time, I'm really sorry," I took a sip of my beer to mask my sorrow.

"We want you to train with us to be a therapist instead," Gale's words hit my mind and without any form of control I just let out, "You want me to do what!" And spat a mix of beer and foam over him in disbelief.

"Uh I guess you were surprised by that?" Gale laughed and wiped the beer off his lap. "We will put you on a course which runs in two stages, each stage should take a year to complete and each stage will give you a diploma which will eventually lead to a specialisation in a chosen field."

"Joanne will be your mentor at first, but eventually we would like to run some groups with you hosting them. The world is changing Fae and we are getting more and more people through our doors and they are getting younger and younger too. They have skirted round the system just like you did, who better to help them out than you Fae?"

I was filled with nerves, "But what if I can't do it?"

Gale shrugged his shoulders and laughed, "You matched a diagnosis and assessment of yourself which was completed by someone with 20 years' experience! You will be fine, and I know you won't let us down; how do you feel about these three areas though? Depression, bipolar disorder and cyber related health problems."

I was taken aback. "Cyber?"

Gale nodded, "Just like the girls you and Joanne have been dealing with all week, we are getting more and more applying to come every week, it's a growing problem and I would like us to specialise in it, if you are happy to take that on?"

I felt a surge of energy run through me. "Yes of course, is there anything I need to do before Monday?"

Gale smiled back, "It's the weekend just enjoy yourself and worry about everything on Monday and maybe celebrate what you are going to achieve, oh but one last thing before you go and get drunk."

I sat up and looked at Gale focussed, "We meet every Wednesday afternoon to discuss progress, patients and anything else? Okay? Eventually, your old room will become your office."

I shook his hand, "Sounds fine to me, but are you sure about this?" I looked at him slightly stunned and bemused.

"Absolutely sure, Fae, welcome aboard!" He grasped my hand firmly and shook it. "There are going to be times when this is tough, Fae, your issues aren't going to just go away, and we know that but we will always be here to support you and we believe in you!"

Gale held my hand firmly as he gave this final statement. "Now go and celebrate!" Gale released my hand and with an air of shock, disbelief and thrill I headed back down the stairs and into the main hallway of the Davizioso.

Joanne was standing just inside the hallway waiting for me. "Welcome aboard partner, see you on Monday!" She handed me a large and heavy bag, "Don't try to read them all this weekend, you have plenty of time to read those."

Joanne walked away as I stood looking into the bag of thick books, she had given me. "Thank you, see you Monday!" I headed home happy and jubilant.

Sitting on my couch I eased back when suddenly the reality of what had happened and that I had agreed to really sank in. Pulling a cushion over my face as I screamed out to myself in sheer exhilaration as now, I had a future and a career doing something that I had always hoped to be able to do.

Promising myself that no matter how hard things got, I would just work harder to get what I wanted, I would be able to use my problems to help other people and make their lives better. Nervous and excited but fearful yet determined, there was no way on earth that I was going to fail either myself or the Davizioso.

The weekend celebration had been heavy but barely able to contain myself, I sat watching the clock tick down on Monday morning eager to start the new chapter of my career. Minutes dragged, as the clock slowly and painfully wound its way down before I could leave for work, amid the partying that had occurred I had started to chew another of the books Joanne had provided me with.

Starting to grow restless, I left half an hour early. *They won't mind 30 minutes?* I thought as I strode proudly down to Fabi's coffee shop for my morning fix. Still recovering from the weekend of jubilance, Fabi was not quite awake when I arrived at his shop, he slurred his words and nearly dropped my coffee over me.

I apologised for causing him to be this way this morning, maybe our celebrations were too intense? He laughed it off, "I should have learned by now Fae, have a great day!" as he disappeared to hide from the sunshine.

Arriving earlier than Joanne, her room was locked so I headed to sit on my old bed in my old room next to Shanky's, sitting for a few minutes to gather my thoughts and compose myself a little before the real work began. Tony wandered in as I sat thinking, "Hey Fae, well done!"

He sat beside me and patted me on the back, I looked round at him, "Thank you, but it's you I should be thanking Tony," he smiled but shook his head.

"No, you have done this by yourself and for yourself, I didn't decide if you stayed or not, you did!" I sat up beside him. "Joanne helped me more than people know," I thought deeply about that as I replied, "No she guided you but you read the books and did the real work, though it's not going to be easy Fae, this place is changing and fast."

"The world is different now, Fae, in truth it's more understanding on paper but less forgiving than ever before. People are self-consumed and the world is a strange and isolating place for many people now, but of course that is where we come in. If you are going to be anything, Fae, then be like me that night we first met, just be the hero for that one person." I sat digesting what Tony said as he stood to leave.

"Tony?" He looked round and I asked, "Why did you dye my hair?"

Tony laughed and walked away, "Come and see me for lunch upstairs and I will tell you why!" Tony left me with questions before I began my day.

Joanne came and collected me to start my new career and to train under her guidance, spending an hour guiding me through the course that I was to be undertaking. Confessing to me that the first month would probably be tedious but that I would need to find a case study for my first assignment, I did have the option to use myself, but she recommended that I saved that for the second stage of my course.

During the morning, she got me to make notes on the patients we had and during the afternoon she would show me how to record them accurately and to save their audio files too. During the morning, we had the same two girls from last week, once again I took the lead on the first patient as she wouldn't open up to Joanne, but she would lead the second patient as they wouldn't open up to me.

However, Joanne was keen to introduce me to the ways that she used to reach that kind of patient and rather than her taking over she pushed me to take over and get my hands into the more complex side of therapy.

Nurturing and encouraging, Joanne guided me through a few techniques to try unlocking the second patient along with a couple of backup techniques just in case they refused. Having taken note of her mentoring, I led the second session and within minutes had begun to extract a story from a seemingly unwilling patient. Gently, I pried round them until they let me in and started to talk about themselves and the problems they were experiencing.

Joanne kept notes for me, but I also kept my own just in case either of us missed something important. When the session concluded, Joanne checked over our notes and we had recorded the exact same details, she started to show me how to accurately record the notes we took and collate it with the audio recordings that were taken for every session.

Guiding me through how to start the first assessment for my course, I noticed that she seemed proud of me and sent me away for lunch with my head held high.

Walking through the Davizioso, I started to head to the rooftop garden to see Tony for lunch as he requested that I did. Feeling no anxiety as I wandered out into the garden to find him sitting in the pergola over the pond, he seemed oddly at peace? Offering me a coffee, he started to talk to me about our discussion during the morning which had left me more than a little confused. Sitting back, he started his insight for me.

"You wanted to know why I dyed your hair?"

I nodded back at him.

"Do you know how many people fail our interviews Fae?"

I pondered for a moment. "Not many?"

Tony laughed and sat back, "90 percent."

I sat up shocked, "90 percent? How?"

Easing back into his chair he spoke openly, "Most people refuse the beer or are insulted by it, the thing is, Fae, as a football coach I had hundreds of players who were great on paper just they weren't that way on the pitch. For example, based upon your history at work you shouldn't even be on reception but here you are!"

I sat up to listen harder to him, "If we went purely on people who are good on paper, we wouldn't be running today, we don't employ people who are good on paper we look for something more than that. We want people who become part of people's lives or people that give everything to make that change for someone, saying you can do that is one thing but doing it is something very different. The beer might seem insignificant, but it tells me that one day someone will hand you something and you will take it and do something with it to make them happy."

I sat listening intently to his thoughts.

"Even if that is a bottle of blue hair dye?" He smiled. "Meant the world to you back then didn't it?" I sat thinking about that night. "All you wanted was to have blue hair, you didn't want anything else, you just needed a friend to help give you what you wanted."

As he stopped speaking, I found myself sniffling to myself, "It was so stupid but that meant everything to me back then."

Tony sat beside me and comforted me. "I know it did, now you can do that for someone else, you make me very proud Fae and I know you will make us even prouder soon," he sat back again.

"Thing is Fae, people see the game but they don't see the grind that goes in to get there in the first place. The sleepless nights, the missed birthdays or family moments, the nights you cry in fear, the days when you struggle to go on but that is what it takes. Reading those two books was just your starting point, there's no limit to how high you can go Fae, especially if you really want it, we will support you all the way. Bad times and the good times, Fae."

Tony offered me his hand, without hesitation I shook it, "Bad times and the good Tony," he smiled and checked his watch and tapped the face of it.

Heading back to Joanne's room with a steely determination and drive to go as far as I could, together we ploughed through the afternoon sessions before we came to our last session. During the last two weeks, our last session had been a self-help therapy session for me, helping me understand myself and to identify my trigger signs when a crash might be coming and what to do when those signs flagged up.

Joanne had a new plan for this last session of the day, two days a week they would be for my self-help and diagnosis but two days a week she would help me with my course. Sworn to secrecy by her, she was going to give me a far deeper insight into the career path that I had chosen, I was more than willing to accept this offer.

Having previously worked at the hospital nearby, she used that experience to teach me how to record data which could be used across all health facilities in the country and how to conduct myself if life at the Davizioso didn't pan out. Joanne wanted me to have a backup plan so that I wouldn't be eternally bound to work just at the Davizioso, Joanne was readying me to think far larger than that.

Over the next month I developed a routine for home life, during the week and on Saturday I studied and worked on my coursework, on Friday evening and Sunday I took a break and made time for myself. Night after night, during the first month I compiled my first piece of work for my course, Joanne checked the piece for me before I submitted it.

That first stage should have taken me 7 weeks but I completed it in 3, both Joanne and I were astonished when it came back with a very high pass. Framing it, she proudly mounted it upon the wall near her desk before taking me for lunch by the river during our lunch break. Sitting in a bar by the river she confessed that the next month would be hard as at my next meeting with Gale they were going to give me my first solo sessions on Thursdays.

Joanne and Gale would keep an eye on me during the first few sessions, but they would very much be mine and mine alone. Coupled with this, I was now going to be allowed to lead on some of the more severe cases which were present among the patients of the Davizioso, Joanne would guide me, but things were stepping up.

Exactly as Joanne disclosed at my next meeting with Gale, he unveiled his plan, though it wasn't anything like what I had conceived. Anxiety and minor depression cases were frequenting the hotel more and more, but Gale was more concerned about the people who couldn't afford the care or didn't really know if they needed it. Gale's plan was fairly simple every Thursday I would run two group sessions, anyone could come, resident or not and they would be free for anyone to attend.

Unsure about the idea we talked and discussed but we agreed that after the first two weeks we would review them and change them if we needed to. Over the weekend and the next week, I spent as much time as I could trying to prepare myself so that when the first session began, I would be ready for it. During my afternoon meeting with Gale, we both agreed to meet early so that we could both have time to compose ourselves and be ready for them to begin.

Meeting Gale an hour before I should have been at work in his bar downstairs we sat and discussed the day ahead, the initial sessions only had room for 15 people, so at bare minimum, it would be a light introduction to this new theory.

Joanne joined us both half an hour before we opened the doors to the first group, she ran through my plan, and we got the room ready for business.

Soon enough the time arrived, and the 15 chairs were filled and the session began, nervously I introduced myself and got the session underway. Gradually enticing some conversational flow out of people, the session didn't exactly get off to a flying start, mouths and minds were locked as we sat awkwardly trying to get things moving.

Once people started to open up and share their stories things went quickly but it seemed pained and forced, this wasn't what I had in mind?

During lunch, we liaised and tried a different approach for the second session but the same painful first hour happened again before people shared their stories and things opened up. Undeterred, we would just try again next week? Something wasn't right with the sessions and against Gale and Joanne's advice I spent all weekend thinking about it.

Sitting in my garden on Saturday evening, I just couldn't stop myself thinking of ideas how to make things just work better? Gale and Joanne were both supportive but deep down I knew those first sessions just weren't very good and in truth I wouldn't want to sit through one so why should anyone else.

Mulling away I started to think about that girl that Joanne couldn't reach, that generational gap which created a connection void between them. Thinking of that look on Joanne's face when she just couldn't break a word from that girl I had a thought, was connectability the key to it?

Either way it gave me an idea, a risky idea but an idea nevertheless and in truth anything had to be better than what had happened during the first two sessions. During Sunday, I wrote myself a new plan for the next sessions on Thursday, I would have to run it past Gale, but it might just work?

During the meeting on Wednesday with Gale, I put my idea to him, he was concerned about the idea but agreed a compromise with me. The first session would be run the same way we had pre-planned but if it didn't really work then I was free to try my idea out.

Much to my surprise though he didn't want me to run it past Joanne? It seemed either he was confident the planned idea would work, or he didn't want to make her worry? Maybe he just wanted it to be a shock to her if we needed my plan? I wasn't sure what his real motive was, but I mentally prepared myself and rehearsed with myself on Wednesday night ready to put my plan into action.

Thursday morning's session was just as bad as the sessions from the week before, nothing flowed and much of the time was spent in near silence, this was my chance. Sitting alone in the park near the beach for lunch, I psyched myself up to do something that nobody bar Gale knew I was thinking about.

Determined and motivated, I walked back into that room for the afternoon session and there was no pretending I was nervous about what I was about to do. People gathered and took their seats, settled down, the doors were closed, and introductions were made before I stood up, took a deep breath and began.

Standing before the 15 people sat around me, I introduced myself as "Fae Edwards, 26, Depression and Bipolar suffering," and began to tell one of my stories from my childhood.

Picking an evening where my group of friends had agreed to meet up in some shady park somewhere in Oured; only to bail on me and leave me sitting alone and scared in the dark before walking home alone in the rain. Telling the deep hurt that night caused and the sorrow as I masked how much it had cut into me from my mum and dad and how isolated I started to become, as I just couldn't reach out. Sitting alone drip drying in my bedroom and crying to myself as once again I had spent weeks being built up just so that I could be thrown off my own ladder.

Confessing to my audience that this was the start of a bigger spiral of problems which would lead to me attempting to take my own life multiple times before my parents stepped in to get me help. I concluded by admitting that I needed to tell someone sooner how much people were hurting me and how alone I really was, how I shouldn't have been scared and shouldn't have been ashamed either.

Sitting back down, I felt a lump in my throat as I had just given light to a memory and thought that had been reserved almost entirely for myself but oddly it felt good? Applause began and as the group began to openly exchange their stories discussions flowed and life was breathed into the session.

Emotions flooding the room and stories being shared and openly talked about, Gale and Joanne were both watching intently as the session rolled on. Much to my surprise, the session overrun as people continued to talk and exchange their pasts before gathering at the end to bid each other goodbye.

Standing by the doorway I thanked all my guests for coming before just Gale and Joanne were left stood watching me. Clapping as they walked over to congratulate me, Gale conceded defeat and agreed that he would be happy for the sessions to run that way. Gale however did have one concern that telling my stories might be dangerous for me, but Joanne assured him it would be like a therapy session for me too.

Joanne took me for a drink by the river to celebrate the success of the session, confessing that she was even impressed by the bravery of telling my own stories to connect with people, admitting that it was a brilliant idea.

Over the weekend I prepared another two sessions for the week ahead, deciding upon two very different stories to tell my groups to see if this really worked or if the initial success was a mere fluke. During lunch with Joanne on Monday, I ran through the stories I had picked with her to get her input for the sessions, Joanne however was keen to show me something.

Pulling out a copy of the local newspaper she opened the pages to the readers' letters pages and passed the newspaper across the table. Pointing to a letter that had been sent following the session on Thursday, reading through the letter thoroughly. The reader had written in to inform Ljianstipol about the sessions we now hosted at the Davizioso and paid high compliment to my bravery. Joanne, however, wasn't the only one to notice that letter in the paper, during my meeting on Wednesday Tony attended to show me the letter too.

Pleased to see it had caught his eye but what both Tony and Gale were happiest about was that the groups for tomorrow would have 20 people for both. Seemingly a snowball effect had begun.

Thursday morning's session went fantastically, 23 people attended in the end and I opened with an introduction to me and my conditions and told one of my own stories. Recollecting the night that Barryn had saved me from the bridge which eventually led to me visiting the Davizioso, many people just sat in silence before sharing their own stories and much to my satisfaction I once again received applause for sharing my own past with my group.

However, if the morning session was good then the afternoon session would have been legendary, 27 people attended as I shared the story of Tony breaking into my room to rescue me as he thought I had tried to kill myself.

Confessing that before that night I had just hidden away in my room and had no concept of what was going on in my head until Tony and Shanky had helped me to understand myself. Stories and pasts soon flowed round the group as people engaged with each other, it was phenomenal to see, and it felt so good to be using my own problems to help other people.

Gradually though, Joanne was letting me loose, I was now running my own sessions with her supervision on Tuesdays, starting to tackle the newer type of patients attending the sessions.

Younger guests with problems being caused by internet-based activities whether that was social media, online gaming and even online dating. Eating disorders and anxiety problems were becoming a common theme for my patients and it was something that was largely unknown, it was a new field and one that I was taking a keen interest in.

Many of these patients shared a common theme though, for the most part they had willingly caused their problems and would openly admit to doing so. People had little sympathy for them either as for the most part they had "Engineered their own downfalls." However, the impact that was being felt by each one of them was staggering.

Trapped inside their own secondary life they gradually pulled their own life into two pieces, the real version of them and the digital version of them. Debating with Joanne, I wanted to explore this world more and complete a case study about this very theme, the only problem was I wasn't exactly a social person online? Thankfully though, I knew someone who lived this double lifestyle and I just had to hope she would be willing to let me use her as a case study for my coursework.

Abby was at first appearance the sweetest and shyest girl you could ever meet, hiding behind her glasses behind the desk in reception or by the upstairs meeting room, she barely spoke. Often looking on the verge of a breakdown if she had to speak too much, nobody would have expected let alone believed what she became the second she started playing online games. Working Abby was a quiet and shy receptionist, but online Abby was a demon and a cyber vixen.

Truthfully the night I spent round hers, she had actually scared me; she was ferociously competitive and almost psychotic as she ruled whatever game she played. Dancing round her living room yelling taunts down a headset wearing shorts and a vest, had I not witnessed it with my own eyes, I never would have believed it was her.

Though the idea of watching her gaming frightened me, she was the only person that could help me to start to understand this odd world that she inhabited every evening.

During lunch, I asked Abby that dreaded question, much to my surprise she had no hesitation in agreeing to allow me to use her as a study for my coursework. Together we agreed that over the next two weeks, every evening I would spend with Abby watching her feed this odd monster that resided within her.

Before these evenings began, we spent a few hours together as I tried to begin to understand just what she found so addictive and just why it made her so very different. However, the more she tried to explain what she liked about online gaming so much the more confused the story became, seemingly unable to give any real kind of answer as to why she was so addicted to this nightly passion.

Having consulted with Joanne during my afternoon meeting with her, that evening I would begin trying to unravel the mystery of the internet storm that was engulfing so many people.

Walking with Abby to her place felt odd, this wasn't like a girl's night in or anything like that, this was work but this was also someone I cared about and though there were no underlying problems which marred Abby, I was still apprehensive at best. While her game loaded, my nerves started to tingle just a little bit, as she connected her headset and crossed her legs on the sofa, that other side of her soon came out to play.

Leant as far forward as she could, she balanced perfectly engrossed and consumed as she confidently blasted her way a stream of 'Noobs', her gaze was unbreakable, and her mood was fierce as she easily dominated the first round of her game. Having worried that I might put her off just with my mere presence it turned out that I didn't have to worry as for the most part it was like I didn't exist as her victories started to bring out that harsher side of her.

Strutting round her lounge and yelling at the TV she challenged anyone to take her down! That shy and sweet girl was nowhere to be seen right now, as she taunted every person she came into contact with. Ferociously chanting at anyone who had dared mock her as she blew them away and only broke her affixation to quench her thirst for blood.

Fearfully, I sat watching this demonic performance, gradually pushing myself further and further down her sofa in utter terror as this strange side of her appeared and controlled this game. However, if Abby winning was scary then Abby losing was utterly terrifying, she got taken out by a 'Camper' and she threw her headset and screamed into a cushion.

Storming round her lounge in frustration she yelled to the sky, "Fucking camper noob!" Before she checked her headset, and the odd addiction began again in earnest. Unable to believe the sight I was witnessing as she entered a new game, her focus was even greater, and her aggression was even higher as she fiercely punched her way through the army of 'Noobs' online.

After three hours of utter terror, I came to leave and head home, she was so transfixed that when I said goodbye to her, she just mustered a strange grunt back as I started to leave.

Heading home, I couldn't stop myself shuddering at the thought of what the next two weeks might hold every evening as this was utterly terrifying! Almost as if she was possessed the moment she went into that gaming world, Abby just ceased to exist and this odd terrifying and demonic side of her appeared.

Sitting at my kitchen table, I started to try and assemble notes on what I had witnessed that evening, but somehow, I couldn't find any rational explanation for this unusual side of her. Wondering if maybe I would need to record her or maybe even film her, filled me with dread.

I wondered if maybe she had any idea just how she was once that screen went from loading to game on? Part of our agreement was that any notes I had taken I would allow her to look over, it only seemed fair, without her I couldn't even start this assessment and as such I felt she deserved to see what I was writing about her.

Abby was in total disbelief about what I had written and flatly refused to believe that it was true in any form, so she gave me the go ahead to record her and to prove that I wasn't just weighting out my work. Over the next two evenings, I recorded her, only audio files, but recordings nevertheless, on Friday as we both had Saturday off, I would stay around hers and witness the full session.

Walking to hers, I treated us to a takeaway; it only seemed fair as she was giving me this valuable insight into the world, she was so deeply engrossed in. Most evenings during the week, I had left Abby's at around 10pm but tonight I wasn't going anywhere and tonight I was going to discover just how addicted she truly was.

When she finished her dinner, she changed into a pair of shorts and a short vest, tied her hair back and the headset went on. Abby filled a sports drink bottle with as much energy drink as she could force into the cup and the screen went on and her eyes focussed ready for the first round.

Engrossed so heavily as the first steps and shots of the game went in, she lost all form of spatial awareness and leant closer and closer to her screen. Taunting wildly and screaming away with each kill, she was so engrossed that her house could have been on fire, and she wouldn't have noticed until the power went off. Her gaze never strayed from the screen as she instinctively guided that drink to her mouth without so much as looking to see where the straw was.

While Abby drew closer to the final stages of the round, I began to film her and capture that terrifying moment when she won or lost the game. Yelling bits of words to herself she was so engrossed that her eyes widened, and she moved even closer to her screen as each kill drew her closer to the victory she desired. Her voice became sharper and her attention fixed more heavily as the showdown began, unable to speak as she flung all of her mental strength into beating her final opponent.

Abby's body tightened and her breaths became shorter as the thrill and exhilaration took full control in this last stage. Searching and questing a single shot rang out and within seconds she leapt from her couch and yelled wildly, "Fuck yeah! How do you like them apples! Noob!" She danced on the spot and yelled taunt after taunt at her headset.

She strutted round her lounge like she had just won the lottery, jubilant and drained, she tipped her head back and raised her arms to the sky, "Who's the winner babies!"

Sitting back down and folding her legs again the cycle began again, with every passing shot or step she became more engulfed in this world on her TV screen. Intoxicating her as this double-sided girl proudly haunted every person who dared to cross her path in that virtual world. Menacing and intimidating, it was almost impossible to believe that this girl right now on Monday would be the shyest and politest person that anyone could ever meet.

Filming every moment of the final stages, I caught video footage of her highs and lows as the evening turned to night and the night turned to morning. Almost as engrossed in watching this strange display which terrified me, I couldn't even keep track of time, only when I looked at my phone did I notice that it was 2am!

Seven hours had passed and beyond the odd break to go to the toilet or dance round her living room Abby hadn't so much as left her sofa. I headed to bed and left her to indulge her passion, however in the morning, I got an even bigger shock.

Walking into her living room, she had simply keeled over at some point during the night, limply laying with her headset still on her head, I checked her pulse as I wondered if she had suffered a heart attack. As my fingers touched her throat, she jolted awake and looked up with a look of total exhaustion upon her face, while she headed to bed, I headed home to gather my thoughts and start compiling notes.

Trying as hard as I could I just couldn't understand the cause of Abby's addiction, was it purely because she won most of the time? I mean, who doesn't want to be good at whatever they do? Surely that is the drive behind it all? Abby winning was scary but her losing was utterly terrifying, I wondered would her relationship be different if she didn't win all the time? What if she played something where she didn't win much at all? During Sunday I went shopping for her to test my idea out.

Walking into town I headed to the only shop in town that could help me put my idea into action, the only shop which sold video games. Walking around a shop filled with teenage boys and hyper nerds, I actually felt kinda awkward as I started to look for a game for Abby. Thankfully for me those nerds and boys were only too keen to offer me assistance, whether it was genuine or because I was a 'hot chick' made no difference to me.

Selecting her two games after the assistance of the inhabitants of that shop I wandered home and wondered just how different they would make her when she played them. One game was a new version of the one she had played during the week, but as she didn't have it, I hoped she would be starting from behind with it and more likely to lose. The second game was an open world building type game, with no winning or losing possible.

I wondered what her behaviour might be like in that? Of course, that was if she would play it, from what I had seen she liked to shoot people so maybe building a house or farm and fighting monsters with other people wouldn't have the effect on her that I hoped? Whichever the case, it was the sort of game I would have wanted to play so I just hoped that maybe she might want to play it too?

During Monday morning, I spoke with Joanne about my findings so far and she flatly refused to believe what I had written about Abby. With Joanne being so suspicious about my finding, I showed her one of the videos that I had taken of Abby on Friday night. Sitting in disbelief as she watched the sweetest receptionist who had ever greeted her and smiled as she walked through, she couldn't believe that within that girl lived this animal.

Watching a few of the videos of Abby both winning and losing; she just was staggered at what she witnessed as each video passed by. Running through my plan with her, she thought that I was thinking logically about trying to understand something that neither of us could rationally explain.

Something else I wondered about though was Abby met guys online, and often her dates were people she had been playing games with? Wondering to myself during the day just how a bond with anyone could develop through a game which was almost entirely a solo experience. Maybe I would see this during the week too?

Presenting Abby with her two presents as my means of thanks for helping me with my course she was only too excited to get home for another evening owning dudes online. However, during that evening her excitement turned to frustration as she wasn't quite up to speed with this game. Similar to her other game of choice but there were just enough tweaks in the game to make it almost impossible for her to actually win at all.

With every defeat, her voice got louder and her language got more colourful as each and every game she got killed. However, with every death she got grittier and more determined to get that final shot in, going back for more and more pain as she slowly learned this new game's nuances.

While she was losing, I noticed a name kept popping up on screen, a partner in crime, I had seen the name last week and it seemed this was someone she regularly played with online. Between rounds they would talk, she was different to how she was at work, but she was more like Abby when she spoke.

Whoever the guy was he also lived in Ljianstipol and seemingly the pair had actually met each other at some point? Yet their conversations were almost entirely about slating each other for being noobs or about other people being noobs? During the next few evenings, they met online and in-game pretty much every night, they spoke about work and general stuff before going to kill each other in-game.

Thursday night however Abby's frustration became a source of utter terror as she lost every single round she played, sometimes barely taking a few steps before she died. Eventually, the pain of losing was just that little bit too much and the game was switched off for the night. Almost sulking to herself she sat forlornly looking at her TV, leaning back and sighing a deep and loud breath as she looked at the case of the other game, I had gotten her.

As it was getting late and we had all tomorrow night, I decided to head away early and leave Abby to console herself after a disappointing night's gaming. Feeling slightly guilty, I walked home and wondered if she would just go back to her usual haunt but what was strange was, she was so gripped to win that even amid her deepest rage she just went back for more? Comparable to just letting someone punch her in the face repeatedly, I couldn't help but wonder why this was so addictive?

Friday evening once again I would be staying with Abby and as a final thank you, we had takeaway again, she was different tonight though? Calmer and less fidgety to get in-game? Sitting talking we slowly enjoyed our dinner before she changed ready for tonight's action, shorts and a vest were all she was wearing tonight. Sitting herself comfortably, she turned the console on and to my utter shock instead of going back to her normal killing fest, she had spent the rest of last night playing the second game I got her?

Abby began in a small house she had made before wandering over hills to a farm she had also made, while I sat watching she admitted she had been up very late last night. Her headset went on but she was actually quiet and pleasant when she spoke, she smiled as she built things and laughed as she killed monsters but the biggest shock was when her friend appeared.

Sitting in awe as she and her virtual man that probably lived next door started to carve out a river and pathway to join their houses to the farm together. Speaking to each other kindly and with no slating they spent hours just digging stuff and then making things to adorn their homes or make other things for decoration.

Mesmerised by her, she did have a moment of rage as she got killed and had to start without the things, she had spent much time collecting, but a different kind of rage, more subdued rage than normal. Despite the game's more casual nature, she became equally engrossed, slowly moving closer to her screen as she created this world for herself.

Calmly and coolly, she made her way through this strange environment that she crafted, her odd satisfaction with every single thing she did was pleasant. Where she was so relaxed it in turn made me relax too, unlike the last Friday we spent together, I wasn't on edge or nervous as she came up against and lost to a myriad of virtual monsters.

Thinking as I watched her dive deeper into a virtual fantasy, why was she so different for this game? Surely death carried the same anger and disappointment with both games? Once again, I headed to bed to find her passed out the morning after in almost the exact same state as the week before.

Walking home in the morning with more questions than answers, it was a complex and confusing thing as the first game had driven her mad, but she kept going back? However, the second game almost calmed her to the point where she was more like Abby and yet she became equally engrossed?

Analysing and thinking all weekend I wrote my findings and thoughts down ready to present them to Joanne for advice on Monday morning. Inviting Abby over on Sunday afternoon I allowed her to review what I had written about her as per our agreement.

Carefully studying my assessment of her, she didn't realise just how enraged she became sometimes, and she did get a shock when she watched some of the videos of her. Abby however was satisfied with me submitting the work and even the videos of her for my course and when Joanne reviewed my assessment and case study, she also seemed happy with my work. However, every Thursday evening I spent with Abby afterwards, she missed me sitting watching and in truth I had grown to quite enjoy seeing this more savage side of Abby.

While the year ticked away the popularity of these new and exciting sessions, we had started to run at the Davizioso were getting noticed not just by local residents but by a wider audience. Word was being spread about the service we had started to offer and the two sessions on Thursday were reaching their capacity, along with the Davizioso my reputation had been spreading too.

Reviews and the odd secretly shot video on social media were drawing larger crowds to my sessions, originally, we hoped to have 40 people per session but now we were struggling to keep numbers below 60. Joanne was astonished and proud of how well my sessions had been going and during a meeting with Gale and Tony everything was about to change. After lunch, I headed to the garden on the roof for my weekly meeting with Gale, but as I walked out into the garden to discover them arguing with each other, it was what they were arguing about that was of concern.

Tony and Gale had heard and seen reviews circulating about my sessions on Thursday, with the local healthcare system being unable to provide any real assistance, we were the only place outside of Usted that offered this kind of service. With my sessions reaching and exceeding capacity, both of them wanted to expand the sessions and run another two one on Tuesday and another on Wednesday morning.

Naturally, I was only too happy to agree to run the sessions, but this wasn't why they had been arguing when I arrived. Joanne had informed them that I was now working on my final piece of work for my course, with Christmas rapidly approaching the pair had booked the assessors to come to the Davizioso in January.

Over the course of a week, they would follow and observe me as well as getting me to complete two written exams, it made me slightly nervous but if I wasn't ready by January then I would never be ready.

Christmas was the next point of discussion, many of the residents went to stay with family or friends over the festive period so a skeleton staff would be needed, me, Joanne and Abby would run the day shifts over Christmas. Gale was going to visit his daughter Ellie, having only recently begun speaking to her again, he was keen to visit her and make up for the lost time when they didn't speak.

Tony and Mona would be going away for Christmas, he was confident that we would all be fine in their absence as there would only be 3 guests staying over the festive period. Finally, we moved onto the source of their arguments when I had arrived, I will confess to being nervous when Tony looked at me and said, "Fae, there is something we need to discuss," with a stern look on his face.

Tony handed me a letter which had been sent to them, it was about one of my sessions, an attendee had written a hearty letter about how my story had reached him and encouraged him to start to resolve some of his own problems. The letter wasn't the problem though, its writer had also written to the local newspaper and the journalists from the paper wanted to come to the Davizioso in January to do an article about the hotel and what we did.

Gale was keen to have them come but Tony wasn't keen on them coming but after his son had killed himself after being stalked by journalists for two years, I couldn't blame him for being apprehensive. The pair had been arguing all day about this and it was up to me to have the final say on the matter. Sitting between them we began to discuss what to do and how to proceed for the benefit of both the Davizioso, staff and the residents and patients within it.

Gale was arguing that the publicity might finally take the place into the wider view of many potential people who could benefit from being within our walls. Many of the people here and myself included, had been through and largely let down by a system which simply wasn't up to the task of handling the middle ground of patients we catered for.

Like me, many people either were left to fend for themselves, misdiagnosed, undiagnosed or even worse sent to prison like asylums where they just fell to pieces. Countless residents had endured the same pain and misery as me, in some cases even worse, some had been institutionalised only to then be flung out when the space was needed. While Gale fought to have the spotlight finally shine on the hotel and all the things it did for people, Tony wanted no such thing to happen.

Tony was fearful that the publicity stunt Gale had in mind would backfire partly through bad press but also because if the journalists turned up when my assessors were here, they might jeopardise my exams. Tony and Gale had argued enough and as there was a risk they would be here during my assessment and exams; they gave me the final decision on the journalists.

Sitting with their eyes gazing upon me I started to think about the options, with their gaze boring into me I took myself for a walk around the garden. Walking through the winding paths to Tony's cabin at the other end, I sat inside and closed myself in to gather my thoughts. Would journalists ruin my assessment if they turned up at the same time as them?

After all, they would be doing an article about the hotel, surely, I would be left alone as they focussed on Tony and Gale or our residents? What effect would the journalists have on the patients here? Would they aggravate their conditions or cause bigger problems further down the line?

Consuming myself with these thoughts the door opened and Tony walked in to join me. Tony cautiously walked in and sat beside me, he knew I was unsure what to do, I wanted to promote the Davizioso and what it really did for people, but I didn't want to risk my career to do it.

"Not sure what to do Fae?" Tony spoke softly as I tried to console my thoughts.

"I want to help us grow and show the world what we really do, what you guys have done for people like me," I sat forward and rested my head in my hands thinking, "I'm biased Fae, I hate the press after what they did to David but this is about far more than just me, I just don't want you to be used as a scapegoat by anyone, you have worked too hard to be treated that way," I looked round at him, "What do you mean Tony?"

He sat back and sighed. "You remember when you started that course?"

I nodded back at him, "Of course I remember."

He smiled a little. "You should have been assessed next July, if you pass or in truth when you pass the first stage, you will have done it in six months. People will say you were helped by Joanne or anyone else, but they didn't give up the time for it you have or been working as hard as you have."

"Joanne didn't make you read your books or do a case study on anyone, you did all that yourself, the only reason those sessions on Thursday worked was because of you! Without you those sessions would have been cancelled and there would be no interest at all in what we do, that's why it in my opinion is your choice."

Tony patted me on the back and stood up to leave me to think, "Tony?" He looked round, "What did you do when you had to make decisions like this?"

Tony smiled a little. "Flipped a coin or went with my gut instinct, thinking for too long is a bad thing sometimes." Tony gently closed the door and left me to dwell.

Deliberating with myself I made a decision, standing I slowly walked back down the paths of the garden to Tony and Gale both sitting waiting for me. Pausing, I thought one last time, before I delivered my answer to them both confidently, "Let them come."

I let out a deep breath of relief as the words fell out of my mouth and mind, "Let them come and show the world what we really do here, let them tell the stories of all the people that have found a home here." Tony smiled and tipped his head to me, Gale looked over at Tony and stood to leave.

"Where are you going?" Tony quizzed him.

"To call them and give them the news that they can come in January," Gale said as he turned and left us behind.

Tony grinned at me. "You took him by surprise, he thought I had talked you out of it!" I laughed with him as I left to head home. "Surely he knows better by now?"

December began to roll along and as it did more residents began to leave to spend Christmas with their families or friends, bar 2 residents the hotel was silent. Gale had gone to see his daughter Ellie and Tony and Mona were sunning themselves abroad while me, Abby and Joanne fended for the hotel during the day.

We agreed that Joanne wouldn't come in to work Christmas Day as she should spend that with her husband and children and with the bosses away it wasn't like they would notice her absence? Abby and I would both be alone for Christmas, after my breakdown last year I invited her over for a few days as it was her first Christmas without her parents around and I didn't want her to feel that same loneliness that brought me to Ljianstipol.

Abby brought her games console round, I just hoped she wouldn't play that game that turned her into that monstrous alternate version of herself as when she turned into that girl, she scared the crap out of me.

During the build up to Christmas Day, the days at work just dragged and dragged, with only two people to tend too, it was a long day, but if we had it bad, I couldn't imagine how long the night shifts must have felt! On Christmas Day, our boredom got the better of us and we organised an all-day pool tournament in Gale's bar, I'm sure he wouldn't have minded too much.

We did at least share some festivities with the two residents that were still here, though the evening was quite hard on Abby as it was her first Christmas without her parents around her. Together though we had a good day and evening although she did terrify me during the evening when she played her console and killed some noobs.

Jumping around my living room like a wild animal and screaming at anyone who fell to her pistol, she was scary when she played but oddly addictive to watch.

While Christmas gently whittled away into the past and the new year dawned on new year's eve, just like everyone else I made empty promises to myself that would last only a few days. Resolutions about eating less garbage food, exercising more or drinking less, all things that I knew I couldn't stick too but said anyway, however buried among those empty words was one promise to myself that I was going to keep.

Home alone on New Year's Day, I sat looking at that picture of me and my mum, over the next year someway and somehow, I was going to start to turn the tide with my own battles and get that girl back for both my mum and myself. I knew the road would be long and hard, at times I would beg to give in, but deep down inside me I knew somewhere over the next year I was going to start to get better and maybe I could finally start to beat my problems.

Chapter 4
Working Therapy

January began as it does for everyone with the quick and pain free death of those empty promises to myself, on New Year's Day I was less than able to cook so takeaway and a bottle of beer washed away the first two. However, they didn't die in vain as I spent the day thinking about the only promise I had made to myself that I had every intention of keeping. Most of New Year's Day, I spent looking through the books Joanne had slowly been gifting me over the last 6 months, looking for potential solutions that would help me get back to being that girl my mum missed so dearly.

Having a few days before I was back at work, I was going to make a plan and work out how to start that process alongside studying before the new working year began. Joanne had agreed to keep running a one-hour therapy session with me each week to help and I was going to start tackling my issues myself too.

January either way was going to be a testing month, my assessors could turn up at the Davizioso anytime without warning as could the journalists, we just hoped they wouldn't show up for the same week. My assessment would be over the full week at work, for the first four days I would be shadowed and monitored and on Friday my exams would be run.

Assessors would be present for every single thing I did at work including my hour with Joanne and the therapy session that I performed upon myself. Over the next few weeks, I needed to start thinking about the next stage of my qualification, either I could continue to cover many subjects or start to specialise in a chosen field.

Although I didn't need to decide for another six months, I was already almost decided about specialising in cyber related disorders as in some ways the stories of those patients reminded me of the hell that me and my mum went through.

Most patients would have gone through the health service but had every door shut to them or been disregarded entirely and by the time they had found the Davizioso, a minor anxiety had exploded into something far more dangerous. Just like me and my mum they had been largely shunned and passed around with almost the intention of forcing them into believing that they were fine when they really weren't.

My mum went through hell to finally get me a diagnosis, but that hell was just a warm up compared to actually getting help for me, either I was passed off with 'Growing pains' or 'That girl time of the month' it wasn't until years later I really discovered what my mum endured to get me help.

Every single person that attended my sessions reminded me of the effort that she had made to get me help and it had made me think more about the sessions that we ran at the Davizioso. Gale had also been thinking about them over the festive period and we had agreed to meet and look to change them so that it would give an open door to people that had endured a similar treatment to my mum and me.

During the first two weeks of January, we started to change almost everything about the sessions. We agreed to start publicly advertising them and they were now entirely free for anyone and everyone and funded by the hotel and in addition we would set up a support network similar to the one that Tony and Gale had set up for me. Apprehensive as we knew we would have to actively monitor the group to keep it free from trolls or anything else, but my group had been a lifesaver for me and maybe it could be for someone else?

During the second week of January, the support group went live on social media and by the end of the week we had 200 members joined into the group. We realised that we had hit upon something that was affecting far more people than we anticipated, and the groups would need to be larger to cope with demand.

During the week Gale planned to meet again and further discuss and develop our plans to cope with our increased demand but it turned out the universe had other plans for us this week.

Walking through the door to work on that Monday morning I should have just done a 180 and walked back home, the journalists had arrived ready to do the short story for the local paper. Tony was less than composed when I met him and Gale upstairs to get a briefing for the week's plan, however our meeting was interrupted when the assessors turned up just before 9. Our worst nightmare and greatest fear had been realised but there was no walking away from it now, we had to appease both parties.

Tony and Gale would try and keep the journalists away from me so that they wouldn't jeopardise my assessment but they couldn't guarantee anything, I had to be ready for anything to happen. Before the assessment began, we had a briefing where they told me what they would be doing and how they would conduct the exams at the end of the week.

Nervous but confident, I began the week with a joint therapy session with Joanne before I would host my own session with a new patient before lunch. Almost blending into the background, the assessor's distant but attentive approach helped calm my nerves, it was a shame that the same couldn't have been said for the journalists. During lunch, I caught sight of an agitated Tony leaving the hotel, incensed and furious about the invasive nature the journalists seemed to have taken in regard to getting the content for their story.

Gale met me during lunch and informed me that he had told Tony to stay away until the journalists left at the end of the week. For Tony, the memories of what the press had caused to happen to his son David were clearly present in his mind and clouded his thoughts far too much. However, this gave me a slight fear as now half of my defensive shield was gone but I guess I just had to ride the wave and hope it didn't break too soon.

During Tuesday morning, the journalists attended the morning group session that I ran, they were oddly invasive jostling for position to get pictures and almost harassing my group members. However, the group ran well despite their almost paparazzi approach to being in attendance, I opened with one of my stories as usual and soon enough the group was openly talking and discussing their own stories.

Forgetting that my assessors were present was pretty easy but missing those journalists was far harder as they interrupted stories and disrupted the flow people had built up. When the session drew to a close, I had a quick word with them to ask them not to be so disruptive if they attended anymore of my group sessions as those guests would be back next week after they had long gone, and we became old news.

Just before lunch I had a quick meeting with Gale to inform him that I had spoken with the journalists and to fill him in on the reasons as to why. I left the hotel to get lunch and the journalists were talking to Shanky, I laughed to myself that he would keep them entertained and had more than a few stories for them.

Stressed and angry about my session being disrupted I went for a quick walk along the prom to cool off and think about my afternoon group's meeting. It is strange how just the sound of gentle waves and soft winds can ease the mind, walking along the prom I relaxed, let my anger go and composed myself for the afternoon.

However, something had changed during that brief hour I had been away, I wasn't sure why, but it seemed like those journalists were now almost stalking me? Initially, I just put it down to paranoia or maybe guilt after having spoken to them about their conduct, they attended my afternoon session and were slightly better than during the morning.

During Wednesday morning, they were back to themselves but now it was obvious their focus had shifted from the Davizioso and its patients and guests to me? Invasive, goading and borderline harassing me during the entire morning session, my assessors were now the least of my concerns as my group was almost entirely snuffed out by their actions.

Once again under the watchful eyes of my assessors I had stern words with them about their conduct and how they had just destroyed my group session though rather than apologise they seemed to almost be prying? Suddenly, I understood and empathised with Tony's hatred for the media and journalists as these guys didn't care how they got their story so long as they got it no matter who paid for their actions!

Once again, I headed to lunch frustrated although I soon found out why their focus had been shifted when I saw Shanky in the marketplace during my lunch hour. Every Wednesday, a market is held in Ljianstipol and Shanky would head there to sell prints of his artwork and during my lunch, I would go and catch up with him. During yesterday afternoon, they had been pestering Shanky when he had dropped them journalistic gold and let slip that I was a former patient of the hotel.

Shanky apologised but it wasn't his fault really, I was certain that they twisted it out of him I just hoped he hadn't filled them in too much! Gale had cancelled my meeting with him and instead I would have a therapy session with Joanne before performing one upon myself afterwards. My assessors followed me to Joanne's room, unfortunately so did those journalists, once again disruptive and intrusive my temper was starting to fray as Joanne threw in the towel and ended my session early.

Leaving Joanne's room, I apologised to the assessors who now were almost a second party to the journalists who almost forced themselves between my assessors and me. Pestering and hounding they were now asking for an interview just with me, extorting and badgering me as I tried to find anywhere, I could get a silent moment to compose my mind.

Fearing that my coursework and all the effort that had gone into it had been thrown away at this last hurdle and all my patients who must have been let down this week. Pitying my assessors who were now largely being forced aside by a pair of hack journalists my temper waned further and I started brooding as they hounded harder. Finally, I snapped, with the journalists barging my assessors out of the way I turned and yelled, "Fine! I will do an interview just leave me to do my work, leave my patients alone and let my assessors do their jobs!"

Wry and almost smug bullying smiles greeted me once those words fell out of me however they did at least leave and let me go and find a moment alone.

My assessors followed me onto the rooftop garden, I guided them to the empty pergola and sat them down to apologise for the way the journalists had treated them. Sighing as I admitted that they had ruined both of my group sessions I offered them both a bottle of beer and to my surprise they took them while I tried to compose my mind.

Having failed to even get half an hour with Joanne, while they watched on, I eased back as much as I could and started to deliver myself a light dose of therapy. Zoning myself out as much as I could, slowly I started to cycle through my own mind and soothe myself and talk out problems in my own mind but unsure whether I was really speaking or not.

Either way I brought myself back and much to my surprise the assessors were both sitting quietly and contently working their way through the bottles of beer I had given them. Rather than just sit in silence I started to talk to them about my past stays at the hotel and how the treatment that me and my mother had received encouraged me to choose this career path.

Actively recalling the trouble my mum had to source help for me and how it was now my sole ambition to stop others enduring that same dislocating treatment that drove me to suicide attempts. Although I wasn't sure if I should really be feeding them beer and just talking so openly to them, by this point I figured the assessment was a failure for me so it wouldn't matter anyway.

Thursday was my final day of assessment before my exams tomorrow and much to my shock and almost disbelief the journalists kept their word but they had already won their prize so it shouldn't have been a surprise really? They attended my morning group session but stayed quiet and out of the way allowing me to fully open up and deliver possibly my best session to date.

During the afternoon I had three one-to-one sessions with new patients of the hotel, all of which went well and with no journalists around for them, I hoped they would be enough to save me from a big failure. Friday and the exams would be the final stage of the assessment, the morning exam was easy enough and I felt confident for the second one too. Halfway through my second exam we were interrupted by Gale, Joanne had been trying to get through to a new patient and was having serious trouble with them and Joanne needed my help.

Gale asked if the assessors could stop the exam but they were unable to, with most of it complete I left the exam took the assessors with me and went to help Joanne. Sitting on the floor in a sorrowful state the young girl had opened up to Joanne only to have a searing anxiety attack, crying her eyes out and bawling as she had come to realise the state she had gotten into.

Joanne, Gale and my assessors watched on as I started to try and calm the girl down but mindful that I was now battling the clock too. Gradually I found mutual ground with the girl and she started to calm down but now I had to race back to the exam and hope the 20 minutes I had were enough to finish it in time.

Rushing my way through the questions in the exam I wrote furiously and mindfully, finishing the last question with seconds to spare but as soon as the exam finished, I headed back to Joanne. Thankfully, the girl had fully calmed and Joanne was working her magic when the assessors both came to join me and shake my hand before leaving having completed their task, my future now was in their hands.

Gale took me to the rooftop garden for a celebratory beer and to apologise for how the journalists had compromised my chances during the assessment. Neither of us had anticipated just how those journalists would behave, Gale did say it was just as well Tony had stayed away as he might have stepped in to stop them hounding me so much.

Gale was quite mindful of what I had agreed to with them too, he had to break that news to Tony, while I had to mull in my own mind over the weekend about what I had been pushed into agreeing to. Walking home it started to hit me what I had just put myself forwards for, saddened as that was a sacrifice that I had made for both my patients and for my career. During that quiet Friday night even pizza and beer couldn't shake the sorrow I felt at being pushed into something that frankly terrified me in every way.

However, hidden amongst the sadness and disappointment was a strange glimmer of hope and almost an inconceivable idea of how to use this opportunity to do something far larger. I needed someone else's input, someone impartial and willing to tell me just how good or bad my thought was and there was only one person I thought could give me that opinion or insight.

While I dwelt and mulled about how disastrous my assessment would probably be, I sent a text message to the only person I knew would give me a 100 percent honest opinion. Responding almost immediately and without any hesitation, in the morning Francois and his razor tongue would come over to talk to me and pass on his honest thoughts, even though that idea was equally as terrifying.

During the morning, I applied more thought to the strange idea. Tony popped over having been informed by Gale what had gone on. Angry and disappointed with the journalists just like I was he apologised for not being around to shield me from the pair as they wrought havoc on my groups and assessment.

While Tony apologised, I put my idea forward to him, he was both stunned and seemingly inspired, before he left, he promised to manage the interview and photoshoot for me. Promising to almost shield me in the way he wished that he had been able to do for David, before Tony headed away his single comment of 'Brave' meant so much to my mind.

Francois turned up around an hour after Tony had left, he brought a little bottle of wine with him and we headed into my garden to discuss my idea with him. Despite how much Francois' honest opinion might just destroy my thoughts and ideas on this occasion, that razor tongue of his would give the most realistic answer which I desperately needed.

Sitting almost on a cliff of terror in his presence, I poured us both some wine and took a deep breath and readied myself for his potentially damning response.

Francois sat intently focussed on me while I ran him through what had happened during the week with the journalists destroying my assessment and potentially my career to get an interview with me. Disgusted and repulsed at what I detailed to him, Francois was obviously angry and appalled at what had taken place, his venom marking how annoyed he was until I stopped him to explain my idea to him.

Sitting observing his fingernails he lit a cigarette, he said, "So tell me what you plan to do, Fae? They might have ruined your career!"

"The thing is, Francois, the only reason they want to do an interview with me is because of what I am? So, what if I used the interview to showcase what people like me are actually capable of being if they are given some kind of chance?"

Francois barely broke his attention as I began my pitch to him. "Maybe they have ruined my assessment but I can do that again, this is the only chance anyone will ever give me to actually make a difference for people?" Francois sat nodding to himself but didn't yet respond.

"Just maybe them potentially ruining my career will give me the chance to use my conditions to help hundreds or even thousands of people like me see that there is hope and maybe I will just change one life for the better?" I sat anxiously awaiting Francois' response.

Without so much as even looking up, Francois poured me another glass of wine and sat back and thought deeply and hard before his mouth even opened in response. "This is one of the stupidest and most reckless ideas I have ever heard, you might have lost your career but instead of fighting for that you are planning to use an interview you don't want to do to help people?"

Francois' words cut me down quickly before he sighed. "If this was anyone else Fae, then I would be telling them not to even consider doing this but you are different no?"

I looked up at him, "Fae since you have come here, I have realised just how brave and determined you are, you have made your own path, we have all helped you but for the most part you just needed to be pointed in the right direction?"

Suddenly, a strange smile was on Francois' face. "Fae, if anyone else said that to me than they would fail before they tried but with you, I know you can do this, it will be hard no? But me and Colette will support you when you need as would anyone else."

Surprised and stunned I keep my focus upon him, "Fae, we believe in you and I know you are the only person in Ljianstipol who can even think to do this, so my answer to you is to go ahead and do the interview to help other people."

Francois lit up a cigarette and poured the last of the wine into my glass. "You might need some help though Fae?" I looked over as a wry smile came onto his face, "You will need some more trousers to mask that backside of yours, but I can help you with that," he winked and sat back and chuckled to himself.

"Francois!" I joined him laughing.

"It is pretty round isn't it?" He laughed even harder.

Touched by his words, "Thanks Francois, it means a lot to me to hear your thoughts."

Francois composed himself and looked up, "I know, you are the bravest girl I have ever met, just don't tell Colette that!" Francois patted me on the shoulder and left me to think.

Spurred on by his supportive words I started to think about how to explain to Gale about what I planned to do when the interview finally happened, thankfully I wouldn't have to wait long to project my idea to him.

Motivated and determined, I headed to my meeting with Gale on Wednesday afternoon to find him and Tony both sitting awaiting my arrival. While they handed out the beers, I introduced my idea to them both and both were supportive and encouraging that I had turned a potential disaster into something positive.

Together they agreed that they would arrange the interview for me and Tony would manage all aspects of it. Knowingly Tony would expect they would want to do the entire thing in a single day in their studio on the outskirts of town, he would negotiate to have the shoot split into two sections.

The first part would be held at the studio in the manner they would want, the second part however would be outside at two locations of my choice in the format that I would prefer. Gale would manage my time before and after the interview, arranging time off for me and providing any other support I might need leading up to the interview.

Heading away from the meeting, I felt encouraged and overwhelmingly touched that people seemed to think that there was a real chance that I could turn something so negative into something potentially life changing for someone. Wondering if my mind had awful images for me about what the interview would be like, I imagined some kind of barbaric interrogation method being used to extract information from me.

Shuddering at the idea of a black room with an illuminated chair just waiting for me among the blackness and two journalists ready to torture my life story from me. Almost laughing to myself all weekend about the hellish thoughts my worst imagination had begun to dream up for me. Motivated and amused by the thought of the interview I had resumed my studies just in case by some miracle I hadn't failed my assessment.

Two weeks after the journalists had arrived at the Hotel Davizioso our article was released in the local newspaper, everyone in the place bought a copy of the paper hoping to see themselves donning those sheets. Giving them credit where it was due, it was a pretty nice article and there were some good stories about both our patients, residents, staff and a little bit about me too.

Initially, Tony and Gale were pretty happy with the article and it generated a little bit of attention for the different free group sessions we now offered. Social media even started to briefly talk about us and our efforts before a week or so after the article came out, we fell back into the darkness of people's minds.

After a nearly painful month since my assessment had been spoilt by the journalists, I was called to a meeting with Tony and Gale for my results, nervously I headed to the rooftop garden to the pergola to learn my fate.

Walking out both of them seemed happy enough, they were more relaxed than I was, Gale handed me a beer and Tony handed me a large sealed envelope. Shyly I looked at both, fearful about how low my grade was going to be, I took a deep breath and opened the envelope and pulled out a large document.

Both leant forward to hear the result. "Well? What does it say?" Tony asked.

"Come on Fae we will be proud no matter what you got!" Gale chipped in as I sat in silence, gently starting to cry to myself.

Thumbing through the document brought on even more tears and Gale came and sat beside me. "Show me Fae, there's no shame you know," Gale took the document and started to read through it.

"What does it say Gale?" Tony asked, looking concerned, Gale didn't respond and simply handed him the document. While Gale consoled me, Tony flicked through the pages, stopping and looking up at me with each page. "What the fuck!" Tony yelled as he reached the final page. "Fae! How did you?" Tony asked, looking astonished.

"I have no idea," as my eyes erupted into tears. "Wait there's a handwritten note attached?" Tony took the note and handed it to Gale.

Gale looked and read the note to me. "Don't let your flame go out Fae Edwards, well done!" Gale smiled equally stunned into silence. "Fae this note is written by the head of the board!" Gale said, handing me the little note which I began to soak in tears.

Tony proudly handed me another beer. "Well done, Fae, how did you get 100 percent plus two commendations for duty of care?"

Gale handed me the document back, "Guess you will need this too then?" Gale pulled out a heavy wooden box from behind his seat and flicked it open. Inside the box was a heavy and thick cut glass trophy, black glass made up the centre with three sets of wings coming off it in the same colours as my hair to indicate my specialisations. Hoisting the trophy to look at the plaque on the front.

"Fae Edwards, 100% never gave up and never gave in," I smiled at them both and rushed to hug them both. "Thank you so much," I bawled at the pair of them.

"Don't thank us, that is your hard work that earned you that!" Gale declared proudly.

"Hard work begins next week right Fae?" Tony laughed at me. "Now go and celebrate would you before you make us cry too, but let me get a picture to go next to my other favourite one on my desk."

Tony had me stand with Gale accepting my trophy from him and headed off to get it printed and framed while Gale looked over the document again. "Just incredible Fae!" Gale smiled proudly at me.

"We need to talk to you about the interview too but that can wait for a few days, just go and enjoy yourself for a few days and you should be incredibly proud of yourself, someday soon you will put us all to shame!" Gale smiled and handed me the wooden box for my trophy along with my results. Hugging him one final time before I began to head home for the weekend, Joanne congratulated me at the bottom of the stairwell with a smile so unbelievable that she set my tears off again.

Leaving work for the weekend so highly charged, I was going to celebrate just as both had recommended and Alyssia, Fabi and Francois and Colette were only too willing to take me for a celebratory drink by the river. Drinks openly flowed from my assortment of friends as did my eyes every single time we spoke about my assessment results, it was obvious how much passing that had meant to me.

However, with the assessment out of the way and the small article in the newspaper behind me my mind and our conversations turned to the interview I had been coaxed into doing. Equally supportive in every way, my friends spent the evening reminding me how brave I would be to attempt what I had in mind when the lights and cameras fell upon me in that studio.

Deep down though as much as the thrill and drive to do something of such magnitude was gripping me so too was an underlying fear and apprehension. Almost always camera shy and very lacking in self-confidence, the idea of openly exposing myself to the world utterly petrified me but the ambition to do something for a greater cause than myself was driving me along.

Starting to plan I began writing myself notes and answers to any questions they might ask but something I hadn't fully decided was how much of my past I should really expose to them. Sitting in my garden during Sunday evening, I made a simple but concrete decision within my mind that I would openly talk about every single moment where my life had turned sour.

Warts and all, I was going to expose and disclose fully the true extent which my conditions had hampered or in some cases destroyed my life or elements around me. Fearful, I started to write notes about my past and the catastrophe that had befell my parents and their marriage as a result of my problems along with every single terrible minute of my life from the day my depression had become my master.

Whether they really wanted to hear these stories or not I wasn't sure but if I was going to tell my story in a hope to inspire or help others then in my mind, I had to be fully open and transparent about how living my 'life downside up' really was.

However, adamant I was, my mind didn't always see things quite that way, though fortunately for me things were currently busy enough to keep it slightly at bay. Since the little story about the Davizioso in the local paper we had seen an increase in attendance to our free groups we had been running.

A slow but steady increase in numbers was an excellent byproduct of the few days of glory we had enjoyed in the sheets of local news. However, right now my own article was a serious point of discussion and on Thursday the boss of the two journalists came to agree to the terms of my interview and article.

Tony and Gale had the meeting room ready and waiting for him to arrive in anticipation of a long afternoon of negotiations, thankfully Tony was pretty good with the media following his years as a footballer. Prepared as we were, there would always be that odd question that would or could come up that we had no expectation to hear asked. The studio wanted to run the interview in a single day at the studio in April, a full day sitting in a blacked-out studio with a host of different electronic backdrops being shown behind me.

Tony began to press my case with him that a single full day would more than likely set off a crash in their studio almost begrudgingly the studio agreed to split the interview process as we hoped. Gale pressed for the date to be moved to June to give me more time to prepare myself and so that the second part of the interview could be conducted outdoors as per my wish.

Bitter negotiating took place but eventually the agreement was made and the second part would be outdoors exactly as I wanted, a contract was signed and I was given the number of the boss to talk to if needed. Truthfully, I placed no faith in him to honour anything that we privately discussed which Tony and Gale both agreed with me upon, any further negotiations would be hosted by the pair.

One final stipulation was that my full details would be withheld by the studio and any contact with me by external sources would be made through Tony and Gale in hopes to protect me. Handshakes were exchanged as the studio boss headed away happy with the agreement, suddenly I noticed that my hands were shaking profusely as he walked away from that meeting.

Reality had hit me, and it hit me hard but determination and ambition was going to drive me forwards and I was going to show the world just who I was and what anyone else like me was capable of doing.

During the evening after that meeting the first anxiety attack hit me about the interview, it had suddenly gone from being a thought to an actual thing that was going to happen and even this early on it started to affect me. Trying to take my mind off its slowly self-destructive path, I decided to try a little walk out to the thrift store that Abby had introduced me to.

Walking out to the store, my head began to fill with hopes of what I might find, maybe I would finally get lucky and find a Colette special amongst its treasures today? Arriving at the car park soon began to soothe the demons in my mind and in their place were hopes of finding gold with the store.

Walking around its aisles always felt rewarding, most of the time I just found odd little things for my house but with things having been going well I was hoping to ride my luck. Exhilaration and joy struck when sifting through the trousers in the store buried amongst them, I found a cool looking skirt and I instantly recognised the handiwork of Colette.

Almost jumping with joy as it fit me perfectly, there was no way I was leaving this behind, even if it meant begging Colette to adjust it for me! The skirt was one thing but the top buried in amongst all the jumpers was something else, they weren't exactly a pair but given both were of Colette's making I didn't really care too much, I mean, how wrong can you go with a black skirt and a nice top? Guarding them with every ounce of my energy I came to the checkout to pay when I was stopped by the store owner Shaun.

Asking me if I could go to his office, I was slightly nervous as to his reasoning but as we walked through the hidden areas of the store, he started talking to me about his daughter Jess? Jess wasn't an unknown quantity to me, I had met her a few times and found her pleasant, she was a polite and well-mannered girl, she's a little shorter than me and quite pretty. Jess was also an aspiring social media influencer and cosplayer; it was pretty common to see her out with her best friend Gwen and sometimes Leanne getting content for their social media profiles.

Cosplay was one thing, but they also did quite raunchy pictures on the beach and at the studio together as both seemed to be hoping to be models but for different reasons. Jess had attended a few of our social media groups before Christmas due to cyberbullying over some of her posts but I hadn't seen her in attendance since, in truth I hadn't seen her at all since Christmas? Reaching Shaun's office, he offered me a chair and locked the door?

"Sorry to lock us in but I don't want what I discuss with you to go any further than these four walls," Shaun sighed and sat himself behind his desk. Shaun looked at me. "Can I trust you not to disclose anything that I show you?"

I felt quite shocked by his request but willingly agreed. "Of course not, but why have you brought me here?"

Shaun turned a laptop around and offered it across the table to me with one of the social media sites Jess used opened and waiting for me to look at what it contained. "Jess doesn't know yet that I know about what you are about to see, I know you might be able to help her after reading the article in the paper."

Shaun seemed slightly sad? Scrolling through the site he had opened for me; it was full of her cosplay pictures and a few bikini shots from the beach and a few studio ones, but it didn't seem to match Shaun's tone?

"Am I missing something Shaun?" I asked unsure what he was asking me to really look at, then I noticed some blurred icons hidden up the top of the site, Shaun pointed to them too. "That's one part of what I need your help with," I clicked on the first blurred image and a couple of pictures of Jess topless appeared, but I could only see a few before I had to pay for them?

"This is what they have started to do to make money," I clicked on a different set and yet more nude pictures of Jess appeared when I noticed something.

"Shaun where have these been taken?" I asked fearing his response.

"My house and my bathroom, I thought these were taken at the studio but I went to have a word with them and they confirmed these haven't been taken using any professional equipment, most likely a mobile phone has been used to take them," he sighed as he pointed to another set, he wanted me to open.

"Master and Slave? Do I really want to click this?" I asked him.

"Probably not, but a friend showed me them," nervously I clicked on the image to see Gwen with Jess on a chain, naked, bound and gagged as her slave. "Oh Shaun, what has happened to Jess?" I sighed in shock and closed the images. "But who took the pictures if it wasn't the studio or either of them?"

Shaun shrugged his shoulders, "I have no idea."

Sitting quietly, "Is that everything?"

Shaun shook his head back, "No unfortunately not, she has been getting more abuse online and she has stopped eating properly to try and lose weight, my girl is ill Fae and she is making herself ill with this stuff!" Sitting back and taking in everything Shaun was disclosing was hard. He clearly loved his daughter and would do anything for her but slowly watching her pick herself apart filled him with the same sadness my mum felt about me in my late teens.

Mulling about the best course of action, I put the question to Shaun. "So, what do you need me to do to help? I'm guessing the group sessions won't work so are you thinking about having her come and stay with us?" Mentally debating with himself and pondering, "But she is 19 now, she can actively choose not to go?"

I nodded, "She can, unless you think she is in danger or maybe if I think she is in danger?" Shaun looked over at me. "Why don't you get her to come here and I will arrange a room for her?" Shaun phoned Jess while I phoned Gale to ask him to make a room available for Jess from Monday.

While we waited for Jess to arrive. "How did you find out?"

He looked at the floor. "A friend found them."

Feeling sorry for him, "I will say I have found them, it's okay if she hates me for a while but you need to focus on getting them taken down for her." Shaun tried to smile but that wasn't happening anytime soon. Jess appeared and didn't seem too keen to see me sitting with her dad in his office, Shaun sat her down and I got myself ready to take the blame.

Shaun put his hands to his chest, "Jess I need to talk to you about something," innocently she sat waiting for him to ask when I interjected.

"I found something by accident Jess, well someone told me about it in truth," I opened the laptop and spun it around, Jess began to blush and her face began crumpling up in defence. Starting to cry she looked at Shaun, he couldn't look back at her just yet. "What have you been doing Jess?" He asked her, still avoiding eye contact with her.

"They're only cosplay and beauty shots, Daddy." She smiled back innocently at him.

"What about these ones?" I asked and pointed to the blurred out pay per view sets.

"Just playing around," she snorted back at me.

Shaun suddenly looked up enraged, "Jess these sets are disgusting and why have they been shot in our house!" He raised his voice to her as she began to cry.

"Fae, wants to help you; I know you aren't doing these by choice and you have lost so much weight Jess that I am worried you will hurt yourself! Is selling every inch of yourself to perverts online for a few euros really that important to you!" Shaun was growing angrier with each word as I raised my hand to him to ask him to calm down.

"Jess, I want to help you any way I can, has the bullying gotten worse too?"

I sat beside her, "Jess?" Suddenly, she erupted into tears and handed me her phone, she opened up the messages of abuse and requests for even dirtier images for me to scroll through. While she cried, I looked through countless vile messages that had all slowly been driving Jess into the darker world to get those few likes she was so desperate for.

Shaun having composed himself a little stepped in again, "I'm going to send you to the Davizioso for a month, Jess, while I try and sort out this mess," sighing as he confessed, he needed to send her away for help.

Jess looked up in outrage. "But you can't do that!" She scowled at him and me. "He can't but I can if I think you are in danger of hurting yourself, Jess, and after seeing those messages, I think you are at risk."

I sighed at her, "Jess, I want you to avoid going through the hell I did and sometimes still do, please just come with me for your parents?"

I softly spoke to try and talk to her but she just scowled back, "Daddy, you can't be serious?"

Shaun sighed at her, "Who has the original pictures Jess?"

She went oddly quiet. "I don't know who took them," she wept slightly replying.

"Jess, I need to know! I have already spoken to the studio about them and they say they were shot with a mobile phone so who took them!" She broke down again, "I don't know I thought it was Gwen but she doesn't have them, Daddy please believe me!"

Shaun sighed. "Then on Monday morning you will be going with Fae and Gale to the hotel for a month while I try and put an end to this, I don't mind the cosplay and I can live with the bikini stuff but that I can't see you doing to yourself Jess!" He put his foot down hard.

Scowling and huffing Jess stood up, "Fine! Thanks very much Fae!" She snidely said as she stormed out of the office and slammed the door. "Fae? Whatever you do? Don't have children for fuck's sake!"

Shaun laughed as the dust settled. "I can't see it being something I need to worry about anytime soon Shaun, are you okay?" I replied, he smiled.

"After taking the blame for me, I'm okay, thanks by the way!" He said and shook my hand.

"No problem, we'll pick her up at 9 on Monday, maybe she will have calmed down a bit by then?" I smiled at him and went to leave.

"Hey you forgot something!" Shaun handed me my prize catches. "Just slip out the back of the warehouse with them, okay? Take them as thanks for taking the blow from Jess?" Shaun put them into a bag for me and handed me my goodies.

"Are you sure? I don't mind paying for them," I replied, a little surprised that he was giving me a free hand to leave without paying. "If you help my Jess, get out of her hole then the debt is paid for many times over!"

Shaun handed me the bag and guided me through the warehouse to let me slip out with my rewards. "Hope you have a good weekend Shaun!"

I smiled at him as I started to walk out, "She will be mad for most of the weekend, but she might thank me someday Fae!" He chuckled as I headed back into town.

Walking back through the streets and towards the old part of town I kept thinking about all the abuse and pressure that Jess had been receiving, it was oddly familiar to me. Reminiscent of the abuse and torment that had driven me to try suicide a few times, deep down I felt a heavy sorrow for Jess, she was a nice girl and smarter than what she was being encouraged into doing.

Just like me though people knew exactly how to push her just far enough to get her to almost willingly do anything for their attention or affection. Jess's battle for me felt personal and I hoped that maybe I could help her fight herself out of the corner she had been smashed into over months of continual abuse and pressurisation. Hopefully by Monday, she wouldn't hate me quite so much and maybe I could help her the way the hotel had helped me in my teen years?

Walking along, I needed to see Colette to ask her to adjust the goodies I had just been given, I just hoped she wouldn't object to knowing where they had come from though, I wasn't going to tell her they were freebies. Colette's soft smile and gentle pecks on each cheek greeted me into her shop as always, her kindness was always something I adored her for.

Colette and Francois had turned into almost a strange second set of parents, after every crash they would come to see if I was okay a day or two after, gently keeping a careful eye on me and my health. Colette was also like my personal dressing assistant, adjusting my clothes and trying to help me look my most beautiful, she was far better at that task than me!

Starting to talk about my shopping trip she sneaked a little eye onto the contents of my bag and pulled out the skirt and top of her making I had found at the thrift store. Smiling as she held up the skirt. "Oh Fae, you will look stunning in this!"

I felt kind of bad as not only had they been given away by the original owner I had got my hands on them for free. Colette however didn't seem too fussed either way as she turned the sign on her door around, "Let's make sure it fits you," she softly spoke as she led me to a changing room and opened the curtain.

While I changed into the skirt, she continued to speak to me. "I hope you don't feel bad about finding them at Shaun's shop, as long as someone loves my work, I am happy for them to come and see me," I wandered out in the skirt and Colette gently ran her hands around the waistband.

"A little loose for you, I will fix that there is a blanket to cover yourself if you want to take a seat while I work on this for you?" Colette guided me to a small chair beside her desk and handed me a small blanket to cover my legs while she adjusted the skirt for me.

My wandering eyes gazed at the beautiful garments adorning her walls, dresses so beautiful that they looked like the dresses from children's fantasy films, anyone who wore one of these would look like a queen. Lacy and serene long flowing dresses, corsets with ornate patterns and stitching on them and the odd little taste of the youth of France with subtle soft flowing tops and trousers.

Colette's shop was both my idea of utter heaven and hell, the garments she produced tickling every element of my clothing fantasies, I just wished I had the income to own any of these pieces of utter indulgence. Colette called me over and I wandered to her complete with my shielding blanket as she fitted the skirt back onto me.

"Perfection, look at those curves Fae!" She said and smiled and patted the waistband on the skirt.

"Thank you, Colette," I smiled at her as she lifted the top out of my bag, "Now Fae! This is almost made just for you!"

Colette smiled sweetly at the top as she held it out, "I told him that she wouldn't be happy with it, but her loss is your gain no?" She chuckled softly as I took my top off for her to fit this masterpiece to me.

Colette paused and grinned. "Fae this is designed to not need underwear, so, could you? Don't worry yours won't be the only ones I see today." Slowly I took my bra off too as she wrapped me in the top.

Softly, she adjusted the sides to hold me firmly in place. "I might have to adjust these often for you but I don't mind helping you with these," she smiled as she checked the fit, "Fae it is as if I made this just for you and you will break all the boys' hearts in this," winking as she stuffed my top and bra back inside the bag I had brought with me. "Thank you, Colette."

She gently patted my sides and gave me two pecks. "Au revoir Fae, now you look like a princess," Colette smiled as she sent me away.

Wandering back through the marketplace my mind turned back to Jess and maybe more importantly how she might be with me come Monday morning. Vividly I remember the car journey from Oured to Ljianstipol with my dad, we barely spoke for the whole duration of that trip, I was so angry with my parents for sending me here.

Even my dad, who seemed to be the only person that understood me or really gave me any kind of respect at the time, had sent me away to this place. That first stay at the Davizioso was to be the start of the undoing of our relationship with each other as this place made me realise just how hard my mum had been working to try and give me any kind of shot at life in Oured.

Tony, Shanky, Gale and countless others made me see just what my mum had been putting herself through while my dad buried his head and acted as if there was nothing wrong and in doing so hiding away from the reality of my conditions.

Though the memory that was on my mind right now was the isolation and loneliness that I felt when I first arrived at the hotel and found myself among strangers. Despite their well-meaning nature, the people here were totally new and the nerves and apprehension of being surrounded by these people stopped me from being able to speak to anyone.

Wandering home along the river, I didn't want Jess to endure that same alienating feeling when she stayed, the same feeling that had kept me hidden away in my room for a month when I first arrived. When I got home, I started to pack a suitcase, I was going to stay for the first two weeks of her visit to the hotel, only two doors down from her too, she wasn't going to be alone, and I wanted her to know that. Packing everything I might need, I started thinking about how in time I made friends for the first time in the Davizioso, it was a slow process.

Over time, I developed strong bonds with people like Shanky and Gale but Tony was my real hero, he almost took me under his wing to bring me out of my room and out of my shell. Tony was like my best friend and almost a second father amongst all the gloom and torment that flowed around my head. I have never forgotten that look on Tony's face as he finally allowed himself to sleep after staying up for nearly three days to help me feel welcome and at home in Ljianstipol.

Almost 10 years on, he still speaks to me just like he did that first night when he stepped in to help me, even now as my boss we still are just like old friends. Joking, laughing, going for a drink by the river together, he always keeps pushing me along and I guess I might be the only person whose boss has ever dyed their hair for them.

Zipping my suitcase closed, I sent Gale and Tony a text to tell them I was going to be staying in my old room for at least two weeks, neither minded as they had kept that room free for me for almost 8 years now. During Sunday, I started to mentally prepare myself to pick up a no doubt quite angry teenager in the morning, wondering if maybe now I regret taking the blame?

Though the main reason I had spent so much time mulling over Jess during the weekend is she was my first true guest and this battle she was starting this morning somehow felt very personal. Strolling along, dragging my suitcase like a hopelessly lost tourist around the outer edges of Ljianstipol; my nerves began to creep up the closer to Shaun's house that I got.

Fearful and mindful of just how long this short wander into the town might feel I couldn't even mask my nervousness before I had to puff my chest out and be the strong girl to walk Jess to her home for the next month. Taking a deep breath, I knocked at the door and within seconds it was opened by Jess, though she didn't look angry she did seem kind of nervous as she put her suitcase outside the door. Shaun came to the door. "Hey Fae, thank you and look after my girl for us!" He smiled as he gave Jess a goodbye hug, Jess went and gave her mum a hug before coming back outside.

Standing nervously, she looked up at me. "Thank you for helping me and my family," she said pensively smiling.

"You're welcome, come on let's go," I replied as we started to walk into town.

Jess looked at my suitcase. "Why have you brought that with you?"

Smiling back at her, "Well I thought you might like at least one friend at the hotel when you arrive, I remember how scary and lonely it was when I first stayed at the place when I was 17." Jess smiled to herself as we quietly walked together.

"I'm only going to be two doors down from you, so knock anytime you feel alone," I softly spoke attempting to assure her she would be fine.

"Thank you, Fae," Jess spoke back as we neared the Davizioso.

Abby greeted us and got Jess checked in while I went to get her a wristband made for the duration of her stay; Tony was panicking in the meeting room while we waited for it to spit out a turquoise wristband for Jess. Unknown to us, someone else had seen the article about the Davizioso and found its way to the eyes of someone far more influential than Shaun.

Gale started the machine up and started to attempt to calm Tony down, feeling almost flustered by the strange nature of Tony.

"Guys what's going on?" I was fearful of the answer. Gale looked at me. "That article found its way to the head of the health authority for the region and they are coming for a meeting with us on Wednesday."

Tony was still flustered by the events. "They want to run sessions here! They are coming to negotiate with us on Wednesday!" Tony sat down. "Fae, we need you to help us? Can you attend the meeting with us on Wednesday afternoon?"

Gale and Tony both looked at me and I started to feel how important this was to them both, "If you think I can help? I mean, I'm nobody special?"

Gale smiled a little. "But to your patients and guests Fae you are everything! You are probably the best person to represent us, these sessions are your creation and who better to decide how they run here? That's if they agree to that of course!"

Tony smiled a little. "Fae this is a huge moment for this place and it's all because of your hard work, you should be representing us for this meeting!" Feeling encouraged and as their motivating words seeped into my mind I replied, "Well if you are sure then of course I will help."

Both smiled and Tony had calmed down as the wristband emerged from the machine. "Your first guest, Fae?" Tony winked.

"My first guest," I smiled at him and started to gently rub the wristband, "It's a personal one too."

Gale patted me on the back, "Your first chance to deliver to someone what you promised to use your past for?" I nodded and thought as I headed back to Jess.

Cheerfully chatting with Abby in the entrance hall of the Davizioso, Jess waited patiently for me to lead her to the room she would be staying in for the next month. Leanne seemed to snub Jess for some reason? Almost avoiding any form of eye contact with her?

We started to wander through the main hallway to the elevator and upwards to our rooms. Jess's smile had gone a little as we walked. "What was that about?"

I asked her, "Nothing, Leanne has been funny with me for a while now."

Jess replied, "We haven't exactly been friends either so I know what you mean."

I smiled back at her thinking about my first meeting with Leanne. Anxiously, we stood waiting for the elevator to come down. "You okay, Jess?" I asked nervously and wondering if the reality of what was happening had hit her, she smiled awkwardly back as the elevator door opened.

Standing inside with the door closed Jess let out a breath of relief, 'Terrified'.

I thought about my first ride in this elevator. "Yeah, so was I back then too, gotta admit it still gives me a shiver sometimes even now," I replied.

Gently, I laid my hand upon her shoulder as the elevator ground to a halt and the doors opened and I waited until Jess took her first step out into the top floor of the hotel. Guiding her down the hallway to my room.

"This is my room, so I'm only a few doors away from you and my door is always open to you, Jess," I opened my door and gave Jess a guided tour. Jess wandered around in awe, "They kept this room just for you?" She smiled as she looked at the huge bathroom.

"Yeah, they have kept it just for me," I sighed back, "I appreciate them doing it, things were hard at home when I first came here but come on, let's check out your room!" I guided Jess past Shanky's door and to her door.

Jess tapped her wristband against the lock and opened the door into her accommodation, her face lit up in awe, "It's almost as big as my house!" She beamed as she took in the vast space. "I did make sure you got a good room," I smiled and gently encouraged her in.

Jess checked out the enormous bathroom before gasping at the vast lounge and bedroom in the room she had been given for the next month. "Well if you want to unpack and then I will show you around the place? Joanne is taking my appointments for the day so we have all day for you to get settled in."

Jess smiled. "Thank you, Fae."

Jess gave me a hug.

"It's okay, your band will unlock my door too so you can let yourself in anytime," I headed off to unpack my things and left Jess to get settled in. Laying my suitcase on the bed, I started to think about my very first visit all those years ago and how I never thought that I would need this room again. Memories of all those days I shied away from anyone and locked myself in my room, at least Jess wasn't going to feel that isolation and loneliness during her stay, while I thought Tony gently knocked on the door.

Tony sat on the end of my bed. "Bet you didn't ever think about staying here again?" He said, patting my duvet.

"No, I didn't think I would either," I sat down on the bed.

Tony sat beside me. *Why are you staying Fae?* I thought for a moment. "I don't want her to feel how I did when I first came here, the loneliness and isolation or the fear, I want her to feel like she has at least one friend here that she can just talk to or sit with," I whispered back to him.

Tony didn't reply but I looked round and saw a strange smile on his face, "That's why you will be the best this place ever has Fae, it's personal for you isn't it?"

I nodded back, "Her story is different but just like mine, though if anything I learned this from you all those years ago Tony, you were my first real friend and I have never forgotten that." Tony smiled.

"Still are too," I chuckled at him, "Yeah, you have been good to me Tony, I don't think I can ever repay you for that?" Tony sat back, "You doing something like this for Jess is all the payment I could ever want and isn't this exactly why you wanted to be here?" I smiled and nodded. Tony stood back up and went to leave.

"Jess, will never forget what you are doing for her you know? But that's not why you are doing it Fae and that's what makes you special." Tony smiled as he walked away and left me thinking about what I was doing and how similar it was to what he had done for me all that time ago.

While I sat thinking to myself, Jess knocked and let herself in and walked across the room and sat beside me. "Leanne hasn't spoken to me for two months now, she's mad because I wouldn't do the photo sets anymore," Jess sighed as she confessed to me. "Leanne hasn't spoken to me since my first day at work nearly a year ago, she made a comment to me about this place employing patients on my first day, we haven't spoken since."

Jess looked and sighed. "She really said that to you?"

I nodded my head. "That's what life was like in Oured too, people just saw me as a problem and not as a person," I sighed. "Life here is good though, the people here are good, well, all of them except Leanne!" I chuckled, "Come on let's show you around, we can talk more later."

Jess followed me to the stairs and I started to show her round the hotel. Walking her down to Joanne's room and gently knocking before Joanne let us in, "You must be Jess? Fae has told us all about you. I'm Joanne you will be seeing Fae during your time here but I'm always around if you need to talk."

Jess was given a quick tour of Joanne's room before we headed to the first communal room. Wandering just down the hallway from Joanne's room we entered the first communal area filled with plush sofas and bean bags. "People just come here to get some quiet time," I proudly told her as we wandered deeper into the Davizioso.

Guiding her to the large room where my group sessions were hosted. "You will know this room, you have been here a few times, it's mostly just for the groups now though," I declared like a proud tour guide with every single spot in the hotel filling me with pride as I showed Jess around. We reached the main dining hall and the adjoined communal area and stopped to get some lunch, a few residents came to introduce themselves to Jess, including Shanky.

Different staff introduced themselves to her too as we began our final stage of the tour towards Gale's bar, at my request Jess had been given access to this special spot in the hotel. Gale was ready and waiting as we entered the room, ready and eager to claim another scalp on his pool table as he introduced himself to Jess through competition.

Once Gale had introduced himself, we sat and had a cold beer with Gale and Tony, both were keen to look after Jess and to make her feel welcomed to the hotel. During the afternoon, we stayed and chatted to Tony and Gale before we headed up to our rooms, I felt content as Jess headed into her room for a shower and we agreed to meet up for dinner in my room.

Soon enough Jess arrived ready for the evening, though oddly she brought her phone with her? After dinner, we sat on the sofa in my room and Jess started to talk about the social media world that had been slowly eating her alive. Scrolling through some vile requests for pictures and almost disturbing abuse that she had received as she started to come clean, no wonder she had been having such trouble.

Endless streams of dirty and abusive messages and the hardest part to read the personal insults and abuse she had been receiving since Christmas. Jess had lost a lot of weight since I had last seen her, reading through the messages began to explain why, as she was openly being called fat and ugly, she had lost all her confidence and started to starve herself.

Jess was a pretty girl and I couldn't believe that anyone could call her fat but that message wasn't just from people online, some were from people that she knew very well. Leanne and Gwen had been orchestrating the naked picture sets that they sold, when Jess refused to do anymore Leanne had turned into a vindictive little bully attempting to coerce her back into selling the pictures.

I pulled out my phone and opened up a file which had all my old abusive text messages from friends and boyfriends during my teen years in Oured and let her look through them. Messages of abuse and hatred that had pushed me over the edge and nearly cost me my life, the world was different in some ways, but our paths were similar in too many ways.

Jess seemed disgusted by what she read on my phone but then made her realise why I had been so keen to help her, "You are starting from the same spot as me, Jess, the system didn't want to help me or my parents and the only people I thought I could trust were the first to turn on me. I remember how alone I felt and how far down I had been pushed, I can't let that happen to you," I sighed to her as she stopped reading.

"Did they really push you that far?" Jess asked in shock.

"Yeah a few times but this place saved me from that end," I smiled slightly as I said that to her.

We spent the remainder of the evening talking about our experiences, even though the means by which we had been treated were different, the outcome was the same. Gradually, we had both been crushed and pushed into becoming more and more desperate to feel any kind of interaction and the harder we tried the higher the bar was set for us to fail.

During the next day we began the process of finding the source of Jess's issues and how they had caused her to fall so far. Jess on the surface looked like she had the sort of life anyone could envy; her social media showed her being happy and showered with love and gifts from all over the world but reality was very different.

Free gifts were paid for either with money or degradation and sometimes both, the affection she received was largely perverse and she had been almost encouraged to starve herself to become thinner. Jess had been using the money from the photo sets to fund the gifts she promoted, when Jess tried to put a stop to it was when things had become vicious for her.

Just before Christmas one of the sites she used changed their algorithm and suddenly she and Gwen lost their much-needed reach and likes, this was when they started to sell the photo sets. Questing for appreciation and likes, Jess had gradually been manipulated into delving further and further until she could sink no lower, like so many of the people who attended my groups Jess was an addict.

While the addiction became stronger, Jess became more desperate but was being openly used by anyone after a cheap deal from her including her friends Gwen and Leanne. Leanne had shunned Jess after she refused to do more photos, but Gwen had stuck by her, though Jess could see that she was being used she was almost powerless to stop the manipulation.

Jess knew something was wrong and just like many other people in my groups she had been largely ignored when seeking help and when that happened, she went silent. Having lost almost all of her confidence and resolve she was an easy target for anyone who wanted a cheap laugh online and with her friends pushing her aside she was alone.

Jess ended her first session with me in a flood of tears as she finally set the truth about herself free, most people would have seen what she was going through as self-induced or petty, but I knew that feeling she was facing only too well. Once again, we spent the evening together talking about my past problems and about Jess and her battles, despite having very different sets of issues we had a lot in common.

Jess ended the evening by confessing to me that she was determined to beat her demons and leave the social media party that caused her such pain, I just hoped her addictions weren't too strong. While Jess headed to bed, I started thinking about the stories she had been telling me and the messages she had shown me during the past two days. Something worried me about it all, in some ways it was like Jess had two completely separate lives, one people got to see and one that she kept hidden away, I didn't fully understand why this was the case?

While I pondered about her, I wondered if Shaun had made any progress trying to have her pictures removed from the internet, I couldn't imagine that was going to be an easy task for him. Jess and Shaun were however starting to assist me make a decision about my future, maybe I should really push for this cyber related mental health?

It was grey ground for many specialists and very new, but it would allow me to cover gently a mix of every kind of condition there was? Would many people really see the internet as such a rampant source of problems amongst people? Just maybe that lack of understanding and willingness of many to tackle it was an even bigger reason to specialise in it?

During the morning, Jess was calmer and happier than she had been for the first couple of days of her stay, it was just a shame the same couldn't have been said about Tony or Gale. Today during the afternoon, the board for the local healthcare authority would be visiting to negotiate the possibility of working together to tackle the growing cyber related mental health problems in Ljianstipol.

Most of the people that were being actively affected had seemingly such minor symptoms that they simply didn't really suit the treatments available to them. However, having been through that system myself, I knew just how inadequately it was able to cope or deal with anyone who needed their help.

While the hours ticked away, we prepared the meeting room for the entire board of directors to arrive, Tony and Gale both dressed up nicely and even their table had been cleaned but as the first members arrived a box of cold beer awaited them. Tony stood beside me peering out of the window as the first. "Offer them a beer when they come in Fae."

I was surprised by his request. "Are you sure it's a good idea, Tony?"

Tony grinned, "Not really, it depends how this goes, these people see us as cowboys anyway so there's nothing to lose on our side of the wall."

Tony and Gale stood awaiting their arrival and as the first steps echoed in the hallway, I made myself ready. Abby escorted the 10 directors to the top of the stairwell before assembling them all and waiting for me to open the door and begin the afternoon of debate.

Once silence fell outside, Tony gave me a nod and I opened the door and greeted each member of the board, offering them a bottle of beer and a bottle of water. Looks of disgust and shock greeted me as every single member refused the beer including two assistants, I wasn't surprised in truth though I did wonder what their plan was? Each seat filled with the members of the board for the local health authority, with their neat and expensive suits and equally well-dressed assistants and the meeting was ready to begin.

Tony had saved me a seat beside him as the meeting began in earnest, these influential and important directors had seen the article about the work we had been doing and were here to capitalise on that. The chairman presented the reasoning behind the meeting and visitation today, in short, the board knew they were failing the local area and wanted to start to change that by hosting their own groups right here at the Davizioso.

Collectively we sat quietly listening to them argue their case and I started to notice that I was getting a few odd looks from the assistants that were in attendance, I guess my hair maybe was my problem? An almost endless stream of databases and charts were being presented to us showing how the sessions being run here would aid the local healthcare system but there was a catch that neither Tony or Gale were happy about.

The board of directors fired across an offer that was almost insulting to not just myself but every single person who had ever visited or worked at the Davizioso. Their group sessions would be run at the hotel but staffed and run entirely by the local healthcare authority, once this suggestion went out, Tony and Gale went to war.

Tony sat upright and furiously said, "You have to be kidding? You have come here to insult us even more?"

Gale didn't hesitate to support, "So your plan is to run sessions here under our name, so that if they work you look like heroes but if they fail you can pass the blame onto us?"

I sat quietly still noticing the rather barbed looks I was receiving from the chairman's assistant. A member of the board sat back.

"Well, you already have the facility and the footfall for it to work just we would want our own staff to provide these sessions," he replied smugly.

Gale paused briefly, "But you already can't cope?"

The chairman suddenly took an interest, "Don't you have sessions which are run by your patients?" He smirked back and as he spoke his assistant smirked at me.

Tony went red and I wondered if he might blow when Gale put a hand on his shoulder to calm him down. "So, who will you draft in to run these sessions here if we let you run them?"

Another member of the board interjected, "We have a couple of people in mind."

Gale grinned. "Not in Ljianstipol, you don't!"

Suddenly the smug grins were disappearing from the faces of the board, "We know the nearest specialist is in Usted and they are a private clinic so you aren't drafting them in to help you anytime soon," Gale finished his point with a deep cutting blow.

Two assistants noted the time and called a brief respite break, while the room emptied, I stayed behind with an enraged Tony and a plotting Gale, "Those bastards all they see is numbers!"

Tony scowled and headed out to get some fresh air. "Don't worry, Fae, we have numbers for them, but he is right they don't see names or faces they see a number."

Gale sighed and handed me a beer.

"You sure about this Gale?" I asked him as I accepted the bottle.

"Not really, we don't want them running anything here anyway, but we are obliged to entertain this shit as a courtesy," I sat down.

"Why is Tony so irate?" Gale sat down.

"The chairman let David out of the healthcare system the day he killed himself and Tony knows it too," I sat back saddened by Tony being insulted by a man that had effectively helped to take his son's life.

"Thing is, Fae, you have been in that system and know what it's like, as long as they see figures and not people or stories then they will never change. Year in and year out we take in all the people that they leave to rot or fend for themselves, just like you and everyone else in this place and they couldn't care less about them."

Gale was irate. "Will Tony be okay for the second part of this?" Gale chuckled, "Yes, he has his secret weapon here and I have numbers for them too!"

Tony walked back in, having calmed down. "How long have we got until they're back?" He asked Gale.

"Five minutes?" I replied.

"Good, then enjoy that and get ready for our pitch!" Tony seemed to have a plan in mind? Soon enough the congregation assembled back outside the door and yet again all refused the cool bottles they were offered on entering the room, as they sat down Tony unleashed his plan.

Tony rested his hand on my shoulder. "Could you get me the picture on the left-hand side of my desk please?" I didn't hesitate to collect the picture but much to my surprise it was the picture of me and Tony from my first visit to Ljianstipol.

"That's the one, could you pass it round the table?" I handed the picture to the first of the board members and as they started to pass it round the table Tony explained the significance of the picture to them.

"That girl was our first true patient, we already had people here but most of them had been through all the establishments you had to offer but she hadn't. She was 17 years old and had been diagnosed with bipolar disorder and depression at the age of 12, her mum had been trying to get her help, but she couldn't get any help."

"Slowly the impact of her conditions was tearing her and her parents' marriage apart. Over a few years, they were largely shunned and left to try and figure things out for themselves but for that girl things had turned deadly."

"Being bullied almost constantly and alone she tried to take her own life by jumping from the bridge in her local town Oured, a passing stranger caught her as she tried to jump. Had she succeeded, the impact of hitting the freezing water beneath her would have been like falling 100 metres onto concrete and if she had survived that fall then she would have likely died from hypothermia."

"Had she somehow by some miracle survived then she would have been quadriplegic at best. Her parents didn't know just how hard life had gotten for her until the stranger took her back home and explained what she had done but he did at least tell her mum about this place. That girl's mum phoned here begging us to help the girl out but we hadn't taken in anyone so young, but the situation was desperate for the girl and we had to help her."

"Over Christmas, we spoke almost daily with her and getting a room ready for her and arranged for different people here to look out for her when she arrived in the new year. She arrived with her dad in January, they hadn't spoken since she found out they were sending her away to this weird place in a strange town, she was so angry with them."

"Over the first few weeks she didn't really seem to meet anyone or leave her room very much, she was so nervous and almost ashamed of herself? One night, her neighbour called me claiming there was a strange smell coming from her room and he hadn't seen any sign of her for a couple of days. I rushed through the hotel to the floor where her room was and the entire floor stank of bleach, I called at her door but there was no response."

"After three tries, I broke the door down and found her collapsed on the floor, rolled over on her side and completely motionless. Panicking, I rolled her over and to my relief she was still breathing but she was an emotional wreck, her face was red from crying and her hands were blue where she had been trying to dye her hair. Gale drove for 3 hours to find her some hair dye and I spent that night cleaning her up and dyeing her hair, we talked a lot and I discovered she had barely left her room let alone the hotel."

"During the next day we changed that, I took her out and introduced her to Ljianstipol and slowly I managed to pull a little smile out of her that day, we got someone to take this picture of me with her. We talked a lot over the next few days and her story was terrible, she was alone, scared and so nervous until that day, we became friends and slowly we started to help her turn a corner."

"What saddened me the most though, was that she knew she was bipolar and suffered from depression but at no time had she been told what it really meant for her, we explained it for her and by the end of her stay she was a different girl."

"She stayed with us for six months before she went back home, she had her 18th birthday with us too and went back like a different person. Although her parents' marriage didn't survive, she came back when she was 19 so that she wasn't around during their bitter divorce. Life had been tough during her time away and we did a lot of rebuilding and soon became a little helper around the place too."

"We lost contact for a few years but last year she returned for the final time, life in Oured had been bad and she had found herself alone and returned to the hotel for the final time. Uprooting her entire life and moving back to Ljianstipol, once again she has turned her life around entirely, she makes me very proud every day if helping her is all I truly ever achieve here then it will be a job well done."

Emotional, Tony sat back up as the picture returned to his hand and he handed the picture back to me.

"Can you get me the other picture please?" Tony smiled at me.

The chairman of the board smirked, "Well why don't you introduce us to this miracle patient of yours?"

Gale grinned as the chairman fell straight into their trap. "You already have, you all shunned her twice," Gale grinned as I handed the second picture to Tony.

Suddenly, the entire congregation were staring at me. "Look at the eyes if you don't believe us!" Gale smiled as Tony looked at his next picture.

"If you want to run sessions here at the Davizioso, then it will be Fae that runs them," Gale grinned.

The chairman looked at me. "But she is a patient too?"

Gale went to answer but I stepped in, "Yes I am a patient here too, my group sessions are my therapy too and right now I have a girl a few doors away who I'm trying to help avoid the mess that my early life became," I smiled back at him Gale interjected, "She had been through your system and yes she is a patient so unlike everyone else in this room she is more qualified in this field than all of us."

Tony turned around the picture and passed around the photo of me with my award along with a copy of my results including my commendations for care. "Fae is the only person in all of the region qualified in this field and check out why she got her two commendations, she agreed to do an interview to protect her patients and she left her exam and risked her entire qualification to help a patient in distress." The congregation handed round the photo of me, each one looked up to check it was really me.

Gale confidently sat upright, "You like figures? Here are the ones we care about; 15 is the number of patients lost in Ljianstipol's healthcare system as a direct result of their mental health problems, 0 the number of patients we have lost in 11 years and finally, 1 the number of specialists in the field of cyber related health problems in the entire Ljianstipol region, if you want us to even entertain allowing you to runs group sessions here, then it is Fae who will be running them," Gale smiled at me as he finished his final statement.

The chairman looked back at me. "Is there anything you would like to add?"
I thought for a moment and collected a bottle of beer, opened it and took a sip.

"When you came here today, you were all offered a simple gesture to welcome you here and you all refused, here at the Davizioso we need people that don't refuse the bottle or just take it, we look for people that become a part of people's lives. One day that bottle of beer might be a game piece a pencil or even a bottle of blue hair dye and what we do with that item is what really makes the difference to someone's life, just like mine," I finished my speech as the congregation began to deliberate with themselves.

Their deliberation died down and they all began to leave, this time however I received a handshake from each member and no dirty looks either, though we were clueless as to their decision. Tony followed them out while Gale stood beside me watching them leave.

"You think they'll be back?" I asked him.

"Hopefully not, I guessed the price for our sessions and tripled it, if they want to use this place as somewhere to lay blame, they can pay well for that honour," Gale smirked as he turned and left.

"Good job by the way, Fae, you made them respect you," Gale said as he wandered away.

Meeting completed I wondered if Jess would be up for going for a walk by the beach and grabbing something to eat by the river. However, and much to my pleasant surprise Jess had been befriended by two guests of similar age to her and they were going to be spending the evening together, I was alone again but for a happy reason. Jess was apologetic but I was only too happy to see her make some friends and find people to help her feel normal again in the hotel.

Alone I went and got something to eat by the river before going for a walk along the promenade and sitting on the wall overlooking the sea with the setting sun illuminating the world in oranges and reds. Happy to be alone for the first time, I felt an odd sensation within me, almost with pride as I had hopefully helped Jess on her journey to beat her demons.

Leaning against the railings when they began to reverberate with gentle tapping noises coming from above me, I looked up to see Tony standing waiting for me to look round.

Smiling at him, "All alone again, Fae?" He asked.

"Not if you sit down?" Tony smiled back and sat beside me. "I figured you would be here; how do you feel after today?" He said as he offered me a beer.

Taking a moment to think before I replied, "Odd, I'm really happy Jess has made some friends even if that means me being alone." Tony smiled. "That's called pride, Fae, there's no shame in it, you might help turn her life around, she may never really like you but she will never forget what you have done for her," he started to look over the horizon with me.

Tony's words sunk down into my mind. "Same way you did for me?"

Tony nodded, "Exactly the same way, you know today those people sneered at you for most of the day, they weren't sneering when they left."

I listened intently to him, "I don't know Tony, maybe they are right?"

Tony turned quickly, "No they aren't! They sent my son away with no help just like they did with you and your mother. They see numbers and not people! Where you and I see people and stories, Fae."

I paused, "Can I ask you something, Tony?"

He nodded his head.

"Did you really mean everything you said?" Tony smiled. "Every word, if you are the only person, I truly help like that then I will be happy," I began to well up a little. "How hard was it? Helping me, I mean?" Once gain he smiled.

"At first, pretty hard but once we had that day out round Ljianstipol, easier, you were just alone and scared, not just scared of other people but you were scared of yourself Fae, but once I got a little smile out of you, I just kept pushing to finally get you out of yourself."

Tony rested his hand on my shoulder. "It's exactly the same thing you have been doing for Jess, that's what makes me proudest of you Fae," smiling I looked round at him to see him also welling up, "Thank you for all you have done for me Tony," he smiled. "Just watch the sunset before we both wind up crying all night, Fae."

I laughed at him as the sun finally dipped below the horizon and we wandered back to the Davizioso.

During the remainder of that week, Jess and her new friends became partners in crime spending most of their time together and that sense of pride just grew stronger each day. Sessions with Jess also went well as she began to try fighting off her demons and with her new friends to support her, she just grew more determined with each talk we had.

However, during the evenings, I was now spending alone that pride was being disrupted by a steadily growing fear and nervousness about the article as it grew closer to being reality. With Jess being settled at the Davizioso, I packed my suitcase and headed home to the comfort of my bed and own four walls, however a letter had come from the studio confirming the date of the shoots and my brain went haywire.

Shaking as I read through the letter my hands were almost uncontrollable and a crushing anxiety attack hit me, mentally imagining a metal chair under a spotlight in a blackened world terrified me. Talking to myself to calm myself down, initially did the trick but during the next morning the shakes and anxiety returned to haunt me.

Studying for a while took my mind off that photoshoot but I couldn't stop it creeping into my thoughts and invading every single minute that I spent alone. Abby popped round to see me and helped to wash the thoughts away with her optimistic and sweet thoughts. Those first fleeting anxiety attacks and fears became a near constant during the next month, causing me a few small crashes at home anytime I went anywhere near the drawer that the letter laid inside.

Throughout her stay Jess became a completely different girl, self-respecting and she put some weight back on and just like Tony said, that strange pride I felt the day she left the Davizioso was my proudest day at work so far. Watching her walk away when she checked out as a changed 19-year-old girl gave me a deep smile that I had never experienced before.

Over that weekend though with the photoshoot looming ever closer, just as I reached my living room my mind went into utter overdrive. Stumbling to the floor, my thoughts turned in on themselves as my mind fell downwards, deeper and deeper into the abyss, erupting in tears of sheer terror I needed to think seriously about cancelling the shoot.

While my crash deepened, I sent a sad face on the messaging group but asked people to give me space too, within seconds support messages had come through but I needed to be alone right now.

Laying in a heap on my living room floor saturating the thick rug with my tears and crumbling emotions as the reality of what I had agreed too really sunk in. Debating continually all that night, part of me just wanted to throw in the towel and cancel the whole thing but deep within me a strange resolve just wouldn't let me make that phone call.

Deep down I was determined to go through with the shoot and raise awareness about countless people who suffered just like me and continued to suffer in silence. My inhibitions however just wanted me to quit, years of shaming and a lack of confidence were becoming a high mountain to scale to even contemplate going through with the shoot.

Raging away inside me a full-scale war between my strongest beliefs and deepest fears was beginning to take its toll on me both mentally and physically. Almost sulking to myself looking at the few old photographs I still had, my darkest moments were haunting me far too vividly, bad friends and cruel boyfriends who had slammed me into the ground during my teens.

Shamed for being a retard or fat and ugly; my confidence within my own skin had never healed in the slightest as a result of what for most just seemed like name calling and bad luck. However, when you are battling your own mind and a constant rain of abuse and shaming is heading your way it doesn't take long for you to start believing what you are being called is true.

Remembering only too well the 'Friends' who had set me up just so that they could laugh when I fell or the guys who toyed with me just to see how hard I would hit the deck when the rug was yanked from beneath me. Memories that I wished that didn't haunt me still were the only thing I could focus on during that entire day, chipping away at what little self-esteem I had, I needed to get out of my house and give myself some room to breathe.

Darkness had descended both in my mind and over Ljianstipol, I took a coat and a flask of coffee and began walking through the town towards the park by the beach. Wandering the deserted streets of Ljianstipol in the dead of night and wading through the desolation of my thoughts as each step drew me closer to my spot of reflection and salvation.

Feeling the gaps between the cobbles told me exactly where I was in town even with my eyes closed, I knew exactly where I was as each little gap offered me a free face first trip to the ground. Walking through the dimly lit marketplace and into the park towards a little spot just away from the paths by a few trees.

Moonlight became stronger with each step I took deeper into darkness as suddenly the path was clearly visible right down to my place of refuge. Finally arriving at the little spot, I sat down and crossed my legs, poured myself a warm drink and started to try and shift the dimensions of my thoughts from destruction to creation.

Looking up at the sky and the glowing moon began to soothe my thoughts as I erupted in an unashamed outburst of loud cries and growing tears. Each passing hour under the moon's gaze began to settle my mind, the tears stopped falling and finally my thoughts allowed me to start thinking about whether I went through with the shoot or not.

Gently, the sun began to illuminate the park and in the distance a figure began to appear, I knew who it would be, only one person instinctively knew when I would be here. Emerging from the light haze his tall and thin stature cast an ominous shadow across the park as he walked with his mood lifting gifts in hand, finally sitting down next to me Francois had come to see me.

Many of my friends had been fantastic since I first arrived in Ljianstipol but when I was at my lowest, Francois almost had an odd sixth sense for exactly where I would be and what I needed. Happy to just sit and talk or just keep me company for a few minutes he quite simply just knew that a coffee and one of his croissants would be a welcome gift.

Never objecting even if like today I just didn't have it within me to talk with him, whenever I had a hard crash, he would appear wherever I might wind up, leave his gifts and thoughts and leave me to think.

Often after one of these meetings I would apologise to him the next time I saw him but he always refused the apology and just wanted to make sure I was okay no matter where that might be. Francois knew why I was here too and rather than talking and expecting a reply, he was happy just to talk today.

Proudly he spoke to me about how brave I was and how nervous I must be feeling, my responses were just to nod or shake my head, Francois was happy with these as replies. Gently talking me through the thoughts that both he and Colette had about the shoot as he tried to help settle my mind and encourage me not to give up.

Francois knew me too well sometimes, I found myself thinking as he started to talk more about the fears about myself, I was fighting with but his support was greatly appreciated but we both knew that it wasn't helping me today. Calmly he stood to leave me to think, gently patting my shoulder before he walked away, while I watched him exit the park, I got a whiff of the cognac in the coffee he had left behind.

Alone but surrounded by moral support I sat under the trees drinking the mix of coffee and cognac and started to really debate what I would do. Slowly tourists began to appear, some would drop change thinking I was homeless, others would try talking before they gave up and left me to sit and dwell alone.

Amidst the mix of happy beach going tourists, I sat glumly under my trees having turned away from any kind of active assistance by the well-meaning passers-by. Consumed with my own sorrow and self-pity, it turned out that today was going to have a very big shock in store for me.

Chapter 5
A Mystery Girl

Every story has a curve ball, that sudden change of direction or crucial moment where everything changes, for me that curve ball just happened to be a petite girl with curly red hair.

With the interview for the magazine article looming, it had started to severely affect me, small anxiety attacks had started to hound me as I found myself crashing again with terror about the whole thing. Feeling low I had been off work for a few days and as my fears surfaced, I took myself to sit in the park near the beach, I often came here if I felt really low. Friends came to see if I was okay, but I just needed to be alone right now, Francois left me a coffee and croissant after he tried to speak with me about the article.

Debating with myself I was deciding if I should call the studio and cancel the photoshoots as they were causing me so many issues now that I didn't think I could go through with them. Sitting on the grass near a tree just away from the path, sometimes people would stop and see if I was okay before they carried on and left me behind or dropped change.

Drowning in my own self-pity, someone was walking past but to my surprise they stopped and stood beside me, they didn't say a single word and for the most part I ignored them entirely. After a few minutes, they sat down beside me, sitting in silence before putting their hand on my shoulder, I looked and could see some odd flowery trainers, but I continued to ignore them.

Without warning they pulled my shoulders towards them and held me, gently wrapping their arm around me but still in total silence, well nearly silence. Breathing slowly and deeply, they sat holding onto me and gently pulling me towards them all the while their breaths were audible and deliberate.

Tugging me again they pulled me even tighter to them and kept a hold of me, I looked up and saw a girl dressed in a green outfit with the curliest ginger hair I had ever seen and a backpack. Continuing to ignore her, eventually she stood up and I thought she was going to leave but it turned out she was unwilling to give up on me and my mood and she had a plan in mind.

Wrapping her arms around me and pressing herself against me, she tried to get me to look at a butterfly on her fingertip, every time I looked, she tickled my nose or ear before pressing her face against mine and smiling.

Every time I looked at her finger, she tickled me until she eventually broke my frown and her chaotic smile with her sweet giggles lifted my mood with this odd game she made up. Whoever she was it was obvious that she never gave up and she never failed to rise to any challenge.

Sitting back down beside me, I started to talk to her about the article and how much it was affecting me, she just sat there listening to me, but she didn't speak until I asked her what she thought. Speaking softly but chaotically but with a soothing tone, she was very soft, suddenly I found myself sharing my problems with her, problems which I hid from everyone and found myself sharing them with a total stranger.

While I sat bleeding my heart out to her, something had happened. Something so unexpected that I couldn't really believe it, my crash had just stopped. Quietly holding me, she just sat and listened to me for hours before she confided in me that she had come to Ljianstipol to find and forgive an old friend from her past. When I asked her where she was staying, she went very quiet.

Having spent all enduring my worst qualities I offered her a bed at my place, it seemed like the least I could do after she had spent all day listening to me pour my heart out to her. We headed through town towards the outer reaches of Ljianstipol and onwards to my home. Seemingly excited as we embarked on a little tour of Ljianstipol and the thrill of the mystery of my town filled her mind.

We walked along the streets, she kept nearby at all times and watching out for danger. "You are quite safe here, there is pretty much no crime at all," I tried to assure her.

Though she calmed a little she still held my hand all the way home, as we rounded the paths and streets that led to my house, she became more excited the closer we got.

Leading her round the final corner, I took out my key and handed it to her, "You wanna let us in?"

Smiling at her and pointing her towards my front door. Cautiously she placed the key in the lock and turned, turning the key as if life depended upon it, she opened the door and peered in, leaning over her I turned the light on, she stood there while I headed in. "Come on in," she cautiously crossed the boundary but seemed oddly nervous as she peered round.

"Come on, it's okay," I tried to softly assure her she was safe as she carefully walked into my living room, she seemed to be quite taken by a rug on the floor near my sofa. Sitting on my sofa she nervously took in her new surroundings, like a kitten the first time it is let out of a cage in a new forever home.

Gradually she started to come out of her shell a little, her face smiling softly and confidently, just as she had in the park while she sat with me. Taking her backpack from her as I led her upstairs to show her the room, she was welcome to, though I didn't think much of it at the time, her backpack was quite light? Showing her the bathroom and where my room was before I took her into the room she would stay in while she found her friend. Putting her backpack on the bed for her before we went downstairs to the living room when I remembered that we hadn't done something.

"Oh, I'm Fae by the way." She smiled softly, "Evelyn, it's good to meet you and thank you for giving me a bed for the night," she spoke softly but kinda chaotically.

"Thank you for supporting me today, Evelyn, stay as long as you want, the company would be appreciated! Not many people sit and listen to me when I'm like that." I was saddened by my own thoughts.

She sat forwards and smiled softly at me. "I couldn't leave you there like that, what kind of friend would I be if I did that?" I sat down next to her.

Sitting looking round the room admiring some of my strange things and looking at pictures on the wall. "Do you like pizza, Evelyn? I meant to get some shopping, but you know where I wound up," her little face lit up and she nodded at me, I ordered a delivery and went to run a bath.

"Do you want the water when I'm done?" She nodded back at me, still looking round my living room while I headed to wash away today's problems.

When I came back downstairs to call her, there she laid curled up on my sofa, fast asleep, her legs dangling over the side adorned with her funny little trainers while her curls rolled back and forth as her breaths caught them. Silently turning off the main light and putting on a side lamp so that I didn't wake this exhausted sleeping angel, though I did take a sneaky picture of her as she was so cute!

I managed to head off the delivery driver so that he didn't wake her up, sitting opposite her as I tucked into our dinner and wondering if she would wake up in time to get some while it was still hot. While dinner cooled down, I carefully took off her shoes, gently placing them on the floor next to the sofa, softly taking her socks off and neatly folding them inside her shoes.

Sitting next to her I folded her little legs onto the sofa with the rest of her and just sat looking at her as she slept. Her trousers and top were made from a deep and rich velvety material that was so soft to the touch, wherever she got this from it was incredibly well made and suited her so well.

Almost unbelievably petite, tiny in truth as she just about came up to my chest standing up, her delicate and fragile little hands and feet were so cute. Sitting on the sofa next to her, watching her rest and gently playing with her little curls, she was breathing so shallowly that you could have believed she wasn't breathing at all.

She started to whimper a little, I stroked her little face and she stopped whimpering and curled herself as much as she could, letting out a little sigh of relief as she curled up.

Gently I lifted her up and carried her upstairs, softly placing her on the bed and covered her with the duvet and put her backpack on the floor by the bed. Sitting on the bed next to her, I put my hand on her side and stroked her curls and spoke to her softly, "Thank you for today, I don't normally open up to people but you are different, but I don't know why I know that? But thank you and stay with me as long as you want."

She smiled to herself and snuggled herself among the duvet. Turning off the light but leaving the door slightly open for her I headed to my room to go to bed but left a light on for her in case she woke in the night. During the night I woke and needed a glass of water, as I walked down the stairs, I was shocked to see her back on the sofa curled up fast asleep just like before.

Stunned I sat down next to her before she started clutching me, holding onto me tightly as she dreamt, what a sweet girl I thought to myself and pulled her onto my lap and held her like my life depended upon her being there.

Thinking about this curious little angel that I suddenly found sitting with me, she appeared when I was at my lowest and unlike many she hadn't just walked off or left me there. Sitting listening to me for hours just slowly breathing to me and letting me spew my problems out to her, I never even asked her name?

While I crumbled in her arms, she held onto me, holding onto a total stranger in a town she didn't know, never attempting to leave or move until I was ready. Whoever this girl was, she was magical for me, she stopped my crash dead in its tracks, not just stopping it but transforming it into a good mood. Though the thing that I found the most amazing was that she seemed to have no hidden agenda, the people of Ljianstipol had been good to me but this was another level entirely.

Soon enough, I drifted to sleep with her resting on my lap, holding her hand to comfort her, it was a strange but beautiful evening. Ljianstipol once again had seemingly given me a new friend but she was different somehow, but I just couldn't understand why I thought that? Somehow though, I knew she wouldn't go anywhere no matter how hard I tried to push her away or how heavily I crashed, she wouldn't walk away.

Morning soon came and I woke with her still curled up on my lap and holding onto me tightly as she had pretty much all night. I couldn't help myself and got a few more sneaky pictures of her while she slept to show people at work my new friend. She gently stirred, stretching herself out before she looked up at me and smiled softly, "Morning Fae, I had a nightmare that you weren't real!"

I couldn't help but smile at her, "I'm very real Evelyn, did you sleep well?" I asked her gently and stroked her cheek.

"I did eventually, I had a dream that you wrapped me up in your arms and we just slept here together."

I chuckled at her, "That wasn't really a dream Evelyn."

She stood herself up and stretched herself out again and I gave her a little hug while she yawned. It was a sunny day and it would be my first day back at work after my crash, I sent a smiley face on that group Tony and Gale had set up and within minutes got a thumbs up reply.

Generally, within half an hour pretty much everyone in the group would reply, whether it was because I was feeling low or because I was good and pretty much everyone replied.

Supporting messages or even just smiley faces helped me to feel good about things and it meant that I didn't have to try and explain myself to people as in truth most of the time I couldn't explain what was happening easily.

Spending the morning getting ready, I gave Evelyn my spare key and a tourist map of the town, showing her how to get into town and how to get back and giving her total freedom of my place so that she could resume her search for the friend she was looking for.

Hugging me before I left for work, "Have a good day Fae, see you later," she waved as I headed out of the door and down the street to work. Being ushered along by the sun I felt good as the morning air filled my lungs, these streets felt different today and a big smile had emerged on my face as I stopped at Fabi's to get my morning fix.

"Same as always, Fae?" Fabi asked from behind his counter.

"You know me too well, Fabi."

He looked over. "You look different today, Fae."

I smiled thinking about my new friend. "I met a new friend in the park yesterday," I showed him the picture of her sleeping on my sofa, "She's cute! You met her in the park?"

I nodded at him, "Look after her Fae and have a great day too," he waved me off as I resumed my journey with coffee in hand.

Walking along the river and towards the divide where the new town became the old town with its carpet of cobbles, the expensive part of town. Here I could only afford to window shop at the array of boutique shops and cafes surrounding the market square with its buskers and aspiring artists. Wealthier tourists loved this part of town as did the daydreamers who promptly left shops after daring to ask the price for items within the shops here.

Every day I would drop my change to a different busker and share what little wealth I really had, most of them I had grown to know since being in Ljianstipol. Heading through the streets and to the Davizioso to be greeted by the ever-snide Leanne, we hadn't really gotten along since my first day here.

Most of the day I spent smiling and thinking about my new friend back home, residents and colleagues were happy to see me back at work too. It didn't take many of the residents long to figure out how happy I was, and I soon began telling them about my new friend and how she ended my crash and then stayed with me for the night.

Every resident seemed to take an interest in my story about her, but we had gotten to know each other well since I had started working there. Some of the residents live here full time, so we quickly developed long and deep bonds with each other. Using my experience of my conditions to help them and they did the same, like kindred therapists helping each other resolve our problems.

While I was showing her picture to a resident, Leanne had overheard me and came over asking to look at the picture. I wasn't keen on Leanne at all, and neither were Tony or Gale, after she got fired from somewhere else in town about something she had done in her past, though no one seemed to know what that was? Her parents had bought her a swanky apartment near the river, and she sneered down her nose at many of the residents and at me too.

Getting in trouble the day I started after, she uttered, "We employ patients now?" Under her breath when I came to start my first day, Abby had overheard her and she nearly got fired for it, she had been resentful about it ever since.

Begrudgingly, I showed her the picture of Evelyn laid on her side sleeping on my sofa that I had sneaked, she hesitated and snorted, "She's tiny like a child," before she wandered off, though her voice was soaked in jealousy?

I couldn't help but shake the feeling that she recognised Evelyn? But how and why? Though there was no way on earth I would ask her. Abby asked to have a look at her picture, "Awww she's so cute! No wonder she is jealous!" smiling from behind her desk when I got a text from Tony?

A smiley face and code 1604 meant that Tony was upstairs in his garden and waiting to see me, sometimes we held meetings up there and discussed patients, other times we just chatted, it was a little bit of extra support they offered me. Walking down the hallway I got a text from Gale, "Bring beer!" With a panting face, I chuckled and went to get some beer from their office and headed up to the rooftop garden.

When I walked round the corner to their pergola. "Fae, you little hero!" Tony beamed as he grabbed the box of beer and handed them out.

"How are you doing today, Fae?" Gale asked.

"Really good, Gale," I started to explain my story to them both about my mystery friend and her sitting with me in the park and lifting my mood and stopping my crash. "Wow that's really cool, Fae!"

Tony smiled at me. "She stopped your crash?" He asked looking confused,

"Totally stopped it, she's at mine right now, the least I could do was give her a bed for the night." Proudly I showed them the picture of her on my phone.

Tony took my phone and looked at the picture, pausing and removing his glasses, "Is that…? No, it can't be?" He handed my phone to Gale who studied the picture carefully, "Is that John's little girl, Tony?" He looked over at Tony. "My daughter used to be friends with her, but she's younger than my girl, what was her name?"

Tony said to Gale, "I will ask Ellie, she will know if that is her, but I'm sure that is John's little girl? How long has it been Tony? 17 years?"

Gale handed back my phone. "I'm sure that is John's little girl, she must be 22 now? But she still looks just as she did all those years ago," Gale spoke softly about her. "Why don't you bring her to meet us tomorrow after your lunch, Fae? We can meet her upstairs and bring her out here to sit and chat with you and us?" Tony smiled at me.

"I'm sure she would like that," I replied.

"Is she going to be staying with you Fae?" Gale asked.

"I hope so, she is here looking for an old friend, but she wound up helping me instead," I responded to him softly and hopeful she would stay.

"She sounds pretty good for you Fae, keep an eye on her and look after her, she can always come and sit out here if she wants to."

Tony offered, "She would like that, she likes trees and parks," I sat thinking about her clinging onto me during the night.

Gale took a look at his watch, "Whoa Fae it's nearly 4, you better get home to her!" I stood up and went to leave.

"Take one for the road and one for her with you." Tony handed me two bottles of beer.

"Thank you and see you tomorrow," I waved at them and headed out of the garden, through the Davizioso and through the town to my awaiting friend.

Walking down past the river and through the town past the shops and out towards the outer edge of town where Fabi had his coffee shop. He was packing away for the day as I passed by. "Hey Fae? Take this for you and your friend."

He offered me a bag with two chocolate cakes inside, "Thanks Fabi, have a good night and say hi to Alyssia for me!"

With his bag in hand, I started to walk the winding paths and roads that led to my front door, slowly walking but excited to see how my new friends' day had been. It was still light but the house seemed to be really quiet? I opened the front door.

"Hey Evelyn, I've got a surprise for us both," when I stepped in, I heard a crunch under my foot. Looking down and just inside the doorway was my spare key? Had she left without saying anything? It didn't seem like she would have done that?

Panic set into my mind as I rushed into the lounge to check out the sofa she had slept on the night before, but she wasn't there. I put the beer and bag of cakes down beside the sofa and headed into the kitchen, but she wasn't there either?

"Evelyn where are you?" I called out for her, but my heart was sinking as it seemed like my new friend had just left me behind? Rushing upstairs but she wasn't here either, her bag had gone from the room I had given her to stay in too? I even checked my room and the bathroom, but she had seemingly just vanished? While I rushed round looking for her, I did notice that my house seemed tidier than before, had she cleaned up and then left?

With my heart crashing, I started to debate, sending a sad face to Tony and Gale, heading back to my living room I sat upon the sofa looking at her picture, "Where have you gone?" I asked my phone as if I expected it to answer me back.

Feeling low I headed into my garden and started to wander down it when something grabbed me from behind and covered my eyes with their small hands, "Surprise!" She squealed at me.

"I thought you had left me, Evelyn," I said as I turned around in shock.

"Without saying goodbye? What kind of friend would I be if I did that?" Thoughtfully and softly, she replied and gave me a hug. "Come and look! I made something for you." She took my hand and excitedly led me down my garden to a tree at the end and pointed to a little spot she appeared to have dug little furrows into. She pulled her backpack from behind the tree and removed a little green packet from one of the pockets and gently laid it in my hand, a few leaves which were tightly bound with grass strands.

Softly, I unravelled the package to find some seeds within the leaves, she pointed at the little spot she had made, 'Sprinkle them'! As I knelt down and sprinkled them into the furrows, she gently covered them over and patted them down.

Dribbling a little water over them, "They will grow soon and you will love them! They will look great, they are my favourite flowers from my home, whenever you look at them you can think of me and how much I love you!" Speaking gently as she caringly patted them a little more.

While she spoke, my emotions got the better of me and a tear ran down my face, "I love it Evelyn, thank you!" I leant over and pulled her back to give her a hug and just held my thoughtful little friend.

"Oh no! I didn't get any shopping Evelyn! We might have to go out and get something for tonight!" I told her, disappointed in myself for forgetting to get anything on the way home. Smiling, she handed me her backpack, confused I looked inside and she had gone and got some shopping for me. "Ooh bacon! We have to use this tonight; didn't you find your friend?" Pausing, she smiled at me.

"I was going to but I remembered you saying that you didn't have anything in the house last night so I went and found the supermarket instead, someone in town gave me directions to get there," she smiled at me. "Anyway, how was your day, Fae?"

She was looking intently at me and spoke so calmly. "It was great and my bosses want to meet you, I told them all about you and they have invited you to go and meet them tomorrow? Did you wanna come? They have a cool garden on the rooftop and I think you will love it?" Evelyn paused thinking, "You want to take me to work to meet your bosses?"

I nodded back at her and smiled. "Are you sure you won't be embarrassed by me?" She replied sounding quite cautious.

"How could I be embarrassed by you, Evelyn? You are gorgeous and sweet." Pausing again she smiled sweetly, "Okay, sounds fun!"

While she sat on the sofa, I started to unload the groceries from her backpack when I noticed something, she hadn't unpacked her things from her backpack but beyond some spare underwear it seemed she had nothing to her name? I leant round the corner of the living room door. "Hey Evelyn? Where are your spare clothes?"

She looked at the floor. "I'm wearing them," she sounded sad and embarrassed, "Did you want to borrow something to sleep in?"

Taking her up to my room I found her a couple of t-shirts to use as nightdresses rather than living in her green outfit, and a skirt she could adjust down to her waist. Being so tiny, all my clothes drowned her but as she was only going to rest or be seen by me in them, she didn't seem to care too much.

Sitting together with her drowning in fabric she started to tell me she had come by bus from Zyvala, though she didn't claim this was her home? Zyvala was a town near the mountains to the north of Ljianstipol, flanked by mountains Zyvala was somewhere people went to reconnect with their youth or fuel their adrenaline.

Surrounded by adventure holiday companies there was nothing else nearby. So, I did wonder where she actually came from if it wasn't Zyvala? Fighting with herself to stay awake, she kept fading and then trying to perk herself back up before she finally succumbed and fell asleep, just as the night before.

Hanging half off the sofa with her little legs dangling down once again I took her shoes and socks off and folded her up onto the sofa to sleep. Carrying her upstairs to bed, she clung onto me a little before I gently laid her down and covered her with a duvet, wondering why she fought to stay awake as I headed to bed. Disrupted sleep was a common by-product of my crashes and episodes, almost routinely after one I would wake during the night and need an hour or so before I could fall back to sleep.

I wandered downstairs to find her back on the sofa, almost exactly as I had the night before, laid on her side facing the doorway? Curious and wondering why she wanted to sleep on my sofa I went and got her duvet and brought it down for her, covering her back up before I went back to bed. Laying pondering why she wanted to sleep on my sofa instead of the comfier bed, part of me didn't really mind, at least she was still here with me and she was welcome to stay as long as she wished.

Lunchtime soon came around and I walked home to collect her. Evelyn was sitting looking excited on my sofa, she couldn't disguise how excited she was feeling. "You ready?" I asked her, nodding she bolted to her feet and a huge mesmerising smile came onto her face.

Proudly wearing her green outfit and those flowery trainers she seemed so proud of, her mind seemed to be racing as we set off. Starting to walk down the roads from my home and towards town, it was a glorious day, the sun was shining and a gentle breeze kept refreshing our faces with a gentle and cool touch. Evelyn was leading us like an excited puppy at pace when Fabi appeared leaning against his coffee shop wall.

"Hey Evelyn and Fae, how are you both?" Stunned by his call.

"How do you know her name?" I quizzed him.

"She stopped to ask directions to the supermarket, we had a little chat and she likes my mochas too," he smiled at her and ruffled her hair. "She won't let me touch her curls though," he winked at her as she giggled back at him. "So, are you meeting her bosses today?"

Fabi leant down to talk to her, "Yes, they have invited me to sit in their garden!" She smiled back at him, "Here take this for the walk there," Fabi handed her a little mocha with a marshmallow on top. "Here Fae we can't be forgetting you either," as he handed me a mocha just like Evelyn's. "Look after each other," he waved us off and took one last ruffle of Evelyn's little curls.

"Thanks Fabi," I smiled at him as we headed off, "So you have made a new friend already?"

"He sure talks a lot but he is a nice guy," she chuckled back at me. We walked through the town and along the river before heading up the steps to the old part of town along the cobbled streets and towards the Davizioso.

Abby greeted us on reception as we walked in, she stopped and gasped as she caught sight of Evelyn and leant over the counter to speak to her, "Oh my goodness! She is even more beautiful in person, Fae! Aren't you just too cute, you can call me Abby, if you ever need anything just come here and ask!"

Evelyn walked up to the counter and smiled back at her, "It's nice to meet you Abby, I'm Evelyn and thank you."

Abby smiled at her, "Tony and Gale have been talking about meeting you all day! They are upstairs waiting for you both," she said proudly to Evelyn.

Leading the way with her close behind me following me through the hallways and communal areas of the Davizioso, I could feel her excitement as we passed Shanky, he bowed his head to her, tipping an imaginary hat and smiling. We headed upstairs towards the foyer and the adjoining meeting room which neither of them really used, walking to the desk to find Leanne.

Eyeballing Evelyn before she asked why we were here. "She has a meeting with Tony and Gale," I proudly said back to her.

Rolling her eyes at Evelyn and snorting back, "Didn't know we were going to start employing children now too," I could feel Evelyn slump as she heard Leanne's barbed assault upon her. Just as Evelyn turned to respond to her, a hand landed softly on each of our shoulders. "Is that any way to greet our guests on their first visit Leanne?"

Tony's voice asked her in a deep condescending tone, the door to their meeting room opened. "Especially a VIP Leanne?" She started to panic.

Tony started to usher us to their door. "You must be Evelyn," he asked gently as he guided her softly with his hand resting on her shoulder. "Fae has told me all about you, I couldn't wait to meet you in person."

Suddenly, he stopped and turned around, "Leanne? Did you bring a coat with you today?" She looked confused and sneered back, "No it's warm, I didn't bring one."

Gale interjected, "Good! Then it's one less thing to forget when you leave, consider this your last day, take your things and go!" Gale pointed at the doorway.

Backing up, "But what will I do?"

Leanne yelled at him, "The supermarket always needs staff, you might be better suited to their way of doing things, now get out!" Leanne huffed, turned and stormed out.

"Sorry about that Evelyn and you too Fae, that girl has been trouble since she came here, finally she gave me an excuse to get her out, though if you need a job Evelyn as you can see, we now have one available."

Tony chuckled at her and lead her towards the room and Gale, guiding her in and offering her a chair. Tony slumped into a chair behind their desk with his feet on their dusty meeting table, Gale opened the fridge and pulled out some beer, he offered one across their table to Evelyn. Smiling sweetly, she took the bottle and took a little sip and offered her bottle to ching with Gale's bottle.

"Ah Fae! I love this girl already!" He grinned and laughed as he passed the other beers out to me and Tony. "Come on let's go sit in the garden!" Tony smiled and started to lead us through the hallways to the rooftop garden, gently guiding Evelyn with his hand resting on her shoulder, as we approached the door to the garden.

Tony pointed at the lock, leant down beside her and whispered to her, "1604," she looked at him, he smiled at her and pointed to the lock. Evelyn pushed the numbers and the lock undone, as she pushed the door open.

"You can come here anytime you like Evelyn, would you close your eyes for me please?" He softly spoke to reassure her that it was okay to do so. While she covered her eyes, he gently guided her through the doorway and out into the rooftop garden, gently he took her wrists and softly moved her hands away from her face.

Gasping in disbelief with an almost unimaginable smile struck her face as she took in the intricately created and winding garden, its aesthetics were stunning. Tony led her down a bamboo pathway through plants and exotic ferns towards the pergola sitting proudly over a little pond.

Offering her a seat as she took in what she was seeing, me and Gale soon joined them, "So what do you think?" Tony smiled at Evelyn; she closed her eyes. "It's so beautiful," her green eyes opened as she replied, "I'm glad you like it and now you know the code you are welcome to come and sit here anytime you like, let me show you something."

Tony leant down and pushed one of the handles hidden on the pergola, reaching inside he waved beer and chocolate at her, "You are welcome to anything in here too," he smiled at her.

"We hear you came to find an old friend but found a new friend instead?" Gale asked her.

"I found a new friend in the park, Fae needed me more," she smiled at him and spoke softly. Tony smiled at her, "Not just anyone can do what you did for Fae, you know? Thank you for helping our girl out."

Gale leant over to her, "If there is anything we can do for you just ask! Oh, that reminds me! We have a little present for you," Gale handed her a little white wristband.

"It has a chip in it, if you go in any shops, cafes or restaurants, just scan that on the card reader and your bill will be paid, we call it paying it forward, think of it as our thank you for helping, Fae."

Carefully putting the band on her wrist, she stood up and presented them with a gift, "It's for your garden," she waved a little green package at Tony and then placed it in his hands. Handing him a folded leaf wrapped with grass just like she had given me the day before, she took Tony's hand and led him to a spot under a tree. "Here would be good?"

Tony opened the package and saw the seeds. "They are the prettiest flowers from my home, you will love them, they are beautiful," she smiled sweetly at him, Tony paused and thought. While we sat watching as Tony led her further down the garden to another tree, his son's tree with David's plaque underneath it, he pointed at the spot.

"What about here, Evelyn?" Looking at the plaque and the surrounding ground before she nodded at him and gently put her hand on his, quietly acknowledging Tony's request. Slowly she excavated just enough earth to sprinkle the little seeds into the ground and covered them back over and poured a little water over them. Evelyn touched David's plaque and looked at Tony.

"He will love them," she gave Tony a little hug and whispered quietly to him. Together they stood and chatted for a few minutes while me and Gale watched them, "She's something else Fae, look after her, she can come here whenever she wants to," Gale said quietly as we watched Tony and Evelyn slowly walk back towards us.

"She really is special Gale, she is changing my life in a good way," I quietly spoke as we watched the pair slowly walk back to rejoin us.

"You okay, Tony?" Gale asked, sounding concerned, Tony sat down holding Evelyn's hand to guide her back onto a chair nearby. "I'm all good," he replied and winked at Evelyn. "Seems our little meeting has overrun Fae, we've made you late, again!" Tony chuckled at me.

"Well, I'm in good company today so it doesn't matter too much!" I laughed back at him.

Sitting we chatted for a few hours and they slowly learned a little about Evelyn and how she found me in the park and had brought me out of my crash. They seemed to be quite taken by her, but so were many people, this odd jewel of a girl, all she seemed to want was to see people happy, in my case she was slowly making me a better person.

Since she had appeared my moods had settled and I felt good, I did find myself curious about her though, I wondered why she slept on the sofa and had those odd battles with herself to stay awake? Before we left, Tony asked, "You remember the code to get up here Evelyn?"

Smiling sweetly at him, "I will never forget it," she gave him a little hug.

"One for the road Evelyn?" Gale offered her a bottle of beer; she clinked the bottle with Gale and smiled at him and we headed off home together. Leaving the Davizioso in good spirits as we headed back to my house, Tony and Gale enjoyed their first meeting with my mysterious new friend and now that she had a wristband, she could get pretty much anything she wanted.

Placing more value in what people did rather than what they said, I think is why they like both me and Evelyn, we did things rather than talking about them. Though I didn't pay much attention to it at the time as we enjoyed that evening together one thing, I did wonder about was the wristband they had given her. White seemed to be an odd colour for her band. The only person I had seen in the Davizioso wearing a white wristband was Tony.

During the evening Colette and Francois came to pay me a visit, they always did this a few days after I had a crash to make sure I was okay and see how I was doing after any slump. Bearing a bottle of wine and some of Francois self-made croissants, as they wandered into my house Evelyn was laying on the sofa on her chest, giggling to herself about something.

Colette caught the little girl in her sight and her face lit up as she quickly walked over to introduce herself to this new little friend. Kneeling down to look at her, Evelyn shyly gave the cutest little smile I had ever witnessed as she introduced herself to the subtle and petite Colette. Gently sitting down next to her Colette began to speak to her solely in French and to my shock Evelyn responded in French, sitting talking to each other, the room was filling with little giggles.

Colette had fallen utterly in love with that girl and her sweet smile and deep green eyes, soon enough Evelyn was rising to the occasion and they sat gladly enjoying her company. Standing proudly, she showed off her little green outfit to Colette with her little belly on show, Colette poked her belly button when she let out a single, loud and uncontrolled laugh.

Standing with both hands covering her mouth and a look of sheer fear as she awkwardly smiled at Colette who now grinned wryly at Evelyn and began to tickle her stomach. Wriggling and writhing she fell back into Colette's tickling arms, laughing wildly and squirming to free herself, before Colette stopped tickling and she just rested with her head against Colette.

Calming down, she seemed to start to relax and just rested holding onto Colette gently, me and Francois watched the pair in disbelief at what we were both witnessing. They continued to speak quietly to each other until Evelyn went and got changed for bed and resumed her position lounging against Colette.

When Francois and Colette left, she gave Evelyn a little hug and kissed her on her cheeks before they headed away, she seemed to have something in mind as she walked away?

Evelyn didn't really tell me what they had talked about during the evening, just saying that Colette was nice and that she had asked her to go see her at her shop sometime soon. While we relaxed for the evening, I couldn't resist the urge to tickle her, laughing away with that infectious laugh of hers as she tried to escape but soon enough.

Like every evening since she had arrived, she lost the battle with herself to stay awake, collapsing onto her side laying in a heap hanging over the edge of my sofa. While I folded her up onto the sofa, I found myself wondering about her? Why had she come here with so little to her name? Where did she come from if it wasn't Zyvala?

Carrying her to bed, I sat next to her as she tucked herself up amongst the duvet and started thinking to myself. Was this girl my chance to pay it forward for someone? I wondered if I could find her some clothes during my lunch hour or maybe take her shopping on Friday as my thank you for her help? Either way, I headed to bed with a plan and maybe the chance to give her something back as my way of thanks for her just being her.

Coming down in the morning to find her back on my sofa was no real surprise, laid there happily dreaming to herself with her hair rolling around the sofa under the weight of her breaths. Soon enough she awoke upbeat and happy, she now had friends in this new land and she spent most of the morning talking about how lucky she was to have these new friends.

Looking up at me and smiling, "How lucky am I Fae? I have you and Tony and Gale, Francois and Colette? Oooh and Fabi too! I have six friends, Fae!" She was bursting with excitement and bouncing round my kitchen floor. "They like you because you are yourself too, Evelyn!"

I felt happy for her but wondered how someone so charming could have so few friends around her? While I put my shirt on for work, I remembered it was Wednesday.

"Hey Evelyn? It's Wednesday!" I said tucking my shirt in ready to go to work.

She looked round at me. "What's special about Wednesday?" She looked curious but intently.

"It's market day, they have a load of stalls in the market square and near the galleries, Shanky will be there selling his pictures, you could go and meet him and make another friend? He liked you when he saw you!" She smiled and looked excited. "Sounds good to me."

I put my shoes on and gave her a hug to say goodbye. "Well, I better get going Evelyn, but if you want anything just ask them to put it on my tab and you know where to find me if you need too," I started to walk out as she went to get herself dressed.

"Have a great day Fae!" She called as I walked out of the door.

Walking down to work I stopped to see Fabi as I did every morning. "Morning Fae, how are you today?" He called out to me as I approached his counter.

"Good thanks, Evelyn is happy too, she has made friends here, she has six now!"

Fabi turned around, "Six friends? Just here?" He looked sceptical as he spoke.

"Yeah, just six," I replied with sadness in my voice, "Hmmm I can't imagine that she is unpopular, she is a wonderful person maybe she just needs the right people around her?" Fabi replied, trying to rebuild the positivity.

Fabi popped my cup on his counter. "Oh, if she drops by can you put it on my tab and I will pay you later?" I asked him, "Will do, Fae, is she going to the market today?" He smiled back at me.

"Yes, she might go and see Shanky," I replied to him.

"I will ask Alyssia to keep an eye out for her, just in case you know but I'm sure Shanky will keep her busy!" Winking at me before I headed off to work.

"Thanks Fabi! I appreciate it!" I replied to him cheerfully heading to work with my morning fix in hand. Part of the way through the day I got a text from Gale asking me to go and see him and Tony, though oddly there was no request for beer this time. I felt a little concerned, what had I done? Was I in trouble or had Evelyn said something? I headed to their meeting room but Abby was there sorting a mountain of paperwork. "Hey Fae, they are having a meeting upstairs in the garden, go right up."

In her usual soft tone, "Hey can you believe they finally got rid of Leanne? I can't believe what she said to you and Evelyn, it was about time they got her out, she was a nasty piece of work!" I looked at the normally shy and timid girl looking angry.

"Yeah, she was horrible to her, though I don't know why? Thanks Abby," I replied to her. While I walked away, I wondered if Leanne had done something to Abby at some point as up to this day, I had never heard her say anything bad about anyone?

Concerned as to the nature of this impromptu meeting I wandered cautiously into the garden, we met regularly on Wednesday afternoons anyway to discuss patients and plans, so why this unexpected meeting? Rounding a corner in the garden to see them sat in the pergola above the pond. "Hey there she is! Our little star!" Tony declared to me as he took off his glasses, I let out a sigh of relief as clearly, I wasn't in trouble.

"Whew. I thought that I had done something wrong!" I laughed as I sat down to join them on the seats. "Fae we just wanted to see how you are feeling about your photoshoots, we know they aren't far away now, our girl is going big time!" Gale smiled away as he offered me a beer and relaxed back.

Thinking to myself as I sat back, "I'm quite nervous about it, I hope I don't portray here and myself in a bad way," I replied thoughtfully and thinking about all the things that they had done for me.

Tony looked over at me. "You will be great, you can't make us look like idiots, we don't need help with that!" He laughed and Gale joined in, "What are you worried about Fae?"

I sat and thought while Gale waited for my reply. "I'm worried that I will look like a desperate model and not a carer, at the end of the day I'm doing this for everyone else who suffers in silence," Gale paused.

"That's a lot of weight you have put on yourself Fae, but you will be great, you are a pure hearted girl," he was very frank as he spoke.

"Yeah, they will see that and capture it too, Fae." Tony joined in supportively. "Just don't try dying your own hair this time." He chuckled and slapped me on the back gently.

"No, I will get you to do that for me Tony," I joined him laughing.

Sitting and chatting about the photoshoot and the article that would follow with me unearthing my fears about it and how they had been affecting me before. Tony paused. "Where is Evelyn today, Fae?"

I turned to him, "She has gone to market day, she is going to see Shanky and get to know him and see his stall," he sat back laughing and put his hands behind his head.

"Shanky will keep her company and look after her, he is a great guy," I sat back up, "She was excited this morning she has six friends here now."

Gale leant in to join us. "She is a fantastic girl; I'm surprised that it's that few! Though after today I am sure it will be more, I hope she remembers to use her wristband,"

Gale looked over at Tony and nodded, "Fae, I need to tell you something?"

I looked over at him slightly concerned. "Sure?"

Gale sat up and pulled out his phone. "I sent that picture of her to my daughter, Ellie knows her, I won't tell you her story as it wouldn't be right, but look after Evelyn, she has been through a lot Fae."

Gale looked at me intently and Tony joined him, "Keep an eye on her Fae, we know you will do the right thing."

I looked at both with their compassionate expressions. "Of course, she is my friend, I will look after her," I wondered what they knew? Gale's daughter was a few years older than me and lived in another town somewhere, but I didn't know where that was.

Gale looked at me again, "You better get going, guess we might not see you tomorrow as you have your group sessions so have a good weekend if we don't see you," I stood and started to leave to find Evelyn at the market.

"Say hi to Evelyn for us," I looked round and smiled at them. "Will do, see you soon!" I started to head down the stairs and through the Davizioso and out onto the market place.

Heading up the steps that led to the market place in the old part of town, there sat on the floor as always on Wednesday was Shanky. "Fae! Where have you been!" I looked at him sitting on the floor on a little blanket surrounded by his pictures. Kneeling down beside him, "I had a meeting with Tony and Gale about the photo shoot."

Shanky smiled at me through his bushy beard. "You will do great! Hey Evelyn is with Alyssia in the gallery if you are looking for her, she's a great little character isn't she?" He smiled while he spoke about her. I headed to Alyssia's gallery to find both of them stood in total silence at the far end of the gallery staring at a picture on the wall, I walked over to them quietly.

"You get it Evelyn?" Alyssia asked, Evelyn paused. "No not yet, you?"

They stood intently looking at a picture on the wall, I didn't know why but I felt obliged to join them doing so.

Standing next to Alyssia who was looking ahead of her with her arms folded and one hand on her chin, "Hey Fae, we are trying to understand why five of these have sold this morning."

Before them was a framed painting, an entirely black background apart from a little yellow square in the left corner. I studied the picture before I noticed the price tag down the bottom. "Five thousand!" I called out in disbelief. "Yeah, this is the last one, me and Evelyn are seeing if we can see why they are so popular?"

They stood staring before Evelyn looked up at me. "Hey Fae? Is Shanky still outside?" I nodded to her, maintaining silence for them, "I don't get it Alyssia, I'm going to see Shanky," she turned and headed out to see Shanky before he packed up for the day.

Alyssia turned around as Evelyn headed off, "I don't get it either but people seem to like them," shrugging her shoulders, "She has been here with me for an hour," she smiled. "Sorry about that Alyssia," she turned round confused, "Sorry for what? She is great company and so adorable, she has been with Shanky and Francois too, does she live with you now?"

A smile returned to my face as Evelyn hadn't been too much trouble for Alyssia, "Yeah, she is looking for an old friend but she found me instead, have you really sold five of these?"

She nodded back seeming equally amazed. "I hear that Tony and Gale finally fired Leanne? Did she really say that to her?"

I thought about Leanne unleashing her vile comments at Evelyn, "Yeah, and without any reason?"

Alyssia sighed. "Well at least she is someone else's problem now, she used to work here you know, but she got fired over a similar thing, they took pity on her and gave her a chance. When Tony's daughter came down over Christmas and met her, she told them all about her past, she bullied some girl at school to the point where they stopped going to school, the girl she picked on got suspended and punished when she stood up to her."

"Leanne however got away with everything as her father was some powerful council member, she used that as an excuse to pick on the girl even more. Real life and school life are different things though, she moved down here because of her reputation, her parents got her a nice apartment near the river but she goes from job to job as she hasn't grown up, people don't want that kind of thing going on at work."

I looked at Alyssia, "Wonder what happened to the girl she used to pick on?"

I pondered that poor girl being pushed to that point where they had given up on school and were punished if they ever dared to stand up for herself, "Hopefully they became a bigger and stronger person."

Alyssia looked at me and nodded at me. "Hopefully."

I headed out of the gallery and there she was sitting with Shanky, helping him to clear away his unsold pictures. "You have made a new friend and worker Shanky?" He looked up and laughed at me.

"She can drop by my stall anytime she wants, especially if she helps me to clear away for the day," he winked at her as she rolled up his final picture and placed it in his carrying tube and handed the tube to him as he stood to leave. He placed a little envelope in her hand, "Same time next week, Evelyn?" He smiled before he turned and headed back to the Davizioso.

"Sure," she replied as he wandered away. We started to walk home and Francois tipped his glasses to her as we walked by. "Have a good evening my little friend," she waved at him as we walked past.

"Eight friends now, Evelyn?" I smiled at her striding along confidently.

"Eight friends now, Fae," we wandered along by the river and up the streets to my home.

Evelyn spent all night telling me everything and anything she had done during the day, telling me the same story a few times as she grew more excited about her memories of the day. Following me upstairs as I went for a bath, she sat on the toilet telling me about her day.

It was strange but quite sweet as she stalked me round the house to tell me everything that had happened. Slowly losing her battle to stay awake she flopped over on the sofa as she had every evening since she had been staying with me.

187

Sitting, I watched and wondered why she did this every single night without fail. What was driving this bizarre battle she fought every night with herself and why did she sleep facing my door. Collecting her up and carrying her upstairs a strange guilt came over me as I took her to bed.

Standing on the stairs I looked at her little exhausted face, sleeping contently in my arms. "If you want to sleep on the sofa, then I won't stop you Evelyn," I stroked her face and took her back downstairs and gently laid her back on the sofa facing my door.

While she adjusted herself back to the spot, she seemed to have made for herself I went and got her a pillow and a duvet and covered her up. Sitting watching her nestle herself among the duvet that guilt didn't pass, for whatever reason I just couldn't bear the idea of her waking up alone in a strange place?

Sighing to myself I laid beside her and held onto her, sharing her pillow and the duvet she was covered with, she nestled herself tight against me and I joined her sleeping on my sofa. Whatever her reasons were for this odd behaviour, I was now part of it and given that I had a few quirks of my own, who was I to question her reasons for this odd nightly routine of hers?

Waking in the morning she had rolled onto my chest and laid holding my face and with her head pressed firmly under my chin, however she had helped to give me my first full night's sleep for a week. While I laid there with her still happily snoozing away, I wondered about seeing if I could find her something at the shops this afternoon so that she didn't need to drown in my t-shirts at night.

Gently freeing myself from underneath her I started to get ready for my last day at work for the week, Thursdays were my busiest days, I hosted two group sessions during the day and held a few one-to-one mentoring sessions. Rarely on Thursday would I see either Tony or Gale unless they decided to attend one of the group sessions, but both were confident in me and just left me to it, which we both liked as it assured me that they trusted me to do my work.

Getting myself ready alone as she continued to sleep on the sofa, she must have worn herself out yesterday.

Time soon came to head to work and I gave her a little kiss on the cheek and left her to sleep, walking down to work I wondered if she would go and look for her friend today. Maybe she would just go and see Fabi? Or spend all day sitting there like a puppy waiting for me to come home?

I laughed to myself wondering what she might be like if she just sat watching the window all day waiting for me to come back?

188

During my morning session on Thursday cyber related ailments were the topic for these weekly sessions, attendees of all ages were welcome though for the most part it was normal for me to be the oldest person attending. Even at 26, I felt old sometimes as the group of normally 30–40 people would congregate and many of them would be late teens or very early twenties. However, their problems were largely anxiety-based and often if they were guests of the hotel, they would be short term visitors, though the problems that they discussed often were hard hitting.

Since my qualifications had come through, we had started to run two of these sessions each week, one on Tuesday morning and one on Thursday morning as this type of issue was skyrocketing. Unable to cope or understand the effects that the social media or internet as a general was having, this was almost like a detox more than a therapy session, however it was something that I had grown passionate about helping people to tackle.

Linked to my own bullying during my teen years, I felt a connection with many of the people who attended and shared their stories with me and the group. If they had told friends or family, they might simply be laughed at given that for the most part they were causing their own problems but either way the dangers were quite serious when things got out of hand.

During my lunch I went into town with Abby to see if we could find some pyjamas for Evelyn, though it turned out that wasn't easy, we did find a set for 12–15-year-olds but decided against it just in case she read the labels in them. Abby seemed to be quite charmed by Evelyn and they were of similar age so I had no doubt they would probably get along quite well as time went on.

Abby asked me if I had her number and I paused to think about it, "I don't know if she has a phone?"

Abby looked kinda shocked, "Really?"

I shrugged my shoulders, "I haven't seen her with one?"

Walking back to work we debated how likely it really was that a girl of Evelyn's age wouldn't have a phone? During the afternoon my group session went pretty well and I had a one-to-one session with Jess, she came to see me for an hour every Thursday afternoon after her brief stay after she had a problem online which gave her an anxiety-based eating disorder. When Jess left, it was time to head back home and enjoy a few days off with my new friend, walking home I had big plans for her surprise day out tomorrow.

Evelyn had been staying with me for around a week and in that time my mood had lifted and I felt more myself again, I had noticed that she didn't appear to have too much to her name but today that was going to change. As thanks for her help and company I was going to take her shopping and for a little tour of Ljianstipol then at least she wouldn't have to live in her green outfit and trainers.

Since she had been around Evelyn had developed an odd ability to seemingly control and moderate my crashes so getting her something to wear seemed a fair exchange for those skills she had. Once she woke up and slowly got ready, I revealed my plans to her, she was quite excited and quickly got herself ready to go and together we went exploring and shopping for her.

Beginning in the newer part of town with all its new and flashy shops we wandered the streets searching and questing to find something for her but soon hit a problem that I hadn't anticipated. Standing all of 4 foot 8 tall, Evelyn was tiny and just in case that wasn't hard enough she was so petite that everything we found that she liked was so baggy or large on her.

With every garment that failed to fit her properly, our disappointment grew as each passing shop had little or nothing to offer my little and disheartened friend, slowly my plan was becoming a disaster. Amid the wall of disappointment, she did at least find herself some shorts and vest tops to wear as pyjamas, at least it wasn't a total failure.

Like me Evelyn seemed to have quite eclectic tastes which in truth made finding her anything even harder, not willing to give in, I took her for a cake and coffee at a café by the river. We sat talking about the sort of things she liked when she started asking about my top and where I had got it from as she liked the clothes that I wore daily. I started to tell her about the thrift store that Abby had introduced me too, tales of wandering its aisles searching for hidden treasure and that most of the money went to charity, so it was a double win.

Sitting in this rustic boutique café Evelyn clung to my every word as her imagination let her dream about finding some treasures for herself among it items, as her excitement became too much she squealed. "Can we try there!"

Grinning from ear to ear with excitement, I paused taking joy in her anticipation. "Sure, we can go there after we finish up here," I offered back and felt her joy. Eagerly she munched her way through a large piece of cake and almost consumed a cup of coffee in a single large slurp and sat looking at me with wide eyes that would break the stoniest of hearts.

Together we began to head out of the main town and to the supermarket where the thrift store was located, she was like a hyperactive puppy all the way, "This way?" She would point as she tried to lead us there quicker.

While she dragged me along, part of me wondered if Evelyn needed reigns to keep her under control, but she was sure making me smile as with every passing street, she became more excited. As we reached the car park for the supermarket, she stood pensively at the doors to the thrift store as they opened to beckon us in.

The doors opened and lured us in to discover today's treasures, I could sense her excitement as she held my hand walking round the first aisles filled with toys and household goods. Evelyn stopped and pointed at a microwave and then a TV. "People give these away?" She seemed puzzled.

"Some people don't like to see good things wind up in a trash centre," I offered back to her as we delved deeper. Continuing our adventure into the deeper reaches of the store, passing by a section filled with tables, cabinets and sporting goods until we entered through another set of double doors into the clothing area.

Evelyn's face ignited as we walked through the doors, brimming with excitement and clasping my hand tighter as her palms began to sweat at the thought of what treasure she might find began to hit her.

Wandering through racks of clothing, she found a couple of tops and a pair of velvet trousers and a white silk dress before she called me over to show me a blue dress she had found, I walked over to her to see what she was so excited about, "Isn't that a bit big for you?" I asked her and quizzed her, she just smiled.

"It's for you, come try it on." Evelyn dragged me to the changing room with the light blue dress with flowers on it, it wasn't the sort of thing I would have picked for myself. While I went to try on the dress, she searched a little more, though Evelyn was struggling to find things that weren't too big for her, when I walked back over to her, she smiled at me in the dress she had found me.

"You look as beautiful as I think you are Fae," I blushed a little as she took me to a mirror to check myself out. Giving her credit where it was due, I did look pretty good in the dress and her smile told me that I was getting this dress as we resumed our adventure.

We continued to hunt for her when suddenly Evelyn stopped dead in her tracks, staring across the store, I wondered if she had seen her friend that she was looking for? Evelyn started to wander across the store, focussed and determined to get somewhere without breaking her gaze, walking towards a pillar with a rail on it and what looked like a sailor outfit on it, like the ones in Japanese TV shows.

Evelyn walked up to it totally transfixed and sucked in by it, gently stroking the arms of the tops before she felt the fabric, she looked round in a panic. "Fae! Fae! Isn't this just beautiful!" She grinned at me.

"This is very cute Evelyn," I smiled at her, lifting the outfit down to offer it to her, "It's still got its original tags in it too! Wow, someone paid a lot of money for this!"

I was surprised as I handed the outfit to her. Excited, she rushed off to try it on, when she appeared she was so excited and grinning like a child at Christmas that she walked right by me before she turned and rejoined me.

"It fits Fae." She was so excited and she looked very cute in it too, it even had the little tie around the neck. "You better get this then, you can't turn down looking this good," I said to her as she did a little twirl for me. "But there is one condition!" I said to her as she stopped and her face dropped a little. "We have to find you some shoes to go with it," I winked at her as her face lit back up and we walked proudly with her in her new little white, blue and black outfit.

Wandering round to the shoes in the store I soon had more success here with her clothes as I found a set of blue cat eared pumps to go with her outfit, "Here Evelyn! Try these on," I called her over, Evelyn wandered over and I slipped them onto her feet and asked her to go and stand up and walk round in them, "These are the cutest things ever!" She beamed at me and smiled like a child. "Here, these ones too, Evelyn!" She came back over as I swapped the blue pumps for a pair of turquoise ones.

Grinning, she put them into our basket before she went to get changed back into her green outfit, she came back but looked concerned as she put the outfit into the basket. "You don't have to get these for me Fae," she said slowly pulling them back out of our basket, I put my hand on top of hers to stop her removing the items.

"Evelyn, for all you have done for me in the short time I have known you, it would be the least I can do to say thank you," I gave her a hug and she whispered, "Thank you," softly into my ear.

Heading to the cashier, we started to put all of our items out for them to scan, the cashier found the sailor outfit and called Shaun the store manager over, he took a look at me and Evelyn.

Terror struck her face as he collected the outfit and wandered away with it, "He got that for his daughter and he paid a lot of money for it too, but she never wore it, he got her the wrong colour apparently!" The cashier sounded disappointed with Shaun's daughter.

Evelyn stood looking heartbroken and saddened while we waited for the cashier to resume tallying our goods, when Shaun came back. With the outfit in hand, he looked at Evelyn looking up and down her before he leant down and spoke to her, "You can't have that outfit without this bag that goes with it."

Shaun winked at her and put a little cat bag over her shoulder. "Don't worry it's part of the outfit so it won't cost you anymore, I'm just glad to see someone will love it how I hoped my daughter would have."

Evelyn's face returned to normal as she stood bemused with the little cat bag in her hands, "Look after your little friend Fae," Shaun said to me as he walked away.

Together we walked back into town to browse the older part of town, though this area was window shopping territory for me because the prices were terrifying. Guiding her round the back alleys we found ourselves at Colette's shop, "Didn't Colette say to go see her, Evelyn?" She smiled and nodded her head.

"Yes," I opened the door to the shop and behind a desk sat Colette. Gently smiling as we walked in, she came over to greet us both and started to show Evelyn around her shop, guiding her through all the clothes that she makes and sells. Evelyn told Colette about the dress she had found me and Colette took me to try it on and show her, walking back through she carefully studied the dress before making a tiny alteration for me just above the hips.

Changing back into my usual top Colette walked over with her head tilted to the side and patted a chair for me to sit down, she started to readjust the straps on my top. "The thing is Evelyn all my clothes come with a guarantee, if I can still use my hands then I will repair or adjust the item for its life time, just like Fae's top," she smiled as she finished adjusting my straps for me.

Colette handed Evelyn a bag, "This is for you little dove."

Evelyn peered inside and smiled back at her, "Thank you," and gave her a thank you hug.

Walking home through town we wandered by the river, normally I didn't take this route home as it was almost exclusively reserved for young couples showing their love for each other. The bridge that crossed the river was another thing I didn't like too much, adorned with padlocks, the modern sign of unbreakable love there was a part of me that often wondered how many of them still belonged there?

Smiling as we slowly walked home, I looked round and pulled her to my side. "What are you doing tonight Evelyn?" She looked around confused, "Spending it with my best friend?" She smiled back, "Do you want to wear that little silk dress and go for dinner?" She thought hard and replied, "Only if you wear your new dress too," smiling as she replied.

Heading upstairs we began to get ready for the evening, I put on the blue dress she found me, I felt good and somehow, she made me feel more confident with little or no effort. Excited at the prospect of a good night out, I sat anxiously in my living room waiting for her to appear and once she did, I couldn't help but just stare at her, she was stunning!

Dressed in the white dress she had found along with those turquoise pumps, she almost floated into the living room with her mass of ginger curls set free and cascading down her shoulders. Evelyn pulled out an odd-looking purse from her bag and offered me what money she had brought with her, waving it at me and smiling innocently. Gently I took her money.

"Tonight is on me, as thanks for all you have done for me," I said as I put her money into the cat bag, she got with her sailor outfit. Nodding to acknowledge the gesture, she offered me her arm and smiled softly, I ruffled her hair a little and locked my arm into hers and together we headed out into the night.

We headed back down the riverside towards the trendier end of town where the artisans wandered, both of us would be out of place here but then again, I guess we were both accustomed to that feeling? I took her to a nice little restaurant just off the river, we sat overlooking the river on a little table with a candle and a pergola over it. Everyone seemed to look twice at Evelyn, but she did look stunning though she was quick to point out that she wasn't the only one attracting attention.

Giggling and pointing out to me every single guy that was looking at me. "Must be my big arse," I laughed back at her as she giggled away. Together we enjoyed a good meal by the river, though it was dessert that excited her the most, but Evelyn wasn't alone in that, nothing brings a smile like a big glass of ice cream topped with cream and some flakes in it.

With the candlelight diminishing, we sat looking at each other smiling, I couldn't help but feel deep inside that this mysterious girl was going to become an enormous part of my life. "Fae?" She said quietly.

As I looked up at her the candle light caught her eyes and illuminated the deep green of them, "Thank you for today, but thank you most for the future times we will share," she gently offered her hand across the table as her words sank in.

Evelyn's words hit the deepest parts of my mind and heart, as I took her little hand and felt the emotions flowing from her. "You are the first person who ever sat with me Evelyn and the first who just listened to me, it's me that needs to be thanking you, you have helped me so much."

A little tear was falling from me as I thought how in all these years that no one had ever just sat and listened to me, let alone been able to soothe my problems like that. Evelyn brushed my tears away and offered me her little finger, she didn't say a word as she softly smiled, I put my little finger with hers and I locked together in body and soul with my new friend Evelyn.

As we walked home along the river, she started to talk to me about how she had come to make peace with an old friend from the past but finding a new friend in me was far more important. We approached that bridge I loathed so much with its collection of padlocks upon it, Evelyn stopped to look at a few of them and called me over. "Fae! There's one here with your name on it!" She called out excitedly.

I looked around surprised and sighed back, "No one has ever stuck by me long enough for that to happen," As I walked over and bent down to look at the padlock she had found. Evelyn placed a luminous green and purple padlock in my hand, inserted the key and opened it, softly smiling at me in the moonlight.

Taking my hand and putting the lock on the railing and guiding my hand so that we closed it together, she gave me one key and she took the other, together in unison we threw the keys into the river. Continuing our journey with me holding her beside me and her holding me in reply, as we slowly wandered home together.

Evelyn stopped and bought us both a bottle of beer, "We can't go home without toasting to celebrate our new friendship," she chuckled as she handed me a bottle of beer. Sipping and giggling as we walked, sharing little tales of our lives with moonlight helping to guide us home, it felt like an entirely new and very unexpected chapter of my life.

Evelyn was a curious and very shy girl to most people but she was utterly magical for me, never turning or shying away from my worst moments as she caught me when I fell. Never asking for anything in return and she never took anything in return except for my friendship and that was something that I was only too happy to give her. While we reached my house, I couldn't fight the feeling that today and that sailor suit was going to become a huge turning point in my life.

Somehow, I couldn't help but feel that today was a total change of direction in my life and for maybe the first time I genuinely felt that I had found someone that I could trust with anything. Adrenaline was fuelling us both as we got into my house, the excitement of finding a kindred spirit was keeping us both going as we both went and changed into something comfier. Chocolate and beer soon came out as we settled on the sofa for a long night exchanging our life stories with each other.

Evelyn came from Zyvala—a small mountainous town a few hours away by coach, she had come to forgive an old school friend who had done something in her past, though she hadn't had any luck finding them yet. Evelyn settled down and started to tell me about her childhood, though more accurately her lack of one, her parents had died when she was very young, her grandmother moved in with her after their death.

Unfortunately, though Evelyn's grandmother didn't like her very much. "She tried but she just couldn't get along with me for very long, though I was challenging at times," she said sadly with her shoulders dropped. The only person who seemed to have stuck by her for very long was a babysitter called Ellie, she was there with Evelyn the night her parents died, though Evelyn didn't seem to be sure why Ellie had stuck around her.

Evelyn started to tell me about her life after her parents had passed away, though I tried to discourage her as I could see it was upsetting for her to talk about her life so openly. However, my therapist mind set in and just as she had listened to me in the park and let me release my thoughts to her, I was going to do the same for her, if she wanted to tell me then I was going to listen to her.

Evelyn slumped back in the couch looking sadly at her fingers. "First they picked on me for being an orphan, then being ginger and finally it was because I just didn't seem to grow, as the other girls got bigger, I stayed the same size, the only thing that grew was my wild hair!" She giggled as she fluffed her hair and put the almost afro of tight ginger curls back into its usual bun.

She started to tell me how people used to pick on her in school, the girl Evelyn had come back to meet and forgive did an impression of her mother dying in the accident that took her parents away. Evelyn had lashed out at her, pinning her down and hitting her, crying her eyes out and screaming at her until a teacher prised Evelyn off them.

While Evelyn was suspended for standing up for herself, the girl's father was some bigwig in the local authority and swung the sword for the school funding, so she got off with no action being taken.

Problematically though the girl used her immunity to pick on Evelyn even more, gradually grinding her down more and more but what made things worse was that her grandmother also sided with the girl. Slowly becoming more isolated as friends turned on her, she started to work hard to get out of Zyvala and away from it all and give herself a good chance somewhere new.

Unfortunately, though when she came home one day from college her grandmother had died and having to choose between keeping her home or her education was only going to end one way. Evelyn had to give up her college and started working at the school in Zyvala as a poorly paid receptionist and librarian, the problem was that her old life followed her to work too.

Lying with her head in my lap, she started sniffling. "No one ever gave me the chance to see who I really was, I think it is why when I found that world, I had to leave and go back there. I tried to make things work in that town, but in the end, I went back to my world," she whispered as she started to drift to sleep in my lap.

As she started to drift to sleep, I started to stroke Evelyn's hair as her eyes grew heavier. "Will you tell me about you tomorrow Fae?" She whispered as she looked up thoroughly exhausted. I looked down at what felt like a child slowly passing out in my lap.

"Of course, I will, we can sit in the garden and talk all day Evelyn, get some rest," I whispered and gently eased down next to her and held her in my arms. Evelyn put her arms around me and gently drifted away into her dreams, I held her just a little tighter, playing with her hair unable to imagine anyone disliking this girl.

Thinking to myself about the day we had met and her just instinctively coming to sit next to me and slowing her breathing to calm me down and then just sat and absorbed anything that I said to her. How could anyone dislike this girl? Let alone use her parents dying against her? Or her ginger hair or even her tiny size? While she began to sleep, I couldn't help but feel that her story sounded familiar somehow. Though it saddened me to hear her story she was strong, determined and almost fearless, soon enough I drifted away beside her.

Stirring in the morning at some point I had rolled onto my back and she had come to rest gently laid on my chest, cupping my head softly with her hands, she was so peaceful. I held Evelyn and smiled to myself at the thought of her being so peaceful and serene, she let out a little whimper and clutched me before she settled back down. Lying there silently, feeling her softly breathing as she clung onto me, Evelyn brought an odd calmness to me, like a soft continual presence keeping a soothing hand on my shoulder.

During the night, she had mentioned a few things or places which stood out in my mind and I kept wondering more about them. Where or what was this other world, she spoke about. She didn't really go into too much detail about it. Like it was a dream of some kind or maybe she was protecting it.

Perplexing as Evelyn was, she must have placed a high degree of trust in me to open up about her past and her parents in particular especially after years of bullying over just that. Yet this world that she spoke of was very secretive, almost mythical though maybe someday she would tell me about it someday or possibly it was just a strange dream?

I found myself thinking about a tree she had talked about near the school that she used to work at, spending hours sitting in it looking out across the horizon, dreaming of a different world. I could imagine.

Evelyn sitting there in all weathers, night or day just fantasising about a different life in this strange and secretive place she spoke of. It gave me an idea, maybe when she wakes, we could go to the beach? There were some big and interesting trees there? As I waited for her to wake up, I started thinking about her sitting in a tree just dreaming, though maybe I just wanted to sit beside her and do the same thing?

Gently, she awoke from her slumber and her face lit up with a sweet smile, "I thought it was all a dream and you weren't real Fae," she softly spoke as she yawned.

Hugging me tightly. "I'm glad you are real though Fae," I smiled back at her, "I'm glad you are real too, Evelyn."

I stroked her cheeks and hugged her back, "Do you fancy going to the beach with me? It's my day off and I want to spend it with you Evelyn," she smiled. "I can tell you about me too," by this point she was grinning and nodded back at me.

"Are there trees there too Fae?" She asked pensively, I smiled at her, "Big trees too," she leapt down and grinned.

"Great! I could teach you how to climb." She ran off hyperactive in excitement to get changed.

Evelyn came back downstairs dressed in the black top and velvet trousers that she found on our shopping adventure. "Don't you look adorable, no sailor outfit today?" I asked her.

"Not today, I'm saving that for a special day together," she smiled as I went and found my skirt and the top that she liked to go with it, "You look beautiful, Fae!" She said as I walked across the living room, she came over and hugged me.

Shyness came over me as she held me and hugged me. "Nothing special today, Evelyn?"

She shook her head. "You are special every day, Fae," she whispered and held me just a little tighter. With the sun filling the air with a deep warmth, we headed out through the town, down the riverside and towards the park, the same park where we first met, walking through it and out the other side to the beach.

Walking along the promenade we soon came to the sandy dunes scattered with the large trees that I had promised her. Today, she was going to learn all about me, though I hoped maybe she would share some more about this magical world she spoke about and hopefully I would get to feel that same magic when we sat and gazed out across the world dreaming.

Having left the park and its pristine grasses and the promenade we headed into the more tortured plant life that fronted the beach, those twisted and gnarled trees, she stopped and pointed at one of them. "It's like the trees in the Hollow!" She was quite excited by it, though I had no idea what the 'Hollow' was that she spoke of.

Evelyn stood beneath the tree, carefully analysing it and the branches and studying it, "It's no good for climbing though, the branches are too brittle, they will break under anyone's weight." We continued through the spattering of trees before she stood beneath another of the warped and distorted trees, excitedly pointing at it, "This one is good Fae," she smiled as I walked behind her chuckling.

"Even for me to climb?" I rested my hand on her shoulder as she looked up at me. "I picked this one just for you Fae," she took my hand, "I will show you later, show me the beach!" She asked in excitement.

Clasping her hand, we started to walk through the last remaining trees and out onto the vast dunes, Evelyn's eyes lit up as she saw the vast expanse of sand with the sea in the far distance.

Carefully she took her top off and laid it under a tree, her upper body exposed to the world bar a little lacy black bra, she had such confidence that I joined her and did the same. Casting my top down next to hers and wearing an almost identical bra to hers. Together we walked bathed in the midday heat along the beach. While we walked along, she started to tell me how she never would have ever shown her body off this way before but someone had built her confidence, teaching her to love herself as she was.

Whoever this person was, she had clearly made a huge impact on Evelyn and helped to turn her from a shy, little and timid girl that she spoke about when she was growing up into the woman that walked beside me today. I could identify with her, it wasn't like I had ever oozed confidence either, I told her how little confidence I had about myself in the past though I was still nowhere near as confident as her.

Evelyn did enjoy the story of me wearing a beanie hat for six months after cutting my own dreadlocks out after they had started to smell really bad but was too embarrassed to go to a hairdresser.

As we walked along, I started to tell her about myself, "It wasn't my body that was the problem or anything like that it was my crashes and episodes," I sighed to her as we wandered.

"Crashes and Episodes?" She asked back.

"My dad used to call them that, my swings, when I was low, he called it a crash as I would just have the world fall on me and I couldn't get back up, he said he used to see me falling through the world towards the depths of despair."

"Episodes were the worst though, that was when my moods would become erratic and irrational, I get incredibly angry and moody, I often become argumentative or obtuse with people. At first, my dad seemed to handle it better than my mum, but I pushed her really hard more than a few times, I still loved her just she became a vent for me, but eventually their roles switched and I grew closer to my mum after my first stay here." Evelyn held my hand tightly, not saying a word as she listened while walked.

One night though my parents' already crumbling marriage finally gave way, my school had been letting me do my exams from home, it was very stressful but they were being supportive. My dad was trying to push me on my last exam. "You need to push harder, Fae!" He kept saying to me.

I backed up instantly. "I'm doing the best I can!" I yelled back at him, we had a huge argument at the table, shouting and yelling at each other. He disappeared outside for a little while, him and Mum had an argument and I stood up for my mum, I sat in a heap by my bedroom door listening to them argue.

While they argued, he said something to my mum and I went back down to stand up for her again and yelled at him for leaving everything to do with me and my problems to my mum. My dad was saying that someone would just give me a chance, but my mum was being more realistic and as much as it hurt me to admit it, she was right.

"After, I put in my final shots to him, he left us both behind, I didn't really see him until they were going to get a divorce and Mum wanted me to come back here so that I wouldn't endure their divorce. Me and Dad didn't speak for years afterwards, then just after I moved here, I called him and slowly started to rebuild things with him, he should be coming down for Christmas too, I'm looking forward to it as I haven't seen him since I was 19."

Evelyn stayed silent while she listened to me.

"My dad moved far to the north and remarried and my mum moved to Usted with her new husband Ash, they are pretty good to me. They still speak from time to time and they let me keep all the proceeds from selling our family home to move here and start afresh. I moved down with a little chunk of money so that I didn't have to take the first crappy job I found."

Alyssia got me an interview at the Davizioso, not for one second did I think they would even entertain having me work there. Somehow though they saw my depression and bipolar disorder as a strength and gave me a chance, my dad was thrilled when I told him, "I told you JaffaCake, just one person needed to see what you can do!"

"He was always optimistic, even if he rarely lived in the real world. They have been good to me, training me up and helping me to use my own conditions to help other people and are putting me through qualifications to become a specialist therapist. Like an expert I guess, but they understand why when I crash sometimes, I just need to stay away, like the day you met me in the park."

"You are brave, Fae," Evelyn said back to me having stayed silent the entire time. "Though what is this Jaffa Cake?" She asked quizzically.

"My dad called me that, he loves them, they are these little cakes with orange in them that people argue about whether they are cakes or biscuits, he would proudly say. 'Some things aren't meant to be one thing or the other Fae,' he used to say that when I was really low. 'I really miss them being together, they were great when they weren't arguing,' I sadly said to her, 'Parents argue about their children because they both love you,' she said back with confidence."

"Yeah, that's very true, Evelyn," I offered back to her.

We started to make our way back towards the trees and the one she had marked with our tops. "Come on Fae, let's get you up in those branches!" She was so excited by being able to teach me how to climb.

She lifted herself up and offered me her hand, "Just pull yourself up Fae," she started to help me get up into the tree with her. Evelyn moved further along the branch letting me have the end nearest the trunk, suddenly the sandy dunes just a few metres below me suddenly felt very far away.

We sat in those branches above the dunes, at first in total silence as she just pointed across the horizon and rested her head on her knees as we sat overlooking the horizon. Watching waves lap the shore, the sand gently blowing round the dunes and the clouds drift in and out of each other in a strange celestial dance. I looked across at her as she sat on the branch, she seemed different?

Totally at peace with everyone and everything, almost mesmerizingly peaceful. I felt that I had to ask her something but I was scared to ask her, while I thought about how to ask her, "You can ask, I trust you, Fae," she said softly almost as if she knew what I was thinking?

"It's just like it was when I sat looking over my old town, I knew deep down I had to get out of that place, I had left what I thought was hell and gone somewhere I hoped would be better, but it wasn't at all. It was my hometown yet I had no one to turn to and no one cared that I had gone, let alone cared that I had come back. I got so lonely, I started dreaming about leaving there and just heading back to the mountains and beyond. Fae, I know how you feel here all on your own, I felt that way too for far too long." She spoke softly periodically stopping to compose herself again. I noticed she was welling up a little bit as she spoke.

"Hey it's okay Evelyn, you don't have to do this!" She smiled at me. "Yes, I do, you have told me about you and now I will tell you about me, you are my friend Fae and I trust you."

Evelyn smiled and paused before she started to tell me about what she called her last night in her old world. I moved as close to her as I could so that I could support her how she had supported me.

"I went to a staff dinner; it was one of those things where you don't have to go but they use it against you should you dare to miss it! I hated every second of it, everyone looked down at me like I was some kind of idiot with my stupid stories. What they didn't realise is that the Evelyn they had known and the one who sat among them that night were very different people!"

"She had made me stronger, much stronger; I believed in myself for the first time ever, I even felt proud of my little body and ginger curls. I had only been back in their world for four months but was already thinking about getting out of there, it had been snowing, there was a cold snap, and the ground had a gentle dusting of snow upon it."

"As the night wore on some of the teachers had been drinking heavily and they started prying about my past and my parents in particular. Unlike before, instead of just running or crying I stood up for myself, 'How dare you ask something so callous and stupid,'" as I went to leave a teacher grabbed my blouse and pulled it hard, so hard the buttons popped off and I stood there with my blouse open for all to see.

"He muttered something, the other teachers acted disgusted but did nothing to stop his assault, but this Evelyn wasn't the one he knew, I wasn't ashamed of myself anymore. While they argued I left to get a cab, but was so enraged that instead of waiting I walked home with no coat and an open blouse which was only protecting my back now. I came to a park that I sometimes went to, and it started to snow again and I had an urge to take my shoes off for some reason."

"That snow reminded me of the forest floor after the rain, the soft wet grass and moss between my toes, as the snow hit my chest, melted and ran down, I suddenly felt warm and alive. The snow between my toes and hitting my chest was somehow making me feel warm, I started to run home."

"I didn't know why but that night I was going to go back to the mountains and back to my world and my forest. I took what I could carry in my backpack and left everything else behind me and left for the mountains that same night." Evelyn sounded oddly positive by the end of her story.

I looked over as she smiled softly to herself, "What were your parents like, Evelyn? Just you don't talk about them which I understand but..." I was so scared when I asked her but she once again rose above me.

Evelyn sighed and just rested her head sideways on her knee and closed her eyes. "Honestly? I can't really remember much about them, I was so young when they left me, I struggle to remember what they really looked like," she started crying.

I pulled her over to me and held her, "Until she took me back to get that picture of them I had all but forgotten what they looked like, though I remember Dad used to fly me around the garden like a fairy, Mother hated him doing that, she was scared that I wouldn't ever grow up," she smiled a little through her tears.

"They used to argue about that a lot, they had been arguing about me the night that they left, I used to blame myself for their death, but she helped me see that it wasn't my fault, she helped me to forgive myself." Evelyn spoke so softly as she revealed this mystery woman to me?

I placed my hand round her shoulders, lifting her back up a little. "Sorry Evelyn, I'm so sorry," I felt so ridden with guilt after asking her about her parents.

"It's okay, Fae, I have a good life now, I have people who love me and I love them too and I have you now too Fae," she smiled sweetly and pulled herself as close to me as she could. "I'm glad we met, Evelyn, I don't know why you stopped that day but I'm glad that you did," I spoke back to her softly as the sun began to set.

Evelyn had never really discussed her past, her parents or this strange world she claimed to be from, today was significant as it was the first time, she went into any real detail about any of it. Wondering about this strange woman and the Hollow and forest she spoke about as we sat in silence watching the world slowly turn to darkness. Watching the sky turn deep blue it also then dawned upon me that this was the first time I had seen any hint of sadness from her during all our time together.

Chapter 6
Wednesday Afternoon Delight

Around two weeks had passed since Evelyn had moved in with me and taken up residency on my sofa and I had grown quite fond of having her around. Lively and spritely she kept me entertained and on my toes most days, her biggest influence though had been an odd ability to seemingly calm my crashes and episodes? Somehow since she had appeared they had all but stopped, no warning signs and generally I was pretty stable, my swings were still there but those were like the weather, continually changeable and unpredictable.

Somehow though Evelyn was like a constant soothing hand on my brain, her soft and often heart-breaking sweetness just calmed me down and slowed the inevitable. However, she was having a far larger impact on me than simply calming my mind, she would almost continually do and say little things that made me feel kinda good about myself. Complimenting me on how I looked and telling me how brave I was, she was helping me to accept myself in truth a big part of me would be lost without her presence.

Evelyn in short was helping me turn the tide with myself and slowly giving me a tiny piece of her self-belief and confidence each and every day. Openly admitting that she was nothing too special and happy to confess that she had only really learned this lesson in life herself recently, however for me she was becoming utterly magical.

Evelyn had also rapidly established herself as a much-liked visitor to Ljianstipol, everyone seemed to love this strange and mysterious girl. Tony would ask me daily when she was next going to visit him, even though they had struck up a deal to meet every Wednesday afternoon during my meeting with him and Gale.

Evelyn would dress her best to go to these meetings with Tony, wearing that sailor outfit and Tony even wore nicer shirts for their afternoon walks around the rooftop garden. Tony however wasn't alone in his fondness of Evelyn, Fabi had grown quite fond of their morning meetings too, even though sometimes he wasn't quite sure what she was actually talking about.

Able to talk for nearly all of Italy, Fabi may have finally met his match in talking terms at least however he also wanted to do something with those ginger curls and as of yet Evelyn had flatly refused to let him touch those precious locks of hers. Every morning she would go and visit Fabi and get him to make her a coffee that she had dreamt up, marshmallows stuffed inside a cup with a rich mocha poured inside, it sounds gross because it is!

The coffee would melt the marshmallows creating a thick sugary gravy, but Evelyn loved them, Fabi had even bought jumbo marshmallows just to make this vile creation for her.

From Fabi, she would then walk to see Francois and sit outside his boutique with him, together they would talk for around an hour, he would even top her coffee up for her complete with marshmallows. Anytime she ventured near his door, he would top her cup up for her, normally razor tongued at every given opportunity, Francois simply couldn't resist that sweet smile and those green eyes of hers.

Francois thought that she was sweet, Evelyn just thought he was strange, but they chatted most mornings nevertheless, though Evelyn did quite enjoy the insults that would spew from that curious and often angry Parisian's mouth. Once she had finished her meeting with Francois, she would head to the Davizioso and spend some time with Abby, only a short visit while Abby took a quick break but both were good friends really.

Abby was one of the sweetest people I had ever met but next to Evelyn's mind she was even sweeter, well when she wasn't playing games online anyway. Evelyn most mornings got a rundown of all the dudes that Abby had owned during the evening, recounting each and every humiliating kill she had gained during the night. Though Evelyn didn't fully understand Abby's fascination with this online bloodbath she did quite enjoy the stories and often the re-enactments that went along with them.

Once Abby's break had finished Evelyn would head to see Alyssia at the gallery in the marketplace, together they would try and figure out different art pieces. Normally quite rigid but considerate Alyssia enjoyed their morning ritual though it turned out neither really understood most of the art pieces but they seemed to enjoy trying to figure them out.

Though the final visit she would make during the morning was possibly to the person who loved and adored her the most of all, even eclipsing Tony's affection for the mysterious and petite redhead.

Colette from the moment she had seen those little curls and green eyes had fallen hopelessly in love with Evelyn, she utterly adored her and after her very first week in Ljianstipol she had been starting to slowly gift something to Evelyn that no money could buy.

Colette had invited Evelyn to visit her shop the first night she had met with her, at first, I thought this was to give her the clothes she had made for her on our shopping trip, Colette however had a far bigger gift to give. Colette had an almost legendary status as a seamstress, Francois admitted that they couldn't work together because she simply put his work to utter shame.

People from far and wide came to sample her exquisite designs and handiwork and more than a few times I had hoped to get lucky in the thrift store, just to be able to afford her work. Until Evelyn came home one night with a simple looking bracelet that she had made for me, before this I had no idea what they did together every morning before we met for lunch.

Colette was teaching Evelyn her skills and every morning for a couple of hours they would work together on different pieces as Colette slowly started to pass her skills to her new best friend. 'Little Dove' was the name afforded to Evelyn by her mentor, surpassing even Tony's affection for the strange girl, Colette's heart simply melted anytime she was anywhere near Evelyn.

Speaking almost exclusively in French to each other, I never really knew what they spoke about, I guess Spanish wasn't so helpful anymore? But I assumed it was fairly kind in nature as neither of them had any real capacity to be vindictive or cruel.

Often Evelyn would bring little pieces home to practice whatever skills she had been learning during the day, I didn't mind either as she was giving me some cool things as she moved onto her next piece to practice upon.

Once my lunchtime arrived Evelyn would head to the park by the beach and together, we would talk about our days and what we might do in the evening or who's garden we would be visiting on Sunday. Within our friend network, we had a simple routine, on Saturdays we would meet in the park just north of my house and on Sundays we would meet in each other's gardens during summer for barbecues or just to catch up.

During her first week in Ljianstipol that honour befell Francois and Colette, they had a nice garden and a cool hanging chair that Evelyn had fallen asleep in during the afternoon.

Evelyn though would have been devastated to find out that she had slept straight through one of the Parisian pairs' almost hilarious arguments, both happily bit at each other in a strange display of verbal abuse towards each other. Francois and Colette were bickering like children while Evelyn gently swung and slept in the background, what a first Sunday in Ljianstipol for her.

After my lunchtime had ended, Evelyn would go and explore the outer reaches of Ljianstipol for a place she had seen on her bus journey into town. We had agreed early on during her stay that every Friday would be our day, we wouldn't see anyone else but each other, and every day Evelyn hunted for places to visit on Friday.

Seemingly unable to locate exactly what she was looking for and incapable of explaining what she had seen, every afternoon she went questing for this place she had seen. Daily I thought that if maybe she could tell me a little more than "I saw a beautiful place out of the bus window," that maybe we could have located the place sooner, however she seemed to be quite enjoying hunting for this place.

Evelyn's passion burnt bright for our Fridays together, she was quite excited about them, however this excitement was nothing compared to her utter delight for another day during the week.

Wednesday is market day in Ljianstipol and Evelyn had grown to like market day very much, all the unusual shops, buskers and Shanky sat in the marketplace selling his prints. Market day was the only time during the week that she would be awake before me, Evelyn would rise from that sofa supercharged. Coffee would be ready, she even made me toast on Wednesdays, I know it's only burning bread, but small things!

When I came downstairs or woke up on the sofa, she would grab hold of me and hug me as hard as she could, a few times I was sure I heard my ribs pop as Evelyn hugged me that hard. Evelyn's mouth would accelerate as she spoke in a total craze of everything and anything that she was going to do that day, stopping periodically only to catch her breath or laugh wildly at herself.

You couldn't help but be taken in by her sheer excitement, the other reason Evelyn loved market day was that she had agreed to go for her walk with Tony every Wednesday afternoon. Both Evelyn and Tony spent all week looking forward to these meetings and walks and both would spend all week telling me about them. Almost as hyperactive as each other, as they would list each and every step they took and how much they were looking forward to their next meeting, it was sweet.

Though I never knew exactly what they discussed as they slowly made their way round the rooftop garden, Evelyn had a strange effect on him. Tony was calmer than normal but oddly focussed too? Almost like she was helping him to finally release something that had long been bothering him?

Together we would walk down, in truth she would almost drag me down the streets of Ljianstipol. Sometimes I contemplated getting a set of reins for her, but it was quite sweet to see her so excited as she all but dragged me to Fabi's coffee shop. Evelyn and Fabi would almost have a competition with each other while I stood and waited, both eager to get that last word in with each other before we headed into town.

Walking slowly by the river, her excitement would grow as we crossed the bridge and followed that winding path by the river. We went our separate ways as she bolted up those steps into the old marketplace and I headed to work.

Chuckling to myself as we always intentionally walked slowly down by the river to build her excitement and anticipation just a little bit more. Evelyn's smile would grow anxious and almost desperate as she tried to hurry us along the banks of the river so that she could sample the delights of the market.

Walking into work I was greeted by Abby, hiding behind her glasses with heavy eyes behind the reception desk. "Morning Fae, Gale is upstairs, he needs to see you about something?" I looked up at the shy, timid and normally exhausted receptionist in fear and concern.

"Morning Abby, Okay, I will head up now," Concerned I began to head up to the meeting room. Tony and Gale weren't exactly meeting people, in truth they preferred to be less formal than that, meetings were normally a beer and a talk in the garden on the roof. Their meeting room was disused most of the time and the meeting table was normally dusty and strewn with paperwork that they hadn't quite found homes for, so a meeting in there was unusual at best.

Walking up the stairs to their meeting room I was greeted by Gale standing at the top of the stairs.

"Hey morning Fae, come on in," he seemed quite cheerful, which made this more concerning? However, the meeting format made things even more concerning as there was no Tony today, just Gale? Slightly fearful I broached the subject. "I'm not in trouble, am I?"

Looking round seemingly shocked by the thought of it he replied, "No of course not! I just wanted to take a few minutes to see how you are doing!" Gale offered me a chair and sat me down. "I just want to see how you are feeling about that photoshoot too, I know it's a big thing and I know it's affected you, I just wanted to check that you are okay!"

Gale sat opposite me brushing crumbs off their meeting table to make a clean space for his feet.

Relaxing and sighing in relief I eased up and tensions left me. "I'm still nervous about it but feeling good, Evelyn seems to have helped me with that? I was going to cancel it but she has convinced me to go through with it somehow?" I paused, smiling and started to think deeply about what I had just aired.

Gale sat relaxed with his feet resting on the table, "What does Evelyn think about it?" I thought and smiled to myself, *She thinks that I will be fine and that I just have to remember who I am and everyone will see me for who I am and not what I am?* Once again, I found myself dwelling on this open airing of Evelyn's active encouragement to me.

Gale paused and took in what I had said to him, "She's a great influence you know? She sure has stabilised you since she has been around, not just you though Tony too."

I felt quite surprised by his remark but before I could reply he sat up. "Why don't I come and sit in on the session you have this morning and then we can chat some more upstairs in the garden?"

I smiled at his gesture. "Sure, maybe you can see if there is anything more, I need to do with the sessions?" I felt pleased and encouraged as we headed to the room where each Wednesday morning, I hosted an open to all talking therapy session about social media related problems.

Gale and Joanne often attended these sessions, and I liked them doing so as they helped me to slowly improve the quality of each session and develop myself just a little bit more as we refined them. Honing the blade which we hoped to finally cut through some of the problems and issues that the local healthcare system was totally incapable to tackle as the problems were either too diverse or too minor for the services they actively offered.

With the session concluded, we headed to the rooftop garden to discuss the session and any improvements or amendments that we might be able to make to improve them. Every meeting with Gale however, always ended with a cold bottle of beer, like a full stop to the meeting separating the business and serious aspect of our work with the more social and friendly aspect of Davizioso work life.

Many of the staff here were friends both in and out of work and these little bread breakers were often a large part of that as the work head came off and the real head came out, we knew a lot about each other. Seemingly reckless in its concept these little informal get togethers were possibly the single best idea the pair had during their conception of the Davizioso and how it would run. Actively used to filter out the right kind of staff for the most part, these brief moments gave a clear indication of the way in which life was led in the forefront of this odd but ground-breaking care establishment.

Gale handed me a bottle of beer as we sat in the pergola overlooking the garden, the sun warming the air and a cool breeze gently rolling over the garden from the beach made today a very pleasant day for a meeting. While I sat back and relaxed, Gale joined me in relaxing, easing back and looking over the rooftop garden, "Can I ask you something Fae?"

I felt quite surprised by his request, "Of course Gale," he leant back even further than he had been before.

"You have known Tony for a year or so now?" I thought about what he was really asking. "Yes, about that in any real capacity anyway?"

Gale nodded at me. "Have you ever heard him talk about David to you?" I sat up and thought about it, "Beyond telling me that he passed away due to depression? Not that I can recall?"

Gale nodded again, "Me either, but that's exactly what they talk about every week when they walk around the garden," Gale smiled a little as that thought came out of him?

"In all the years since he passed away, he barely mentions his name, almost as if he is ashamed somehow, not of David, he has never been ashamed of David but ashamed of himself. Evelyn shows up and gives him some seeds to plant under any tree in his garden and he takes her to David's tree to plant them and spends hours talking to her about him, not just once but every week."

"Forgive me if I sound really jealous but I'm just astounded by it, it's like Evelyn had breathed life back into Tony, the sad thing is he did everything to keep David safe, especially from the media. Tony even kept his family hidden away in Zyvala so that the press would leave them alone but it didn't work. When

Tony made the national squad, the entire world wanted a slice of him and his family became their easiest targets."

"Being 17 and having the entire world press on his back all of the time is what really killed David. Tony blames himself for not protecting him more, not that he could have done anything more to protect him than he had already done. Though I sound jealous talking about it, I'm glad that Evelyn has started to extract that from him and so are Mona and Sophie, it's almost like David is back again in some ways?" Gale paused and smiled to himself at the thought that his best friend had found solace in Evelyn.

I sat back and smiled thinking about what Gale had just told me. "He's not the only one either, she has even broken Francois! He loves her, they talk every morning, Evelyn just thinks he is a funny Frenchman but she does enjoy some of the comments he makes at people!"

Gale looked round at me and laughed in shock, "She even broke that French viper?" I joined him laughing at the sheer thought of it. "There is one curious thing about her though Gale. The first night she stayed with me she fell asleep on the sofa and I took her to bed, laid her down and covered her up in my spare room. Partway through the night, I went downstairs for a glass of water and she was back on my sofa, curled up in the corner facing my door, almost as if I had imagined taking her to bed?"

"I laid beside her to keep her company as I felt kinda bad about the idea of her waking in a new alien place alone but for the next 4–5 days we did the same routine every night until one night I was taking her upstairs and felt really bad about it and just put her back on the sofa to sleep. Now I just fold her up on the sofa with a duvet and normally stay with her as I don't like her being alone, I know she is 22, but I feel really bad leaving her alone."

"I have grown quite fond of it in truth, Gale, but it's something that I have found odd since she has been staying with me. Most mornings I wake with her either laying on my chest holding my face or nestled in my arms, it's very sweet really. Gale, you have children, do you have any idea why she might do that?"

Gale sat back and thought for a while. "How well do you know Evelyn?" I looked at him and thought deeply before answering.

"Pretty well I think?" Gale nodded, "I mean, has she spoken about her past to you?"

I thought harder. "She has told me about her life," Gale sat back up and passed me a beer.

Gale opened himself another beer and sat back, "You remember how me and Tony met and became friends Fae?"

I sat up and smiled. "Didn't you guys get into some fight over a girl and then became friends?"

Gale smiled and chuckled, "Yeah, that's the one! Marie was her name; she was my age and she was stunning. Tony and I had spent weeks chasing her, outdoing each other week in week out trying to attract her interest before we got into a huge fight with each other. Unfortunately for us, that fight sank us both in her eyes, but we became friends and she eventually married our friend John."

"Tony missed a big cup game to go to their wedding, he nearly got thrown out of the team he was playing for over that! Tony's family, my family and John and Marie were really good friends and my daughter Ellie was about 7 years old when they had their first child, a girl."

"Ellie used to craze them to let her look after their little girl especially when she took a shine to fairies, Ellie got me to make a little door to put on a tree in their garden. John and Marie's daughter used to sit there for hours just dreaming and believing that someday she would finally see a fairy come through that door for the first time. Eventually, they let Ellie become their babysitter, every time they went out, she would go and look after that little girl and Ellie sort of saw her as a sister of sorts."

"John and Marie paid her nicely for her time too, but Ellie would have been happy unpaid, she loved that girl, one night and quite late I got a call from Ellie, John and Marie hadn't come home yet and it was getting quite late. Ellie was only 12 at the time and it was nearly half ten when she rang me, she went to see if the girl might know why they were late, but beyond saying that they had been arguing just before Ellie arrived, she had no idea."

"Ellie phoned me about an hour later saying the police had turned up at the house, I went over as quickly as I could, John and Marie had been in a car crash. The police were trying to explain to the girl what had happened and what it meant but she didn't understand. John and Marie's daughter, Evelyn didn't understand that her parents were gone, so they gave her some fuzzy cat toy and her mother's necklace before they left," Gale sighed and leant back shielding his mouth with his hand momentarily, before raising his bottle to John and Marie.

"Did you know the whole time, Gale?" Gale looked over and shook his head.

"No, I hadn't seen her since she was maybe eight years old, I wasn't sure and neither was Tony, I hope you don't think that we have lied to you Fae?"

214

I sat back and shook my head back at him, "No I don't think that. Speaking of Tony, where is he?" I probed Gale gently.

"He has gone to get things for this year's party, especially the lanterns, he has ordered an extra two this year, he even went to find her in the marketplace so that she can go shopping with him," Gale sighed and lifted his bottle, I looked over and joined him, "To John and Marie."

Gale smiled a little and spoke back, "To John and Marie." Gale eased back into his seat.

"I'm sure you now know why Tony gave her that white wristband," I nodded sadly looking at him, "A few months after her parents died, we went to see her, her grandmother had moved in with her and was looking after Evelyn. Her grandmother complained that she wouldn't go near her own room and had started sleeping on a sofa and always facing the doorway. We reasoned that Evelyn just needed some time to adjust to her new life without her parents around, but it seemed like she was waiting for them to come back?"

"Her grandmother had been slowly falling out with Evelyn more and more, locking her in a backroom with a fold out sofa bed anytime we went over. Around a year ago, Ellie phoned me up saying that she had seen Evelyn and that she had gifted her family home to Ellie, we were suspicious at best."

"Ellie had been with a guy who had totally changed her, she lied a lot and we fell out and didn't speak for a good few years until she finally broke off from him and we had started talking again. What was strangest to Ellie though wasn't that she had given her the house, but that Evelyn's room was still completely unchanged and exactly as it was the night her parents died."

"Every single thing exactly where it was, dust free and all clean but trapped in a never-ending cycle of the exact same night for 18 years now. When I sent a copy of that photo to Ellie, she phoned me nearly four times a day to talk about her and asking me to thank her for what Evelyn had done for her and to make sure she was looked after but I guess, Evelyn is now looking after all of us."

"The saddest thing though is that if we knew just how bad her grandmother was to her, we would have adopted Evelyn or Tony's family would have taken her in," Gale wept a little as he finished speaking to me about Evelyn.

I sat back and looked over at Gale, "She can't remember her parents, at least not very well, she told me about that when she told me about her past, imagine not being able to remember them?" I sighed to myself at the thought of that.

"Tony has a surprise for her, he still has photos of Evelyn's parents, he is going to give them to her at the party, just keep it a secret!" Gale sat back up and we tipped our bottles one final time to John and Marie before Tony and Evelyn arrived for the Wednesday afternoon ritual.

Gale and I sat awaiting the pairs arrival and sure enough and right on time, in walked Tony softly ushering Evelyn into the garden, with her neck turned almost a full 180 degrees to keep talking to him as they walked into the garden. They both looked really happy today, but they looked like this every Wednesday as they went for their walk around the garden together and little meeting with each other.

While me and Gale discussed current patients and new patients arriving or ways to improve things at the Davizioso, they walked together. Tony had now fully entrusted this side of the business to both Gale and me, it was a nice gesture to be so involved in the deeper running of the Davizioso.

Before they began their walk around the garden in the glorious sunshine, Tony would hand a beer around to everyone before they headed off. While out shopping, Tony had found some new beer for us all to try that he planned to get for the party at the end of June, the bottle was nearly as big as Evelyn though!

With near 30-degree heat and that soft breeze rolling off the beach they couldn't have picked a better day for their walk if they had tried to. Evelyn softly held her hand out to Tony and he gently took it, and off they went slowly walking their way down the garden towards the first corner of the rooftop.

Tony had a new shirt on today and almost all the buttons were done up on it too, Evelyn was in her sailor outfit as they wandered away dressed to their best for this weekly special occasion. Taking a bottle each, they gently wandered hand in hand like school children, talking and giggling to each other all the way, it was one of the sweetest things I had ever seen.

Gale sat back and laughed at me. "It's just like magic you know? He's a different man around her, like everything has just worked out, it's beautiful to see!"

We both chuckled away as we watched them slowly wander hand in hand down the path and round the corner to David's tree, "I don't know how she does it? She does it to everyone! Francois, Alyssia and even me? I haven't had a single crash since she had been around me, I've had twinges but Evelyn stops them!"

I looked over at a surprised looking Gale, "She stops them?"

216

I nodded at him and smiled. "A few times I have started getting warning signs that one is coming but almost the second they show up Evelyn leaps into action. The first time I was on the sofa with her, and she put my shoes on without even saying why and took me down through the town, past the river and the bridge that I hate. Leading me through the old part of town and the park and out onto the beach, she never said a single word as she dragged me through town."

"Almost the second we hit those dunes, Evelyn stopped and climbed up onto my back and held me tightly as she pushed her face against mine, I could feel her smiling as she clung on and made me watch the setting sun drop beneath the horizon."

"Together we stood into the darkness, never saying a word the entire time until she gently climbed down and hugged me so tightly that I thought that she might break my ribs. She pulled her head next to mine and whispered into my ear, 'I need you Fae and I love you,' over and over, she held on for what felt like an eternity before she let me go."

"Offering me her hand she walked me slowly back through town, stopping at the bridge to show me our padlock and giving me another hug. 'I love you Fae,' she whispered but nothing else and she led me home, Evelyn stopped that crash dead in its tracks."

Gale looked at me surprised. "The first time? What about the second time?"

I sat back and smiled again, "The second time we were in the garden at home and I started to have one of the short and hard crashes that I get sometimes? As I started to fall to my knees she caught me in her arms, pulling my head tight to her chest, Evelyn rested her lips on my forehead and we just stayed there."

"I could feel her lips twinging as she spoke and whispered but I couldn't hear what she said? Evelyn never let go though, she kept hold of me and softly ran her hand through my hair and around the back of my head as she held on. Soon the moment passed, and the crash went away, I just stood back up and grabbed hold of her as a mighty cry fell out of me, but no crash and no tears? But do you know the strangest thing about all of it, Gale?"

He looked around at me. "No, I couldn't guess?" Gale seemed puzzled.

"She has never mentioned a single word about them, almost as if they are so normal and trivial that we just don't mention it. If I thank her Evelyn just replies with, 'Fae you are my best friend and I love you,' and we move on?"

Gale looked quite stunned. "She is quite magical really, isn't she?" We chuckled together as Tony and Evelyn reappeared on their route around the garden.

Tony and Evelyn reached the turning point of their walk, a little fountain near the pergola and every week they went round it 4 times before they retraced their steps back down the garden. Every time they did this, me and Gale would sit and giggle to each other as they made this odd turnabout 2 metres from where we sat watching.

Gale looked at me with his hand on his face trying to mask his laughter from the delightful pair of walkers as they made their way back down the same path they had just wandered.

"Hey Fae? You remember Leanne?" Chuckling with him at the pair.

"Yeah, sure I do, after my first day here how could I forget her?" Gale composed himself a little.

"Ellie knows of her, Leanne has got a job at that American diner by the river and according to Ellie, it was Leanne that used to bully Evelyn. Leanne used her father's position in the local authority to keep herself out of trouble and get Evelyn into more trouble for reacting to whatever she did to her. Just so you know, it might be worth steering clear of that place, though Ellie did say that Evelyn is more than capable of defending herself!"

"Apparently, Evelyn gave Leanne a few black eyes over the things that she did or said to her, imagine that snooty brat being floored by that little angel!" Gale laughed but he was being quite serious.

While we watched Tony and Evelyn disappear back around the corner behind the lush grasses and oriental bushes of the rooftop garden. "You think that she hasn't said anything because she is worried that she will have to leave if she tells me?" Gale shrugged his shoulders at me.

"Who knows? Maybe me and Tony got to her before Evelyn did when Leanne said those things to her?" While Gale's thoughts sunk in, we watched their shadows slowly vanish behind the plant life.

"I know Evelyn told me that a girl did an impression of her mother dying in that accident and she wound up on top of them and hitting them before a teacher prised Evelyn off them?" Gale shrugged his shoulders again, "No idea but I can imagine that Evelyn is far tougher now than she was back then." Together, we waited for the pair to reappear at the opposite side of the garden.

Soon enough the pair slowly came walking back down the garden towards the pergola, hand in hand and still talking away before casually joining us on the pergola. Gale checked to see if his buddy was okay while Evelyn started to tell me about their shopping trip together. Seeming to be thrilled at her little jaunt round some of the less visited shops of Ljianstipol on their quest for different beer and delights, though I'm sure more time with Tony was a big part of her joy.

Equally elated as we headed home, she seemed vaguely suspicious at times during the night, almost as if she was either probing or hiding something?

May the twentieth was my birthday, my 27th birthday and for the most part I wanted to keep it very low key but Ljianstipol and its residents had other ideas about that. Fabi started the proceedings with a little cake and a card from him and Alyssia in the morning, feeling quite humbled as I wandered to work. Abby greeted me with a card and a small gift too, though she did understand I was quite shy about my birthday so she did wrap it in brown paper, which kinda made it look suspect in truth but thoughtful nevertheless.

During the morning, my group therapy session went pretty well and I headed to meet Evelyn for lunch only to be greeted by Colette instead? Colette took me for lunch at one of the bistros by the river and she and Francois gave me a beautiful silk scarf as a present and I noticed it had all Colette's hallmarks in it. When I headed back to work, I was summoned to the rooftop garden by Gale as a matter of urgency, in truth I should have known it was a set up but it didn't even cross my mind as I walked up the steps to the garden.

Walking into a wave of birthday wishes as I was taken down to the pergola to be greeted with a huge birthday cake and pastries for this little surprise birthday party. Shanky had drawn a picture of me with Evelyn in a nice little frame to go on my wall, Joanne had conspired with Tony and Gale to give me a voucher for Colette's shop.

Throughout the day, small gestures had appeared and as much as I wanted to keep my special day as low key as possible their decision to make it less secretive filled me with a nice contentment as I wandered home. Not for one second though did I expect to arrive at an empty house when I reached home? Evelyn was nowhere to be found? A note was on the bookshelf in my living room.

"See me in my tree," I looked down the garden and could see little candles flickering away in and around the tree at the end of the garden.

Walking down the garden towards the tree there were two chairs and a table set up, but these weren't mine and in truth I had no idea where they had come from? Without warning Evelyn came from behind me. "Happy birthday Fae!" She called out as I turned around to see her standing shyly with an apron on and holding a large paper bag. Standing with her feet pointed inwards she offered me the bag with her arms outstretched and a sweet smile to seal the deal. Inside the bag was a soft but wrapped gift with "Happy Birthday Fae, Love Evelyn," written across it.

Ushering me upstairs so that I could open her gift, it was quite obvious she was just a little excited as she almost dragged me up the stairs. Sitting on my bed to unwrap her gift while she stood watching me pensively in excitement as I began to gently tear away the wrapping paper. Opening the gift unveiled a large and flowing white dress, upon holding it up I noticed the unmistakable stitching of Colette on the back on the inside of the dress.

Stitched in golden thread on the inside was "As beautiful as I think you are." I gasped in shock at the undeniable quality of the dress.

Evelyn was almost jumping up and down. "Come on Fae! Try it on!" She was so excited that her normally soft voice was almost squeaky in delight. Gently lifting the dress over myself and threading the halter over my head and gently patted the dress down while she offered me a mirror to get my first look.

"Evelyn it's beautiful," I said to her in sheer awe at the thoughtfulness and sheer beauty of her gift. Following my lines and curves beautifully but leaving my shoulders exposed I actually looked quite divine in it?

Reflecting upon the sheer generosity of her gift and standing almost in awe of myself as she stood cautiously awaiting my judgement. "Evelyn, this is beautiful, you really didn't have to do this."

Evelyn grinned back at me. "Yes, I did and Colette helped me to make it for you."

I turned in shock, "You made this?" I was staggered.

"Colette helped me but now you can be as beautiful as I think you are," she smiled so sweetly that it was obvious how much making this gift had meant to her.

Both calming she took my hand and led me back through the house and outside, gently offering me a chair and sitting me down as she vanished back indoors. Returning with candles and beer for me before she appeared with our dinner and she had my favourite pizza for me too. Together we sat outside and enjoyed my candlelit birthday dinner together under the stars, although I think she enjoyed it nearly as much as I did.

Throughout the evening we chatted away and she thanked me for looking after her since she arrived in Ljianstipol and how she looked forward to spending more birthdays together. As far as I could tell Evelyn had no plans to go anywhere for very long and seemingly my little visitor had become my housemate.

Evelyn was keen to show me the fruits of her exploration over the weekend, she had found a small park near my house that I didn't even realise was there. Enthused to take me and show me some of the places she had unearthed since arriving in Ljianstipol, we headed out early on Friday morning ready for a long day in the sun together. Walking out towards the edges of town and along the roads that skirted along the now bollards off town centre we came to our first stop.

Up a little hill a nearly fully enclosed park, not especially large by all accounts but intricately maintained, though Evelyn wasn't that interested in the paths. Evelyn would take her shoes off and walk barefoot through the grass and moss, she often said it reminded her of the forest floor as the grass gently tickled the soles of her feet and toes.

However, these moments seemed to many it was when she was almost at her most magical as she almost serenely floated along at full peace with nature and herself. Wandering slowly through the maze of little paths and trees we came upon a neatly created concrete plaza which overlooked the town, walled off with ornate concrete fencing and a little walkthrough fountain in the centre. Sitting in the park and occasionally going to dip our toes in the cool water of the fountain, we had certainly picked a good day to visit this place today.

Together we remained well into the evening and watched the sunset from the concrete walls of the plaza, it was stunning as the oranges and deep purples of the sky slowly encapsulated our minds.

Walking home however was something rather different entirely, with darkness having descended, the park felt menacing and ominous for me but for Evelyn it felt just like home. Growing fearful I was keen to depart the park once the daylight had fully faded however Evelyn encouraged me to wait for just a little while longer? Sitting on a bench in the plaza she was almost unnervingly peaceful as we waited.

Minutes rolled into an hour as she waited for just the right moment to make her move, she took her shoes back off and encouraged me to do the same as she gently held her hand out to me. Slowly she guided me towards the paths that would lead back to civilisation, however she had no intention to wander along those soft concrete paths as she guided me into the trees themselves.

Gently holding my hand with just her fingertips, we started to enter the myriad of trees and when we did, we paused for a brief moment though she didn't explain why, but once I looked at her face, I understood why we had waited.

After a few moments, my eyes adjusted to the light and suddenly the ground was illuminated almost like daytime but in a soft blue and purple light as the moonlight broke through the canopy of the trees. Evelyn's eyes were just a tiny bit greener and her curls slightly more orange as she started to walk me barefoot through this grassy wonderland.

Grass gently tickled and soothed my feet as each step grew more magical and the light seemed to grow just slightly brighter as I followed behind the seemingly enchanted Evelyn. Mystifying during the day but utterly magical by night was all that kept flowing through my mind as she led me slowly through the trees, for what felt like an eternity. Stopping before me she turned to look at me and smiled.

"Your eyes are prettier in the dark, Fae," in the softest and calmest tone I had ever heard come from her. Suddenly, I understood that look that she had when she sat overlooking the world at night from the tree in our garden or at the beach. Evelyn was hopelessly in love with the world and that forest had fully enriched her soul and every chance she had Evelyn took it to feel that same magic that tonight she was showing me.

Like an almost angelic presence in the world, I felt a sorrow that for the most part her world hadn't loved her anywhere near as much as she loved it, but I took joy in the fact that she had found happiness in the darkest of places. Somewhere among the trees and flowers of the forest that she spoke of Evelyn had found a place which fully encapsulated her wildest dreams and filled her soul with happiness.

Reaching the end of our journey through the trees filled me with sadness but a strange feeling of happiness as Evelyn had just shown me a magical place right on my doorstep. Walking home with this strange and new sensation flowing throughout my mind and body in utter silence with my magical friend, I hoped she would show me this world again soon.

Over the weekend, people were quite scarce so we made the most of the time together by going for walks and little adventures in the parks or on the beach. During Sunday we started to notice a change coming to Ljianstipol as trucks and lorries began to arrive and campsites were being prepared all over town in any available space. Ljianstipol was a town which very much liked to do its own thing and often hosting events that were very different was a big part of that puzzle.

Over the next week a circus was going to be visiting Ljianstipol but this would be no ordinary circus and this was also the sole reason for the scarcity of our friend network this weekend. Preparation was well underway in the town for the four-day event that would begin on Thursday, banners were being erected and the town was getting a light makeover ready for the opening day.

Francois was dressing his shop to suit the expected waves of customers and had been keen to try and get me attired in an outfit that he was making just for the special occasion. Turning up at my door on Sunday morning he presented me with a free outfit if I was happy to wear it during the week at some point. Knowing the value of his offerings and the quality of his work, who would I have been to have turned down such a generous offer?

While Evelyn helped me to try out the new outfit, Francois had gifted me in the safety and comfort of my garden the circus began to roll into town. Ljianstipol for the next week would be home to a steampunk bizarre, gradually the parks were filling with campers and different businesses began to set up stalls in the town in preparation for the launch on Thursday.

Throughout the next week Ljianstipol slowly grew more and more? Well steampunky? Neither me or Evelyn really understood what it really was and looking for an answer on the internet made things even more confusing. Seemingly an odd splice of science fiction and early industrial design neither of us really quite got the fascination but day by day the towns population skyrocketed as more people arrived daily to sample this steampunk bizarre.

Each evening, I spent trying to get used to the outfit that Francois had given me, the top was pretty cool with a nice leather corset and black silk shirt top but the shorts were kinda different. Quite body shy, I wasn't accustomed to having anywhere near this much of me on show and certainly not quite so much of my quite large backside out on public display.

Evelyn was very encouraging and kept complimenting me on how the outfit made me look though no matter how good her compliments were, I couldn't tackle the boots which went with the outfit. There is a good reason that I wear flat shoes or trainers with almost no balancing skills, every few steps in those beautifully made high heels sent me crashing to the floor like a toddler taking their first steps. Francois would just have to live with trainers going with the outfit unless he was going to keep taking me to hospital over the duration of the bizarre!

While the week slowly wore on, more strange people and stalls started to appear in Ljianstipol, Evelyn's market day was unusual for her to say the least as the marketplace was filled with so many stalls that her and Tony had their walk around the market instead this week. During Wednesday evening, we sat in the garden and could hear the crowds that were camping in the two nearby parks partying late into the night and bands played into the early hours ready for the grand opening during the morning.

During my walk to work on Thursday, the mass of people that had already descended upon Ljianstipol became very obvious. Walking down to work Fabi had a large queue already forming by his coffee shop, thankfully as I am kinda like clockwork every morning he had it ready and just left it near the bench by his shop door for me to take with me.

Panic stricken as he laid the cup on the bench for me to take, he didn't even contemplate taking any payment this morning, I left him the money just inside of his door and left him to fight his way through the crowds gathering by his shop. Walking by the river an entire mass of people were congregating ready for the grand launch in just a few minutes' time, almost having to force my way through a sea of oddly dressed people just to reach the Davizioso.

Almost having to battle my way to the front door of the Davizioso through the mass of oddly attired people who had arrived in Ljianstipol for the next four days of steampunk madness.

Panting, as I finally landed at the safety of the reception desk to an almost entirely empty hotel, Abby was talking to a resident who was about to depart and see all that the bizarre had to offer. "Hey Fae, can you believe all the people! Tony has headed home but Gale is around here somewhere he is having another insomnia week!"

Abby smiled as shyly as ever through those frames marking out her sweet smile. Wandering to the room where we held our Thursday group sessions to find just Gale sitting and waiting for me. "Morning Fae, it might be a slow day for us!" He gestured and waved his arms around the emptiness of the room.

"Looks that way, getting to work was a nightmare, there's people everywhere!"

I laughed back at Gale, "Well everywhere but here!"

Gale sat almost nervously on a chair near the door as I leant with my bum on my hands against the wall as we waited impatiently for anyone to show up. Every time the door rattled with the wind, we both perked up on high alert and ready to greet nothing, I looked over at a deflated Gale who looked at his watch, sighed and started to rummage around his pocket.

While I stood looking out of the window, I heard a short and sharp. "Fae! Think fast!" I looked round and saw something hurtling at speed towards me.

Catching the object in mid-air as Gale declared, "Well caught," he chuckled.

"Thanks, Gale," I laughed back and looked at the offending item and paused. "A cube of chalk?" I quizzed Gale feeling a little suspicious of his intent.

"You got something better to do right now?" Gale smirked back with a competitive edge in his voice. I looked around the vast and empty hall.

"No, I guess not?" And Gale started to lead me to his bar downstairs, Gale shut the door and poured me a cool fizzy drink and handed me a cue. Gale often came to this little haven he had tucked away in the hotel, though it wasn't exclusively his own, not many people ventured into it as Gale is quite a shark at a pool table. During the weeks where he couldn't sleep, it wasn't unusual to find him playing against himself well into the morning hours.

Gale always said he was in the bad books either way at home when he had these weeks so if he was going to be in trouble he might as well do the crime to go with it. Since his teenage years, Gale had struggled from time to time with sleep, sometimes going days on end without getting so much as an hour of rest, though a few times he had been found asleep in the chairs in his bar by the morning cleaning team.

Gale was a curious person really, the quieter and more reclusive of the pair, though he was never behind the game much to the contrary more often than not he knew instinctively what to do and where to be at almost every opportunity. Gale of course, had pushed for me to be moved from a support worker in the hotel to be a trainee therapist and consultant, I didn't fully grasp his unwavering faith within me but I appreciated how hard he was pushing to give me a career.

Almost from the first day I had been working at the hotel he had been actively monitoring every single move and decision I made, he never had any bad intentions.

Gale had a vision of where I could go, something that I lacked when I had first wandered these halls as a member of the team rather than a patient and something he was slowly teaching me with each meeting and pool session. Between his gloating and sledging during the games, would be little drops of information, sometimes really small and subtle and other times monstrous, delivered in a way to keep me slightly off the scent of what his mind was doing.

Tony was quite open to admit that Gale really ran the Davizioso and he was just a caring front man for the enterprise but Gale heavily refuted that idea as he willingly admitted that without Tony there was no dream or vision to chase. Each frame we played he would drop tiny little pieces of information and I lapped them up, though I wasn't sure what he always was getting at today he was spilling something big, very big.

Gale and his daughter, Ellie, had fallen out and not spoken for years until recently but as the games wore on it started to sound like she was going to be coming to Ljianstipol and this time she would be staying.

Gale would never directly give this information to me but he would give me just enough pieces to paint a picture for myself, his trust in me was always highly appreciated. Sometimes I wondered why he placed such high faith in me that I couldn't see any reason for his justification yet his faith made me believe in myself more. While our time together slowly drew to a close, he was dropping chunks of details to me about something very large but almost so large that I couldn't really quite work out what he was indirectly telling me.

Leaving to find Evelyn for my lunch his little drops kept playing over in my mind, I couldn't assemble them into anything as it just didn't seem to make sense or maybe I had just misheard him? Gale was hinting at a fundamental change at the Davizioso that maybe only he really knew about and Tony had just said yes to it.

Either way that change was going to be huge if it was true and in truth I couldn't quite understand where I fit into it? Evelyn hadn't been into town today, instead she had been sitting in the tree in my garden watching the cars and trucks roll into Ljianstipol and expand an already huge population of visitors to Ljianstipol.

After heading back to work after lunch me and Gale again sat alone in the hall of the hotel, alone and bored, he just took me to his bar for a beer before just telling me to head home.

Today, the Davizioso was almost entirely empty bar a few staff all standing round the halls of the hotel bored senseless, feeling slightly guilty as I walked away early but soon, I forgot that as I attempted to plough my way through the huge crowds of people that had flocked to Ljianstipol.

Friday was me and Evelyn's day together, we went for walks or just lounged around the house in our comfiest and sloppiest attire. However, with this strange mechanical circus in town tomorrow we were going to go and sample a little slice of this curious affair. Everyone would be meeting in the park on Saturday to watch the bands, entertainers and just relax over the weekend so rather than visit the parks we were going to plunge ourselves into the bizarre.

Feeling slightly self-conscious I just wound up wearing the white dress Evelyn had made for me and would wear the gift from Francois tomorrow when we all met in the park. Together we headed into town during the morning, there would be no coffee stop this morning as Fabi's queue was nearly all the way to the edge of the pedestrianised zone.

Walking past all the fancily dressed men and women patiently waiting for a coffee at his stall, his panic yesterday seemed like nothing today as he rushed round trying to keep up with demand. Rather than be disappointed with a poor coffee, we got ourselves an ice cream instead, it's not quite a substitute but there was no queue for that this early in the morning.

Together we began to wander around all the curious stalls in the marketplace, selling strange but beautiful clothing, odd hats and cool but unusual sunglasses. Evelyn had worn her sailor outfit today and she was drawing far more attention than she seemed to be comfortable with as people asked her for pictures and selfies with her. Evelyn didn't refuse many, but she didn't look comfortable at all as each person seemed to want a shot of the cute little creature and her outfit.

Feeling her anxiousness with each picture we wandered to the beach instead to sit in the park together, but even the park was no place for peace today. Lining every single path were stalls or entertainers eager to impress and deepen the impact of this strange event.

Trying to flee the crowds flocking and enclosing every single space we walked by the promenade instead, thankfully here was quieter. Standing together we looked over the beach to see it was packed with people in their strange but intriguing outfits when a call came from behind me.

"Fae! Can I get a picture for the paper?" I turned around to see Karl with his camera looking to get pictures for the local paper about the bizarre. "Hey Karl, um I'm not sure about that?" He raised his camera anyway and took a picture. "It can be like a warm up for the shoot in a few weeks, you are still going to do it aren't you?"

Trying to build myself up for him and Evelyn, "Of course, I'm ready for it!"

Karl just took another picture, "Great! Could you stand with your arms folded looking over the beach?"

Almost instinctively, I followed his every instruction while Evelyn watched on with a strange smirk on her face? Karl took his picture before asking if I could go stand in the park for him but Evelyn stepped in, "No you got your pictures now leave us alone!"

Karl looked at the 4 ft 8 redhead and instinctively backed off and left us be. I looked at Evelyn with her face filled with anger. "He just didn't know when to stop!" She said to me as we started to head back to the park and market place.

However, surprised that I was with her she did have a good point, he just didn't leave us alone, as we walked around the park, he still chased to get that one extra picture. Agreeing with him almost purely to get him to leave us be, I stood by a stall in the market so that he could get another picture before he finally left us alone.

Walking around the market stalls one last time as both of our tempers were waning, while I looked at a dress on a stall the selfie brigade descended upon Evelyn again. Some of the pictures she had no objection too but with shop owners eager to promote themselves she was having hats shoved on her head and I could see her slowly becoming agitated by them. While she was innocently looking at some scarves, a shop owner pounced upon her, taking pictures of her looking at his stall before imposing different garments upon her.

However, when he started to mess around with her little sailor top, she changed, she tensed up and you could see her growing angrier by the second as he played with her top. I started walking to her rescue before she finally snapped.

"Why don't you just fuck off!" Evelyn yelled with such venom and volition that the entire market went silent. Evelyn however didn't back away as she unleashed her fury and willingly stood fast against an enormous and towering man, her body was rigid and her eyes transfixed upon his menace.

A passing stranger stepped in to help her, putting himself between her and the shop owner. "Hey leave her alone!" He yelled at him before he turned to check that she was okay. He leant down and gently helped to turn her around and walk her away from the menacing shop owner; before Evelyn rejoined with me and just hugged me sadly. "Can we go home, Fae?" I sighed and thanked the passing stranger.

He leant down to her, "Sorry, some people just don't know when to quit but don't let it ruin your weekend," he smiled sadly at her and handed her a little necklace with a lightbulb on the end. "You take care now little sailor," he smiled at her as he walked away.

Stunned by her sheer anger and the odd terror in her voice, I gently placed my hand on her shoulder and guided her away from the marketplace. Slowly we walked along the river together before we walked over that bridge and onward home. Evelyn was sniffling angrily to herself all the way home. "He just wouldn't leave me alone," she seemed really disappointed that he just didn't leave her be?

I took her for a beer in the newer part of town, but it was very busy so we just got a couple of bottles and wandered home quietly. Slowly wandering and sipping away I hoped that she wouldn't lose heart in her sailor outfit and that she would be okay to go to the park tomorrow. Wandering and worrying, I started to think that maybe he had reminded Evelyn of that last night in her old town? We headed into the garden to chill out under the tree together, sitting quietly she slowly started to come back and become her usual self again.

Feeling sorry for her as she had spent most of the week looking forward to going to the festival on Friday, it was a shame that it had almost been ruined for her by an overly keen shopkeeper. Hopeful that she would be okay come the morning and we could venture to the park to listen to the bands and sit in the comfort and safety of our friends.

During the night I stayed on the sofa with her, as much as she probably wanted to be alone, I couldn't bring myself to leave Evelyn to her own thoughts alone during the night. Stunned into silence when that 4-foot 8 tiny girl had stood up and fronted up to a towering 6-foot man, she was utterly fearless and steadfast until the adrenaline had been sapped out of her.

However, my fears were soon quashed in the morning when she awoke as happy as ever almost as if the previous day's events had never happened, though I was wary as we headed to the park together. Feeling encouraged and knowing that both Francois and Colette would be in attendance today, I did dare to wear the outfit he had given me, though Evelyn today wore her black outfit that Colette had given her.

However, concerned I might have been, her confidence was clearly back and in abundance as we walked through the morning sun to meet our friends in the park and to watch the day unfold.

Heading through the entrance of the park filled me with dread as once again the entire park was filled with more stalls and entertainers. Although after her performance yesterday, I was fairly sure that if the stall from yesterday was in the park that there was no chance, he would dare to harass her again.

Colette soon greeted her and took her for a little walk and though part of me was apprehensive but aside from me or Tony there was nobody more likely to stand in anyone's way for Evelyn. While they disappeared off round the park as Alyssia and Fabi arrived to join us for the afternoon, just in time for the first entertainers to begin their acts for the afternoon.

Sitting together as more members of our party arrived and Colette returned with a seemingly refreshed Evelyn, whatever they had spoken about seemed to have settled her mind again. Together we sat before we decided to go and have a look around the stalls, with her at peace I finally relaxed as we went walking round the park.

Wandering through the stalls was calmer here today, the atmosphere was friendlier and less frantic too which further settled my mind as we wandered around. Evelyn was at peace too which helped and much to her surprise the guy that had stood up for her yesterday spotted her and came to see if she was okay after her encounter yesterday.

While Evelyn spoke with him, I once again was collared by Karl and his camera, eager to get another few pictures for the paper. Keen to snap away Evelyn had clocked his presence and once again that odd smirk appeared upon her face as he took his pictures. While Karl finished his little photo session with me in the park, Evelyn rejoined me with a slightly jubilant, "He likes your bum," she grinned as she took my arm and we walked around the stalls together.

However, those two little photo sessions had flared up my fears and inhibitions about the interviews coming up in just a few weeks' time. During the afternoon, the thought of it started to encroach upon me more and more as the day wore on, while most people didn't really seem to notice, Evelyn was fully aware of what I was thinking.

Evelyn gently offered me her hand, "Come and get a drink with me, Fae," she gently lifted me up and we walked along the paths and through the trees.

Stopping at the bar, rather than heading back to the group of friends sitting together in the park, she guided me out of the park through an alternative exit so that we didn't get stopped and we wandered alone to the park she had taken me to the weekend before. Quietly walking through the trees and heading towards the plaza and the concrete fence that overlooked the town.

Evelyn leant against the wall and I sat on the wall as together we sat quietly contemplating together, though she didn't really try to force the conversation she was only too happy to try and build me up. Fortunately, the park was largely empty as everyone had gone to either the park we had just left behind or the town itself, the silence of the park was a pleasant environment for us to both gather our thoughts.

Sitting on the wall together, we overlooked the town together and started to watch the day turn to evening as we recharged our minds. Evelyn had learned early on that night-time and moonlight seemed to help me to recharge and calm my mind, she had however slowly been giving me something much newer to help my often-jagged thoughts.

Nothing fulfilled Evelyn more than just walking barefoot through the forest at night, with moonlight gently lighting the path through the world she described as home. A few times during her stay I had watched her walk around my garden barefoot just after the rain and wondered quite why she did this, until she introduced me to the feelings and sensations that this simple act caused. One afternoon she almost dragged me outside after a passing shower and walked me down to the tree down the end of my garden.

Initially, quite shocked and bemused by this strange action only to find that with each step and every single touch from the wet ground beneath I became calmer. However, this simple act was never more potent for me than during the night, at first when she had made me wait for the darkness in this very park, I became anxious and fidgety to get home.

However, once we set off through the trees each gentle stroke along the soles of my feet by the grass eased and soothed my mind and thoughts, the light made this feeling even more enchanting as a soft and gentle bluish hue guided us through darkness.

Tonight, Evelyn was going to give me that sensation again but tonight it wasn't just my mind she was looking to soothe. Evelyn's encounter yesterday with that trader had hit her hard, possibly stirring images of that night when she was assaulted in Zyvala before she abandoned her home for the forest. While we walked in darkness through the trees, it was obvious that this gift from the forest that she had given to me wasn't just a coping mechanism for just me, it was also one for her own mind.

Together again, we slowly wandered home, quietened and at ease with ourselves again through the winding streets and back to the safety and comfort of my home. Heading to the tree down the end of my garden Evelyn was talking to me so softly that even the air leaving her lungs was cooling my mind as I readied myself for my last week at work before the photoshoots that were filling me with such dread.

Almost from the very first moment that we had met, Evelyn had been building my confidence for the photoshoot, telling me that people would love me and that I wouldn't be seen as a desperate wannabe model but the dedicated training therapist that I truly was. Continually rebuilding my confidence and talking me into feeling a deep sense of pride in what I was undertaking she had become a magical force for me, a living and breathing comfort blanket.

However, I wasn't alone in feeling that strange magic that she so easily instilled within me, Tony had been slowly starting to talk about his departed son with her. Gale openly confessed to being jealous as his best friend of nearly 40 years had never once truly opened up to him about David and yet he found a deep solace and trust in the mysterious passing petite redhead.

Francois, normally a man to openly insult and attack everyone had yet to so much as pass a bad word her way, he adored her as did, Abby, Shanky Fabi and Alyssia. With the exception of Leanne, I was yet to meet someone that didn't just crumble to her green eyes or ginger curls.

While the evening wound down, we got ready to visit Francois and Colette during Sunday afternoon for a quieter catch up before the impending final week at work. A week that would be the start point of something very different for me but also, I expected to see Evelyn's hyperactivity and addictive happiness hit an unbelievable peak on Wednesday afternoon.

Colette had been keen to have everyone round their garden for some time but with different events they had to wait to host everyone but finally they could have everyone over again. Francois was fond of Evelyn and me, he never put a bad word her way and in truth aside from the odd snipe about my trousers exaggerating my curvy bum he was pretty good to me too.

Colette however, was utterly in love with her new little friend Evelyn or as Colette called her, 'Little Dove' from the moment she met her, she had fallen hopelessly in love with that girl and her little curls. Most mornings she would speak with Evelyn while teaching her some of her more than legendary skills.

Thus far, Evelyn had only made a few bracelets and a very nice scarf under her stewardship and of course as it turned out she had also helped make the white dress that she had given me for my birthday. Evelyn of course, was only too eager to spend nearly every morning that she could with her friend; they shared some kind of deep bond between them, an odd kindred spirit with each other that aside from her bond with myself anyone would be envious of.

Colette and Francois were in on the real reason that my shift on Thursday had been moved to Friday, we had agreed to keep the real reason very secret as Evelyn was about to experience the same strange wave of care from this tight knit group of friends that I had when I first moved to Ljianstipol. When we walked into their garden and Colette smiled and gently patted a spot beside her on their hanging chair for her little dove, Evelyn was oblivious to what would happen on Wednesday afternoon after her walk with Tony.

Fabi and Alyssia of course were in on the set up and neither of them gave any hint of what was coming, even as Fabi tried once again to talk Evelyn into letting him try anything on those ginger curls of hers. Evelyn however was adamant and resolute that he wouldn't be allowed anywhere near those curls with his scissors or straighteners, I smiled to myself wondering if Evelyn's decision and thoughts on letting Fabi touch her hair would change soon?

Colette had been sitting in that hanging seat with Evelyn most of the afternoon talking, Colette spoke to her almost exclusively in French and though I wasn't really sure what they spoke about it seemed to mean a lot to them both. Maybe Colette had unlocked a hidden facet of my little sofa surfing friend? Evelyn either way had brought the normally very shy and reclusive Colette out of herself.

Truthfully, before she had met Evelyn she rarely seemed to speak very much, since they had met, she had spoken more in the last few weeks than she did in the previous year, not because she was rude or anything like that she just rarely spoke too much, Colette left Evelyn lounging in that swinging chair of hers with Francois talking to her.

Colette had taken me inside to speak to me inside about my photo shoots next week and asked how scared I was about them; I couldn't lie to her; I was petrified about it. Colette sweetly assured me, I would be fine and readjusted the straps on my top for me.

233

"Fae, your bosoms are certainly heavier than they look, but this is not a bad thing, if you were like me and Evelyn you would have different concerns with them," she smiled to me as she liked to see my figure look its best, even if she was better at maintaining it than I was. Colette though rare to really speak in any depth was often almost motherly to me and I really trusted her deeply as in truth I did Francois too, they had both been pretty good to me since I moved to Ljianstipol.

Just like Evelyn, Colette was keen to stress that the world wasn't going to see me as a cheap wannabe, though I still had my doubts about that, it did feel nice to hear it from another person. Colette openly confessed that she saw me as being very brave for doing what I was and that I should be deeply proud of myself and she actually shed a little tear when she confessed her admiration of me, it was a touching moment with the petite Parisian.

Once we headed back outside, we were greeted and shushed by Francois, his 'Petit Oiseau' had passed out on their swinging chair, Colette smiled sweetly at her sleeping friend.

"Did you bore her to sleep too?" Colette smiled at me as she began another of their nearly legendary arguments and all while their little friend slept right through it. Evelyn gently swayed in the breeze as the pair locked into another of their bickering arguments as their passions fell out of their mouths in the form of loving and affectionate insults, Evelyn would have been devastated if she knew, as she quite enjoyed their arguments.

While the afternoon slowly wound down and turned into a warm evening, we made our way home, Evelyn well rested having spent most of the day gently sleeping in the garden chair and me content with reassuring support from my group of friends ready for my last week at work before the moment I had been dreading would finally arrive. My deepest fears were allayed, when on Wednesday morning Evelyn changed into her sailor outfit ready for her walk with Tony, I breathed a sigh of relief as at least that market trader hadn't tainted her love for that outfit she loved so dearly.

I headed into town and down to the beach to collect Evelyn ready for her afternoon walk with Tony, knowing full well what him and Gale had planned for her, fortunately she seemed to have no idea why I had swapped my final day at work either. While they began their walk together, me and Gale mentally prepared ourselves for just how she might react, Evelyn was excitable at the best of times and today we fully expected an utter explosion of chaotic joy from her mouth and mind.

Tony had supplied Evelyn with his final beer that he was trying out for their walk today, as he handed her yet another new beer for her to try; she was still blissfully unaware that she was being set up. While they wandered away around the rooftop garden, Gale started to ask about what had happened with her in the marketplace during the steampunk bizarre.

News had spread fast about the diminutive redhead facing off to a towering 6 foot plus vendor that was far too keen to try and impose his will upon the plucky and very much self-confident Evelyn. Gale also mentioned that Jess had suffered a similar problem during the event though Jess was normally quite eager to encourage that kind of attention when her social media influence needed that sort of content.

Gale did however disclose that the steampunk bizarre had been an enormous success and would return next year, though maybe with a few tweaks, I didn't mind as aside from that moment for Evelyn, it was pretty fun. While Gale began to laugh at the mere thought of Evelyn standing willingly face to face with the looming and menacing vendor in the marketplace, our attentions turned as in the distance two figures appeared.

Walking hand in hand as always and both with almost empty bottles they wandered back laughing and giggling like little children having almost completed their walk. Evelyn was still completely unsuspecting as the pair joined us to share a final beer for the day in the glorious sunshine on the rooftop. Tony sat down and handed around a final bottle to each of us, Gale nodded at Tony, "You okay buddy?"

Tony sat back and smiled. "All good," and gently patted Evelyn on the back.

Tony offered Evelyn a bottle which with her usual sweet smile she took quite willingly. "Fae are you ready for the big photo shoot next week? We've given you the week after off too just in case you need it."

Tony smiled at me and winked as the plan started to be put into action. "You didn't need to do that, Tony, or you Gale?" I said acting surprised.

"We didn't need to give you Friday off either but we have," Gale interjected.

Tony shrugged his shoulders, "You are working for us by advertising for us and given what you are doing for the wider world; what difference does two weeks make?" I smiled as that part of the plan I didn't know about their thoughts on.

Tony smiled and raised his finger. "On a more serious note, though, you are coming to our party yes?"

I chuckled back at him, "Why would I miss that?" Tony handed me a little card, which Evelyn followed its full journey from Tony's pocket all the way to my hands, with her eyes perking a little as I opened the little card invitation. While I opened my card, she looked at Tony and Gale confused as to what was going on, Tony was rummaging around his pocket, making some odd faces as he failed to find something.

"Ah! There it is!" Tony pulled a little envelope from his pocket and handed it to Evelyn with her eyes widening as his card neared her little fingers.

"Open it!" Gale smiled at Evelyn, carefully and cautiously she prised the envelope open and pulled out a thick white and cream folded card. Evelyn's eyes flicked from side to side as she read the card when suddenly her face ignited and her eyes widened and the largest grin, I had ever seen smothered her face.

Evelyn jumped to her feet in a sheer fit of delight, excitement and bliss, "Yes! Yes! YES!" She erupted in a loud and high pitch squeal. "Thank you, Tony and Gale!" Evelyn ran to Gale and gave him a huge hug.

"It's my first ever party!" She almost yelled into Gale's ear before she headed for Tony and grabbed him so hard, I heard a crack. "And it's with my best friends!" She yelled again with her eyes starting to well up. While me and Gale looked at each other wondering if maybe we should have worn earplugs, she gripped Tony harder. "Thank you so much," she was so excited and happy.

Evelyn eventually let go of Tony and sat sipping her beer in silence smiling to herself without removing her glowing eyes from the words on that little card. Casually, we finished our drinks and began to get ready for the no doubt very fast paced walk home, Evelyn hugged them both once again, Tony's ribs took another pounding from her vice-like grip.

We turned to leave and Gale called out, "Have a good time off little star and see you on Wednesday?"

I nodded back at him, "Yeah, don't worry about making us look bad, we're pretty good at doing that ourselves so you don't need to worry!"

Tony laughed as we headed away.

Together me and the fully delighted Evelyn began to make our way through the hallways of the Davizioso and began our journey homewards, she couldn't mask her delight as she waved that card at every single person, we passed on our way home. Skipping home in her sailor suit with that card flashing it up and round all the way home, she ran at Fabi to show him while he packed away for the day.

"Look Fabi! They invited me to their party! I've never been invited to a party before." Evelyn was speaking so frantically and chaotically that Fabi had to pause before he fully ingested what she was saying, as she waved her card at him.

Fabi leant down and took a look at her little card. "You lucky girl! They don't invite just anyone to that party you know! Do you and Fae get to go together?"

Fabi smiled as he spoke to the more than hyperactive girl. Evelyn paused and looked at me. "We both get to go don't we?" She squealed in excitement, I walked to join her and Fabi. "Yes, we both get to go!"

Fabi smiled at me. "What are you both going to wear for it?" He asked both of us.

Suddenly, Evelyn stopped almost on the spot, her face dropping as she thought, *Fae! What am I going to wear? I've never been to a party before let alone a special one! I can't go like this, can I? Can I?* Evelyn was expelling her thoughts so frantically with barely enough time for her to even breathe between them.

Pausing to think for a moment. "What about this?" I pointed at her sailor suit.

"I can't wear this to a special party, Fae!" She said back, sounding concerned.

Fabi walked up to the now slightly subdued Evelyn and gently rested his hand on her back, "Go how you feel comfortable, they want to see you there not some fancy-dress Evelyn," he was so kind as he spoke to her. "I know but it's an important party for them and I need to respect them both in person and in dress for it."

Slightly saddened Evelyn replied, Fabi nodded at her in agreement with her thoughts, "What about Francois? He might be able to help?"

Evelyn and I both looked at him in shock, "That funny Frenchman?" She sounded confused.

"He's strange but he is a wizard with clothes, why not give him a go?" Fabi replied to a quite shocked Evelyn.

Evelyn looked round at me. "What do you think Fae?" She asked and gave me those puppy dog eyes that she was so masterful with "Couldn't hurt to try him, he sorted me out before, he is eccentric at best but he is good at what he does," I replied to her and tried to reason with her.

Heading home she gradually began to calm down from her previously quite chaotic and nervous state, sitting on the sofa she let out a huge sigh. "I know it seems silly Fae, but I've never been to a party before and they have been so good to me and you Fae that dressing correctly seems the least I can do to acknowledge their generosity," Evelyn spoke looking at the floor with her shoulders slumped forwards and twiddling her thumbs.

Looking over at her to see Evelyn looking so downtrodden by the thought that she would mortally insult her new friends at their special invitation only party. "Have you really never been to a party before?" Sceptically and almost in disbelief as I asked her.

She looked across at me sadly and just shook her head. "Not one single party, my prom at high school but that didn't end well," she sighed back.

I moved down the sofa and sat next to her and put my arm around her, "Then let's make your first party the only one you will ever need to go too and one that you will never forget," I pulled her tight against me and started to wait for her to perk back up.

Calming down we started to chat about Francois, and I told her how good he was with clothes though I knew nothing would prepare her mentally for when he was working. Soon enough she drifted off as always having lost another battle to stay awake as long as she could, while I sat thinking about her shunning a cosy bed for my sofa.

My mind couldn't help but feel a deep sorrow for my little friend, was this really her first party? I often found myself thinking about how hyperactive she was and how excited she became over things that just for most were kinda normal? While I took her shoes and socks off for her and folded her up on the sofa to rest it dawned upon me that maybe she was so hyperactive as it sounded like she had barely had any kind of childhood at all?

Starting to wander upstairs I looked over at her one last time and was hit with the same enormous sense of guilt that I felt the final time that I attempted to get her to sleep in a bed. Stopping and feeling my sorrow for her it was obvious that tonight as much as my back needed a proper bed, I couldn't leave her alone, slowly I found myself settling down just behind her and pulling her tight against me.

While she snoozed away blissfully unaware, I wrapped my arms around her and held her gently but firmly against me as I drifted to sleep beside her. Morning soon arrived and unlike normal she was up and waiting for me, already dressed with her green outfit on and sitting next to me with her feet resting on the cushion and her chin pressed to her knees smiling at me.

"Good morning, Fae!" She said sweetly and excitedly as I got a whiff of my coffee sitting on the table, ready and waiting for me to awaken.

"Morning Evelyn," I chuckled back at her eagerness. Evelyn rolled onto her knees and gave me a hug.

"Thank you for staying with me last night," she whispered gently into my ear.

I held her just a little bit tighter, "You're welcome, did you sleep well?" I whispered back.

She tilted her head just a little bit, "Better than ever! How did you sleep?"

I smiled at her, "Really well, though I keep finding red hairs in my mouth."

Evelyn let out a little laugh and fluffed her hair up. Sitting beside her having gone to get changed we drank our coffees as she put her trainers on ready to go. "Ready, Evelyn?" I called to her as I finished my coffee.

"It's going to be a great day, Fae!" She beamed and led me to the front door.

"First stop, Fabi?" I asked her as we started to wander through the morning sunshine. "Sounds good to me," she declared as once again I questioned if those reins might be a good investment.

"Good morning you two, usual for you both? Marshmallows today, Evelyn?" Fabi called to us as she almost dragged me to his shop. Fabi had started to keep jumbo marshmallows just for Evelyn, 3 of them just about fitted inside of his cups, he bored a hole in them and filled it with a rich mocha, creating a strange sugary coffee mess but she loved them.

"So, are you going to see Francois?" Fabi asked us.

"Yes, I am taking her to see him and get her something nice for the party," I replied as Evelyn waved her invitation card at him which she had been proudly carrying ever since it had landed in her hands. Fabi smiled at the quite happy and excited Evelyn before he reached inside his pocket and pulled out a little folded card and handed it to her, "Can you give that to Francois for me Evelyn?" He asked kindly.

Evelyn looked at him and gently took the card.

"Of course! What is it?" She replied and started to study the fold along the card.

"It's a secret, don't look or you will spoil it!" Fabi said to her and winked at her.

"You better not be setting her up, Fabi!" I felt slightly defensive, but I knew what was going on as he looked at me and laughed.

"I would never do that to Evelyn, I might do it to you but not Evelyn!" Fabi smiled and winked at her again. With the trap now set, we headed off to see Francois, "See you both later when you look fabulous!" Fabi called as we started to walk into the depths of town and towards Francois boutique in the marketplace.

We crossed the bridge and started to wander along the river with Evelyn still studying that folded card in suspicion of what it might contain, just ahead of us was the looming figure of Alyssia. Surprised to see her, I called to her, "Morning Alyssia, you are late this morning?"

Alyssia turned and gestured with her hands in the air. "That idiot was up late and I barely slept, I've woken up late but they can wait another 10 minutes for their paintings!" Her deep British accent carried the sincerity of her thoughts! Alyssia walked alongside Evelyn, "Morning Evelyn, how are you?"

Evelyn smiled at her, "Good thanks," she handed Alyssia her invitation that Tony and Gale had given her, "Well look at you! Getting invited to the most important party in town! Are you going to Francois?" Alyssia probed and Evelyn just nodded back.

"Yes, but I'm nervous as he is kinda crazy."

Alyssia laughed back at her, "He is definitely unusual but Francois will fix you up, right Fae?"

Evelyn's focus turned to me. "He sorted me out before," I assured her. "Could you do me a favour, Evelyn? Can you give him this for me?" Alyssia handed her a little envelope, Evelyn looked at it carefully, "Sure? Of course, I can," she shrugged.

"You little diamond! I will see you later when you look beautiful and ready for your party!" Alyssia began to march off to open the gallery that she should have opened 30 minutes ago and now the trap was fully set.

Entering the old part of town with its soft cobbles and just at the end of our journey, leaning up against the wall of his boutique stood Francois. With his shirt half open and a loose tie hanging down, looking as moody as ever with a cigarette in his hand. "Bonjour, Fae!" Francois called as he caught us in his gaze.

"Bonjour Francois!" I called back to him, "Ah the lovely Evelyn! How is my little red-haired friend today?" She smiled at him.

"Good, how are you?" He paused and leant back against his wall and studied his fingernails. "Well, I'm disappointed you didn't come and talk with me like you do every morning but today is good now as I get to see both of your lovely smiles," I blushed a little as he spoke, he certainly could charm!

"So, what brings you both to me today?" He wryly smiled.

"Show him, Evelyn," I pointed at her as she handed Francois her invitation card.

"Oh, my Evelyn, this is a very special party and you are lucky to have been invited!" Evelyn smiled at him as he spoke to her.

"Evelyn needs a dress, it's her first party and she wants it to be special for her and for Tony and Gale," I answered for her, slightly nervous about what his reply might be.

Francois threw his cigarette to the ground and stamped on it, "Surely this cannot be your first party, Evelyn," he seemed quite shocked as he spoke to her.

Shyly Evelyn stood before replying sadly. "Nobody invited me when I was little, I mean, younger, I've always been little," and looking at the floor. Francois paused for a moment.

"They don't know what they have missed Evelyn, so we will have to show them what they have missed!" Francois stood in front of his doorway and waved her into his shop, "Come, Come!" He ushered her through his door into a fantasia of clothes, linens and terrifyingly priced lingerie before Evelyn paused.

"Oh, I nearly forgot," she passed him the two notes that she had for him. Francois studied Fabi's note, carefully opening it and reading it before he shoved it into his pocket and then did the same with Alyssia's note before shoving that into his pocket along with Fabi's.

Francois stood studying Evelyn before he asked her to walk up and down the shop, waving her towards him and ushering her back before getting her to walk again. Standing transfixed upon her as she walked around his little shop, waving his arm to get her to walk and turn just as he needed so that he could see just how her shape and body moved.

Pacing the floor, Francois began to talk to himself, Evelyn looked at me and shrugged her shoulders, I just did the same back to her, he was certainly different in the way he approached things.

Suddenly, Francois stopped dead in his tracks. "Evelyn, you have such a subtle and curved shape, I am trying to work out how to show you off without losing your beautiful figure," he explained himself to her.

Francois pulled out a little tape and started to work his way around her and measuring different parts of her, noting his measurements down on a scrap of paper and measuring her again. He started to pull out little bits of fabric and started to make a little template for her.

"Fae, could you turn the sign around on the door for me and close the blinds?" Francois asked as he removed his glasses from his pocket. "Maybe you could lock the door too for me?" He requested. Evelyn seemed a little nervous.

"I need to give you my full attention Evelyn, I don't want anyone interrupting us, just relax as much as you can, there is a coffee pot and some marshmallows for you in the back of the shop if you want to refill your cup."

This wasn't the Francois that I was accustomed too? Evelyn sat on a little chair in the corner of his shop as Francois assembled his template periodically, he looked up at her over his glasses, smiled at her and began to hum something to himself?

Evelyn looked at me as I wandered his shop admiring some of his garments adorning the walls, I found the same bras he had given me when I first moved to Ljianstipol, I was glad it was a gift as there was no way on earth, I could have afforded one! Francois stood up still humming to himself as he walked towards Evelyn, she stood up in response to him walking over and he offered up his template and pressed it against her.

"Beau cygne blanc," he said and smiled before taking it back with him. Resuming humming to himself as we sat bemused by him, Francois had started to assemble a little garment to check against her and started walking back to Evelyn. "I need you to take off your top, Evelyn, don't worry I'm sure it will not surprise you that a man as charming as I am, has seen many breasts before, so you don't need to be afraid," he softly asked her.

Evelyn looked over at me before she obliged and removed her green top for him exposing her little body and bra, as she looked up at him, "Frappant, frappant, petites mains, beau," Francois smiled back at her and pulled his template over her.

Waving his hands at her, Evelyn stood up and walked a little, up and down, backwards and forwards and finally back towards him, "Vole, vole, petit oiseau," he smiled at her again.

Frantically he started to pull down the fabrics that he had chosen for her garment before he turned around, "Could you come back this afternoon? I need time to get this right for Evelyn," Francois asked us both. We looked at each other. "Sure, is 3 okay?"

I responded to his question, "3 will be fine," he replied and as we headed off out of his shop he shut and locked the door behind us. Evelyn looked at me breathing a sigh of relief, "He is nuts!" She laughed.

I joined her laughing. "That is him being calm too!" We started to walk towards the river, "Lunch Fae?" Evelyn asked as we started to wander down the river towards the main town, "Sounds good to me."

We headed across the bridge with its locks and back into the heart of the main town and towards a little bar she had become fond of. We sat together and had a nice lunch before we headed to one of the bars by the river for a quiet drink watching the waters gently flow by. My curiosity peaked. "What was he saying to you, Evelyn?" I asked hoping she knew.

"I'm not sure in truth, I don't know all the words but it sounded happy?" She smiled back sweetly; Francois certainly could charm people I thought as Evelyn smiled softly. Having finished our drinks and relaxed by the river we started to make our way back to Francois and his boutique.

"What do you think he is going to make for you Evelyn?" I asked hoping to gain an insight, she thought deeply, *If it's as pretty as his songs then I don't really mind*, that sweet smile was back as she responded.

I tapped on Francois' door; he slowly opened it just enough to peer out of the crack. "Ah you have returned and just in time too!" He opened the door and let us both in before shutting it and locking it again. Francois smiled at Evelyn, humming again, "Come, come!" He waved her towards him, "Fae, I need you and Evelyn to trust me? Okay?"

I looked at him slightly surprised by his request as Evelyn replied, "I trust you Francois."

Carefully he sat her down and started to remove her shoes and socks, gently placing them on a nearby table, "You certainly have eclectic tastes, petit oiseau," he smiled at her as he placed her shoes down and turned back around.

He removed her little trousers, exposing her legs and lacy underwear, "No, no! This will not do Evelyn!" He said as he handed her a little bag with some underwear inside, he shrouded her with a huge piece of fabric and looked over at me while she changed for him. When she was ready, he placed the big piece of fabric over a large mirror in front of her, he took her top off for her and gently placed them on the table along with her other clothes.

Francois asked her to turn around, "You trust me yes?"

She nodded and stood facing the shrouded mirror. "Frappent, frappent, petite mains, beau," he spoke softly and calmly as he took her bra off for her. Francois looked over at me and raised his finger to tell me to stay calm as he folded her bra and gently laid it on the table with her other clothes.

While Evelyn stood waiting, he collected a bag from behind the table and walked back over towards her, when there was a knock at the door. "Fae could you?" He asked me.

I opened the door just enough to see outside. "Alyssia is here, Francois?" I called over to him to see if it was okay for her to come in.

"Ah the wonderful Alyssia, she can come in but lock the door behind her!" He called back across at me, without hesitation I let her in but locked the door again.

Francois started to remove something from the bag, he placed his hand on Evelyn's shoulder. "Close your eyes for me and do not open them, until I say it is okay? Yes?"

She nodded for him. "Alors qu'elle se tenait fierement au soleil," he spoke softly as he lifted the garment up and over her little arms pulling it down. "Elle a realise que meme un cygne petit," he pulled it down over her body as he continued to speak, "peut devenir un beau cygne blanc," he proudly said as he stood back and tweaked the dress.

"What are you saying to her Francois?" Alyssia asked in her strongest accent, he turned around stunned. "3 beautiful women and yet none of you speak the language of love and romance?" He replied as he unveiled the mirror.

Francois returned to Evelyn, placing his hands over her eyes. "As she stood proudly in the sun, she realised that even an ugly duckling can become a beautiful white swan," he spoke softly as he uncovered her eyes and revealed to Evelyn the dress.

Evelyn started to cry as she saw the long flowing purple dress that he had made her, she turned around and gave him a soft hug, Francois gently smiled at her, "Vole, vole, petit oiseau!" She smiled.

"Fly, fly, little bird," he smiled happily at her. Francois began to talk her through the dress.

"Come, come, walk to me," as she walked to him, the dress flowed and followed her curves perfectly. "Look, the straps mean that you don't have to wear one of those things but they will keep you supported and secure," as she walked away from us the dress ran deep down exposing all of her back from her shoulders down to just above her bum with an adjustable belt to keep everything together.

Francois asked her to stand in front of him and he knelt back down and finished it off with a pair of handmade white sandals. "Promise me you won't wear the trainers with this, okay?" He smiled at her as he did the straps on the sandals up for her. "Francois, you have really outdone yourself on this!"

Alyssia was stunned, he shrugged his shoulders at her, "It's her first party, let's make it special!" Evelyn carefully removed the dress and Francois shielded her so that she could dress herself before he gently placed it inside a bag for her. Francois gave her one last hug before he handed over two large bags and two smaller ones. "Payer en avant petit oiseau."

Evelyn smiled and hugged him back, "Un jour," she whispered back to him.

Francois guided us back outside and resumed his usual stance against his wall and lit a cigarette, "I will see you in the morning petit oiseau?"

Evelyn nodded back at him, "I will have your marshmallows ready for you!"

Alyssia smiled at her as we walked away, "You have broken him?"

Evelyn looked at her and chuckled, "No he is still a strange Frenchman but he does make me laugh when he says things to the badly dressed as they walk by," I laughed at her.

"That razor sharp tongue of his!" Evelyn smiled as we headed along the river. While we headed home for the evening, I started thinking about how kind Francois and Colette had been to me since I moved to Ljianstipol, to see them openly pass that along to my best friend made their actions feel even sweeter and kinder.

Evelyn woke in a state of utter bliss the next morning, guiding me upstairs so that she could show me that beautiful purple dress as she pretended to dance with herself. Pressing it against herself and twirling round with herself as she laughed and smiled with each turn and twirl, she gave, it was the happiest I had seen that blissful girl.

Her dress of course wasn't the only reason that Evelyn was so excited, she had been invited to the biggest and best party in town, but not merely invited, she was a VIP too! Francois had made her a dress so stunningly beautiful but she still needed to go back and see him for some reason? Suspicious and curious as to why but as he had marshmallows for her, she didn't mind as she wanted to go and see what he had for her and to listen to him insult people.

Tonight, also Fabi and Alyssia would be coming over for the evening and staying, Evelyn was excited by that too but her biggest cause for excitement? After my meeting with Gale today I had the next two weeks off work, all morning she beamed about what we would get up to in my time off, she was also excited about the first part of the photo shoot.

Evelyn was the sole reason that I hadn't cancelled the whole thing after it caused the breakdown which had brought the strange girl into my life and onto my sofa.

When I was ready to give up, she stepped in, "You need to let the world see you Fae and they will see how incredible you are!"

Though I wasn't fully sure if she was right, she did at least encourage me to go through with it, despite my big fear that I would be seen as a hopeless wannabe model and not a girl trying to make a difference. Evelyn wore her sailor outfit and talked to me the whole time as we got ready to walk down town where I would meet with Gale and she would head to the marketplace.

Morning sun bathed us as we walked into town and our first stop at Fabi's to get our morning coffee and the air was soothing and wonderful, it felt good to be walking today even with Evelyn in full hyperdrive. Fabi was ready and waiting for us.

"Morning you two, how are we today?" He said as he placed our cups on his counter and leant over to look at Evelyn, "Hey come and see me after you have finished with Francois? We can get ready to take Fae for our afternoon in the park?"

Evelyn smiled back, "Sounds good to me, Fabi!"

With coffee in hand, we headed off, I saw Fabi wink at me? Like he was signalling that he had a surprise for me, though I wasn't sure what that could be? We wandered by the river and I had a few minutes to spare before I met with Gale so I walked Evelyn to the waiting Francois. "Good morning my two wonders of nature, how are we this morning?"

He seemed off key this morning? Not one insult? "Good Francois, how are you?"

He smiled, "My petit oiseau has come for my morning chat so I am well, of course I get to see you too, Fae!" My mind wondered about him sometimes, normally by now he had found at least one snipe to throw my way? As I headed to see Gale, Francois sat on the little patch of grass in front of his shop proudly telling Evelyn about the disasters he had seen this morning. I could hear Evelyn chuckling as he repeated to her what he had ejected from his mouth this morning as I walked out of the marketplace and towards the Davizioso.

Tony and Gale had texted me late yesterday as they needed help to prepare a room for a new resident that would be arriving while I was away, after they had willingly given me time off for the photoshoots, I was only too happy to help. Our new resident had been recently thrown out by his long-term partner after they couldn't cope with him or them in this case.

He had a personality disorder, 27 of them in truth, the dominant ones were quite arty and crafty so we planned to prepare a room for them to be like an art studio. With my absence over the next two weeks, we were going to get as much done today as possible to make the space ready for the new and intriguing resident. When Tony and Gale had first told me about him, I had my apprehensions, I had never dealt with someone so complex as of yet but in truth I was quite looking forward to meeting him or them?

The apartment was like a studio adorned with crafting and art materials and a couple of cameras so that he could film his work. Tony looked at his watch, "Whoa we have made you late Fae, go on get going! And have a great couple of weeks!"

Gale smiled at me. "We will see you on Wednesday anyway right?" I nodded and started to leave.

"Hey Fae, we are both proud of you for doing this!" They both said as I went to leave.

"Thanks guys, I couldn't have done it without you!"

Gale smirked, "Yeah, you could have, you just needed a supporting hand." Both waved me off as I rushed out of the Davizioso and headed to meet Evelyn outside.

As I headed out of the doorway of the Davizioso there stood Alyssia and Francois? "Hey, what are you guys doing here?" I questioned them.

"Fabi and Evelyn have gone on ahead with Colette, we have come to collect you and walk to the park with you, there's a band playing on the gazebo today too," Alyssia spoke for them both, she was one lady who Francois didn't insult! Together we walked up and through the town and towards a park just outside of town, the same park they had taken me to after my crash at Alyssia's.

With the sun basking the world in all its glory, it was so warm as we headed into the park, you could feel the heat emanating from the ground as we walked to the main plaza with music playing in the distance.

Ljianstipol and its park often attracted bands from all over the place to come play pop-up gigs, some of the biggest bands would turn up and play gigs to a handful of local residents. Walking through we headed to an opening on the grass just below the welcoming shade of some trees with Colette sitting waiting on a blanket for us.

"Where's Fabi and Evelyn?" I quizzed.

"They have gone to get us some drinks they will be back soon," Colette softly replied. Soon enough, Fabi walked round a corner with Evelyn following close behind but almost as if she was being shrouded by Fabi? As they drew closer Colette covered my eyes.

"Ready?" Colette asked in her soft French tone, I nodded and she removed her hands and before me stood Evelyn in her little sailor outfit, but her hair wasn't exploding all over the place. Evelyn's normal mass of ginger curls had been straightened and neatly plaited into a single braid which ran from the front of her hair all the way to the back. Nervously, Evelyn stood with that sweet smile of hers, I stood up and gave my little friend a big hug.

"Oh, you look so beautiful!" She smiled and hugged me back, "You like it?" She said looking up pensively.

"I love it!" Evelyn held me again.

Fabi smiled to himself. "Evelyn finally let me have a go at those curls! It's only a trial run and will only last a couple of days but doesn't she look great!" I looked over at Fabi, understanding what the little wink was for.

"Francois has made me some more clothes too," Evelyn smiled at me as Francois looked over. "Payer en avant Fae!"

Evelyn stood looking so proud of herself, "You have broken that Parisian Evelyn!"

I laughed with her, "She is more charming than you, Fae!" Francois smiled and laughed at me, there was the Francois that I knew! We spent the entire afternoon and evening in that park and we got lots of pictures of the new and improved Evelyn with her two newest fans, Francois and Alyssia.

Easily two of the most intimidating people that I had met had been broken by that girl and her curls. They loved her and adored her; they respected her but most importantly they had made her feel like part of a family in Ljianstipol.

While our group slowly began to disperse, we headed back to mine for the evening, Francois and Colette headed back to theirs for the night while Fabi and Alyssia came with me and Evelyn. Together we spent the remainder of the evening talking and enjoying ourselves, soon enough Evelyn began to drift to sleep, her legs dangling off the end of the sofa as they always did.

Without even thinking about it I took off her shoes and socks while still talking to Fabi and Alyssia as they both watched me with their mouths open in either disbelief or shock at what I was doing. Continuing my routine, I gently lifted and folded her legs onto the sofa next to me before gently moving her down and resting her head on my lap as Evelyn began to cling onto me. Alyssia was watching almost with that look Evelyn could do.

"That's so sweet! She must really trust you, Fae!" as Evelyn folded herself up like a cat next to me.

"Did you need help getting her to bed Fae?" Fabi asked, I sighed. "No this is where she sleeps, she won't sleep in a bed for some reason?" Alyssia and Fabi both smiled as they headed up to my spare room to sleep for the night.

Evelyn laid there dreaming away happily as I laid down beside her and wrapped her in my arms and whispered to her, "You have some fantastic friends now Evelyn, and they love you just like I do, sleep well my little friend." She pulled herself tighter and let out a sweet whimper.

Alyssia woke me up in the morning as she stood over us admiring the sweetest thing she had ever seen, with Evelyn nestled into my arms on the sofa still fast asleep. Fabi started to walk down the stairs and Alyssia shushed him as he carefully crept down the stairs before getting me a cup of coffee and sitting with Alyssia opposite watching us both and waiting for Evelyn to stir.

Suddenly, her green eyes appeared with a sweet smile as she took in the sight of Fabi and Alyssia before tilting her head back and smiled at me.

"Morning, Fae, did you sleep well?" She held me tighter.

"Morning Fabi and Alyssia did you sleep well?" Alyssia popped a coffee down in front of her and gently stroked her little nose. "Aren't you just the sweetest thing!"

Evelyn smiled and rose to give her a hug before she sat upright. Fabi looked at her, "What are you doing with the next two weeks, Evelyn?" She paused.

"Spending it with my best friend," she gave Fabi a hug before they left.

Chapter 7
The Bipolar Coaster

That night, I barely slept as I laid there thinking about the interview for the article, while Evelyn dreamt the way she did every night, I sat dwelling on my own fears. Periodically I would get some brief respite and get a few hours of desperately needed sleep, my mind and heart pounded all night long. All I could feel was the total and utter terror of what I had really undertaken and what I was about to put myself through today.

Deep down, I questioned whether I really was the right person to be standing before the world to try and show what life is liking living with conditions like mine. Every now and then Evelyn would whimper before she eased back and fell deeper into her dreamworlds, my little friend believed in me, even if I didn't believe in myself, she certainly did. Watching her softly breathe in and out, I started to think about the stories she had been revealing to me about her strange world she claimed to have come from.

That dark, concussive and fear inducing forest that she had made her home, truthfully, I couldn't really imagine her choosing to live somewhere like that? For the most part it sounded horrible, during the day it would be so gloomy that I could readily imagine it slowly destroying the soul of anyone. Evelyn however had learned to endure its constrictive ways to see the glory of that place in the moonlight. Maybe I just needed to be more like Evelyn and overlook the very things that I found terrifying to see some kind of light on the other side of it?

More than a few times I had imagined what Evelyn would have been like in that dark and dangerous place which she proudly called home. More often than not I imagined her walking cautiously through a never-ending maze of old beaten trees with little or no light to guide her. Eternally fearful and on edge as she tried to make some vague form of existence for herself in that unforgiving and vicious place.

Evelyn however whenever she spoke of the place did so with a deep and often loving smile on her face? Evelyn's early days in that forest had indeed been very similar to what I imagined but at some point, she had figured something out about that place and her living amongst it.

Merely four feet eight in height and diminutively petite, she had realised that the very things that had made her a target for most of her life, in that place those things made her stronger? Trees and their branches were brittle and often frail but with so little weight to her it meant that she could utilise them to stay clear of any threats on the ground with almost complete impunity from harm.

Having spent many of her early days in the forest living at night she had become very adept to living in the forest in total darkness which she used to her advantage too. Evelyn's lack of height and weight also meant that she could make a tree her home and reside there in comfort and safety.

Truthfully, I had often wondered about the tree she spoke about having made her home? Deep down I just wasn't sure if she could really have found anything like what she described though truthfully, I also didn't care too much.

Whether other people believed her or not, Evelyn, that strange and now almost eternally loved girl, was far stronger than anyone I had come to know. Maybe to do this whole article and interview I just needed to be more like this girl who had taken up residency on my sofa?

When the sun began to slowly encroach upon my living room it dawned upon me just how long I had been awake, while Evelyn dreamt away, I had sat mulling over the day ahead. Daily, I found myself wondering what she dreamt of as she looked so blissful and serene as she slept. Maybe her forest or the mountains she loved so much? Maybe the strange people she had slowly introduced me to from this odd world of hers? Just maybe this was the only place where she remembered her parents?

Hoping for her that her dreams were the place where her daddy flew her round the garden like a little fairy and her mother read her stories before sleepy time. Imagine being unable to remember people you loved so dearly and that had been taken away while you were so young?

Sometimes seeing her dream made me hope that she was with them and for those brief moments she got to feel what she had so sorely missed growing up. Indeed, if her blissful smile was rooted in that kind of dream then I would willingly sit and watch her rest every night just to see that look on her face as her curls rolled around under the power of her breaths.

Today however I was going to be like Evelyn, I was going to face my terrors and fear and make this interview count for everyone, that is what I was telling myself now I just needed to hope that my mind would take notice of me!

Carefully, I got myself out of her grasp to go and make myself a coffee, standing and looking at my little friend while it brewed before I went and rejoined her on the sofa. Blissfully unaware that I had even moved she scooted up the sofa and laid on my lap, letting out a little soft noise as she bedded herself back down.

Sometimes these mornings were like a strange and heart-warming start to the day, maybe these were part of the reasons my conditions had largely calmed down? Sipping away I started to think about what I was going to wear for the shoot, my work uniform was of course on that list but what about the other outfits they had asked me to take? They wanted to get some studio shots of me in my normal clothes, that Colette top and skirt was an obvious choice, Colette after all had readjusted the straps for me again yesterday afternoon when we had been at their place? Colette did make me chuckle though.

"Fae, your bosoms seem to be heavier than they look, though don't worry about that, if you had bosoms like me and Evelyn, you would have bigger concerns." Ever sweet, Colette made sure my top showed off my figure which both her and Francois adored so much, Colette from time to time was almost motherly to me? Colette and Evelyn however were something totally different to that, Colette adored her, from the moment she met Evelyn she had made every effort to look after her, 'Little Dove', it was sweet, though sometimes I felt a hint of jealousy over it, it was so damn cute!

While I pondered, a little voice spoke.

"What about the white dress?" Evelyn mumbled, I looked to see if she had actually been awake or had she just told me that in her sleep? Her eyes were still closed and she hadn't budged, if anything she was actually more supple than before? Even in her sleep she gave good advice, though I knew she would like it, as for her it was Karl's favourite dress as it showed my curvy bum off for him.

"Thanks for that, Evelyn!" I said to her as I giggled to myself about how much she would grin when I put that dress on.

While my coffee began to go down, I found myself thinking about my little friend, more specifically about her laying on a log in that dark forest. She had often told me about little places she liked to go and sit in the forest, a few stumps by little pools in the depths of the forest. Tree branches through which she could see the moon and stars at night along with the mountains which she loved so much in the far distance.

Somewhere near her home she had found a long-fallen tree trunk, half buried in the dirt, she laid on it during the evenings and it is where she found the flowers she had planted in my garden. During the week the first one had come out and true to her word, they were beautiful, little orange and white flowers, she picked the first one and put it in my hair.

Smiling sweetly as she tucked the little flower into my hair. "Like a little princess," she smiled making no attempt to mask her excitement at seeing the first of these flowers rehomed in my locks.

Wondering and daydreaming about her laid on her belly on that log, I wonder if she got any visitors? Did she give them that sweet puppy looks like she threw me and Colette's way from time to time? That same look that guys had hoped for from her when we went out in the evenings? Imagining her in that forest offering one of her flowers to passing strangers with that deeply sweet look on her face; I couldn't imagine man or beast refusing to take that flower from her. Suddenly, my dreaming was halted by yawning and Evelyn stretching herself out like a cat before those little eyes opened and her smile ignited upon her face.

Ethereal green eyes soon opened and the almost fixed smile she wore appeared as the new day began for Evelyn, "Good morning, Fae! I had a dream you couldn't decide what to wear today," she smiled at me as she wrapped her arms round me to give me my morning hug. Holding her and hugging her in return.

"Morning Evelyn, did I pick the white dress?" I smiled at her knowing what her answer would be but much to my surprise she didn't say anything, though that grin did appear on her face.

"Did Karl like it?" I asked her as she started to giggle at me with that ever sweet smile.

Sitting looking at me she paused and smiled softly, "Did you manage to get any sleep Fae?" Her eyes analysing me and my empty cup, "Not much, but some."

She placed her hand on my trembling hand, "You will be fine Fae," she leant against me and held me. "You are great Fae and everyone will love you," she whispered to me as she clung on to me knowing I was scared about today.

Evelyn topped my coffee up for me and sat back down with me holding my hand, softly smiling to me and rubbing the palm of my hand to calm my nerves.

Sitting in silence she kept a calming eye on me as she pulled me over and we switched roles as I laid with my head in her lap, holding her.

Playing with my hair as I laid shaking with fear, she whispered to me as I laid in her lap, reassuring me while we waited for noon to arrive. Placing her hand on my shaved hair. "We have nearly five hours if you want to get some sleep, Fae; don't worry I will be right here with you," she stroked my hair to soothe me. Slowly, I began to drift away as she soothed me, she knew I was terrified about today and she knew some sleep would help me too.

Evelyn woke me a few hours later having sat with me in her lap and soothing me to try and help me get some rest and to calm my nerves. Waking to her sweet smile and that look she did every so often, I felt better about things and calmer as she got me another coffee. While I sat and sipped away, she had gone to prepare something for me to further soothe my nerves.

Slowly she took my hand and led me to my bathroom and opened the door, having run me a bubbly bath to help further ease my mind. Leaving me to relax and calm my nerves, "We have over two hours Fae, so take your time."

As she began to walk away, I called her back, "Thank you Evelyn, stay and chat with me? Please?" She smiled at me.

"Okay, how are you feeling now Fae?" She sat on the toilet to keep me company. Sitting there proudly in her little green outfit, she knew I was scared when she came over and knelt down and began to wash my hair for me. Pouring shampoo into my hair and massaging it into my scalp.

"You will be fine Fae, I'm going to be right there with you too, you have nothing to worry about," she kept talking to me as she washed my hair for me. While her little fingers massaged my scalp, it dawned upon me how I could never be like this girl, this magical little friend who had come into my life and changed it so dramatically.

When I had been ready to quit multiple times since she had appeared just over a month ago, every time she had picked me back up and stopped me picking up the phone to cancel the whole interview and article. Somehow, she was making me realise just how important it would be for me to go through with it, even though just like this morning it was taking a heavy toll on me.

As the water rinsed the last suds out of my hair, her calming and soothing affections had eased my nerves, my hands were stable and my mind was easing back. Evelyn took her seat back on the toilet while I finished my bath, she stood waiting with a towel open ready for me to be cloaked in its soft fabric. Standing on the toilet so that she could wrap it over my shoulders, as I turned round, she held my cheeks and looked into my eyes.

"You will be great Fae," her words soaking into the very fabric of my mind, I grabbed her and picked her up spinning round with her, my head rested against hers, "Thank you," I said over and over as I spun this little hero round my bathroom floor.

Carrying her with me into my room so that I could get changed and ready for the impending photo shoot which has caused me so much mental anguish. Gently I placed her on the foot of my bed as I started to get the clothes ready, I was going to take with me.

Packing a little bag to take with us with my workwear and two personal outfits in, she headed towards me with the dress she had found me on our first shopping adventure together. Smiling at me as I took the dress in my hand, "You are beautiful Fae, everyone is going to love you," she said, a little tear was forming in the corner of my eye as her supporting words sunk in.

While I stood transfixed with that blue flowery dress in hand, Evelyn had walked over and wiped my tears away, resting her hand on my cheek again and just smiling as I looked back at her. While I stood, "Come on, let's get you ready," she smiled as I started to put the dress on, I bent down so that she could put the halter round my neck.

Standing back up she smiled sweetly again, "Beautiful Fae," I held her hand and together we headed downstairs to get ready to head to the studio.

Putting my shoes on, Evelyn gave me one last piece of encouragement as she took my hands one last time. "You will be great, Fae, I believe in you," she smiled as her encouragement took hold.

Rising up still holding her hands, "Thank you Evelyn, at least you believe in me, even if I don't!" I smiled back at her. Time was approaching as I took my bag and we started to make our way to the studio on the industrial estate in Ljianstipol's outskirts.

Ljianstipol's industrial estate was slightly unusual as it was set inside a former airbase, when the old regime collapsed the former base was abandoned and soon became home to some of the expanding businesses in town. Lumber yards, factories and car lots filled most of the base along with the printing press for the local newspaper and magazine, the hospital was also on the old base along with the studio inside one of the former hangars for the airbase.

Jared and Karl had invested wisely to acquire the hangar at a cheap price, though were rather surprised to discover their new business enterprise came with an unexpected gift. When the pair arrived to start converting the base into their studio, they didn't expect it to come complete with a helicopter which had been left in the hangar.

Unwillingly, the pair now found themselves the quite surprised owners of a Hind attack helicopter that had been abandoned along with the hangar. They contacted the seller of the hangar who said, "We did suggest you come and look at the asset," they contacted museums to see if they might take the helicopter as a display exhibit.

Museums would have taken it but under the proviso that the pair could get it to the museums, how exactly do you transport something like that across the country to another museum without flying it there? Eventually, the pair decided to just park it out the front of their studio, thanks to a few local farmers they managed to tow the Hind to a spot at the front of the studio, where it now proudly sits.

Despite not really wanting the surprise they received they also didn't want to see it be vandalised, the pair hatched a plan. Every year they would offer one side of the helicopter to artists to paint, the other half would be offered separately, this year one side has the Power puff girls on while the other side has a grey camouflage scheme with a tiger hidden in the grey striping. The former piece of Soviet hardware proudly sits outside as a little photo point for military enthusiasts and artists, in truth it looks pretty neat.

Walking out of town and towards the industrial estate, my nerves were still ever present and Evelyn knew it too. Most of the walk she held my hand to keep me calm and maybe to stop me quitting at this final hurdle as she wandered alongside me. Soon enough, we approached the gates of the former airbase and down past all the other business sat the Hind, proudly marking the studio.

Terror was starting to fill me once more as we stood at the doorway to the very thing I feared so heavily, Evelyn took my hand and led the way. Walking over the threshold of the former base and onwards to the studio and my destiny.

"Maybe we should have got another coffee for the walk?" Evelyn commented, taking a deep breath, "I think a beer might have been more helpful right now!" I laughed at her.

Slowly we approached the gunship, Evelyn had a look around it, "Imagine how much fun it would be to own this," she declared to me as I took a picture of her with it, she picked the tiger side of it.

Standing at the doorway of the studio Evelyn looked at me. "You okay Fae?" She said sweetly to me. "Terrified," I offered back, she smiled. "I know," she said as she took my hand and we opened the door and walked through together.

A receptionist greeted us as we entered the ultra-sleek waiting area of the studio. "Good morning, you must be Fae? Karl has told me all about you!" She said politely.

Evelyn giggled at me. "I bet he did too."

Rolling my eyes at her, "My bum?" I said to her as she giggled away. The receptionist smiled at us again, "I've heard what you are doing today, Fae, you should be really proud of yourself, not many people would be brave enough to go through with this and most of those people don't have anything like you do!" A deep sincerity was in her voice.

"Thanks, it hasn't been easy, she has kept me going," I pointed at Evelyn who was still giggling to herself, the receptionist smiled at her, "We all need a helping hand sometimes Fae, are you nervous?"

I took a deep breath, "Absolutely terrified."

She smiled at me and walked round and put her hand on my shoulder. "You will be fine; Jared and Karl are both great at what they do and it's me that will transcribe what they write so you are perfectly safe! They are just finishing a shoot but you can head down if you want? It might be less scary than waiting out here, it's like a dentist surgery here," she pointed to a doorway.

Together we started to walk towards the doorway, we opened the door which led into a long corridor with another door down the end. Walking down the corridor, the walls adorned with photos the pair had taken for the magazine, newspaper or other things, Evelyn stopped at one. "Fae! Come here, there's one of you here!" I looked round slightly surprised and walked back down to where she stood.

Sure enough, in front of her was the picture from the steampunk festival that Karl had taken of me standing on the promenade overlooking the sea. Strangely though seeing my picture on their wall seemed to slightly ease my nerves, it was a great photo too, of course Evelyn had her suggestions why it was there!

"Thanks, Evelyn!" I giggled back at her before I put my hand on her shoulder as we headed to the doorway to the studio. Opening the door to the incredibly vast and dark hangar that now served as the photo studio for the pair, Jared sat at a desk with a laptop while in the far corner of the studio Karl was photographing two girls.

Jared offered us both a seat and a coffee, while the two girls finished their set with Karl, Jared sat down with us and started to show us the studio, not that much of it was visible. Huge in size the studio seemed to go on forever with different areas set up to do different types of shoots.

One corner had a large green screen which the two girls were being shot in front of with a beach scene behind them, a few set up props were on the other side along with an old metal bed frame with long drapes over it. I looked at Jared.

"I hope you don't think I'm going to go on that!" I said as I pointed to the bed frame, he laughed.

"No, no, your set is in the middle just there," he pointed to a metal and wooden chair in the middle of the studio with a digital background behind it. Turning round his laptop. "These are the backdrops I have for the first part of your shoot, are you okay with these?" Jared started to scroll through a stream of green ribbon backdrops before he moved onto a few others for later on.

Jared looked up, "Are you nervous?" I gulped a little.

"Terrified," he smiled.

"Did you see the picture in the corridor?" I nodded back at him, "You will be fine, me and Karl will look after you, what you are doing today is an incredible achievement, if you anywhere near as good as the picture in the corridor, the world will be glad they read about you Fae," he smiled as he continued to get his set ready for the shoot.

Karl whistled at Jared as the two girls he was shooting started to get dressed, having finished their set, Karl headed over to us and just in time to see my hands starting to tremble again.

Evelyn held my hand to try and steady my nerves, Karl saw me trembling and took me into the corridor to show me that picture Evelyn had seen. Standing in front of the picture, he pointed at it, "You looked great that day and you look great today, Fae, Jared is going to take good care of you, we have the studio just for you, so you don't have to worry and of course your friend is here too," he said to me trying to steady my nerves, it wasn't working.

Nervous and emotional, Karl led me back into the studio and guided me back to the table to sit with Jared and Evelyn. Sitting down just in time to see Jess and Gwen leaving. "Digital influencers," Karl said.

Jared smirked, "They come every week with new stuff they have, most of the time they have paid for it, not that you would think it if you see their posts!" Karl grinned. "One way ticket to rehab," I sat thinking if only they knew how close to the truth they really were.

Karl headed to the door to check that Jess and Gwen had left before he called the receptionist and told her to lock the door so that we couldn't be interrupted. Sitting down they started to go through the plan for the next 5 hours, we would do an hour at a time with a little break between the first two before a half hour break to split the afternoon up before the final two. How much of the plan I really took in was anyone's guess, their words seemed to merge into a big mess as fear took a vice-like grip of me.

My mind was firmly shaking itself down as they started to illuminate that chair in front of that screen and rolled the first backdrop, Jared looked over at me. "You ready Fae?" He asked.

"Fae? Are you okay?" He asked, sounding concerned. Jared walked over to me and put his hand on my shoulder, he took my coffee cup out of my trembling hand, "Hey Fae?"

I looked up at him, "I've seen the stuff you do for people, compared to what you do for people, this is nothing to be scared of."

Deep down I knew he was right. Evelyn walked over to me. "Fae?" I looked at her.

"I believe in you Fae," she smiled and took my hand and walked me over to the chair and stood there with me.

Suddenly, I took hold of her and hugged her so tight that I might have popped her ribs for a change. "I can do this can't I?" I asked her.

"Easily!" Was her response.

Jared walked over. "If you need to stop at any time Fae, just say so and we will stop, okay?" I smiled at my little supporting friend.

"I'm ready," Evelyn went to walk away, "Wait one second!" I grabbed her from behind and pulled her back to me.

"I couldn't have been here without you," Evelyn looked up at me.

"Yes, you could have, you just need to believe in you!" She smiled and went to sit with Karl again. Jared scrolled the first backdrop round, "You wanna start with this one Fae?"

I looked round at it and suddenly a determination came over. Like some bizarre shockwave running across all of my body, suddenly I was driven and determined to do this, I looked at Evelyn as she sat looking at Karl's laptop, I smiled to myself before I nodded to Jared to signal that I was ready to start.

Jared changed the backdrop to do a warm up shoot, sure enough I stood with my hands on the back of the chair, he took a few pictures before he came over to show me. Jared took a good picture too. "See you are going to be fine!"

I went to change into my work clothes before I sat down and waited to begin the shoot. In my mind I had a plan of what I was going to do and say, but as the set began that plan had completely left my mind. Jared took the first few photos for the first session while I sat awkwardly in silence, periodically giving odd short answers to any questions he asked.

Evelyn and Karl were jointly reviewing some of the work he had just done with Jess and Gwen, she kept giggling at him and periodically she would glance over at me and smile. Jared was probing a little to try and coax me out of my shell but my mind was almost transfixed on Jess and Gwen and their shoot.

Over the next half hour, I languished on that school chair in front of that ribbon backdrop, Jared looked over at Evelyn and Karl, when he asked a question, I wasn't ready for in any way.

Jared smiled as he saw the two happily flicking through all of Karl's handiwork, he sat up and looked at me. "Do you remember your first boyfriend, Fae?" I looked at him kinda shocked that he asked me that when suddenly and without warning, I just opened up.

"My first boyfriend?"

That's a weird question?

Sure, I remember him, but he was the first guy to dump me, though it wasn't that he dumped me that was the issue, more how and who dumped me.

I was 16 years old and just after new year this guy, Toby, took an interest in me, I had never had a guy be serious about me before, so naturally, I kinda freaked out a little, but he kept grinding away and eroded my suspicions away. Two weeks of bliss with a boyfriend, his family were nice and my parents didn't mind him either, he told them how. "He could handle anything," when my dad asked Toby if he could handle my mood swings.

We were out on a date at the cinema when I had a little episode over some popcorn, this guy knocked into me and my popcorn went flying as did my temper shortly after. I yelled at the guy while Toby shied away into the blackness of the cinema hallway, the dude apologised, he even went and got me some more popcorn.

Later that evening the crash came, stricken with guilt over what I had said to that guy and the things I had called him, my mind crumbled a bit as did Toby and his promises to my dad. Laying on my bed crying about how nasty I had been to that guy just for bumping into me, Toby went home to 'study'. A few hours later I got a text, not from Toby but from his mother! "Sorry Fae, but Toby needs to get off your Bipolar Coaster."

My Bipolar Coaster? What does that even mean? I wasn't surprised in truth, maybe just disappointed that he got his damn mum to break up with me for him!

Of course, that sort of thing is normal for most people with my kind of conditions, that first introduction to what now would be classed as cyberbullying has actually worked in my favour though. It's one of the newest problems we deal with now at the Davizioso, victims of cyberbullying and social media pressure victims, it was a part of my qualifications and now is one of my specialisations that I am studying for.

As the pressure mounts on them for new, exciting and extreme content, the pressure on their mind ticks away, anxiety, depression, eating disorders and a general lack of self-worth are the most common outcomes. Boys tend to do progressively more stupid things and girls tend to start flashing more and more of themselves, it's quite sad really when you think about it.

Shaun? The guy who runs the thrift shop? His daughter Jess, yeah, the one with the dark hair you have been photographing every week for the digital influencer thing she does? She stayed with us for a month as the mental pressure of that life took its toll and gave her an eating disorder and anxiety problems. Problem of course is that she is over 18, so she can do whatever she wants? Of course, you could also argue that she is the victim of her own self-created world?

No one made her decide to start flashing her body and sharing it with the world? What started for Jess as a simple cosplay soon escalated into something far sleazier, as her, 'Fans' called for more and her content had to get riskier and edgier. Jess and Gwen, the girl with her, started to do sets that people could buy, as they got calls for more, they soon descended down until they did a set called 'Master and Slave' where Gwen had Jess as a naked slave in chains.

Jess couldn't go down any further and when Shaun found out he was outraged, he tried to get them removed from the internet, but with both girls being over 18 he couldn't do anything. What actually upset him the most though wasn't what Jess had done, nor that the sets had been shot in his home, what really upset him was that whoever had held the camera for them, now had power over his family.

Jess came to the Davizioso for a month to try and break the cycle while Shaun battled with social media companies who would do nothing and in truth could do nothing about it, the pictures belong to the person who took them and without their permission the pictures couldn't be removed. Jess went clean for a little while, she even stopped using social media, but soon enough she got back into her old habits.

Truthfully though? Part of me envies them and part of me pities them, they are confident in themselves but is that level of exposure worth the few hundred likes they actually get? All for a free pencil case or some panties? They are almost trapped in a merciless cycle with people and algorithms choosing for them how much they can like themselves today.

It's also why a big part of me admired Evelyn. How many 22 years old girls do you know who don't have a phone stuck to their hand or face? Let alone a 22-year-old girl who doesn't even own a phone? I didn't know one either until I met her!

Just don't get any ideas though!

"There is no way I would show my well-rounded arse off! Not for a million likes!"

I looked up and saw Jared smiling as he shot away when from in the distance. "Karl would like it," Jared erupted laughing as Evelyn sweetly yelled that across the room.

"Thanks Evelyn!" I laughed at her. Jared called our first break early so that both he and I could recompose ourselves after Evelyn's interjection. Returning to the table where she and Karl sat looking through his laptop, she was giggling with those puppy eyes she deployed when she needed them.

Chuckling to myself, I grabbed her from behind and gave her a big hug and blew a raspberry on her head as she squirmed trying to escape. Without her there was no way that I would have gone through with this damn shoot and she was keeping Karl and Jared entertained too. During the first stage of the shoot, she had started to play peekaboo with Karl and his camera, both seemed to be enjoying this game they were playing too.

Soon enough I returned to the seat to begin my second hour, this time I spoke about the Davizioso and my time in Ljianstipol since having moved here. Going into detail about how Tony and Gale had shepherded me into becoming the professional that I found myself being today. Of course, I had to go into detail about my qualifications which also meant exposing how close the pair had come to jeopardising my career when they did their article for the local paper about the Davizioso.

Discussing at length the group sessions I now ran and how they had become one of the biggest parts of the Davizioso and of course my career path. Before we resumed, Evelyn came over as I stood next to that chair to give me a little pep talk. "You are doing great Fae, just keep going!" Before she went to torment Karl some more. Jared got me to sit down and rolled a new backdrop on the big screen before we began.

Jared looked at me. "So, tell me about your past?" Having eased into the whole thing I started to unfurl my story to him.

"At first, my mood swings and depression weren't too bad, but as my hormones began to rage so did my flares and slumps, the target eventually just became my mother. It's a strange by-product of my conditions, you find a natural vent, this vent generally winds up being whoever is closest to you?"

"In my case it was my mum, whenever my temper flared, she just happened to say that one thing and all my worst qualities would be unleashed upon her. We argued nearly constantly and after I vented at her she would in turn vent her fury on my dad."

"My dad was laid-back and easy going but she somehow managed to hit his sore spots and get his other side to come out on show. They wound up arguing nearly constantly, but to make things worse, when she had finished with my dad, I would then go back at her for laying into him."

"My mum heard about the Davizioso in an article she saw at work, given that my conditions and life had been steadily getting much worse, she spoke to my dad about it. Three weeks later he was driving me to Ljianstipol, he wanted to give me a break from life and also give them a chance to save the marriage I was slowly destroying."

"Hardly speaking to each other in the weeks leading up to my journey, I was so angry at them! Mum was sending me away to a strange place, we just about managed to say bye to each other as I left on that morning in the car. Truthfully though the car journey wasn't much better, I was fuming about being taken to this place, like a dog being taken to a kennel."

"At first, I hated it here, I barely left my room, surrounded by strange people and being trapped, even though you could come and go as you pleased, I felt trapped."

"Gradually, I started to make friends, well more they made me their friends really, I suppose? Tony, Gale and Shanky in particular, as they helped me understand myself, I started to make more friends too. Though I was pretty bitter about spending my 18th birthday here, they had a party for me, but in the company of strangers, it wasn't the birthday I had in mind."

"Whatever my parents hoped for saving their marriage, it didn't work, I had driven an irreparable wedge between them. Two years later I was being sent back to the Davizioso so that I didn't have to witness their bitter divorce with me out of the firing lines. For the next 4 months, the Davizioso would once again be home, meaning I would also be celebrating my 20th birthday here."

"Both of my parents eventually married again, my mother moved to the city to the north of my hometown, she moved to live with her new husband. Dad met a new partner and moved in with her, leaving me with our family home but with no family, 3 years after my parents' divorce, I had a house of my own, just I was completely alone."

"After 2 years of nearly total isolation, I decided to move to Ljianstipol after meeting my mother to go shopping just before Christmas. I spent that Christmas Day looking for a new home, my decision was Ljiastipol and in a few months I would be starting the journey of my life to a new home."

"My dad let me use the house as collateral, meaning I wouldn't have a mortgage to pay and I could take my time to find my feet in Ljianstipol. Becoming ever more popular due to its proximity to the coast and its laid-back and romantic charm it was my natural choice. My reason for moving was far simpler of course, I wanted to be somewhere new where my past wouldn't be looming over my head."

"Not long after I moved to Ljiastipol, I met my first friend Fabi and his wife Alyssia, then it turned out that my past hadn't forgotten me as Tony and Gale interviewed me for the job at the Davizioso. Both remembered me only too well, they asked what happened to my dreadlocks, imagining the embarrassment of telling them I had to cut them out after they started to stink!"

"Tony and Gale gave me a break to work as a carer and to then train to become a specialist consultant at the Davizioso. Their continued and unwavering faith in me, a depression and bipolar disorder suffering, former patient, is the only reason I have been able to move my life forward at all."

"Every single person in Ljianstipol has helped me, Tony, Gale, Fabi and everyone else, but the biggest help, especially for my mental health and self-confidence has been Evelyn. Ljianstipol and its people have changed my life but it was that mysterious little girl who arrived by bus one day that has changed me the most. That day she found me in that park, I was going to phone you guys and cancel this whole thing, but she talked me round."

"Yeah, that same girl who is now playing peekaboo with Karl, talked me into going through with this whole thing. Evelyn talked me round to telling my story and to do this to help all the people who don't get the chance to be seen or heard."

"That charming and enchanting petite girl made me realise just how much I needed to do this for both myself and everyone else who suffers in silence. Evelyn is the reason I am here in this studio today, even this morning I was still thinking of giving up on this all."

I looked round and Evelyn was toying with Karl, while Jared walked over to me and gave me a pat on the shoulder before he called for lunch. Walking back to rejoin Evelyn as she tormented Karl, she smiled at me before she resumed her play. The door to the studio opened as the receptionist brought a tray of sandwiches and pastries in for lunch.

Karl looked over at me. "How are your nerves now, Fae?" Noticing that my hands were still shaky.

"Not so bad now, but still going."

Jared walked over and popped a beer on the table for me. "That will calm them for you, well done too, you have been doing great Fae," he smiled as he went outside to get some fresh air.

Having reached the halfway stage of the interview it was time for me to change into something a bit more 'Fae' and less work uniform. Evelyn brought that bag of mine to the chair I had been sitting on and pulled out my white dress and offered it to me with that sweet little smile of hers. Like most women I had a very bad body image and was very self-conscious, Evelyn stood beside me to shield me as I started to change out of my work clothes and into my dress.

While I stood in my underwear, she stood at my side to help mask me from the eyes of Jared and Karl before helping me to get into that dress she claimed Karl loved seeing me in. When I knelt down to let her attach the halter for me, she gave me a little hug and whispered, "You look great!" Into my ear.

Before I stood up, she gave me one last hug which I returned in an equal manner, holding my little friend as if my life depended upon her being there. Evelyn patted my dress down for me before she went back to sit with Karl and no doubt, she would torment him some more for the next hour.

Jared took up his position and we resumed the shoot, this time we were delving into my deeper past, my personal stuff you know? The bullying and generally nasty things that had happened because largely people didn't get me for being different.

"Truthfully, I think a big part of my problem was that people couldn't understand me because I didn't really understand myself? At least not until I met Shanky at the Davizioso, he helped me to learn about myself. My parents didn't really help with that though, as supportive as they tried to be, my mum almost pretended my conditions didn't exist and my dad being so laid-back probably just aggravated my conditions."

"While my mum tried to get my diagnosis reversed and by doing so hiding her head, my dad on the other hand just acted like it was nothing and let me run wild, maybe in some way they engineered their own downfall?"

"Their approaches being so different that there was no common ground between them, like my conditions, they were at totally opposite ends of the scale. At least unlike me they were two separate people, whereas I was just one but exhibiting the very same opposite ends of the spectrum."

"When I returned home after my first visit to Ljianstipol and the Davizioso, at least I had some idea why people had been how they were. Not that it really made me feel any better about that but at least now I knew why it happened, not that it prepared me for when just as before it happened again and again. The worst part was that no matter how cruel people were to me, I often blamed myself for what they did and my mind sided with them about how I deserved no better."

"This self-destructive and self-consuming trait was becoming a serious issue, with little or no self-esteem, unwillingly I had put a target on my head for people to get a quick shot in on me. You may think you learn? But in truth you really don't, being so lonely and isolated makes you grovel more and more for their approval and attention."

"Each and every time I allowed people in, they did crueller and crueller things to me, eventually I just started to shut myself off from everyone. Two years later, when I returned to Ljianstipol for my second stay at the Davizioso, I had no friends of any nature."

"While my parents battled their way through their brutal divorce, I was back at the Davizioso learning more about myself again with Tony, Gale and Shanky. Here at least I had some human contact and people here didn't leave me alone in darkness or dump me in the park alone for a quick kick. Maybe they made me realise just how bad things in my hometown really were? When my parents eventually moved out and moved on with their lives, even they seemed to have left me behind?"

"I think that is why I decided to move here in the end? I hoped for a fresh start here, away from my past and my parents' story? The real root of my parents' lack of understanding was rooted in a healthcare system which couldn't actively explain my issues to them, I'm not badmouthing my parents, just so you realise that!"

"People here were different to what I had become accustomed to, they were genuine and meaningful in their approaches? It was an alien feeling and way of life when Fabi and Alyssia befriended me, I was waiting for the fall which has never come. Instead, I found myself in a life which had meaning? After Fabi swiped my hat off my head which had been masking the sorry mess, I had made for myself, rather than laugh he invited me over and sorted my hair out for me."

"For maybe the first time, I had actual friends and gradually they introduced me to their friends and before I knew it, it seemed like I had an entire world of friends who had been waiting for me to walk into their lives. Most significant of them all though turned out to be Evelyn, that strange, hyperactive, petite, ginger curled, four foot eight, mystery of a girl."

"What makes her so special? She is totally unfazed by me and my conditions, if anything she enjoys the challenge of it? It was a strange thing when she slowly opened up to me and started entrusting me with details of her past, how she had been bullied pretty much continuously since her parents died."

"The strangest thing I wondered about her was how someone so beautiful could be considered ugly? I figured jealousy was the root cause of that. I knew she had come to find Leanne and forgive her for the cruel things she had done to Evelyn in the past, maybe it just proved how much stronger than anyone Evelyn really was?"

"Though the thing which makes her so special for me and maybe just for me, was the other side of her, that side of her she keeps very much for us. Buried deep among the giggling and ginger curls is an almost angelic little creature, considerate, affectionate, supporting and compassionate. Encouraging and supporting she often goes to extreme lengths to try and make me see myself the way she sees me."

"Evelyn is more confident in her own skin than I could hope to be and she knows it too, she spends so much time complimenting me and my figure, encouraging me to be proud of my body and my shapely curves. That day we visited the beach together was the first time I had ever dared to walk a beach in just my bikini top, the confidence she has in herself and her body is contagious. Whenever I struggle, she picks me up and gets me back on my feet, she never lets me suffer alone as she wraps me in a cocoon of love and care."

"Though there are things that I see in her that maybe others don't? Underneath that childish demeanour is a soft, caring and loving girl, a girl who has been shunned through life. Having had little or no childhood by anyone's standards and having no confidence or self-belief of any kind, somehow though she has become the strongest person I have ever met."

"Having taken up residency on my sofa of all places, often I found myself resting with her on that sofa, after I started to join her sleeping on the sofa, her true power really came to light. Suddenly, I noticed that my crashes and episodes seemed to have stopped?"

"She soothed me and slowly started to help me turn a corner in my own mind, I sleep better when she is around me too. My life changed the day she walked into it; she is slowly making me a better version of myself."

Jared signalled to me to take a break, in truth I was relieved as I was starting to well up heavily, as it turned out I wasn't alone either. Karl had exited the hangar to get a few moments, while Evelyn stood waiting for me with another hug, red cheeks telling me she too was emotional about what I had just discussed with Jared.

Thankfully the last part of today's shoot was just pictures and no more talking or storytelling, while I sat with Evelyn, I put my hand on hers, "I couldn't have done this without you," she smiled and just sat quietly thinking to herself. Jared came over to join us.

"I will give you both a few minutes before we do the final part, you are doing great!" He walked outside to join Karl and get a few moments. Evelyn sat next to me with a deep soft smile on her face, calmly thinking away to herself, with her little reddened cheeks catching the odd bit of light from the studio lights.

Noticing on the laptop that Karl had managed to get a few pictures of my little friend as she tormented him from that little chair she sat upon, at least today I wasn't the only person feeling that girl's magical power.

Jared and Karl, both rejoined us as I went to get changed for the final session, Evelyn once again came with me to help me change and shield me from view. Evelyn had suffered from very negative body consciousness after being bullied almost all of her life about her soft and subtle figure. While I slipped out of that dress, she shielded me again and reassured me that I was attractive and that I shouldn't be ashamed of myself.

Carefully she gave me my skirt to change into and then my top in turn, as I stood there in my underwear, she complimented me and my curves.

"You should be proud of that shape Fae," she said in her sweet tone. Jared and Karl both watched as I got changed with Evelyn shielding me from their full gaze. Before we resumed, she gave me one final hug, resting her nose against my chest and telling me how proud she was of me for being so brave.

Jared stood up and retook his position while Evelyn went back to sit with Karl, looking at the laptop he had, I wondered what he was showing her? While Jared started the final session, getting the portrait shots he was after, Evelyn started to play round on that chair again. In the dimly lit corner of the studio, she clambered all over that chair tormenting Karl and his camera again.

Karl was utterly fascinated by her; I could understand why as she was certainly a pretty thing and of course entertaining too. While me and Jared clawed our way through those first awkward few pictures where I probably grimaced more than smiled or relaxed for him, the air started to fill with giggling.

Evelyn had introduced a new game to Karl, saying words backwards and then growing into entire sentences, if Karl got the word or sentence right, he got a picture of her, however if he got it wrong then she got chocolate from their gratuity bowl. Soon enough the air was filled with their laughter as they played this odd game, the receptionist arrived to see what was going on.

Walking into the studio to be greeted with 'Gninrom doog', she looked at Evelyn in confusion before she repeated back, 'Uoy ot gninrom doog' to a smiling Evelyn.

Briefly she stopped and rested her head in her hands, looking at me with that sweet little face that she unleashes every so often. While my heart melted as she caught me in that gaze of hers, she resumed her game with Karl and the receptionist stayed to join in with them.

I had become so transfixed with what was going on and that little smile of hers that I didn't even notice that Jared had carried on shooting the whole time, I swore deep down that she did that to make me forget the camera was there! Though both me and Jared would thank her for that, during that final session he got the best pictures of the day, he even caught a rare glimpse of an actual smile from me!

Just like most people, they loved her, this bizarre and strange girl just somehow seemed to make people's hearts stop for a brief moment? Deep down she just enjoyed being herself, when Jared finished my set, Karl and the receptionist had their pictures taken with her. Karl gave her a box to stand on so that she would be nearly the same height as them, though in truth, she was a giant by comparison to us all.

Evelyn had cut a deal with Karl though; she wanted a picture or two of me and her together in that studio in exchange she would give him the picture he craved as compensation for the string of images of her hair as she hid behind that chair. Together we stood there as Karl and Jared both took our pictures, some nice portraits of us together, though I did see that he had also been encouraged to get a picture of me changing by my little friend!

Evelyn tried to scurry away as I wrapped my arms round her stomach and lifted her back towards me, they both took pictures of that moment too. Jared sat with me at the table with the receptionist to discuss the second stage of the shoot in a few days' time.

Evelyn though true to her word walked with Karl to the middle of that studio, she had one condition for him though. Whether good or bad, he was only allowed to take one shot of her, he of course agreed to this term. She turned that chair round and knelt upon it, laying her hands over the back of the chair she unleashed that look for him.

Gazing lovingly at him like a little puppy with her green eyes glimmering away, he gasped a little as she unleashed this deeply hidden beauty, he took one final deep breath and took his shot. Confidently, he strode over to her and showed her the picture on his camera, her smile said that she was happy with it and she gave him a hug to say thank you. Karl disappeared through the corridor as we sat talking about the next stage in three days' time.

Karl soon returned with a large cardboard tube which he handed to her along with a bar of chocolate, she gave him another hug. Karl grinned as he whispered,

"There's a surprise in here for you both," and winked at me before we headed to the door and back out into the sunlight.

Striding through the evening sunlight, she proudly carried that tube of hers as she indulged her chocolate craving as we walked home. With the shoot overrunning, I figured we could get a takeaway and go sit in the park near my house which overlooked the town and beach, to unwind from the stressful and chaotic day we had.

Heading to my place, we dropped off her tube and my bag of clothes and headed to the town to get some burgers and fries and go to enjoy them by the beach. Evelyn brought her backpack and brought some beers for us too as we wandered down towards the little park. Heading through the gate of the park and towards the plaza where we could sit on the wall and overlook the beach as we enjoyed our dinner. Sitting on the walls we enjoyed our food and toasted each other for a good day with a drink.

Evelyn had spent all day building me up and supporting me, truthfully if she hadn't been there today that interview would have been a total bust! We sat talking, she was telling me how great I looked and how much people would love me when the article came out when suddenly she just stopped. Sitting looking over the beach and almost deathly quiet; like something had suddenly hit her.

She seemed odd, her normally cute smile had gone and she looked sad? Looking over at her, "You okay Evelyn?" She looked round and nodded and laid chest down on the wall looking over at me, she seemed to be crying? I moved over to her, "What's wrong? Evelyn?" She laid her face down.

Concerned about my little friend I started trying to think what might be wrong with her, I decided to take a guess. "Is it about Leanne?" She looked and nodded. Moving her hands next to mey knees she looked up at me. "I didn't want to tell you I had found her, in case you wanted me to leave," I put my hand on her shoulder. "Why would I want you to leave?"

She looked up again, her cheeks puffy and red. "I found her but she is worse than ever, worse than she was in school, she's nastier now, when Alyssia told me what she had said to you on your first day at work, I knew I couldn't forgive her, but I didn't want you to know in case you wanted me to go away," I lifted her sad little face up, tears running down her cheeks.

"I never want you to leave Evelyn, stay for as long as you wish, you are my best friend and I never want to be without you." Trying to smile, something was bothering her, it was much more than just this?

Scooping her up and sitting with her in my arms, she rested her head back and started to spill her stories, stories that up until now I no idea nor suspicion of.

"Leanne bullied me almost continuously, since she did that impression of my mother dying in the car accident, for being an orphan, ginger, having freckles before she turned to my petite figure. People sided with Leanne too, her near impunity from the school rules made her a valuable person to side with, where I had nobody to stand up for me."

"Though what made it worse was that my grandmother also sided with Leanne, so not only was I being bullied at school, that same gauntlet was a constant threat at home too. She used to send me up to my room and just ignore me all night while she drank and gambled online. We fell out soon after she moved in, I started to sleep on the sofa, facing the door in some vain hope that one night my mum and dad would just walk back in, alive and well, she got really angry about it."

"In the end, I started staying in our spare room with a pop out sofa bed in it, she used to lock me in that room sometimes for the entire day, she was quite nasty." Tears were rolling freely down her face and landing on my arms before continuing their journey down my arms and onto the ground.

"The only person that stuck by me was Ellie, my babysitter, she and her friends let me hang around with them, though being only 12 with those 18–19-year-olds, my grandmother was nasty about that too. 'You'll wind up a drunken whore!' She used to yell at me when I got back home.

"When she bumped into Leanne was the worst though, that girl would tell her lies about me and she just believed her. I thought about suicide a few times, but I didn't want to give them the satisfaction of beating me, instead I started to study harder and harder. Things were going well in college when she died, in truth it was freeing for me but what was a problem was that she had accrued a huge debt against my house through her gambling."

"Having to choose between my education or my family home was fairly easy, I chose my family home! My boss was just as bad as them, he constantly commented on how boyish I looked or how feral my hair looked, I used to straighten and bathe it in hairspray to try to control it." She seemed to start calming down as she unleashed her darker past.

"When I came here, I was going to make amends with Leanne but when I found out what she had done to you, I knew I couldn't forgive her, she doesn't deserve it. I know she works at the burger place by the river, I thought about popping by to make amends there but when I spoke to Colette about it, I decided not to do it."

She smiled a little bit, "I hope you don't think I have lied to you Fae," I held my little friend.

"You haven't had much luck in life have you, Evelyn?" She smiled and closed her eyes.

Holding her little hand as she eased herself back into me, it was quite odd, where we spent so much time together, I hardly noticed how small she really was. When she hugged me, I had just gotten used to her head resting on my breasts or when we walked anywhere, I just saw her as being normal, but holding her hand and her little stomach reminded me just how delicate she really was.

My hands were easily twice the size of hers, her subtle little figure too, she was very attractive but maybe for some people, Leanne included, she was an enviable girl, was jealousy the real fuel to the fire of Evelyn's past?

While she relaxed after spilling her torments, I couldn't help but wonder? How had she been so brutally treated but wound up so resilient and strong? Maybe those strange people she spoke about? I didn't really know if I believed her stories about them, they sounded like some dark and bizarre fantasy story? Though maybe it was all true?

One thing I knew for certain was that she wasn't going anywhere, I wanted her to stay around me, I needed her and somehow, I felt that she needed me too. Soon it started to get cold so I put her on my back and carried her back home as she held on. "You could put me in that backpack if I get too heavy?" She chuckled at me, that was my Evelyn.

Like an oversized baby, I carried her down the street to my home, I took her indoors and sat her on the sofa, it didn't take too long for her to slump over, legs dangling over the side like always. Starting to take her shoes and socks off, I smiled to myself as at least now I knew why she slept on that sofa! I went and got her some bed clothes and changed her into them, like my own little child, she never stirred either!

Today she was really tired tonight, she had been so strong all day, she had kept everything going for me, I decided tonight she deserved company. Changing into a vest and shorts I took position with her on the sofa and wrapped her in my arms. "Stay forever Evelyn," I whispered to her as she snuggled herself up a little more, soon I fell asleep with her in my arms.

My phone rang and woke me during the morning, Karl had tried to ring me a few times, when I rang him back, he asked if he could send me a few sneak previews from the shoot yesterday, of course I said yes! Minutes later, a few emails from him came through, Evelyn had woken up by this point and sat with me as I looked at the emails on my phone.

Karl forwarded a few of the portrait shots Jared had taken along with that picture of Evelyn he worked so hard to get. Though it was the final email which he sent that I liked the most, pictures he had been taking during the shoot of Evelyn giving me those little pep talks. Each image showing that side of her I tried so hard to explain to people but just couldn't tell them what it was like.

This little series of images however caught that perfectly, he also sent the picture of me grabbing Evelyn after she had helped him get a booty shot of me. Me smiling with that giggling girl flying through the air and back towards the tickle monster!

Smiling deeply to myself as I sat looking at those pictures, Evelyn was the real hero of the day, from the moment she woke up she just kept me going, without her that shoot wouldn't have happened let alone gone so well!

Today we had agreed to have a lazy day, comfy clothes, no bras and just binge watch rubbish on TV. Evelyn gave me her cardboard tube, upon opening it I found 3 copies of that picture of us she had begged Karl for. Taking one out she gave it to me to put on my wall, she put the other 2 back into the safety of that tube. While she watched something, I put that picture on the wall above the sofa she liked to sleep on, what a great picture too.

Both smiling away as we stood side by side with our kindred spirit in the blackness of that studio, thankfully with the exception of Friday to review their images, I had no need to visit their studio again.

Part of the other reason for having a lazy day was so that Evelyn would also be refreshed for her favourite day in Ljianstipol, Wednesday was market day and of course walking with Tony day and she was looking forward to spending market day together too, we hadn't been able to do that since she arrived and we both were looking forward to it. Hours soon whipped away while we consumed junk and watched the endless stream of crap on TV.

Day soon turned into night and night soon turned into hyperactive Wednesday morning as Evelyn's pulse and mouth both accelerated in sheer delight for market day! Evelyn led the way down to Ljianstipol town and the marketplace ready for her favourite day of every week in Ljianstipol.

Fabi greeted us as usual with his charming Italian smile, of course he was only too happy right now, on Friday night after weeks of trying to negotiate with Evelyn, she had finally agreed to let him touch her little curls with his scissors and brushes. Fabi was quite chuffed for finally breaking her hair based standoff with him and on Friday night he and Alyssia would be having us over so that he could work his magic on those ginger curls.

Evelyn of course, had agreed as she wanted her hair to look special for Tony and Gale's big party next week. Fabi whether he realised it or not was under a lot of pressure as Evelyn was very fond of her rolling sea curls, I'm sure if he messed it up, she would talk him to death every morning while she had breath in her lungs. Having collected our morning fix we wandered along the river and over that bridge before we came upon the marketplace.

Shanky was sat as always carefully laying out his prints on his blanket, wandering over he smiled as his little helper started to assist him setting out his prints. I sat with Shanky while Evelyn went for her first stop for today, heading off to see the notorious French viper and no doubt giggle at the insults Francois had for unexpecting passers-by today.

While she walked off, I noticed her stop at a stall and talk to the owner before collecting a little envelope from him? Shanky smiled at me and we sat and chatted while I put what I had just seen to the back of my mind. Shanky was one of my favourite people in this place and of course as far as I was concerned, he had largely helped to save me from myself.

While we talked, Evelyn reappeared to make her next stop at Alyssia's gallery, when she once again stopped at a stall and collected another envelope? What was my little friend up to? Shanky smiled at me. "She's smarter than people think."

I looked at him confused, "What do you mean Shanky?"

He laughed a little. "Go and have a look on their stalls."

Feeling bemused, I walked over to the stall I had seen her visit first, I couldn't see anything special on it, just pictures the guy had painted? Shanky called over. "Look harder!" as he sat watching me try to figure out what he was on about? Looking over the pictures again when I noticed something strange hanging on the side of the stall, I pointed at it as Shanky nodded at me, walking back over to him and sitting back down. Shanky smiled at me.

"She has been pulling that since she got here, they asked her to pose for them and she agreed as long as they gave her a cut if they sold any pictures with her in them," I smiled thinking about her cutting a deal with all these artists. "What does she do with the money?"

Shanky pointed to Alyssia's gallery, "She takes it to her, I don't know what she has planned for it?" He said thoughtfully back. Evelyn appeared again and stopped at another two stalls before she handed the envelopes to Francois this time? Evelyn went to see Colette before she reappeared and came back to join us, having completed her rounds for the morning.

Sitting, smiling away with Shanky and selling pictures for him too, he always paid her but she always gave him back his money before he would give it back to me to give to her instead! Pondering to myself about what she did with the money she was getting from them, deep down I knew it would be something so adorable that I had no reason to ask her what she was doing.

Lunchtime soon came and while we sat with Shanky, she had become super excited when Tony appeared in the market square and simply offered his hand to his little walking buddy. Running like a child towards him before she clasped his big hands with both of her little paws, we began to walk to the Davizioso, her smiling the whole way as we headed up to the rooftop garden.

Collecting a beer each they headed away hand in hand for their walk around the roof while me and Gale chatted about my photo shoot. Filling him in on the whole thing and how Evelyn had largely helped to save the entire thing before I showed him the pictures Karl had sent me. Gale sat scrolling through the images before he stopped on one of Evelyn shielding me from their view.

"She's so sweet," he smiled while continuing to look through the pictures. Gale looked to me as he paused on another image. "She has helped your confidence hasn't she?"

I looked over at him, "What do you mean?" He turned my phone round and showed me an image I had missed. An image of me stood talking to her in my underwear with her holding my hand.

Turning red, Gale smiled at me. "No need to be embarrassed Fae, it's good to see how much your confidence has come on," I smiled back at him.

"She has helped with that, she was great at that shoot, I would have crumbled if she hadn't been there," Gale smiled back.

Deep down however there was something I was itching to ask Gale; our new resident Hugh had moved in this week and I had been eager to meet him or them? Hugh had come to us as the system had largely just moved around until everywhere had been exhausted for him to live, with at least 27 personas to his name. I had been keen to meet this new guest.

Gale started to talk to me about him, "You will love him, he's really cool, though I was talking to him on Monday and he switched and it was like we had to start all over again? It's a new one for me but I like him, Shanky does too."

Knowing full well in advance that the guy was going to be a new experience for us all, we had been keen to set him up next to Shanky in the make shift art studio we created for him. Evelyn and Tony came to join us after they had finished their walk and Tony asked about my shoot, Gale showed him that photo. "Well look at you go, Fae!" He smiled and laughed.

"Thanks Tony!" I chuckled along with him.

"Are you ready for tomorrow, Fae?" Tony asked caringly, smiling and grabbing my little friend.

"As long as she is there, then yes!" Evelyn smiled back, "Karl likes her bum!" Giggling the whole time.

Wryly smiling Gale joined her, "Going by that picture yes he does!"

Tony joined them chuckling away, "Thanks Evelyn," I said as I fluffed those curls up for her. Together we sat for a couple of hours talking about tomorrow's photoshoot and the party next week, Evelyn eagerly excited of course with her secret session with Fabi on Friday to trial a hair do just for their party.

Time soon passed and we walked through the town and home, market day had been nice and it turned out Evelyn had been making full use of those dreaming artists. Maybe she hit them with that look and took control of their minds, though to give her credit, I never would have thought of that. Though I did wonder why she gave the money to people to hide? Maybe she had something in mind for it that she was going to surprise me with? Whatever it was I had no doubt it would be considerate as that was her all over!

We reached the comforting walls of my home and sat together on the sofa as we did most nights, chatting away about tomorrow's shoot, which as per my request would be shot outside. First, we would visit the small park that overlooked the beach and from there we would head down to the beach itself during the sunset and into the darkness.

Trying to time things just right; I ran my friend a deep warm and bubbly bath as a small thank you for how good she had been with me on Monday. Seemingly I timed things well as she was still awake at least as she headed to have a long soak while I got tonight's gourmet ready for us both. Evelyn emerged almost glowing where she had soaked for so long in those warm waters, wrapped in a towel like a mummy, her little curls dripping themselves dry.

After dinner, we resumed our spots on the sofa before she soon passed out, though tonight I felt okay, things had been good this week, largely thanks to her in truth! Though I did wonder how long that wait before tomorrow's session started would feel as we weren't starting the shoot until nearly 4 o clock, those hours might feel all too long!

Tonight, though I needed the comfort of my bed, as much as I hated to leave her alone my back needed a rest from the stiff cushions on that sofa. Relishing in the softness of my duvet and mattress, I rested my head into my soft pillows and fell away to that sleepy world. Though through the night as always, I woke up needing some water, almost at that exact same time every night this would happen.

While I started to head downstairs, I could hear Evelyn giggling? Heading into my living room to see her still curled up fast asleep and giggling away to herself. Carefully I sat on the sofa opposite and watched her giggle away to herself for the next hour, maybe she was with her dad tonight?

Though I imagined there was just as much chance she was with Karl giggling about his love affair for my rear! I chuckled away to myself as I wondered what she might be laughing away at in her clearly very happy dreams.

Having watched her for an hour I headed back to the comforting cocoon of my bed, though something very strange happened the next time I woke up. Much to my surprise and amazement when I stirred someone's green eyes were waiting for me to wake up. Her smile grew the instant my eyes opened and her beaming face told me that today would be a good day, she had brought coffee and toast for me too, though I wondered why she seemed so excited today.

Smiling away as she sat on the foot of my bed, I checked my phone to see a message from Jared. "Karl will do your shoot this afternoon Fae, I've had some problems and can't get in, sorry!" I replied to thank him for letting me know and tell him not to worry. While I was typing I couldn't help but notice someone's smile seemed to have grown larger.

Looking at her grinning to herself as she waited for me to tell her the news, just as she had in her sleep she sat and giggled away when I told her Karl would be doing the shoot today. Smiling sweetly, "He can get some more of his favourite photos of you," as she giggled away at herself, I turned and patted my rear, which made her start to cry with laughter.

Today to pass time before this afternoon I was going to go with Evelyn and do her morning rounds which she did every day when I went to work. Starting with Fabi and coffee, we spent nearly half an hour with him as he started to dream about what he was going to do with those locks of hers tomorrow night. Leaning against the wall of his shop, as he played round with her precious curls, talking in a progressively more excited tone as he spoke about it.

Evelyn however seemed unsure still though she was quite keen to see what her new friend might do with her curls. Onwards we headed and to Evelyn's most unlikely of friends Francois, the near legend status of his vicious tongue. Every morning they would sit and chat, Francois topped Evelyn's coffee up for her as he would fire insults the way of anybody passing by whom didn't dress correctly.

Evelyn enjoyed the comments he sometimes made as his passion for the female form and fashion conspired to force him into ejecting insults at unwary passers-by. Alyssia would be the next stop on her little day trip, they would discuss the new pieces in the gallery, generally both seemed to have little idea why these pieces sold.

Alyssia was quite fond of Evelyn too which was quite a surprise in truth as Alyssia had quite a firm approach to most things, so to see her bend to the excitable Evelyn actually shocked me a little. After her visit to Alyssia, she would pop and see Abby as she took her morning break near the river, they talked about gaming of all things?

Abby often seemed utterly exhausted every morning having been up into the twilight hours beating guys online gaming. Evelyn enjoyed hearing the stories about how she had destroyed some poor guy online last night, Evelyn's final stop however was her favourite by far. Leaving Abby behind she would walk through the small streets and to Colette's boutique in the backstreets.

Colette had fallen hopelessly in love with Evelyn the moment she met her and ever since had taken Evelyn under her wing, providing her with clothing and teaching her some of her well renowned skills. Colette adored this little girl, naming her, "Little Dove," she had shown that affection on Sunday when Evelyn passed out in their swing seat.

Colette's eye lit up when her little dove walked into her shop, she walked over and gave us both a big hug as she welcomed her little trainee back. Speaking to each other almost exclusively in French whenever they spent time together, I often wondered what they talked about and wished I had picked French instead of Spanish lessons at school. Colette had been teaching Evelyn to make a simple dress over the last few weeks and today she was finishing the seam to the bottom of the dress.

Colette would guide Evelyn through the process and sit with her while Evelyn learned Colette's incredibly unique skills. Colette had helped Evelyn to make me that white dress she gave me for my birthday and of course, I loved that dress. Watching Colette mentor her little dove was oddly touching as she calmly guided her in finishing the seam on the bottom of the dress she had been making.

Evelyn's stitching was pretty good for a novice and Colette seemed to be quite proud of her work too, after just over an hour it was time to head home. Colette adjusted my top for me again ready for this afternoon's session before she gave me a smile and wished me good luck for today's shoot. Evelyn took me for a burger and beer by the river before we would head to the park for the first part of my shoot with Karl.

Meeting Karl at the gated entrance of the park, Evelyn giggled at him, "Gnineve doog," he smiled in return. "Nyleve gnineve doog," she giggled and gave him a hug. Karl walked along with us through the park until we reached the plaza which overlooked the town and the beach. Karl checked I was ready and we started shooting away, maybe the rehearsals we had at that steampunk festival helped me today? Either way unlike Monday, I felt good and confident today, his camera bearing down upon me wasn't daunting me either.

Willingly telling him about my work and my life as he worked his camera magic, from time to time he would head over to show me his work. Karl's pictures for me had a better feel than Jared's seemed to though I suspect this might be my bias for being outdoors instead of in that studio?

Evelyn was being oddly calm too, still very much here and as supportive as always, but she knew I felt good today and she was respecting that. Our time in the park soon passed and Karl got some fantastic shots of me and a few sneaky ones of Evelyn too. While he flicked through the pictures, he had got of me and Evelyn; I smiled at her, "Guess he likes your bum too!" She blushed a little before just giggling back, "He likes yours more," as she patted her rear for me.

Karl gathered his gear together and offered to drive us as close to the beach as he could get, but with the evening being so warm and me feeling so good we chose to walk to the beach instead. While we headed to the beach, I started talking about how good I felt today and how confident I felt today, in truth I was almost as hyperactive as Evelyn as we wandered through town towards the beach.

Evelyn smiled at me. "You are beautiful Fae, people will love you," as she held my hand as we continued our journey and rejoined Karl at the entrance to the park which led to the beach. Karl led us to the promenade so that he could get a few shots of me from there set against the falling sun.

Karl took some pictures similar to the one he had hanging on the wall of the studio, though set against the oranges of the sky, these pictures looked incredible. Once we finished on the promenade, we headed along towards the tortured trees that lined the entrance of the beach.

Evelyn took up residence in the tree we had sat on the night we chatted about her past, with my confidence rising along with the warm temperature of this June evening. Karl took a few pictures of me among those trees while I prepared myself to head out onto the dunes, he got the shots against that setting sun which again looked great. Evelyn sat overhead quietly watching me like a little owl, Karl was going to stay just under the tree nearby to get his pictures.

Confidence rising, I took off my top and passed it to my little friend, she took it and smiled at me, as I turned, I took a deep breath as I started to walk out towards the dunes of the beach. Striding out with confidence and happiness, the evening felt so incredible, as I cleared the last trees, I started to crash.

Stumbling just as I hit the open dunes, this wasn't just a crash, more like a trainwreck, all happening under the very public eyes of Karl and his camera. Suddenly, I stopped as my mind started to fall in on itself, slowly falling through the fragile layers of my very being as I plunged towards the darkness of my own mind. My body language started to change as I started to fall to my knees, panicking and starting to lose the capacity to do anything, she leapt into action. Evelyn jumped from that tree and ran past Karl.

"Stop shooting! She's crashing!" I looked over to see a look of sheer terror and despair across his face as Evelyn sprinted past him barking orders at him. Evelyn was running towards me at full pace, while my mind went into full self-destruct mode, I was falling to pieces on those open dunes of that beach.

As she drew closer I turned to look at her, she jumped at me, hugging me for dear life, she hit me so hard that she almost knocked me from my feet. Wrapping herself around me she began to whisper into my ears as she clung onto me and rested her head against mine.

Soon I just erupted into a flood of tears as my emotions fell out of me, crying uncontrollably she just held me even tighter and whispered, "I love you no matter how broken you feel Fae," over and over again. Pulling my head into her shoulder I just bawled my eyes out, she never once let go or made any hint of doing so until I was ready to move.

My grimace turned slightly as she picked me back up and led me to a nearby bench just behind the trees, Karl collected my top and followed us, his face in a state of shock and disbelief in what he was watching unfold. Evelyn stood on the bench and got me to kneel on it with her, she pulled my head to her chest and just held me there.

Pressing my face against her chest and whispering, "I want you to feel how much I love you and how much I care about you," over and over. Holding me for what felt like hours, never letting go and continually telling me how much she loved me and how she always would.

While we stayed locked in that embrace, she told me that she would come out with me to help me finish the shoot, she was determined that I had to finish this. Evelyn asked Karl if he would be happy with her joining me for the final part of the shoot, he agreed though he was more concerned that I was okay than he was about getting those pictures. Gradually I began to come back to life and hugged my little friend.

"Thank you," I said to her, my voice being muffled by the fabric of her top.

Resting her chin on my head. "Let's get those pictures of your bum for him," she giggled and smiled at me, I couldn't help but giggle along with her.

Evelyn took my hand as I stood back up, she took her top off and handed it to Karl.

"Are you okay Karl?" She asked him, looking slightly bemused, "I'm okay, how are you, Fae? We don't have to get any more pictures if you feel bad?" Concern saturating his voice, I looked at him with tears still running freely down my face, "I'm okay, sorry about that," he paused. "As long as you are okay, I'm glad to shoot you and Evelyn," Evelyn smiled at him.

"Get a nice one of her bum for me," he chuckled at her as she led me back through the trees and out to the dunes. Together we stood at the edge of the treeline, she took my hand and started to lead me out onto those dunes. Passing the exact spot where a few moments earlier, she had once again saved me from my own very much self-destructive and crushing mind.

Initially, she stood right next to me, her little body exposed to the world as a kind of moral support for me, that subtle figure of hers proudly on show. Initially, she stood just far enough away so that Karl could get shots of just me, however I didn't want that for these last few moments. Each time he got ready I stood closer to her until eventually we just wound up hugging each other for the final pictures, we both laid on our chests as I thanked her for saving me on those dunes.

Karl's terrified look had turned to a strange and content smile as he caught the final few images for us. While we laid and chatted, he wandered over to us both and sat down next to me, laid his hand on my back, "You are the bravest person I have met Fae," he showed me a few shots he had just taken before he stood to leave.

"Evelyn?" She looked up at him.

"I do like her bum," he winked at her, she giggled at him, "I know you do, see you tomorrow." Karl gave us a thumbs up as he began to leave.

"Hey Fae, call me when you are ready tomorrow!" He called as he began to walk off the beach.

Looking over at Evelyn as she sat smiling to herself, I pulled myself next to her and just held her, "Thank you so much for tonight," she smiled back, "You are my friend Fae, I would never leave you like that."

Sweetly and as considerate as ever, we stayed for probably an hour, not really talking but just together. While the moon and stars began to move across the sky, we came to leave the beach, walking back towards the park and into town. Evelyn put her top over her shoulder and feeling motivated by her I joined her doing the same as together we slowly wandered along the river.

Striding along with confidence it was hard not to feel sucked in by her sheer will and self-belief as she wandered quite content through the heart of Ljianstipol with her entire upper body on show bar that lacy bra she was fond of. Together we certainly drew attention as the wandering eyes of men and women glanced at us, she chuckled a few times as she caught guys looking at me twice.

Gradually but surely, we found our way to my front door and into the loving embrace of the sofa, Evelyn went and ran me a bath. While I soaked away the memories of the day kept giving me little pumping moments of joy as I dwelt upon that crash and how she once again had rescued me from it.

I went and laid down on my bed thinking away to myself about today and feeling worried about tomorrow, soon enough I drifted to sleep. Right on schedule part way through the night I woke, though my duvet seemed to be heavier than normal? Curled up next to me and laying on top of my duvet, she laid like a guardian angel to keep me company during the night.

Still facing the door just like she did on the sofa, but tonight she had come to make sure I didn't have any terrors during the night too, I stroked those little curls of hers and kissed her on the cheek. How fortunate was I to have this strange girl appear in my life? Every single time the situation demanded it, she simply rose to the occasion and tonight was a prime example of the magic she brought into my life.

When I woke the next morning, she was still there curled up and dreaming away with that soft and blissful look she had almost every time she slept. Today was going to be my thank you to her, though I didn't know how I felt about going and seeing Karl or Jared? Evelyn would help me with that, this I know only too well, she would lead me to that studio and hold my hand the entire way, realistically I had done the hardest part?

This would just be looking at their pictures and maybe sifting out the odd one that I really didn't like, how hard could that be? Truthfully though my main concern really was that after watching Karl endure a brief vision of the hell my mind puts me through I was a little embarrassed. Karl and Jared would no doubt be cool about it and probably concerned that I was okay, but I wasn't thinking that right now.

I could hear my phone pinging away as message notifications sounded out, I rummaged around to find it being kept warm by Evelyn's little bum. Carefully and cautiously, I prised it out from underneath her, to see a whole chain of support messages. Guessing that Karl and Jared had notified Tony and Gale about my crash and they in turn had notified that group they set up for me. Buried among them though was a message from Karl.

"Call me when you plan to head up, it's important!" I sat wondering what was so important, I know we have to go through the pictures today but surely that's not a major problem is it?

While I sat wondering about that my thoughts shifted to Evelyn and her date with Fabi and his scissors tonight. Genuinely I was surprised that she was going to let him anywhere near those precious curls of hers but I know Fabi will do something great with them for her. Just like her body she was very proud of her locks, those curls would explode when she took that hair tie out of them, bouncing all over the place in a dance that almost defied gravity.

I manoeuvred my way out of the bed without disturbing my sleeping friend to go and have a coffee in the garden while I waited for her to wake up.

Taking my cup, I went and perched myself in the branches of the tree at the end of the garden when a calm sensation came over me as the breeze rolled through my hair. As I sat looking over Ljianstipol, some more of Evelyn's flowers had sprouted out, like her they were very pretty. A knock at the door interrupted the moment of serenity as I discovered that Tony and Gale had come over to see if I was okay. Inviting them in they had come bearing coffee and pastries while checking up on me.

Evelyn appeared still half asleep as she lumbered down the stairs and came to rest leant up against me on the sofa. Tony smiled at me. "She saved the day again?"

I smiled while looking down at me. "Right now, she is saving every day," he smiled as she slowly started to come to life. Her sweet little smile slowly emerged as she realised that her friends had been to Fabi to get her that vile sugary creation, she was so fond of.

Gale offered her a croissant, "When are you going to the studio today?" She smiled at him.

"Can't they just come here today? I'm tired," he laughed at the sleepy Evelyn and her heavy eyes. We chatted for a little while before they headed back to the Davizioso leaving me and sleepy Evelyn to enjoy our day. I headed back to the tree to sit; Evelyn came along too and once again rested, leant up against my side as we sat and looked out over the world. An hour or so later we headed back indoors, my phone started to ring when I answered it Karl claimed to be outside with Jared.

Opening my door, they both stood there with a bunch of flowers in hand and their laptops. "We thought maybe we could bring the studio to you today?" Karl said with that concerned tone back in his voice. Inviting them in they had also come bearing gifts as they set up on my kitchen table to start going through all the pictures that had been taken during the photoshoots.

Jared was speaking to Evelyn when Karl looked at me. "How are you today, Fae?" His concerned voice resonating.

"I'm okay, just embarrassed in truth, sorry you had to see that."

He seemed taken aback, "Sorry? What for? You can't control those, I'm just glad you are okay, it was scary to watch that," he said reassuringly.

Evelyn came through to join us as they opened their laptops and began to show me all the pictures they had taken. Navigating the seemingly endless stream of excellent pictures they had taken; it became apparent that this might actually be harder than the photo shoots had been! Gradually we narrowed things down and agreed what they wouldn't use rather than what images they would, Karl looked at me. "Forgive me Fae but there is one last folder I want you to see."

Karl plugged a memory stick into his laptop and opened the folder, he clicked on the first image. While Evelyn had been saving me from my crash last night Karl had carried on shooting, capturing every single moment on camera. Starting from the moment I stumbled to the moment Evelyn walked me back out to the dunes to complete the session.

Scrolling through the images of her rescuing me from my mind, with my face red where I had been crying my eyes out, they were a chilling reminder of just how destructive my problems could be. Oddly though, they were actually quite beautiful? The incredible dedication and love that she had used to help bring me back from my own brink?

Images with sorrowful and emotionally tortured looks strewn across my face as my world caved in on top of me? While I scrolled Evelyn put her hand on my knee to support me. Karl shielding his mouth with his hands, "I thought you needed to see these," he said as he removed the memory stick and gave it to me.

"I haven't got any copies of this, so they belong to you," he placed the memory stick on the table and pushed it across to me. Taking it in my hand I sat looking at it and thinking about all those harrowing images and how it must have been terrifying for him to stand there helplessly and watch as my world fell apart.

Suddenly, a very strange and odd notion came over me. "Use them." Karl and Jared looked at me confused, "Show them what it's really like, these pictures show what it is really like for me, not just me but thousands of other people just like me, use them for the article, you have my permission to show the world what it looks like when my world crashes," Jared looked at Karl.

"Are you sure about this?" I looked over at Evelyn.

"Yes, it might be the only thing I am sure about," Jared and Karl packed their things and started to leave.

"I'm glad you are okay Fae, see you soon," Karl said as he left me and Evelyn to await our visitors this evening.

Soon enough, Fabi and Alyssia arrived carrying takeaway and Fabi had his hair dresser bag with him, Evelyn gulped as she realised the threat to cut her hair had become all too real. Enjoying dinner together Fabi spent as much time talking to Evelyn about what he planned to do with her hair as he did eating.

Soon enough, the time came as Fabi sat Evelyn down on a chair in the middle of my kitchen and started to unpack his bag. Alyssia and I went into the living room to leave them to it, periodically we could hear Evelyn cry out as locks of her precious hair were placed into her hands.

Periodically we would check in on them, Fabi with straighteners in hand was fighting the goliath like monster that resided on Evelyn's scalp, he would shoo us out of the kitchen so that he could work. Eventually, though he called us through to unveil his handy work, when we joined them in the kitchen, I couldn't believe what he had done with Evelyn's hair.

Straightened and with a thick neat braid running around the front, she looked so different, somehow, she actually looked cuter? I mean, Evelyn was one of the cutest things that I had ever laid my eyes upon but that haircut somehow just heightened that aspect of her. Her sweet cheeks and neckline fully exposed with little odd bangs running down the side of her face, she smiled contently as Fabi wandered around her with a mirror showing her his handy work.

Evelyn gave him a hug and thanked him for his work. "Now you look like a princess," Fabi simply smiled back at her as she held onto him and squeezed away. Alyssia sat and chatted with her about what she had planned for the weekend when Evelyn unveiled her plan to take me to another place she had found.

Evelyn had continued to search for the place she had seen from the bus window that she wanted us to visit together and it seemed she had succeeded in finding it. Alyssia and Fabi soon departed and left us to enjoy the remainder of our evening before Evelyn would take me to this place she had spoken about so often.

Excited as ever, she wore the outfit Colette had gifted her little dove and I wore that white dress that Evelyn claimed that Karl was so fond of. Evelyn brought her backpack along so that we could have a picnic, today was going to be a very long day it seemed! Together, we headed out further from Ljianstipol than I had ever ventured on foot, the June sunshine soon had the temperature rising up as we embarked on this journey that Evelyn had been so eager for us to make.

Leading the way, we seemed to wander endlessly further and further until we arrived at a crumbling wall and she led us through an equally crumpled gate into an enormous expansive park. Evelyn took her sandals off and put them in her backpack, she liked to walk barefoot in the woods as it reminded her of the forest where she claimed to live.

Feeling ever encouraged by my friend I joined her and put my sandals in the backpack along with hers as she joyfully led me deeper and deeper into the trees. Stopping at a little meadow with a picnic table we sat and had a snack and a drink before we resumed her quest to show me what she had seen from the bus window when she first arrived in Ljianstipol.

Having walked for what seemed like hours the trees began to thin and before us was a vast meadow which overlooked the mountains and surrounding farmlands. Glorious in every conceivable way the lush grasses were adorned with little flowers as bees flew in and out of the flowers collecting nectar.

Sunshine bathed this incredible land as we continued to walk at a slower pace further and further into this oasis of grasses and flowers. Before us, the landscape began to roll away as the lands rolled onwards to the base of the mountain range which she had always said marked the dividing line between our world and hers. Amidst the open expanse of grass sat an old tree stump, the tree itself having been long since cleared away it sat like a beacon in the sea of green.

Together we sat and enjoyed our picnic we had brought with us, relaxing in this utterly blissful and tranquil environment time simply seemed to stop as the sun floated over the sky. Evelyn was sitting on the tree stump looking over the horizon to the mountains when I could hear her sniffling?

Approaching her slowly and softly from behind she turned her head to reveal her red cheeks where she was weeping about something? Standing next to her, I started to try and help my little friend, she seemed to be struggling to tell me something and whatever it was, it was clearly something very big? Eventually, I sat on the stump with her in my lap and started to try and extract from her what was bothering her so much.

In truth, she had been quieter than normal today? Something was affecting her and whatever it was for her it was very important to her, a few times she had seemed to be staring endlessly into space? Gradually I managed to extract from her what was upsetting her so much, Evelyn had chosen a very private and touching moment when she unveiled her plans to leave after the party and return to the place where she hailed from.

Evelyn was struggling to tell me why she needed to leave, trying to explain that she needed to leave so that she could come back sooner? She just couldn't tell me how soon that might be? Almost inconsolable as her emotions took full control of her and she broke into tears trying to explain herself to me.

Pulling her back and laying her across my lap I started to support her, whatever her reasons for leaving where I was going to make her last week with me extra special. Telling her the truth how my life had been so much better since she had been with me and that she would always have a friend and a home here with me.

Equally devastated at her plans we just sat and chatted; I would really miss my little friend but felt deeply touched that she had chosen this private moment to unveil her plans to me first. She would tell everyone else at the party of course but she felt she owed it to me to tell me first, I thanked her for telling me first. Evelyn's news devastated me but when she said she would return I had no reason to doubt this as in the two months that this odd girl had been in my life, she had never lied to me.

Sitting with her in my lap we started to plan our final week together before she would catch that bus back to her hometown and venture onwards to the mountains and beyond to her home. While the sun began to dip below the mountains, we agreed to come back to this park on the day before she left, alone we would spend one last day here together.

Amidst this last plan she asked one strange request, she wanted us to both wear the clothes we had worn the day we met, though I couldn't quite understand this odd stipulation, I agreed to it. Together we wandered back to my home, a quieter walk back as both of us seemed to be thinking about the time we had spent together and how much we would miss each other. One thing in my mind was very certain though.

Whatever happened until she would return, I would miss her, in truth I couldn't imagine my life without her, she needed to do this for herself and of course she promised to come back and as of yet my little friend had never lied to me.

Over the next week, we simply spent as much time together as we could, evening walks, visits to the beach and the bars along the river, together we had a wonderful week. Days passed seemingly faster and faster as we headed towards Saturday night's big party, Evelyn had been so excited about this party since they gave her that little card and of course she was eager to finally wear that dress.

From time to time, I had sad moments as I realised how quickly our time together was passing and that soon it would come to a very abrupt and sorrowful end. Though I didn't let this affect our week as we crammed in as much time together as we could muster. Karl had popped round during the week to check I was okay after that crash during our photoshoot, Evelyn was quite amused by his unexpected visit.

Evelyn spent the next few days telling me how Karl must really love my bum to keep popping over to see it, "Thanks Evelyn!"

I would laugh at her. We planned for our final week together too, she wanted to have a big meal with everyone that she liked, she would announce it at the party along with her plans to leave. Maybe the only downside to her final week here would be that I would be working but either way we would cram in as much as we could that week. Saturday was going to be tough for her, not only did she have to announce her plans to leave and arrange this meal but Tony had a surprise for my little friend.

Wondering how she would feel when he gave her those pictures of her parents? Would it make her happy or sad? Being able to glimpse at the parents she lost when she was so young that she struggled to remember them in any real detail, maybe if nothing else it would at least give her some form of closure?

Either way at least she would be surrounded by all the people who loved her so dearly, the almost endless stream of people who just fell in love with her. Every single one of them would be there tonight to support her when she received her gift from Tony and they would be more than happy to console Evelyn if she needed them to.

Soon enough, Saturday morning arrived and Evelyn and I both woke excited like little children as this was the night, we had both been looking forward to. We spent all day getting ourselves ready for the big night in Ljianstipol, pampering each other throughout the day while the hours ticked away and our excitement grew ever stronger.

Evelyn put on the dress Francois had made and she looked incredible in it! Her soft and subtle curves being heightened by that soft purple fabric, that deep cut in the back showing off her beautiful skin and shoulders. Evelyn looked utterly dreamy as she proudly donned this beautiful piece, if people didn't find her attractive before tonight, she was certainly going to blow them away!

Having spent much of my time debating between the blue floral dress or the white dress she gave me for my birthday or 'Karl's Dress', as she had come to call it. Eventually, I went with the blue floral one, for me it was because this was the dress, she found for me on our first real adventure together in Ljianstipol.

I came downstairs dressed and ready to go, Evelyn looked over at me. "You look beautiful Fae!" With her usual sweet and encouraging tone. Blushing a little I smiled back at her, "Would Karl like it too?" She giggled and came over to pat my rear for me. "Yes, he would like it," she continued to giggle as she patted my bum.

Just when she thought she had gotten away with her little amusing gesture, I turned and unleashed the tickle monster on her little belly. Trying to escape she fell back onto the sofa as my tickle onslaught continued, wriggling, writhing and crying with laughter as my fingers tickled her little stomach before I stopped and smiled at her, "Thank you so much for everything you have done, Evelyn," I paused to reflect before I gave her a hug.

"Thank you too Fae," she said back as we embraced one final time. Taking her hand, I helped her stand back up and together we headed to Tony and Gale's party on the outskirts of Ljianstipol.

Chapter 8
The Missing Mystery

Together we walked through the evening sun towards the conjoined homes of Tony and Gale for the big party, they had bought them after a property developer ran out of money. They paid the developer to finish both homes with a minor adjustment to the garden, they removed the fence from the garden and created a single huge garden. Every year, they host a huge party to thank the people who have helped them in their journey since they arrived in Ljianstipol. People from all walks of life attend, business owners, people who randomly helped out and even a few residents of the Davizioso come to this no expense spared thank you party.

Walking along we were turning more than a few heads as we confidently wandered through the streets towards the party. Evelyn was certainly drawing attention but in truth that was no surprise as she looked phenomenal tonight, though she was equally happy to point out that I was getting a lot of attention too.

Sauntering along with a happy and carefree demeanour as the journey began to draw to a close and we could hear laughter and talking as we approached the driveway to their homes. Mona caught sight of us and walked out to meet us.

"Fae and Evelyn, nice to see you both, you both look great! Come on down!" She smiled as she guided us down the driveway and through to the garden. Walking through the smiles of Tony and Gale appeared as I wandered through with Mona and Evelyn just behind me. When Mona stepped aside to let Evelyn pass, silence struck as people caught sight of her in all her majesty.

Tony raised his arm to her and she headed over to let him give her a welcoming hug, they were so adorable! Tony loved that girl, if them walking the garden wasn't enough to break the stoniest of souls then this little hug certainly was, as Tony turned to mush the second, he got hold of that girl.

Together we sat with Tony and Gale and chatted for a little while, Tony gave Evelyn one of those huge beer bottles he had found just for her, I'm sure he found the biggest bottles ever for her, they were nearly as large as her. Mona soon came to join us; she also had a large affection for Evelyn as she seemed to be helping Tony to finally bring their passed son David back into their lives.

Sitting and chatting about my photoshoot and the article that would soon follow, the evening was certainly pleasant as more guests began to appear. Alyssia and Fabi came to join our little group, Fabi was keen to point out the wonders he had worked with Evelyn's hair. "The dress could make anything you do look good, Fabi!" Alyssia declared as she attempted to curb his enthusiasm.

Barbeques flamed away and the wonderful smell of cooking meat over hot coals filled the air as the sunlight began to fade away into the deep blue of the night. Lamps around the garden began to flicker into life as it became very apparent to Evelyn that this would be a very long night for us both. An almost ceaseless stream of guests continued to arrive, including Shaun and his wife with Jess in tow, she stopped on the spot when she caught sight of Evelyn wandering the garden with Mona in that beautiful dress of hers.

Francois and Colette were the last guests to arrive, Colette's jaw nearly hit the floor as she sped over to greet her little dove. "Look at you little dove! You look incredibly beautiful," smiling to her little sweetheart as she spoke.

"A beautiful little swan thanks to yours truly," Francois said as he winked at his little friend.

Colette smiled. "At least you can do this one thing right, Francois," their usual love for each other in full swing tonight as Colette winked at her little dove.

As the evening drove on, the first part of Tony's gift to Evelyn was approaching as he disappeared to get all the floating lanterns ready to be released to remember all the people who had passed out of their lives. Over the next twenty minutes everyone in turn lit their lantern to remember their fallen family, friends and loved ones who had sadly passed away.

This seemingly morbid moment meant a lot to Tony as he released the lantern in honour of his fallen son David, Evelyn stood with him and held his hand as he let the lantern float up into the air. Tony took her hand and guided her away, looking over and signalling me to follow him as he led Evelyn down a secluded path to a hidden garden.

Tony gave Evelyn two little lanterns and a lighter, shielding the lighter he helped her light the first lantern, she waited before releasing it off into the distance. Taking the second lantern and letting the fire ignite and take hold of it before she let that float away to join all the other lanterns. Whispering to herself as the lanterns floated away into the sky, she rubbed her eyes, Tony turned and left.

"I will give you a few minutes," he said as he walked away and smiled at me. Evelyn stood in silence, gently rubbing each eye and whispering to herself as she watched the lanterns float away into the distance and illuminating the sky. Suddenly, I noticed she was crying, I slowly walked up behind her, she looked up at me and just rested her head against my chest and held onto me as her emotions fell out.

Quietly she stood there holding onto me tighter and tighter and weeping to herself when Colette came walking down the path, saw us together and smiled softly. Colette smiled. "Petit oiseau come here."

Colette offered her arm to Evelyn who softly flopped over to her, continuing to cry. Colette put her hand on Evelyn's hair and held her softly, "Our petit oiseau has just said goodbye, is that right, Evelyn?" Colette looked down at Evelyn, still weeping but with a little smile appearing.

Colette pulled her tighter, "Let it all out my little dove, you have waited a long time for this, we will be here all night if you need us to be, isn't that right Fae?" Colette looked at me.

"All night, Evelyn," I replied as I joined Colette comforting Evelyn and wrapping her in a little cocoon of love and support. Tony and Francois came heading down the path but Colette waved them away, she knew Evelyn needed a few minutes of just silence to let what she had just done sink in.

Colette held onto Evelyn with her eyes closed and whispering French poems almost silently into her ears before she seemed to feel Evelyn relax. Colette looked at her and noticed her tears had gone, she gave her a little kiss on the cheek before she hugged her one last time.

Colette wiped her eyes anyway and gave her a little peck on the nose. "Are you ready to go and listen to Francois again petit oiseau?" Evelyn just nodded back. Colette gave her one final hug before she took one hand and I took the other as we walked her back to the party, like three sisters. Francois offered Evelyn a beer, when she took it, he raised a glass to her, silently acknowledging what she had just done.

Francois patted the chair next to him, "You idiot! Why would she want to sit next to you!"

Colette bit at Francois with a wry smile, "Because I am the charming one no?" Evelyn giggled and sat between the Parisian love birds as they argued and traded insults.

I went and sat with Tony and watched as Evelyn chuckled away at her two warring friends in a glorious display of verbal abuse. Evelyn had waited for 17 years to finally say goodbye to her parents, maybe deep down she had been waiting for that moment to finally happen? After all the years of being abused for being an orphan, being ginger or for being small, she had never had the chance to just say goodbye to her parents?

Just as she had helped Tony to talk about David, Tony had helped her to finally let go, something that maybe nobody else could have thought to do? Symbiotically they had helped each other move forwards.

Tony of course still had one last gift for Evelyn, with many people having left as the evening drew to a close. Mona came to rejoin us with a bag in her hand, handing it to Evelyn as Tony smiled at her, "Open it," Evelyn opened the bag to find a little wooden box.

Upon opening the box, once again she was moved to tears as she discovered a plethora of pictures of her parents and her as a child with them that Tony, Gale, Mona and Ellie had provided for her. Mona sat next to Evelyn as she started to thumb through the pictures, putting her hand on her back as she pulled one out, Anna joined them. Anna took the picture and smiled. "I remember this day, it's the day they came home with you Evelyn, look at your little curls!" She smiled sweetly at the weeping Evelyn.

Continuing to go through the miscellany of pictures Anna stopped at one. "Gale took this picture in our garden, look at you with Ellie!" smiling away as she reminisced with Evelyn.

Gale looked at Evelyn, "If we knew what she was like, we would have taken you in Evelyn, Ellie always wanted a little sister," he smiled sadly as he thought about the hellish life Evelyn had endured. Over the next hour, we sat sifting through Evelyn's largely forgotten past, each image making her smile and cry as she caught glimpses of her much missed but now unforgotten parents. Hugging them all harder than ever before it was time to head home, Gale gave us both a beer for the journey home.

Smiling sweetly to herself as we walked through the darkness and back towards my home, the moonlight caught the little angel as she wandered along. Light glimmering over her cheeks and down her back highlighting just how magical this friend was, she seemed oddly at peace. Maybe finally having the chance to just say goodbye was fuelling a slightly more content look across her face as we wandered along quietly?

Quite possibly having those sneak glimpses of the past she couldn't remember was driving the little angel tonight. Whatever it was, she certainly was pleased, she had thoroughly enjoyed her first party in Ljianstipol and rather selfishly I hoped we wouldn't have to wait long to have her second party here.

Evelyn spent most of the next day just going through those pictures, not that I blamed her in truth it was nice to see her slowly look back at her past. Eventually, she put them all back in that box and placed them on the chest of drawers in the room I had given her when she first arrived. Oddly though she kept one out and put it in her backpack? I didn't really ask her why but for some reason it seemed that this sole picture she would be taking with her when she caught the bus on Sunday?

During that day we planned our final week, we would visit the beach during the evenings after I finished work. Friday we would go for the big meal she had planned and Saturday we would have our final day together alone in that park before she caught the bus on Sunday morning to return home.

Evelyn started packing ready for it, she took her green outfit and on the day, she would leave she would wear the black top and trousers we found on our shopping trip when she first arrived. Everything else would remain here and await her return, we spent the day neatly folding and hanging her clothes up so that everything would be ready to go when she came back, whenever that might be.

During the party she had unveiled her plans to leave to a largely devastated audience of people, they loved this little girl and her leaving was something they had hoped wouldn't happen anytime soon. Life of course, has a way of throwing obstacles in your way, the obstacle this time was the group sessions for the healthcare system that Tony and Gale had intentionally pitched to lose, they had won and this Wednesday and Thursday night we would run the first two trial runs of these sessions.

Evelyn was okay with losing those few precious hours together in her mind as I would be doing something of great importance so losing a few hours together was a sacrifice she was happy to make. While I was at work, Evelyn had arranged the big meal on Friday night and invited all the people she wanted in attendance, nobody refused her invite.

Evelyn's chosen venue was the American diner that Leanne was now working at, when she told me I spent most of Monday and Tuesday trying to get her to change this venue. Evelyn though was insistent that Leanne wouldn't be given the chance to spoil this last glorious and special night in Ljianstipol.

Wednesday afternoon would be Evelyn and Tony's final garden walk together until she returned, out of respect for them both me and Gale held our meeting in the largely unused boardroom of the Davizioso. While they wandered round the garden, we held our meeting at that dusty table, though even through the thick walls we swore every now and then we could hear them giggling to each other as they wandered those garden paths.

While Evelyn went home to await my return, together me, Gale and Tony made ready for tonight's first pilot session, Tony was angry about hosting them. Tony asked Gale with fury in his voice, "How did we win this?"

Gale shrugged his shoulders, "I have no idea, I tripled our actual price to try and lose the contract." Tony's reason for not wanting these sessions was fairly simple, the chairman of that delegation who had largely shunned me and their work, was the same man that discharged his son a mere 6 hours before David committed suicide.

Both pilot sessions would be 2 hours long and in truth both actually went pretty well and it seemed like every Wednesday and Thursday night I would now be running these two sessions. Strangely though both evenings when I returned home, Evelyn was sitting in the tree at the bottom of my garden talking to herself? Given what would be happening in a few days, I figured maybe she was just talking things out with herself and gave her the space to work these things out in her mind.

Friday soon came and with it that final last hurrah that she would spend with all the people that she had come to know and befriend in Ljianstipol. During the morning, we did one last final iteration of her morning rounds, naturally with this being the last time she would do this it was a very emotional morning.

Francois was oddly quiet and his normal razor tongue had been put away for their final morning coffee together. Alyssia simply stood holding her while they wandered that gallery trying to figure out what people saw in these art pieces that people paid so heavily for. Colette though was the hardest, unable to hide her sorrow that her little dove and trainee was heading away, she spent most of their final hours disappearing to mask her tears.

Colette threaded a little bow through Evelyn's hair before we departed to get ready for the evening meal, simply put the entirety of my friend group was preparing themselves to mourn.

During the week people had been trying to get Evelyn to change the venue for tonight's meal, people were more than aware of the role Leanne had played in Evelyn's tortured childhood. Evelyn however was stoic and resolute in sticking to her choice for tonight's meal, surrounded by her friends, Leanne wasn't going to have any chance to spoil this celebration.

Everyone gathered for this special moment with their new friend, a table of 16 no less and highlighting just how adored she really was. That diner was packed with all the tables outside also being full, Colette made sure she got to sit next to her little dove, but of course Colette adored her, so it was no real surprise.

Spirits were high and the evening was joyful with so many people being there to show just how much they liked this strange girl. Leanne had clocked Evelyn in her sailor suit, sneering at her every time she walked past our table, when our meals came out, she plopped a children's meal in front of her with a plastic dog toy.

Leanne smiled at Evelyn, "A child's portion for a child," Evelyn calmly and slowly stood up.

"I think you have made a mistake Leanne," Leanne turned round, "No, 15 adults and one child, it's correct," she walked over and fronted up to Evelyn. Colette stood up to support her little dove but as it turned out, it wasn't Evelyn who needed the back up!

Leanne stood towering over the calm and composed Evelyn, "Enjoy your meal, child," Evelyn smiled back at her, "I will but can you change the toy for the cat please?"

Leanne stared down at her and slammed her hand on the table, "Why have you come here you little freak!" Evelyn looked round the restaurant.

"Your mum and dad aren't here to protect you this time Leanne, though why do you need to ruin all these other people's evening?"

Before Leanne could respond to her, "You had an entire school and your parents to back you up and you didn't break me. Unlike you, I have grown and look at you now, all the people in this restaurant are disgusted with you and the way you are, so maybe you should have the toy?"

Leanne started to back away, looking round to see her boss waiting for her, "I'm going to lose my job because of you!"

Evelyn smiled at her, "No Leanne, you are going to lose your job because of you," Evelyn sat back down to the applause of every single person in the diner with the exception of Leanne who walked past our table crying after being fired for her performance. The owner of the diner replaced Evelyn's meal and gave her a dessert free of charge, the evening was fantastic aside from that odd standoff moment.

Evelyn proved during that stand off just how large she truly was, even after years of abuse, abuse that would have broken many, she proved just how strong she truly was. Evelyn had grown to be proud of herself, her size and her figure and her courage was something to behold as she rose above everyone that ever doubted her.

The truth was that Evelyn actually pitied Leanne, with the entire world behind her and Mummy and daddy using their influence to keep her clean. Unlike Evelyn, Leanne had never grown as a person mainly because she had no reason or need to do so. Real life though is very different to school life, what might have been funny to a group of mid-teens was not funny to the average 20–40-year-old.

Quite the opposite in truth, where the world now saw Evelyn as a beautiful petite girl only Leanne still saw her as an object to be picked on. Fortunately for Leanne though, Evelyn had grown out of physical defence as in the past Leanne had lost out to her in this area despite her popularity and vast near 6-foot size compared to the 4 foot 8 Evelyn.

The sun rose and illuminated the June sky for the final adventure that me and Evelyn would spend together before she caught the bus tomorrow and headed off into the distance. While she still slept, I started to get a bag ready to take with us on our final jaunt to the park we had visited last week and we planned to eke out as much time on this last day as we could manage.

Wandering out towards the park I caught fleeting glimpses of that girl's magic quality as she strode happily along in that strange green outfit and flowery trainers, she was so proud of. Sunlight kept dancing over her eyes and skin, exposing just how attractive she truly was in that little outfit, her delicacy and intricacy all masked in that petite figure of hers. Barefoot as always, we wandered through the vast park and out towards that meadow that overlooked the rolling hills and mountains beyond.

Chest down, we laid in the ocean of flowers and soft lush grasses near that stump from where she would sit and stare over the horizon seemingly dreaming as she looked across the world. We talked about all that had happened and as always, she was continually reminding me that she would be coming back just she couldn't tell me how soon it would be. Though she did manage to explain better why she had chosen this moment to leave, the flowers she planted under my tree seemed to be linked to this decision?

Colour changes on those flowers seemed to give her some kind of warning sign? In truth the light orange flowered had darkened as they grew but what link could this have to her leaving me? Evelyn became aware that I was deeply saddened by her impending departure, she pulled out a tourist map of her home town and started to draw on the map inside it.

Drawing a line from the town and mountain range depicted in the map, she drew a line through the forest to a little opening? Pointing at it, "If you really need me before I return, this is where you will find me," she smiled as she handed me the little map. Sitting looking at the amended map she had given me, she came over and gave me a huge hug.

"Mother would love you too," she whispered as she drew the line to this opening in the forest. Smiling away she stayed next to me as the sun began to set across the mountains and rolling hills in the distance, her little cheeks reddened as she let a few tears go.

Sniffling away to herself, I unleashed the tickle monster on her one last time, furiously tickling her little belly one last time, as she wriggled to try get free, I caught her and held her, "I'm really going to miss you, come back to me soon," she smiled as I held her, "I will, let Karl look after your bum until I come back."

I looked at her smiling face, "I will," as I patted my bum for her.

Through the night we stayed up and talked, extracting every precious minute from our last hours together, she would keep telling me where to find her if I needed her. Precious hours passed as the inevitable end of this chapter approached, when the sun came up, she began to get herself ready, carefully packing what little she was taking with her. Crying from time to time as she put each item into her backpack for her journey, she took a bath before she appeared with her green outfit and flowery shoes ready for our walk to the bus station.

We shared one last private hug before we began the journey for her to get her bus, as we walked, we were joined by an unexpected friend for her final moments. Colette had come to join us and to bid farewell to her little dove. "I couldn't stay away little dove," she said to us both as we walked towards the bus station. Soon enough the bus that would carry her away arrived and she shared her final moments in Ljianstipol with us, hugging us both and telling us she loved us before she climbed on the bus.

If this had been a film, halfway up the road the bus would have stopped and she would have jumped off and ran back down the road towards us. However, this wasn't like a film, the bus didn't stop, Evelyn didn't jump off and run back to us, as the bus drove away it simply turned a corner and disappeared into the distance carrying our little friend away with it.

Colette hugged me and walked me back to her and Francois home where we spent the day sharing our cherished memories of Evelyn, Colette and Francois both adored that girl.

Emptiness filled their garden that day, though I appreciated their support in this dark moment, it did nothing to lift the sorrow that we all felt after she had gone. Early days without my little housemate around were tough, really tough; during the first few nights after she left, I found myself waiting for her to appear when I got home from work.

Fantasising about her running at me and giving me those back breaking hugs or trying to scare me as she jumped out of a closet, the house was oddly quiet without her around.

Every time I woke for water during the night, I came downstairs and looked at my sofa hoping and dreaming that maybe she would be back there, curled up asleep in her spot. However much I dreamt about it, night in night out, she wasn't there with her little curls rolling under the ebb and flow of her breath or giggling as she dreamt.

However, it was the first Wednesday after she left when it really hit me about just how big the void her departure had left in Ljianstipol. Heading down to work without the hyperactive girl at my side was slightly odd and quite painful in truth, our padlock was still on that bridge which just served to remind me of what I felt I had lost.

Evelyn loved Wednesdays in Ljianstipol, the market made her utterly psychotic in the mornings but also, she and Tony both looked forward to their walks together. Heading up to the rooftop garden after my lunch break for my meeting with Gale, it was then that the true magnitude of her departure really struck me. Tony sat ominously quiet as me and Gale held our meeting, every time Tony heard a noise, he would snap round to look at the gateway to the garden expecting her to have appeared for their walk.

Tony left halfway through the meeting, consumed with sorrow and grief that his little friend really had gone away, he disappeared to spend a quiet moment alone. Gale was deeply concerned about Tony and how hard Evelyn's departure had hit him, she had opened Tony back up and her leaving seemed to be closing him back down. Together, we discussed what we might be able to do to try and help Tony, but whatever we thought might help it was clear that Tony just needed time to process her departure.

My evening group therapy sessions went well this week, somehow through my own grief I managed to remain composed enough to host the sessions better than before. Sharing my grief about my newly departed friend seemed to give better flow than before though in truth it might have been a bad idea as picking scabs before the heal can be very dangerous.

Thursday evening's session went fantastically well, after I returned home, I celebrated with a beer in the garden. Looking at those flowers she had planted, their soft oranges had grown into deep and saturated colours, looking at the tree she sat in, I climbed and sat in the branches and overlooked Ljianstipol.

Raising my bottle to her, I shed a tear as it dawned on me just how much she had changed my life in that short time she spent with me. Unexpectedly though as I sat in the branches a voice called to me? A deep German voice?

"Good evening to you," slightly stunned, I looked over the fence to see a man sitting upon a children's slide, with a bottle of beer in his hand? During my second week off work, people were meant to have moved in but having seen no sign of life I assumed that the house was still empty?

He raised his bottle to me. "You are Fae? Yes?" A deep Bavarian accent carrying his words.

"Yes, nice to meet you," I said back and raised my bottle back to him, "I'm Magnus, your friend she has gone yes?" I looked over at him.

"Yes, she has gone," I said back with a sad tone, he raised his bottle again, "She asked me to keep an eye on you when she left, so feel free to sit and chat with me anytime out here."

As I took in what he just said, "Was it you she was speaking to last week Magnus?" He smiled. "Yes, she is a funny girl, but I quite liked her," a softer tone carried this statement from him.

We sat on opposite sides of the fence and introduced ourselves to each other, he was a graphic designer but mostly worked at night, hence why I hadn't seen him since he moved in next door.

Unexpected times carry unexpected events though, as if the first week without my friend wasn't hard, the second week would be devastating. Every day I woke hoping to see her back on my sofa again, my mind blindly wandering and luring me into false senses of hope. With each passing day, I felt more and more alone, my friends had been openly keeping a watchful eye on me as they knew I was struggling with Evelyn gone.

Slowly I had stopped topping up my hair dye, and the normally radiant purple, blue and turquoise was slowly fading away into a washed out mix of blues and sad green whites. Colour was fading out of my hair just as much as my drive and passion was falling out of me. Days started to merge into a smear of largely meaningless and emotionless hours and minutes as my life force began to drain away.

Gale had noticed how much I was suffering and was trying his best to prop me back up and reignite my passion and burn that had stunned an entire world. Colette would pop over some evenings to make sure I was okay; they knew I was falling away in a state of loneliness.

Fabi, Alyssia, Francois and Tony also kept checking up on me as I seemed to start wandering aimlessly through my own abyss, their biggest fear was what might happen when I had my first crash without my friend to help me.

Thursday night after my group session I went back home, as I walked into my empty living room, it came, with vengeance. Looking at the empty sofa, my mind stumbled and went crashing down carrying me with it towards the deepest depths of my own hell. Sitting on the floor, my eyes were flowing fully as every single emotion and tear fell out of my body, suddenly erupting into a loud series of crying fits.

Waning hopelessly on the floor of my own home, my mind was only too keen to remind me just how alone I now was. Unable to think clearly, I began to hyperventilate as this brutal reminder that no matter how in control I felt, my mind belonged firmly to the grips of my conditions. Shuddering as every passing thought began to fill with despair and crying uncontrollably, as I fell onto my side on the floor something strange happened.

Collapsing onto the floor in the shallow pool created by my tears, as I rolled over that picture of me and Evelyn from the photo shoot caught my eye and as it did something very odd and unusual happened. Looking at that sweet smile and the sheer love that girl could emit, my mind started to ease off, as if she was stood there just holding onto me.

305

Suddenly, my mind started flowing with all the wonderful times we had shared together, where she picked me up or caught me when I fell, those times she rescued me from the vice-like grip of my depression or anxiety. Evelyn had never been fazed by either, nor did she mind my often very different personalities, even in her absence, she was quite capable of saving me from myself.

Laying there I started to think about that crash at the beach, that helpless look on Karl's face as he watched me crumble and the look of sheer terror as my mind collapsed into itself. Reminiscing about how hard she hit me when she ran at me to give me that seemingly eternal hug and her constant words of reassurance.

Almost as quickly as my crash hit me, it began to fade away as the thought of her drove it out of my mind and replaced my emotionless face with a very subtle smile. Magnus had heard my crying and came to see if I was okay, walking in to find me sitting on the floor staring at her picture.

Sitting with me for a while I started to tell him about the photo shoot where she got Karl to take this picture and how she had managed to get every single piece of chocolate out of their gratuity bowl as she played that game with Karl and the receptionist. Softly smiling to myself, "Gninrom doog," I uttered and Magnus looked confused, I started to explain her game to him, by the end of the story both of us were laughing about how she tortured them in that studio.

I started to explain my conditions to Magnus, he stayed for a few hours before he went back to his family and left me behind, he gave me his phone number and told me to text him if this happened again. Evelyn even in her absence had gone to great lengths to try and make sure I would be okay while I awaited her return, now I just hoped that wait wouldn't be too long.

However unknown to me there was someone else keeping an eye on me too, very secretively and in the darkness of my circle of friends, just watching over me but keeping a very shrouded approach to this. Sourcing general information about how I was bearing up from my friends, they were watching and all too aware that I was suffering in the absence of my little friend.

Friday morning having recovered from my crash, I had decided that I would go and do Evelyn's normal morning rounds. Slightly reliving her time with me as I started with a longer visit to Fabi, we chatted for a little while as he had started to grow concerned with how my usual zing was fading away.

Fabi sat with me, and we had a lengthy discussion about how I was faring alone before he offered to dye my hair back to its normal radiant colour scheme.

Reasoning with him that I might just let it return to its natural colour, that blonde and brown colour that hadn't seen the light of day since he swiped my hat that morning at his shop. Confessing to Fabi that maybe it was time for a change as I showed him the picture of me and my mum, he would help but he did say I might look a little strange for a time.

Fabi was supportive and he commented that I did have a nice natural hair colour but to let him know if I changed my mind and wanted to dye it again, after all my past attempts to dye my hair myself, hadn't exactly been resounding successes.

Francois was next on my round, we sat talking for a while, clearly, he was sad to see his friend gone, though I did start to understand why Evelyn enjoyed listening to him as he shot his insults the way of the badly dressed. Remarkably though it surprised me that he didn't wind up with multiple black eyes for the comments he made to people, that tongue was certainly sharp this morning!

Alyssia would be my next visit, she was only too happy to spend a bit of time with me, her normally stern British tone was much softer this morning. Clearly, she was concerned about me as we wandered the gallery, a very different Alyssia walked with me today, this Alyssia was filled with fear? Alyssia kept me with her for an hour before I headed to join the ever-sleepy Abby on her break outside the Davizioso, Abby recounted her most recent gaming achievements with me, showing me videos of her, 'Owning dudes'.

I wasn't entirely sure what she was talking about but it made her very happy to have done it. Abby was also quite concerned about me and she quite willingly offered her assistance if I needed company at night. Abby agreed to pop over Saturday night to give me some company and she would bring takeaway for a girly night. Colette would be my final stop of the day; her usual shy and quiet approach today was replaced by a welcoming and heartfelt chat.

Colette locked her shop and she took me for lunch at a bistro she was fond of, together we spoke about her little dove and how much we both missed her. While we spoke about Evelyn, I told Colette about my crash the night before, she smiled as I told her that Evelyn's picture helped me overcome it, "Even when she is not here my little dove is a guardian angel," smiling as she held my hand and checked if I was okay.

Colette told me to come and see her any time, she didn't want me to suffer alone, everyone in my circle of friends was carrying the same message.

After my morning rounds though, I wanted to take some time out and to just sit alone and process things and think about things. I headed to the beach to sit on the promenade and just sit alone and try to smooth things out in my mind. Sitting at the very front of the promenade, I sat down on the wall leaning on the railings looking over the beach and sea.

Looking over the horizon as I dwelt upon our time together as the sun slowly made its way across the sky. Almost as if she was there with me, I took my top off and sat in my skirt and bra with my upper body being warmed by the sun's warming glow. Periodically, people would tut at me. "Don't be so stupid!" as if they thought I might jump from the wall to my death on the sand and rocks below the spot where I sat.

Slumping over the railings with my face down as I watched the sky begin to turn orange and red, I felt something grab the railings. Vibrations from tapping fingers making me aware that someone was standing there, almost disapproving of my chosen position to reflect upon my current state.

Growing agitated by the continual tapping on the railings my temper began to fray, just as I grew the nerve to look round and tell them where to go, they spoke. Tapping away, "You okay?" A softly spoken voice breaking the sound of tapping, before I could look round—"I thought you might be here," in the same soft and considerate tone as before. Slightly stunned by this sudden voice, I looked round to see Karl stood against the railings, he looked at me.

"I was worried about you, so have been looking for you," I looked at him as he started to look over the horizon. "I'm okay, I just needed to think and work things out," he smiled as if he knew I wasn't being honest. I turned to look back over the horizon. "Honestly, Karl? I'm doing really badly; I'm struggling to sleep and my motivation and enthusiasm has drained away since she left."

Karl put his hand on my shoulder. "I know, I'm worried about you Fae," he said as he squeezed my shoulder softly.

Leaning my head over to his arm. "You can see the spot where it happened from here, can't you?" Karl pointed over the beach to that spot where I had my crash during the photoshoot.

Sighing, "Yeah, that's the spot, sorry for you having to see that, Karl." He smiled a little. "I'm glad I was there, I had no idea how dangerous those crashes you have really are until that night, in truth it gave me a few sleepless nights after seeing it," he held onto me.

"You miss her don't you really miss her?" He squeezed a little tighter. Failing to find words to really respond, I just nodded and smiled as a little tear rolled down my cheek, "Me too," he softly said.

Standing still holding my shoulder he stayed with me for a few minutes just supporting me silently, holding my shoulder before he sighed. "She would be happy though."

Feeling surprised by this remark, I questioned him, "Why's that, Karl?"

Karl sat down beside me and passed me a bottle of beer, he smiled at me. "Imagine how much she would smile if she knew I was sitting next to you," as the words left his mouth; I started to laugh softly at the thought of that grin on her face if she knew.

Laughing to myself, "Told you he likes your bum," he smiled as I took the bottle from him and he sat next to me.

"She would love it wouldn't she!" I looked back at him, "She would have that smug sweet smile on her face."

I chuckled as how much I missed her hit me. "I really miss her you know," he put his arm on my shoulder. "I know you do," he softly said as he held onto my shoulder.

Together, we sat watching the sun fall into the horizon and the sky change from orange to deep blues. Leaning over and into him, "Thank you for coming tonight, Karl," he smiled.

"Don't suffer alone Fae, I'm worried about you," I smiled again at the thoughtfulness of him.

Looking over at him, "How did you know, I would be here?" I questioned him.

He smiled. "Evelyn said this was your favourite place to come and think so I guessed you would be here," he held me slightly tighter.

"What's happening with your hair Fae?" I ran my fingers through it as I thought about what to do with it, "I might just let it go back to its real colour, it's been blue long enough now."

Karl let out a soft smile, "We all have to move on at some point Fae, bet it will look nice too," he stood up and offered me his hand to stand me up. Taking his hand as he pulled me up, he pretended to struggle. "Sorry my bum is heavier than it looks," he chuckled as he hauled me up and handed me my top.

Walking along the promenade, he held me as we walked along towards the park and back into the town. "What are you doing Tuesday Fae?"

I looked at him slightly surprised and blushing a little. "I'm not sure? Why?" Karl smiled at me.

"How about I meet you here at say six o'clock and we can chat again?"

Thinking as a strange feeling came over me before I replied, "Sounds good to me, I will bring the beer next time though."

Standing in the park I put my top back on while he responded, "See you on Tuesday, text me if you feel low and look after that fine bum of yours."

Smiling to myself as he let those words loose, I gave him a hug as thanks, "Thank you, Karl," oddly though he held me differently? Feelings started to flow round my mind as he held onto me, before he let me go, I had held his hand before we headed our separate ways.

Walking back home through the town a strange emotion was filling me, a new emotion a very different emotion? Thinking to myself, how did he know how I was? Why did he come and just happily stand there with me? Wandering back through the last streets which took me to my front door as strange and menacing thoughts hit me.

Had Evelyn been right the whole time? Buried in her jokes and laughter was there some kind of actual meaning behind her fascination with Karl and his love of my bum? Whatever it was for the first time since she had departed, I had a smile on my face and those good feelings about myself had come back.

Part of me over that weekend debated and doubted that Karl would keep his word, it's not like I hadn't been told that kind of thing before. Pretty much, every guy that had shown interest in me faded away fairly quickly if they showed up at all. Somehow it felt different to those times? My mind seemed to trust him to be true to his word and maybe as he had clearly been watching from the distance, he must have some degree of dedication to me?

At least, unlike other guys he had witnessed first-hand what really happens when my mind collapses in on itself, the poor guy had a front row seat for that! Though I couldn't quite see why he had any interest in me at all, deep down I trusted him to be true to his word and that little hug and momentary piece of affection had filled me with a hope.

Over the course of the weekend my lust for life slowly returned and during my Saturday evening with Abby she hinted that it seemed like a good thing for me. Evelyn had often told me how I just needed to let someone see who I really was and that they would embrace me and love me how I hoped someone would?

Sunday in the park with my friends, people seemed to also hint that there was something behind this and not just mere words and empty hopes or dreams. Colette in an almost mothering way took me aside while we sat in the park. "Karl has been keeping an eye on you Fae, this only means one thing, you should let him try," she reasoned with me in private and almost mentoring me.

Colette could see a sparkle had come back into my eyes and she was only too keen to step in and tell me why it was there. After all her jokes and jibing giggling with me about Karl, was Evelyn right all this time? If she was, how did she know?

Continually debating with myself and truthfully doubting the sincerity of Karl and his promise to meet me again on Tuesday evening to sit once again on the front of that promenade. Despite all my apprehensions and fears, I headed down to the beach with the beer that I promised and waited, after an hour had passed it seemed like my fears were correct.

With my hopes and dreams fading, much to my surprise a soft hand placed itself on my bare shoulder and squeezed it tightly. "Sorry I'm late," came Karl's soft voice. Bolting to my feet in exhilaration and turning and hugging the apologetic Karl, as he held me back all the fears and concerns, I had melted away as he held me in his arms.

Starting to blush a little as he took my hand and guided me to sit with him again on the wall, I handed him a beer, he opened it and passed it back to me then opened the other bottle for himself. Karl began to explain his reason for being late, something had happened with my article at work and they had been stuck in some massive meeting for hours?

Karl took my hand and looked at me. "Your article has been pulled from our magazine Fae, I'm really sorry, we did everything we could," he sighed as he told me this devastating news.

Looking at him, "Will all the photoshoots and interviews come to nothing?" He smiled sadly.

"For our magazine, unfortunately yes," I started to cry thinking about the hell I put my mind through to try and tell my story and to raise the awareness for people just like me.

Karl wiped my tears away and held onto me as I cried, "There is something important that has come from it though Fae," he sounded odd, positive almost. After losing the article they had worked so hard to produce, what sliver of joy could be taken from this? Karl raised me back up and looked at me.

"I need you to be brave, Fae." His words confused me.

"Brave? Why do I need to be brave?" I asked him back.

"Your article was picked out by our bosses, they are going to publish it in the big national magazine instead of ours," Karl smiled as he unleashed his news on me.

Shocked to the core, I covered my mouth in disbelief at what he had just told me, he took my hands and looked at me again, "You are going to be on the front cover too, your story is going to be their cover story for August's edition of the magazine Fae!"

Still in total disbelief, I stammered as I tried to speak to him, a continual stream of noises emitted from me as I failed to find any words after his shocking news. Karl smiled and pulled me towards him and rested my head into his shoulder. "You are going big time Fae," he held my head as his words sank in and I wrapped my arms around him and started to cry out of joy.

I sat back up and just pointed at myself, "Me? Really? Me? They are going to have me on the front cover? My full story? Me?"

He smiled and nodded, "Yes you Fae and that wonderful bum of yours."

I flung my arms back round him and said, "Thank you so much!" as I held him and cried again, "I can't believe it, Evelyn would be so pleased!"

Karl supported my head again, "She's going to be in it too, those pictures from the beach? They are using them too," he smiled. "Guess it's a good job I kept shooting, no matter how hard it was to keep doing so."

Smiling and thinking about that crash that he had witnessed, though my thoughts about it had become happier thoughts.

Karl seemed to have been deeply moved that night and it now seemed that unlike so many guys in my past, he was genuine? We sat overlooking the beach into the darkness, when we came to leave, we walked slowly back to the park, he held my hand as we headed back towards town. Once we reached the entrance of the park and the place to head our separate ways, he held my hands again and gave me another of those emotion fuelled hugs.

While his hands held me tightly and my head rested in his shoulder, it became obvious just how right Evelyn had been about him. Before he headed home, Karl lovingly put my top back on for me, carefully lifting over my body and held me one last time.

Karl resting my head on his shoulder, "See you again soon?" A deep smile came over me. "Sounds great to me, see you soon," I squeezed him tight before he let me go.

While we headed our separate ways, he sent me a text, "Have a good night, Fae and thank you," I smiled deeply as I walked through town in a jubilant daze.

Walking alone in the moonlight felt good, a rich and deep sensation was flowing through me as I strolled smiling to myself all the way home. People started to notice that I seemed more myself, more 'Fae', more like the girl they had grown to know. Colette knew exactly what was going on and was quite keen to encourage me to let Karl in, oddly enough Magnus agreed with her too.

Every Wednesday and Thursday evening Magnus would sit on that children's slide and I would sit in the tree and we talked about things through the fence. Our unusual means of discussing our trials and tribulations throughout the week was quite pleasant and it did mean he didn't wake his children. Everyone in my circle of friends was happy to see glimpses of Fae as she seemed to be returning to their lives.

Over the next few weeks these emotions intensified and a light state of happiness had come across me, things were good again, though it didn't mask the hole Evelyn had left behind. Slowly I started to drop my guard with Karl and almost exactly as Evelyn had promised, he responded in kind at first then an odd silence descended?

He would eventually reply but almost begrudgingly? As confusing as it was, that wasn't what was on my mind as deep down, I was still mourning that part of my life that now sat vacated by my departed friend.

While I began to return to life in Ljianstipol over the last days of July, something however was brewing, a few people seemed to know and were almost powerless to stop what was happening to me. Unknown maybe even to me was that rather than being held in the normally sharp and violent crashes I had become accustomed too, I had fallen into a much larger and subtle crash.

Gently simmering away in the comfort of my own home, my loneliness was giving me daily reminders of just how I really felt. On one of the last evenings in July it was going to give me one last brutal reminder that I was far from okay, in truth much further from okay than most realised. While the final hints of blue eroded into the light browns and blonds of my natural hair colour, at the end of my Thursday evening group session the crash started.

While Gale helped me clear away the glasses, my mind went into hyperdrive, stumbling and falling to my knees, my mind violently collapsed into the abyss as everything finally just fell in on me. Gale caught me as I stumbled and moved me to a nearby chair as every emotion fell out of me, he rang Tony and screamed at him down the phone. "Get down here! Fae needs help now!"

It was the first time I had heard Gale raise his voice, moments later Tony appeared and sat with me. "Come on Fae, come back to us!" He repeated over and over, terror came over both of them as they tried to bring me back from my own abyss.

Hours passed as they wrestled with the demonic thoughts slowly consuming my mind, however unlike any time in the past, nothing it seemed would bring me back. Shanky came to try and help but even he with his years suffering from worse variations of my conditions was powerless to stop this monstrous crash. Tony vanished as Shanky sat talking to me with Gale slowly trying to coax Fae out of darkness and back out into the light.

Tony emerged with a large picture in his hand, he rushed over, tripping and falling casting the picture across the floor as he fell to the ground. Standing back up he collected the picture and stumbled back over towards me, limping and holding his arm in pain, he turned the picture round. Tony showed me a picture he had found in the market of Evelyn crouched on a tree branch, under moonlight in a forest.

I held that picture, paused. "I miss her so much," and bawled my eyes out at my beautiful and wonderful friend who I missed so dearly. Tony held me as every emotion fell from my eyes and I cried out loudly and uncontrollably as her beautiful green eyes stared back at me, glistening in the moonlight. Tony joined me crying as just like me he missed her dearly too, Gale had contacted Karl to let him know what had happened to me, but he didn't even reply to them?

However, someone else was only too quick to reply to them and turned up in minutes still with a gaming headset on and in shorts and a short vest top. Not even stopping to fetch her glasses Abby had come running, in her slippers to come to my aid.

Something became obvious to them all, no matter how hard they tried tonight, Fae wasn't going to come back tonight and not here either. Between them they started to plan how to get me home, with a pedestrianised town, this wasn't going to be easy. Tony had very possibly fractured his arm in that fall,

Gale asked Abby if she could run to his house and fetch one of the golf carts, she took a key and ran off into the darkness.

While Abby headed to Gale's house, our attention turned to Tony, clutching his arm. "You might need to go to the hospital Tony," Gale said to him, "Not until she is back home and safe!"

Tony bit hard at Gale while we awaited Abby's return. Tony sat beside me. "I really miss her you know Fae; she helped me to talk about David again and bring him back to life for me and Mona. But I can't imagine how much you miss her and I guess that journalist is just a damn journalist after all."

Tony spoke in a sullen tone as he confessed that to me. "Guess he just wanted his moment of glory huh?" I looked at him.

"I promised that wouldn't happen again." Tony patted me on the back.

"It hasn't happened yet Fae," as he tried to stir my mood. Abby soon returned having lost one of her slippers, Gale looked over at her, "Can you help me get her to the cart, Abby, and maybe we could go and find you some clothes before we try this?" Gale took her through the hotel to a room out the back where the chefs kept spare sets of clothes, they weren't exactly gratifying for her but they did give her some coverage at least.

Abby took one side of me and Gale took the other, gently lifting me up and walking me out of the Davizioso and to the golf cart outside. Tony came following behind us still clutching his arm and limping as he slowly made his way to the cart to come with us. Abby drove us out past the Davizioso and away from the town to the streets that would lead to my house, with no need for a car, she wasn't the most gifted of drivers and Gale winced a few times as we had near misses along the way.

"Is this the scenic route, Abby?" Gale asked as she got lost on the way, he started to give her directions as we slowly wound our way round the outer edges of Ljianstipol to my house. Stopping outside of my house Magnus came out to see what was going on as Gale was shouting at Tony to stay on the cart, he took one side and helped Gale to get me inside.

Putting me down to rest on my sofa, Abby sat next to me and Gale, I noticed had brought the picture of Evelyn with him and rested it gently against my wall so it stood up for me to see. Gale checked to see if Abby would be okay alone with me but Magnus offered to help if she needed it and gave her his number to ring in case he was working upstairs.

While Gale drove Tony to the hospital, Abby sat talking to me when I offered her full use of my wardrobe so that she didn't have to look like a chef. While Abby headed to my room, I sat mulling still slowly crumbling into my own mind, Abby came back downstairs and sat beside me quietly talking to me about everything and anything she could think of.

Slowly though she was losing a battle to stay awake, letting out a single loud snore as she woke herself back up before she finally succumbed and crashed out for the night.

While Abby slept, I looked at that picture Tony had bought at the market, it must have been one of those guys Evelyn had been taking a cut from. While I sat drowning in my sorrow and tears, something seemed odd about that picture. Not the picture itself but the tree she was on. The trunk of the tree had an enormous hole in it. Surely whoever drew it couldn't have dreamt this up, she hadn't disclosed anything about that other world to anyone but me.

Not even Colette knew about this strange world she often talked to me about and if they didn't know about that world then they couldn't have known about the tree she spoke to me about calling home. I tried to get some sleep alongside Abby, as I looked over at her sleeping, I felt sorry for her, that was the second violent crash she had witnessed.

Knocking at the door woke us both up, Abby looked round slightly dazed before smiling at me. "Glad to see you are okay, Fae."

I smiled back at her as she sat making odd faces as she woke up, "I'm okay I think and thank you," Francois and Colette had turned up to check I was okay, they came in to join us and we sat and chatted.

Francois brought along some of the pastries he was so adept at making, while he and Abby grilled each other, Colette took me aside to the safety of my kitchen. Colette gave me a hug and started to ask how I was after hearing about my crash at the Davizioso, looking concerned as we sat down at my kitchen table to talk.

Starting to tell her about my crash just after that final group session of the week before Tony, Gale and Shanky tried to bring me round. Colette came over and adjusted the straps on my top as she often did in her odd motherly ways. "Let me adjust these for you Fae, your bosoms are heavier than they seem." She gave me a little hug when she finished her adjustments and sat smiling at me again.

Colette peered through the doorway to the lounge where Francois and Abby were chatting. "She really saved the day, Tony and Gale wouldn't have been able to get me home, I'm pretty sure Tony has broken his arm from the fall he took trying to help me."

Colette looked at me. "Possibly, but he did that out of love for you Fae, they did it because they love you, the same as me and Francois love you too." Sniffling as her words sunk in, she came back over and hugged me again when Francois appeared, she looked at him, "Why do you always time things so poorly, Francois!" He made a hasty retreat as Colette scorned him.

Francois and Colette came to leave and I rejoined Abby still sitting on the sofa, clearly still exhausted both physically and mentally, sitting together and we began to talk about the previous night's events. Heading upstairs I ran a bath for her so that she could clean herself up, while she soaked upstairs there was another knock at the door as Alyssia and Fabi had come over to check that I was okay, Fabi had brought his hairdressing bag along with him?

While Alyssia and I chatted about the crash I had, Fabi started trying to restyle my hair which I had let fall into ruin over the last few weeks. Clipping the end to make it look slightly less of a mess, he did offer to reshape the sides but I wanted to get back to how I had been hair wise before all of this mess began. Gradually Alyssia and Fabi came to leave along with the hero of the day Abby, I thanked her before she headed home dressed in that chef outfit again.

With my crash having passed, I returned to work on Monday but was surprised to find that Tony was still in hospital and having surgery after breaking his arm during his fall. Gale for this week at least would be flying solo for the first time since they opened the Davizioso over 11 years ago. Monday and Tuesday I ran my group sessions as normal; Gale though was struggling trying to run the Davizioso solo.

Feeling responsible for the predicament that Gale was suddenly thrown into on Wednesday I would step in to try to help him out. Wednesday morning, I helped Gale out with some paperwork before my session ran, again after my session I helped him before my lunch.

During my lunch, I went to the market on my lunch to see Shanky and see how he was doing and thank him for helping me last week. While I was walking round the market, I saw that picture of Evelyn which Tony had given me during my crash, I figured the least I could do was replace his picture for him?

Turning round to see a budding artist maybe a little older than Evelyn, was smiling away as I stood holding his work.

He took the picture from me and held it out to admire it, smiling to himself, "Truly beautiful," he said as he started to wrap it.

"Wait? Can I ask you about this picture?" I asked expecting no response of any real worth, much to my surprise he smiled gleefully and unwrapped the picture again and held it out.

Pointing to the painting, "I remember doing this with her, she sat on the wall near the beach so that I could get the pose just right, her little curly hair kept blowing all over the place so it was hard to get her hair right." He smiled as he pointed at the curls he had given Evelyn, he paused and pointed at the tree she was crouched upon.

"Can I ask you about that tree?" He looked slightly surprised that I was more interested in the tree than Evelyn, but he smiled again, "What was strangest though was that she was very specific about this tree, everything in the background she gave me total freedom with but that branch and the opening in the tree had to be just right, I had to do this picture 4 times until I got that just right, she wouldn't let me sell them until it was exactly right, it was a curious thing, the tree mattered more to her than even she did?"

Slowly he began to wrap the picture back up, "I miss her you know Fae; she was fun and these pictures of her sell better than my work does," he said with sadness in his voice, "How do you know my name?" He smiled. "She asked me to give you my envelopes for her if you stopped by my stall, she used to talk about you all the time when I was drawing her," smiling as he closed the wrapping paper around her, "Please take it and these are hers too, say hello to her for me if you see her," he said handing me the picture and 5 envelopes?

I looked at the envelope, "Thank you," as I offered him the money for the picture, he raised his hand to me. "No this one's on me," he refused my money?

Wandering back to the Davizioso I found myself wondering why the tree in the picture was so important to her, more important than anything else? Heading to see Gale for our Wednesday meeting in the rooftop garden, thinking about that painting all the way until I arrived at that pergola over the pond on the roof. Gale sat mournfully looking over the garden, handing me a beer bottle his sullen mood resonating. Gale looked at me.

"I'm so sorry Fae," he said sadly looking at the floor.

"What do you mean? It's me who should be sorry for causing the problems I have," I joined him looking at the floor.

Gale shook his head. "No, no Fae! We should have been more careful with you; we knew we were pushing you hard with those extra sessions during the evenings. After Evelyn left, you haven't even had time to fully process or recover from her leaving you, I mean, she was a huge part of your life, it's like losing a parent or child. While you suffered, we all just let you wander alone in darkness, we set this place up to stop that sort of thing happening, so to find ourselves doing it to one of our own is shameful."

"We should have stepped in sooner and helped you, we have given you the next two weeks off so that you can grieve and process things properly, maybe then we can get our Fae back. Were sorry we didn't help you Fae," Gale sat back up sighing in disappointment at himself.

"No that's not true Gale, I should have told you what was going on, what about the evening sessions?"

Gale looked at me and smiled. "Always thinking about others, truthfully we didn't want the stupid evening sessions, we pitched to lose them and hosted the meeting out of courtesy, frankly if they take them away, we don't care, we would sooner lose them than lose you Fae," he smiled a little as he sat back up.

I looked over at him, "What about tomorrow?"

Gale smiled. "I cancelled your session so that you can help me with paperwork, it turned out Tony was better at that than me," Gale chuckled when we heard the door to the garden open.

Wandering through with one arm in plaster came Tony, with one arm in the air. "They finally let me out!" Walking smiling away, almost ecstatic to be free. "Get me a damn beer!"

I stood to greet him with an open bottle in hand ready for him. Hugging him, "I'm sorry I broke your arm Tony."

Tony smiled back, "Ha! I broke my arm trying to help you! I have broken 3 bones in my life and all 3 of them have been for you!" He laughed as he took his beer and joined us.

Tony sat down proudly waving his cast around when I presented him with the replacement picture, I had gotten him, he smiled. "We better put her where she belongs."

Tony stood up and offered me his hand, I took his hand and took the picture as we started wandering down the garden, replicating his walks with Evelyn. Walking along he was smiling softly to himself, "Has Gale told you were giving you two weeks off to process what has happened since Evelyn left?"

I nodded at him, "I'm just sorry I didn't tell you people I was struggling."

Tony looked over. "Thing is we should have known, you are just so strong that we weren't ready for you to be weak, we are sorry for that."

We approached his little cabin at the far end of his garden, Tony opened the door and took me in, just over a little stove was a hook ready and waiting for the picture of Evelyn.

Tony smiled as he hung it back up and levelled off, "I really miss her you know Fae; she helped me talk about David again," he smiled a little as he stood back and looked at the picture, he did a double take. "Sorry Fae, I can only imagine how much you miss her."

I stood beside him and smiled. "Every day I think about her and I keep hoping she's just going to turn up on my sofa again."

Tony put his hand on my shoulder. "Someday she will be back, she promised that she would and I know she will be back, I just hope it's soon."

I put my hand on his, "Me too, maybe then I won't break anything else."

Tony smiled and together we walked back down to Gale as he sat waiting for us to return. Gale smiled as we joined him again, "Fae is going to do your paperwork for you tomorrow, so don't worry about that."

Tony smiled. "I'm not worried about Fae doing my paperwork but you on the other hand I'm worried about," Gale laughed at him,

Gale presided over my Wednesday evening group session, staying nearby to make sure I didn't become overwhelmed or stressed, I stayed in a spare room at the Davizioso to have a night away from things at home and to try to keep my stress levels down. During the night I couldn't sleep and wound up wandering the halls of the Davizioso, during the early hours of the morning the place was eerily quiet.

Night staff were walking around keeping a check on things and the only sign of life I could find was in Gale's Bar and pool hall on the ground floor. Gale often suffered from insomnia and often would come and play himself at pool into the twilight hours of the morning. Gale was almost as shocked to see me wandering the corridors as I was to see him as he offered me a cue, "But I can't play well?" Gale smiled.

"Seems like a good night to learn?" I took the cue from him and he started trying to teach me how to play pool. Through the early hours of the morning, we played and chatted about life since Evelyn had gone, like everyone else he missed her too, but his gravest concern was the effect her departure had taken on me and

Tony. Tony had started to close back up after she had gone, David slowly vanishing back inside Tony as he locked back down.

Gale was also gravely concerned about how I had slowly faded away but what was really bothering him was that nobody seemed to notice it happening. Gale conceded that warning signs had been flagging up before I had my crash last week and yet despite the signs, they hadn't acted and helped me before things took a severe turn. Gale spent hours talking about how this was his biggest single disappointment since they had opened the Davizioso, even more shameful than the two-year long fallout with his daughter Ellie.

Together we sat in those plush seats near the window as he confessed this major disappointment to him, I conceded that I should have done something to help myself before things got so bad. Equally sharing blame for the state, I had wound up in last Thursday eventually we just smiled at each other and sat in silence as the sun came up.

Gale smiled at me. "Well, I managed another sleepless night, you wanna help me sort paperwork?"

Looking at him and thinking about his bizarre request at sunrise. "Why not, it's not like we've got anything better to do."

Gale brought a large pot of coffee up with us as we headed to the boardroom filled with paperwork strewn everywhere and got to work. Thursday, we spent most of the day sorting that paperwork and stopping periodically to check on guests and staff. Gale sat in on my final evening session to keep his eye on me.

Sitting thinking to myself I wondered what I would do with the time off I now had I hadn't spent this much time alone since way before Evelyn showed up, so this would be a new experience? Thinking long into the morning hours when I got a strange urge to tidy my house, while I was clearing up the front room, I noticed something poking out underneath the sofa?

Something small and white seemed to be stuck just underneath it at the back of the sofa, kneeling down I found one of Evelyn's tiny socks had been stuck at the back of my sofa. Wondering and pondering how long it had been stuck there I started to think about her, I wandered up to her old room and sat on the bed looking at the sock almost as if I thought it might talk to me. I took her sock and placed it in her drawer along with her other socks and underwear, opening the drawer below it to sit looking through all the little tops she had left behind and the memories started to flood back.

Sitting holding a little black top she found on our first shopping adventure together and of course that sailor suit she loved so dearly. Sitting on her bed, every little garment brought back a very real and vivid memory of my little friend, those pictures from the steampunk festival just above the chest of drawers!

Evelyn loved those two days and walking back through those dark trees with her, she was so incredible, that picture she loved of me overlooking the beach. "He likes your bum," I found myself impersonating her and laughing.

Taking that box full of photos that Tony gave her at the party and sat on her bed looking through the pictures of her and her parents when she was a child. Evelyn dressed as a fairy sitting in front of a tree in their garden, Evelyn and Ellie and her parents. Sitting looking through her past gave me a strange and quite bizarre thought; I went and found the map she had drawn me and started to dream about going to find her?

Evelyn had told me if I needed her to go and find her and she had drawn me a map to show me the way, all I had to do was catch a bus? Even if the forest was a strange dream she had, I could at least start in the town she had come from? Surely there would be someone there that knew her and could help me find her?

Thinking about it more and more, I decided that today I would visit the park we spent our last day together in and make my decision what to do there. I got a few hours' sleep before I would get myself ready to go and sit in that place and think about going to find my friend.

Having spent most of the night up thinking I overslept and wound up leaving the house later than I hoped, rushing to get as much sunlight in as I could. Strolling through the streets and far out of town, feeling almost like I was in a race against time itself to spend a few hours in that meadow overlooking the mountains and rolling hills.

Soon enough, I found myself at the crumbling walls that marked the entrance to this vast park, walking through the trees barefoot to try and feel that sensation that she talked about. Feeling the grass and dirt between my toes and the soft blades tickle the soles of my feet as I walked the endless maze of trees and out towards the meadow, we had spent those final precious hours in. Sunlight was baking me as I cast my top over my shoulder and let my torso breathe in the warm air.

Sunlight disrupted by the shadows cast by the trees and leaves kept flickering across my eyes as step by step the trees slowly began to clear away and opened out onto that meadow. Rapidly approaching that tree stump, surrounded by the ocean of flowers where we had spent our last day together. However, my happiness soon turned to sorrow as it became clear to me just how much I had really lost when she went away.

Laying belly down on the sea of flowers and lush grasses I started thinking of all the time we had spent together and thinking about how empty life had been without her around. Sitting on the tree stump overlooking the mountains I started crying as the impact of that girl leaving really sunk in. All my friends have been good to me since she had left and so had Abby and yet none of them filled the void she had left.

Whether it was going downstairs in the morning to find her dead to the world on the sofa, giggling to herself as she dreamt or those Wednesday mornings where she was so hyperactive that I often had no idea what she was talking about, she created such a huge presence in this world and nobody could fill that.

Everything else aside though it was those moments we shared very privately, where we would share our darkest and deepest secrets that had meant the most. Evelyn had been through hell as a child and into her young adulthood, yet somehow became strong and determined.

Every time we talked about her past, I started to admire her more and more for her sheer resilience to a world that didn't love her anywhere near as much as she loved it. Evelyn underneath it all though was simply a girl who fell in love with a forest, she spoke with such passion about that forest and those trees, the flowers and everything else in that dark world.

Sitting overlooking the mountains as the sky started to turn orange it became obvious to me, I had to go and find my friend, even if that might mean blindly following the map she had drawn and wandering into that world she spoke of. Jumping down from the stump, I put my arms out and started to fly round as if I was a fairy, flying round with my eyes closed and crying about my little friend.

Standing with my head held high and tears streaming down my face I yelled to the sky, "I'm coming to find you Evelyn!"

As those words left my mouth, I began to run home, whatever happened I was going to get that bus on Sunday morning and go find my friend.

Saturday I headed into town and after visiting Fabi to get my morning coffee before I went to find some clothing suitable for hiking. I went and found a backpack in one the shops near the river in the new part of town, a couple of pairs of walking trousers, a blouse and a pair of walking boots, I found a copy of the same map Evelyn had given me and went home to start packing for my journey to find my friend.

Furiously, I started picking out things that would be good if indeed I found myself following that map, she had drawn. Loading up the backpack with everything that might be good for trekking too and across the mountains, I was ready and composed, looking at myself in the mirror with a determined smile, I wondered if she would like my hair now it was its actual colour and not my usual purple, blue and turquoise and it now looked kinda kooky too?

I had a long soak in a hot bubbly bath before I headed to bed, as it would be a long day tomorrow when I caught that bus. I had told a few people I was heading out of town for a few days but I had told no one why I was going or where I would be heading. Rather than sleep in my bed I slept in the bed I had given Evelyn when she first appeared, sitting looking at those pictures of us on her bedroom wall as I drifted into a serene sleep.

Morning soon came as sunlight flooded the room and I woke up charged and ready for the adventure that today would see me go hunting for my little friend in her hometown and beyond if needs be. Grabbing a coffee before I started to make that long journey to the bus station, I had walked her too when she had left us all behind to return to her world. Wandering along, I couldn't stop myself daydreaming about finding her, maybe she would be sitting in that tree near the school she used to work at?

Daydreaming I soon found myself at the bus station and boarding the bus that weeks ago had carried my friend out of Ljianstipol and out of my life. Waiting eagerly and anxiously for the journey to start, soon relief filled me as the bus started its voyage through the streets and out of Ljianstipol.

Passing by that park where we had spent so much time and just days ago, I had decided to go in search of my little friend, I smiled to myself as we passed that stump proudly sat in our meadow.

While the miles passed by, I planned and dreamt about finding my friend happy in that town I found myself heading towards. Steadily the time passed by and in the distance the mountains were growing larger and a large town was looming as this first phase of my journey to find Evelyn drew to a close.

Studying Evelyn's map, I started to try and figure out where to start my search, but being a tourist map it didn't offer much insight into where the school might be? Evelyn had spoken about working there in her past and it seemed an obvious place to start my search. Passing by a large industrial estate, the open roads soon turned into the winding streets of a bustling town. Eventually, the bus drew into a station in the middle of the town and I took my first steps in her world.

Stepping off the bus into the bustling streets of that town, sunlight caught my eyes as the new and alien town unfolded itself before me. Standing on the pavement, trying to get my bearings, I started to notice people looking at me? Not just looking but staring in some cases?

Maybe me standing there spinning a tourist map round trying to figure out where exactly I was had drawn their attention? Looking around I started to look for anywhere that might be able to help me figure out where to start looking. Along the street I could see a newsstand, I started to wander towards it figuring it would be a good place to make a start.

Walking towards the stand it became obvious that I seemed to be drawing a lot of attention, though I was clueless as to why that was? People were stopping and looking at me strangely, becoming a little self-conscious I walked quicker to try and escape their odd glaring looks. Walking past a digital billboard on the side of a bus stop, I discovered the reason for these odd and unnerving looks.

As the pictures flicked through up came the front cover of the magazine, with me on the front cover. "Life Downside Up, Fae's fighting depression with depression." It was a cool title though I wasn't sure how true it rang with me. The billboard changed to that picture of me and her together, I leant my hand against her and rested my head on the billboard and uttered, "Gninrom doog," smiling to myself as I thought about her torturing Karl and that receptionist.

Walking further along I approached the newsstand and saw the top shelf of the back row, full of copies of this magazine I was on the front cover of a magazine normally reserved for celebrities or politicians, but for August it was my face on that front cover. Stopping I got two copies, one for me and one for Evelyn, the cashier looked at the picture on the front and double took as she looked at me.

Taking one last look at the front cover, "You are very brave to have done this, please take them free of charge for what you have done, for speaking out for others in your situation."

Humbled by the offer I refused and paid anyway, though she did ask me to sign a copy of the magazine for her. I stood thumbing through the magazine, there was that picture of me and her, I asked the cashier if she had seen her, she shook her head, but she did give me directions to the school, even drawing them on the spare map I had.

Wandering through the streets following her directions and drawings I soon found myself walking towards the school and found that tree she spoke about. Truthfully, the tree was magnificent, no wonder she was so fond of it, though I couldn't get up to the branch she sat on a gazed over the horizon dreaming about a better life elsewhere.

Wandering into the school felt strange, stranger though was that when I asked at reception and showed them a picture of her, they acted almost as if they had never heard of the girl? Dismissively and almost shunning the idea she might have ever worked there at all?

When I left the receptionist followed me out and asked to look again, she proceeded to tell me that most of the staff had been laid off following an incident some time ago. Most of the staff had only been at the school for two years or less, the girl had worked there but had vanished over two years ago?

Worse was to come though as I started to wander from shop to shop asking tirelessly, but every answer was the same? I even found a shop that sold those flowery trainers that she adored, but they had no clue either? It was almost as if this girl didn't exist? Searching high and low my approach changed as I started asking everyone and anyone only to find the same answer each time I asked.

With my hopes fading, I asked outside a bakery, only to receive the same answer, as they left someone approached asking if they could help me. I opened the picture on my phone that I had been showing people.

"Have you seen her?" She gasped and uttered, "Evelyn!" In a soft and sad tone as she stroked the picture of her.

Stunned into silence I rummaged through my bag and found the magazine and found that picture of her and showed her it, "Evelyn is so beautiful isn't she," her soft tone and almost seeming to cry as she thought about her.

Vague hope filled me. "Do you know where she is?"

She smiled at me. "I might know where she is, but it's getting late, where are you staying tonight?"

I looked at her, "I hadn't really thought that far ahead, I guess I could find a hotel?"

She shook her head at me. "No, you don't have to do that, why don't you stay with me tonight I have a spare room?"

I smiled at her generosity. "Thank you, I'm Fae, it's nice to meet you."

Smiling back, "Nice to meet you Fae, I'm Ellie, my car is just over here," she started to walk to a car park and I followed her.

Ellie led me towards a car park and drove us home, though she claimed it used to be Evelyn's home, claiming she had given it to her before she left with a strange woman, she had started calling Mother or the queen. When we arrived at the house, she led me in and we sat talking, she spent an hour or so probing me, checking to see how well I knew Evelyn before she started to tell me about herself and how she knew her.

While we probed each other, it dawned upon me who she was. Suddenly hitting me.

"You were the babysitter?" as I asked,

She looked at the floor and nodded, "You knew her well enough for her to trust you then," she said back, lifting her head and wiping away a small tear.

Handing her my phone so that she could see all the photos of us together or just of her while I started to explain how she had helped me with my problems. Ellie sat going through the photos when she stopped one of her asleep on my couch that I took the first night she arrived.

Sighing, "She is so beautiful isn't she, like a little angel?" She said as she showed me the photo, nodding back I started to tell her some of my cherished memories of her. Telling her how she used to wait for me to get home before she would run through and jump at me to give me a welcome home hug or how I would wake with her lying with me.

Smiling to herself, "That's Evelyn for you! She is such a fantastic girl, it's just a shame that this world didn't love her as much as she loved it," her tone suddenly changed.

Offering her the map Evelyn had drawn me, she took it and pointed at the little gap Evelyn had drawn. "That is where she went, if you want to find her then I can get you close to the mountains but the rest you would have to do alone."

She offered, "You don't have to choose right now, though sleep on it and see what you decide to do tomorrow?"

Smiling at me. "Sounds fair to me, have you been to the mountains?" She laughed.

"No! I'm not as brave as she is!" She smiled to herself.

Leading me upstairs she took me to a spare room at the back of the house. "You can have this room, the beds comfier than it looks!"

I dropped my bag down as Ellie led me down the hall to show me the bathroom. Before we headed back downstairs, I caught a glimpse of another bedroom just down the hall. "My room is down the end on the right, if you need me in the night."

Ellie pointed down the hall. "There's a spare towel in here if you want a shower."

I went and had a shower, thinking to myself as I washed away the smells and dirt of the day I kept wondering if she knew where I had come from? Walking down the hallway before I went downstairs, I entered the wrong room.

The room was curious, it seemed largely untouched for many years, there were old posters on the wall trapping the room in a continual cycle of the exact same year which the room had been vacated in. The seemingly only new addition to the room was a picture of Evelyn dressed as a fairy on the side table.

Picking the picture up to look at it, "This was her room when she was a child, she never slept here again after that night," Ellie said softly as she took the picture from me, smiled and placed it back on the side table.

I looked at her, "Sorry I took the wrong door."

Ellie smiled back, "It's okay, it's a curious room, sit on the bed, I want to show you something," as requested I sat on the end of the bed.

Ellie walked to a closet and opened it before removing a white dress with a set of wire wings hanging over it, "She wore this on her prom night, she looked stunning too, the other girls threw cola over her out of jealousy, that little girl they picked on her and made her feel ugly and unworthy, she was beautiful, more importantly she was beautiful without trying to be, they didn't like that," Ellie spoke in a saddening tone as she looked over that dress.

Ellie sat on the bed with me and sighed. "We went back to my place to clean her dress up, she didn't want her grandmother to know that she had left the prom early, she didn't want to give her the satisfaction of knowing she had been right to say that Evelyn shouldn't have gone to that prom, we got pizza and we gave her the first beer she had ever had that night as we sat talking and watching bad horror films."

Holding her thigh as she spoke about this memory. "They did everything to try and break that girl, but she kept fighting back and never let them win, not that there was much they could have taken from her, I don't think they understood that? Her grandmother passing away might have been the best thing that happened to her in some ways, as not only did Evelyn get bullied in school her grandmother was no better either, her death set Evelyn free in some ways," Ellie handed me the dress as she finished speaking.

Sitting feeling the fabric and looking at the tattered wings Ellie spoke to me again, "The thing is though Fae, they never beat her, she never gave up and in the end, it was Evelyn that put us all to shame," she started to smile again.

She went and picked up the picture before returning to the bed with me. "The last time I saw her I was dropping off this birthday card for her, the picture is from when she was just four in our back garden, she loved fairies, really loved them, she used to dress up as one and my dad made her a fairy door for the tree in their garden."

"My mum took this picture of her when they came over to see my parents during the summer before her parents died, she was so cute! Her dad flew her round our garden for hours, she laughed and giggled the whole time, that day I discovered she had a tickly belly too, she nearly wet herself when I tickled her, she would laugh so loudly and wriggle trying to escape."

Ellie smiled. "The tickle monster."

I laughed back at her, she smiled. "I started babysitting her whenever her parents went out, I loved doing it too, she was so much fun! Almost tireless, she would play peekaboo with me, even if she had nowhere to hide," she smiled speaking of these fond memories to me.

Sighing again, she looked over at me. "I used to give her this card every year, for her birthday and a different one at Christmas, Evelyn would give me a card back every year until just after her 20th birthday the cards stopped coming. Irrespectively I took the cards round year in year out, we hadn't spoken much as I was still trapped in a bad relationship, so we hadn't seen each other much."

"The day of her 22nd birthday I came to give her that card and hoped to see her, with that relationship being over I hoped to see my friend again. I came to the door and I was greeted by a strange woman, a menacing and fearsome woman. When she saw the card somehow, she knew who I was and demanded that I take her shopping to get her daughter Evelyn a gift for her birthday."

"Fearful and confused, I agreed and took her to find a present, we stopped at all sorts of places before she found a dress and necklace for her, she presented the shop owner with a huge piece of gold to pay for them. That gold was probably worth more than the entire shop but she traded it anyway claiming that seeing her daughter happy was worth more than any gold was."

"While we were out, she confided in me that the real reason she had come back was to collect a picture of Evelyn's parents so that she wouldn't forget them. When she told me I helped her hide that picture to get it back without Evelyn knowing she was carrying it, I didn't know why or how, but somehow, I knew she would care for her?"

"Though she had crossed the mountains with Evelyn, pretending to want to see this place just to smuggle a picture back? Though I didn't understand her motives for adopting Evelyn, she gave her the family she has needed all along and I couldn't question her love for her." Ellie wept a little, as she spoke of her friend.

Ellie sat with me for another hour talking to me about her relationship with Evelyn before she got up to leave and I asked her, "Why did she give you the house?"

Ellie smiled and sat back on the bed. "Evelyn found out about my bad years with that guy and gave me the keys to here to start my life again, like her in that new world I got to start this whole game again," smiling as she thought of her.

Ellie stood to leave. "Whatever you decide will be hard, but that road to the mountains is really hard, beyond I can only imagine but if you have come this far then I'm sure you will keep going, good night, Fae."

I smiled at her, "Good night, Ellie and thanks."

She waved her hand to gesture it was nothing. "Just one question?"

I looked back up at her, "Sure?"

Ellie pulled out her phone and showed the picture of Evelyn sleeping on my sofa.

"Did you take this?" I smiled back.

"Yes, the first night she stayed with me," she smiled.

"Thought so," and left me to rest. Sitting and thinking as she left me behind and headed to her room, I couldn't imagine how much it must have meant to be given this house to make a fresh life for herself. Gale had said they didn't speak when she was with that guy who had been bad for her, I guess we both knew who each other were just we hadn't yet admitted it to each other?

Looking at Evelyn's map she had drawn for me I started to question just how tough it might be? It would be hard to reach the mountains let alone beyond them, so I needed to think hard tonight. Either way, in the morning I would answer Ellie's question and decide to head home or head to the mountains to find my friend.

Ellie woke me in the morning, gently knocking on the door. "Fae, are you okay?" Before she went downstairs. Slowly as I came to my senses I realised where I was, the bed was facing the door and I could see a lock on the handle, was this that spare room Evelyn's grandmother used to lock her in?

Getting dressed I couldn't help but wonder if this was the room Evelyn had been confined to so often in her childhood? Rich and aromatic coffee smells kept wafting upstairs leading me nose first downstairs to find Ellie waiting for me at the doorway to the kitchen, "I've got coffee ready, it's not as good as the coffee you are used to, but it's drinkable!"

She smiled a little, seemingly amused with herself? Ellie offered me a chair at the table with her and poured me a coffee, she watched as I took my first sip. "How is it?" as she saw me grimace a little.

"Not bad at all," she chuckled in uncertainty.

I started to look around the kitchen. "It's quite a nice house Ellie and thanks again for putting me up for the night," she turned round and joined me at the table, "Your welcome and sorry if I grilled you a bit too much, just I'm still used to people picking on Evelyn, so I am wary when people ask me about her."

She seemed almost disappointed in herself for defending and looking out for our friend? "No problem, I'm sure I would be the same if someone asked me about her."

Suddenly, I noticed an extra copy of the magazine with that article in it. While I sat drinking my coffee, she posed the question, "What are you going to do then, Fae?" She looked at me expectantly awaiting my answer, my answer was instantaneous.

"I'm going to find her," she smiled at me. "Then we better get you ready to go, we will get you supplies this morning and I will drive you as close as I can tomorrow, plus then I can show you this old town too."

Feeling encouraged and cheerful, "I wondered what this place is like?"

Ellie refilled my cup and sat down to join me and looking at the map I had brought with me. "You are going to need a better map than this for starters, Evelyn said it took three days to walk from the mountains to here, I can take a day or two off that by getting you closer to them, what clothing have you brought with you?"

I headed upstairs to get my backpack before re-joining her to show her what I brought with me. Ellie started looking through my backpack. "You will need warm clothing too, it gets cold out there at night and there is pretty much no shelter, there are adventure clothing stores in town. We can get you some better clothing for your journey and a better map too and a few snacks for the journey, I have no idea how long it might take you to find her so you might need a lot of food and water."

Ellie finished her coffee and sat looking at the cover of the magazine. "What happened to your hair?"

I shyly replied, "I have been pretty low since she left, so I lost interest in keeping it dyed," I sighed running my fingers through it.

Ellie smiled. "Shame but that colour suits you too, but sorry to hear you have been doing badly, Fae." She put her hand on my back, "Come on, let's get you ready for tomorrow, Evelyn would be proud of you Fae," I looked up at her as she smiled sweetly at me.

Ellie took me out to the car and began to drive us towards the town to get supplies ready for my journey. Walking the streets with her we stopped by a few shops set up for the clients of the various mountaineering and adventure holiday companies near the town. Ellie spoke to me about Evelyn and their past growing up together in further detail, buried through the sorrow Ellie seemed to feel was a sense of pride and admiration in her for overcoming all odds and becoming so strong.

Ellie took me for lunch at the restaurant where Evelyn had attended the work party where she was assaulted on the night, she decided to leave this town and return to the forest. However, what Evelyn didn't know was that someone had reported the incident and most of the teachers and staff at that meal had wound up being fired for failing to report or act upon her assault.

Leanne's parents had been in attendance for that meal as guests of the school and they also wound up losing their jobs due to the incident. Ellie smiled while she told me about it as Evelyn finally got some justice, even if she wasn't around to see it be served. After having lunch, Ellie drove us back to her home to help get me ready for the long journey to find Evelyn that I would start tomorrow morning.

While I sat trying to translate Evelyn's little map onto the bigger and more detailed map, Ellie was thumbing through that article, she stopped and smiled at the picture of me and Evelyn. Studying the place where the mountains descended to the forest, I started to get some vague feel for how treacherous this journey might be, the incline if this map was accurate was almost vertical.

Just at the base of the descent the land levelled out before rising again and then falling back away, dropping down to a lake at the foot of the mountains. Marking out my potential route to reach the mountains Ellie glanced over at me. "He's really proud of you, you know that?"

I looked over at her, "Who is?"

She smiled looking at the front cover. "Dad is proud of you; I hope he has told you that!"

I looked over at her slightly surprised. "Gale?"

She nodded back, "Every time we speak, he tells me how well you're doing for yourself and for your guests, he's really proud of you, in truth given where you came from so am I Fae," she sat looking at the front cover.

Feeling slightly shocked I folded the map and looked over to her, "I remember, you helped to dye my hair the night we met, I tried to contact you a few times but didn't hear back," I sat up intently to listen to Ellie.

Ellie closed the magazine cover and sat back, "Given the way we met how could I ever forget you Fae, though you look better without the dreads! You were their first real patient you know? Most of their guests had been through the system but were older, you were the youngest patient that they had taken on. Dad wanted me to come and see you to see if I could help you come out of your shell a little, of course that was the night I wound up dying your hair."

"The strange thing for me is that to me you just looked like anyone else, nothing obviously odd about you, the hair maybe but other than that to me you just looked normal? I helped Dad and Tony to try to help you before I went home, of course not long after I got back to Zyvala I fell off the radar myself with a string of bad relationships. Controlling and bad guys, me and Dad didn't speak for years, that's why I kinda vanished, can I ask you something, Fae?"

She looked over at me oddly. "Sure?" She looked at the cover again, "Are you really going to find her and take her back with you?"

I smiled and looked at that picture on my phone. "Yes, the guy in the shop told me there's nothing out there but I know her too well for that, I'm going to get her home."

Ellie smiled. "I want to show you something," she walked out of the kitchen before returning with a little box. Ellie sat back down and opened the box pulling out some old pictures and handing them to me. The first picture she gave me was a picture of Evelyn dressed as a fairy with Ellie flying her round the garden.

"She was four when this was taken, she came to Dad's barbeque to celebrate Tony retiring from playing football, Sophie and David were there too, but I spent most of the time playing with her. I had spent some time with her before and found out she loved fairies, so me and Mum got her that fairy outfit, her dad had been flying her round and I took over when he gave up. We would fly round, heading towards the realm of the fairies at the end of the garden under a tree, there was a door on the tree where the fairies would hide away."

"However, to get there, she had to fly through the dandelions where the trolls would hide and guard the entrance to the fairy world, she needed to knock the seeds off the dandelions so that the trolls couldn't hide away and try to catch her. However, it was dangerous as from time to time the trolls would catch her, crashing and rolling onto her back trolls would swarm her and try to capture her so that she couldn't reach the fairy world."

"Kicking, wriggling and laughing ecstatically as she tried to squirm her way free from the tickle trolls that attacked, tickling her belly and trying to stop her reaching the fairies. Eventually, she would wriggle free and we would go off flying again as she broke down the trolls' dandelion defences and finally reached the fairy door and the gateway to the realm of the fairies."

"After a few hours, she started to wear out, she fell asleep on my lap and resting against me, Marie took her and changed her into some different clothes and laid her down to sleep for an hour or two. Minutes after being laid down to have a nap, she came wandering out, bleary eyed and still asleep, she came and climbed back onto my lap and went back to sleep. Marie and John, both thought it was the cutest thing ever, so did I in truth, she also started calling me her big sister too, we spent a lot of time together over that summer."

"Our age difference didn't bother her parents and it didn't bother us either, we spent hours sitting at the end of her garden watching the fairy door we put on the tree in her garden for her."

"Rain or shine she was happy to sit under that tree for hours, sometimes I just sat with her holding an umbrella to keep her dry, she started calling me sister Ellie. Evelyn loved her new big sister and in truth her big sister loved her too, I started babysitting for her during that summer too, her parents knew I would look after her so they were quite happy for a night off."

Ellie handed me another picture of her sitting with Evelyn fast asleep on her lap. "That was the same day, we spent all day flying round and she was fearless, no matter how many times she got caught by the tickle trolls she kept coming back for more. Every time she would laugh louder and squirm more but she was almost tireless and I loved playing with her, it was fun and we had a great time together."

"Late in the afternoon she started to flag and drifted a few times as we flew; we sat down and she drifted off in my lap. Marie took her indoors and changed her clothes and tried to put her to bed for an hour, they used my bed for her. Maybe ten minutes after they put her down for that nap she wandered back outside, still half asleep and groggily made her way back over to me. She raised her arms for me to pick her up and gave me the sweetest look."

"I want to sleep with my sister," she asked in the sweetest and saddest little voice. I leant down and picked her up, gave her a hug and lifted her back onto my lap, she leant against me and drifted back to sleep in my arms. John and Marie thought it was the cutest thing they had ever seen, Evelyn and her new sister sat together happily in the evening sunshine.

This last picture is of her that night her parents died, at four she had wanted to be just like me, John and Marie found her this outfit for her fifth birthday so that she could dress like her big sister. Evelyn liked me babysitting her, she stayed up late with me on the sofa watching films and playing, she was so adorable too, so sweet and innocent. Even that night she was brilliant and fearless, even if she didn't really understand what had happened that night, she almost supported me?

When her parents died, we still spent time together just in a different way, her grandmother didn't approve of our bond, maybe she didn't like our age difference? Often, I went round and she said Evelyn wasn't well and was in bed, but I grew suspicious about it, me and Dad went round and while they talked, I spoke to my sister about what was really going on.

Evelyn had started sleeping in a backroom on a pull-out sofa bed and her grandmother would often lock her in that room, like her own prison in her own home. Whatever the reason was, she just didn't seem to like Evelyn very much and she quite willingly made Evelyn aware of that, bullying her just like the kids at her school.

"We started to meet at school and out of school, I found a way to get to her window and eventually her grandmother had to let me see her, there was no way she was going to stop us spending time together."

Ellie sighed as she finished telling me about her long relationship with Evelyn, "Can you promise me one thing, Fae?"

I looked over at the watery eyed Ellie, who sat with her head on her hands looking sorrowful. "When you find her and take her back with you, give her the forever home? Give her the forever home she has needed since she was five years old? I know you love her, otherwise you wouldn't be risking your own life to find her but just give her the home she has deserved for so long."

Without hesitation I responded in the most Fae way I could. "She always has a bed in my home and even if that is my sofa I don't care as long as she is sleeping on it every night."

Ellie smiled through her tears and took my hands, "When you find her tell her that I will see her at Christmas and don't forget the 13th of October."

I looked to her, "It's her birthday, it will be her 23rd birthday." I smiled at her and memorised the date.

We spent the rest of the evening talking about their past and how Ellie wished that Gale and Anna had adopted Evelyn. Ellie did break one last piece of news to me that evening too, she was moving to Ljianstipol and Evelyn's old room was the last thing she needed to sort out before the sale went through. Trinkets and fond memories were all she was going to keep, that fairy outfit, her jewellery box and some other things she placed value in would be going to Ljianstipol with Ellie and I guess she would give them back to her little sister.

When I headed to bed, my head was filled with all the stories Ellie had told me about their past and of course my own fears of the mammoth journey ahead of me. Fearful as the guys in the adventure clothing shops had told me that there is nothing beyond those mountains and no one had been known to return from descending the mountains.

Though they did say that adventurers don't tend to share their failures, but they did say there was an abandoned prospecting building in that forest. Having been abandoned for over 150 years as the mine turned out to be barren, maybe that was where Evelyn lived? Though I kept wondering about that strange woman Evelyn spoke about and the strange people that she claimed inhabited that desolate and dangerous place?

Maybe these people are real? And if no one ever explores that place they could remain undiscovered and hidden from view for eternity. Maybe the people that had ventured into those trees had simply been killed by the tribes Evelyn spoke of or maybe they just became a part of those tribes. Soon enough I would find out for myself just how far this world had really pushed Evelyn and just how dangerous the route to her world would be.

Chapter 9
Mountains of Hope

Ellie woke me early so that she could drive me as close to the mountains as she could manage, she wanted to give me as much daylight to make that long walk to the mountains as she could. Leaving under the cover of darkness we drove out of Zyvala before the sun rose, driving from the paved road on the outskirts of the town onto empty wasteland. Vibrations heading from my backside all the way up my spine reminded me just how rugged the terrain was becoming as we ventured further towards the mountains.

Sunlight began to unmask the route ahead, revealing the torturous nature of the landscape surrounding me, even in Ellies 4x4 the route was getting harder. Gentle vibrations turned into shockwaves as the route began to get perilous and Ellie's car was struggling to go much further with unwavering determination she pressed ahead.

After five hours of driving, however, she could go no further as deep troughs and large rocks in the terrain made the route impassable for her car. Having packed as much food and drink as I could carry it was time to walk, Ellie gave me a last hug.

"Bring her home Fae and good luck," she hugged me tight before she watched me start my journey.

Walking through growingly more undulating and hard terrain the route was tough and growing more and more so as the mountain range loomed ever closer. Hours passed as I walked through ever tougher and more barren wastelands towards the mountain range. Sitting on a rock formation to take a break and get some much-needed food and water down myself as the heat of the early September sun took its toll on me.

Sweating profusely, I ventured ever deeper before the terrain changed vastly and the dry earth became rocky and increasingly harder as I encroached upon the mountain range. With daylight fading, I continued at pace towards the edge of the range that dropped away and marked the gateway to Evelyn's world.

Eventually, I reached the edge of the range where just as she told me the mountains fell away in a near vertical drop and down into a deep basin. Under the cover of darkness, I found myself at the edge of the two worlds, in the darkness behind me I could see the faint light of Zyvala on the horizon against the night sky. Ahead of me and far below the vast and thick forest Evelyn called home; searching tirelessly, I found the path she marked on the map.

Standing and peering over a near vertical drop of almost a mile down the mountain range and into the realm she dwelt in and called home, suddenly it hit me just how brave Evelyn truly was. Sitting on a verge among the edge, I sat overlooking the terrain below me, lit by faint moonlight it was both majestic and imposing.

Evelyn told me how she had ascended that almost vertical path in a thunderstorm, however I was going to wait until the morning to even attempt that deadly descent. Searching I found a little spot to bed down for the night, between two large fallen pieces of rock and a little shelter to get some much-needed sleep.

During the night the temperature had plummeted as autumn made its presence known, sleeping sporadically cut short by shivering to keep warm. Waking, freezing just before sunrise I topped my fluid and food levels back up and sat upon that verge again to await the sunrise, even with warmer clothes on, I admired my little friend's determination and sheer bravery.

Sunlight slowly started to unmask the world which laid beneath me, moment by moment exposing the sheer majesty of the view and scenery below me. A vast and endless body of trees hiding in a deep basin in the countryside, a near sheer drop off the side of the mountains to the floor below. Fearful as the dangerous path below in daylight was clearly nearly a death sentence, I found my thoughts shifting round as I tried to muster the courage to make the descent.

As the sunlight began to reveal its beauty I found my mind thinking about Evelyn and her childhood in particular. Evelyn gave nearly full credit to a mystery woman she had met in the forest seemingly being adopted by her and mentored into being the woman she had become. However, for me I laid almost every single part of Evelyn's development in her hands alone, she might have been guided but it was her that had changed things for herself.

Professional Fae started to analyse Evelyn's childhood, those moments Ellie spoke about in particular, how did she see herself when she was in fairy mode?

Was she a tiny fairy fearlessly fighting her way through giant dandelions and trolls to reach the realm of fairies? Did she make these journeys alone in her mind or was she helped along the way? Imagining her wandering through a maze of giant dandelions in total darkness with terror continually at her back when suddenly my thoughts changed.

Were the trees now just like the dandelions? Were the trolls now the people of Zyvala who had made her life a living hell? Was the realm of the fairies now the forest? Or Ljianstipol? While my mind pondered about these odd questions, I found myself asking my thoughts turned to the Hotel Davizioso and Shanky in particular.

Ljianstipol had been a good thing for me, having spent years wandering in the darkness of Oured and the clouds which shrouded my past, I had found a new way of life entirely for myself. People had been good to me not just good in truth but utterly inspiringly generous and welcoming, from my earliest days I found friends who were willing to give everything to see me happy and succeed.

Shanky had made me understand myself all those years ago which in truth probably saved my life and now his health was failing and I needed to return that favour? All my guests for my therapy sessions needed me too, I was their supporting hand in the darkness and they needed me?

Realising that I needed to be there for my residents and guests made me realise that as much as I wanted to, there was no way I could descend that slope to Evelyn's forest. Everyone had placed such faith in me in Ljianstipol and if I went down that slope and just vanished then all their faith in me would be unjustified. Suddenly, something became horrifyingly obvious to me, just like my past life, Evelyn had spent years wandering in the darkness searching for the one thing she needed so desperately.

The realm of the fairies wasn't the forest or Ljianstipol, the realm of the fairies for Evelyn was the spot on my sofa or a bed in a home. A home where she was loved and where she belonged surrounded by people that loved and adored her and a place where she could just be that hyperactive and goofy little wonder that she was.

Whatever her reason for vanishing, just like the people of Ljianstipol had placed their faith in me, I needed to place my faith in her to return just as she promised she would. Heavy heartedly it was obvious that I couldn't go down that path no matter how much I wanted to, I needed to wait for my housemate and best friend to just come back whenever that might be.

Evelyn had said she would be back before Christmas and now I needed to place my total and utter faith in her and as I readied myself to walk back to Zyvala, I stood and looked over the forest below me one last time. Looking out across the vast expanse of trees below me, I yelled out, "I love you Evelyn, come home soon, I will be waiting for you," crying as I turned and began the long walk back to civilisation.

Whatever people thought wouldn't matter, if the forest and that edge of the mountain range was real then Evelyn had never lied to me, I just had to wait for her to deliver exactly what she promised, and I had every faith in her.

Walking slowly and thoughtfully through the terrain my mind was splitting about my decision to abandon the mission I had set myself, part of me felt like I had failed myself and Evelyn, the other part was in the middle of an epiphany. Maybe that moment on the ledge of the mountains was the first truly selfless and faithful thing I had done? Realising that I simply had to let nature take its course and await the outcome so that I could be the person that people believed I truly am.

Since Evelyn had gone away, I had hardly been exemplary in any way, locking my emotions away and shielding myself from everyone, what kind of inspiration was I if that was how I conducted myself? Even small details like my hair had fallen massively, all the colour had washed out and I hadn't let Fabi touch it for 2 months, maybe it was time for another change?

A much simpler change but a change nonetheless, my mum loved how my hair was in those photos from that holiday all those years ago, maybe Fabi could help me find that again? Evelyn had helped me find the girl in that picture that sat with my mother so maybe that final little tweak would be the cherry on the Fae cake? Dawning upon me just how much Evelyn had changed me and realising that in the time since she had left, I had let her down, it was time to change that.

Promising myself and arguing with myself all the way to the outskirts of Zyvala, through the barren wastelands and the darkness of the night, when the sun rose, I was going to tell the truth about how hard the last two months had been. Willingly I was going to tell people how much I missed my friend and willingly I would tell them how I found the mountains and forest where she lived but had come back because I owed it to them to be the person, they believed me to be.

People might not understand and see it as me failing or giving up but I didn't care about that, returning to the Davizioso and Ljianstipol without Evelyn would be proof that I wasn't about to let everyone down. Fae Edwards today was going to be the woman and the professional that had been through hell and come out the other side laughing.

Today, I was going to place my total faith in the mere words of a friend to fulfil their promise and today I was going to finally start repaying the gratitude, faith and friendship that the people of Ljianstipol had given me. Touching my foot on the asphalt road that marked the true outskirts of Zyvala today Fae Edwards was a different person to the one who had lived for the last 27 years in their own shadow.

Walking back through the outer limits of the town I started to make my way to Ellie's house to see if she was around, she would be the first person I was going to tell. The driveway was empty and there was no sign of her, I headed to the place where she told me she worked but she wasn't there either?

Walking back into town I made my way to the bus station, wandering past billboards with my picture on, pictures of yesterday's Fae upon them. With the bus station in sight, a familiar voice came from behind me, looking round I couldn't see the source until it came again and stood next to a car in the street stood Karl.

Slightly surprised I did a double take as he waved me over to him, "I wondered if I would find you here, did you?"

He looked at me and offered to take my backpack. I sighed and nodded at him, "I'm just going to be honest Karl, I really miss her but I know she will come back, I just have to believe in her and also sorry, Karl."

Karl took my backpack. "Sorry? What for?"

He looked odd, surprised almost? "Sorry I have lied to you for the last 2 months."

I slumped my head in shame, he walked round the car and shook me gently. "Hey, everyone knew, maybe we should have stepped in sooner to help you, Fae," he held me and hugged me tightly. "Come on let's get you home. I assumed that is where you want to go, Fae?"

I looked up to see his concerned face looking for an answer. "Can you take me back home to Ljianstipol?"

He opened the car door and let me climb aboard. We began the drive home, leaving the streets of Zyvala behind us.

"How did you know where to find me?"

Karl laughed. "Shanky guessed you might be out here, he misses you."

I looked out the window thinking, "How's he doing?" Silence filled the car, "He's better but still has bad days." Sorrow hit as I felt awful for abandoning my friend and saviour, "I'm glad he's better but I shouldn't have left."

Karl looked over. "You needed to know though, right? No one blames you Fae, don't be so hard on yourself."

I placed my hand on his, "Can we get you a shower though, Fae?"

He laughed and I sniffed myself, "Wow I smell really bad! Sorry about that!" I laughed back at him. Karl seemed to smile a little to himself as we continued our journey.

"What's with you?" I asked ever so slightly concerned.

"Well, there's something I need to show you Fae, back at the studio, there's a shower there too if you are up for seeing what I need you to see?"

I looked over. "Please tell me it's not another picture of my arse?" Tutting at him, "No, no, it's nothing like that, just I don't know if you will understand it better if you see instead of me telling you about it." Curious as to what this might be, I agreed to go with him.

During the journey it dawned on me that he was a good guy, I mean, he had driven out here just on the advice of Shanky to come and find me. Maybe Evelyn was right about him? It seemed a strange thought to have, but she was insistent that he had some interest in me. Strange thoughts kept me smiling as we drove the continuous miles of highways towards Ljianstipol and the studio he partly owned.

Wandering through the door he led me down the walkway to the main studio, there proudly on the wall was the picture from the article, not the front-page picture but the picture of me and Evelyn, "That's my favourite picture Fae, two best friends just being best friends," he smiled as I stood looking at it.

"She's so beautiful, isn't she, Karl?" I said as I looked at her deep green eyes and that cute little face.

"Both of the people in that picture are beautiful," Karl said as he started to wander back down the hallway and through the doors of the studio. Karl pointed to a side door and guided me through to an apartment hidden in the hangar. "There's a bathroom with a shower in there, I kinda used to live here when we first started out."

Taking my backpack he went back into the studio, "I will meet you back out here Fae, take your time." Walking round the luxurious apartment I found the shower and washed away the days of sweat that had tainted my skin. Dirty filthy mud and grime flowed off my skin as the warm soothing water washed away four days of torment, the smell of sweat was replaced by sweet smelling soap.

Taking a look in the mirror at my former pride and joyful hair, I was happy with what was peering back at me for a change, in time maybe Mum could get her little Fae back too?

Wandering back into the blackness of the studio down the far end on a bed prop was Karl with his laptop, carefully walking through the studio to join him, he laid on the bed with his laptop open.

Patting the bed, "Come join me Fae, it's comfier than those wooden chairs," I got onto the bed and laid next to him, he offered me a beer too.

Karl started to flick through emails. "I have to find it first but it will be worth the wait Fae," as he started sifting through pages of emails.

"Didn't think you wanted to lay on this bed," he sniggered.

"Imagine what Evelyn would say if she knew!" I chuckled back at him Karl smiled and offered me his laptop.

"Check out all these emails of support about your article," I started to scroll through a continual stream of emails from all over the world from people who had been moved by my article. People from countries that I had never heard of had seen my article and written to thank the studio for publishing the article. Laying utterly stunned.

"Pretty impressive huh? The world loves you Fae, but that's not what I wanted to show you," Karl took the laptop and scrolled to another email and looked at me.

"You ready?" I nodded still dazed but what I had just seen, taking the laptop I began to read a very formal email. Skim reading before I read some words, stopping to read them again I turned to Karl and just pointed at my face, "Me?"

He nodded as I read the email again but fully, "Really? They want me?"

He smiled. "Yes, they want you, Fae!"

I was shocked, "Me? Really just me?"

He laughed as he closed the laptop. "Yes Fae, they want you to be in the calendar for next year twice, for May and December."

The same fear that had gripped me before the article took hold of me again, "But I'm nothing special, I'm just a care worker, I'm not special in any way Karl, how can I be a calendar girl!"

Karl shuffled over and laid closer next to me, he pulled out his phone and opened the picture of me and Evelyn that he had on the hallway of the studio. "She thinks you are special and so do a lot of people Fae and in truth me too, I think you are special Fae," he was calm and collected trying to reason with me.

"But I look like shit, my hair is awful, and I haven't looked after myself for two months now, there's no way I can be in a calendar, all those other girls look phenomenal but I just look terrible."

Karl sat up and sighed. "You look great Fae, you are attractive, kind and caring and people like you, you can easily do this, it's just two pictures and you look better than almost everyone that comes through those studio doors."

I sat up with him as my doubts clouded me. "You're just saying that to get me to say yes!"

Karl looked over and had a strange look on his face, "I mean it Fae, if you want, I can grab a camera and show you right here right now!"

My hackles went up a little. "Fine then we'll do just that! Where are we doing this!" I snapped a little at him.

Karl pointed to a black screened area in the studio and wheeled a single light over for this moment of truth, I was determined to prove him wrong. "You are going to regret taking these Karl!"

He smiled back, "No I won't." His collective nature was incensing me, determined to show him he was wrong, I took my top off and stood in trousers and my bra. Calmly he adjusted the light changing the colour of it, "It won't help Karl!" He carried on through my flaring temper, smiling each time I let out little remarks.

Taking the first photo's he smiled more which made me angrier, he called out posing changes to me but when he realised, I didn't understand him he came over to manually pose me. While he manipulated me into the positions he needed, his calm nature was driving my temper onwards, bubbling away as he seemed to be enjoying this?

I turned round and looked over my shoulder to a spot just beside him, "Yeah, get my fat arse in there too!" I scolded at him and he just laughed to himself, "Oh yeah? Then try this!"

Without thought I took my trousers off and stood in just my underwear, "Get that full moon in there Karl!"

He erupted laughing and stepped back before taking some more pictures. Walking towards me, he was still chuckling away as he offered me his camera and put his arms around me and gave me a big hug.

"Thought you didn't want to do underwear shots Fae," he laughed away as I looked at the back of the camera.

"These will all be awful," I started scrolling through and even with my awful hair and fat arse, as much as I hated to admit it, he was right, Evelyn was right and even bloody Francois was right, I looked pretty good? I looked at Karl and just laughed at him.

"I'm sorry Karl, what a bitch! You were right and I don't look that bad," I shyly conceded defeat.

Karl laughed. "Come on let's go look at them on the laptop."

I chuckled at him, "It's not widescreen is it?"

He put his arm around me and walked me back to the bed at the end of the studio. My temper was receding as I became a little embarrassed at what I had just subjected the poor guy to, he just laughed it off though as he loaded the pictures on the laptop.

Laying back on the bed next to him, "Didn't you want your trousers Fae?" He chuckled as I lay next to him in my underwear.

Scrolling through the images just made me feel even worse for being so short with him, "Wow these are good Karl, I'm sorry, my temper gets the better of me sometimes, though look how thin I have gotten?"

Karl sighed. "Not eating much Fae?"

I nodded back, "Sorry I haven't been around much for you Fae, you needed help and we weren't there for you."

Apologetic in his tone, sighing to myself, "It's okay, I'm as guilty as anyone else, I should have told you all what was going on, I've done this to myself."

Karl just put his hand on mine and smiled. "I'm here for you if you need me, Fae," a strange sensitivity was emanating from him.

"Was Evelyn right about you?" I asked quietly almost as if I thought the walls might hear me, he didn't answer he just smiled to himself. Each picture he had taken was perfect, the light set to enhance my pale skin and bring out my freckles and eyes. Every pose he forced me into made me look elegant and delicate, I was stunned to see myself this way, even with my natural hair colour, even that looked stunning.

Lying alongside him in near silence as he seemed to rejoice in his little victory, suddenly feeling at ease next to him, "It's really late, Fae, I should get you home, you must be tired."

I checked the time to see it was 2am! I collected my trousers and looked at Karl before I put them on, I turned round and pointed at my backside. "Did you want one more picture for the road?"

He just laughed at me. "Come on, we'll save that for another time." Leading me back to his car, my temper flared a little again as he drove me back home. "Can I ask you something Karl?"

He looked over at me. "Sure?" I took a deep breath as I built my confidence. "If you like me, then why haven't you taken me on a date?"

He chuckled and shrugged. "Tuesday night good for you?"

My hackles went back up, "Yeah, Tuesday is good for me, glad you didn't wait too long to ask!"

He laughed it off again as he dropped me outside my house. "See you at 7 on Tuesday?"

I turned round to him, shyly, "Tuesday at 7 is good, thanks for today and putting up with my temper," watching as he drove away.

Light anger had filled me as I walked back into my empty house, arguing with myself, "Who is this jerk asking me on a date on Tuesday at 7? Just who is this guy!"

When suddenly I listened to what I was saying to myself and erupted in shock, "Oh my fucking god Fae! You have a date on Tuesday at 7," talking to myself as I began pacing up and down my home.

"But what do I wear, my hair looks like shit and I've never been on a real date before? Who can I ask about it? Alyssia?" Pacing faster and crashing face down on my sofa, "But what if it doesn't work out? I need help from someone who won't talk about it and someone who knows how to make me look good?"

Looking at the ceiling with names crashing in and out of my mind, Mum maybe? Eventually, I figured out exactly who to ask, someone who would help me look way better than I could achieve on my own and someone who always gave good advice. As much as my mind couldn't believe it the obvious choice was Francois, he knew exactly how to bring out my shape and he gave good advice even if sometimes it was quite barbed!

Somewhere along the way I had lost all track of time and found myself thinking about walking to find his shop locked up as it was every Sunday, my mentor wouldn't be available today. Thinking how I had lost all track of time, when a knock came at my door and much to my surprise there waiting stood Gale?

We had an awkward moment as I sheepishly invited him in, he had brought goodies with him, not that in my mind I deserved them, he had come to check on me and see how I was doing. Sitting at my kitchen table he exposed that Ellie had told him she had seen me and taken me to the mountains to find Evelyn, Gale was pleased to see me back safe and well.

Looking at my concerned boss I started to unravel myself to him and apologise for keeping both him and Tony in the darkness about just how hard Evelyn leaving had really hit me. Apologising for letting myself, him and the Davizioso's guests and residents down but from today everything was going to change.

I wanted to reactivate the sessions I had been running in the evening and I was going to use myself as a full case study for my course and for my group therapy sessions. Gale however only had one reason for coming to see me, he wanted to apologise for pushing me too hard and not noticing the state I had gotten into before I had my crash which had broken Tony's arm.

Gale seemed odd today, remorseful and subdued almost as if he was ashamed? We spent an hour or so talking in raw terms about the past two months before we came to a mutual agreement that they should have stepped in soon but also that I should have told them how bad things had gotten for me.

Agreeing the best way forward before we turned to the future and what we would do to stop anything like that happening again, when I told him about the moment on the mountain edge where I had turned back as my professional mind stepped in and I wasn't going to let them or my clients down by walking away. Times had changed for me and I had come back driven and determined to go further than before and to repay Gale and Tony's unwavering faith in me.

Gale asked if Ellie had given me her big news? Ellie would be moving to Ljianstipol and joining the team at the Davizioso as Tony's injury exposed just how much the pair needed new help, of course Gale was happy to have his family back together.

Maybe somewhere amidst the disasters of the last two months, some good had come from it all, I knew how happy Gale was at the thought of Ellie being around him again, he couldn't mask that smile every time he spoke about her working at the Davizioso alongside him.

Conversation soon turned to more important things, like the sorry state my hair was in and our next late night pool session together, Gale found the picture on my bookshelf of me and my mum when I was little. Smiling at me, "Why don't you try this for your next hairdo, Fae? You looked really cute like that."

As I smiled back, he seemed to sense something. "Did Karl find you? He came looking for you last week about another photo shoot?"

My little blush gave the game up, "He found you then?"

Gale laughed and stood behind me. "Don't worry, your secret is safe with me but maybe work on your poker face, so that if anyone else asks you don't go bright red!"

I relaxed a little. "Imagine what Evelyn would say if she knew he was taking me out on a date."

Gale smiled. "She was right then?"

I nodded my head at him, "Give yourself the chance Fae, he might be good for you, if he cared enough to come find you in Zyvala then he can't be all bad?"

Gale stayed for half an hour before he headed back to the Davizioso.

After Gale left, I sat looking at the picture of me and Mum together and sent Fabi a text to see if he could sort my hair out for me, it was short notice but hopefully he could come and help? Fabi soon texted back a thumbs up, while I waited, I ordered a delivery to thank him and Alyssia for being there for me so many times since I had arrived in Ljianstipol.

Soon enough they both arrived, he had his hairdressing bag with him and Alyssia had brought a crate of beer just in time for the takeaway to arrive. We sat in my kitchen and just like with Gale, I apologised for being so terrible over the last two months and just like him they also felt responsible.

Friendship is a curious thing though, we shared responsibility for the failings and successes of the last few months. I showed Fabi the picture of me and my mum and asked if he could do my hair just like that, he seemed surprised that I was going for something quite so tame and not really the Fae he had become used to.

Alyssia sat talking to me as he got to work, I spoke to her about the moment on the mountains where I had decided to place faith in Evelyn to come back and how I couldn't abandon my new home and the friends that went with it.

Alyssia logically talked with me about my decision and how my new renewed faith in myself and the people around me was heavily evident in my mind, like a new version of myself. Openly admitting to her that I shouldn't have locked down in the first place and how I had created a vicious cycle for myself almost hiding myself away from everything.

I started to reveal to her that I was going to use myself as one of my case studies for my course, Alyssia thought it was a great idea but wondered if it might be hard to write so openly about myself. Part of me agreed with her, it would be odd to write about myself as both a professional and patient. But maybe this was my true strength and the best way to help me rationalise the past.

Alyssia offered to be a case study for me in place of doing a self-assessment but I was certain that it would be a good idea and that it would be therapeutic too. Fabi soon finished working his magic and when he offered me a mirror, I couldn't believe the girl that sat looking back at me, just as Evelyn said I looked stunning. My little flyaways and the bun showing off my sweet face and my natural colour proudly on display.

"No more hats," Fabi chuffed at me.

"Never again," I smiled back at him.

After a few hours together, they left me to myself for the evening and my mind turned to Tony and Gale, both had been so good to me over the years and in the last two months I hadn't been the best. Willingly putting me onto an expensive course to give me a bigger chance for my future, it was time to get stuck back into it and really push.

My course needed two additional case studies Shanky had been an original case study but I needed two further to demonstrate my understanding of my profession. Something dawned upon me, I needed two examples of people that either had been failed by the health system or somehow and against all odds had found a way to overcome undiagnosed problems.

Thinking harder gave me two real options for this, my first would be myself, accurately accounting how destructive the last two months had been and how I had failed myself by closing up. Finally, I would analyse Evelyn, somehow, she had managed to overcome all the problems which marred her childhood and rise above all of us, I was sure she wouldn't mind, though it would mean delving into her past and without her present it might cause me problems to think about it.

Determination and drive had returned to me and while I thought about my course and how hard I was going to work at it, my mind returned to my date and seeing Francois in the morning. Part of me genuinely dreaded what answers and insights he might give but one thing I knew was that no matter how much I might not like what he said it would be utterly truthful.

Francois wouldn't say anything vaguely deceptive and neither would he let anyone know why I had gone to see him or what we discussed. Willing he would even withhold that information from his dear wife Colette, one thing he never had done to me was share anything we had ever discussed in truth neither had Colette.

Oddly, both placed high value in keeping certain things between us only and in truth I admired that side of them both, Colette had never shared what she and Evelyn ever discussed, anytime I asked she just smiled sweetly and talked about something else. Most of that evening I spent slowly writing down parts of Evelyn's past, the stories that she and Ellie had told me, ready to start analysing and evaluating her for my course.

Periodically, my mind turned to my date with Karl and that calendar that I had been offered two spots in, I looked at pictures of Evelyn on my phone and decided that I would do them for her. Had Evelyn been here, she would have talked me into doing them and assured me that it would be a good thing for me to do, no matter how long it would have taken her to talk me round, she wouldn't have wavered or given up on convincing me to do it.

Sitting looking at the picture of us on my wall. "If you are here, you will be in those pictures with me you little shit!" I sat talking to myself and smiling as I made my decision for the calendar pictures.

Evening turned to night and night soon turned to morning as the time arrived to go and brave Francois and his sharp words of advice. Walking down feeling refreshed and anew with an odd step of confidence in my step as I walked down by the river and up onto the cobbled streets which marked the entrance to the market square.

Francois was standing as always leant casually against the wall of his boutique smoking away, however unlike normal he dropped glasses as he caught me in his eyesight. An odd smile came across his face as I approached him, he seemed oddly happy and content. "Fae, you look incredible! You were beautiful before but now you are just stunning!"

As his words sunk into my mind, I just smiled at him, blushing a little. "Why has my beautiful friend come to me today?" He stood waiting for my answer.

I took a deep breath and plucked up the courage, "Francois, I need your help with something."

He looked at me concerned. "Come in and lock the door Fae," Francois guided me through his door and bolted it closed behind us. Walking me through his shop and offering me a seat.

"So, tell me what you need my help with Fae?" He fetched a cup of coffee for me and sat opposite with a fearful look on his face. Sitting looking at the floor, he came over to me and put his hand on my shoulder.

"Fae what is wrong?" I built up the courage to talk to him.

Looking up at his concerned face, "Francois, I have a date on Tuesday, I haven't been on a real date before, what do I do? What do I wear?"

Francois looked stunned. "Really? A girl as attractive as you should be fighting the boys away." Like a father he sat down to talk to me. Softly smiling, "Where are you going?" He smiled.

"Dinner, I think?" He sat up and looked at me again, "The answer to your question is simple."

I looked at him, "How so?" I questioned him.

Francois sat back and relaxed. "Wear the white or blue dress depending what you want from the date," thinking as he spoke to me.

"What I want from the date?"

Francois laughed. "If you want to have sex on the first date, wear the blue dress, if you want another date then wear the white dress."

I sat up in shock, "Francois!"

He laughed a little. "If you wear the white dress, he will meet you again, as he will be devastated if he doesn't see you again, the blue dress will get you a night in bed but not a second date, that is how men's minds work I'm afraid Fae," Thinking away as he gave his insight.

"What if we meet more than once, Francois?" He smiled at me.

"He will be an idiot to turn down a lady as beautiful as you Fae and you must never date idiots!" I smiled as he gave his insights into me.

Shyly I asked him one last question, "How will I know if he is serious?"

Francois came over and gave his shy little girl a hug. "If he meets you more than twice for the fourth date tell him you will meet him but don't tell him where, if he is serious, he will know where to find you, Colette did it to me. There is a little cafe in the heart of Paris she loved, you couldn't find it by accident, that is where we had our fourth date and we have been together ever since."

"Fae, me and Colette, both love you and I have always tried to bring out your beautiful lines with my clothing, you are stunning to look at and any man would be lucky to be with you," Francois put his arms around me. "We will always be here for you."

I cried a little as that softer side of this perplexing man came back out, "You really mean that Francois?"

He held on. "Why would I lie to you now?" Francois offered me a tissue and offered me his hand to help me stand back up, he stood back analysing me. "I might have something that will make you unforgettable? If you want to try it?"

I dried my eyes. "Me? Unforgettable?"

Francois smiled. "Turn around."

Behind me I could hear him looking for something and swearing at himself as he approached me again, "Close your eyes and no peeking!"

Trusting him entirely I closed my eyes and awaited his instruction. "Open your eyes, Fae."

Stood in front of me was Colette with a mirror, "You are perfect as you are Fae," she smiled sweetly and came over to give me a hug, she held me and stroked my face, "You look incredible Fae, you don't need special dresses or anything else as you are perfect as you are."

Colette held me like her own daughter, she smiled at me. "Your secret is our secret Fae, now go and win his heart or crush his dreams!" Colette let me go and helped me out of the shop giving me a little peck on the cheek as I left.

Walking home filled with optimism and the wisdom of my strange new parental figures, I felt good and hopeful, the Parisian pair had touched my emotions deep inside and just maybe they would prove to be right? Tony and Gale were still on my mind, I made a detour and headed to the Davizioso, Abby greeted me, seeming surprised to see me back.

Venturing up to their conference room I found them talking about paperwork, Tony looked round with a huge smile, "Fae! Come here it's so good to see you back!" He came across the room to shake my hand, "Look at you! Don't you look beautiful now! Did that photographer find you?"

I grabbed Tony, "I'm so sorry, can we meet on Wednesday and talk about everything and make plans?" Whimpering like a badly behaved child.

Tony held onto me. "We knew times might get tough for you, we should have stepped in and helped you and yes we have big plans to discuss with you."

He smiled at me and pointed at his arm. "No sling or cast anymore so be gentle with me Fae!"

I couldn't help but laugh at him, "No hair dye either right?"

Gale looked at us both and smiled. "We'll see you Wednesday, usual time Fae?"

I walked to him and shook his hand too. "Usual time Gale."

He tipped his head to me. "Now get out of here before you start helping sort my life out again, see you Wednesday, Fae." He began sifting through the mountain of paperwork strewn round the office as I headed back home.

That night I started my self-assessment and began to document all the events over the last two months, I was going to hit this course harder than before and make amends with myself. Spending all that night sitting typing on a laptop under the picture of me and Evelyn together, I smiled to myself as I thought how even in her absence, she had changed me.

I wondered what she would think or say if she knew that tomorrow night I would be going on a date with Karl. Cross analysing myself and where I had failed myself in regards to care. Writing down all the moments and times where I had masked my problems and feelings from everyone including myself and assessing where my conditions had been the deciding factor and where a lack of understanding had been the deciding factor.

Ruthlessly assessing all the points at which I should have asked for help and where I should have stepped in to help myself. Words began to flood out of me and I began to realise just how dangerous that cycle really was and just how volatile the situation became. Where normally I would use my own troubles to kickstart my group therapy sessions and by doing so deliver myself therapy, by locking down I had cut my own therapy out which led to the implosion of my mind.

Realising and bullet pointing every step of the scenario which led to an almost catastrophic lack of care, time scaling the day-by-day account of the last two months. What I soon began to see was an all too familiar pattern which so many of my residents and guests had in their stories.

Locked up and secretly my conditions had slowly grown worse and I became better at masking them, until my crash most would have been unaware just how far I had fallen. Tony and Gale felt responsible for what had happened that night but the reality was that it was almost entirely my own fault and as such I should have acted far sooner.

Whether I was sitting at the beach alone or just hiding in my house, rather than helping myself I had been aggravating my conditions by hiding away from them just like my dad had done when I was growing up.

Finding the similarities between me and my dad's behaviour I picked up the phone and rang him to talk, I owed him an apology as deep down it turned out I was capable of being just as bad as him. My dad answered with his usual optimism, and we spent the next hour talking, talking in ways we hadn't done since I was 17 years old.

Forgiving him for how he had handled my problems when I was younger, I found myself crying a few times and I heard him sniffle a few times, I guess it was good to finally get it out in the open and talk about it? I finished by inviting him to Ljianstipol for Christmas, we hadn't seen each other for years now and this seemed like the right time to see him and show him the world I now inhabited.

Heading outside I took a few moments to gather my thoughts in the cool night air, autumn was coming and though it was cooler at night somehow it felt warmer than summer? Sitting in our tree watching the horizon and the darkness engulfing the world I decided to phone Mum too and apologise for being so bad to her as a child. Nearly an hour passed as I sat in my tree and spoke to her, telling her about speaking to Dad and I invited her to visit for Christmas too, she accepted without thought.

Feeling better about myself I began to wonder how Evelyn would feel if I told her what I had just done, I'm sure she would be proud of me for forgiving my dad and mum. Evelyn though would probably be happier to tell me that by forgiving them that I had started to forgive myself for what I had done to them in the past.

Magnus appeared below me and sat talking with me for an hour, we did this evening chatting quite regularly now, he used it as a break from his children, I just enjoyed the company and he was quite funny too. I remember the first night his voice came from behind the fence, how he startled me and yet all he really did was keep an eye on me and be a soundboard for my thoughts.

Possibly against my better judgement I asked his advice on dating but his advice was similar to the advice Francois had given me, he advised the white dress unless I wanted a simple night in bed.

I spent hours getting myself ready for Karl to pick me up, I adjusted the white dress so many times to make sure it sat right on me and brushing my hair to be just right, clearly this date meant more to me than I wanted to openly admit. Nervously waiting, as the hours ticked away, anxious and excited about the prospect of the night ahead, I wondered where he was going to take me.

Running over the conversations that we might have in my mind; this was nearly as hard as preparing for the interviews for the magazine article. I tried to steady myself and calm down as the hour drew closer, I had a beer to try calming myself down a little before a knock came at the door and excitedly, I answered to find Karl dressed up awaiting his girl for the evening.

Karl walked me to his car and opened the door to let me in before we drove to a little restaurant just out of town. Karl knew I would be nervous and wanted to take me somewhere away from anyone we might know and he hoped it would help calm my nerves.

Awkward conversations kicked off the candle lit dinner in this remote little place, he kept laying his hand on mine to try steady my mind a little, it didn't really work too much and he noticed. Looking up at me he put his hand out to me. "Just relax and be you, Fae, even if it's the angry bitchy version of you."

I looked up and saw his concerned face and as his words seeped into my mind I laughed, "You bastard, you wonderful bastard."

He smiled back at me. "That's better," he laughed back. Conversations began to flow, and I relaxed into the evening and everything felt different and better somehow, a little smile became fixed to my face and I wanted the night to never end. Karl drove us back to the park just round the corner from my home and parked up, feeling nervous.

"Why have you stopped here?" He just smiled. "So, I can walk you home," he offered me his hand. Walking through the park in silence together I pulled myself closer to him and held his hand, he put his hand on my waist, and we walked along slowly.

Silence felt golden as our minds seemed to be talking for us, I looked up a couple of times and saw him just smiling as we walked along together, I stopped and he followed suit. He looked at me in concern. "Are you okay?"

I smiled at him, "I will do the calendar pictures."

He looked surprised, "Really?"

I nodded, "Really, But under two conditions?"

Karl just nodded, "No underwear shots and if Evelyn is back before you send the pictures away, she is in the pictures with me." Karl smiled back, "Sounds fine to me," he took my hand again and we walked back to my house.

We stood at my doorway, and I held his hands, "Thank you for a nice night."

Shyly looking at him waiting for him to ask about another night. "Next week?"

He smiled at me. "Tuesday night is good?" He smiled. "I will pick you up again," he placed his hand on my back and gave me a little hug, I gave him a little kiss, he looked up in shock before relaxing and running his thumb down my cheek before kissing me in return. "Good night, Fae," he kissed me on the cheek before he turned and left.

Standing on my doorstep I watched him walk away and vanish into the night as my heart began to pound and exhilaration took hold of me, I ran inside giddy like a little girl, smiling and grinning away to myself. Sitting on my sofa, "He loves your bum."

I laughed at myself as I thought about all the times when Evelyn had told me he liked me, I slept in her spot on the sofa for the night, smiling to myself throughout the night.

Colette woke me the next morning, her sweet smile was a warm and welcome sight as was the cup of coffee she brought with her. Inviting her in she sat down as softly as she spoke, looking at me her innocent little smile and wise eyes knew how my evening had gone. Running through the entire evening with her, she rarely spoke, just listening happily to me telling her about my first real date. She put her hand over the table to me.

"It will be the first of many wonderful evenings for you, did you call him a bastard?"

I nodded at her, "Me and Francois insult each other a lot, to many it looks like we rarely get along, but the truth is that we are comfortable to be around each other. Some may not approve of our ways, but it works for us and we very much love each other, maybe this is also the way for you?"

Her soft accent carried her sentiment. "I hope he will be the man for you Fae, you are a beautiful lady and you deserve a good man and I hope that he is that good man," smiling at her in almost full mother mode.

Colette promised to keep everything to herself, I said she could tell Francois if she wanted as I trusted them both implicitly. Colette departed and went to open her shop for the day as I got myself ready to go for the big meeting with Tony and Gale.

Arriving at the rooftop garden just after noon, both sat waiting for me in unison they stood to greet me. "Fae! It's good to see you!" Tony smiled at me and gave me a hug, Gale stood smiling at me. "Good to see you Fae, hope you slept well?" He winked at me.

Tony clocked Gale's remark and pushed me back and looked at me in shock, "Did you go on a date last night?" My face couldn't hide the truth, he laughed. "He did like your bum then?" He hugged me again, "Yes he did, thanks Evelyn!"

I held onto him. Tony sat me down and Gale passed me a beer, we clinked our bottles. "We have big news for you Fae, but first are you seeing him again?" Gale smiled at me.

"On Tuesday," shyly I answered his question.

Tony patted me on the shoulder. "Fourth date is when you let him play!" He laughed at me.

"Tony!" Gale smiled. "Hey she might play with him first Tony!"

I sat back, "You guys are both awful!" I smiled and laughed to myself.

"We are just toying, it's nice to see that smile back Fae." Tony looked at me the same way he did that night he broke into my room.

"We want to start by apologising to you Fae, we pushed you way too hard and when Evelyn left, we should have stepped in and made sure you were okay," Gale looked at me with shame in his voice, "We knew you were struggling after Evelyn went away and we didn't act upon it, we let you carry on walking into darkness alone. We will never let it happen again; we know you feel responsible but really, we should have done more to take pressure off you."

Tony sounded remorseful. "I should have told you how badly I was doing, I shouldn't have locked up and maybe I should have turned down those evening sessions to take weight off myself, I'm sorry I let you both down," Gale leant over.

"No Fae! It's all our fault, we should have done more for you," I looked up at them both and smiled.

"Can we just agree to talk more openly in the future? As Gale you are shit at paperwork."

Gale laughed at me. "This is actually what we want to discuss with you, we have realised that we need to make some big changes for the future."

Tony handed me a sealed envelope, "Don't open it just yet, but you know that we have dropped the evening sessions? They see numbers at those sessions and not people and stories, we have never seen our guests or residents as numbers and we won't start that now. Gale will tell you the big changes we have coming and I have a few smaller ones to list too."

Gale handed me another envelope, "You know Ellie is coming to Ljianstipol?"

I looked at him, "Yes, over Christmas?"

Gale nodded, "Ellie will also be joined by Sophie."

Tony added, "They both will be joining us in the new year, we won't be around forever and since your article came out, we are busier than ever, but we need to take weight off you too, so how do we do that?"

I looked over at him, "Will Ellie and Sophie be joining me?"

Gale laughed. "No, that night you crashed someone else stepped up to the mark and someone we never suspected would do so."

Thinking away, I tried to recall all who had come to my aid, "Abby?"

Gale smiled. "We want you to mentor and train Abby, she will take over some of your sessions and we will be employing two more members of your team. With you getting your qualification soon, we need you to officially do something that you have been doing for some time and in truth until you weren't here, we didn't realise just how much you had been doing it."

Tony passed me another beer, "We want you to lead our business, you have been driving this place forward for a year now, just now we want you to officially be part of that and recognised for doing so."

I sat up, "What do you mean?" I said to them surprised as to what they meant.

"Open the envelopes." Tony said.

Cautiously I prised open the first envelope and pulled out a contract. "What is this?" I started to look at the contract.

"It's your new contract, starting in the new year, you will be our head of practice if you want to be of course, you will be fully qualified by then and this will recognise what you have done for us and this place since you have been here." Tony smiled at me.

"What's in the other envelope?" Tony looked at Gale.

"Something a bit different."

I opened the envelope and pulled out a strange looking document? "What is this Gale?" He came and sat next to me.

"Read it carefully Fae," as I sat reading the document. "Holy shit! You have to be kidding me!"

Gale put his hand on my shoulder. "No, I'm quite serious, here's a pen, sign it!" Placing a pen in my hand, I started to shake. "You are really sure about this?"

Tony came and sat the other side. "Absolutely, sign it."

I handed Gale the pen back, "I can't sign this."

Tony handed me another pen, "Yes you can, we can recruit anyone we need but most people don't get this place, but you do and there is no one better to sign this document."

Gale put his hand on my shoulder. "There is nobody else I would offer this to Fae, just sign it."

I sat thinking, "But this makes me a business partner?"

Tony smiled. "Yes, you will own 20 percent of the Davizisoso and as such you will be a deciding voice in how it moves forward, just like you have been for over a year without us ever noticing."

Gale handed me back the pen. "Your article showed us just how much you had really done for us, so please sign it and become our partner, you will even have a swanky office on the top floor, on the corner where your old room was."

Welling up, "You turned my old room into an office?" I looked at Gale.

"Well, it's still a work in progress but yes, it should be ready after your holiday in October, well sort of?" Laughing to myself, I signed my name on the document and handed it to Gale and signed my new contract and handed it to Tony.

Tony looked at me. "There is one last thing Fae," I looked at him as he handed me yet another beer. "You need a case study for your final assessment, don't you?"

I nodded at him, "Yes a posthumous one?"

Gale looked at me. "I will leave you two alone for a few minutes and go and get these ratified and bring Abby back with me." Gale walked away and Tony sat next to me. "My proudest achievement is that we have had zero deaths at the Davizioso which have been caused by the conditions our residents have, but for your course and qualification this is a problem?"

Tony seemed more thoughtful than usual, "Fae? Look at me."

I looked at him, "I want you to use David for your posthumous case study."

Stunned by what he had just said, "Tony, I don't know if that is a good idea?"

Tony looked over the horizon. "Yes, it is, take these diaries and we will talk about him until you have everything you need to make your assessment about him, you will be my therapist Fae."

I looked at him and put my hand on his shoulder. Tony smiled. "I hate journalists Fae, but he came looking for you and drove to Zyvala to make sure you were okay, that makes him okay in my books, did you agree to the calendar?"

I sat up, "Yes I agreed but only if Evelyn can be in the pictures if she is back."

Tony smiled. "I hope she comes back soon Fae; did you really go to the edge of the mountain range?" He looked round at me. "Yeah, I went there, but I realised that I needed to trust she will be back and I can't leave my residents behind either, I owe it to them to be the person they believe that I am." Tony gave me a hug.

"Good girl," Gale appeared with Abby following him, she sat down and I handed her a beer. "Welcome to the team and thank you for helping me," we clinked our bottles and she smiled.

Gale handed Abby a new contract which she had no hesitation to sign. Gale looked round, "About that Fae, we have ditched their sessions and will be running our own in their place, but only if you are happy to run them?"

I paused and thought, *Can I use the sessions to start training my new partner?*

Gale looked at Tony who just shrugged his shoulders, "Why not? If Abby is happy to do that?" Gale looked round at Abby.

"Sounds good." We shook hands and discussed our plans for when I returned to work on Monday before time came to head back home.

Most of the week I spent reading through the diaries that Tony had given me about David, his own diary, Sophie's diary and a stream of social media posts and documents about his care. Tony came over on Saturday night to talk to me about David and start the therapy sessions which he was doing purely to help benefit me and my career.

Ploughing through the mass of documentation surrounding his stays at different clinics all of which had failed catastrophically to prevent his death. Every single piece of information seemed to point to him needing long-term help and assistance but he was released not once, but three times far too early from care.

My mind returned to the day we had the meeting with the healthcare authority, one of those practitioners had signed David's release paperwork the night he killed himself. Openly stating that his conditions presented no threat to life, it seemed almost as if the real reason behind David's death was simply the system, he was in didn't care at all.

Tony came back on Sunday at my request to read through the case study I had done for David, he brought Mona with him and together they sat and read the full document. A few times Mona cried as she processed what I had written and a few times I left the house and sat in my garden to give them space to breathe and grieve David and his early death. Mona came outside and just walked over to me and gave me a hug.

"Thank you, Fae," I held her in return.

"Sorry, this happened to you both." Tony came and joined us shaking my hand to thank me. "See you tomorrow Fae," they left with a heavy heart but happy with some kind of answer, even if it was just my opinion.

My mind turned to work and more importantly my new apprentice, I was surprised that Abby would be training to become a therapist as it didn't seem like her but the more, I thought about it, the more it made sense. During my first week at the Davizioso she had befriended me and when I had my first crash, she even abandoned her date to come to my aid.

On multiple occasions, she had come to my aid and never hesitated to be there for me, now I could repay her and give her a career just like I had been given, I was going to work my hardest to make her succeed. While I sat thinking and planning, there was a knock at my door, it was a chilly and wet night? Who had come to see me tonight? Much to my surprise a wet and nervous looking Abby stood at my door.

I invited her in and sat her down, she was physically shaking and struggling to speak, it seemed obvious just how nervous she was about tomorrow. Offering her a beer to calm her down we sat talking about her training, she was petrified, not about being a carer but about letting the guests down. A few times she cried as her fear unleashed, truthfully, she reminded me of myself in a lot of ways, that had been my biggest concern when I started at the Davizioso.

More than once I had considered leaving as I didn't think I could do a good job and help people, of course this was a quality that is needed for this career as caring about how well you can help people is almost as important as helping them at all. We sat chatting as I tried to assure her that she would be fine, it was an awful night the rain was almost constant, so I offered her a bed for the night so that she didn't spend a night in fear alone.

Walking her to my spare room, she looked in the room I kept for Evelyn wandering in and she sat on the bed looking at the pictures she kept on the wall. Looking at the sailor outfit still proudly hanging on the wardrobe door.

"I really miss her you know; she was such a funny girl," she gently stroked the arm of the outfit and sighed. "I miss her every day, her crazy talking in the morning, her passing out of the sofa with her little legs hanging off the side," I picked up a picture on the drawers and sat on the bed with Abby.

"Sorry, I didn't mean to upset you, I know how much her leaving affected you," she looked at me. "Ah it's okay, though sometimes I wonder what would have happened if I just crossed the mountains instead of coming back. Maybe I would have found her? Maybe I would have just slipped and fallen to my death? Who really knows but I just couldn't do it."

Abby leant over. "But you tried you shouldn't feel ashamed."

I smiled. "I'm not ashamed, I'm proud in truth, I turned back because people believe that I am a better person than I am, I turned back because I can't turn my back on my guests who need me, I turned back because somehow this stupid, bipolar and depression suffering girl inspires people like you to be more than they already are and how can I turn my back on that? Only a coward would have walked away, maybe what Evelyn taught me the most was to have faith in people and I do believe she will come back."

I found myself weeping, the more I spoke to Abby she just smiled sweetly, "You inspired me Fae, I look at you and think if you can achieve what you have with your conditions then there is no reason, I can't do the same."

I looked over at her smiling like Evelyn would have been. "You will be better than me Abby."

She shook her head. "No one will be better than you Fae." We sat and talked for most of the night, a mutual respect for each other carried between ourselves.

Abby would be spending all week shadowing me and learning the ways of The Davizioso, so for me it only seemed right that we start our day with coffee from Fabi. Together we made our way down to his little shop before we ventured down and through town to start our first day of work together, one thing no one had told me was who was replacing Abby on reception. I was shocked to find Jess being mentored by Abby's friend and coworker on reception showing her the ropes and I figured she would be a good fit here, she had experience of the place too.

Tentatively, we spent the morning visiting different residents and Abby largely stayed out of the way but in the afternoon, we visited Shanky and she seemed to ease up a little. Slowly coming out of her shell and starting to almost enjoy herself as we listened to his stories and enjoyed some time with him, he was doing better too, I was quite relieved to see him well again.

363

Next door to his room was my old room or what would soon be my office, Tony was inside waving at the walls with Gale holding his hands on his head, they seemed stressed so we left them to it and visited Hugh instead. Hugh was preparing to do a blog about a painting he had done, Abby started to help him out when suddenly his persona switched, she seemed quite surprised to find herself being introduced to a new name by the same face she was chatting with just minutes earlier.

Whether she was in shock or not she carried on and seemed to overcome her fears a little in the face of something very unique. While I kept an eye on Abby, my mind was starting to think about my date tomorrow night, wondering where we would go and almost phasing out for a few moments. "Fae? Are you okay?"

I snapped out of my daydream. "Sorry Abby, yeah I'm fine."

We started to head back down to hand over to the evening teams. Walking home she seemed concerned but had a strange smile on her face, "Thinking about your date?"

I looked at her in shock, "How do you know that?"

She grinned. "You can't hide that lusty stare Fae; don't worry I won't tell anyone." Dropping her at her doorstep, I ventured back home and sat pondering about tomorrow night.

Karl had started to send me goodnight texts most nights now, it felt nice, odd and touching to know someone was thinking about me and cared, each one gave me a little smile when it arrived. Tuesday was mostly a daydream, Abby shadowed me for two group sessions, observing and learning, though she did try to join in, but my mind was focussed on tonight. Soon enough that knock came at my door at 7 and Karl once again stood awaiting me, he gave me a little hug to greet me before he walked me to his waiting car.

Driving out of town again we headed to a large park out of town to go for a walk in the falling leaves under the cover of darkness. Walking together hand in hand talking about ourselves and slowly revealing our true selves to each other, the moonlit paths were luring us further and further. Reaching a bench on a hill which overlooked all of Ljianstipol gently glimmering away in the distance, it was quite romantic, something felt obvious though?

Unlike anyone, I had been dated by before this was no attempt to simply woo me, this was deeper than that? A mutual respect and deep bond? I leant against him and he put his arm around me and we sat in silence for an hour before we started to wander back, my arm around his waist and his hand rested just on my hip. Slowly walking suspended in soft blue light through the trees and fallen leaves of autumn, we reached his car and he opened the door for me to get in before he drove me back home.

Parking round the corner so he could walk me home again, his hand returned to rest on my hip as we sauntered towards my doorstep. He hugged me differently? His hands resting just above my hips and my hands around his waist as he gave me a deeper and more powerful kiss than before.

Every moment of that kiss felt magical and as he pulled away; I returned the kiss in an even more potent manner, seconds felt eternal as our lips connected fully. His eyes looked at me differently as he said good night and gave me a parting kiss and hug, in truth that look set my mind on fire as something new took hold deep inside me, was I falling for him? Had stupid Fae finally met someone that actually wanted to be with her rather than just wanting a quick laugh or thrill?

Everyone now noticed that something was happening to me as my normally glum look had been replaced with a small yet very noticeable smile. Abby was shadowing me again during my group session and she was far more involved in today's session, every now and then she looked over and smiled at me wryly.

During our lunch break she sat just smiling at me. "What?" I asked her.

"I would ask how last night went, but going by that little smile, I'm guessing pretty well? When is the next one?"

I blushed a little but tried to contain my excitement. "Next Wednesday, we might meet for a drink over the weekend but he is away doing another article next weekend, so we want to meet before he heads to Usted for that."

Abby smiled. "Good for you Fae, I hope he works out for you."

I smiled back, "Yeah, me too."

She headed to the market place to see Shanky while I went for my afternoon meeting with Tony and Gale. Both had spent most of the week starting to convert that room into my office and it was obvious that neither were exactly cut out to be tradesmen. Both were pleased to hear how Abby was doing and I was happy to tell them I was pleased with her initial progress.

Discussing how we would train her to take over some of my groups so that I could start to help them build the business Tony smiled as he sensed the same thing Abby had. Like a smug child he kept grinning away, "Date go well, Fae?"

Gale winked at Tony, "Yeah, pretty good."

I smiled at him, "We know, you really can't hide that little smile, can you? It's sweet and were happy to see you happy again."

Tony sat next to me. "All we want for anyone who ever comes here is for them to find happiness but especially you Fae, you deserve to be happy," I smiled and looked at Tony.

"Thanks guys, I don't know how it will go but it feels different and special somehow?" Gale came and sat beside me. "It's called love, you'll grow to enjoy that feeling a lot Fae," he put his hand on my back, "It's good to see you this way, just think how you were only a few weeks ago! We thought we might lose you for good."

I sighed at the thought of how far I had slipped. "I know, I can't believe how far I slipped away, but I'm back and stronger than before!"

Gale smiled. "We know."

Tony looked over at Gale, "Hey and now she is my therapist!"

He laughed. "Guys really?"

Tony patted me on the back, "Ah you are the best girl for the job."

I sat up and shook my head. "Second best for that job."

Tony smiled and held my hand, "Evelyn?"

I nodded at him, "How's my office coming along?" Tony showed me his black finger where he had missed the nail with a hammer. "This well!"

We sat and shared the laughter we often did at these meetings, always half business and half messing around, almost like little self-contained therapy sessions.

Nothing prepared me for Thursday however, Abby came in refreshed and with a determination to deliver during our morning visits to residents she had started to push herself into the fold. Stepping out of the shadows and fully immersing herself into the new career path she was walking down, throwing aside her fears she grew confident.

During the afternoon we spent time again with Shanky and Hugh, helping Shanky with his artwork and then helping Hugh finish up his blog, she was so focussed that she was inspiring. During the new evening session though was when she really started to shine, I opened the session with a story about my life after Evelyn left.

Openly breaking down in tears part way through my story as I told the world for the first time just how deeply her absence cut into me, she sat quietly just watching. One by one people began to share their tales and stories of loss and how it had affected them when suddenly Abby opened up to the group about her own past. Abby started to tell a story about someone who she loved and respected falling through the cracks, falling deeper while the entire world ignored the warning signs until it was too late.

Weeping as she told how deeply her friends fall from grace had affected her and how she should have stepped in to help sooner, somehow her story felt familiar? Somehow, I couldn't tell why but I knew this story, but I wasn't sure why it was so familiar to me? Abby concluded by telling the group how her friends fall from grace had inspired her to train to become a therapist.

Placing her hand on my shoulder she smiled softly, "I should have stepped in sooner Fae, but thank you for inspiring me to be better than I was."

The group applauded her. Weeping a little I stood up and gave her a hug.

"Thank you, Abby," I cried into her ear, "No thank you Fae, for inspiring us all to be better." Applause filled the room as she held onto me.

We walked home together, walking her through the streets to her door. "Why don't you stay tonight, Fae? We can celebrate our first week working together?"

She smiled at me sweetly, "Well okay, why not, it has been a good week!"

I joined her in her lounge. Intentionally kept nearly pitch black for her online gaming prowess we celebrated a week with a few beers. Like carefree students we indulged ourselves before we fell asleep in her front room on her couch waking with that pasty mouth feeling with her slumped over, gently snoring to herself. Reminding me of Evelyn as she smiled away to herself in her dreams, I moved her so that she was laying down and sat thinking about how she had just emerged from shadows to become a beacon of hope for people.

Like Evelyn she was a curious thing but incredibly attractive and sweet to boot, well when she wasn't playing video games anyway! Inspiring in some ways as she had never really seemed to have any interest in work at all but her story had moved many people during that evening session, myself included.

Unlike Evelyn, though she was very shy and incredibly timid, often shying away and hiding behind her glasses, maybe there was a bigger reason she had decided to do this? Wondering about her and the motivations she had found to develop herself further she began to wake up, with that soft smile she normally had but the dark eyes to match her normal look. We spent the morning talking and recovering from our evening drinks before I headed home and wondered if I would hear from Karl?

Fabi and Alyssia came over to see me during the evening partly to catch up with me and to ask if I would keep an eye on their house while they were away for the next two weeks. Saturday morning, they would fly to the UK to visit Alyssia's family for a week before they headed to Italy to see Fabi's large family for the second week of their vacation.

They were both quite excited to see their families too, though Alyssia did seem concerned to leave me alone for two weeks but when she saw a little smile creep over my face as a text hit my phone she pounced.

Sneaking a peek at my messages, "Well maybe you won't be entirely alone," snatching my phone and reading the messages, periodically smiling as she read them, "He sounds good Fae, I'm pleased to see you happy too."

Alyssia handed my phone back, "Just don't give yourself up too easily, girls as good as you have to be earned and worked for."

Fabi offered to do a little trim on my hair but I turned it down, I was happy with how it looked and so was my mum. Reminiscing on the phone with me about how I looked just like I did when I was a little girl, she sounded so happy when we spoke and I was pleased too, at least my natural colour didn't fade.

Fabi left me a bag of his coffee, at least this way there was no threat to him from this customer's loyalty though I would miss our morning chats on my way to work. I wished both a safe journey as they departed and I texted Karl to agree to meet tomorrow night for a drink or walk somewhere, not quite a date but just a short meet up.

Walking down by the river at Karl's' side as we went for a drink on the promenade to watch the sunset, every step felt special and every moment glorious as the sun dropped below the horizon. Autumnal air should have chilled us both but in his company, I felt warm and content to sit on that bench all night long.

Stopping at a bar along the river and sitting at a candle lit table, life felt good though I was sad that he wouldn't be around for most of next week while he was away with Jared working. Glistening eyes and a nearly magical smile kept me feeling lucky during the evening and as we walked back to mine with his hand resting softly on my hip, that feeling I kept wondering about was growing.

Blossoming in my heart and mind was a resounding feeling that I had never really felt before and it was magnificent but sometimes confusing as my head argued about these feelings. While we wandered up the streets to my house, I was debating inviting him in for a drink, my head raged in an internal battle or pros and cons. Alyssia's advice was strong though and in the end, I decided that tonight was too soon, I guess he would understand and if he was serious then he wouldn't mind waiting?

Sharing another deep and long kiss before we went our separate ways, his touch was causing new sensations within me but tonight was not his lucky night. Seeming disappointed he headed away after agreeing to meet again on Wednesday night before his trip, though I didn't hear from on Sunday night?

Contractors had started appearing at the Davizioso on Monday, Abby continued to shadow me throughout the week and was growing more and more confident with every passing day. During our meeting on Wednesday, I tried to get out of Tony and Gale what the contractors were doing, but neither would tell me? Like it was some inner circle secret?

Meeting Karl in the evening should have been a light relief but neither of us were in good form that night, it was kind of awkward, he apologised that work was on his mind. Though I wasn't doubting myself, yet I felt like maybe making him wait had disrupted our flow but if that was the case then I had made the right decision.

Sensations still surged through me every single time he touched me, or cast a glance and that smile appeared on my face every single time he sent a text, but I felt apprehensive for some reason? Muddled feelings and emotions were flowing round my mind all Wednesday night as with the sparkle seeming to dull, I was doubting myself again.

Trying to take my mind off things, I set back to work on my course, trying to finish my last assessments and finalise some further writing but my mind wasn't playing tonight. Thursday was a monumental day for my new trainee as much to everyone's surprise not only did, she rise to the occasion but actually took the lead during the evening session. Abby was turning into a rising star and she had a connectability with people which was almost addictive to see, that shy receptionist was gone and replaced by a confident young woman.

Though for the next two weeks she would be training Jess to fully assimilate her role on reception and as an aide to Tony and Gale. Abby came to mine this week to celebrate her second week in training, we sat together and she took an interest in my case studies, sitting looking through and trying to gain an insight into the behind-the-scenes stuff she didn't know about.

Once again, we had a pleasant evening together and we slept in the living room after watching TV into the early hours of the morning. Abby headed away happy with herself and I openly admitted to her that I was both proud and amazed at how quickly she had developed and come out of her shell.

Friday however was a miserable day; I hadn't heard anything from Karl since Wednesday so maybe it wasn't meant to be? This was being compounded by September ending soon, the nights were darker and cooler. Evelyn's little flowers had turned from sweet orange to a mix of blackening browns as they slowly withered and died before they would return in spring.

This night was the loneliest I had endured since she had headed back to her world, any vague hopes of her reappearing had gone. No longer did I check the sofa every morning for her or await her to jump at me when I came home before we fell asleep on the sofa together, these thoughts fading into the bleak reality that she wasn't coming back.

A few times I wondered what might have happened if I just went down the mountain and wandered into that forest? I was far from alone in missing her though Ellie missed her as did Abby, Alyssia and Fabi, Francois missed their morning chats, her sitting their giggling while he insulted people. Gale missed her chaotic mind and smile, Tony had spoken to me a few times about her, little heart-to-heart sessions where we spoke about our loss.

Colette was different though, just like me she didn't just miss her, for Colette it was like her own child had passed away, a dress they had been making sat gathering dust as Colette found herself crying when she tried to work on it. Just like me she utterly loved and adored her little dove, between her and Tony they would have moved heaven and earth to find her, that was why I didn't show them the map.

Whatever the reasons, Evelyn was protecting the people in that forest and given how Tony had protected me in the past so I knew how far he would go for someone he cared for.

Tonight, though I needed to be alone, Tony had been in contact with me as he was worried about me, he was a great man and almost like a father figure to me but tonight Fae needed something simpler than that. Settling down to watch a crappy film and shovelling ice cream down my throat in some vain hope to perk myself up, like it was really going to help?

I heard a car slowly driving round, stopping a few times before carrying on? In a quiet street this was unusual at best, hearing a door open and footsteps sounding like they were walking to my house? Were Tony or Gale coming to check up on me? A distinct and resounding thud hit my door multiple times, I ignored the first two rounds, consumed with my dairy indulgence, when the pounding continued, "I'm damn well coming!" I yelled at them.

My temper flaring, I stormed to the door and flung it open. "What the hell do you want?" I yelled at them out of the door.

Before me stood a tall and very imposing woman, deep skinned and dressed in a long white dress with a gold crucifix around her neck. Her mere look stopped my rage and, in its place, came a fearful respect. "You are Fae?" I stood stunned into silence. "You are Fae?" She spoke louder and with an angrier tone. Tutting at me. "Are you simple?" Her face was starting to scowl. "Fae!" Her stern look commanded my reply.

"Yes, I'm Fae," she seemed to change but walked into my house.

Pulling me along with her she headed into my lounge. "Evelyn stayed with you yes?" I looked behind me and could see another figure outside? Her look returned as she awaited my response.

"She told me about your eyes but she didn't tell me how beautiful they are, though your hair isn't how she said it was," she wandered in and sat on my sofa. Stunned into silence I walked through behind her as she gazed round my living room.

"Nice little home you have," she spotted a picture of me and Evelyn on the wall. Standing up, she walked over to it, smiled. "She is so beautiful, isn't she? You are too but look how happy you both are," she stroked the picture before she returned to my sofa. Sitting opposite her, "What is going on? And who are you?"

She eased herself back, "You don't already know?"

I shook my head at her though it felt like I should know her for some reason? Sitting back up she looked sternly at me. "You can call me Vitsa or mother if you prefer."

I snapped my gaze to her in awe, "You? You are real?" I stuttered as I spoke in disbelief.

She was standing looking at a picture of me and my mum. "I have something for you Fae, but I must know that you will look after my gift to you, not just now but forever?"

She stared through me as she spoke. Nodding back, she disappeared outside, I sent Tony a text for help, before she reappeared in my doorway, seeming to hide something. Hidden just behind her, shielded by a backpack and a large hooded cloak, the mystery gift was being shielded by this terrifying woman. Noticing her little shoes and curls falling out of the hood.

"Evelyn!" I ran at her and grabbed hold of her, lifting her high into the air.

Pulling her tight against me. "I missed you so much!" She held me in return. "I missed you Fae!" She was crying. "I tried to find you, but I couldn't cross the mountains."

I was crying my eyes out as we fell onto the sofa together. Stroking her little beautiful face, "I came back for you Fae,"

She giggled at me. "I guess she was telling the truth about you Fae!" Vitsa smiled at me. "Thank you!" I cried back at her. My front door flung open.

"Fae? Are you okay?" Tony came hurtling in to be greeted by Vitsa wielding a dagger at him, he stopped and looked past her, "Is that?"

He palmed her dagger away and walked past her, his face shocked and put his hand out, "Evelyn, is it really you!" She smiled and walked up to him stretching her arms up at him.

Bending over he scooped her up in his arms. "I missed our walks Tony; can I come and see you on Wednesday?"

She smiled and cried as he held her tightly. "Every Wednesday is yours Evelyn," he gently put her back down.

"1604?" Vitsa asked him, he looked at her slightly surprised.

"1604," she patted him on the back to acknowledge his loss. Tony looked at me and winked, "At least you are okay now, see you on Wednesday," he waved at his little friend as he walked out in silence.

Returning to our rightful spots of the sofa, Evelyn propped herself against me as she slowly started to drift to sleep, without thought I took off her little shoes and socks, neatly putting them down before folding her up onto my lap.

Retaking her spot laid across my thighs as she drifted away, retaking the spot where she belonged in my house and in my heart, sleeping sweetly as I started to stroke her little face and curls. In front of me Mother, now had a sweet smile, "You have answered my question Fae, I know you will look after my little girl."

My gaze never broke from Evelyn, "Of course I will, I just wish I could have come and seen her in that forest but I'm not as brave as her or you," she came a knelt before me. "Most people can't cross the mountains but she has told me all about you and now that I know you will look after her, she can live here with you," stroking Evelyn's little curls.

"I would love that; would you like to stay for a few nights? I have a spare bed?" Mother smiled at me as I gently placed Evelyn on the sofa and took her to my spare room. Leading her into Evelyn's room to show her the purple dress Francois had made for his petit oiseau. "It's nearly as beautiful as Evelyn's friend."

Sitting together on the bed, I looked at her, "Are you really going to leave her with me? I am no one you know and then there are my problems."

Mother took my hand, "If you were truly no one then I wouldn't be here and I wouldn't have brought my daughter back to you."

She pulled me over to her side. "She told me all about you and your mind problems but she also told me how you looked after her when she stayed here, as much as I love her, she belongs here in this world but now she has people like you and that man, she will be looked after and have the home she needs and you will give her the family she has needed for so long."

Turning she looked at me and stroked my face, "You have such beautiful eyes and such a beautiful soul, I know you will look after my girl like she is your own and I know you love her and she will be happy here with you."

I cried in doubt at her, "I can't even get her to sleep in a bed, how can I look after her when I couldn't even cross the mountains to reach her?"

Mother looked at me. "Your strengths lie elsewhere, look at what you give to people especially with your problems you give so much and that is your strength. For her sleeping in the bed, have you tried staying in there with her? She sleeps next to you, yes?"

I paused and thought, *Why don't you try it tonight? Go get her,* heading back downstairs to my little friend back on my sofa where she belonged.

Carefully I stroked her little curls and lifted her into my arms, she wrapped her arms round me as I carried her upstairs and down the hallways to our bed. Mother was waiting for us, she pulled back the covers. "Come on, Fae, put her to bed," she was standing holding Evelyn's backpack and pulled out a night dress and handed it to me.

Carefully, I changed her clothes, the limp little body flailing as I put her into the silk dress for her to dream in, laying her down and arranging her on her side facing the door. Mother watching us smiled as she pulled out a photo of Evelyn and placed it onto a bookcase next to a cat toy she had placed there.

I went to look at the picture, "It's her parents and look at their little girl," she smiled as she pointed at her in the photo.

Quietly she wandered to the bed and stroked Evelyn's nose. "Join her Fae, there is room for you too," patting the space just behind Evelyn, I laid down behind her and wrapped her in my arms and pulled her closer to me.

Mother smiled and tucked us both in and gently stroked my nose too. "Sleep well, we will talk more tomorrow as there is something I need to tell you," she stood to leave.

"Welcome to my family, Fae," she turned out the light and left us to sleep, it didn't take long for me to drift away with my little friend in my arms either.

That night we both slept soundly, I had a dream about me and Evelyn in a strange log cabin by a lake surrounded by trees and mountains, I was stunned when I woke in the morning to find her still nestled in my arms. After all those months where she had slept on the sofa, maybe all she needed was me to be there with her a few times and then she would be fine to sleep in the bed?

Laying thinking about her, the door softly opened and mothers smiling face peeked out from behind the door before she winked and left us both lying here together. Quietly, I slithered out from behind Evelyn and crept downstairs and joined her sitting on my sofa, "I told you she just needs company, after so many years alone all she really wants is company."

She leant over and shook my arm gently. "I know you will look after her, she is very proud of you Fae, she missed you and I know you will love her and give her the home she needs and she will be happy," her soft smile echoed her words and thoughts, "I missed her so much, but are you sure you want to leave her here with me?"

My doubts clouding the air. "If the rest of the people here are like you or that man from last night, then this is the best place for her, she doesn't belong in the forests, she belongs here with you," she gave me a comforting hug and just as she let me go little footsteps started to come down the stairs.

Yawning away and having changed into the pyjamas we found her during her last stay, her little belly on show and her green eyes glistening away. Wandering slowly to the sofa she came and gave me a hug.

"Thank you for staying with me last night Fae, I missed that, good morning," she wandered over to Mother.

"Will you stay tonight?" She held her tight. "Tonight only, then I need to make my way back," she touched the tip of Evelyn's little nose. Spending a few hours just relaxing on my sofa as Evelyn showed Mother the house, her clothes and then my garden, like a little tour of my four walls, it was quite sweet in truth.

Mother came back inside as Evelyn was reunited with her talking friend Magnus and she sat in her tree talking to him as he sat his children's slide to talk through the fence. Sitting next to me she leant over. "I need to tell you something Fae, I will leave early in the morning before you both wake, if she is awake, she will try to come with me, she needs to stay here."

She started to stroke my hair. "When she fell asleep with you, I knew she was telling the truth about you, when you caringly took off her shoes and socks before putting her in your lap it was obvious how much you care about her and that you are the one, she needs," she seemed almost pained.

Looking at a picture of Evelyn with her parents she smiled. "She has barely had any life at all, when she came back talking about this place and all these people but after seeing the people in that place she was from and how vile they were to her I couldn't believe her but I was so wrong, Fae. You look after her in a way I couldn't have expected and even started to sleep with her on the sofa, didn't you? So that she wouldn't be alone?"

I smiled at her as I thought off all the nights, we slept on the sofa together. "I didn't like her waking up alone or feeling alone in her sleep."

Her smile grew. "You even tried to come and find her?"

I nodded, "I wasn't brave enough to cross the mountains," she laughed.

"Neither was I, if it wasn't for her, I never would have set foot in these lands," shaking she handed me a package.

"This is for you but open it tomorrow, if you wouldn't mind?"

I took the heavy linen wrapped package from her, "What is it?"

She smiled, "it's my parting gift to you for looking after my little girl, from one mother to another."

Reasoning in my mind, "But I'm not a mother?" She smiled again, "You became one they day you took her in and cared for her," she held my sides. I took her gift and placed it on the kitchen table, she followed me into the kitchen looking down the garden at Evelyn happily sitting in the tree talking to Magnus.

"Tomorrow will be hard for her, but she has you to be there for her and I know you will do everything to make her smile again," looking round at her, she was weeping as she watched out the window. Spending an hour talking before Evelyn came back in, darkness had descended and we enjoyed dinner together before Evelyn began to fade on my lap on the sofa.

Evelyn took herself upstairs, slowly wandering up the stairs before silence came, Mother looked at me. "Come Fae, let me put my girls to bed one last time." She took my hand and led me up the stairs.

Evelyn sat on the bed awaiting us, yawning away, her eyes nearly shut, she had neatly folded her socks into her shoes and changed into pyjamas, sweetly smiling to herself. Mother opened the covers for her and she soon climbed in and nestled herself into the duvet, slowly going supple and drifting away with that serene smile she wore when she slept.

I tucked her in and Mother sat at the end of the bed smiling at me. "What beautiful girls you two are and thank you Fae."

I felt confused, "What for?"

She wiped a little tear from her face, "For giving her a good home," she put her hand on top of mine and sat smiling away. She took my hand and led me down the hall to the room she was staying in, guiding me as she opened a strange looking bag which was sat on her bed and pulled out a garment.

Closing the door behind me. "Evelyn asked me to make you something, a welcome gift, could you take off your clothes for me?" Feeling nervous and apprehensive, she smiled. "Don't worry Fae, as a mother to four girls I have seen most things," her calm voice soothed my mind as I slipped off my top and skirt.

Circling me and gently running her hands down my sides. "She told me you were beautiful but she didn't tell me just how beautiful you were," she circled me again and undone my bra and slipped my briefs off, "Utterly beautiful Fae!"

She touched under my armpits to get me to raise my arms and started to thread a dress over me and pulled it down, offering me a skirt. Gently lifting it up my legs and resting it just over my hips, she wrapped a sash over my shoulder and resting it on my stomach, joining the short skirt to the top.

Stepping back from me and smiling, "Just beautiful Fae," she rubbed down the sides and walked me to a mirror and unveiled me to myself, "Welcome to the family Fae, my fifth daughter," she held my side and smiled at me.

Feeling oddly at peace I changed into some shorts and a vest top and joined her as she led me back to the sleeping Evelyn, opening the cover softly, "Come Fae, let me put my daughter to bed."

Gently sliding in next to Evelyn and cuddling up next to her. Gently stroking my face, "Rest well Fae as tomorrow will be tough for her, she will need all of your strength."

I nodded at her, "I will look after her, will you come back to see her," she didn't really reply, she just winced a little as she walked away.

"I love you both," turning out the light and closing the door. Pulling Evelyn closer to me. "I will be here for you no matter what, Evelyn."

I held her a little tighter and pulled some cover under her little chin to keep her warm. Maybe we had more in common than I thought, both of us needed something simple in life from people but both of us had been largely deprived of it.

Before I fell asleep, I promised myself and her that she would always have a home here with me and that she would never be alone again, she belonged with me. It should have been hard to fall asleep given that I knew what was coming in the morning but somehow this was the easiest it had been for me to sleep for months. With my little friend tucking herself into my arms and clutching me, it really didn't take long for me to drift away and to start dreaming again.

Morning soon arrived and I woke alone. Jumping out of bed and running to check the other rooms but she had vanished. I ran downstairs but the house was silent and the rooms were empty. There was a note on the sideboard in the living room but it had been opened. "To my daughters," I looked upstairs again but there was no sign of her.

I stood at the kitchen sink panicking when I looked down the garden on that rainy morning to see her down the end of the garden under the tree near the flowerbed she made. Walking down the garden, she sat in the rain slumped down with her head in her hands looking at her dead flowers, I slowly walked up behind her and put my hand on her shoulder.

Crouching down next to her, she looked round, her little cheeks were bright red and shimmering where she was crying, soaked through and trying to smile before I just pulled her towards me and held her.

Whimpering, "She is gone, Fae," she started crying again, "She didn't say goodbye."

I put her head onto my shoulder. "She left me behind without saying goodbye," I turned her round and held her as tightly as I could.

Pulling her tight and lifting her up, "She wanted you to have a home Evelyn," she wrapped herself around them as much as she could. "I have you now Evelyn and she wanted you to have the family and life you should have had in your old home town; she was going to take you back if I wasn't good enough for you."

I put my hand on the back of her head to soothe her, she tried to smile but couldn't. I rubbed her little nose to try and get her to smile, she was trying but she was hurting badly. "You are home though Evelyn; you belong here with me and I love you."

She smiled a little bit and leant back a bit, "Evelyn?" She smiled and wiped a tear from her eye.

Thinking how to try and help her, "Though you timed coming back pretty well Evelyn,"

She looked puzzled as I pulled her closer to me. "How come?"

I put my head beside her ear, "I have two weeks off work and I want to spend them with you, think of all the things we can get up to together."

A little smile appeared on her face, "Two weeks off work?"

I smiled at her, "I would love to spend them with my best friend, we can go to market day, you can have your walk with Tony?"

She smiled a little more, "Shanky too?"

I touched her little nose. "We can even sit and listen to Francois insult people," she hugged me hard, driving her head onto my chest. "I missed you, Fae," smiling deeply.

"I missed you too Evelyn, come on let's go inside and spend all day on the sofa watching garbage on TV." She stood and held my hand, "Ice cream and takeaway too?"

I started to lead her back inside, "Sure, why not?" We headed indoors and went and got changed into some comfies and together we sat on the sofa, her between my legs with her head resting on my chest watching whatever trash we could find. Spending most of the day twiddling her little curls round my fingers as she slowly came back to life and her normal chaotic but loveable self-emerged.

Slowly building her back up as evening approached and while she was barely awake, I picked her up and carried her upstairs to bed. Gently laying her down and climbing in next to her and covered us with the duvet, she nestled herself up to me and I wrapped her in my arms. "Welcome home Evelyn," I whispered to her, "I love you Fae and thank you for taking me in."

She whispered back, "I never would have turned you away Evelyn," I held her tight.

Suddenly, a strange thought crossed my mind, "You know who else missed you Evelyn?" She looked up at me. "Who?" I grinned.

"Tickle trolls," my fingers started to tickle her little belly and she laughed and tried to escape, wriggling and writhing as her laughs grew louder and uncontrollable. Slowly stopping, I just held onto her, "I really missed you," she hugged me. "I missed you too, really missed you," she tucked herself back against me as we drifted away together.

That day was hard for Evelyn but quite wonderful, she lost her mother but gained a home and a place with some kind of future for her, which she so desperately needed and sorely deserved. It was much simpler for me though; I got my best friend back and this time she wasn't going anywhere!

Chapter 10
A Gift from the Forests

Soft breaths tickled my nose and woke me from my slumber, it was the first week of October and though cooler the rains had stopped patting on my windows and sunlight was bathing the room that me and Evelyn had slept in. Slowly stirring I soon noticed something strange and unusual? Unlike every night since I had known her Evelyn had slept in my arms as normal, but she was facing me, still with that serene look on her face but not facing the door?

Evelyn always slept facing the door in any room, still awaiting her parents to return even after 17 years, I found myself wondering why she had suddenly stopped watching the door. Lying watching her sleep, I rested my hand on her little hips, since she had been gone, she had become thinner, her normally soft lines were more chiselled, either she had been working out or she had starved since she had been away.

Holding her in my hands, I waited to see her wake up for the first time since she had returned, waiting for those magic green eyes to open and her mind to just accelerate into fits of love and laughter. Whimpering on occasion as she dreamt, today we were going to go and reintroduce her to the people who had sorely missed her since she went away.

Fabi and Alyssia were still away so they would have to wait but Francois and Colette in particular would be dying to see their little friend. Like a little python, she wrapped her arms around me and held tight, holding her in return I started to wonder about Karl, I hadn't heard a thing since that night I didn't invite him in. Had I offended him that mortally? We were meant to be meeting tomorrow night for date number four, but I guess maybe that is now off? While I wondered, a little lumbering giant awoke, yawning as her glistening eyes emerged, she pulled herself tight against me.

"Morning Fae," I could feel her smile as her head was pressed against my chest. Putting my hand to her head and hugging her in return.

"Morning Evelyn," I gave her a little kiss on the forehead as she stretched herself out and got out of bed, stretching and reaching the ceiling as she slowly came round.

Lying on the bed I watched her carefully fold up her little green trousers and top and gently put them in a drawer, softly smiling to herself as she pushed the drawer closed. Almost as if that part of her life was now over and this was a new chapter of her life, while she stood almost transfixed, I wrapped my arms round her little belly and held her, "Welcome home," she rested her head back against me and held my hands gently.

Looking up at me and smiling softly at me, she just stayed there in silence for a moment, thinking away to herself but she was happy. "It's good to be home," she said as she looked at the picture of her parents.

Lifting her gently onto the bed with me, we sat looking at the picture of her mum and dad, somehow it seemed like for Evelyn her journey had gone full circle. Eventually, we headed downstairs and sat at the kitchen table drinking our morning coffee, she seemed calmer than normal and even sweeter.

Telling her about the photoshoot on Thursday for the calendar and when I told her that she would be in my pictures, at first, she didn't want to steal my thunder, but I told her if she wasn't in the pictures with me, then there would be no pictures of me in the calendar. Noticing that I kept smiling if Karl was mentioned, she extracted from me about tomorrow night's date, Evelyn noticed and started to coax out of me what had happened with him in her absence.

Telling her the story of what now appeared to be a short-lived romance, she giggled as she had been right about him liking my bum. Slowly telling her the story and about our dates, she clocked that this would be date number four and a wry smile crept onto her face as she knew what happened on date four.

Sitting smiling at me. "You're going to wait for him at the bench near the beach aren't you?"

I looked at her in surprise. "How did you know that?"

She shrugged her shoulders, "It's your favourite place, closely followed by the park that overlooks the town at night," smugly grinning to herself.

Evelyn refilled my cup and sat next to me holding my hands, "Where are you going to go after you meet him? Because the fourth date is when you let him…you know?" Blushing a little.

"How do you know that?"

Evelyn went very sheepish. "Well, it's kinda complex?"

I perked up as something dawned upon me. "Wait! Have you? Here?"

She went bright red. "Not the artist!" She shrugged her shoulders, "Well maybe once or twice," her grin didn't disappear though and she had a strange look on her face as she seemed to be fantasising about him, "You little minx!"

I smiled at her, "He was good with his hands," she shrugged her shoulders and smiled at me.

Looking at her, "What did it feel like and how did you know you were ready?"

She put her hand on top of mine. "You don't really know it just kinda happens, suddenly an urge takes over your mind and you can't think about anything else. It feels amazing and addictive, all of your body tenses up and then tingles afterwards. Like after you kiss but a deeper and longer sensation before a huge sudden release of energy," her distant smile told me what words couldn't. Though she avoided letting me know who she had spent those times with during her summer visit but clearly, she still fantasised about them.

While she sat dreaming about her conquests, I started to explain about the night me and Karl met up last week and how I hadn't heard from him since, she seemed disappointed with him. Though we did wonder if maybe work had just got in the way of things, and he would show up but I was nervous as hell that he was going to blow me off.

Together we drew up a plan, if he didn't show up then we would make sure he regretted it on Thursday, of course Evelyn was concerned about me being left for dead. We had a plan for if he didn't show up, though she encouraged me to go on the date anyway, if nothing else to put my own mind at ease and give myself some kind of answer of whether he was interested in me or not. Though I didn't know if it was a good idea, I could see good logic to her thoughts as either way I would have a clear and simple answer and I could adjust my mind accordingly.

Together we walked down to the town, bathed in the early morning sun of October, though not as warm as the mornings of summer, it was pleasant as we walked past Fabi's closed shop. Stopping on the bridge as we started to head to the old part of town Evelyn wanted to see if our padlock was still in place, which sure enough it sat proudly nestled among the other locks of love.

Walking along the river amongst the slowly falling red and orange leaves of the trees that adorned the rivers bank, I got a new glimpse of my little friend. Her sweet little orange curls buffeting in the breeze and her energetic little smile all packaged into that petite little figure as we wandered along the river and up the steps into the old part of town. Dressed in a little crop top and black hip huggers, she looked very sweet and as we turned the corner she was soon scoped by Francois. Astonished, he cast his cigarette down and ran towards us.

"Petit Oiseau!" He called as he scooped her up and lifted her high and gave her the most loving hug I had ever seen. Holding her aloft he spun round with her and spoke to her in French, I didn't understand what he was saying but his tone and the little tears he was shedding told me how happy he was to see her.

Gently placing her down he held her hand, "Fae! You have brought my friend back, oh wait until Colette see's you both she will be so happy!" He was grinning in a way I had never seen, almost as excited as Evelyn got on market day morning as he spoke to her and smiled away at us both, clearly, he had missed her very much!

"Look at you both, you are both so beautiful and how fortunate am I to be paid a visit by two wonderful ladies, especially now that Fae looks so amazing," he smiled away to Evelyn, "She looks really pretty with her hair like that Francois."

Smiling sweetly at him. Francois led us both inside his shop and handed Evelyn a little envelope, "I promised to look after it until you came back," she took the envelope from his and he presented her with a cup of coffee and a jar of marshmallows. "It's not Fabi's coffee but it will be good for this morning."

Evelyn started to make herself that vile sugary mess she loved so dearly as Francois watched her every move. "How happy are you now Fae? You have your little friend back!"

Almost bursting at the seams, "I'm really pleased she is back and she is staying this time!"

Francois looked surprised. "How long for?"

I exploded with joy, "For good!"

He walked over and gave me a cup of coffee followed by a soft hug. "I'm happy for you Fae, it's good to have you both back too, Colette will be ecstatic too!"

I looked at Evelyn concocting her vile drink. "I know she will, but she's not the only one!" He smiled and we sat by his work bench to talk.

Francois didn't have a single bad thing to say as he discussed with Evelyn about her time away and the effect that her absence had on me. Sitting happily talking to each other as I pondered about Karl and that envelope Francois had given Evelyn, I always wonder what they contained. Shanky had told me she pooled money she made from him and the artists that sold pictures of her and left the money with Alyssia, Francois and Colette?

Maybe this was one of those envelopes? But if so, what was she using them for? Truth was, I needed to see Colette anyway, Evelyn didn't realise I knew her birthday was next Friday and I could think of no one better to make the perfect gift for my little friend than Colette.

I knew that she wouldn't be cheap by any stretch of the imagination but what price could I put on the friendship and the love that I had for my friend? Unusually for me I even knew exactly what I wanted her to make for my little friend and she was the only person I could trust to deliver this gift!

Two hours passed as Evelyn and Francois caught up with each other and we headed off to the backstreets of this end of town and towards Colette's boutique. Slowly wandering as Evelyn smiled softly to herself, step by step we grew closer to the only woman that possibly loved Evelyn more than me, we opened the sticky door to Colette's shop and without warning Evelyn was accosted from behind by a very happy Frenchwoman.

That 5ft 2 Parisian easily lifted Evelyn to the heavens as she was reunited with her little friend, crying and talking in soft French as they hugged and embraced. Today Colette didn't need any words to explain how she felt that soft face and rich smile said everything for her as she grinned away at me. Shaking as adrenaline fuelled her into a stream of affectionate hugs and kisses, she had missed Evelyn nearly as much as I had.

Evelyn had been training with Colette before she left, learning Colette's skills and abilities, slowly learning to master a skill which couldn't just be learned; it had to be passed down, like a cat teaching a kitten to hunt. Together they renewed Evelyn's training and began work on the project which they had been working on prior to Evelyn's departure in summer.

Never knowing just what they had been working on, I knew it was large and very important to both of them, Colette had refused to divulge what they had been working on. While Evelyn began to work a sewing machine, I took my chance to put in my request and order with Colette. We stood outside the shop so that our words wouldn't be heard as I asked if Colette could make a special dress for Evelyn's birthday next week, I knew the timescale was short but Colette said she could do it easily.

Colette had a strange wry smile as she discovered that Evelyn's birthday was coming up, though I just figured she felt determined to deliver something so perfect that it would even make Francois look awful. Evelyn completed the piece she was working on but asked if she could come back tomorrow to work on the piece some more, not that Colette was going to object to spending more time with her little dove!

Agreeing happily that Evelyn could spend all day there working before we headed home, I had wondered about telling her what was happening at the Davizioso, but figured that Tony or Gale would tell her on Wednesday when she went for her walk with Tony!

Wandering back through town, the world felt good again, my friend was back and her friends were more than happy to see her again, Abby would see her Wednesday and so would Shanky for market day. Evelyn though seemed different to before? Calmer and at peace with things, her mind didn't seem quite so chaotic, like she had found herself or something in the darkness?

Serenity was something that had now started to adorn that girl and in truth it made her even more majestic than she had been in summer, though I was pretty sure she would still be excited come Wednesday morning! Walking those last few turns before arriving at my front door, she was almost floating rather than walking, something had taken over my little friend and whatever it was, it had fully encapsulated her.

During that evening I was going to try and get on with some work for my course, Evelyn ordered a takeaway for us while I sat trying to finish my final assessment. Struggling away at my kitchen table, she watched from the living room before she came to join me with our pizza delivery in hand. Sitting watching me as I struggled to finalise anything she came to try to help me out, I hadn't told her that I was using her as a case study, thankfully she just thought it was a cool idea.

Spinning my laptop to face her she read through the notes I had on her, "Can I make some amendments?" She asked calmly.

I just nodded back, "Sure if it will help me?"

She sat and started to type and fill in some voids in her story. Pulling myself beside her, the more she typed the sadder her story became as she plugged all the gaps that nobody knew about, parts that not even Ellie had any idea existed.

Devoid of any form of parenthood beyond the age of five, it was a miracle that she wasn't dead or a gibbering mess in an asylum somewhere.

Friends were non-existent, her grandmother hated her and she had been assaulted a few times including that final evening in Zyvala at that work party. Once she finished typing, she smiled at me and headed into the lounge to watch TV, having gifted me the valuable information that I needed, the hard work began. While she giggled at trash on TV, I finalised my assessment of her, I asked her to read my conclusion, she just smiled and pressed send for me.

Not even discussing what I had written or anything she had just detailed in my assessment; she just led me into the lounge to join her on the sofa. My assessment was about her being an enigma, a beacon of empowerment and hope for everyone as she had risen above everything life threw her way and came out as the strongest person I had ever met. Assisting me that night to help drive me forwards and progress in life, all she really seemed to want was to make me happy?

Evelyn soon tired and as she began to drift away and much to my shock, she kissed me goodnight and took herself slowly to bed! No flopping over on the sofa and even putting her shoes neatly by the sofa. Watching her slowly climb the stairs, I sat in total disbelief as her little footsteps stopped as she found her bed for the night, what had happened to my friend?

Partly through intrigue I went to join her soon after and there neatly tucked into her bed, she laid, not asleep just yet but her little face showing the signs of exhaustion, she smiled sweetly as I sat on the bed with her.

Gently stroking her sweet cheeks as she yawned away to herself, "Fae?"

I looked at her smiling away, "I'm really sorry about how much I upset you by going away," leaning down to her.

"It's okay, you're here now, that's all that matters," she wept a little. "But you have gotten really thin and your mind was bad when I went away," lying beside her on the duvet I looked at her dwelling in her shame.

"I needed to lose weight anyway, my arse was pretty large," she smiled a little. "I'm not going anywhere now though Fae, I love you and this is my home," I snuggled up next to her and toyed with her little curls. "No, you belong with me, Evelyn."

I headed into my room and dressed for bed, going back to join my little friend. Lying beside her, I put my hand on her hip and held her stomach as she nestled herself into my arms, her little smile telling me how happy she felt as she drifted to sleep. Evelyn shouldered all responsibility for the state I wound up in while she was away, the truth was that it was entirely down to me, but she wouldn't let me believe that. While she started to dream and that serene look came onto her face, I thought about how gifted she was, sometimes like a sister but when needed she became almost motherly.

Continually assuring me about myself and encouraging me to let people in, she was slowly turning me into someone very new and different, her thoughts were always beyond her years. Giving her one last kiss on the head before I fell asleep with her, it seemed to me that she was at peace with something? Something that she couldn't explain but she was very different to the girl that slept on my sofa during summer.

Tuesday morning, we spent discussing my date that evening with Karl, if he showed up that is! And Christmas, my parents were both promising to come down before Christmas and in truth I was really looking forward to seeing them. Evelyn was keen to meet them too and I had no doubt both of them would love my new little friend and had no qualms that she would make Christmas magical for all of us.

Riddled with doubts about my date that evening she kept urging me to go ahead with it even if he didn't turn up. I would know if he was truthful and faithful or not and as much as I hated the idea of him bailing on me, it would give me mental peace? Filled with caffeine she headed to see Colette for the day and work on that project they had been colluding on.

While she headed down the street, I headed to sort my room out and the clothes she had brought with her in that backpack she had shielded behind. Sifting through the backpack to find a selection of warmer clothes, a pair of boots and some odd green shoes, I started to put them into drawers and the wardrobe for her.

Cool little dresses with stars on them and stripey warm jumpers and a few strange looking dresses, each found their own spots in her room. Heading into my spare room I found that parcel that the queen had left me, having forgotten all about it, I picked it up. Whatever it contained was heavy and very solid?

The queen had also left a backpack behind, which contained more of Evelyn's clothes, cute tops and a strange blanket with an odd wooden tree wrapped inside it? Carefully assembling it to discover it was some kind of Christmas tree, I took it into Evelyn's room and put it beside her cat toy and that picture of her parents. Whatever that tree was, it was quite old and I guessed it was very sentimental to her, I sent a picture of it to Ellie to ask her if she knew about it?

Collecting that heavy package, I went back downstairs to unwrap my unexpected gift. Sitting at my kitchen table I untied a couple of bows which kept the package wrapped up neatly, slowly unfurling the fabric covering to discover another parcel once again wrapped in fabric. A single large leaf tightly tied with grass strands was shielding something very heavy, solid and cool to the touch.

Slowly unpicking the grass strands my jaw hit the floor as a solid gold crown fell out, encrusted with jewels with a little note wrapped around it. Stunned into silence I held the crown up and looked at my reflection in its central jewel before unrolling the note and holding it out to read.

Loosely written on handmade paper, "To Fae, look after my Evelyn for me and make her happy, from one queen to another, love Mother," I sat stunned and wondered if Evelyn knew she had gifted me this. I took the crown upstairs and placed the crown neatly on the set of drawers in Evelyn's room as I sat in utter silence and wondered if she would see Evelyn again? Thinking heavily, I wandered downstairs to await the returning Evelyn, after spending all day with Colette I was sure she would be excitable at minimum.

Evelyn soon returned with a huge bag in her hands and an even bigger smile on her face, grinning to herself as she stood with her arms outstretched to offer me the large bag. Shaking in excitement as I took the bag from her with that sweet smile on her face and her green eyes twinkling away, "Open it!" She beamed at me standing with her feet turned inwards and her knees bent as she waited for me to open the bag.

Inside was a 2-piece dress wrapped in paper, a soft black corset with silver and white trimming with a long flowing silk skirt, elegantly stitched and with all of Colette's hallmark handy work. This dress was what she had been working on with Colette before she went away and since she had been reunited with her mentor.

Almost dragging me upstairs she helped me into the dress, highlighting all my curves and shape, I couldn't believe what I saw in the mirror. Silenced by the sheer beauty and craftsmanship that had gone into the dress. "If he doesn't turn up tonight, he will know what he has missed out on," she rested her head against my chest while I stood in sheer awe.

Shedding a little tear as I couldn't behold the beauty, she had turned me into. "I love it, Evelyn! Thank you so much!" She smiled at me. "You are the most beautiful girl in Ljinatipol now, Fae," she guided me back downstairs so that I could make my way to the venue of my date.

Hugging me gently, "I hope he turns up Fae, if not we will show him on Thursday what he has missed out on," I held her little hand and gave her a little hug and smile before I headed off.

Walking through what remained of the evening sun I couldn't help but notice that heads were turning and eyes were looking as I walked by. Feeling good about myself as I glided my way through the streets of Ljianstipol and down through the little park and along the promenade to the spot where I would wait for Karl. Picking the bench where he had witnessed my crash the night, he did my photoshoot back on that warm June evening. Sitting in the oddly warm October sun looking over the beach my mind kept fluttering every time I saw a shadow or any hint of a human shape, odd gusts of wind blew my hair round, it was a nice evening.

However, it would have been nicer if I wasn't sitting alone waiting for someone to show up, slowly wondering if maybe the whole thing had just been a way to get me to agree to doing the calendar shoot.

Darkness began to cloak the sky as the sun dropped below the horizon, it was clear that Karl was another name to be consigned to the arsehole list of guys I had encountered in my life. Slouched on the bench, I didn't shed any tears because I wasn't sad, more just disappointed in him, while I watched the darkness cloak my world, footsteps drew closer.

Silence descended once again as a soft hand rested on my shoulder and two little arms wrapped themselves around me. "Sorry Fae," Evelyn pressed her head against mine and squeezed me hard. Pulling me back towards her and pressing her entire body against me as she held onto me and rested my head back into her arms.

Looking up at her she tickled my nose as she did when we first met but no butterflies on her fingers this time. "I'm okay Evelyn, can we go get a drink?" Evelyn smiled and helped me stand up, she checked my cheeks for tears with her thumbs before we wandered back through the park and to a bar by the river.

Evelyn got us a couple of bottles each and walked me up to the park that overlooked the town, slowly walking holding each other as we wandered the streets and through the pathways that led to the wall, we sat on during the steampunk festival in summer.

Sitting together on the wall overlooking the twinkling lights of Ljianstipol behind us, Evelyn kept holding my hand to console me. Evelyn seemed really angry with Karl, maybe even angrier than I was, with him having witnessed one of my crashes he knew what he might cause if he messed me around too much.

While we sat in silence, a guy was walking past with a dog, Evelyn called him over to ask him to take our picture, he seemed a little surprised but he agreed. Evelyn handed him my phone. "Dressed up like that for a beer in the park seems a bit elaborate?" He quizzed.

"I was meant to be going on a date but he didn't show up," I said sullenly.

"Didn't show up when you look like that? His loss!" He took a couple of pictures and went to hand my phone back, "Wait aren't you that girl from the Davizioso? The one who does the evening sessions?"

He stood looking at the photo he had taken. "Yeah, that's me," he offered me his hand, "Nice to meet you, Fae? My friend comes to those sessions, you have really helped him out, I'm Dario by the way." He shook my hand and handed me my phone back, "Is he yours?" He smiled.

"No, my friend isn't well so I'm helping him out, did you really get stood up?"

I looked at him and just shrugged my shoulders, "Hmm what a jerk, did you go to the bench near the trees on the beach?"

Evelyn looked at him, shocked, "How did you guess that?" He smiled at her, "I read the article, it seemed like the place she would go, hey weren't you at the steampunk festival in summer? By the beach in that white dress?"

I smiled a little thinking about the wind blowing my hair by the beach. "Yeah, it was a fun event," he looked at me. "You looked good then but are stunning now with your hair like that, anyway have a good drink and I hope he hasn't upset you too much Fae," he turned and started to walk away, stopping after a few steps. "Hey if he hasn't put you off dating guys, how about I take you for that walk on the beach someday?"

I got down off the wall and looked at Evelyn, she smiled at me. "Sure, she will, are you going to turn up?" He walked over to her, "Why wouldn't I turn up when she looks that good? Here take my number and It's nice to meet you."

Evelyn put my number in his phone and sent him the picture he had just taken, he smiled at it, "Thanks and see you soon Fae," he sent me a text with a picture of me and Evelyn as he walked away, "Night," I called to him as he waved us goodbye.

As he disappeared, Evelyn held my hand and smiled at me. "Night Dario." She pretended to kiss me laughing at herself while she did her impression. "Must be the dress?" I smiled at her and grabbed hold of her and hugged her.

We started to walk home through the darkness when she stopped in her tracks and turned to look over the horizon. "Fae?" She stood awkwardly and nervously cupping her hands, "I know I'm kinda annoying but can I stay with you?"

Her face was full of nerves and her words hit my heart hard, I walked over and touched her arm. "Why wouldn't I want you to stay?" She looked at me. "What should I do?"

I looked at her confused, "For work I mean, I can't let you bankroll me forever?" She was being quite serious too.

Pausing to think, "Why don't you come work with me? Tony and Gale said they would give you a job if you wanted?"

Evelyn thought deeply. "That wouldn't be fair on you Fae," I thought again, *What about those drawings of you people sell, you made good money off that?*

She smiled a little. "It's a good start I guess but I need to find a job so that we can have more takeaways without you having to pay,"

I held her hands gently. "Take your time Evelyn, I'm sure you'll find something easily," we started to walk home, she had an odd smile on her face as we reached home, we sat on the sofa for a while, Evelyn kept smiling at me saying how Karl really messed up.

Truthfully, I wasn't too bothered, Karl just became another in that string of guys who messed me around, I had hoped he would be different but after I refused him that night, I wasn't shocked he didn't turn up, maybe he was just after more pictures all along?

Waking early, I could feel a heavy weight on my chest, as my eyes open staring crazily at me was hyperactive Evelyn waiting for me to wake up for Wednesday and market day. Prising her off me I rolled her over and threatened to tickle her stomach, when I noticed a cup of coffee and some toast waiting for me, my heart melted at the gesture even if it should have been insignificant.

While I enjoyed my breakfast in bed, her mind accelerated as she started to talk about what we would be doing today after all market day was Evelyn's favourite day in Ljianstipol. Already dressed she was super excited to get going, I could see the tortured look on her face as I sipped slowly away at my coffee, mentally urging me to drink up so we could go and start our day.

Gradually getting myself ready, like a hyperactive puppy she was itching to get going, she was looking forward to seeing Shanky, they hadn't met up yet and of course her walk with Tony would be today too. Fabi and Alyssia were still away so we made our own coffee to walk down into town with, slowly wandering the streets as her mind and thoughts expelled themselves in crazed outbursts of energy.

Walking by the river among the falling leaves she calmed down a little, maybe that subtle hint of the forests made her relax a little. Serene flowing waters and orange and red leaves seemed to soothe her chaotic mind as we reached the steps that led to the old part of town, at least she was calm until she saw Shanky sitting on a stool in the market.

Hurtling towards the poor old guy with her little curls flowing behind her as she yelled his name at the top of her voice before she crashed into him and grabbed hold of him. Shanky smiled and embraced his little friend for the first time in three months, Evelyn started to talk to him in such excitement that even she couldn't keep up with what she was saying.

While I joined Shanky, she went to do her morning rounds and collect her takings, she approached three stalls collecting envelopes from each of them before she headed to listen to Francois. Together they sat on a little blanket in front of his shop, he made her a coffee and gave her a croissant and they began their favourite morning hobby, scouring the horizon for people for Francois to insult.

Shanky had been given a stool by the same artist who I found selling those pictures of Evelyn, though he didn't appear to be around today but it was nice to see Shanky out and well again. With his life catching up with him, Shanky had been in a bad way for a few weeks and I was really worried he might be gone far too soon, so I hoped to spend as much time as possible with him.

Ever upbeat and optimistic he had been doing a lot of work with his new neighbour Hugh and collaborated on a few pieces together, as we sat talking Evelyn disappeared to visit Colette in the backstreets. Wandering around the market stalls, today was different for some reason however I became freaked out when I came across a guy who had painted a picture of me from my article.

Standing looking at the portrait of me he wandered over and double took as he realised that I was looking at his painting of me, he offered me the picture, I asked him to sell it and give the money to charity. Whatever his motives, he did capture the colour of my hair and my purple eyes pretty nicely, walking back round I bumped into Evelyn's artist of choice, Zach.

He smiled as he saw me. "Fae! Look at you! I love what you did with your hair, maybe I should draw you next?"

I blushed a little. "Nice to see you again Zach," I shook his hand, "Hey I gave Shanky a seat so he doesn't catch a chill on the floor," he smiled away.

"Yeah, he told me, thank you for doing that for him, how's business today?" He frowned a little. "Not too good today but there is still time I guess, catch you later!" He wandered off to his stall. Sitting back with Shanky helping him to sell his pictures when he nudged me and pointed.

"Look Fae!" I looked over and saw Evelyn sat with Zach on a little wall. Her legs crossed and sat facing Zach as he sat with his hand on hers talking to her, giggling away to each other like school children, maybe this was her guy she dreamt of? Having seen Evelyn on a few nights out I knew the faces she made when she wasn't interested in guys who approached her however when she liked someone she changed entirely.

Evelyn's smiles would become slightly softer, her eyes fluttered a little and she became almost transfixed upon them as she gazed at them like a lustful kitten. Zach right now was getting the cutest and sweetest look I had ever seen on her face as she stared lovingly at him, softly holding hands and giggling at each other. I couldn't help but feel a smile come over my face as I saw her so happily engrossed in her first meeting with her dream guy, though he looked just as sweet.

They shared a little hug as he climbed down and then took her hand to help her down from the wall, hugging and smiling one last time before she wandered back over to me and Shanky. Evelyn's little cheeks were slightly red as she came back to join us, every other step she would look over to catch a glimpse of her man. "He's cute."

I grabbed her from behind. "I like him," she smiled and rested her head to the side.

"He likes you too, is he why you have your belly on show today?" I started to make kissing noises into her ear, she just giggled at me.

Together we headed to the Davizioso for Evelyn's afternoon walk with Tony, I hadn't told her about all the upcoming changes as I figured Tony and Gale would tell her. Walking in through the doors we were greeted by Jess and Abby on reception both came to greet Evelyn, Abby was pleased to see her back in Ljianstipol as they had become quite good friends during her last stay.

Wandering up the hallway and out onto the rooftop garden Gale picked Evelyn straight up as she approached the pergola. "Good to see you again," he handed her a beer and put her back down.

Evelyn sat down next to Tony, he looked out of the side of his eyes at her and offered her his hand, she jumped to her feet and smiled as he slowly stood up and off, they went down the garden for their walk. Gale smiled as they walked down the path. "Like she never left."

He passed me a beer. "Exactly like that," I took the bottle from him and we watched them vanish round the first corner of their route.

Gale sat up, "How are you then Fae?"

I eased back into the chair. "Pretty good, I'm so happy she is back and I think she has found love?"

He smiled at me. "Good to hear that you are happy now she is back, I'm not surprised she is just as beautiful as her mother was, though how did your date go last night?"

My lack of response gave my first part of the answer. "Sorry Fae, did he show up?"

I shook my head. "Arsehole, but his loss only an idiot would turn down a girl as stunning as you," a little smile came across me.

"It wasn't a total loss though Gale," I showed him the picture of me and my dress.

"Evelyn made it! With Colette!" He looked stunned. "Evelyn made that! Wait, who took the picture?" He looked at me as I smiled. "A guy was walking past and Evelyn asked him to take it."

He patted me on the back, "Good for you, please tell me you sent an 'accidental' message to that other guy who stood you up?" He meant it too? "No! Of course not! Evelyn is mad as hell at him, she has some kind of plan for him at tomorrow's shoot?" He paused. "What kind of plan?"

I shrugged my shoulders, "No idea, but she is angrier at him than I am."

He smiled a little. "Maybe he will get the punch she didn't give Leanne?"

We laughed thinking about it, "Have you told her what's happening here and about Ellie?"

I shook my head. "No, I thought you could tell her that?"

He laughed. "Management has gone to your head already?"

I snapped round at him, "No definitely not, I just figured you might want to tell her about Ellie?"

He smiled. "I was going to let Ellie do it at the get-together we are having next Saturday night, you're both going to come right?" I smiled as Evelyn and Tony reappeared hand in hand walking back towards us.

"Yeah, we'll both be there," he smiled as they reached their roundabout which they always went around 4 times.

Handing me another beer Gale eased back into his chair. "It's good to see him like that again, he was doing better after you had been talking to him, but she somehow just breaks that guy down," he smiled as they wandered back down the path together.

Gale started to tell me about Abby and how she was doing this week before he discussed Ellie and Sophie's arrival in two weeks' time, both had bought a house together, the old childhood friends would be living together again. Contractors had been working at the Davizioso but I still wasn't sure what on, they couldn't have been doing my office?

Surely, they would have finished that by now? Gale however wouldn't tell me a thing about it, what was the big secret? I knew they had bought another place right next door which was being converted for more residents, but these contractors were working in the main hotel, whatever were they doing? Tony and Evelyn rejoined us and Gale led her off into the hotel, curious as to why Gale was taking her away, "Where are they going Tony?" I probed him a little.

"He just wants to show her your new office," shrugging off my inquisitive nature. "How are you now that she is back?"

I smiled at him, "Great! I'm happy to have her back."

Tony rested back, "Sorry that journalist blew you off though Fae, but I hear you found a new guy the same night."

I showed Tony the picture, "It's okay, I kinda figured he wasn't going to turn up, but check out the dress Evelyn made with Colette!"

Tony smiled. "You look amazing in that, did Evelyn really make that?"

I grinned at him, "Yep she made it for me," I put my phone back away, "I hear she has a plan for him too?"

I shrugged my shoulders at him, "She is really angry with him, though I don't know what she has in mind for him?"

He laughed. "I hope she gives him the punch Leanne deserved!"

I laughed at him, "You really didn't like that guy did you?"

He shrugged his shoulders, "I hate journalists!"

Gale appeared with a grinning Evelyn, "Your office looks good, Fae!" She smiled as she sat back next to Tony.

"You going to come to our little get-together next Saturday Evelyn?" She looked at me. "Is Fae coming too?"

Gale nodded at her, "Then yes! Another party? That's two in a year!"

She grabbed my arm. "Hey can we meet next Wednesday evening for our walk Evelyn?" Tony asked her, offering her his hand, she paused and thought, "Why don't we just meet in the evenings from now on?"

She put her hand softly on his, "Do you like hot chocolate?" She smiled.

"I'm guessing that is a yes then?" He smiled at her.

Time came to head home and both gave her a hug goodbye before we wandered back through the halls of the Davizioso and out onto the streets of Ljiantsipol to head home. Wandering back up along the river I tried to get out of her where Gale had taken her but she wouldn't say a word, whatever the secret was she was now helping to keep it for them.

Slowly wandering up the streets she spoke about Abby being my student, I started to tell her how she had come to my rescue the night I had a big crash at work. Evelyn seemed oddly proud of Abby coming to my aid and rising to the challenge of my ever-dangerous mind though she didn't seem surprised which seemed strange?

While we approached my home, Evelyn had something on her mind, not something huge but it was clear she was thinking ahead of herself. Coming to rest upon the sofa, she began to talk about our future together as house friends and more importantly how we would give each other space?

That of course, wasn't the only thing on her mind, Karl was on her mind too, she was incensed that he didn't turn up for our date and disgusted that after refusing his approach he had just ditched me after he got the calendar pictures arranged. Evelyn though had a plan, not a vile plan but a simple display of what he had thrown away and to show him that neither of us needed him, it was him that needed me.

Their article about me had gone around the world and been seen by thousands of people and generated a level of interest in them that they couldn't maintain easily. Simply put, that single piece had been seen by more people than all their other articles combined, and they had been given another huge opportunity which they needed me for.

Truthfully, I was in two minds about the calendar pictures, I didn't really want to be in that dark and imposing studio again but at the same time I liked the idea of being in a calendar for May and December especially as Evelyn would also be in the pictures. Sitting on that chair in front of that bluescreen again terrified me and I hated the idea of it but somehow with her there it would be okay, not fun but bearable.

Evelyn however wanted to go to the beach for one of the pictures, to the spot where he should have met me for our date, the same spot he did my last shoot at, where he knew I would be waiting for him. Karl had enraged Evelyn though, she was filled with anger after he didn't turn up for our date on Tuesday night, though I was kind of thankful in hindsight. Maybe Karl just went somewhere else? Or of course, maybe he got me to agree to his calendar pictures and for him that was all he really wanted.

Since her return Evelyn was different most people probably wouldn't have noticed her subtle changes but for me some of them were quite stunning. Evelyn was always affectionate and caring but since her return this had been heightened and she was somehow softer than before too. Her thoughts and mind had calmed, she was still very excitable but aside from Wednesday morning her normal almost psychotic morning talks had almost ceased.

Evelyn's biggest change though was something that only I would notice as it happened in my house at night and in the morning. Previously she always passed out on the sofa, almost as if he stayed up as late as she could until she just flaked and wound up strewn over that sofa with her little legs dangling off the side facing the door.

Every night she had done the same, if I took her up to the bed, she now slept in she would take herself back downstairs to sleep on my sofa facing the door, Ellie shed light on this odd trait of hers. Ellie thought that she was simply waiting for her parents to come back, even after 17 years she still slept every night facing a door as if they could walk through at any moment, yet since her return this had stopped.

Waking every morning with her facing me cuddled up as close to me as she could get herself it almost felt like she had simply made me her family. Truthfully, I loved her very much and couldn't imagine living without her again and now that she happily slept in a bed was quite nice, I never minded her sleeping on my sofa but it was nice knowing she would be calmly dreaming away somewhere more comfortable than my couch.

Rather than passing out on my sofa she had started to take herself to bed when she felt tired, she would lie and wait for me to come and see her before she fell asleep but clearly now, she wanted to sleep in her own bed. Tonight, I was going to try and leave her alone and see if she would still be there in the morning or if she would be back on the sofa at sunrise.

Laying with her in my arms with my hand gently resting on her hips I made her a promise that she would always have a home and family here with me and I had no plans to break that promise anytime soon.

Whether her relationship with Zach took off or not she belonged here with me and as far as I was concerned, she was like my little sister and I was certain my mum and dad would love to meet her. Both had been happy to hear about my little friend and how she had helped me calm my issues during summer and with both coming down before Christmas, soon they would meet my guardian angel.

Mum always said she wanted another little girl and maybe with Evelyn she would get that wish. I was convinced she would love her, aside from Leanne I was yet to meet anyone who didn't love that girl. Slowly waking up her little eyes glistened and I couldn't help but hold her a little tighter as she yawned herself awake and softly smiled away at me.

Evelyn was so soft during the mornings gently holding onto me as she woke up, affectionately cuddling me until she knew when to let go of me, it was part of her gift. During her last stay she had helped to calm my episodes and all but stopped my crashes, with her constant blanket of love and affection she kept my conditions at bay.

While we were getting ourselves ready, she started to talk to me about working and jobs again, she was worried about paying her way now that she would be living with me. Offering me her little envelopes as payment, each one crammed with money, I just put them all into one envelope and gave them back to her, "Use it for something nice for you," I smiled at her gesture.

While the morning ticked away, I asked about her green outfit she had consigned to that drawer, she smiled softly and just said that girl belonged to the forest and this girl now belongs to Ljianstipol. Seeming to have consigned the forest to her past she started to tell me about the queen's crown and how it was an enormous gesture for her to have given it to me.

I told her how the queen had said it was a gift from one mother to another, she smiled when I told her that. Casually we got ready to head to that studio on the outskirts of Ljianstipol, Motivated, we walked out to the old airbase and hangar where the pictures for the calendar would be taken. The receptionist smiled happily when she saw Evelyn, recounting their last meeting and that game Evelyn had invented, to distract me during the photoshoot.

Walking down the hallway Evelyn saw that picture of us proudly on show on the hallway wall, smiling and pointing at me. "You look even more incredible now," we walked into the blackness of that studio but only Jared was there. He walked over to greet us.

"Sorry he didn't show up for today either, jerk!" Shaking our hands, he guided us to a table set up in the studio and started to show us the backdrops he had for the shoot.

Jared walked over to Evelyn, "You don't need to show him what he has missed out on, I'm going to do that for you, he knew better than to do that to Fae," seeming ashamed of his colleague's behaviour. Evelyn looked at him, "You sound sad?"

Jared offered her his hand to help her up. "He knew what might happen if he didn't turn up, I hope he didn't upset either of you too much, but it's his loss! Look at Fae now!" He smiled at me as he pulled Evelyn off the chair.

Flicking the first backdrop on, he put a large soft chair in the middle of the studio, we sat upon it, Evelyn lounging back into me and he took a few pictures of us together. Looking at the photo he had just taken.

"What an idiot," he smirked at us as we got ready for his next picture.

Jared was odd. He was quite angry with Karl and his treatment of me but it seemed to make him take even better pictures of us together. Like Evelyn he was being fuelled by anger at his comrades' behaviour and his pictures got better and better as if he planned to make sure it hit Karl hard on what he had done.

While he got another set ready, me and Evelyn sat on the side of a bed talking, while we sat chatting unknown to us, he carried on shooting and showed us the pictures. Truthfully, they were better than the setup shots so he asked if he could take more pictures like that which we naturally agreed to. Walking round the hangar talking and stopping to rest on different props he stalked us with his lens, slowly getting more and more evocative pictures of us together.

We walked back down the hallway, and he followed us to get pictures as we stood looking at their handiwork proudly hanging on the walls, this was nothing like the other shoot, this felt almost easy? Jared seemed to have found a magic formula for this session and his pictures were showing it, everything looked effortless and less staged than before, our expressions were softer and sweeter.

After an hour or so wandering around, we sat back at the table with him and he ran through the pictures with us, we decided to give him total freedom and submit whichever he felt would be the best. Jared however wasn't finished. "Now can I get some to show him what he missed?" He grinned wryly.

Evelyn looked at me before she replied to him, "No those will do that for you, but would you come to the beach with us? I would love a picture of us together down there in the trees?"

Jared looked at me. "I would like that too if it's okay?" He smiled. "Strong girls, come on I will drive us as close as I can get." Heading to his car he drove us into Ljianstipol and as close as we could get to the beach before we continued on foot. Walking down through the little park and along the promenade we walked to the spot on the beach with all those gnarled old trees, Evelyn took my hand and walked me to one of the trees.

Smiling, I took her hand and we walked to the tree she liked to sit in, she climbed up and offered me her hand to help me up to join her, pulling me up we sat on the branch together overlooking the beach and sea. Jared took a few pictures of us.

"Hey Jared? I hope that's a wide-angle lens to get all my fat arse in!" He laughed.

"Looks fine to me Fae," we came down and wandered down towards the edge of the treeline. Lying on the sand together on our stomachs we just talked to each other as Jared took picture after picture, standing up we stood side by side, holding each other and he took his last picture.

Jared stood smiling at me. "Magical, thank you both, I will email them to you, Fae," he waved and walked away, me and Evelyn sat down on the sand looking over the horizon.

Walking home though Evelyn was more interested in seeing if I was going to text Dario and give him a try? Part of me wanted to but I wasn't sure yet. Evelyn had long wanted to see me happy with someone and although Karl had turned out to be an arse, she was certain Dario wouldn't be, but I wasn't sure why she was so confident about that.

Soon enough she started to tire and took herself off to bed, neatly tucking her socks into her shoes in the exact same manner I had whenever she had passed out on the sofa. While she dragged herself upstairs, I waited to see how long it would take for her to fall asleep, tonight she would be sharing that bed with her thoughts alone, soon guilt took over and I went up to see her.

Barely awake she had been waiting for me to join her, softly I stroked her face and tucked her in, "It's time you share this bed with you Evelyn, but I am only next door, I love you," I gave her a peck on the cheek, she smiled and closed her eyes.

Sitting watching as she started to dream with her eyes fluttering and that majestic smile over her face as she rolled over and faced the wall rather than the door. Heading to my own bed, I wondered if I would awaken to find her with me or on the sofa? Stunned awake by my dreams, I found myself alone, wandering to her room where she still laid majestically dreaming to herself.

Little hands clinging to her duvet she looked so peaceful and was resting so serenely, I wondered if she was dreaming about Zach while her lips moved as if she was speaking to herself. I headed downstairs and made her a coffee for when she awoke, returning to sit and wait for her to wake up, soon enough those green eyes appeared and her smile grew.

Offering her that cup of coffee, "Dream about anyone nice?"

She smiled. "Maybe?" Sitting grinning to herself and fluttering her eyes at me, there were no prizes for guessing who she had been dreaming about last night!

Evelyn stayed home while I went to visit Colette to see what she had started to make for Evelyn, stopping at Fabi and Alyssia's to scoop up their mail before they returned tomorrow morning before I wandered down past Francois and onto Colette's little haberdashery in the backstreets. Colette was jubilant today. While she started to show me what she had drafted for Evelyn's birthday gift, she let slip that she was arranging with Tony and Gale for a surprise birthday party for her.

Realising that this was the get-together they invited us too she made me promise not to tell Evelyn and confessed that she was going to ask Evelyn to join her as an apprentice two days a week. Colette however had also arranged with Francois for her to work with him two days a week as well after Evelyn had let slip that she was looking for work.

Having seen Evelyn's handiwork I wasn't surprised that both were quite happy to take her on as their apprentices and train her up, I knew she would love working with both of them, she loved them both and they loved her. Evelyn had firmly planted herself in Ljianstipol and this was now definitely her home, people adored her and she loved them.

While Colette offered me different fabrics for Evelyn's gift and we picked colours for her, Colette was sweetly smiling away speaking about her little dove and her new trainee. Together we opted for a deep blue colour with a white skirt, we felt this would look stunning on Evelyn but Colette also showed me something else she was making for her little friend.

Showing me an intricate and elegant dress, she had been making for Evelyn, admitting it was by far her best work she had ever done and it looked incredible and I knew Evelyn would love it. All those little lacy parts and all the bows and ribbons adorning the little dress, it would show her off in such a way that the entire world would bow before her presence.

We started to plan for winter thinking about how to spend time together now the weather was getting colder when Fabi and Alyssia came to visit after returning from their trip to see their families. Both were thrilled to see Evelyn and Fabi soon agreed to do Evelyn's hair for her just how he had in summer, although she loved her curls, she also loved what he had worked with her during summer and she wanted that for her Saturday night.

While Fabi worked away at her hair, Alyssia found out about what Karl had done. "I'll kill that bastard if I see him! How dare he do that to you!" She was outraged about him standing me up but was quite pleased that he hadn't upset me, I showed her the picture of the dress Evelyn made me. "You look incredible Fae! Did Evelyn really make that?"

I smiled and took her to show her the dress. "Evelyn made it with Colette!" She smiled as she touched the fabric. "How happy are you to have her back."

I paused and thought, *Ecstatic, I really missed her, but she sleeps in her bed now!*

Alyssia smiled. "Because she is home and where she belongs!" She gave me her hand. Downstairs Fabi had finished working his magic on Evelyn's hair and once again she looked just as she had in summer, she was pleased too, all ready and set for her date tonight, when Fabi and Alyssia departed.

While the air started to turn cooler during the day, we started to venture back to the places we had wandered during the summer, rising early on Sunday so that we could venture to that park to the north of town. Dodging the showers that tried to dampen the mood of the day as we walked along the dirty paths in that park, just as before though she cast her shoes off so that she could feel the earth between her toes.

Walking on the wet grass with blades licking at the soles of her feet she seemed oddly energised by the sensations running along her toes, just as in summer I took my shoes off to try and feel that same magic. Somehow the soft and moist embrace of the sodden ground made me feel alive and sent the odd shiver down my spine and we approached that meadow we had visited all those months ago.

Questing through the wet grass and dirt until we found that exact spot where she had told me she was leaving all that time ago but today she had no news of that kind. Perched on that tree stump she just smiled away to herself as she rolled her toes around the edge of the trunk beneath her, intricately adjusting herself until she sat perfectly upon it. October afternoons cast a strange glow and light upon her little face, the oranges and reds of the leaves seemed to embolden her red hair and deepen that exotic looking skin.

She made room for me to sit with her and I came to rest with her between my legs holding her stomach softly as we talked about the future. Unknown to her as she didn't yet realise that I had met Ellie and knew what was important about Friday, while she presented that she would treat me on Friday as a means of thanks, I knew why she would be doing so.

Evelyn would be turning 23 on Friday, it was strange when I think about it as when I first met her, I assumed she was an early teen due to her size and shape with her petite stature masking her years. Oblivious to the real motive behind the 'get-together' that Gale had invited her too I did wonder how she would receive Colette's surprise party for her, she was excited about the summer party but this would be solely for her.

Colette was throwing her heart and soul into making her stay I guess like me she truly loved her little dove and at that party she would also invite Evelyn to become her trainee. Deep down I felt Evelyn would love training with both her and Francois and if that dress, she made was anything to go by then she would be good at it too.

Just like me when I moved to Ljianstipol the universe was conspiring to help Evelyn stay in her new home and of course I was pleased too, as once again just as in summer my conditions had almost ceased. Something that she hadn't discussed since her return was the forest, almost avoiding talking about it entirely as if it now somehow hurt her to speak of it.

Early warning signs were coming in that this winter was to be brutal, heavy snowfall and some of the lowest temperatures ever recorded were a daily feature of the weather reports. Though she never fully explained why she left Ljianstipol in summer she did mention it having something to do with the flowers she planted being some kind of warning beacon about the winter.

While the sky began to turn orange, she started to talk about her brief return visit to the forest, when she came back, she had grown very thin and now she began to explain why that was. Tribes in the forest were often in conflict with each other, fighting over claims of land or hunting grounds, however this year was very different as the hunters were struggling to find food to feed everyone these little spats turned into full blood lusted wars.

Evelyn when she saw the queen's crown knew that she had left it as she didn't expect to survive the winter, her tribe had splintered while Evelyn was in Ljianstipol and both of her daughters were now dead having been killed during fighting. Evelyn one day had been crying into the lake near the home she had in the forest and when the queen learned about me and Ljianstipol she knew what to do.

Rather than letting Evelyn be killed or starve to death in the forest she had insisted upon helping her get back to Ljianstipol accompanying her so that she knew she was safe in my home. Simply put the queen threw all her efforts into setting Evelyn free and bringing her back to a place where she knew she would be looked after and cared for and have some hope of life.

All of this explained why she left in the dead of night with no trace of her having ever arrived in Ljianstipol bar that crown she had left behind. Evelyn didn't begrudge her leaving her behind but she knew she wasn't going to see her again which made her sad, but she did believe that she had a forever home with me, which was true.

Walking back through the dwindling light towards my home, Evelyn was filled with heavy emotions as she missed the forest, but she belonged here now and she was right about the forever home too, she wasn't going anywhere unless she really wanted to.

Over the course of the week, we went for walks all over Ljianstipol together, during the day or evening recounting almost the exact routes we had taken during the summer. Evelyn met up with Zach one evening and she came home with a sandy bum so I kinda assumed what she had been up to with him?

Tony, of course, met her on Wednesday evening for their weekly walk, they walked round the garden through the sunset and then sat in that cabin with the fire going into the late hours of the day. Agreeing among themselves that they would meet like that every week now instead of during the day, while they went for their walk, Gale hustled me at pool in his bar downstairs.

Gale was always looking for blood when he offered anyone a game, his ferociously competitive nature just took over, he had been teaching me however so a few times I beat him, not that he minded as he was getting the game time he loved. While we played, I tried to extract from Gale what the contractors had been doing while I was away but just like last week, he wasn't budging on that, whatever they had been doing seemed to be a surprise of some kind?

Gale did discuss one minor change that had been agreed in my absence and that was that for the first time the staff being inducted to the Davizioso would have to participate in my evening sessions to gain experience in the same way Abby had been doing. Gale reasoned that they would learn more in a few of those sessions than in any classroom, they had also now fully binned the local authority and decided to pursue their own routes of care again.

Abby dropped by on Thursday evening to see how I was and to have a catch up with me before we resumed her new role on Monday. Her confidence had skyrocketed since she had started training with me, and she was no longer that shy receptionist hiding behind that desk although she now was Hugh's assistant for his podcasts.

Waking early on Friday I sneaked out of the house to meet Colette and collect Evelyn's birthday present before she woke up. Walking through the streets before the sun rose, even the birds weren't awake yet as I reached Colette's shop, she stood just inside the door waiting for me. Carefully wrapped was the long dress jacket I had asked Colette to make for Evelyn and I had no doubt it would be made with every ounce of love she could put into the garment.

Since seeing the initial draft for the gift, I hadn't actually seen it yet so it would be a surprise for me too when she opened it. Quietly I sneaked back into the house just before the sun began to rise, hiding the gift in my wardrobe until I would have a chance to either move it or surprise Evelyn during the day. Sitting on her chest I sat over her waiting for her to wake up, as her bleary eyes opened. "Happy birthday Evelyn!"

I rubbed my nose against hers and gave her a hug. Smiling away in surprise as I wished my little friend a happy birthday. "How did you know it was today?" Her sweet little voice questioning away, "The Queen told me."

A little smile came over her face, "So what do you want to do today Evelyn?"

She paused and thought deeply. "Can we just spend today together and alone?" I nodded my head at her, "Whatever you want, today is your day!"

We sat downstairs and I made her one of those vile sugary coffees she was so fond of. While she sipped away, I went and ran her a deep and rich bubble bath and got ready to give my friend a pampering session, helping her into the bath, I sat with her and washed her hair for her while she soaked away.

Slowly massaging oils through her hair while she rested back like a queen, I sat on the toilet talking to her while she finished her bath before covering her in a huge towel and wandering her down to my room. Pointing to my cupboard, "I found something in there."

Evelyn looked puzzled. "Found what?" She walked towards the cupboard and opened the door to find a present neatly wrapped on a hanger.

Carefully she plucked the hanger from the wardrobe. "You didn't have to get me anything Fae."

I wrapped my hands around her stomach. "Sure, I did! You need at least one present for your birthday!"

Sitting on my bed she gently unwrapped her present before she gasped, "Fae! It's beautiful!" She held the long dress out and smiled. "A friend helped me with this one for you." Standing up, she pressed it against herself and pretended to dance with me. "I'm glad you like it, Evelyn," she bowed to me before she sat back down and marvelled at her new outfit.

Smiling at me and hugging me, "Thank you Fae, I love it but comfies and ice cream today?" She looked up at me with that puppy face of hers.

"Of course," I stroked her hair and we headed downstairs to spend a very lazy day together. Spending nearly all that day just cuddling on the sofa, she kept smiling and squeezing me every so often, while she smiled to herself, I wondered how she would feel tomorrow night? Unlike any other evening together, tonight we both fell asleep on the sofa, she rested on my chest holding my face to gently support my head as she laid on top of me.

Wandering down into town we both needed a Fabi fix this morning, all that sugar had caused us both to crash massively and it was a nice morning too so the fresh air didn't hurt too much. Evelyn of course ordered that horrid mocha and marshmallow thing she was so fond of, he gave her a little bun he had made for her too, she was happy she did have a pretty sweet tooth.

Chatting to each other it often seemed like they had a mental battle to get the last word in every single time they spoke, normally exhaustively they battled this way every time they met up. Wandering round town to see what delights the shops held for us today yielded very little, she did find a strange wooden box she was fond of but beyond this the shops held no treasure today.

We popped to see both Francois and Alyssia both were quite jovial today too though neither let on about seeing her again tonight our next stop would be Colette. From the very first moment she laid eyes upon Evelyn, she fell hopelessly in love with her little dove, normally shy and timid around everyone she opened up to Evelyn, they were like soul mates. Never discussing anything they spoke about; both kept a very secretive grip on anything they talked about, nor would Colette disclose anything Evelyn had been working on at her shop.

Colette, of course, also stood to back Evelyn up when Leanne picked on her at that restaurant, not that Evelyn needed backing up as it turned out. Diners watched in awe as the 4ft 8 Evelyn faced up to the nearly 6ft Leanne and put her to shame in that standoff, Leanne lost her job that night and moved back to Zyvala to her parents as nowhere in Ljianstipol would employ her.

Colette fought hard not to expose her surprise party to Evelyn before we left to get some lunch by the river at the same place, we visited on our first ever day out together. Sitting watching the water flow by as the last of the leaves fell into the waters before we crossed that bridge, I hated so much and Evelyn pointed out our padlock as she did every time we crossed that bridge. We arrived home and began to get ourselves ready for tonight's little get-together, she wore her sailor outfit as she didn't want to spill drinks on her new outfit but she looked as cute as she always did!

Together we began to make our way to Tony and Gale's places on the edge of town, she was quite excited, but her deeper smile seemed to be about her birthday present. Reaching Tony's gates to be greeted by Mona who walked us through to the garden, fire pits were going to keep everyone warm round the patio, it wasn't the warmest of evenings, but it was dry. Ominously though, Gale wasn't there yet? "Gale is running late; he will be here in a few minutes." Tony handed us both a bottle and sat down to talk to us.

"How has your week been Fae?" Tony asked.

"Pretty good thanks, I'm looking forward to next week!" He smiled. "How are you, Evelyn? It's good to see you both back together again!"

She smiled sweetly at him, "Good thanks Tony, how are you?"

He smiled at her, "Good now you are both here," his sincerity echoed in his voice as Gale walked through the gates shaking his head.

"Sorry I'm late, I got held up by a tourist or two," he laughed as he walked into the garden followed by everyone who Colette could have invited to tonight's little party. Evelyn looked confused as they stopped and turned.

"Happy birthday Evelyn," they chanted at her as they came over to see her.

"But? How did you know?"

Gale patted her on the back, "Blame Colette for this one, this is all her doing."

Colette marched over to Evelyn and grabbed hold of her, "Happy birthday little dove," she handed her a little bag, "From me and Francois, my petit oiseau," slowly being moved to tears as people handed her gifts and birthday wishes were exchange with her, "Your second party Evelyn!" Tony smiled at her, "This one is just for you though," Gale joined in, "Thank you."

Gale put his hands up, "This is all Colette's work not ours," Evelyn wandered over to Colette and threw herself around her, crying away, "Thank you Colette."

Colette smiled softly and lifted her up and held her, "You are welcome my little dove," they stood against the backdrop of fires, holding each other before Evelyn returned and sat down smiling to herself. Wiping her tears of joy away a card fell into her lap, as Evelyn looked up, "Happy birthday little fairy."

Her face lit up, "Ellie!"

Leaping up and holding her, Ellie lifted her up and swung her round, "Dad said they were having a party for you and there is no way you can have a party here without me, Evelyn."

Ellie smiled at the teary Evelyn, "Hey Fae!" She smiled at me; Evelyn looked surprised. "How do you know each other?" She asked me.

"Someone stayed with me for a few nights, remember this?" Ellie held out Evelyn's old fairy dress, she gasped and held it, "My dress!"

I stood to join them, "No tickle trolls tonight?" Evelyn smiled at me while Ellie held onto her, "Have you told her yet Dad?"

Gale shook his head. "Told me what?"

Ellie grinned. "Guess who's moving to Ljianstipol?"

Evelyn's face lit up again, "No way!" Ellie nodded, "Guess we'll have to practice flying again?"

Tony walked over to us.

"I have something for you Evelyn," he handed her a neatly wrapped box. "You might want to come over here and open it though, you coming Fae?" Tony took her hand and walked her down the path to the summerhouse where he had given her the photos of her parents. Following them as Gale came to join us with Ellie in tow, Tony sat Evelyn on a soft chair and put the box back in her hand.

Looking at him and smiling as she opened it, inside was a new phone in green, her favourite colour, she gasped, "Thank you so much."

He smiled and looked at her, "The phone isn't the gift,"

She looked puzzled as Gale turned it on for her and handed it back to her.

"Look at the videos," Ellie said to her. Evelyn scrolled through the phone to the videos and pressed on the first one, a video of people from town wishing her happy birthday, she smiled.

Gale sat next to her and scrolled through the videos. "Try these ones," he played one of the videos and as it began, she started to cry, with my concerns growing. "What is it, Evelyn?" She handed me the phone.

I looked down to see a video of her dad flying her round their garden. Crying her eyes out, she watched videos of her and her parents, giving her back the memories of them that she couldn't recall.

Tony put his arms around her, "John and Marie were good friends of ours," she rested her head back against Tony and watched another video of her and Ellie at the bottom of Gale's old garden. "That is my favourite one,"

Gale leant over to join them and watched his own memories of his little girl playing with Evelyn, "Thank Magnus for fixing these up for you, we hope you like them."

Evelyn looked up at them both, her face still running with tears. "Thank you both, I miss them every day."

Gale smiled at her, "We know you do but there is one video I think you will love!" He scrolled through the videos to the very last one and played it for her. Evelyn and Gale both chuckled at secretly shot footage of Evelyn standing up to Leanne in the restaurant including the applause that she got from the diners and guests as Leanne left the restaurant after getting fired.

Tony leant over her again, "You made her look stupid again, she never beat you, in all those years she never beat you."

Evelyn smiled a little. "She is stupid and thank you again." Tony and Gale gave her a little hug, Tony sat with her while she calmed down, composed herself and got ready to go back to the party. Walking back to the party hand in hand and giggling away to each other just as they did anytime, they ever went walking.

Tony and Gale, just like the rest of this town and the procession of people who loved her wanted her to know how welcome she was and how important to each of them she was. Colette and Francois went to every effort to show that girl how adored she was, and they weren't alone in that either but Colette's soft spot for Evelyn was only just smaller than mine. Evelyn had been through hell but somehow like me she had found a home in Ljianstipol, not just a home but a future and a hope, the sort of world where she had belonged all along.

Had it not been for the death of her parents so early in her days, her life would have been very different, these people she found herself surrounded by wanted to be that difference for her. Evelyn's second party was a very personal evening for her, suddenly she had discovered the same thing that I had in Ljianstipol, just how much people cared about her. While we walked home that night, she had a smile on her face though she kept looking at an odd key that Gale had given her as a gift. Though he had given her the key, she had no idea what it was for.

Evelyn was up early on Sunday morning, laying on the sofa watching those videos on her new phone, though she wasn't that interested in the actual phone itself. Quietly sipping away watching her old and largely forgotten memories being played out before her eyes, it was quite a sweet sight as she smiled watching her parents. Whenever she wasn't watching the videos, she would study that strange key that Gale had gifted to her, she asked me about it, but I had never seen it before and just like her had no idea what it would unlock or why he had given it to her.

Ornate and seemingly made from precious metal it was obvious it wasn't for a car or anything new, this key had history to it but with no context we could only guess what it was for.

Carefully, she had put her old fairy dress with its wings in the wardrobe hanging next to her green outfit from the forest, both seemingly fond memories now consigned to her past life. Calming and becoming less hyperactive each day she now was even more magical than before, her gentle mind washing the world in a soft blanket of love and affection. Something had changed within her massively and it had made her even more mystical and mesmerising to be around, her hugs were firmer and her thoughts deeper than ever before.

During the party Colette and Francois had broken their news to her that both were happy to train her as an apprentice, in truth if her work thus far was anything to go by, they would be stupid to refuse her. Evelyn had made me two pieces since she had been in Ljianstipol, she helped with the white dress that she got me for my birthday and then there was that two-piece dress she had given me for that night Karl stood me up.

That black two-piece corset and skirt made me look so good that even I couldn't believe just how different I looked when I wore it, the world stared as I walked by in that dress. Evelyn would work with Colette on Monday and Wednesdays and with Francois on Tuesday and Thursday, she was quite excited too as she would work with two of her favourite people in Ljianstipol.

Tomorrow morning, she would walk down to work with me for the first time ever, she spent some time picking out what she would wear to work, putting thought into how she should look for her new career path. While the hours ticked slowly by, she sat outside talking to Magnus through the fence, they had become quite good friends over time, sharing more with each other as they sat on opposite sides of the fence.

While they chatted, I went to check over my work for my course, I had committed myself harder to working on it and was grinding my way through case studies, my final study was about myself. Self-analysing myself and writing so openly and honestly about how my life had been shifting and changing during the last six months seemed to be slowly soothing little scars.

Scars long since forgotten but never actually gone, just buried down in the deeper parts of my mind and masked from view by my now quite well-established array of disguises. However, when Evelyn had vanished those disguises fell away, and my worst memories and scars were left exposed for all the world to see as I simply seemed to forget how to look after myself. Finally typing my final notes on my assignment, I submitted it and now I just had to wait to see how this final piece of my work would fare against the judges.

Evelyn rejoined me just in time for my dad to call me to have a chat with me, still planning to come down before Christmas though he was concerned about the weather reports and forecasts. Living far to the north and near the mountainous region of the country he was at high risk of being cut off if the snow being predicted hit as hard as they were suggesting, we both hoped this wouldn't be a concern.

Soon after Dad hung up my phone rang again and my mum was more than keen to speak to me, Evelyn sat quietly listening to us talking as Mum promised to come and visit for Christmas.

Having booked a hotel for a week she would be a welcome guest; we hadn't seen each other for nearly two years as work or other issues had stopped us from visiting each other.

Evelyn's biggest concern was that my parents wouldn't like her though I assured her that like everyone else they would love that chaotic mind and sweet smile of hers. Chilling together before we headed to bed to start our new weeks together and apart as we both would head to work in the morning. While I tucked her in, she told me she was going to see if she could stay with Abby on Wednesday night so that I would have the house to myself to do my coursework.

Slowly she drifted away with that sweet smile, her outfit for work hung carefully on the drawer ready for her to start her day from the moment she woke up. Turning out the light I smiled as I thought about my friend dreaming away to herself about her parents, settling down and drifting to sleep ready to start a new chapter at the Davizioso.

Waking before my alarm it was obvious just how much my new role at the Davizioso was exciting me, slowly walking downstairs to find Evelyn sat on the sofa already with a coffee waiting for me. Double taking as I caught her in my sight, she was even dressed and ready to go as she sat waiting for me to come downstairs with a big smile and her eyes alight. Sitting together sipping away we had a slow and relaxing start to our morning before we got our coats and started to walk down to get our morning fix from Fabi.

Walking along the river together, through the sea of fallen leaves that now blew round the paths before landing in the river, the air had shifted and it was far colder than just a few days before. Arriving at the steps where our journeys separated, she gave me a little hug and smiled as she bound up the steps and on to start her new job with Colette. While she vanished out of sight, I walked up the road to the Davizioso and much to my surprise I was greeted at the doorway by Abby.

Dressed in a neat shirt, waistcoat and skirt she was clearly making sure that I knew just how serious she was about her new adventure, that shy receptionist wasn't this girl anymore. Looking so confident and professional we walked into the hotel together and I walked up the stairs to my new office and an awaiting Gale stood smiling as we walked up the stairs.

Walking past Hugh and Shanky's rooms to my old room from way back when I had been a resident at this strange facility where I now was a part of the managerial team. Tony was waiting at the door to my office, with his hand on the handle, "You ready?"

I nodded confidently at him, "Ready," he turned the handle and pushed the door in. Gale covered my eyes and walked me through the doorway, "Ready?" He quizzed.

"Ready!" He uncovered my eyes and my room had been transformed entirely.

The bathroom was still there as was the kitchen but the far part near the window no longer had my bed near it, a couple of bookcases and a large desk with two high-end chairs. Two large monitors sat proudly upon my desk as did a picture of me and Evelyn on the wall flanked by my award and certificates along with an empty frame?

Wondering, "It's for your next qualification to go in." Tony smiled as he guided me to a large machine. "You can make wristbands here too and also actively monitor every single one which is still in use."

Gale opened up the tracker and dots appeared all over the map of the town showing every single band which was still registered to the system. Gale zoomed the map out, "You can even see people who have left and still wear their bands!" He rotated the map and found active wristbands from the hotel all over the world. Over the other side of the room was a communal area with tables and chairs near the double window on the corner of the hotel which overlooked the beach.

Stunned into silence as I walked around my new office, they sat in the chair waiting for me to join them with a stack of paperwork for new residents who would be joining us over the next month.

Tony handed over the thick file, "These are all coming because of that article, that is why we owe you so much."

Gale handed me another file. "These people want to be cared for by you but this file contains something else."

Quizzically opening the file, I found a letter requesting another article but not from Jared and Karl this was the big magazine that they lost my article too. Taking a deep breath, "You really want the press back again?"

Tony looked at me. "No but they want to see you and show what you really do, we are happy if you say no but they would be working around you, and it won't be like that last article."

Gale leant over. "They won't be allowed to do anything like those two did the last time they came, they will shadow you and Abby to show the work you really do here," I sat reading through the letter and the proposal and thought to myself.

Standing up, I stood looking out of the window overlooking the beach. "No studio stuff?"

Gale stood up, "No studio." I leant against my window, "No more telling the story of my shitty past?"

Tony stood beside me. "No stories or history, just your future and the work you do."

I wandered behind my desk and looked at the picture of me and Evelyn on the wall. "I'll do it but no Jared or Karl!"

Tony walked over and smirked, "We won't let that bastard back in here after what he did to you," he shook my hand, "The world wants to see you Fae," Gale shook my hand.

Together they walked away, Abby came and stood next to me. "You don't want to do it do you?"

She looked out of the window, "Nor do they but if the world wants to see what we really do then I'm only too happy to show them," I sighed thinking how I had just agreed to a rerun of that article which nearly cost me my qualification. Settling in my office, we began to plan the week's sessions; Abby was going to be taking the lead for the first time tomorrow and we were going to use Hugh and Shanky to check she was ready.

Hugh was a good testbed as his persona could shift at any moment and with him having 27 of them, it was a lottery who you might be speaking to as he switched, Shanky was often insightful and would help Abby fill voids in her work. Sitting at the table she ran through her plans with them both, they helped her change a few parts of her speech and general idea before they headed off to do another podcast.

During the afternoon I hosted my first session purely for social media related problems focussing in particular on anxiety, we had run evening sessions for this, but this was the first time it had been run during the day. Residents' problems had been evolving even in the short time I had worked at the Davizioso, guests were getting younger and from further afield.

Less people came because they had largely known problems like me or Shanky did, now our guests generally had anxiety or depression being induced by the internet. Abby stepped in a few times to share her own experiences with our group, but the session went really well and I was confident that she would excel tomorrow when she flew solo for the first time.

Evelyn finished work just after me so I went to meet her outside Colette's shop, she walked out with an enormous smile upon her face. Spending all the time telling me about her day as we walked home it was quite clear she enjoyed her first day of work and indeed she spent all night telling me the same story about her day. Glistening eyes and that sweet smile kept me happy all night as she explained every second of her day in that same chaotic tone that she had for market day or her walks with Tony.

While she excitedly told me every detail of her day, I wondered how she would fare with the slightly more cutting Francois tomorrow. Francois like Colette adored Evelyn and as of yet he had never said a single bad word about her, his flamboyant style would suit Evelyn though I just hoped she didn't pick up that venomous tongue of his.

Taking herself to bed early so that she could start her training with Francois quicker it was obvious that she was only too keen to learn from them both and I couldn't help but feel happy for her as she wished me goodnight and took herself to bed.

Once again, she was ready and waiting for me the next morning, eager to get to work and spend her day with her mentor Francois, walking so quickly through Ljianstipol she almost jumped up the steps as we went our separate ways. Abby had spent all night rehearsing ready for her first solo session today, she was keen, and she was nervous as hell, we had a coffee in my office to steady her nerves before the time came.

Projecting herself strongly she began her session, I stood at the back of the room to keep an eye on her, but I had no doubts as she started to tell a little story and the group started to share their own tales. Growing in confidence with every single little story emanating from different members of her group her own fears and self-doubts were quashed and set aside as her voice became stronger.

Feeling pleased with her I slipped out of the session to go and start sorting through those files Tony and Gale had left me. Three hundred new applicants had applied to visit the Davizioso and each needed to be sorted through and slots allocated for them at some point in the near future. Buried among the applications were the odd fish, people or undercover journalists looking to get a cheap expose about either me or the hotel, these files I referenced back to Tony and Gale.

My article had caused a surge of new applications for the Davizioso and we were happy to help anybody but we also knew just how much of a double-edged sword it could be. Aside from Abby, two new members of staff would be joining my team soon with my career changing, I was being sought out by other facilities in the country for advice and insight into their patients.

Tony and Gale had started to take the pressure off me so that I could focus upon assisting the other facilities in the country and deliver better one-to-one care. Jess had come to visit me and stood nervously at my door. "Can I come in?" She gently knocked on my door frame.

"Come in Jess, it's good to see you! Take a seat," I walked over and sat down by the coffee table and she joined me.

Nervously cupping her hands as she sat awkwardly. "I just wanted to thank you."

She looked and smiled sweetly, "What for?" She pulled out a copy of the magazine with my article in and opened it,

"For making me realise how stupid I had been," she pointed to the story I told about her, "You weren't stupid Jess, just misled," she pensively smiled.

"Can I ask are all these stories you told true?" I took the magazine gently from her.

"Every single one," sighing as I look at the story about my first boyfriend dumping me. "You made me realise that I needed to do something," she smiled. "That's why I joined here."

I leant over and handed her back the magazine. "You made a good choice! Did you ever get the hard copy of that photo set?"

She grimaced a little. "No but Gwen got them when Leanne left, they are gone now."

I smiled at her and cupped her hands, "Just don't ever do that to yourself again Jess and welcome aboard, it's good to see you here!"

Jess smiled and stood up to leave. "Thank you, Fae," she offered me her hand.

"For what?" She shook my hand.

"Being an inspiration to me," she walked away and smiled before she wandered back to reception. Jess's little visit touched me deep inside, though I wasn't sure what being an inspiration to her really meant it felt good to have changed her life just enough for her to give herself a second chance.

Meeting Evelyn just after work and she was just as hyperactive as she had been the day before, we sat in the park near the beach and she told me all about her day with Francois. Recounting every little thing he had taught her during the day her mind chaotically raced to cram in as much information as she could, before she wandered off home. Staying behind I sat on the promenade looking over the beach, it was a nice night, quite cool but dry.

Reflecting on the events of the last two weeks filled me with an optimism that I had lost when Evelyn went away. Hours ticked away as I sat and just felt the air moving in and out of me as my breathing became calmer and more relaxed. Allowing myself to dream about the future and my thoughts were calmer than ever before, though I did wonder how Evelyn would fare staying with Abby tomorrow night.

Abby would often be up late playing online games, her other persona came out when she was online, ferociously competitive and menacing as she ran rings round dudes online. Evelyn was about as opposite to that as she could be though I imagined that maybe she would just enjoy listening to Abby yell at guys online?

Walking home alone late with the air now oppressively cold still felt good, the lights illuminated my route home and much to my surprise Evelyn was already in bed fast asleep? Leaving her to dream I took myself to bed and pondered about tomorrow night and what I would get up to alone? I had plenty of work to do. While I sat working on my coursework Evelyn would sit at the table with me practising different stitching that Colette had been teaching her.

Mentoring Abby during Wednesday morning but I was surprised when I arrived for my meeting with Tony and Gale to discover Evelyn there waiting for me? Sitting in the pergola with them sipping a beer with a strange smile on her face? "What are you doing here?" She smiled sweetly and sipped away before Gale handed me a bottle. Gale sat down and looked at Tony.

"We made a promise to you a long time ago?" Gale handed me a little box. "We don't break our promises," he added as I took the box from him.

Evelyn smiled at me. "Open it!"

Curiously I opened the little box to find a key exactly the same as Evelyn's? "What is this for?"

Gale stood up and Tony joined him, "Come with us," he offered me his hand and helped me stand as they started to walk back into the hotel.

Guiding me back down the stairs and to their office Tony pointed at a section of the wall. "You know this place has history? Some good and some not so good?"

I nodded confused as to what was going on. "But it's just a wall?"

Evelyn stood next to me. "Look harder," she walked over to the wall and laid her hand on it, walking to join her I looked but just saw a wall? Evelyn gently

418

pushed against the wall and it moved? Joining her I pushed the wall to discover a hidden doorway leading to a heavy sealed door. Evelyn put her key into the door and turned it to reveal a very elaborately adorned elevator. "Only me and Tony have ever seen what you are about to see."

Gale guided us into the elevator and pulled a solid gold lever. Whirring into life the elevator began to move as I stood in silence while Evelyn smiled away, coming to rest Tony opened the elevator door which led into a long passageway with yet another heavy door. An electronic lock was on a heavy door at the end of the hallway, Tony stopped us.

"You have your wristbands?"

I nodded and Evelyn waved her wrist at him, he took my arm and put my wristband against the lock. Beeping as my band touched it the door unlocked. "Only you two and us can access this place." Tony opened the door which led to a hallway with three doors.

One door had a keyhole with an electronic lock upon it, the door in the middle had two key holes and the third door had another keyhole with an electronic lock on it. Gale looked at me. "Left or right?" He pointed to the doors. "Left?" He put my band against the reader and I put my key in the door but it didn't open? "Oh this is the wrong door?" He put my band against the door lock on the right and as I put my key in the door unlocked and opened. "This one must be yours Fae," he encouraged me to open the door.

Pushing the door open it revealed an enormous apartment contained in a hidden floor within the hotel, stunned into silence. "We always said you would have a room here Fae." Tony smiled at me.

Dumbfounded and lost for words as I looked round an apartment bigger than my entire house. "It's all yours now, this is where me and Mona were going to live." Tony guided me through and walked me round the vast expansive apartment. Sided almost entirely by glass wrapping round the side of the hotel only the bedrooms and their respective bathrooms had real walls.

Gale smiled as I stood by the huge windows overlooking the beach and sea. "Don't worry you are set back just enough so that nobody can look in and see you, it's also two-way glass," he led me to a set of doors which opened onto a large balcony which was hidden behind the same glass as the main apartment. Guiding me back into the apartment they walked me to another hidden door which opened into an enormous lounge and entertaining room, complete with an enormous, wrapped sofa and a pool table?

"Why is this here?" I pointed at the table.

"Well, it was harder to get out than I thought, so you can practise here for our games," Gale smiled at me.

Wandering out onto an even larger balcony, "This is for you both and we might come here every now and then, if you don't mind of course!" I shook my head in silence as they led us back towards a door at the far end of the room.

"You can both get into this one through this door," we put our keys in and opened the door back into the hallway. Gale took Evelyn's hand and put her band against the lock and she turned her key opening the door to her apartment. Almost mirroring my apartment, the vast place filled a third of the entire floor plan of the Davizioso, "This one is yours."

Tony smiled and took her hand walking her through the apartment to show her the rooms and leading her to the door to the joint lounge area. Gale and Tony stood proudly watching Evelyn look around her rooms. "These are yours forever, we promised that you would always have a place here and with you now, both having guys in your lives maybe you can stay here instead of lurking around the beach in the dark alone."

Tony winked at me and I smiled at him, "You don't have to live here but they are yours now."

Gale smiled away I walked over to them both and hugged them both, "Thank you, but what about Ellie and Sophie? Couldn't they have had these?" Gale looked at me. "They didn't need them, and they haven't earned them the way you two have."

Tony gave Evelyn a hug. "See you tonight?"

She nodded her head at him. Gale started to leave.

"Oh, try the other door in the elevator!" He smiled as he walked away, I looked at Evelyn, "When did you find out about this?"

She smiled. "About an hour ago," grinning away to herself we walked to the elevator. Stepping in we pulled the lever and as the elevator came to rest, I tried a door the other side which opened to another hallway, wandering down we opened the door and found ourselves in my office! Touching the wall as it closed. "I didn't even notice it."

Evelyn smiled. "That's the idea, look," she handed me a famous picture of the old leader giving a speech from the balcony we now shared.

October soon turned to November and when it did winter hit Ljianstipol harder than ever before, as the days shortened the cold began to bite, really bite, during a Thursday evening in the middle of November the snow finally arrived. Watching it fall we decided to visit that park on the outskirts of Ljianstipol that we loved so much during summer. Dressing up warmly, we wandered through the darkness and found ourselves at the entrance of the park just as daylight finally broke.

Lightly dusted with snow the park took on a new character entirely, with sounds deadened by the white miracle and the ground frozen there would be no barefoot walking today. Gently walking through the trees and paths, revealed the place to be a winter wonderland as we reached the meadow that overlooked the rolling hills in the distance.

Covered in snow, the place looked like something off a Christmas card and the hills in the distance all blended into a single white mass. Spending an hour sat in the majestic whiteness before the snow began to fall again and fall harder than it had during the evening. Feeling the cold, we both agreed that it was time to go home, and we began to walk through the flurries and freezing winds that brought them back to the safety and warmth of my home.

During the time it took to reach the entrance to the path the snow had doubled in depth and was still falling heavily as we made our way through the streets back to my house. Evelyn was shivering heavily as we grew closer, but she wasn't alone either, despite being heavier and thicker set than her the winds had chilled me to the bone too.

Walking quickly, we soon arrived at my door and with my freezing hands fumbling the keys as the cold truly bit away at me, shaking as I got the key in the door, we both rushed in and stood by the radiator to warm up. Making us a hot chocolate to warm ourselves and take the shivering away we sat together staring out of the window as the snow grew heavier.

Warming ourselves we sat watching until the snow stopped falling just before bedtime and we figured that would be the end of the flurries. Putting Evelyn to bed we both figured that Ljianstipol had seen all that winter could throw at it, just how wrong we would both be proven to be.

Chapter 11
New Horizons

Waking in the morning the house was freezing, my alarm hadn't gone off and the house was oddly quiet? Fumbling around my house in pitch blackness I opened the curtains and couldn't believe my own eyes, shutting them again as I thought it was just my imagination. Evelyn sat downstairs shaking on the sofa, her hands and legs pale with coldness as she shivered away waiting for me to come downstairs. During the night the power had gone off and when I opened the curtains, I soon realised my mind wasn't lying to me.

Opening the curtains displayed that the snow had come again and drifts almost a meter deep flowed across my garden and the streets were just as submerged. My locks had frozen and little icicles hung off my key in the back door, I went and got a wool blanket to wrap Evelyn in while I hunted for an old camping stove to make us something warm to drink. Snow was still falling heavily as I found the stove and warmed some water to make a hot chocolate, Evelyn sat shaking almost uncontrollably wrapped in that blanket.

Sitting beside her, I pulled her next to me. "Use my fat arse to keep warm," while we waited for the water to boil, she slowly started to shake less but colour wasn't quite returning to her just yet. I placed a warm cup of cocoa in her hand and as she sipped her colour returned slightly as the rich chocolate soothed her from the inside.

Together huddled up and wrapped in the blanket we sat watching the snow continue to fall, my phone was no use either with no signal, if this kept up it would be a long weekend. I found an old radio with some batteries and turned that on to keep us entertained while we shivered away, soon turning it off as the report was pretty bleak. Warnings were played every other song as people were advised not to leave their homes as the weather was expected to turn even worse throughout the day.

People tried to make paths down into Ljianstipol but they weren't winning any battles with the snow and their reward would be hypothermia if they weren't careful. Temperatures had shattered during the night, and they were expected to keep falling as the wall of snow grew larger and taller, only the Davizioso and hospital would have power courtesy of backup generators.

Evelyn looked at her key and pondered, "Could we go there and stay?" With the snow growing deeper we debated into the night whether to try the journey or not, as darkness descended, we cooked anything that would give us a long-lasting warmth.

Lighting candles in the smaller room in my house we moved every single blanket and duvet we could find into there and would sleep together to keep warm; we blocked off every gap in any door to keep the warmer air in.

Shivering away, we bedded down together cuddling each other for heat, sleeping sporadically as the cold bit harder and more ruthlessly during the night. Listening to the radio, if we woke just made things harder as the temperatures had fallen to minus 30 and the river had frozen over.

People were being removed from the streets though some had made little alleyways through the snow, fearing what would happen to my guests, together we pondered trying to reach the Davizioso. Fortunately, with the warnings most of the people in the hotel had been evacuated only a few residents and some staff were still there.

Gale was trapped there as he was having an insomnia week, I just hoped he could keep himself entertained while he was there. Looking out the window the next morning made us realise that we were going nowhere soon, the drifts had grown, and the paths people had attempted to make were caving in.

Attempting to reach town through those little alleys would probably be a death sentence but thankfully we had plenty of things to cook and the snow could easily be melted for warm drinks.

Spending all that weekend huddled together in that small back room had its challenges, we both were very cold and every time we opened the door, we would shiver profusely for half an hour before we warmed back up. Evelyn being so small really suffered with the cold, wrapped in every spare blanket or duvet I had, her small size wasn't helping her too much right now.

Keeping each other's spirits up though was fairly easy as we talked about ourselves in greater depth than we had ever discussed before. Rebuilding the bonds that had brought us together the first time we met and even deepening them to some extent as the torment rolled on. Evelyn kept inventing silly games to keep our moods up too, catch the bumblebee, bad liars and dirty trolls kept making her giggle away to herself and her little laugh is pretty contagious.

Even at the very worst of times she just seemed unconcerned by anything and just as she did with my episodes and crashes, she soon quashed any fear of boredom, Evelyn never got bored! Like squatters we stayed together in that small room all weekend and we quite enjoyed it too but the sense of relief we both felt was unimaginable when on Tuesday afternoon the house lit back up and the power came back on. Just having a warm house again and being able to see instead of falling over things as we moved around the house, what a relief!

Snow continued to fall throughout the week and when I got a very sad phone call from my father, Evelyn once again rose to my challenges. Dad called during Friday evening, living far to the north he had been entirely cut off from the rest of the country and with the population there being so low it was unlikely that unless winter simply went away that he would be down before Christmas.

Dad cried while he spoke to me, Evelyn sat at my side quietly listening to him spill his sorrow down the phone, gently with her hand on my back to support me. When tears fell down my cheeks, Evelyn had heard enough and took my phone to speak to my sad father.

He sounded surprised when her soft voice said, "JaffaCake would rather see you when it's safe for you to come," he quizzed her about who she was. Evelyn started to play games with him down the phone, like most people he didn't quite seem to understand her games, but he tried to join in. Soon she got me to join in and a new voice came onto the phone, I had never spoken to Dad's new wife until that day, she had been a mystery to me.

Sounding quite sweet she was quite keen to meet me finally whenever that might be, Evelyn started to get her to play her games and much to Evelyn's surprise she understood her games? Spending hours giggling away with my confused sounding Dad she broke any sorrow that had preceded this game, and she sent a picture of us huddled together to my dad.

Dad, of course, adored her but then who didn't? We agreed to meet as soon as we could and with moods and spirits lifted, we returned to wait for the snow to finally set us both free from winter's firm icy grip on Ljianstipol. Evelyn did cause a little stir as Dad didn't know I had a friend living with me but then we had never really had any reason to discuss that?

Snow ploughs had been drafted in to free the road leading to Ljinastipol and teams were now cutting paths into the town. Problematically with the town being largely pedestrianised all the work to free the town had to be carried out manually and on foot.

Teams worked tirelessly through the day only to have some of the effort taken away during the night as this cold snap just didn't let Ljianstipol go but slowly they were winning the war. Snow was being piled into the river to free the town from winter by the start of December the town was accessible once again and with that my mother would be able to visit.

Finally able to get back to work after nearly two weeks trapped in my house, I gladly hugged every person I came across in the Davizioso, though winter wasn't done by a long way. Mum and Ash were going to stay in a hotel in town and they would be driving down next week from Usted, me and Evelyn were both quite excited to see them.

Ljianstipol had been getting itself ready for Christmas illuminated walkways and lights were going up everywhere and rapidly followed by huge trees scattered throughout the town. Just like the winter wonderland that we had walked through during November with the deep snow still lying around Ljianstipol looked magical especially at night.

Evelyn had also been keeping a good hand on my swinging moods, stabilising me and calming my mind, life with her around was great and I felt like things couldn't get better. While she worked on her stitches, I worked on my qualification, ploughing every evening I had into it and my results were showing it, my final piece was given a full 100 percent with two commendations for it.

Tony and Gale couldn't mask their delight when they found out that come the new year that empty frame on my office wall would be filled with a new qualification.

Something however that Tony wasn't keen on was the lights being put up in the Davizioso ready for the journalists to descend again. Throughout the week every light in the hotel was changed to be just a bit brighter and to have a different light ready for the journalists to arrive on Monday.

Tony still utterly hated journalists and after my little debacle with Karl and the way he used me to get me to agree to the calendar pictures, he was even more agitated about them being here again. Gale and myself understood however that we needed to make the most of this second chance as soon enough the hotel and me alike would be old news and forgotten.

During a meeting with the journalists on Friday, we had a good hope that they would at least be more professional in their conduct while they got their story. Gale was happy after the meeting; Tony was less angry, and I was ready but somehow not as nervous as before?

Continually Tony tried to get Evelyn to join the hotel as a member of staff but much to everyone's surprise she instead dropped a day with Colette and took up an extra day with Francois? Colette had taught Evelyn well but counteracting Francois and his flamboyant ways she really shined; her choices of colour were always perfect for anyone. Evelyn's test pieces are in my wardrobe which made me surprised when she kept bringing pieces home for me to try out. She told me that she needed the perfect body to try them out upon, I guess she was learning some of Francois charm?

Colette, of course, didn't mind that she went with Francois, her little dove was still learning her masterful skills but Francois was the showman and that suited Evelyn's chaotic mind better. Walking into his boutique when both were there, they offset one another like a good cop and bad cop kinda deal, Francois put people on edge but Evelyn wrapped a soft comforting blanket around them.

Sitting in the shop one day I watched them argue over a shade of purple, both were very passionate about their craft and Evelyn had been learning how to master colour through Colette. Arguing just like two kids they stormed outside and then just stopped and laughed at each other, if being in that shop wasn't odd enough before it was definitely very strange for people now.

During Sunday evening, she laid on the sofa quietly, she didn't yet know that my mum was about to visit, laying on her chest in her pyjamas, she had no clue what was about to happen when there was a knock at the door. Running to the door my mum kept quiet as she walked through the doorway and into my lounge, Evelyn still laid oblivious to her new admirer. "Who was it Fae?" She asked, still looking down.

My mum stood closer to her, "Who is this, Fae?" My mum asked softly and Evelyn looked up stunned but with that adorable puppy look on her face, "Fae's mum!" Her face came alive and she sat up to greet my mum.

Kneeling down my mum picked her up, "You must be Evelyn?" Gently she asked her and touched her little nose, Evelyn blinked and scrunched her nose as Mum tickled it.

"I'm Evelyn," she giggled at her.

My mum sat her back down and held her hand, "I hear you have been looking after my little Fae?"

Evelyn nodded at her, "Are you spending Christmas together?" Evelyn just smiled at her, and those gorgeous green eyes came out to play. "It's nice to meet you, doesn't she look pretty now, she is just like that photo of you both!"

Mum smiled at her, "I like her hair like that." Mum and Evelyn sat talking as Ash arrived after parking their car. Sitting together me and Ash talked about Ljianstipol and my life here while Evelyn and Mum bonded, what Evelyn however didn't realise was that my mum knew all about her.

During my meltdowns after she had left, we had discussed her many times and Mum was quite inspired by the mysterious girl and what she had been doing for me. However, my mum wanted to offer my little friend something that she hoped would fill a void in all of our lives.

Happily chatting away my mum started to play with Evelyn's little belly and just like Colette, Ellie and I had found that tickling Evelyn was quite fun. Evelyn giggling and wiggling to escape my mum's fingers it was clear my mum like everyone else had been intoxicated by her charm. While she calmed and rested on my lap, Mum handed her a little envelope, Evelyn looked up at me. "What is it?"

My mum smiled at me and nodded, Evelyn looked at my mum and sat herself up, "Evelyn, you haven't had a very good run in life, have you? But here you are, and you have helped and saved Fae for me."

Evelyn sat silently just nodding and looking at me and her voice softened "She's my best friend," as she cuddled me. "Evelyn?" She looked up at me. "Open the envelope," she looked at my mum and gently undone the envelope, reading the letter contained within, "Would you like to become my daughter?"

My mum smiled softly at her. Evelyn looked up at me. "You don't have to sign them Evelyn, either way you are my best friend and I love you no matter what."

She looked back at my mum who leant forwards and spoke softly to her, "Your parents won't be forgotten, Evelyn, just I would love to give you back the family that was taken from you."

Ash looked over at Evelyn and walked over to her leaning down he looked at her and gently spoke, "Fae isn't my daughter Evelyn, but I love her just like she is and Fae loves you that way too, Fae's mother also loves you that way, but take your time to think about things, it's not an easy decision." He gently patted her on the shoulder before returning to my mum's side.

Evelyn sat thinking to herself in silence, while we chatted about Christmas, she thought away to herself about what to do.

Mum and Ash left to go back to their hotel in town and Evelyn laid in bed thinking, I sat beside her as she tried to make her decision. Emotionally confused, she looked nervously at the letter, "Fae?"

I looked down at her, "I'm scared I will upset your mum if I don't sign it?"

I sighed sitting beside her, "Evelyn you are my sister in my mind whether you sign that paper or not, I love you and can't wait to spend Christmas and new year with you."

She looked filled with mixed thoughts, "Would I be Evelyn Edwards, like you?"

Wondering myself the answer to that question, "I guess you could pick that or her new name?"

Gently she rested her head and laid on her side staring at the letter, softly I patted her side. "You don't have to sign it Evelyn, either way you are home whether you are Evelyn Edwards or Evelyn Mariconi," she looked at me with that sweet face she could call upon at any time and smiled. "Good night, Evelyn, sleep well."

I gently stood and started to walk away from her, "Fae?" She called out softly as she rolled over. "What would you do?"

I paused and thought hard and honestly before answering her, "Honestly? I have no idea, if I was sitting there having to pick, I couldn't decide either, but just go with what your heart says," Evelyn rolled back over and I turned the light off for her, I did wonder if she actually got any sleep that night?

During the day we were going to take my mum and Ash into Ljinastipol and show them the shops and they were going to visit the Davizioso too. Tony and Gale were keen to meet her properly for the first time and I wanted to show her my office and all my certificates on the wall.

Evelyn was happy as usual but she was still mulling over what she should do, should she sign her name away and become my official sister or did she just stay as she was? Together we walked down to meet Mum and Ash and every so often she would just seem to stare into the distance, she wasn't upset, just the decision she found herself making was big.

Meeting my mum and Ash in the market square we took them round all the shops and galleries, Evelyn was only too pleased to take them to Colette's shop, almost dragging my mum along by her hand. Showing my mum some of the work she had been doing under Colette's guidance, though I saw the look on my mum's face when she saw a price tag on a dress they had made together.

Francois was the next place she dragged my mum too in her excitement, though Francois was well behaved today, not a single bite from that razor tongue of his. Visiting Alyssia in her gallery before we crossed the river and headed to the Davizioso. Gale and Tony had both spoken to my mum many times before I came here as a 17-year-old and of course Gale had seen her briefly when he picked me up to come back at the age of 19.

Yet they had never actually met in person until today, Tony dressed up for the occasion, it was the second time I saw him with a shirt that had almost all the buttons done up! Like excellent hosts they guided my mum and Ash around the hotel, showing them all the different communal areas and some of the rooms in the hotel. Taking them for a little tour of Tony's rooftop garden before we headed to show them my office and all the awards and different things inside.

We sat together at the coffee table in my office, when my mum spotted a picture on my desk, she went and collected the picture and sat next to Evelyn with it. Mum handed the photo to Evelyn and pulled out her purse and opened it to show her the same photo of me and my mum from the holiday when I was 11 years old.

Explaining to Evelyn that it was her favourite picture of me, from before my problems began, she recounted every single detail of that holiday we spent together. Evelyn took the picture back for my mum but when she went back to sit next to her again my mum showed Evelyn another picture she had in her purse. Evelyn welled up as my mum showed her the picture, she looked at my mum and hugged her, quietly crying to herself as my mum consoled her.

Heading over to see what was wrong with my friend my mum showed me the picture she had shown Evelyn. "It's my favourite picture of you," Mum said to me as she showed me the picture of me and Evelyn from the night after Evelyn had come back to Ljianstipol, us standing together hugging each other after months of separation.

"Evelyn brought me back my little Fae." Mum smiled and I took Evelyn from her and hugged her as we joined together for an emotional family moment. We chatted and composed ourselves ready for the afternoon together, Tony and Gale bid them a safe journey as we set off.

Taking them both for lunch by the river before we showed them round the newer parts of Ljianstipol and its shops. Together we sat overlooking the river as it flowed by, and we enjoyed a nice meal together before we ventured to the shops. Walking around the shops in the newer part of town we were in for a shock, Ash called me over, as I walked round the corner of the aisle to be greeted by a picture of me and Evelyn.

The calendars for next year were out and on sale, having forgotten all about the thing, I had no idea we were also going to be on the outer sleeve of the calendar. Looking on the back of the calendar to see something strange, Jared was mentioned but not Karl? Was this the revenge that Jared planned, or had they gone their separate ways? Jared was pretty angry at Karl for what he did to get me to agree to the calendar photos so maybe the pair had split up? Either way we bought one each.

"At least four people have bought them," I joked to Ash as we headed out of the shop. With the day drawing to a close, we headed home and Mum and Ash headed back to their hotel for the night, we would meet tomorrow for dinner before they made their way back home.

Evelyn sat during the evening on the sofa looking at the letter my mum had given her, still unsure what to do, with the letter in one hand and a picture of her and her parents in the other she was in limbo. Silently, she sat mulling to herself, almost in a world of her own as she contemplated whether to sign or not. Sitting next to her she came to lean on my side as she pondered, I put my arm around her but let her enjoy some quiet time as she thought away to herself.

Colette popped over to drop off a card for us both before her and Francois would head to Paris to visit their families there. Sensing Evelyn's limbo status she sat beside her little dove and they spoke in French for a little while, as their conversation wore on Evelyn's mind seemed to ease and her usual self came back out.

Colette left and as she did Evelyn took herself to bed early, sitting alone I wondered what they had spoken about? When I headed to bed, Evelyn was already fast asleep, clutching that letter in her hand as she dreamt away to herself, whatever they discussed it had certainly eased Evelyn's mind.

Mum and Ash came to meet us earlier than we expected, Evelyn had only just woken up when they arrived, she wandered downstairs bleary eyed and with her belly on show in her pyjamas. Much to my surprise, she went and leant up against my mum as she slowly woke up and began to fill herself with coffee, it was quite sweet to see. After we had all woken up and got ourselves ready to go to dinner, Ash drove us out of town to one of the restaurants on the outskirts of Ljianstipol.

Together, we enjoyed a very nice meal as the time ticked away on my mum's last day with us and Evelyn was back to her usual self too, her sweet smile and that chaotic mind in full flow. Emotions began to run high on the drive back to my home, as Mum handed me a bag with Christmas presents and smiled sweetly at me.

"I'm so proud of you Fae," as her words entered my mind I cried and hugged her, "I'm glad to be back to being Fae again."

Evelyn waited before she handed my mum a sealed envelope and gave her a hug and wished her and Ash a safe journey, though I didn't know if she had signed the letter or not? As their car drove away, we returned to the sofa to spend the evening together, quietly we sat and watched films, Evelyn was herself again too after a few days being slightly quieter than usual.

Mentally I prepared myself for my last week at work before the Christmas break, it should be a calm week, with many of the residents heading away for the holidays. Evelyn was flying solo at Francois' shop, he told her not to go in if the first few days were bad, Ljianstipol is still a tourist trap and when it's freezing cold and snowing, people don't tend to visit.

Having worked all last Christmas after this week I would have two weeks off work, and I was looking forward to the time off and to spending Christmas with Evelyn. As the day grew ever closer, I wondered how excited she would be on Christmas morning? If how excited she was on market day was anything to go by then I needed ear plugs. Excitement was building as the countdown began on Monday morning as we walked to work, all I had to do was survive four days with the journalists.

Walking down to work my heart started pounding at the thought of those journalists, I remembered the last visit we had, staff getting hounded for stories and guests being menacingly stalked for snips of information. Truthfully the last time we had journalists at the hotel it was like letting wild animals roam free, they hounded the assessors too but in the end that worked in my favour.

Evelyn wished me good luck as we went our separate ways at the pathway to the market square, my breaths became shorter and sharper as I reached the entrance to the Davizioso. Composing myself at the doorway my mind cast back to the last time the journalists descended upon the hotel. Shaking and trembling I put my hand on the handle and took one last deep breath, before firmly opening the door and walking inside.

Unexpectedly though calmness was in the air, I wondered if the crew had actually turned up, I headed to Tony and Gale's meeting room, but they were awaiting me in my office. Together with the crew that would be at the hotel during the week they sat at the table in my office waiting to have a meeting about how the team would undertake interviews and any filming.

Unlike the journalists from before, every day we would have a briefing in the morning, and they would agree with us where they were going to be and what they would be doing at the time. Today, they would be sitting in on one of the sessions that Abby would be hosting alongside getting an interview with Tony and with Gale.

Sceptical about them however my fears were soon laid to rest, they stayed just out of view and were respectful of both Abby and her guests, no interrupting or barging through people to get their pictures. Tony and Gale had their interviews done in my office, borrowing my desk while I started to work through files and paperwork ready for the new year.

Gale was as calm as ever during his interview, telling them how the Davizioso was changing and evolving to move into the future. Even Tony was calm during his interview too, so that crew must have been doing something right, Tony filled in the details which Gale left out. After their interviews were concluded, the team told us that tomorrow they would be speaking with the residents of the hotel, and a short piece on the new staff.

While the team worked their way around the hotel interviewing different residents including Shanky and Hugh, we met for a pre-Christmas team meeting. Ellie and Sophie had slowly been taking more responsibility from Tony and Gale, absorbing nearly all their administrative tasks. Gale was now focussing his efforts almost solely on the financial side of the hotel and recruitment, Tony was starting to just spend time on the floor of the hotel with guests, but he helped Gale still with recruitment and development.

Together we sat and planned for the first few months of the new year, with two more members of staff joining my team, I was going to be spending far more time in my office and mentoring Abby. Thankfully the two new members of staff had come along with experience, having both left their respective hospitals to come and work at the Davizioso.

With work matters planned our conversation turned to planning for new year's eve, with the year having been so testing for each of us it seemed only right to spend it together. Gale and Tony wondered about getting everyone round theirs, but I had a different idea to bring everyone together for the celebrations. Neither me nor Evelyn had used those apartments upstairs and with such a massive expanse of space it seemed a shame to leave it completely empty.

With both apartments being so huge, we could easily all stay for the evening too and everyone could enjoy the night together knowing they didn't have far to go after the party. Decisions were made and the new year's party would be hosted in the secretive parts of the hotel, and everyone could see in the new year together.

During the afternoon, Shanky had his interview with the journalists in his room next door, sitting in with him as the crew learned about him and his past, he accidentally dropped a little bomb. Shanky would be leaving the Davizioso on Wednesday, with his health fading almost daily he had reconnected with an old friend and was heading away to see out his days with her.

When he dropped his news, I stood at the back of the room quietly crying to myself out of both sorrow and happiness, he came over and gave me a hug when he saw my watery cheeks. Having planned to tell me privately and before the interview the crew left us to have a few moments, they didn't even contemplate taking a photo of this final moment we might share together.

However, I simply thanked him for all he had done for me over the years and admitted that without him I wouldn't be around today but most of all I was happy for him, but I would miss him immensely. Calling the crew back in, they were respectful again, one of them even checking to see if I was okay while they finished their time with Shanky.

Once they had finished with Shanky we headed back to my office as they wanted to discuss tomorrow and Thursday with myself, Tony and Gale. During tomorrow they would be spending time with all the other members of staff and guests that attend the group sessions on Wednesday morning.

Thursday however, they planned to spend all day shadowing me, attending my group session in the morning, the session I held with Jess in the afternoon and finishing with an interview with me. Running me through their plan I was actually kinda happy to accept, from what I had seen from them so far, they would be respectful and considerate to me and my patients, so the die was cast.

After work, I met Evelyn and along with Ellie and Sophie we went for a drink at one of the bars along the river, we had slowly been spending more time together and became a close group. Abby and Jess also joined us when they finished their shifts, spending most of the evening together chatting happily when Sophie had a suggestion for the new year.

Sophie and Ellie had been looking at group holidays and found a few deals and options, hoping to gauge our opinions and see if we would go away together as a group. Everyone was interested and wanted to go so now we just had to agree upon where that was going to be? During the next couple of weeks, we would all look and discuss before booking this massive holiday together as a group of friends.

Walking home with Evelyn, she admitted that work was hard this week, barely anyone was coming into the shop, and she was thinking about closing the shop as Francois had said she could. Debating with herself as we reached my home, she spent most of the night talking to herself about when she would shut the shop.

Eventually, she either made a decision or just stopped thinking about it as her mind turned to the holiday planning, we sat at my kitchen table and spent all night dreaming about hot weather and sandy beaches on my laptop.

Winter had bitten again during the night and we awoke to a little dusting of snow, only just up to shoe height but it was the cold that was really doing damage in Ljinastipol right now. Dressed as if we had just embarked on an arctic expedition we headed to work together, Fabi's coffee kept us both warm on the walk by the river, Evelyn was going to come and see Shanky during her lunch break and say her goodbyes to him before he went away.

Today of course was also market day and the last one of the years, only a handful of stalls still turned up as the weather got colder but also and most importantly for Evelyn her walk with Tony. Since her return, they had started meeting during the evenings instead of during the afternoon, walking round in thick coats before retreating to sit in the cabin with a stove going for heat.

Just like in summer both Tony and Evelyn spent all week looking forward to this walk, both were excited about it and would tell me multiple times every day about it, they had become very close.

During the morning, the journalists observed my group session which I now ran with Abby assisting me, it was a bustling group too, I opened as always with a story about me before the group would light up. Conversations soon flowed and even the journalists began to join in and share their own little stories with the group and in truth it was one of the most pleasant sessions I had ever run.

People seemed to be jubilant and joyful, and the room was filled with happy faces enjoying spending a few precious hours together before they headed away for Christmas. Evelyn came during her lunch to bid goodbye to Shanky, she cried just as heavily as I did as he bid her goodbye, he handed her one last envelope before she left. Just after she left it was finally that moment though as Shanky took a little suitcase and walked the marble halls of the hotel for the very last time.

Having been here for nearly twelve years the place wouldn't be the same without him, we shared one final hug before Gale took him away on a golf cart to be collected and driven away and out of our lives. One of the journalists caught our final moment together on camera, he came over and gave me the memory card which made me cry again but he gave me a hug to calm me back down.

While Gale drove Shanky away, I met with Tony for our weekly meeting, though work was the last thing on Tony's mind today. Surprisingly Tony had been handling having the journalists here pretty well given his hatred for the press, he was oddly calm about their presence. Rather than discuss work we spoke about our plans for Christmas Day, mine was fairly simple, me and Evelyn were just going to spend it together on the sofa alone.

Tony asked if I had got her anything, I made him promise not to tell her what I had coming for her, we had both agreed not to get each other anything but I couldn't keep that promise. Tony was going to spend his Christmas at the hotel with Sophie and Mona, now that their family was reunited, they were making the most of the fleeting time.

Our conversations soon turned to Shanky and his departure; Tony was distraught that he had finally headed away but just like me he was happy he had found somewhere for himself. However, we did find solitude in one aspect of him leaving, Abby now had become Hugh's partner for his podcasts and videos, we just hoped he never took up online gaming.

While Evelyn headed to go for her walk with Tony, that evening I started to mentally prepare for a day with the journalists and my last day of work until the new year. Sitting at my kitchen table running through all the things they might ask and what questions they might throw my way, I just hoped they didn't want a full rerun of my past.

Evelyn soon came home with a beaming smile on her face, it wasn't unusual for her to be almost psychotically happy after her evening wander on the rooftop garden of the Davizioso but tonight was different.

Evading every question, I asked as to her happiness she gave me no clue quite why she was so jubilant tonight, I wondered if maybe Tony gave her something? Either way she did help go through my preparation for the journalists tomorrow, though her usual 'Just be yourself' sentiment was as sweet as always. However sweet she was during the evening; it was nothing compared to how she was in the morning.

Having woken before me she brought me breakfast in bed, coffee and actual food not just burnt bread, sitting with me talking to steady my nerves almost exactly as she had during the shoot in June. While I started to get dressed, she stayed with me, reassuring me about myself and telling me how beautiful I looked and how proud of me she was, she was being very sweet this morning.

Together we walked to Fabi's, Evelyn treated me today, getting me a chocolate bun along with my usual coffee, carefully walking by the river avoiding the ice patches left behind by the snow. Reaching the divide in our journeys, she gave me a hug and agreed to come and see me during my lunch to make sure I was okay, she wished me luck as we headed our separate ways to work.

Nerves weren't kicking in too much as I headed up to my office, my hands weren't spilling my coffee all over me at least, I composed myself briefly before I opened my office door.

The journalist team was ready and waiting for me as I walked into my office, they had brought peace offerings with them too, different buns and a big cup of coffee for me. We sat together in my office and ran through the plan for the day while we talked through the plan for the day, I noticed one of the crew members was holding a bag?

I looked over at him and he offered me the bag, "It's just in case your friend turns up."

He smiled a little as I took the bag full of sweets and chocolate and smiled at him, "Hope you are ready to lose all of this if she turns up," he chuckled a little.

Escorting me down to my morning group session once again they were respectful, staying out of the way and avoiding interfering with the group, a few of them joined in with the group too. As the participants of the group session left, I headed up to my office for a one-to-one session with Jess, the journalists came along too. Jess after her issues with the social media which had led to her staying with us for a month, she had kept coming to see me on Thursday and still does now that she works on reception.

Jess arrived and was surprised to find herself in the media spotlight, given the news she had been dying to tell me during her final session of the year it would prove to be an ironic twist.

Jess settled herself down and we started talking about the general things we discussed every week, what she had been posting and why but from the outset things had changed. Incapable of ignoring the strange smile on her face I asked her again what she had been posting this week, she handed me her phone. "Nothing," she smiled as I took her phone and scrolled through.

"Well done, have you finally broken the bug?" I asked her quite shocked as she had admitted to spending 6 hours a day on social media sites and wasn't previously shy about showing herself to get attention.

Jess smiled back at me again, "That's not all either, look let me show you," she took her phone and opened another site where her and Gwen had sold photo sets.

"Here look," she handed me her phone back.

"Am I missing something?" I asked her as I scrolled through her profile page, then I noticed that something had gone.

"Wait a second! Did you?" Jess smiled back, "They're all gone, and I have broken off from Gwen." Jess had managed to get the pictures that caused all of her problems removed. "Wait but how did you get the original owner to agree to remove them?" I handed her phone back and she smiled again.

"Gwen had them in the end, she had told me it was Leanne who had them but when Leanne was about to leave, I confronted her and she told me they were on Gwen's phone. After I started work here, I confronted Gwen too. Eventually, I went to the police and she backed down and deleted them, we haven't spoken since, she was happy to lie to me to sell her own pictures. Gwen was meant to be my friend, but she was happy to put me through hell to make a little bit of money, but it set me free," I could see a deep sense of pride in Jess's mind as she had finally broken her biggest demon and maybe now her family would be free too.

"Is this your last session then Jess?" I asked her feeling proud of her but she shook her head.

"No, I quite enjoy these chats," she smiled and hugged me before she headed back to reception.

"Hey I'm proud of you Jess," I called to her as she left and smiled thinking to myself as she walked away.

Lunchtime soon arrived but Evelyn didn't, the crew seemed a little disheartened that she had yet to turn up, "Maybe she has been held up at work?" I said to try and alleviate the sorrow on the faces of a few of them.

The crew chief sat with me while his team disappeared into town to get some lunch, he started running me through the schedule for the afternoon and then running me through the equipment they had with them. While he ran me through the equipment, I noticed a very different camera set up at the side of the room.

"What's that one for?" He looked round and pointed to it, "That one?"

I nodded at him, "Yeah, what's that one for?" He took me over to the camera. "This one is to film the interviews, so that if we miss anything we can go back through it," he turned the camera on and played a video they had shot this morning.

"Also, if the television companies need footage, we already have it so that we don't have to come back, just in case places don't want us back."

I looked over the videos on the camera. "Have you got any footage of me?"

He smiled and scrolled through. "Here you'll like this one."

Mesmerised I watched the footage of me and Jess from just an hour ago we sat back down.

"What do you think then?" He asked quizzically.

"It's been easier than the last time we had journalists here, much easier! How have you guys found being here?"

I offered him a bottle of water over the table as he thought, "It's different to what we expected, it's true what people say about you though, you are an inspiration for others."

He smiled as I sighed. "You want an inspiration? Wait until Evelyn turns up!" He leant forward. "No, it's true, with your history you should be proud of yourself, you are very brave,"

I smiled a little at the compliment and was thinking about something.

"Is that camera working?" He pointed to the camera he had just shown me.

"Yes, it's ready for this afternoon," I sat wondering if they would do me a little favour later on. "Would you do me a favour later on?"

He looked back at me and smiled. "Of course, what do you need?"

I sat thinking again, "Would you do a video for me, I need to tell a friend something?"

He nodded and smiled softly, leaving the table and patting me on the shoulder. "I think I know who it's for and yes for you of course Fae."

Lunch soon ended and the journalist crew appeared to begin the afternoon session but still no Evelyn yet? "Hope she is, okay?" One of the cameramen asked me.

"She is late? But then if that is all the sweets you have with you, she will have them all off you in one hour!"

The crew settled into their positions, and they began the afternoons interview in my office, with me sitting in front of my desk under their watchful eyes. Rather than covering my history they just started by asking what had changed since my article came out and how it had affected me during and after being published.

I sat back and thought about their question and composed myself before giving my reply. "Honestly? It hasn't changed much, a few people have selfies with me and we have more people now coming to experience our way of doing things but I'm not exactly famous or anything like that but then again, I didn't want to be famous, I just hoped that maybe it would help a few people who suffer in silence or who don't know where to turn for help."

"People that have spent their lives like I did alone and isolated and without knowing who or where they should go to get help or just to talk about things, talking about things helps. That's why I start all my sessions with one of my stories to help other people talk about their stories and of course it helps me to process what has happened in my life too, like symbiotic therapy maybe?"

The crew chief nodded at me and silently clapped as the next question came. "How did the interview and photoshoots affect you Fae?"

I sat back and thought again but all I could think of was the morning before the shoot and Evelyn building me up to go. "Truthfully? It tortured me, I nearly cancelled it so many times as it kept causing me anxiety attacks, but then I met her?" I paused and gathered my thoughts.

"Evelyn, you mean?" The crew chief asked.

"Yeah, Evelyn, I was in the park in the middle of a crash and major anxiety attack, just about to throw in the towel and ring to cancel the article when she turned up and built me back up," I started welling up thinking about that first day in the park.

"Do you need to stop?" The crew chief came over. "No, I'm okay! She made me realise that I had to go through with it all, even on the morning of the shoot I was a mess, panicking and picking myself apart mentally but she just kept propping me back up and making me believe in myself. During the shoot I was struggling and couldn't focus but then she started playing around with one of the photographers and she distracted me enough to let me just forget about everything and tell my story."

"You've read my story, so you know it isn't that pretty, telling it was hard, really hard but somehow, she just made it feel easy? Like I was telling people about something so small and uninteresting that I just found it easy, life was tough when she went away for that little while, I really fell apart but since she has been back, I'm good again," I carried on weeping to myself, "Can we take a few minutes?" I almost begged for a minute to compose myself again.

I stood and went and looked out of the window, leaning against it and pressing my hand to it, consumed with thoughts about how much Evelyn had given me since she had been around. "Are you okay Fae?" One of the journalists stood beside me. "She really helped you didn't she?"

I nodded at him, "Yes she really has, she made me believe in myself more than anything else," I held myself and smiled thinking of all the fond memories from summer and that crash on the beach where she picked me back up.

Composing myself I went and sat back down. "Okay I'm okay now!" I said to them wiping my tears away with a tissue and settling myself back in.

"We read about you having that crash on the beach? When was your most recent crash?" The crew chief tentatively asked.

"That crash was nasty, we had done the first part of the shoot without any issues or problems but almost the second I passed the treeline, I went straight down. Fixed to the spot just staring helplessly at the photographer, my face slowly losing any expression or emotion, while he stared on, she leapt into action though."

"Evelyn jumped down and ran at me so hard she nearly knocked me over, now you know how small she is, so she ran fast to hit me that hard, she just hugged me so hard, I'm sure she popped a rib or two as she squeezed me. Eventually, she took me to the bench near the trees and brought me round from my crash before we finished the shoot. My last crash?"

I paused to think about my last crash before recalling exactly where it was. "Four months ago? Here at the Davizioso, downstairs after a group therapy session, I had been fading away for weeks and neglecting myself when the session concluded as we cleared away for the evening, it happened. It was just before she came back, I went looking for her but gave up and came home after having an epiphany on a mountain side. Wait, that must be wrong? Surely that wasn't my last crash?"

I sat thinking as the crew watched carefully, "No that was my last crash, four months ago, I haven't had one since she's been back not even when that guy stood me up?" I sat thinking to myself as I must be wrong surely?

"Who stood you up? If you don't mind us asking?" The crew chief asked cautiously.

"Ah it's okay to ask that, just after I came back from the mountainside one of the photographers from the shoot gave me a ride back to Ljianstipol and we had a few dates. We were meant to meet up the week they did our photos for the calendar, but he didn't turn up, it turned out he did the dates to get me to agree to do the pictures for next year's calendar."

"May and December's pictures by the way, he didn't turn up, but Evelyn turned up and took me for a drink after he left me at the beach alone crying. I promised myself that things like that would happen to me again when I came to Ljianstipol, but I was wrong," I slumped down a little thinking about that little blemish on my time in Ljianstipol.

One of the crew asked, "Tears for yourself because of him?"

I sat up and looked over to the window, "No, tears for him because he stooped so low that he didn't even show up for the calendar photoshoot that he was so desperate for, so it's his loss." The member smiled at me.

"You know you got the cover too?" I smiled and the crew called time for a little break.

We congregated at my coffee table and started to talk about the last hour of their interview with me when they got exactly what they had been waiting for. My door opened and she walked in, "Sorry I'm late Fae, I closed the shop up for Christmas when a customer came in and spent an hour looking around but didn't buy anything!"

She came and just sat right on my lap. "It's okay, I'm glad you are okay, they have been waiting for you all afternoon!" I smiled at my best friend as she looked around the room.

"Really? But they are interviewing you?" She seemed confused as one of the crew members waved that bag of sweets and chocolate at her "Noonrefta doog?"

He smiled at her, she grinned at him and smiled back, "You will need more than that if you are going to try beating me at that game!"

He took a picture of me and her sitting together and their game began. Sitting back in my office chair as she stayed at my coffee table with two members of the crew. "See what I mean?" I said to the crew chief as they slowly started handing over the contents of the bag to her.

"So, what about the future Fae? What will you do next?" The crew chief asked me and the final hour began.

"The future? I really don't know? We are expanding, the Davizioso is changing to meet the future needs of our guests but for me personally I don't really know? I'd like to get that last frame on the wall filled in," I sat thinking as the game on the other side of the room grew larger, the laughter was saturating the air as the crew started beating Evelyn at her own game. I started to laugh.

"You aren't losing, are you, Evelyn?" She turned and shrugged her shoulders as they earned more pictures of her, "They haven't won yet!" She declared with a wry smile on her face.

"What's she got planned?" The crew chief stood next to me and asked, mesmerised by the strange events engulfing the entire crew.

"Just wait, you'll see," I laughed at him.

A crew member got another picture of her, "Think you are getting burnt, Evelyn!" He laughed at her, she stood and pulled the sweetest smile ever and in the softest tone ever spoken by her unleashed the game winner.

"Cnalb engyc uaeb nu rineved tuep, titep nialiv nu emem euq esilaer a elle, lielos ua tnemereif tianet es elle'uq srola." She put her arms behind her back and grinned at the stunned into silence crew who stood looking at each other, staggered and clueless as to what she had just said to them.

Proudly she put her hand out to them, "Thank you," she smugly smiled as they handed the entire bag over to her, she bowed to them and headed back over to me.

"Come here you little shit!" I walked and collected my friend up.

"I told them they would need more sweets than that to beat you at that game." She smiled back at me. "They did better than Jared and Karl,"

I laughed at her, "Yeah, they turned up too," I patted my forehead to her. I took her back to my chair and sat down with her, "Come on, I need your help for this last bit, Evelyn."

She went slightly shy. "Really?"

I looked at her, "I couldn't have done the last interview without you and I don't want to finish this one without you either, you're my best friend and I want to tell them that."

Evelyn gently wiped a little tear from my cheek, "Okay then, just for you though Fae!"

We sat back together and started the final part of the interview. "You asked about what I was going to do in the future?"

The crew chief nodded, "Yes, please continue."

I eased back and pulled my candy loving friend back with me holding her tightly. "In the future, I'm going to give my best friend the things she didn't have and deserved when she was younger, more importantly I'm going to make sure she is never without a roof over her head and a loving family around her."

"Without her none of my story would have ever come out and without her I wouldn't slowly be starting to win my battle with my problems. Neither of my conditions are going away but with her by my side I can learn to live with them and beat them. Without Evelyn, you wouldn't even know I exist, if you want to call anyone a hero or brave, it is Evelyn!"

She squeezed my hand and looked up at me. "Great speech, Fae," she turned round and hugged me, crushing herself against me so hard that she took my breath away.

"What about you, Evelyn? What are you going to do next year?" The crew chief looked at her, she shyly got down from the chair and stood next to me thinking.

Pausing a few times while she thought about her answer. "Spend it with my best friend and hero, Fae!" She smiled at him and unleashed those puppy eyes on him. Overwhelmed, I stood up and hugged her before we stood side by side for them to get a photo of us together, she knelt on the chair beside me to get her head closer to mine for one last picture.

With the shoot concluding, the crew started to head to see Tony and Gale in their meeting room but the chief stayed behind to grant my request. "Evelyn? I will meet you in the garden in a few minutes. Is that okay?"

I smiled at her and held her hand, she nodded at me and walked away smiling and waving at the crew chief. "She's incredible isn't she?" I smiled at him as he waved her off, still bemused from how she beat his entire crew at that game of hers, "Yeah, just a little bit."

He brought the camera over and set it up opposite my chair. I sat down and composed myself as the red light went on, we recorded the video I wanted for Evelyn, by the end me and the crew chief were both fighting tears off, he gave me a memory card with it on and I thanked him.

Together we headed to rejoin the crew in Tony and Gale's office where we would go our separate ways and I would head to find Evelyn in the garden, but to my surprise she had followed the crew instead.

Tony was laughing his head off as she went for another victory over the entire crew, talking to cameramen in her hyperactive and chaotic way, they laughed or stood puzzled by her.

"I did warn you!" I laughed at the crew as she tormented them one by one into submission, I walked up behind Evelyn and held her to try calming her down a little. We stood together as they discussed with Tony and Gale about the final days filming when the crew chief approached us.

"Would you be interested in coming back tomorrow?" He asked.

I stood quietly, "He's not asking me Evelyn," I patted her gently on the shoulder and she looked up in surprise. "Me!" She pointed at herself, seeming stunned.

"Yes you! Would you like to come back tomorrow, and we can film you too?" He bent down slightly to speak to the amazed Evelyn.

She paused thinking and looked up at me, I shrugged my shoulders at her, "It's your choice Evelyn if you want to do it or not," I gently said to her and softly held her shoulders. Evelyn was thinking deeply about her reply, she looked up at me again and her face changed slightly, she became softer in her expression and gently tilted her head back down.

"No thank you, tomorrow is Friday, that's our day," she smiled sweetly at the crew chief. She held her hand out to shake with him, he seemed disappointed but quite willingly shook with her, she turned her feet inwards and stood looking innocent.

"Sorry," he smiled back at her, "No need to be sorry, I understand, have a good day together and you know where we will be if you change your mind," he winked as he and the crew resumed their discussions.

Walking home felt good, I was now off until the new year and Evelyn had shut Francois' shop as the days with no customers were just pointless and boring for her, the downside of a tourist town in winter. Although the snow had largely gone now, the nights were still bitterly cold, long and very dark, over the weekend we planned to finally decorate my house ready for the big day to come next week.

I was looking forward to spending Christmas with Evelyn but it did keep me worrying about her, though she never really mentioned it, the closer Christmas got the more she became quieter and subdued. Sitting scrunched up as tight as she could next to me most nights on the sofa, quietly thinking to herself and mulling over the days past and days ahead.

Evelyn missed her parents and though I never asked I assumed her grandmother didn't exactly make Christmas a fun time for Evelyn, this year however that would be different. Ever since she had returned in October, I had been planning to make that big day extra special for her, it might be the first decent Christmas that she had experienced since she was four years old.

Though we had people who would have come round as well, this year I wanted to spend it just with my friend, it would be a simple day where she was shown the love, care and appreciation she deserved.

As we walked through the door of my home and back into a world of warmth, the work uniforms came off, the comfies went on and pizza was ordered to celebrate our last days at work. While Evelyn headed for a bath, I started to put my plan for her Christmas into action, I sneaked into her room and found her phone that had slowly been vibrating its way around the inside of a drawer.

Evelyn kept her phone charged so that she could watch those videos of her past if she wanted but that was all she used it for, the rest of the time it slowly did laps of the inside of her drawer as Zach tried to win her back. Having been dumped by Evelyn after breaking a simple rule for her pictures, Zach had been phoning her 20–30 times a day every day to try and get her to change her mind, clearly, he didn't know her at all.

Evelyn didn't really say how she dumped Zach but she did tell me that Tony had found him selling pictures of her dressed in far less than she was comfortable with being portrayed in. Evelyn stormed down to see him and end their relationship; he didn't win her heart, but he did win the black eye that she owed Leanne.

While Evelyn soaked herself in a deep mass of bubbles, I took her phone to my laptop and started to download that video that I had got the crew to make for me, this would be a small present for her on Christmas Day. Sneaking the phone back into her room, I only just beat her as she came in just as I had closed the drawer and replaced her phone. She leant up against the door frame.

"Are you okay, Fae?" She quizzed me looking suspiciously at me.

"Yeah, I was just thinking about putting this tree downstairs tomorrow?" I pointed to the odd Christmas tree she had sat on her drawers.

Evelyn walked over wrapped in her towel and her shoulders dropped a little. "Hmm, that wouldn't be right, Fae," she gently ran her hand over the ornament.

"This belongs to my past," she sat on the end of her bed. I walked and sat beside her on the bed.

"It can be part of our decorations, Evelyn?" I said softly to her.

She didn't say anything, she just sat looking so sadly at her hands, "Evelyn?" I put my arm around her and pulled her closer to me.

"Hey come on, it's okay," she turned herself and hugged me as her little heart finally broke. Pulling her tight to me as her towel started to slowly soak me too, she didn't make any noise, but I could feel her crying as she jolted in utter silence, I put my hand on the back of her head and held her as tight as I could. Evelyn let go and looked back up at me, before she held me even tighter than before as her emotions finally let go.

"Hey come on, it's okay, I've got you Evelyn," I whispered to her as the jolting started again.

A knock came to my door as our delivery arrived. "Wait here Evelyn, I'll be right back!" I went to the door and collected our delivery and took it upstairs with me.

Walking into the room with both balanced on my hands, "Dinner in bed?" I smiled at her as she looked up and smiled softly back and nodded her head. "Okay but could you do me a favour first?"

I stood before her bed with our pizza boxes in hand, "Could you maybe get dressed?" I pulled her towel tighter around her and she chuckled a little.

While I went and got us a beer each, she came downstairs in her pyjamas with our dinner and that ornament with her and placed them on the kitchen table, "Maybe we could have dinner here tonight," she smiled as much as she could manage.

I pulled a chair out for her, "After you," I smiled at her and offered her a seat, she smiled sweetly and sat herself down as I pushed the chair in for her.

Sitting myself down I passed her a bottle of beer. "Cheers Evelyn," I raised my bottle to her as we sat to enjoy our dinner together, she was still quiet though as we enjoyed our dinner. While she finished her dinner, I went for a bath and hoped maybe she would perk up a little by the time I came back downstairs, I wondered if maybe I should show her that video tonight?

Soaking away, I started wondering how many people really knew just how hard that night all those years ago had really affected her? Evelyn masked it well and only seemed to let people she trusted know about her parents, even Ellie didn't fully know just how much it hit Evelyn on occasion. Drying myself with my towel, I started to debate getting her phone to try and lift her mood, I headed back downstairs and hoped maybe she had calmed a little.

Thankfully her little smile had come back and she seemed happier, I sat down beside her and she pressed herself against me and I wrapped my arm around her as we prepared ourselves for a night watching crap on TV. Sitting and thinking as she slowly came back out of herself, gently holding my hand and resting her head against it, "It's okay to miss them Evelyn."

She didn't reply, she squeezed my hand a little tighter. Unlike most nights since she had been back, she fell asleep leant against me on the sofa, gently I eased her over so that she rested against me and the sofa, I guess this would be our bed tonight. While she slept her smile appeared as she dreamt away to herself, I hoped it was her parents she was dreaming of as she serenely slept in my arms.

While she dreamt away, I started to plan for the build up to Christmas, I knew it was going to be a tough time for her and I could never ever dream to fill the void her parents had left behind, I couldn't even fill the void in my life when she had left in summer! Planning and thinking about things that she might enjoy doing before the big day, I knew I had to keep her away from Magnus as he had kindly hidden her present for me.

Having both promised not to go too crazy on each other, I had failed and broken that promise within hours of making it as I found something that I knew she would love so much that I couldn't say no. Part of me hoped that it was just me who had broken that promise but it wouldn't have surprised me if she had too, as I eased my head back on my sofa as much as I could, I soon drifted thinking how to make her Christmas magical again.

Waking in the morning to find that at some point during the night we had wound up laid on our backs, she rested gently on my chest with her arms flung around me, while she continued to dream, I prepared to start putting my plan into action. Finding myself holding her a little tighter as she gently slept, maybe if I could slip out from underneath her, I could go get us a coffee from Fabi? She did love that strange mocha and marshmallow thing she had dreamt up for him to make for her, it might be a nice start to the day for her?

Thankfully she woke briefly and rolled onto the sofa beside me, so I got myself up and got myself dressed and walked to get her day started even if she wasn't awake to appreciate it yet. Walking down my mind was thinking over all the little things we could do to make everything just a bit more meaningful, Evelyn had been an unbelievably good friend and I wanted to repay that favour. While Fabi got our coffee ready, I noticed he still had a few cakes left so I got us one of those too, when an idea hit me.

"Fabi? Could you show me how to make that coffee for Evelyn?" I must have asked in the most pitiful way possible going by the look he gave me after asking.

"Sure? You will need to come round here though," he smiled back, squeezing into the shop behind him he started to talk me through how to make this gross sugary mess for her.

"You need to heat the chocolate but not too much or it will taste burnt, run it through the marshmallows and then put the coffee on top and let it mix," he started to walk me through the process.

"No like this, Fae!" He said sternly as I heated the chocolate up, "You have the right coffee for this?"

I shook my head at him, he sighed and handed me a bag of the coffee, "Take some of these too," he handed me a bag of the jumbo marshmallows he had bought just to make Evelyn this vile coffee thing.

"Thanks Fabi, you are a lifesaver, see you on Christmas eve?" I smiled at him.

"Me and Alyssia will be there waiting for you both!" Fabi waved me off as I headed back home, hoping Evelyn was still asleep.

Finding myself sneaking into my own house was a new experience for me but thankfully it was rewarded as she was still sleeping as I got into the lounge, only when I sat back down with her did she awake. "Hey sleepy, I got you something," I gently said as her eyes fluttered as she came round from her slumber and her little smile appeared.

"Morning Fae," yawning and grinning as she caught sight of her morning treat. Gently clasping her cup, she sat herself up and smiled to herself as the sugary concoction hit her tongue.

"Ah that's good, thank you Fae, did you sleep well?" She spoke so softly with every ounce of her innocence.

"Pretty well thanks, did you Evelyn?" I gently smiled back at her, she rested back with her face to the ceiling and her eyes shut.

"Really well and thank you for last night," she smiled sweetly again, her words hit me hard.

"It's okay, I'm just glad you are happier again," I pulled her to my side and held onto her as she smiled at me.

"So shall we decorate today?" She sat pondering and looked up sweetly, "Can we go for a walk on the beach instead and decorate tomorrow?"

I ruffled her hair. "Sure, but bring a warm coat it's really cold out," I winked at her, "Ugh I sound like my mum," I laughed at her.

Together we got ready and headed down to the beach, wrapped up nice and warm, we wandered along a few of our favourite walks along the beach, it was freezing so enjoyed a largely empty beach.

While the day ticked away, the sun began to set and we stood on the promenade to watch the sun fall below the waves, just as we had in October and so many other fond evenings together during summer. Evelyn was quiet again during the evening but not in the same sullen way as the night before she seemed happier or more at peace with something? Maybe the walk on the beach had laid something to rest within her?

The next morning while I waited for her to wake up, I started to dig out the box of decorations and our tree for Christmas, I wondered about that tree in her room. Maybe she would like to see that up somewhere? Maybe she would want to keep it in her room so that she could have a few select moments of reflection with it? I decided I would just let her make that decision, if she wanted it down here then we would make space for it.

Sitting at my kitchen table, I waited for her to come downstairs and thought about the next few days together, I hoped she hadn't found anything that I had got her for Christmas either. While I sat hoping, she soon appeared wandering downstairs and as she sat down, I tried to recreate that coffee she loved so much, she didn't seem to mind it either.

Together we started to assemble the tree in my living room, she worked on the branches at the bottom and I did the higher ones, we moved it four or five times until she was happy with its location.

While I began to wrap the lights around the tree, she had tinsel duty, laying it over herself like a hula dancer and prancing around my living room giggling away to herself, at least she was back to her usual hyperactive self today.

Tree completed we began hanging garlands, not that Evelyn could help much with those! Though she did direct me a few times while she placed a few candle holders round the lounge. Together we stood back and admired our handiwork, and while she sat on the sofa, I went to check on her presents upstairs, when there was a knock at the door.

"Evelyn, can you get that?" I called out to her as I started to check in my hiding places for her presents, I could hear her talking while I looked for her presents to put under the tree.

Walking downstairs to investigate when I heard an unmistakable voice, "JaffaCake!" I stopped and did a double-take with my mouth open, stunned into silence. "Dad!" I cried at him and ran towards him, he extended his arms out and caught me as I began to cry, "Dad!"

He held onto me. "I'm only here for tonight, the weather is going to be bad again so I can't stay long," he held me out and turned his attention. "So, this is Evelyn then," he smiled at me and I nodded, "Evelyn, this is my dad."

She stood shyly with her hands behind her back but with her sweet smile. Soon enough though the shyness went away, and the real Evelyn showed up and my dad discovered just how excited she could get when she gave him a guided tour of my house. My dad sat down on one of the sofas with me next to him and offered Evelyn his car keys. "Could you go get me the bag in the boot?"

He smiled at her as she took his keys and headed away. "She's great, isn't she, JaffaCake? There's a little something for her in the bag she is getting, it's my thank you to her for looking after you."

Dad smiled as we waited for her to come back in, "Are you driving back tonight?"

I looked over at him and he nodded his head. "Yes, sorry JaffaCake, I wish I could stay longer," he sighed back at me.

"It's okay I'm just happy to have seen you and sorry for the bad things I said to you in the past," he looked over and smiled.

"I'm sorry too, I should have been better to you and your mum," I smiled at him and gave him a hug as Evelyn walked back in with the bag of presents and handed it to my dad. "Thank you, Evelyn," he smiled at her and rummaged around the bag and pulled out a box and handed it to her, "This is for you, no peeking now!"

Evelyn gently took the box from him a gently shook it, "It's my thank you for looking after Fae,"

She smiled at him, "You're welcome, she's my best friend."

He looked at her, "I know she is."

Dad stood and got himself ready to leave.

"Come on, girls, give Dad a hug before I go," he gave us both a hug.

"Have a good Christmas, Dad," I said to him as he headed to his car and left. Evelyn carefully studied her box before putting it under the tree, I put my presents for her down next to it along with the presents that Dad had just left behind.

"Did you tell him, Fae?" Evelyn asked as I rejoined her on the sofa, I looked over at her, "Yes, I said sorry to him." She leant against me again and we spent the evening watching the lights twinkle away on the tree.

Every passing day leading up to Christmas the excitement continued to grow not just for Evelyn but for me too, I was looking forward to Christmas morning and seeing her face when she got her gifts. We walked down to the bars by the river to meet with Alyssia and Fabi for a quick drink before we would meet with Jess, Abby, Sophie and Ellie for a couple of drinks before we went our separate ways for Christmas Day.

Our little group of friends had been expanding rapidly, the only people missing today were Francois and Colette who were both in Paris staying with family for Christmas. Staying for a couple of drinks with our friends before we started to head home, Ellie had given Evelyn a Christmas card to take with her and Evelyn had exchanged one with her just as they had for so many years.

"Same card as always, Evelyn?" I asked her as we walked home, she studied the yellow envelope, "I think so," she smiled away as we reached my house.

"I'll go get some blankets," I headed upstairs to bring down some blankets to lounge on the sofa together. Carrying down the blankets Evelyn sat ready to open her card from Ellie, carefully she undone the card and seemed surprised by it, she flipped the card round to show me.

"When did she get that one?" I asked Evelyn surprised.

Evelyn looked equally as surprised. "I don't know?"

Ellie had given Evelyn a card with a picture of me and her sleeping on the sofa? "No fairy this year, then?"

Evelyn, still bemused, shook her head. "Guess not," I offered her the blanket and went to make us a hot chocolate while the hours ticked away.

Evelyn followed me into the kitchen and sat at the table, "Hey Fae?" She asked, sounding nervous.

"Are you excited about tomorrow?" I looked round at her sitting looking awkward at the table, "Spending all day with you do you mean?"

She nodded her head a little. "Yes, I have been looking forward to spending Christmas Day with you for weeks, why do you ask?" She looked to the floor. "Just I was worried that maybe you would have a better day without me around."

I walked and sat with her, "Why would you ever think that Evelyn?"

Sheepishly she looked up, "Because of all the trouble I caused you when I went away," she said sadly.

Saddened by her fears I sat right in front of her and held her hands, "Evelyn I wound up like that because of myself not because of you, it was my own fault that I wound up in that state, having you home is well one of the best gifts I could hope for this year," I spoke to her as she continued to look down.

Rather than talk to her I just pulled her onto my lap and held onto her, "You really do have a hard time sometimes, don't you?" She rested her head against me. "I'm sorry I left you Fae," she said with sorrow muffling her voice. "It's okay Evelyn in truth you leaving helped me more than if you had stayed but I'm glad to have you home with me," she perked up a little but still rested against me.

Sitting with her resting in my lap I found myself running over that question that I was asked at the interview about my last crash. I wasn't sure why, but it kept rolling around in my head? Like some kind of unanswered or unrealised moment in time slowly though I was starting to assemble a very different truth about that last crash. While we sat together drinking our hot chocolates and readying ourselves for Christmas Day, we both contemplated our own thoughts.

Evelyn took herself to bed ready for the day ahead while I continued to mull over that question from the interview about my last crash. Since coming back from the mountains, I had been telling everyone and even myself that my last crash was at the Davizioso just after my therapy session in the evening but that wasn't true.

While I sat overlooking the forest from the mountains I had a crash, a very small one but a crash nevertheless. Unable or incapable to just head over that ridge and descend into the forest I slumped, consuming myself at my lack of courage and at my failure to try and really find Evelyn.

However, that crash had turned into the epiphany that had brought me back to Ljianstipol and since that day I hadn't had a single crash, not even minor warning signs had really appeared since that day. I headed to bed thinking about that moment on the mountainside and the effect that it had on me and my mind, why had the crashes just suddenly stopped?

Lying, looking at the ceiling I wanted to stay up and just think things out but that was too big to be thinking of right now though I was sure it wouldn't be far from over in my mind.

Waking to an utterly silent house on Christmas morning was pleasant, I quietly checked on Evelyn who had cocooned herself in her duvet, lying with a picture of her parents in her hand. Walking silently downstairs I could hear the joyful sounds of Magnus and his family enjoying Santa's visit, the laughter coming from the walls made me feel happy for them as they played.

Sitting outside to have a morning coffee, Magnus came out to wish me and Evelyn a Merry Christmas and to help pass Evelyn's present over the fence. Together, we wrestled with the very large and quite heavy gift that I had gotten her before he helped me move it into place just below her tree at the end of the garden, while he slipped back to his family, I slipped back inside to wait for her to wake.

While I sat in the silence of my lounge, a message arrived on my phone from Dario, he had stayed in touch ever since he met me that night in October, respectfully building a bridge between us. Feeling touched by his ongoing consideration rather than just reply with "Merry Christmas," I asked if he still wanted to take that walk by the beach? He didn't take long to reply with a yes.

As Darios reply came through, the silence in my house ended, a loud thud followed by heavy and fast footsteps running along the hallway and down the stairs as she ran into the kitchen. "It's Christmas!" She yelled at the top of her voice with her face almost bright red in excitement. "It's Christmas Fae!" She yelled again and ran at me and hitting me so hard she actually knocked me over.

Hugging me and squeezing me so tight. "It's Christmas," she wept as she grasped me harder, I put my hand on her hair and squeezed her back, "Merry Christmas Evelyn," she pressed herself even harder against me. "Merry Christmas Fae!" She squealed in delight.

Gradually she let go and we sat at my kitchen table to have coffee together, she was so excited that market day Evelyn seemed quite tame compared to this one, as she sat grinning from ear to ear. Distracting her as she tried to look down the garden, I led her into the living room to sit and watch some TV together before we tackled the gifts under our tree.

Together we went and got ourselves dressed, she wore her sailor top with her black velvet trousers and I just wore comfy jumper and trousers. It was quite obvious that we were both excited, just she expressed that far better and more openly than me. Excited, we both headed downstairs to sit and have another coffee, both of us were getting twitchy as we waited for someone to finally break the deadlock and deliver a gift into one another's hand.

Every time I moved her face lit up a little but in truth every time she moved so did mine, I pretended to need the loo so that I could start her day by showing her that video on her phone. I walked back downstairs to see her anxiously waiting. "Evelyn, you have a missed call?" I said as I walked down.

"It's probably just Zach begging again!" She said sadly.

"No, it's not! Look," I placed the phone in her hand and started the video. While she sat consumed with the video that I recorded for her during the interview I got her first gift ready, hiding it behind my back and waiting for the video to finish. Evelyn started to weep as the video drew to a close and looked up at me with a quivering lip, "Happy Christmas Evelyn!"

I held her first present out for her. Gently she put her phone aside and slowly moved towards me and wrapped her arms around me. "Thank you, Fae, you really mean it?"

I gently moved her back away from me. "Every word," I whispered back as she took her first gift.

"I thought we weren't getting each other presents?" Evelyn asked as she studied the box. "Yeah, I kinda broke that rule."

I laughed at her, "Yeah, me too," Evelyn wandered off to see Magnus and returned with a large bag of presents that she had hidden at his house.

Evelyn handed me my first gift and together we sat and unwrapped them together, Evelyn smiled when she found a new pair of those funky flowery trainers she so dearly loved, and she got me a large and soft deep purple coat. Together we sat sharing gifts with each other and enjoying how much we had both lied to each other, when it was time to unveil her final gift to her.

During summer, Evelyn had fallen in love with a hanging chair in Francois' garden, she lounged in that every time we went anywhere near their garden. I handed her a pair of shoes and a coat and led her down the garden to her very own hanging chair, suspended beneath her favourite tree to sit in, ecstatic she sat in it, freezing cold in the Christmas Day sun. Patting the cushion beside her to invite me to join her, "Wait one second!" I went back inside and grabbed a blanket and took it out to her, while she readied our seat, I got a mug of hot chocolate for us both.

Sitting next to her she leant on me, "Thank you Fae, here's your final gift," Evelyn handed me an envelope? She sat back and closed her eyes and relaxed as I carefully opened the envelope, "Tickets?" I asked her in surprise, she nodded with a strange grin on her face?

"It's sort of two presents in one," she said softly still with her eyes closed. I studied the two tickets when I noticed where they were for. "Monesta?" I said in surprise. "That's where Mum and Dad took me when I was 11?"

Evelyn smiled still. "Isn't that where that picture was taken?" I looked at her in amazement.

"How did you know that?" She giggled. "Your mum told me," she still had her eyes closed. "Thank you, that will be incredible," I said with my heart flowing fully.

"Have you found the other present yet?" She said quietly.

"Other present? In here?" I looked inside the envelope but couldn't see anything before checking the tickets again, "I don't see anything, Evelyn?" She smiled sweetly.

"Look a bit harder," I looked over the tickets again, carefully studying them but just saw one for me and one for her.

Looking at her confused when I suddenly realised that I had seen something, I studied my ticket thoroughly before looking at her ticket again.

"Evelyn Edwards!" I said in utter disbelief with my mouth open wide.

"No wait that must be wrong," I looked again and sure enough the ticket read Evelyn Edwards, I looked over at her resting back with her eyes still shut, "You signed the papers?" I was in total shock and she knew.

"Yes, you know what that means, Fae?"

My heart began to pound and adrenaline rushed up my spine.

"We're sisters now," she giggled at me.

"You little shit! Why didn't you tell me?" I spewed words out and grabbed her and pulled her to my side. "You gave up your family name for me?"

Evelyn opened her eyes and looked at me smiling, "I will always love my parents and miss them every day but, you are my family now Fae, on paper and in my heart."

I broke and started to cry as she unleashed the biggest gift, she could have given me. Evelyn went and fetched us some more hot chocolate and my phone so that we could wish our family a Merry Christmas, sitting together as sisters for the first time.

We rang my mum and my dad to wish them both a happy Christmas and both were quite eager to speak to their newest addition to the family, though Dad did jest that he might have to give my nickname to Evelyn with her ginger curls.

While the daylight faded, we went back inside and spent the evening snoozing on the sofa and watching films together in almost utter silence. We didn't need to speak during the evening, our minds were both quite content to sit quietly beside each other filled with sisterly love for the first time.

With night-time rapidly approaching, we went back outside to sit with each other in the hanging chair before we went to bed. Enjoying a nice bottle of beer together wrapped up in a blanket of love, it was a dry evening and the moon made the slow wind down from a very exciting day even more pleasant.

Together, we made a plan for New Year's Day too and started to fantasise about how together we would see the first sunrise of the new year sitting right here together as sisters.

Heading to bed that night as the questions stopped running around my mind and answers replaced them, as I drifted to sleep in my home with my sister in the adjoining room, content with life. However, if Christmas Day was a heartful experience, then the week leading up to the dawn of the new year was even more stunning. Slowly we met up with all our friends throughout Ljianstipol and they all were introduced to Evelyn now being my sister.

Everyone was thrilled with the news and Colette was especially touched upon her return as she made a special trip to come and visit us before promising to see us on new year's eve. Together we spent the build up to the big night readying the top floor apartments ready for an almighty party amongst our friends.

Soon enough, the big night arrived and we spent the afternoon getting ourselves ready, we would both go in our best dresses. Evelyn wore the purple dress that Francois had made for her during the summer, and I wore the black dress Evelyn had made for me. Together, we wandered through the dark streets of Ljianstipol with a spare change of warm clothes ready to try and beat the sun in the morning.

Walking with a quiet and deep smile upon my face, I didn't fully understand it fully just yet but over Christmas another epiphany had happened within my mind.

Together we slowly welcomed a nearly endless stream of guests into the previously very secret apartments on the top floor of the Davizioso. Combined with the magnificent entertaining area previously only used by the former regimes top and most elite members; but tonight this was our toy to play with. Spirits were high and emotions flowed as the evening and the last minutes of the year drew ever closer.

As bells rang out and everyone yelled, "Happy new year!" To each other as the year passed into the blackness of the night. Shaking hands, kisses and hugs were being exchanged in abundance as people sang and danced their way into a new year.

Gradually though the excitement and intoxication began to send guests into an emotion and alcohol fuelled slumber. Evelyn headed to one of the rooms where we had stashed our change of clothes ready for the morning, we both set two alarms on our phones and went to sleep ready to chase the sunrise.

Sleeping through our first alarms we woke slightly panicked having lost precious minutes as we aimed to beat the ceaseless march of time. Hurriedly we both got changed into our warm clothes and began to quietly navigate our way through the ocean of slumbering bodies adorning the floor. Stepping our way around and over each fallen comrade as we made our way to the elevator and out through the hotel into the blackness of the morning.

Walking at pace through the streets of Ljianstipol we both were determined and being driven faster and faster to beat that first glimmer of orange on the horizon. Hurrying down the riverside and rushing over the bridge with our padlock still glimmering on its railings as we marched on and up toward the edge of the town.

Rounding the streets that lead to my front door the sky was already starting to change from blackness to blue as the time ticked away. Panicked we raced through the house and into the garden, when as we walked down the garden I just stopped on the spot.

Evelyn looked round at me and came back. "Are you okay, Fae?" She asked.

I put my hand on her shoulder and just gazed at her, staring at her ginger curls and into those deep green eyes. "It couldn't have happened without you, Evelyn," I smiled to myself as we stood together; she cupped my hand.

"Yes it could have," she answered back. "I'm just glad it happened with us together in the end." She smiled with her eyes closed as she spoke.

Just over her shoulder, I could see the first hints of yellow and orange breaking through the blackness of the night. Smiling deep within me, her concerned face changed as she understood what I was thinking; she gently hugged me and took my hand to lead the way. Placing a blanket down, she settled herself into the chair and offered me her hand, smiling as I took her hand and sat beside her. "Here's to our new life, Evelyn." I smiled at her and she looked around at me.

"To our new life, Fae," she pulled herself as tight to me as she could and the new dawn began. Pulling her over to rest against my side as together we watched as the sun finally break through the horizon and witnessed the first dawn of a new life together as sisters.

While we sat watching the sunrise on that first day of a new year, my mind suddenly allowed me to make sense of things. My crashes had stopped entirely since I had returned from the mountainside, but how could this be? I had gone to the mountain because loneliness and heartbreak had sent me spiralling into a darker place than I had ever been before.

Finding myself unable to cross the mountains, I crashed again before having that epiphany on the mountainside which had made me realise what I had here in Ljianstipol. Since that day, I hadn't had a single crash and my moods had lifted and since Evelyn had reappeared, my life had turned around.

Yet it was her absence that had finally set me free. Evelyn had taught me to accept myself for who I was and by doing so helped me finally forgive myself for my past.

Evelyn's real gift to me was far simpler than that; we had both come to Ljianstipol alone and found friendship and acceptance amongst the people here. While the sun finally freed itself from the horizon, it became clear to me that when Evelyn appeared, she made my house a home and with Evelyn around, maybe living my life downside up wasn't such a bad thing.